D0054389

MORTAL DANGER

EILEEN WILKS

BERKLEY SENSATION, NEW YORK

THE BERKLEY PUBLISHING GROUP
Published by the Penguin Group
Penguin Group (USA) Inc.
375 Hudson Street, New York, New York 10014, USA
Penguin Group (Canada), 90 Eglinton Avenue East, Suite 700, Toronto, Ontario M4P 2Y3, Canada
(a division of Pearson Penguin Canada Inc.)
Penguin Books Ltd., 80 Strand, London WC2R 0RL, England
Penguin Group Ireland, 25 St. Stephen's Green, Dublin 2, Ireland (a division of Penguin Books Ltd.)
Penguin Group (Australia), 250 Camberwell Road, Camberwell, Victoria 3124, Australia
(a division of Pearson Australia Group Pty. Ltd.)
Penguin Books India Pvt. Ltd., 11 Community Centre, Panchsheel Park, New Delhi—110 017, India
Penguin Group (NZ), Cnr. Airborne and Rosedale Roads, Albany, Auckland 1310, New Zealand
(a division of Pearson New Zealand Ltd.)
Penguin Books (South Africa) (Pty.) Ltd., 24 Sturdee Avenue, Rosebank, Johannesburg 2196,
South Africa

Penguin Books Ltd., Registered Offices: 80 Strand, London WC2R 0RL, England

This is a work of fiction. Names, characters, places, and incidents either are the product of the author's imagination or are used fictitiously, and any resemblance to actual persons, living or dead, business establishments, events, or locales is entirely coincidental. The publisher does not have any control over and does not assume any responsibility for author or third-party websites or their content.

MORTAL DANGER

A Berkley Sensation Book / published by arrangement with the author

PRINTING HISTORY
Berkley Sensation edition / November 2005

Copyright © 2005 by Eileen Wilks.
Cover art by Marc Cohen.
Interior text design by Kristin del Rosario.

ISBN: 0-425-20290-9

BERKLEY® SENSATION
Berkley Sensation Books are published by The Berkley Publishing Group,
a division of Penguin Group (USA) Inc.,
375 Hudson Street, New York, New York 10014.
BERKLEY SENSATION and the "B" design are trademarks belonging to Penguin Group (USA) Inc.

PRINTED IN THE UNITED STATES OF AMERICA

10 9 8 7 6 5 4 3 2 1

This book is dedicated to my editor, Cindy Hwang,
who is not only brilliant, efficient, compassionate,
and patient beyond the dreams of
over-deadline authors, but has
excellent taste in movies.

Thanks, Cindy. For everything.

PROLOGUE

THE audience hall was vast, hot, and noisy, an echoing oven of a space hollowed out of the remains of an ancient volcano. Gan scurried across the stony floor as fast as its stubby legs would carry it, watching out for shadows. Sometimes the crevices shifted. What looked like a shadow one day might, on the next, send you plummeting. Or make you look foolish, which was almost as bad.

There was no roof. The walls climbed jaggedly up and up to the exposed sky at the rim of the caldera, black and empty. Gan's skin crawled at all that overhead emptiness, though it knew Xitil's pets wouldn't bother it. Not this time.

Courtiers of every ilk fought or chatted among the carved columns thrusting up from the floor—here a fourteen-foot granite phallus, there a set of gaping onyx jaws big enough to swallow an ox.

Not that half these idiots knew what an ox was, Gan thought with a sniff as it rounded a set of rosy labia formed from quartz. Gan did, though. It might be young, it might be small, but it knew more about the human realm than any of them.

Which was why it had been summoned. A shiver of mingled dread and anticipation fled down Gan's spine. Drawing the notice of the Most Feared was not safe.

But oh, it was apt to be interesting.

Gan was so busy mentally chortling over the possibilities that it trotted around a grasping stone talon a little too quickly—and dropped flat to the ground, its hearts hammering in terror.

A long snake of a tail, spiked and deadly, whizzed over its head.

Idiot! Gan screamed at itself silently. Acting like a two-year imp instead of a full demon—daydreaming in the hall! It had almost bumped into one of Xitil's Claws. You did *not* want to startle a Claw. Their reflexes were as swift as their wits were slow.

At least Gan had stopped short of real insult. It hadn't actually touched the Claw.

"What's this?" The high-pitched voice came from several feet above Gan's head. This Claw was female, or mostly, Gan decided. "A bug?"

Gan's field of view consisted of the dusty rock floor, but out of the corner of its eye it saw a scaly foot as long as one of its arms. The claws protruding from the four thick toes were thick and yellow and sharp.

Don't breathe yet, it told itself. The immediate danger was over, but Xitil's Claws were as touchy as they were stupid.

"Maybe." The second voice was raspier, possibly male, and came from the left of the first one. By cutting its eyes as far to the right as possible, Gan could just glimpse another pair of clawed feet. "Or some kind of parasite. Better step on it."

"Great One," Gan squeaked, "a thousand pardons. This one deserves to be squashed, yes, squashed flat for intruding upon you, but I beg you to withhold your foot. I am summoned."

"Summoned?" A clawed foot curled around Gan's ribs. Idly the Claw rolled Gan over on its back, and Gan stared up into the golden glow of the Claw's forward pair of eyes. "You think it's stupid enough to try to lie about that, Hrrol?"

"Looks stupid enough for almost anything. Better step on it."

"Oh, Great One, I am stupid indeed for having offended, yet not brainless enough to lie about the Most Feared. If I do not speak truth, punish me twice, thrice over—punish me endlessly—but for now, allow me to answer my summons." *You great, dumb doff! If I were stupid, I couldn't lie, could I? Not even just with words. And if Xitil's unhappy with me for being late, she'll be unhappy with you for having delayed me.*

"Won't be much left of it to punish if it's lying," the Claw on the left observed. "Better smash it now. Or at least remove that puny excuse for a tail."

Gan bristled. It was quite proud of its new tail—which maybe wasn't as long and prehensile as the Claw's, but was wonderfully strong and had lovely spikes along it.

"No," the first one said regretfully. "If Xitil has some use for this bug, she might wish it to keep its pathetic little lump of a tail. Later," she decided. "I will punish it later. What's your callname, bug?"

"I am called Gan, Great One." *May worms eat you.*

"You are a lucky bug, Gan, for I must bow to the whim of the Most Feared, who may prefer you whole. I release you."

"Thank you, Great One." Gan scrambled to its feet, bowing as it retreated. "May your claws grow ever longer and sharper, the better to rend your prey." *And may your prey not hurt itself laughing at your stupidity.*

Once out of range of the Claws, Gan paid better attention to its surroundings as it hurried to the hottest end of the hall. Here the rocks glowed dull red in their artful tumble around the entrance to the tunnel that led to Xitil's private chambers. No courtiers lingered at this end of the huge hall. If Xitil wished to see her subjects, she joined them. If she didn't, who would go to her uninvited?

Gan was invited. With dread and a chest-puffing sense of its own importance—not to mention very hot feet—Gan crossed the threshold.

It immediately felt more comfortable. The ceiling of the rocky tunnel was irregular, but nowhere was it higher than twenty feet. There was only one sharp defensive twist in the tunnel, a mark of Xitil's confidence. No one had tried to depose her for a long, long time.

The tunnel narrowed at the end; few of her courtiers and none of her nobles could pass into her chambers upright. Gan could, though. It trotted toward the pinkish-purple light at the end of the tunnel, its brow wrinkled. Pink usually meant she was cheerful, or maybe horny. Purple, though . . .

Gan stepped from the hot, dry tunnel into steamy pink mist, as if the air itself were sweating in the heat Xitil craved and created. The floor here was polished obsidian, slippery and wet. And there facing it, lounging on the mounded pillows on her couch, was Xitil the Most Feared—rockshaper and tyrant, weathermaster and prince of hell. A paroxysm of awe and lust froze Gan in its tracks.

"Gan." Her voice rumbled through the mist, an audible caress. "Come here."

Shivering in fear and arousal, it obeyed.

Her immense, undulate form glistened in the directionless light, the flesh as rosy and damp as an aroused vulva. And dense, oh so deliciously dense to Gan's *üther* sense, each roll and fold of her packed with lives. Her foremost arms were bent to prop her up, the jewel-tipped claws partially retracted.

Xitil favored breasts lately. She'd grown six of them, and the upper pair were bare. The nipples were hard little nuggets framed by aureoles as red as her eyes—which crinkled with amusement.

"Gan," she whispered, "you haven't greeted my guest. Do so."

It jolted to a stop, eyes widening. Would it be punished? She'd told it to come to her, but . . . *obey, idiot,* Gan told itself. It tore its gaze away from Xitil, and its eyes widened as it at last noticed who—or what—stood to the left of Xitil's couch.

A human. How odd. They did show up from time to time—many of the courts had private deals with one or more of the species—but why would Xitil want Gan to meet one?

No, it realized a second later. That was no human, whatever form she might be wearing. She'd done something to cloak her energies so Gan read little . . . but what it read made it shiver again.

The rumors were right. Xitil was entertaining a very strange ally.

Or potential meal? Surely even she wouldn't dare . . . but Gan had been told to greet the Most Feared's guest, not to speculate. It cleared its throat and bowed deeply. "Revered One, forgive me if, in the depths of my ignorance, I address you incorrectly."

The girl—for that was what she looked like, a brown-haired, brown-eyed human girl of perhaps fifteen years—smiled kindly at it. "Many from this cycle do not know Me. You are forgiven." She glanced at Xitil. "You are sure? This one looks rather . . ."

"Unprepossessing?" Xitil chuckled, a low rumble that made her breasts quiver. "It's young and weak and too curious for its own good, but you do not require a warrior. Gan has the skills you do need. It can cross unsummoned, and I can use it to pass instructions and information to your tool."

"Ah. And the other tool I requested?" the girl asked.

Xitil ran a claw idly along the great mound of her hip, parting the veils so the lush curls of her pubes peeked out. "That was predicated upon our original plan. You did not open the Gate. Nor have you been willing to honor my one personal request."

Threat—challenge—*power* rippled through the air, power so vast Gan had no reference for it. In one quick, nauseous plunge, it fell into vertigo as gravity tugged, released, and clenched again around it. Its hearts stopped beating altogether.

As quickly as the storm had hit, it passed.

The girl laughed, a light, carefree sound. "Oh, look— we have frightened poor Gan. It would be a shame if we harmed it with our little testings, wouldn't it? But really, Xitil, it is too bad of you to taunt me sexually. You know my feelings about that sort of thing."

Oh. Oh! So *that's* who She was. . . .

Xitil shrugged and didn't reply.

The girl who wasn't a girl at all turned to study Gan. "I suppose such tools are not plentiful, and yet it's so small. The size of a human child. No matter how its form is altered, it won't present the appearance I need."

"You think not?" Xitil's eyes glowed. "Gan."

Gan's attention fixed entirely on its prince, for beneath the syllable of its callname reverberated a tug on its true-name.

"Grow."

Gan scrunched its face unhappily and obeyed—a trifle slowly, perhaps, but she hadn't said to hurry. It was twelve feet tall and very uncomfortable when Xitil spoke again.

"Stop."

Gan obeyed that command gladly and then concentrated on holding itself steady while the nongirl studied it.

"Amazing," she said at last. Her voice sounded distant;

Gan's ears were too attenuated to catch sounds properly. "I had no idea you could disperse yourselves that way." She cocked her head. "I can see through its hands."

Xitil chuckled. "Poor Gan. It lacks the substance to expand greatly, but it will do for your purposes. Resume your usual size, Gan."

Gan dropped back into its normal density with a sigh of relief.

"I have a job for you," she told it. "How would you like to drink a little blood?"

"I would like that," it answered honestly. "Whose?"

"A human's. She will be brought here."

Brought here? Gan's eyes grew large. This, it realized, was why Xitil had allied with the one who looked like a brown-eyed girl. Part of the reason, anyway. Xitil's games were never simple. Xitil's guest would bring a human here for Gan to . . . to . . . Gan whispered, "You wish me to possess this human, Most Feared?"

Xitil smoothed her hair over one breast with a ruby-tipped claw. "There. I knew you couldn't be entirely ignorant. You did eat old Mevroax, after all."

"And—and the human will go back to its realm?" Gan's senses were whirling. To be able to experience the human realm as a human—it would eat and drink and fuck as humans do, and see so much! So much more than it had ever been able to see or do before—

"She'd be of little use to me here. Of course she will be returned. But you will not be able to possess her immediately, Gan. She is a sensitive."

Gan's mouth opened. Just in time, it closed it again. The Most Feared must know some way to get behind a sensitive's barriers, or she would not have brought Gan here. And it was never a good idea to question her.

"Very wise, Gan." Fortunately, Xitil was amused rather than annoyed by Gan's near gaffe. Whatever she planned to do with the human, it had put her in a high good humor. "Your unvoiced thoughts are quite correct, though. Normally breaching a sensitive would present a problem, but my guest will deal with that."

Gan's gaze swung back to the brown-eyed girl. It swallowed. Xitil had earned her title of Most Feared, yes. But this one . . .

The girl smiled at it sweetly. "Don't fret, Gan. What I will use to open the human to your possession won't harm you. Demons are not subject to guilt."

Gan felt a wave of relief. That made sense. Humans, with their pesky, mysterious souls, were always vulnerable to guilt. Even sensitives could be reached that way. Not by demons, of course, but the gods specialized in souls and guilt and worship and such, didn't they?

"You will be directed by another tool of mine," the girl told it. "Xitil, with your permission . . . ?"

Xitil didn't reply, but the rocks near the girl groaned and parted, revealing another tunnel. A few minutes later, a human male stepped out. His face held the usual assortment of features—unremarkable, Gan thought, even for a human. He wore one of those suits that betokened status in the western nations of Earth and carried a black staff that matched him in height.

Gan sniffed. It was to take orders from this man? Why, he was no more prepossessing than Gan was. His energy was thin, not at all powerful.

The staff he held, however . . . Gan squinted at the length of wood, reading it more carefully. Huh. That was odd. The staff had power, but it read as empty rather than dense.

"Most High," the man whispered, his attention fixed on the girlish avatar. His eyes glowed with what Gan supposed was worship. "How may I please you?"

She smiled at him. "This little one is called Gan. It will do your bidding when you return. Gan." She turned to it, still smiling. "This is the Most Reverend Patrick Harlowe. When the time comes, he will assist you."

Gan dared a question of the brown-haired girl, borrowing the mode of address the human had used. One could never be too courteous in dealing with such as She. "May this puny one ask who I will be drinking from, Most High?"

"Her name is Lily. Lily Yu."

ONE

◥

THE Odyssey was large, crowded, and noisy. Built in the seventies, the circular restaurant with its glinting window-walls perched on a promontory by the ocean like a giant disco ball gone flat over the years.

Wedding guests filled two rooms and spilled out onto the patio, which provided a fine view of the sun going down over the western waves. In the main banquet room, music competed with the hum of conversation as couples young and old took to the dance floor. In the adjoining dining room, buffet tables were piled artfully with crackers and crudités, shrimp and smoked salmon, fruit and cheese, and bite-sized cookies. The remains of a towering wedding cake occupied a place of honor at a separate table.

Lily Yu wasn't watching the sunset or nibbling wedding cake. She was too busy trying to keep her second cousin, Freddie Chang, from stepping on her feet and wondering when she could leave.

Not for at least an hour, she decided. Not without

paying a terrible price. Her mother would know if she snuck out early.

Freddie interrupted his monologue on the iniquities of the self-employment tax to say, "You could at least try to look like you're enjoying yourself."

"Why?"

"Everyone is watching. Your mother. My mother. Everyone."

"Does that mean you aren't going to try to grope me this time?"

His chin jutted in the mulish, self-righteous way that had made her spill lemonade in his lap when he was twelve. "You don't have to be crude. Just because a guy tries to be friendly—"

"Ow!" She stopped moving.

"I didn't step on your foot."

"No, you bumped my arm. The one in the sling," she added pointedly.

He looked stricken. "I'm sorry. I'm sorry. I forgot. You shouldn't be dancing." He took her good elbow. "You need to sit down."

Freddie's habit of telling her what she needed was one of many reasons she avoided him whenever possible. It brought out the worst in her. She managed to clamp her lips together until they were off the dance floor. "Thanks for being understanding. I think I'll go graze off the buffet."

"All right. I'll fix you a plate."

"I can feed myself these days, you know."

"You've only got one good arm." He kept hold of it, too, steering her toward the dining room where the buffet was laid out.

Lily sighed. She didn't want food. She wanted to get away from Freddie. From everyone, really, but that wasn't possible, so she might as well suck it up and try to be pleasant.

"Mother tells me you've finally quit that job of yours," he said as they reached the buffet table. "I'm relieved. So is Mother. I'm sorry it took being wounded for you to see that—"

"Wait a minute." She jerked her arm out of his grip. "I didn't quit the force because I got shot."

"Whatever the reason, I'm glad you've come to your senses. Police work is dangerous and exposes you to, ah, the wrong sort of people."

Like criminals, she supposed. Or maybe he meant other police officers. "I guess your mother didn't have all the news. I'm still a cop. A fed, maybe, but still a cop."

"A fed?" He looked deeply suspicious.

"FBI. You have heard of them?" She reached for a plate.

Freddie never noticed sarcasm. His frown was thoughtful, not offended, as he piled food she didn't want on her plate. "I guess that's an improvement. You'll be dealing more with white-collar crime, not murderers and thugs."

Lily's lips twitched at the idea that FBI agents arrested a better class of criminal. She could have told him that she'd taken her only line-of-duty bullet after being re-cruited by the FBI, not before. She didn't. He'd tell his mother, who'd tell Lily's mother, who had jumped to the same conclusion—that Lily was in a safer job now.

No point in rocking that particular boat. She looked at the plate in her hand, which he'd piled with enough food for three people. "I hope this is for you. I'm allergic to shellfish."

"Oh." He glanced at the plate. "Forgot. Well, I can take it and get you another one."

"Never mind."

He didn't listen, of course. He just started filling an-other plate. "There's something I've been wanting to ask you."

"Don't go there."

He paused to frown at her. "I guess you think of yourself as taken right now. By, uh, that Turner fellow. The, uh . . ."

Pig eyes, she thought. Freddie had greedy little pig eyes. "Lupus. It's okay to come out and say it, you know. It isn't a bad word."

"I was trying to be tactful. Tell me, is it true that they—"

"Yes. Absolutely." She glanced around. Who could she use as an excuse to escape?

"You didn't let me finish!"

"Didn't I?" Ah, Beth was talking to one of Susan's doctor friends. Lily managed to catch her little sister's eye, but Beth just grinned, crossed her eyes, and then turned her back.

The rotten little rat fink. Beth always had been spoiled.

"I want you to know that I won't hold your liaison with Turner against you," Freddie announced. "I'm a fair man. What's sauce for the goose and all that. And, uh, I'm aware that his kind . . . well, they exert a certain sexual compulsion. Though I was surprised to hear that you . . . but it's not your fault."

Her gaze jerked back to him. "What the hell are you talking about?"

"Your affair with Turner. Really, Lily, I shouldn't have to repeat myself. It's only polite to listen."

"Oh, I'm listening. I just didn't think I'd heard right, since my personal life is none of your business."

"We're cousins. And one day, when you've finished your youthful experimentation—"

"I'm twenty-eight, not eighteen." She shook her head, exasperated. Once Freddie got an idea into his head, it took a sharp scalpel to get it out. "Read my lips. We are not going to get married. Not ever."

His smile was patient. Tolerant. "Your mother wants it. So does mine."

"My mother wants me to get married, period. You're

the right gender; you're Chinese; you have a good business. That works for her, but she's already married. Give it up, Freddie. You don't want to marry me. You don't even like me."

"Of course I do. I'm very fond of you. You're my cousin."

He meant it, too. Or believed it, which was almost the same. She sighed. "I agree with your mother—you *do* need to get married. Soon. Just not to me." She handed him her plate, patted his arm, and made her getaway while his hands were full.

Relatives could be the very devil sometimes.

She'd dance some more, she decided, heading for the other room. That wouldn't eliminate the possibility of nosy questions, not when so many people here felt entitled—obliged, even—to ask about her shoulder, her new lover, or her career change. But it limited their opportunities.

The DJ was playing "I Want You to Want Me," and the room was crowded. Lily stood at the edge of the dance floor tapping her foot, more in irritation than to keep time.

Freddie was not exactly the soul of insight, which made it all the more irritating that he'd put his finger on the truth. She was taken, all right. Taken over, it sometimes seemed.

Her gaze drifted across the crowded room, past cousins and strangers, acquaintances, family friends, and those newly related by marriage. It snagged on Aunt Mequi, who was dancing with Lily's father.

Mequi Leung was her mother's sister. They ran tall on that side of Lily's family, and Mequi was thin all over—thin body, thin face, and a thin smile that looked like a bandage slapped over something painful. Lily's own lips twitched. Aunt Mequi hated to look ridiculous, and Edward Yu's head barely topped his sister-in-law's shoulder.

He wouldn't be troubled by that, she knew. Her father possessed a marvelous capacity for ignoring things he considered unimportant. He was probably talking about option strike, vertical spread, and other esoterica of the broker's world.

Probably . . . but Lily couldn't know for sure. They were fifteen feet away. She couldn't hear them over the babble of other voices.

Three weeks ago, she would have been able to.

Relief mixed with a wisp of disappointment. For a while, the mate bond had made her hearing as acute as Rule's, but the effect had faded. She didn't know why it had happened in the first place, or why it had gone away. Inhumanly good hearing might have come in handy at times, but so much had changed in her life in such a short time. On the whole, she was glad one thing had reverted to normal.

Of course, it might come back.

Lily touched the small charm dangling from a gold chain around her throat. The *toltoi* was the outward emblem of all those changes, the token she'd been given when she formally accepted membership in Rule's clan. Her foot began tapping faster, losing the beat of the music altogether.

Rule thought the bond had responded to danger by blurring the lines between their separate abilities. Maybe he was right. At the time, he'd been able to draw on some of her own immunity to magic, and they had definitely been in danger. A nutty telepath had been trying to sacrifice them to her goddess.

But Rule's theory made the mate bond seem almost sentient, like some sort of psychic snake—now tightening its coils around the two of them, now loosening them. Most of all, it irritated Lily that she didn't *know*. There were entirely too many mysteries about this bond.

Maybe she'd find out soon. She had an appointment in three days to talk to the Nokolai *Rhej*—Rhej being a position or title. Rule said the woman was sort of a combination of priestess, historian, and bard. Now that Lily was clan, she was supposed to get filled in on some of the history.

She hoped this Rhej person had some answers. She had a lot of questions.

As if the shifting sea of couples hid some arcane lodestone, her gaze was drawn to one spot, near the curving wall of windows.

Rule was there.

She couldn't see him. Lily had inherited her father's lack of inches, and there were too many people between them. But she didn't have to see him to know precisely where he was. She always did, if he was close enough . . . within one hundred twenty-nine feet, to be exact. The effect became imprecise after that. Last week she'd made him test it.

That's how it was now, anyway. Three weeks ago she'd been unable to be that far away—literally unable. She'd nearly passed out when she put too much distance between them. Rule claimed that was normal for a newly mated pair.

He had some weird ideas of normal. But the bond had relaxed, just as he'd said it would. She wasn't sure how far their tether would stretch now, but she meant to find out. Soon.

The music ended, and some of the couples started to leave the floor. In the gap that opened up, Lily saw the man who'd recently moved into the center of her life. Or, according to Rule, had been shoved there by his Lady.

He'd been dancing with someone Lily didn't know. A member of the groom's family, probably, as the woman looked Chinese. She was about Lily's age, with very short hair and a sleek blue dress that set off her figure admirably.

Not a puke-green bridesmaid's dress. Lily grimaced. The mate bond made it impossible for Rule to stray, but his thoughts could still wander, couldn't they?

The woman's hand rested on Rule's arm. She was smiling in a way that was becoming all too familiar. Lily wondered if she looked like that, too, when Rule's head bent toward her the way he inclined it now, listening to his dance partner.

It was an elegant head. Its dark hair was too long for fashion, but it suited him. His face was narrow, the skin taut over cheeks that might have been sculpted by the wind. The angle of those cheekbones was mirrored by the dark slashes of his eyebrows.

He wore black, of course. He always wore black. The expensive suit covered a body that never failed to fascinate her. It seemed somehow more focused than other bodies. Watching him now, she had the fanciful thought that he attended to the world with all of him—listening with thighs and biceps as well as ears, observing with scalp and eyes and nape, with the soles of his feet and the backs of his knees.

The backs of his knees . . . she knew how his skin tasted there.

His head turned, and their eyes met.

Oh. She put a hand on her stomach. That didn't usually happen, not since the first time. But every once in a while she got this little jolt when their eyes met. Like being stroked by a feather, she thought. Startling because she felt it in a place she had no name for. A place she hadn't known could be touched.

Why did it hit sometimes and not others? She grimaced. Mate bond mystery number three hundred seventy-six.

As if he'd read her mind, the corner of his mouth kicked up. Those rakish eyebrows lifted, asking a question. She made herself smile back and shook her head: *No, I don't need you right now. I'm fine.*

"Not like that, dummy," a voice said at her elbow. "Like this."

Lily turned. Beth was making kissy faces at Rule.

Rule grinned and blew Lily's little sister a kiss.

"See?" Beth turned to her. "You have a hunk like that hanging around, you don't scowl him away."

"That was a smile, not a scowl. *This* is a scowl."

Beth studied her. "By golly, you're right. The difference isn't as obvious as it ought to be, though. What's wrong?"

"It's such a pleasure to be asked that by someone I can tell to mind her own business."

"The rellies been giving you a hard time? Rhetorical question," she added, hooking an arm through Lily's. "Of course they are. You've confounded everyone's expectations again. C'mon. Let's see if there's anywhere to hide on the patio."

It was either go with Beth or be tugged wholly off balance. Lily went. "Grandmother's holding court out there."

"Right. The buffet, then," she said, shifting course. "I'm pretty sure I could cram in more chocolate."

"You think it's a good idea for the two of us to stand next to the food? Some people have weak stomachs."

Beth glanced down at her bridesmaid's dress, a match for Lily's. "And to think I always believed Susan liked me. It's not as if she needed help to outshine me. She's done that all my life."

"Maybe she's turned color-blind." Lily's shoulder had progressed from stiff to aching. She could use it as an excuse to leave, she supposed, but her mother and the aunts might start bringing her food again. And stay to tell her all the things she should be doing differently . . . again.

"That doesn't explain Mother," Beth said darkly.

"There is no explanation for Mother. I thought you knew that." Lily reminded herself that she didn't really need to have her arm free. She wouldn't need to draw on anyone at her big sister's wedding. Odds were slim for even a fist fight.

But it was a relief when they reached the buffet and Beth let go to zero in on the sweets. "No chocolate cookies left," she said sadly and reached for a cookie shaped like a pair of wedding bells. "How long did it take Freddie to pop the question this time?"

"He's stopped proposing. He just talks about our marriage as if I've already agreed. You could have rescued me."

"I hate to interrupt a tender moment. Speaking of which, why are you avoiding Rule?"

"You can be intensely annoying, you know that?"

Beth nodded and downed the other half of the cookie. "You don't want to talk about your relationship with Tall, Dark, and Occasionally Furry. I get that. And I understand why you haven't said much about him to Mother. Who would? But you've clammed up with me, too."

Lily heard the hurt beneath the banter and gave up. "We had an argument, all right? Nothing major. I'm just not all that pleased with him at the moment."

Beth gave her a worried glance.

"Not about other women," Lily said impatiently. "If that was the problem, I wouldn't call it a minor argument, would I? And I wouldn't be making smiley faces at him."

"Right." Beth was relieved. "Of course you wouldn't. Though I don't understand why you—all right, all right, don't get huffy. Hey, there's some chocolate sauce left! Pass me one of those strawberries."

Lily knew what Beth was thinking, and why. And maybe she ought to give her sister a better explanation than she had so far . . . but not now.

"So, you going to tell me what you two argued about?"

"No. Are you still dating the octopus?"

"If you mean Bill, he's *so* last week. At least tell me if Rule is as incredible in bed as he looks like he would be."

A grin stole out. "Better."

Beth dipped her strawberry in chocolate while she thought that over, then shook her head. "Not possible, but trying to imagine it is exciting. Did you get those dark circles beneath your eyes because you keep skipping sleep in favor of hot monkey sex, then? Or is your shoulder keeping you awake? Or is something else going on?"

Lily jerked her good shoulder in a shrug. "Bad dreams. They'll pass. Are you going to eat that or make love to it?"

Beth licked more of the chocolate off the strawberry. "The two are not mutually exclusive. Considering what happened to you, bad dreams aren't surprising. *Not* that I know exactly what happened. I don't suppose you want to talk about it?"

"I'm not much for talky-talky."

"No kidding." At last Beth popped the strawberry in her mouth.

With Beth's mouth temporarily occupied, Lily's attention slipped back to the argument she and Rule had tripped over last night. He wanted her to move in with him. He'd been patient, by his lights, but she wasn't ready. She needed time to adjust to all the changes in her life. And she needed to spend some of that time alone.

He didn't get that. Nettie had told her that individual lupi, like individual humans, fell in different places along the introvert-extrovert scale. But on the whole, they needed more touch, more contact, more sheer time spent with others than the average human. The wolf was a pack animal, after all.

Strawberry disposed of, Beth asked, "Since you won't do the talky-talky thing, have you been digging?"

"Waging war on weeds. I can't use a shovel with one arm." Rule had offered to dig a bed for her at Clanhome, but that would have changed everything. She did her gardening at Grandmother's because she didn't have any land of her own, but that didn't mean . . .

"Hey!" Beth's hand passed in front of Lily's face. "Where'd you go? You're pale as a ghost."

"That's appropriate," Lily muttered.

"What?"

She shook her head. "Never mind. I saw . . . I thought I saw someone I used to know." Someone who couldn't be here.

The woman Lily knew only as Helen didn't know

Lily's family, for one thing. For another, she was dead.

"I'm guessing it wasn't someone you liked."

"No." Lily stared in the direction the woman had gone, vanished now behind a cluster of chattering teens. She'd looked exactly like Helen: tiny build, long blond hair, baby face, eyes as cold and empty as a doll's.

There she was again, heading for the exit that led to the restrooms. Lily's heart began throwing itself against the wall of her chest as if desperately seeking escape.

It was crazy to think that she'd seen Helen. Crazy. And yet . . . "I'm going to freshen up," she told her sister, moving to follow a woman who couldn't exist.

Three weeks ago, Lily had killed her.

NANCY Chen obviously enjoyed dancing, and she was good at it. She was tall enough that her steps matched Rule's well, too. She smelled of tobacco, which he didn't care for, and baby powder, which he liked. She had a lively sense of humor.

All in all, Rule would have been enjoying their dance if only she'd stop trying to grope him. "Uh-uh," he said, moving her hand back to his waist. Again.

She grinned. "Can't blame me for trying. It's not as if that pretty thing you're dating would object."

"I think you don't know Lily."

"She can't be such a fool she doesn't know about your kind. More power to her, I say, for having the guts to take you on anyway. I hear you can give a lady quite a ride." She slid him a coquettish glance . . . and slid her hand down again.

Torn between exasperation and amusement, he reclaimed the wandering hand. This time he kept a grip on it. "I suspect you've given quite a ride in your day, too," he said dryly.

Nancy Chen was eighty-two years old, the great-aunt of the groom.

She laughed. "My day isn't over. It just doesn't come as often as it used to. Get it? Doesn't *come*." She laughed again, enjoying herself.

Rule enjoyed her, too, for the remainder of the dance, because he kept her hands pinned. Nancy didn't expect him to take her propositions seriously—though he suspected that, given an ounce of encouragement, she'd have happily hunted up a closet for them to duck into. Mostly, though, she was getting a kick out of being outrageous.

Some women reacted that way. They went a little giddy over the chance to step outside the normal bonds of society with someone who lived outside them. He was used to that, as he was used to the whiff of fear-scent most people gave off when they met him. But both could be wearying.

He wanted Lily. And she was avoiding him.

Rule made his way around the edges of the banquet room, exerting all his tact to avoid dancing with yet another woman who wasn't Lily. The air was ripe with scent—food, flowers, candles, humanity, and a faint note of ocean. But he didn't pick up Lily's scent, or the tug that would tell him where she was.

The directional aspect of the mate bond wasn't as obvious for him as it was for her—another of the mysteries that so plagued her. When they'd discovered this during her little test last week, he'd suggested that she was simply more attuned to the immaterial than he was because of her Gift.

Lily had shaken her head in disgust. "That's not an explanation. That's substituting one question mark for another."

A smile twitched at Rule's mouth as he headed for the other room. His *nadia* did not approve of the inexplicable.

He wove through the crowd, looking for a small, slender woman with hair the color of night, skin like cream poured over apricots . . . and a dress the color of mold. His smile widened. Truer love hath no sister than to wear such a gown.

Still no Lily. Rule paused. She wasn't happy with him right now. Tough. He wasn't too happy with her, either. She had no business being back on full duty. She wasn't healed yet, dammit, and why her superiors couldn't see that, he couldn't fathom. But she wouldn't have—

"Rule." The smooth, feminine voice was newly familiar. He turned to see Lily's mother beckoning him.

Julia Yu was a tall, elegant woman with beautiful hands, very little chin, and Lily's eyes set beneath eyebrows plucked to crispness. She stood with two women about her age—one Anglo, one Chinese, both intensely curious about him and trying not to show it.

Rule repressed a sigh. He'd been glad of the chance this wedding offered to become acquainted with Lily's people. They were part of her, after all, and he was endlessly curious about her. Last night he'd met her parents at the rehearsal dinner, with mixed results. They'd both been very polite, but neither of them approved of him. Her father was reserving judgment, he thought. Her mother liked him, didn't want to, and wished he would go away.

It was Lily he wanted now, though. He was tired of the curiosity, the fear, the speculation. He might be used to being on exhibit, but it was different this time. Personal. *Look, everyone, see what followed Lily home. It walks and talks just like a real person.*

But after the briefest of introductions, Julia Yu excused herself to the others and took Rule aside. She'd tucked a frown between those crisp eyebrows. "Have you seen Lily?"

His own brows lifted in surprise. "I was just looking for her."

"Tch! I'm being silly." She shook her head. "It's Beth's fault, putting ideas in my head, and I've been so busy . . . you have no idea what it is to put on a wedding like this."

Worry bit down low in his stomach. He replied with automatic courtesy. "You've done a magnificent job. The wedding was beautiful, as is the reception. But what ideas did Beth put in your head?"

"Such a silly story! Of course she was imagining things. Beth is very imaginative." It was impossible to tell if she meant that as a compliment or criticism of her youngest daughter. The frown hadn't budged. "I paid it no heed at all."

"What kind of story?"

"She said she saw Lily go into the ladies' room and followed her. They haven't had much opportunity to talk lately, you know, so I suppose . . . but Lily wasn't there." Julia's lips pursed. "Beth swears Lily could not have left without her seeing, but that's nonsense."

It had to be. Didn't it?

Rule stood stock still for a moment. Lily wasn't far. He *knew* that. But he hadn't been able to find her, and the world wasn't as sane and orderly as it appeared. The realms were shifting.

And three weeks ago, Lily had pissed off a goddess.

"I'll find her." He turned away, moving quickly, propelled by an urgency he knew was foolish.

The last place she'd been seen was the ladies' room, so that's where he headed. The restrooms lay off the hall that connected the private dining rooms to the public part of the restaurant. A knot of unhappy women had collected outside the ladies' room. He picked up snatches of conversation.

". . . anyone sent for the manager?"

"Is there another one?"

"Plenty of stalls, no need to lock the door."

". . . some kind of sadist, if you ask me!"

Someone had locked the door to the ladies' room. Rule's mouth went dry. He eased his way through the women, using his size, his smile, and, after a moment, their recognition to part them. "Excuse me, ladies. Pardon me. No, I'm not the manager, but if you'll step aside . . ."

"Shannon," one of them whispered to another, "You dummy! That's the Nokolai prince!"

That silenced them for a moment. "I think I can fix this if you'll . . . thank you," he said as the last one moved away. An odd, faint odor hung in the air near the door. He bent closer to sniff, but he couldn't identify it.

Lily was on the other side. He felt her nearness as a slow stir beneath his breastbone. Heart hammering, he rapped on the door. Hollow core.

"That won't work!" one of the women snapped. "You think we haven't tried knocking?"

The knob turned, but the door didn't budge. Bolted on the other side, he judged.

"We tried opening it, too," the woman said sarcastically.

Rule put his fist through the door.

Wood splintered. Someone shrieked. He reached through the hole he'd made and found the bolt. His blood made it slippery, but he gripped it hard and yanked. He shoved the door open.

Lily lay on her back by the sinks. She wasn't moving.

TWO

"**AND** why," Rule asked with strained patience, "Did you send the EMTs away?"

Lily sat in the middle of the restroom floor in a puddle of muddy green chiffon, petting the white tiles. In the hall by the door, a uniformed officer kept out the curious and the concerned while his partner took statements.

Rule sat on the floor, too—over against the wall, well away from Lily so he wouldn't mess up the traces left by her attacker.

She frowned at the floor as if someone had written an unwelcome message there in invisible ink. "They wanted to take me to the hospital."

He stared at the heart of his heart, the one woman in the world for him . . . the pigheaded, my-way-or-the-highway idiot who'd refused medical treatment. "Imagine that. What were they thinking?"

Her lips twitched. At last she looked away from the fascinating floor. "I'll go later. My sore head is evidence of a sort, but I really am okay. Unlike you, I didn't lose any blood—"

"You opened your wound."

"But it barely bled, and I'm already stuffed full of antibiotics. My sister checked me out."

"Yes, and said you probably had a concussion—"

"A *slight* concussion."

"—and should go to the emergency room and let them run tests."

"Which would confirm that my head hurts, after which they'd tell me to rest. I'm resting."

"You're conducting a bloody be-damned investigation!"

"I don't have much time before the S.O.C. crew gets here."

"You're speaking acronym again."

She rolled her eyes. "Scene-of-crime crew. I wanted to check things out before they show up. Or Karonski." She frowned at the floor one last time, and then held out her hand. "I've learned all I can. Help me up?"

He rose swiftly, crossed to her, and took her hand. With one gentle tug she was on her feet and in his arms. He nuzzled her hair. Her scent reached inside him, easing him away from anger.

Which left the fear standing alone. He drew a shaky breath. "Dammit, Lily. Your face is the color of sweaty gym socks."

"I'm so glad you told me that." But she leaned into him, letting him have the warmth and weight of her—the prickle of arousal and the comfort of connection. He knew she drew strength from the contact, too. She'd come that far in accepting the mate bond. She no longer denied them this out of fear her needs would swallow her.

But she wouldn't live with him. That, Rule promised himself, would change. After this attack, even Lily couldn't continue to insist on warping both of their lives to conform to some notion of autonomy.

"The uniform is staring at us," she muttered.

"Mmm." The uniform, as she put it, was not happy about having a lupus on the scene. The man's first impulse had been to arrest Rule on general principles. Dissuaded from that, he'd wanted to remove Rule from the crime scene.

Reasonable enough, from a cop's point of view, Rule supposed. But he wasn't leaving Lily. Eventually the officer had accepted that, though it was a toss-up whether it was Lily's newly minted federal badge, her past status as a homicide cop, or Rule's simple refusal to leave that had prevailed.

He rubbed his cheek against her hair, trying to breathe her in. And paused. "You smell funny."

"Hey." She leaned away. "No more cracks about sweaty socks."

"Not that kind of funny." Rule bent, sniffing down her shoulder and along the sling that held her left arm, where the scent was strongest.

"Could you try to be a little less weird?"

"Picture me wagging my tail, and this will seem more natural." He inhaled deeply, trying to sort the odd scent from all the others. "I can't place it," he said, straightening. "Not in this form."

"Maybe you're smelling whatever left the traces I felt on the floor."

Lily was a touch sensitive, perhaps the rarest of the Gifts, and an unusually strong one. She couldn't be affected by magic, but she could feel it, even the slight traces left by the passage of supernatural beings. His eyebrows lifted. "What did you feel?"

"It was odd. Sort of . . . orange."

"Which tells me little."

"Doesn't tell me much, either." She shook her head. "Magic feels like a texture, not a color, yet this . . . I can't explain it. I've never felt anything like it before."

She looked troubled, but Rule felt relief. "It didn't feel like that damned staff, then."

Before she could respond, they were interrupted.

"Sorry, ma'am, you can't go in there."

That was the officer by the door. A familiar feminine

voice replied with a stream of Chinese, followed by another familiar voice—Julia Yu. "I told you they wouldn't
let you in. If they won't let her own mother in, they won't
make an exception for her grandmother."

Lily sighed and pulled away. "Grandmother, don't
curse the man for doing his duty."

"I curse who I curse. You will come out now."

The old woman standing on the other side of the burly
officer was less than five feet tall. Her dress was red,
ankle-length, and Oriental style. Black hair striped with
silver was drawn up in a knot secured with twin enameled
picks, and the ring on one finger held a cabochon ruby.
Despite her years, she had a spine like a sapling, supple
and erect, and the hauteur of a queen.

Rule couldn't look at Madame Li Lei Yu without
thinking of a cat. She knew she was in charge, whatever
the idiots around her might think. Right now, she was a
cat who wanted a door opened. Immediately.

Lily gave Rule a wry glance and left the restroom. He
followed.

At the west end of the hall another officer was talking
with one of the women who'd complained about the
locked restroom door. Food smells drifted in from the
nearby kitchen, and the sounds of diners in the public part
of the restaurant competed with the hum from the rooms
occupied by the wedding party.

Here, under the suspicious eyes of the patrol cop,
three women made a triangle, with the oldest and smallest of them at its apex. Julia Yu—the one in the middle—
touched her daughter's shoulder, looking anxious. Lily
gave her a reassuring smile and turned to her grandmother. "I'm here, as instructed."

"Ha! You do not fool me. You come because you are
ready to come."

Two pairs of black eyes met—one wrapped in wrinkles, one surrounded by smooth young skin. The two
women were almost of equal height. Alike in other ways,

too, some of them visible. "You don't want me to neglect my duty," Lily said.

"Pert," her grandmother announced. "Always you are pert." She cupped Lily's cheek. The skin on the back of her hand was as fine and soft as tissue laid over the strict architecture of bone and tendon. Her nails were red and beautifully tended. "You are well, child?"

Lily smiled into that cupped hand. "Aside from the little guy hammering on my skull from the inside, yes."

"Then reassure your mother. She worries."

Julia Yu was indignant. "You were the one who insisted on coming to see for yourself that she was all right. You wouldn't take my word for it. Or Susan's, and she's a doctor."

Madame Yu ignored that, dropping her hand and turning to Rule. "You do not greet me."

"I but await my opportunity." He bent and kissed one whisper-soft cheek.

Her eyebrows shot up. "You flirt with your lover's grandmother?"

"I flirt with *you,* Madame. It is irresistible."

"Good. I like flattery when it is done well. Tell your peculiar friend I wish to see him."

"Ah . . . which peculiar friend would that be?"

She chuckled. "You have so many, eh? The beautiful one."

"She means Cullen," Lily said dryly.

Of course she did. Rule eyed the old woman, wondering if he wanted to know why she wished to see Cullen. Probably not, he decided. "I'll give you his phone number, but he doesn't always answer it."

"I dislike telephones. You tell him come see me when I return."

"Return?" Julia Yu frowned. "What are you talking about? You aren't going anywhere. You don't like to travel."

"Tomorrow I get on an airplane. I fly to China."

In the sudden silence, Rule looked at the faces of the three women. Julia Yu was shocked. Madame Yu was obviously enjoying her daughter-in-law's reaction. And Lily . . . her distress was plain, at least to him. It showed in her stillness, her lack of expression, the change in her scent.

He moved closer to her. "This wasn't a sudden decision," he told the old woman grimly. "You can't get a visa for China overnight."

"Can I not?" Her expression suggested he'd fallen from grace. She shrugged and spoke to her granddaughter. "For years, I have thought of such a trip. I am many years now in America. There are people and places in China I would see again before I die. Or they do."

"You've talked about a trip," Lily said, "but you never made plans. Why now?"

"I am an old woman. I am reminded of this recently."

The unexpected wryness in Grandmother's voice made Rule think she referred to the battle two weeks ago—one involving a number of armed Azá, himself, Cullen, Lily, a handful of FBI agents, several wolves, . . . and one very large tiger.

Madame Li Lei Yu hadn't seemed like an old woman to him at the time.

Lily had herself back under control. "Li Quin will go with you?"

"She, too, has people and places to see. My gardens—" She broke off, turning as Rule did toward the east end of the hall.

Rule knew who was coming by the sound of the footsteps. A moment later the man appeared around the bend in the hall: Abel Karonski, sometime friend, full-time FBI agent, part of a special unit of the Magical Crimes Division. And witch. The satchel he carried wouldn't hold file folders or a change of clothes.

But the person with Abel wasn't his partner, Martin Croft. Instead the agent was accompanied by a long, lanky woman with a butch-crop of silvery blond hair, half a dozen earrings in each ear, a badly fitted gray suit, and deep-set eyes the color of old whiskey.

Most people wouldn't notice the eyes. Not at first. All they'd see were the tattoos.

"Cynna!" Rule exclaimed.

Her mouth tilted up between the indigo whorls looping from cheeks to chin. "Hey, Rule. Fancy meeting me here, huh?"

"**YOU'VE** added a few," Rule said, pulling out a chair.

After a brief confusion, Lily, Rule, Karonski, and the unexpected addition to their task force had adjourned to the restaurant's smallest private dining room. It held one table, six chairs, and a coffee pot.

"More than a few, but some of 'em don't show in polite company." The woman's grin rearranged the designs on her cheeks. "Damn, you look good. Haven't changed a bit. Maybe you'd like to check out some of my new tattoos later."

Lily sat in the chair Rule was holding. She supposed she'd better get used to women propositioning Rule. It was going to happen.

Karonski put down his satchel, pulled out one of the chairs, and sat. "Dammit, Cynna, I told you—"

"And I told you that was bullshit. Rule's a lupus."

"Ah, Cynna." Rule's smile held a definite tinge of regret. "As delightful as such a study would be, I must decline. I'm not available."

The woman's eyebrows went up. She looked at Lily, her expression hard to read behind all the tattoos. But she didn't look friendly.

Lily decided her head hurt too much to figure out how to handle this blast from Rule's past. She knew how she felt about it, though. Pissed. But who was she supposed to be angry with?

Karonski, maybe, for springing Cynna Weaver on her like this. She'd wondered if Weaver was here to execute an AG warrant—in effect, an order of execution signed by the U.S. attorney general. The FBI's temporary director was pushing for one, though so far the attorney general wasn't buying. No surprise there. The political fallout could be huge, since AG warrants had traditionally only been issued against nonhumans.

Like lupi.

But Karonski had assured her Weaver was part of the unit. She was here to help find Harlowe, not to kill him. Lily turned to him. "What exactly did you tell her about Rule and me?"

"That she's to behave. Rule's taken." He looked around. "Didn't someone say something about coffee?"

Lily would have smiled if her head hadn't hurt so much. Karonski was an overfed white male with a severe wardrobe impairment, the stubbornness to outlast a jackass, and a firm belief in the power of caffeine. He was also her boss. "Sure. It's right there. Get me a cup, too."

He heaved a sigh and went after his version of life support.

Their little haven had originally been intended for the use of business types. With cops everywhere, the suits hadn't thought this was a good time to discuss a merger or acquisition or whatever, so Karonski had commandeered the room and the coffee. While the four of them conferred, the S.O.C. team was going through their routine—they'd arrived on Karonski's heels—and other local cops took the names and addresses of everyone in the restaurant.

This included the entire wedding party, much to her mother's distress. Susan and her new husband had been allowed to leave—the only ones, so far, to receive permission. Lily's parents were trying to soothe their guests, and Grandmother had summoned Li Quin to take her home. The local cops would try to stop her, of course, but Lily was putting her money on Grandmother.

It was weird, sitting on this side of the local-federal fence. "So Croft's in Virginia already?" Lily referred to Karonski's partner.

"On his way. It's a major outbreak, the biggest in decades."

"Any fatalities?"

"Two confirmed. The nasty little shits caused a major pileup on the interstate by riding a trucker's windshield." He brought two full mugs back to the table with him. Today's suit was brown, wrinkled, and missing a button. His tie suggested he'd had something with ketchup for lunch. "Here."

"Thanks." Lily wrapped her hands around the steaming mug and took a sip. Caffeine had analgesic properties, right? It was bound to help.

"What about you?" Rule asked the agent. "You're leaving, too?"

"I'll be heading there as soon as I've got things lined out here."

"I don't know much about imps. They've always been rare on this coast. Were they summoned?"

"No one summons imps on purpose. They can't be controlled. But a poorly executed spell can call them up instead of a demon, and most summoning spells suck. That's one thing lost during the Purge that I hope we never rediscover." Karonski took a sip of coffee, sighed with pleasure, and added, "More often, though, imps bleed through some weak place between the realms. We don't know why. Not usually in such numbers, though."

"Hell's restless lately," Cynna commented.

Lily looked at her. "You would know about that?"

"Not directly. I'm righteous these days. But I hear things."

Lily knew that the section of the FBI's Magical Crimes Division called the Unit was more flexible than the rest of the Bureau about any less-than-respectable skills its agents possessed. They had to be open-minded. The Unit couldn't function without the Gifted—witness her own hasty recruitment. And over the years, the Gifted had found different paths for their talents, paths often cloaked in secrecy. The Purge had put an end to making such explorations openly.

But a Dizzy who worked for the FBI?

"All right," Karonski said, "I've got a plane to catch, and Lily here has to go get her head examined—yes, that is an order," he said directly to her. "So let's make it quick. What happened?"

"I saw Helen."

Karonski spilled his coffee. "You're worrying me."

"It wasn't really Helen. I know that. But I'm not talking about a resemblance, either. This woman looked exactly like her—body, face, hair, everything was exactly the same."

Karonski frowned. "A twin?"

"That was one possibility. Or she was an illusion. Or I was going nuts. I didn't think I was crazy, but I couldn't see any way to prove or disprove that right away. The other two possibilities meant she'd been planted to get my attention or Rule's. Since I knew it wasn't an illusion—"

"Wait a minute," Cynna said. "How could you know that?"

Lily raised her eyebrows at Karonski.

"Cynna just flew in. I hit the high points on the way here, but she doesn't know much more than she read in the papers after the big raid."

Okay, so Lily had to explain herself—something she wasn't used to doing. Until last month, she could have counted on the fingers of one hand the number of people who knew about her Gift. "I can be fooled, but not by magic. I'm a sensitive."

Cynna's lips pursed as if she'd bitten into something sour. "A sensitive."

"I never outed people." It was a refrain Lily had used a lot lately. Too often, sensitives had been used by witch hunters both official and otherwise to sniff out the Gifted or those of the Blood. Most of that was in the past . . . but not very far in the past. "It came in handy sometimes in my work, but I was with homicide, not the X-Squad. You going to have a problem working with me?"

"I can handle it. Think you can handle working with me?"

"Let's see." Lily held out her hand.

To her credit, Weaver didn't hesitate to offer a quick, businesslike shake. Then she cocked her head to one side. "So what did you pick up about me?"

"Not about you. I'm no empath. I read magic, not people." She took a moment to gather her impressions from the brief contact. "You've a strong Gift," she said at last. "And complex, like lots of fingerprints on top of each other. I haven't run across your brand of magic before."

Weaver showed her teeth in a smile. "There aren't many like me around."

Rule shifted in his chair. "Let's get back to this woman who looked like Helen. It wouldn't be hard for an uninvited guest to crash the party."

"No. But how did she know there was a party to crash?"

"That's rather my point. You suspected she'd been planted to get your attention. That meant they'd learned enough about you to get her here, at your sister's wedding. So naturally you followed her." His fingers drummed once. "Did it occur to you she might be bait?"

"Of course she was bait. That didn't mean I could ignore her. Harlowe's still missing. So's that damned staff. This Helen look-alike had to be connected to him, it, or both, and someone knew enough to send her to my sister's wedding. What was I supposed to do—let that link walk away?"

"You could have come to me for backup."

"If I'd hunted you up, I could have lost her."

"You lost her anyway."

Because that was patently true, she didn't argue. "Maybe I miscalled it, but I'm the only one who can't be affected by that staff, and I didn't want to take the chance. If it had been there . . ." She started to shake her head, winced, and turned to Karonski. "She went to the ladies' room, I followed, and that's the last I know. Something clobbered me as soon as I stepped inside."

"And locked you in there," Rule said. "Then vanished."

Karonski's forehead knitted. "What do you mean?"

"The restrooms are in the middle of the building. No windows. No way in or out except through that one door—and it was bolted on the inside."

"Get real," Cynna said. "A locked room mystery?"

Lily was tired, hurting, and—if she was honest with herself—scared. They'd struck at her in the midst of her family. How had they known where and when to find her? "Are those tattoos for show, or do you actually know something about magic?"

"I know enough to not buy into vanishing villains. Invisibility was impossible before the Purge. It sure hasn't become possible now."

"The bolt," Lily snapped. "Whoever knocked me out didn't have to disappear. She just had to spell the bolt into moving from the other side of the door."

Cynna's mouth opened—and closed. She grimaced. "My stupid. Sorry."

Anger was not good for concussions. Even minor ones. The throbbing increased, bringing on a wave of nausea. Lily rode out the wave, then said, "We need to—hey!"

Rule had pulled her chair back from the table. "You've played macho cop long enough. We'll be going now. Abel, good to see you again. Cynna, you, too."

"Wait just one minute." But when that gentle, inexorable hand propelled Lily to her feet, the room hit the spin cycle. She closed her eyes and waited for it to firm up again. "Okay, okay. I'll even let you drive."

"The ambulance crew is still here. I told them to wait."

Her eyes snapped open so she could glare at him. He smiled and slid an arm around her waist.

"You're going to the ER, Yu," Karonski said. "Don't be a baby about it."

"I said I'd go." Pride wouldn't let her lean against Rule, but it was tempting. As much as she hated to admit it, determination had about run its limit in keeping her upright. "But this is not an emergency. I don't need to tie up an ambulance."

"They're here. Might as well make use of them. Be sure your phone's turned on, and I'll let you know what Cynna and I find out before I leave."

"You're flying to Virginia tonight?" Lily tried to hide her distress. She was a very new FBI agent. She might know how to conduct an investigation, but she didn't know FBI procedures and resources.

He grunted an affirmative. "I don't know how long we'll be gone. Imps aren't hard to deal with, but there's a lot of them and we have to figure out how they got loose. If there's a leak, I'll have to close it."

"You can do that?" Rule asked.

"Piece of cake." He grinned. "Pretty fancy cake, maybe. I might even need a little help. In the meantime, Lily and Cynna will be handling the hunt for Harlow and that staff. Lily, you've got authority to call on the local office as needed. Cynna, you have seniority—"

She snorted. "As if I cared about that shit."

"No, you're a damned loose cannon. Like I was about to say, you've got seniority, but you're not in charge. This is Yu's investigation. You're to assist."

She was leaning, dammit. Lily forced herself to straighten. "You call it my investigation, but you brought someone in without telling me."

"Blame Ruben. He had one of his notions yesterday. Says he thinks you'll need her soon."

Ruben Brooks was the head of the Unit. He was also

an amazingly accurate precog. When he got hit by a notion, it paid to listen.

Lily turned her head to look at Ruben's latest notion—the woman whose body had been covered, inch by painful inch, with impossibly intricate patterns of power.

Or that was the idea, anyway. The Dizzies had been a big deal on the street about a decade ago, a quasi-religious group based on poorly understood African shamanistic practices. Most of them had been black, connected to gangs, and without enough of a Gift to cause much trouble—or to keep the movement going. It had pretty much died out when it became obvious the leaders couldn't deliver on their promises of power.

Beneath the inky tattoos, Cynna Weaver's skin was white. Lily assumed she was an exception in more than pigmentation. The Unit wouldn't have signed her up if she were as ineffective as other Dizzies. "So how are you going to assist the investigation?"

"I'm a Finder." She bared her teeth in a hunter's grin. "You get me something to work with, and I'll find that Harlowe bastard for you."

Shit. "That may be a problem. His house burned down two days ago."

THREE

CYNNA watched Rule hustle his pretty little cop out the door. He was so careful about her, and it was so unnecessary. That one was tougher than she looked.

She remembered when Rule had been all careful like that with another female who'd insisted she didn't need any man looking out for her.

Her mouth twisted wryly. Such a prickly little shit she'd been! Twenty going on twelve, street smart and cocky and scared of all the wrong things. But no matter how much she'd insisted she didn't want to be coddled, Rule had known better. And she'd eaten it up, hadn't she? Hoarded the memory of him, too, all these years. Rule's caring had fed the hungry child she'd been back then.

Well, she wasn't that hungry brat anymore. So maybe she was disappointed that he was taken. She'd get over it. She turned to Karonski. "So what the hell am I doing here? I can't find Harlowe without sorting his pattern, and I can't sort without something of his to sort from."

He shrugged. "Blame Ruben. He thinks it's a good idea for you to be around."

"And doesn't know why, I suppose."

"Does he ever?"

She shook her head. "Pretty big coincidence, Harlowe's house burning down right before I arrived. How'd it happen?"

"Someone doused the bushes with gasoline."

"Huh. Think the bad guys have a precog, too?"

"Maybe. Or else they were just being careful, and the timing really is coincidence." Karonski pushed back his chair and grabbed his mug. "Come on. Let's go hassle the locals. I'd like to run a diagnostic on that bolt and find out for sure if it was shifted magically."

She stood, too. "Nothing I like better than hassling a few cops."

"You *are* a cop."

"Weird, isn't it?"

Their little dining room opened onto the main dining room. The Odyssey's patrons were still being interviewed by the local cops; from snippets Cynna overheard as they made their way to the back, some were excited about their proximity to a crime, some worried, some angry. The poor waitresses and waiters were still trying to deliver food, but no one was much interested in the meal they'd come here for.

The place must do a lot of private party business, Cynna thought as they made their way through the crowded dining room. The public dining area occupied only about half of the donut. The rest was all private rooms.

The restrooms were in the center of the donut, off the hall that circled the kitchens at the center. A uniformed cop stopped them just inside that hall. Karonski's badge persuaded him they could be allowed to advance to the next sentry, a tired-looking woman in front of the ladies' room. The sound of a hand-vac inside announced that the crime scene techs were still busy, and a quick exchange brought an estimate of fifteen minutes before they'd let the feds have the scene.

She and Abel moved down the hall a short distance to wait. Cynna leaned against the wall and crossed her arms. "That's a lot of hullabaloo for a simple knock on the head."

"Assault on a federal officer in connection with her investigation is a big deal. Try to remember that you're important now."

Cynna just shook her head. She didn't feel like a federal officer, for all that she'd been with the unit five years now. Most of her fellow agents would say she didn't act like one, either. "So who is this Helen Yu thought she saw?"

Karonski took a healthy swallow of his coffee. "She *was* a telepath. She's dead now."

Cynna's eyebrows shot up. "The one who wanted to open a gate to hell?"

"That's her."

Cynna considered what little she knew. The dead woman and Patrick Harlowe had belonged to the Church of the Redeemed, also known as the Azá. Some of those involved in the hell-raising scheme had been true believers; others had been magically bound to the cause with the help of a mysterious staff Helen had wielded. With it, she'd been able to control minds.

Which, of course, was impossible. Or so everyone had always said.

Three weeks ago the Azá, led by Helen and Harlowe, had taken Rule and Lily Yu captive. Somehow they'd managed to turn the tables on their captors, but Harlowe had gotten away. And the staff had vanished. "Seems like the staff should be our primary target."

"We know a fair amount about Harlowe, next to nothing about the staff. Hard to track a piece of wood." He sipped his coffee, watching the activity inside the restroom. "Seabourne tried, right after the staff went missing. Couldn't do it."

"That's the one you told me about. The sorcerer."

Karonski chuckled. "Your skepticism's showing."

"Well, Jesus, Abel, there haven't been any sorcerers

since the Purge! Not real ones, anyway. A few wannabes who know just enough to get in trouble."

"Seabourne's for real, though what he can do is limited."

She tipped her head to one side. "Sorcery's still illegal, last I heard."

He snorted. "And I know how that troubles your conscience."

"It's important to be flexible. Is this guy working for us?"

"Hey, sorcery's illegal. He can't work for us." Karonski grinned. "Call him a friend of a friend. Turner and Yu wouldn't have stopped Helen without him."

"It was the China doll who offed her, though, right?"

"Yep. And if you call her that to her face, I want to be there." Karonski set his empty mug on the floor, pulled a mint from his pocket, unwrapped it, and popped it in his mouth. "So where do you know Turner from?"

"Oh, me and Rule go way back. All the way back to before you arrested me." She grinned. "I was just a big bite of mean back then, all attitude and no sense."

"And you're different now in what way?"

"Smart-ass." She shook her head. "Lord, but seeing him does bring back memories. I used to hang out at a place called Mole's in Chicago. Wonder if it's still around?"

"You met Turner there?"

She nodded. "We hooked up for a while." Now, there was a nice, low-key way to refer to someone who changed your life. "What's this deal about him being unavailable, anyway?"

"None of your business."

"Yeah, but it doesn't make sense. Lupi don't do the faithful bit."

"Rule is. Leave it alone."

He hadn't been when she knew him. He'd made that clear up front, and she'd accepted it. In that respect he hadn't seemed much different from the other men she knew, just more honest . . . but she hadn't exactly hung with a stellar crowd back then.

That was thirteen years ago. Jesus. Hard to believe in some ways . . . and in others, it seemed like a couple lifetimes ago. He would have changed since she'd known him, but this one was a real one-eighty. Sexually open relationships were a moral must for lupi. Something to do with their religion, she thought.

How had the China doll gotten him to change his mind about something that really mattered to him? Not by playing the fragile femme. She might look the part to someone who wasn't paying attention, but Rule paid attention. That was one of—

"Looks like they're about finished," Karonski said, picking up his satchel. "It'll take me a while to get set up. You want to check it out your way while I set my wards?"

"Sure." She straightened and followed him.

Karonski was Wiccan, and Wiccan spells were considered the gold standard. In certain carefully circumscribed situations, what he learned was admissible as evidence in court. But his methods did take a while. According to the authorities, Cynna's spells were unreliable because the accuracy depended on the skill of the caster.

But she was one hell of a Finder. One hell of a lot faster than Karonski's methods, too. Cynna had her head cleared and her energy focused on the serpent maze on her left arm by the time they reached the door to the restroom. While Karonski got rid of the local representatives of officialdom, she started the spell moving through the maze.

Finding was her Gift. She didn't need spells for that. But to be any good as a Finder, she had to able to sort, to find the patterns of things and people. That's what most of the spells inscribed on her body were for—sorting the energy she detected so she could Find its source.

When Karonski gave her a nod, she stepped inside the restroom, turned, and held her hand over the bolt. Energy zipped from her hand to the bolt and bounced back, altered, to slither along the paths of her skin and burn a new design on her upper right thigh.

She dropped her hand, staring at the bolt. "Holy shit."

LILY sat on the examination table with her head pounding and her eyes closed. Her "room" was a curtained alcove that offered all the sketchy privacy of a hospital gown—an indignity she'd been spared so far, though it might have been more flattering than her bridesmaid's dress. Nearby a baby was crying the thin, monotonous wail of exhaustion. The air stank of disinfectant and less obvious odors.

Down the hall a woman was cursing some man. On the other side of the curtain a monitor beeped relentlessly. Lily turned her head. "What does it smell like in here to you?"

"Pain."

Rule sat on the table with her. She'd temporarily abandoned her "don't lean" policy and was glad of the support of his arm and body.

Funny. The way she was snuggled up against him left her good arm pretty much useless, but that didn't make her uneasy. Was that the effect of the mate bond, making her feel safe whether she was or not? Or was she just too tired and sore to care? "And yet you insisted on bringing me here."

She felt his smile in the way his cheek moved against her hair. "Pushed you around while you were temporarily weakened."

"Damn right, you did." There were a few good things about his height, she decided. It put his shoulder at just the right level for her to rest her aching head.

Lily felt guilty over how much she appreciated her parents' absence. Her mother's hovering and need to take charge would have driven her crazy. She'd persuaded them that the trip to the ER was a formality, necessary for insurance purposes. Grandmother, as expected, had left by the time Rule hustled Lily off to the ER, but she wouldn't have been a problem anyway. Grandmother didn't do hospitals.

"Watch it," Lily said. "We aren't exactly private here."

Rule's hand had slid up her rib cage, and his thumb was stroking slowly along the underside of her breast. "I don't know what you're talking about."

"I told you once before: you don't do innocent well." But there was no heat in her voice. Pleasure rose in drowsy waves, stirred by the movement of his thumb, by his simple nearness. Her eyelids drooped. "How can I feel like this when my head hurts?"

He bent and ran his tongue slowly around the curve of her ear. "I don't know. How are you feeling?"

"Distracted."

"Good."

The woman down the hall was yelling about a suitcase now. Someone had stolen it, and they'd better give it back right now.

Lily sighed and straightened. "I hope Nettie gets here soon."

Nettie was Dr. Two Horses, a trained shaman as well as a Harvard-educated physician. She was connected to Rule's clan in some way. Nettie wasn't a lupus herself, of course, because lupi were always male. But their children came in both sexes.

"You're worrying me," Rule said.

"What do you mean?"

"You haven't once complained about my calling her. After all the grief you gave me over my interfering ways with the ambulance crew, I'd expected at least a minor hissy fit."

"I don't like hospitals. I do like Nettie. I guess there are some perks to being involved with a prince. Nettie would be one."

Rule grimaced. He wasn't fond of the press's habit of calling him "the Nokolai prince." He was heir or Lu Nuncio for his clan, but the position didn't really equate with the human version of royalty. "Nettie isn't treating you because of me. She'd have come for any clan member."

"Oh. Right." Lily sometimes forgot that she was clan now. So far, that particular change hadn't had much effect on her life, though the adoption ceremony had been moving. "You know what's weird?"

"All sorts of things lately. From your point of view, that would include me, the mate bond—"

She nudged him with her good shoulder. "Not you. I'm talking about the fact that I'm still alive."

His arm tightened around her. "*Weird* isn't the word I'd use."

"I'm not complaining, but think about it. Someone went to a lot of trouble to get me alone. So what did they do when their plan worked? Bonked me on the head and left, locking the door behind them. Doesn't make sense."

"They must have been interrupted."

"There was a bolt on the door, remember? And that's another thing. Why was there a bolt on the door? I've seen bolts on restrooms in convenience stores or gas stations, but in a restaurant?"

"You think your Helen look-alike brought it with her?"

"Maybe." She frowned. "I wish O'Brien had been running the S.O.C. team. I know he'd catch it if the bolt had been . . . what is it?"

He'd turned to the right, head up, but his body stayed loose. Whatever he'd sensed, it wasn't a threat. "Nettie's here."

Had he heard Nettie or smelled her? Must be hearing, she decided. Rule wouldn't be able to pick out a single scent in the soup of the ER, not in this form . . . would he? "Good. She can tell you I'm okay, and we can go home."

A tall woman pushed back the curtain. Her skin was smooth and coppery; her hair was gray, frizzy, and abundant. The knot she'd made of it at her nape looked ready to unravel at any moment, and her wide mouth looked ready to smile. "You'll have to indulge me first. Professional pride insists that I poke at my patients before I agree with them."

Some of the tension eased from Lily's shoulders. "Hey, you're wearing a lab coat."

"It goes with the stethoscope. For some reason everyone wants to see my credentials if I show up in shorts and an athletic bra." Nettie, like most of the residents of Clanhome, generally wore as little as possible. She came up to the table. "How are you feeling?"

"Tired. Sore. Ready to leave."

"Mmm." Nettie asked a number of questions as she went through the usual medical rituals, checking Lily's chart and shining a light in her eyes. But not all of her examination methods were taught at Harvard.

"I sometimes wonder how anyone gets better in a hospital." She lit a smudging stick, let it burn a moment, and then waved out the flame. A wisp of smoke trailed up from the bundle of herbs. "The energy's always muddy as hell. Can you stand up for a minute?"

"Sure." Lily slipped off the table. Nettie chanted softly as she circled Lily, an eerie sound that did not go with her lab coat at all, using a large feather to waft the smoke toward Lily. The smoldering sage gave off a crisp, clean scent. By the time she'd made three circuits, Lily could have sworn her head didn't hurt as much. "Did you actually do something, or do I feel better because I think you did something?"

Nettie chuckled. "Does it matter? You can sit down again. I want to take a look at that shoulder. You said the wound opened?"

"Probably when I fell." Rule helped her unstick the tabs that held the sling together and slip her arm out. "Didn't bleed much. I'm sure it's okay."

True to her word, Nettie wasn't about to agree with her patient without doing her own poking and prodding. Lily was developing goose bumps, sitting there in her strapless bra with the bodice of her dress in her lap, when her cell phone rang.

Nettie grabbed Lily's good arm when she started to move. "Uh-uh. I'm not finished."

"I'll get it," Rule said. He retrieved her purse from the floor. "Yes?" He paused. "She's being examined right now . . . Dr. Two Horses. Why?"

Lily twitched. She wanted that phone. "Is that Karonski?"

Rule nodded, listening intently.

"Fight crime later," Nettie said. "Right now I've another mystery for you. There's something odd about your wound."

"What do you mean?"

"I'm picking up some kind of . . . *dissonance* is the best word I can think of. Something that doesn't belong. You're the sensitive. Touch it and see if you can tell me what I'm talking about."

Lily shrugged her good shoulder. "All right, but magic doesn't stick to me, so I don't see what . . ." Her voice trailed off when she touched the skin next to her wound.

"You do feel something."

"Yes." Troubled, Lily skimmed her fingertips over the neat, round scab where a bullet had entered her body three weeks ago. She shouldn't be able to feel anything, but she did. "Orange. It feels orange."

"Sonofabitch."

Rule's low-voiced curse had Lily's head swiveling, but he seemed to be responding to Karonski, not her. "What?" she demanded. "Did Karonski learn something?"

He shook his head, still listening. "All right," he said reluctantly. "Though you're wrong." And he handed the phone to Nettie, not Lily.

"If that idiot thinks he has to get a doctor's permission just to tell me what he found—"

"No." Rule's voice was hoarse. He looked at Nettie, at Lily, and then away. "That isn't it."

Nettie's gaze flicked to Lily. She listened a moment, her expression professionally blank, and then said, "I can, yes. The ritual itself doesn't take long, but the prep will take about an hour."

Lily's head throbbed in time with her suddenly accelerated heartbeat. "If someone doesn't tell me what's going on, I may explode."

This time Rule looked at her and didn't look away. "Cynna identified your assailant. Karonski confirmed it. You were attacked by a demon. He wants to be sure it isn't still here . . . inside you."

FOUR

THIS being a weekend, there was a live band at the Cactus Corral. Music ripped through the air and beat against the eardrums, a crashing wail of steel guitar and relentless rhythm. This was music as a battering ram, designed to smash into restraints, making customers eager for the slide into booze, the bump and jostle of bodies on the dance floor. In the pounding darkness, it was easy to dance with a stranger. Easy to forget a lost job or a lost wife, unpaid bills and unfinished dreams.

The only empty spot was at the bar next to a middle-aged man with a mustache the color of weak tea and excellent teeth. He was trim but not athletic, looking rather like an accountant who was as tidy with his body as with his clients' money. Though he was a little older than most of the others, he didn't really stand out. Yet the space on his left remained empty despite the number of customers vying for the bartender's attention. And no one seemed to notice.

They didn't notice the squeaky voice that came from that open spot, either. "Did you see the breasts on that blonde?"

Patrick Harlowe heard the voice. He ignored it.

"Cantaloupes," that voice said dreamily. "Big and firm. Maybe you could get it up with her."

Damned little monster. Why didn't the music drown it out? He leaned across the scarred bar and shouted his drink order at the bartender.

"You had a little trouble with the last one, but this blonde could make a dead man rise. Get it? Make his cock rise." That was followed by a girlish giggle.

Patrick had barely heard his own voice over that miserable excuse for a band, but he heard every word from the creature at his side. "Shut up."

"Ha! You shut up. You'd better, or they'll think you're nuts, talking to yourself."

Patrick looked down. He saw a short, squat *something* with slick orange skin—lots of skin, because it was both hairless and naked. It stood on two legs shaped more like a beast's haunches than human limbs. The tail and the forward tilt it imparted made the creature vaguely resemble a stubby kangaroo. The arms were human enough, though, with five-fingered hands; the head was round with no visible ears and a wide slit of a mouth.

"Stinking hermaphrodite," Patrick muttered. "Why are you looking at breasts, anyway? Play with your own."

"I do. Doesn't mean I wouldn't like playing with hers." The little demon winked at the blond woman who was chatting with her friend a few feet away, oblivious.

Forget it, Patrick told himself. He might have to put up with the ugly little bugger for now, but it was temporary. So was hanging out in dives like this. Purely temporary.

That didn't mean he'd forgotten the chink bitch who'd caused all his problems. She'd get what she had coming. His lips curved up. Oh, yes, she'd pay, and he was the one who would deliver the bill. He'd been angry at first because he wasn't allowed to kill her, but this would be better. This way she'd be paying for a long time.

"Maybe you'd better stick to blondes. The brown-haired ones remind you of Her, huh?"

Patrick's mind went white. His heart kicked in his chest so quick and hard that his heartbeat swallowed everything else—thoughts, memories. . . .

He wouldn't think about it. He didn't remember it very well, anyway. Didn't have to. *She* was in hell, and he was here. He was fine. "Stupid little shit. You don't know what you're talking about. She's Chinese—black hair, not brown."

"I'm not talking about that one. I meant—hey, watch it!"

Patrick had brushed that slick orange skin with the staff, sending just a trickle of power through it. He smiled. It was satisfying to see the little shit jump. "Whoops."

"You'd better watch it with that thing! You fry me, you're gonna be in big trouble!"

"I'll be more careful," Patrick assured it solemnly, letting the demon see how little he meant that. Time to remind the creature who was in charge. "You'll be careful, too, won't you?"

It rubbed its shoulder—which was smoking slightly—and grumbled under its breath.

Patrick turned away, feeling better, and noticed the way the man closest to him was looking at him. As if he was crazy.

Better fix that. He smiled and stroked his index finger along the staff. The man—a cowboy type whose mustard yellow shirt strained over a beer gut—relaxed and smiled back. He said something, but Patrick couldn't hear it over the pounding music. Patrick shook his head, still smiling, and gestured at his ears.

Before Beer Belly could become a problem, the bartender slid Patrick's drink to him. Patrick turned to him, his left hand grasping on the staff, his expression pleasant and friendly. "Thanks, asshole."

The man blinked. He hadn't heard the words, of course, in all this din. Just the tone, the melodious crawl of Patrick's voice . . . augmented by the staff he couldn't see.

None of these fools saw anything that mattered. Not the demon, not the staff, and only what Patrick allowed them to see of himself. Like right now. As the music crashed to a stop, the dazed bartender stammered, "On the house. Your drink's on the house, man."

"You recognized me." Patrick gave that just a touch of chagrin. "I hope you won't tell anyone I'm here. Sometimes I need to get away, you know? Relax with *real* people."

"Hell, no, of course I won't say anything. Wouldn't blow your cover for the world, man."

"Thanks." Patrick turned his back on the man, wondering idly who he thought Patrick was. Someone powerful, of course. Someone the man privately revered, but who would a turd like that look up to?

Didn't matter. It was easier to let them make up their own version of who he was. All he had to do was persuade them he was important, someone to admire and serve. He'd always been good at that. Now, with the staff backing him up, he was invincible.

"Invincible," he murmured into his glass before taking a sip. He liked the sound of the word, the sheer truth of it. The bitch wouldn't win, and he would be the one to take her down. Personally. His hand slid lovingly along the staff.

The band swung into another song—something about boot-stomping, with a heavy, driving rhythm. Patrick's mouth tightened. He hated country music. Bunch of losers whining about their lousy lives, that's all they were.

"So are you gonna fuck the blonde or just do her?"

This time Patrick was able to ignore the mouthy little twit. He continued to look over the crowd, searching for the right one. The staff wasn't picky. It would take whatever he fed it—and it needed feeding often. *She* had done something to it, changed it, while he was in . . . that place. With Her.

But that was part of the plan. All part of the plan, and it wasn't so bad, after all, though he'd been upset when he realized how often . . . but a good workman takes care of his tools. That's what his father always said, and what was the staff but a tool? *His* tool.

There. The girl in the red T-shirt and short black skirt. She was looking for some action tonight, wasn't she? Look how she smiled at that cowboy she was dancing with . . . he'd separate them easily enough. Patrick started for the edge of the dance floor so he could be in place when the current dance ended.

Maybe he'd outlaw country music once he was in charge. *Death to all who worship Kenny Chesney,* he thought, and chuckled.

The girl tossed her head and her hair flew out, a shimmering light brown halo alive with youth, motion, and light. And that, too, was temporary. Quite temporary.

FIVE

FORTY-FIVE minutes after learning she might be possessed, Lily was wearing underwear, a hospital gown, and the *toltoi* on its gold chain. She sat in a hospital bed with the head cranked up, the TV turned off, and a roomful of people.

For a while, it had looked like she'd be thrown out instead of admitted. She hadn't been sure which outcome to root for.

The hospital authorities were prepared to tolerate a certain degree of deviation from scientific methods. Native healers were in vogue—a number of Hollywood types had been singing the praises of shamanistic healing—and Nettie had a quietly powerful reputation among the medical community. But the prospect of a mini-exorcism held within their respectable walls had pushed them past their comfort level.

And that's what it would amount to. Nettie had explained that the best way to find out if Lily had a demon in her was to perform the preliminary steps of an exorcism.

That way they'd be ready to take things to the next level if the answer was yes.

So Nettie had requested a private room for "a more elaborate procedure, which requires privacy," without specifying the nature of the procedure. No point in ruffling feathers if they didn't have to. Unfortunately, a nurse had overheard them discussing the situation. She'd tattled to the head of the ER, who'd called in the hospital's senior vice president.

Lily wasn't sure if the man was afraid that she might really be possessed and wreak havoc in his fiefdom, or that the press would find out about a purported exorcism and the hospital would look foolish. She suspected the latter. A lot of people considered exorcism about as relevant as those old maps with sea monsters in the corners. Sure, demons existed, and every now and then some nutcase managed to summon one, but the gates to hell had been closed for centuries.

Possession? Get real.

Between Lily's badge, Nettie's professionalism, and Rule's name dropping—his clan retained a prestigious law firm—they'd prevailed over the bureaucracy. Just before Lily was moved to a regular room on the third floor, Karonski and Cynna Weaver had shown up. And Nettie had gone to the chapel to pray.

Prayer was a key component of the ritual, apparently. Lily wasn't sure how she felt about that. She frowned at the sheet in her lap. It wasn't as if she had anything against religion. But it was slippery stuff, wasn't it? One person believed this-and-such, another believed that-and-such, and before you knew it they were having a nice little war over their differences. She didn't like depending on something so hard to pin down.

"Is your shoulder hurting?" Rule asked.

He sat in a chair beside the bed, holding her left hand. Lily quickly dropped her other hand. She'd been rubbing her shoulder again, the way you'll pick at a scab or run your tongue over the place a tooth used to be. Not because it helps, but because something isn't right. "Not really."

"You aren't possessed."

He said it so calmly, as if he were completely certain. She grimaced. "I don't think I am, either. Magic can't get inside me, so how could a demon?" And yet she'd felt something around the wound. Something that shouldn't have been there.

"Probably it couldn't," Karonski said comfortably from where he sprawled in a chair by the window, digging into a bag of Fritos. The blinds were pulled up, letting the tattered darkness of a city night peer in. "We'll find out for sure soon."

Karonski was in shirtsleeves, having draped his jacket over the back of his chair. Maybe he'd been too warm. Or maybe he'd wanted to have quick access to the .357 in his shoulder holster in case Lily suddenly turned green and started ripping off people's arms.

Cynna paced. They could have snagged another chair for her, but she didn't want one. A restless sort, Lily supposed. Not comfortable with waiting.

She could relate. "I see why you can't take my word for my condition. But I'd know, right? If I were possessed, I'd be able to tell."

"Maybe." Karonski dug into the bottom of the bag, frowned, and came up with crumbs.

"I'd know," Rule said. His hand tightened on hers.

"Maybe," Karonski said again, and popped another chip in his mouth.

"I got the demon's scent from the door. If it was in Lily, I'd smell it on her."

"Yeah?" Cynna paused. "What does it smell like?"

"Cloves and car exhaust. Sort of."

Karonski shook his head. "If your sniff test was reliable, Dr. Two Horses would have said so."

Lily didn't think Rule had been talking just about scent,

but they couldn't discuss the mate bond in front of Cynna. Would it alert Rule to an alien presence inside Lily? She didn't know. She didn't think he did, either.

She looked at Cynna. "No opinion?"

"Plenty of them, but not about possession." She reached the closed door, turned, and kept moving. "I don't know much about that."

"I thought Dizzies were into demonology."

"Some are." She paused by the window, frowning out at the darkness as if she disapproved of it. "But most of demonology is a matter of finding enough names for a demon to summon it and then control it if it shows up. Exorcism's a whole 'nother bag. That's a job for religion."

Religion. The subject kept popping up lately. Most noticeably with the Church of the Redeemed, aka the Azá, and their former leader, the Most Reverend Patrick Harlowe. He'd tried to sacrifice Lily and Rule to the Azá's goddess. But there was Rule's mysterious Lady, too—the one he believed had Gifted the two of them with the mate bond. The one who, his legends said, had created the lupi a few millennia ago to defeat the Azá's goddess.

It was enough to make Lily's head pound. "I thought the Dizzies were a sort of religion. Ah—is it okay to call you that?" Belatedly she'd remembered that "Dizzies" was a mangling of the original Swahili.

Cynna shrugged. "That's what everyone called us. I'll admit I dabbled a bit in demonology in my young and stupid days. That's how I could recognize the traces left by your demon."

"Not *my* demon."

"Whatever. The point is, it's gone." She scowled at Karonski in his chair by the window. "This whole rigmarole is so not necessary. I picked up two of the demon's names."

Karonski crumpled up his chip bag and tossed it in the general direction of the trash. He missed. "Not enough to Find it, you said."

"No, but I could sure enough tell if it was in the room with me!"

"I believe you, already. But there are procedures for this sort of thing."

That was news to Lily. But she hadn't made her way halfway through the pile of reading she'd been given on FBI and MCD resources, regulations, and procedures. "And yet you delayed your flight."

He looked at her, his eyes gentler than usual. "If I'd left, there wouldn't be a senior agent to oversee the procedure. Can't very well leave you in charge of a major investigation until you've been documented as clean."

Okay, that made sense. Lily drew a steadying breath. She wished Nettie would hurry up so they could get this over with.

"At least," Rule said, "we can make a guess about what they were up to."

She nodded. Her head was feeling better. At first she'd thought that was Nettie's doing, but that was foolish. Magic—even the good stuff, like healing magic—couldn't affect her, so it must be getting better on its own. "They sent a demon to possess me. That required privacy, so someone supplied a bolt for the door and the demon zapped it into place." The S.O.C. officers had confirmed that the bolt had been freshly installed.

"Makes sense," Cynna said. "The woman you followed was the demon, form-changed to look like Helen. It knocked you out and did . . . whatever."

Lily looked out the window. From fifty yards away two windows stared back, one lit, one dark. Like two great eyes frozen in mid-blink. What had the demon done while she was unconscious?

She didn't feel different. There was no sense of an alien presence in her body or her mind, none of the struggle she'd seen in Karonski when he'd fought against the mental tampering inflicted by Helen and her staff.

And yet she'd felt something when she touched her

shoulder. Something that shouldn't have been possible. Lily's fingers twitched in Rule's grip as she thought of the odd, slick feel of her wound. Orangey.

She looked at Karonski. "You know what's required for a demon to take possession?"

He was brushing crumbs off his shirt. "There are plenty of theories, most of 'em contradictory. But because of an incident seven years ago, MCD regs for dealing with demons limit involvement to persons of faith. Doesn't seem to matter what faith, so long as the agent has one."

Seven years ago . . . it took a moment for Lily to place the reference, but the story had been sensational enough to stick. "You mean the shoot-out down in New Orleans? That FBI agent shot by his own team—he really *was* possessed?" Someone had leaked that to the press, but very few had bought it. Too outlandish.

"Oh, yeah. The powers-that-be didn't want to alarm the public with the facts."

"And this guy who was possessed wasn't . . . um, a believer?"

"Catholic, but lapsed." Karonski stretched out his legs and laced his fingers over his middle. "Way lapsed. My personal take is that he was more vulnerable than most because he'd lost his faith, but that's just a guess." He shrugged. "MCD policy is just a guess, too."

"What *do* you know?" she asked, exasperated.

The door swung open. "Proximity is a factor," Nettie said crisply. "The demon must be in close physical proximity to its victim. Possession doesn't happen at a distance."

"How did you do that?" Lily demanded. "Rule can hear me from two rooms away. You can't."

Rule smiled. "You were a little loud."

And a little more rattled than she wanted to admit, dammit. Lily took a slow breath, reaching for calm. There was something different about Nettie. She was wearing the same lab coat and jeans. Her hair was braided instead of hanging down in a fuzzy cloud, but Lily had seen it that way before. So what . . .

"Another thing," Karonski said. "Demons can get into animals, especially birds. I've been on a couple cases involving possessed birds." He shrugged. "Don't know why. Maybe birds are easy for them."

"If you've dealt with possession before, why is Nettie doing this?" Lily glanced at Nettie. "No offense."

Nettie just smiled.

Karonski shook his head. "I didn't say I've performed an exorcism. I haven't. When an animal's involved, the procedure is different. Demons can't hide themselves as well in animals as they do in humans, so we can confirm possession pretty easily. Then we kill the animal. That forces the demon out so we can kill or banish it."

Oh. That was different, all right.

"Another thing," Rule said. "They can't possess cats. Or lupi."

"Cats?" Lily couldn't see behind the surfaces of his eyes. They were dark and glossy in the glare of the fluorescents, reflecting the overhead light and hiding everything else. But he looked tired. "You've been talking to Max."

Nettie snorted. "I take Max's pronouncements with a whole lick of salt, but the part about lupi is right."

"Who's Max?" Cynna asked.

"A friend," Rule said.

"He owns Club Hell." It was Nettie's face, Lily decided. Or maybe just the eyes. They seemed to hold . . . more. Which was a silly thing to think. What did she mean, more? More what?

Nettie nodded at Cynna. "I need you to stand over by Abel, please."

Karonski's eyebrows shot up. "Lupi can't be possessed?"

"No. The Lady made them that way." Nettie approached Lily's bed. "It's time for the rest of you to be quiet."

"This is a religious belief, then? One of your legends?"

Rule answered. "It's fact, though I don't expect you to believe that."

"Talk later," Nettie said, "or you'll have to leave. Rule—"

"I'm not leaving."

"Stand on the other side of the bed, then. Don't touch her until we're finished." She took Rule's place by Lily's bed. "How are you doing?"

It seemed a genuine question, not mere courtesy. And her eyes, those huge, dark eyes . . . darker than Rule's, they were, that deep, bottomless brown people sometimes call black. "I'm okay. I don't know what to expect. Have you done this before?"

"I have, yes. Twice. Possession is as rare as true amnesia, so my experience is unusual. The first time was with a chicken."

Lily grinned. "A possessed chicken. That's . . . I don't know. Like Bunnicula, who drains the juice from carrots. Just not scary."

"The chicken had killed two dogs and attacked a child. The other time was an adult man. He—or rather, the demon in him—tried to kill me."

That cut off any mirth.

"He couldn't. It wasn't allowed. I tell you this so you won't worry. You and I will be protected."

How? Or maybe she meant, by whom?

Nettie smiled as if she'd heard the unspoken question and found it amusing. She sat on the bed by Lily's hip. Her eyes were so dark. Knowing. "This won't be like a Catholic exorcism. My people don't wrestle with a demon spiritually. We connect with our gods through the earth. Demons aren't of our world, so we call on the powers of this realm to expel the intruder."

Okay, that made sense. Sort of. "I don't worship your gods."

"You are of the earth, so you are theirs whether you acknowledge them or not. They do require your permission, however. You must willingly surrender to the ritual."

Lily considered that. "I'm not much at surrender, but I want this to happen. Does intention count?"

"It does. I have your permission to continue?"

"Yes."

"Very well, then. Be calm." Nettie certainly was. Her eyes were so serene, yet vast. Vast enough to hold answers to questions Lily had always wondered about, and maybe some she'd never dreamed of asking. "We're entirely safe. You can relax. Rest."

"I'm not . . ." *Not nervous,* she was going to say, but it seemed rude to finish the sentence. Nettie had started chanting—low, quiet, a soothing repetition of words Lily didn't know.

The sound made her sleepy. She fought it. She wanted to look for those answers, the ones hinted at in Nettie's eyes . . . *the same kind of answers the stars are always trying to give us,* she thought, *when we look up and up at them.* So high above, speaking in gradual whispers about time, about their own flaming hearts and the endless cold that lies between . . .

"Wake up," someone said softly. "Time to wake up, Lily."

Everything had changed between one blink and the next. Nettie stood instead of sitting on the bed. Karonski was on his feet, too, shrugging into his jacket. Cynna wasn't even in the room.

Rule was where he had been, though. Beside her.

Lily scowled at Nettie. "I was asleep. You put me to sleep!"

Nettie smiled. "I put you *in* sleep, yes. With you out of the picture, I could find out if anyone else was home."

"You're finished?"

"All done, and you're not possessed."

Rule laid a hand on her arm. She turned to see him grinning at her. "The ritual proved to be a major anticlimax. Nettie chanted, you dozed off, she asked some questions, and no one answered."

Lily was disgruntled. It didn't seem right. After all that tension and buildup, she hadn't even been around for . . . well, for whatever had happened.

Or hadn't happened, and that was what mattered. Lily caught herself before she could start rubbing her shoulder again. She reached for Rule's hand instead. "All right, then. Everyone clear out. I want to go home."

SIX

ONE and a quarter million people worked, ate, slept, loved, and fought in San Diego's four-hundred-square-mile sprawl. It was never quiet, never fully dark in the city. Tonight, overcast had turned the sky into a dirty brown bowl that sealed in the city lights and shut out the night. Rule couldn't see the moon.

He still felt her, of course. The moon's deep, slow chimes sounded in his blood and bones, growing louder when she waxed toward full, as she was now. But he missed seeing her changing face. He missed the stars and the spangled depths of night. And he missed being four-footed. There'd been little opportunity to run the hills in his other form.

If he couldn't run on all four feet, he might as well find other ways to enjoy speed. The city's streets might not be empty, but at midnight they weren't congested. Rule considered that permission to ignore the speed limit.

He expected to be rebuked by his law-abiding passenger. But when he pulled onto I-5 and brought the Mercedes up to a comfortable ninety miles an hour, Lily remained still and silent, her weapon in her lap.

She'd retrieved it from his trunk as soon as they reached his car. That hadn't surprised him. She'd be feeling the need for it tonight. And she'd be right.

But she wasn't asking questions. Questions were Lily's way of sorting the world into shapes she could deal with, and she'd been tossed some pretty odd curves in the past few hours.

Women were complicated creatures, he reminded himself. Any man who thought he had one figured out simply wasn't paying attention, and his *nadia* was more complex than most. The mate bond didn't deliver understanding along with the physical tie. That was up to the two of them. He'd be foolish to fret over her silence when he had so many more concrete dangers to worry about.

She was tired, after all. He wasn't, but he was still too churned up for sleep to sound remotely possible. Lily was probably craving it by now, though. An injured body needed sleep.

He thought of seeing her sprawled on the floor, unconscious, and anger burned through his blood, hot and vivid. He wanted to howl—and then tear out someone's throat.

"You trying to dig a new grip into that steering wheel?"

"Hmm? Oh." He flexed his hands on the wheel, forcing them to relax. "How's your head?"

"Better." She gave it a little shake. "A lot better. More than makes sense."

"You may notice some improvement in your shoulder, too. Nettie left you in sleep for a while after the ritual was over."

Now her head swiveled sharply. "What do you mean?"

"You know what 'in sleep' means."

"More or less. It's a healing trance, magically induced. I know she said something about that, but I thought she was just using a term I was familiar with to describe something similar."

"No, she meant just what she said. You were in sleep."

"But I couldn't be! That's magic, and magic doesn't affect me."

So that's what was bothering her. "Normally she wouldn't be able to put you in sleep, but for this she was backed by spiritual energies, not magic. Which may have given your healing an extra boost, by the way."

"But that doesn't make sense! It's . . . I can *feel* Nettie's Gift when I touch her, so what she does is magic."

"What does Nettie's Gift feel like?" he asked, curious.

She made a vague gesture, palm up. "Sort of like crumbly dirt or fern leaves—basic, earthy, intricate. The point is, she uses magic. Even if she gets it through prayer, it's still the same stuff."

"Apparently not, since she was able to put you in sleep."

She frowned at the glittering worm of taillights ahead. "At first I was thinking . . . wondering . . . what if my being a sensitive messed things up? She thought I was clean because no one answered, but maybe my Gift kept her ritual from working. But that doesn't make sense, either, because she *did* put me in sleep. Only I don't see how she could."

He made a soft, wordless exclamation and reached for her hand. "You're still worried about it. Lily, there's no trace of the demonic in you."

"I know. I know that, and yet I feel something. When I touch my shoulder, there's still a trace of that orangey texture. The demon did something to me, and I don't see how it could. I need to know that, and I need to know what it did."

What could he say? He knew she wasn't tainted, but his certainty was intuitive. She wanted rational.

He tried anyway. "Even if a demon could somehow

get behind your shields, or whatever it is that makes you a sensitive—"

"One did."

"Maybe. You don't know what that orange feeling means. But even if being a sensitive didn't protect you, the mate bond would. You're touched by the Lady."

At first she didn't say anything. A quick glance told him she was frowning hard, as if he'd presented her with a delicate knot to unravel. "I realize you believe that," she said at last. "But Karonski said people of faith were protected. I'm not of your faith, so your Lady's protection wouldn't extend to me."

She was being so careful to sound respectful of his beliefs. It annoyed him. "The Lady is real, Lily. As real as her adversary—and I know you believe in Her existence."

"The one we can't name. Right. She's real enough." Lily's fingers drummed an impatient tattoo on the crumpled chiffon covering her thigh. "Stipulating that your Lady is real doesn't mean that what you believe about Her is fact."

"We don't claim to know everything about the Lady, but she's spoken to the clans many times down through the centuries. We can be fairly confident we've got the basics right."

"Hmm."

She didn't even ask. She assumed he was talking about some fuzzy business of prophets and faith where logic need not apply, and she didn't bother to ask what he meant. "Don't be so bloody dismissive of anything you didn't read about in school."

"There's a difference between myth and documented history."

"Our oral history isn't myth. Whether you believe it or not, when the clans are in danger, the Lady speaks to us or gives us aid in other ways." Maliciously he added, "She uses one of the Chosen."

She swiveled to stare at him, horrified. "You are not saying what I think you're saying."

He smiled. It was not a nice smile.

At the *gens amplexi* two weeks ago, when Lily had been made officially Nokolai, she'd received a fervent welcome. So many of the clan had been eager to talk to the new Chosen. To touch her. She'd been baffled by the attention, and he hadn't explained. He'd been pretty sure she'd be appalled.

He'd been right.

She swallowed. "You mean they thought . . . they think . . . good God."

"They're hoping the Lady will help us through you."

"You told them different, didn't you?" It was more demand than question.

"What could I tell them? I don't know the Lady's purpose."

"Well, you can't possibly think I'm some kind of mouthpiece for your goddess, some prophet or . . . what's it called? Avatar."

"The Lady doesn't use avatars."

He could almost hear her teeth grinding. "Pick another word for it, then. Good God. I don't even have the language to discuss this. It's obvious I—hey! You missed the turnoff."

"No, I didn't."

For several long heartbeats she didn't respond. When she did, her voice was tight. "I'm not going to your apartment."

"They knew enough about you to get to you at your sister's wedding. They for damned sure know where you live."

"Rule—"

"For God's sake, Lily, be reasonable! You've got a decent lock on your door, but that won't stop someone from breaking that nice, big window in the living room and stepping inside. I can protect you from most things, but if that demon—"

"I haven't asked you to protect me. If you—"

"They tried and failed to possess you. Who's to say what they'll try next? If the Azá's goddess is behind this—and we'd better assume She is—She is not one to give up on revenge. Killing you would be the easiest of their options. Benedict sent a couple of his men to my place for extra security tonight, and that's where we're going."

"Fine. Great. But if you think I'm going to trail body-guards around while conducting an investigation, you need a reality check. And I can't stay at your place tonight. If you'd just—"

"Dammit, Lily, this is not the time to argue about where we live! Or whether we're living together at all, or just getting together every night. Do you have any idea how strong demons are?" he demanded, swerving around a slow-moving van. "You're protected from a magical assault, but that doesn't help much if the demon decides to rip off your head."

"Would you slow down? Your reflexes may be super-sized, but the drivers you're passing have to get by with plain old human response times. You could scare one of them off the road or into another car."

He glanced at the speedometer. His lips tightened as he forced himself to ease off on the accelerator. He'd passed a hundred without noticing.

"You also need to turn around. And listen. I've been trying to tell you—"

"What? What kind of lame-ass reason could you possibly have to refuse to make yourself as safe as possible?"

"Dirty Harry."

Rule swallowed what he'd been about to say and used his breath for cursing her cat—her blasted, be-damned, antisocial, wolf-hating beast of a cat they'd left outside because the infernal creature had been off doing stupid cat things when they left for the wedding.

But Lily had accepted responsibility for the animal, and you didn't abandon a dependent when there was danger. Rule understood that, however little he liked it at the moment. The neighbor Lily occasionally asked to feed her cat was out of town. No one else had a key, and it was after midnight.

He ran out of ways to describe the beast shortly after they left the interstate.

"Feel better?" she asked dryly.

"No." He began winding his way back toward her apartment. "Dogs make sense. They understand hierarchy and the need to cooperate. They come when you call them. A cat though—a cat will take your number and get back to you. Maybe. If he's in a good mood." Not that he'd ever seen Harry in a good mood. "Why couldn't you have gotten a dog?"

"At what point do you think I had a choice? Now that I think about it, being claimed by a cat isn't that different from the mate bond."

"There's no similarity at all."

She just looked at him.

He took a deep breath, trying to get his temper under control. "We'll feed Harry and take him back to my apartment."

"You keep forgetting the asking thing."

"So?" He was being unreasonable. That was all right. He didn't *feel* reasonable.

She surprised him. He hadn't expected her to pout—Lily wasn't a pouter—but he did think he'd get an argument, maybe an explosion. Instead she sighed, unclicked her safety belt, and levered herself onto the console separating the seats.

Automatically he stretched an arm behind her, steadying her. "What in the—"

"Shut up, Rule." She leaned against him.

It couldn't be comfortable for her, perching on the console that way. It wasn't as high as some, but if she'd been bigger than a bite she wouldn't have fit.

Her head was level with his. Normally that only happened when they were in bed. He could smell her hair—she'd recently switched to an apple-scented shampoo he liked—and the musky, indescribable scent that was Lily.

His arm relaxed around her. Her upper arm pressed against his, and the calf of her left leg rested along his right leg. She was warm. So warm.

What the hell. He'd give her suggestion a try and shut up.

For several blocks he drove one-handed, in silence and more slowly. His arm was no substitute for a seat belt.

Gradually his thoughts began to slow, too. He found a measure of silence, the inside sort. Like listening to the wind or letting the slow pulse of the earth seep up through his feet, this was a quiet that soothed even as it made him pay attention to things he'd wanted to ignore.

She was so warm and welcome against him, and he could lose her.

Nearby, a dog barked. A couple blocks away someone honked. He passed dark houses, closed businesses, an old Chevy with the bass blasting. There was the purr of the engine, the shush of tires on concrete, and the quiet susurration of her breathing.

Could she hear his breaths? He was never sure how much humans heard. In his other form, he'd have been able to pick out the beating of her heart, but his hearing wasn't that acute while two-legged.

Of course, in his other form, the sound and scent and feel of her wouldn't have affected him the way it was now. He was aware of his own pulse now, the sound of it in his ears, the heat and heaviness in his groin. Need brushed him with heavy wings that fluttered between desire and panic.

He could lose her.

When he turned onto the street that dead-ended at her apartment complex, she spoke quietly. "I'm scared for you, too."

His hand tightened at her waist. "If you'd go to Clanhome—"

"I can't hunt down Harlowe if I'm locked up somewhere."

"I know. I know, but that doesn't make this any easier."

"What do you want me to tell you?"

That she'd quit her job, stay at Clanhome, let him make sure she was safe. That she'd . . . be someone other than who and what she was: the one for him. The only one, now and for the rest of his life. And a cop.

His instinct was to protect. So was hers. This was going to make their life together interesting. "Nothing," he said. "There's nothing you need to say. I'll deal with it."

He tried not to think about his brother. There was no point in going there, no point in remembering what Benedict's Chosen had put him through. Lily was nothing like Claire, thank God. But she was human. So easily damaged. He couldn't help remembering Benedict's wild grief, the way it had ripped sanity from his brother like skin ripped from the body, leaving the insides exposed, bloody and dripping.

Gods, the sound of Benedict's howl . . .

He hadn't understood. He'd been very young, of course, when Claire died. But even as an adult he hadn't grasped how deep his brother's grief had cut, though he'd seen the effects of that wounding.

Now he'd had a glimpse. For an instant, one tiny slice of a second, when he'd seen Lily's body on that bathroom floor . . .

"Don't *do* that!"

"What?"

"Your eyes have gone all weird. Like you're about to change or something."

His breath hitched as he caught himself. Gods, yes,

he'd been slipping, sliding toward the beast without noticing. Like some crazed adolescent, losing control through
sheer, bloody inattention. "Sorry. I'm sorry. I can't believe
I . . . don't worry. I'm not going to lose control."

"Just don't turn furry while you're behind the wheel."
She brought her leg back over the console and slid back
into her seat.

He missed her immediately. How absurd.

They'd reached her apartment complex—though that
was too grand a name for the U-shaped, stucco huddle. It
had begun life in the thirties as a cut-rate motel and
hadn't been improved by the Pepto Bismol paint job inflicted on it by some deranged manager. The exterior was
well lit, at least—good from a security standpoint, if not
aesthetically.

"How is it that you can always find a parking space?"
she asked as he pulled into a spot directly in front of the
exterior stairs that led to her unit.

"It's not hard at this hour." He climbed out.

The one advantage to Lily's living quarters was the
location—only two blocks from the ocean. The air was
heavy with the sea's complex perfume. Rule filled his
lungs with it.

As usual, she got out without waiting for him to get
her door, her unholstered automatic in her good hand.
"That's not it. You always . . . what?" she said crossly as
his lips twitched. "What's so funny?"

"Your weapon makes an interesting fashion acces-
sory."

She glanced at the gun in her hand, at her wreck of a
dress, shrugged, and started for the stairs. Then stopped.
"All right, all right," she told the huge gray beast twining
around her ankles as he voiced his opinion of the late
hour. "The food's upstairs, Harry. If you want to eat, you
have to let me move."

"He was worried about you."

"He was worried about his dinner. Hey!"

Rule had passed her, moving at an easy lope that was roughly as fast as a human could run. He had no intention of allowing her to go in first, but she was likely to argue about that, given a chance. "You're rearguard tonight."

Her voice followed him up the stairs. "Just get out of the way if there's something in there that needs shooting."

"I'll bear that in mind." There was no sign of forced entry. And Harry, whose nose was keener than Rule's at the moment, was impatient to go in, his tail twitching, obviously unalarmed. Rule put his key in the top lock, then the next one, and swung the door open.

A smell that didn't belong had him dropping into a fighting crouch—then straightening as his brain caught up and identified it. "Bloody hell. What are you doing here?"

SEVEN

LILY'S heartbeat jumped when she saw Rule tense. She rushed up the last few stairs, weapon ready. Then he relaxed and asked someone what they were doing here.

"Good question," she said, slowing to a walk. Dammit, she was too tired for yet another adrenaline cocktail. Her heart was still pounding, but she'd hit shaky soon enough. She just hoped she didn't fall flat on her face. "There's also who, how, and why, but I'm tempted to skip them in favor of 'good night.'"

"I'll do my best to get to 'good night' quickly." Rule stepped inside, and Lily had one of her questions answered.

There was only one chair in her small, spare living room. Her unexpected visitor wasn't using it. Instead, he sat on the floor pillow by the coffee table, playing with the air between his fingers. He wore a dark blue shirt, collarless and only half buttoned. His feet were bare, and his cinnamon-colored hair had gone too long without a trim. With his head bent, it concealed a face she knew to be heartbreakingly gorgeous.

Cullen looked up. "Hello, luv. That is one ugly dress. The blood yours?"

Lily sighed. "I know I locked the door, yet here you are. In my living room. Uninvited."

"Ah, well, I thought you wouldn't want me to wait out on the cold concrete, and I was sure I didn't want me to. I've been here for . . ." His fingers paused. "Good Lord, it must be after midnight." He looked her up and down with brilliant blue eyes she wasn't entirely used to. Three weeks ago, his eye sockets had been scabbed-over hollows. "Looks like you've had quite an evening. Rough sex?"

She growled low in her throat and started for the kitchen. "Come on, Harry." And almost humiliated herself when Rule scooped her up in his arms, swallowing a startled shriek at the last second. "Don't do that when I'm armed."

"She's got a point," Cullen said.

Rule deposited her in the oversize armchair. "You can disarm now. I'll take care of Harry and then get rid of Cullen. And before you blow up at me," he added, dropping to crouch in front of her, "remember that I'm used to being yelled at for my high-handed behavior."

Cullen chuckled. "He means the Rho. The old man's healing, but it takes longer at his age. Makes him great fun to be around. He ripped Rule a new one last week for following Nettie's instructions about the Council meeting."

Rule had told her he had clan business to attend to last Thursday. He hadn't said it was a Council meeting. He didn't have to tell her everything, but she was clan now, wasn't she? Shouldn't he have told her?

She looked at the eyes holding steady on her own—dark eyes, not bright blue like his friend's, set in a face that was striking but imperfect. The nose was too narrow, a little too long. The lips were too thin, and the ears . . . Rule's left ear was set higher than his right.

Funny. She hadn't noticed that before.

She leaned over to place her weapon carefully on the

floor beside the chair, then straightened so she could trace one imperfectly placed ear. Feelings tumbled through her like an acrobatic troupe—bouncing, rolling, piling up on top of each other in precarious balance. And she realized she was smiling. "I'd have to come up with something pretty impressive to compete with one of your father's rants. I don't think I'm up to it."

"You're impressive." He leaned in to give her a light kiss. "At all times."

"Very sweet," Cullen said. "And generally I'd enjoy watching your foreplay, but I did come here for a reason. I'd appreciate it if you could leave off the billing and cooing for a bit."

"I'm too tired to kill him," Lily said. "You do it."

"After I feed Harry," Rule said, straightening. "Who isn't much of a watch cat, apparently."

Cullen shook his head without looking up from the empty space between his hands. "Don't worry about Harry. I already fed him."

Sure enough, instead of glaring at them from the kitchen doorway, Harry sat by the coffee table, staring at Cullen.

"What did you feed him?" Lily asked. Harry was supposed to be on a diet, though the cat disagreed with his vet about the necessity.

"Ham. You had some in the fridge that he seemed to like. He ate enough of it, anyway, before going back out. I had a sandwich, too." He paused to frown at the cat. "Stop that."

Rule shook his head, bent, and scooped Lily up again so he could settle in the chair with her. It was a chair and a half, so there was room for both of them . . . as long as she sat with her legs draped across his lap.

That was the way he arranged her, at least. "We need to have a talk about this new habit you've acquired of moving me around to suit yourself."

"I promise to let you move me around later."

Her mind immediately offered an image of one possible arrangement of Rule's long, beautiful body, and suddenly her body was a welcome place to be in spite of its aches.

He knew, of course. If nothing else, her scent would tell him. His lips turned up, but his eyes remained dark and serious as he tucked her hair behind her ear. "When you've rested, *nadia*," he said softly.

She lifted her eyebrows. "We'll see." Then she looked at Cullen and sighed. "Get to the point. You claimed you had one."

"Half a moment. Bloody interfering beast," Cullen muttered, wiggling his little finger as if he was tugging on something. "I used to have a cat as a familiar," he added, as if that explained things. "They can't resist putting in their two cents . . . there."

"Cullen," she said, exasperated, "what are you *doing*?"

He looked up. His quick grin took him from annoying nutcase to heartthrob. "I've been messing with some loose sorcéri while I waited for you. You've rather a lot drifting around, you know, considering there's no node nearby. Perhaps the ocean . . . but you don't want a theoretical discussion right now. Want to see?"

Without waiting for an answer, he tilted his hands outward, muttered something—and he was holding what looked for all the world like a tennis ball made of wiggly, glowing worms.

A second later it flickered and passed back to invisibility. Lily was impressed in spite of herself. "Those are sorcéri? I didn't know you could make that stuff show up for us nonsorcerous types."

"New trick." He looked pleased with himself. "I haven't figured out how to make it stable, so the usefulness is limited. Makes a pretty show, though, doesn't it?"

Rule didn't sound nearly as pleased. "I thought it was dangerous to deal with them directly instead of through a spell."

"These are pretty weak. And I am pretty good. *Ciao,*" he said, and clapped his hands, apparently doing away with the energies he'd gathered. The cat turned his head as if watching something invisible drift into the corner by the coat closet.

"Cats see them, too?" Lily asked.

Cullen shrugged. "Some do. That's why so many witches take cats for familiars."

She chewed on that a moment. "And what you did just now—you changed something about the sorcéri, right? You did it to them, not to us."

Cullen's eyebrows went up. "You don't usually ask stupid questions. Aside from how annoyed Rule would be with me if I did something to him magically without his consent, directly changing people is damned tricky. I confess I'm not up to it. Neither is anyone else in this realm, of course, unless we're entertaining a faerie lord unaware. And you're immune anyway, which brings us back to the stupid question part. What's going on?"

"Lily was attacked by a demon," Rule said flatly. "It may have left some sort of residue behind."

Cullen went very still. Only his eyes moved, cutting to her.

"I'm not possessed," she said, irritated. "Nettie checked me out. But it left something on me. It shouldn't have been able to, but it did."

"You're all right?"

"Aside from being pestered in my own home when I just want to go to bed, yes."

A smile spread over his face. "This is marvelous. Bloody marvelous."

Lily let her head drop back on Rule's shoulder. "How do I make him go away?"

"Sorry." Cullen flowed to his feet, looking not at all sorry, and began to pace. Cullen was a dancer. An exotic dancer, actually, otherwise known as a male stripper, but however annoying he could be, he was a pleasure to watch in motion, the most innately graceful person Lily had ever seen. "You know what a selfish sod I am. It's just that now you won't be able to turn me down."

"For what?"

Rule answered before Cullen could. "He wants to be part of the official hunt for Harlowe."

She lifted her head and met Rule's eyes. She'd guessed that Cullen might be doing some searching of his own. She'd wondered if Rule knew . . . and hadn't asked. Apparently he had known and hadn't told her.

Their relationship posed some tricky questions of loyalty for both of them. She looked at Cullen. "Why?"

"The staff, of course. I have to find and destroy it."

A pang of pity held her silent. Cullen had suffered terribly after being taken prisoner by the mad Helen. Because he had some sort of sorcerous mental shield, Helen had been unable to use the staff to take over his mind—which she'd mightily resented.

His eyes had been put out. He'd been locked in a glass cage, taken out occasionally in shackles to be questioned. He'd been beaten and threatened repeatedly with death.

Lily didn't blame Cullen for hating, but his hatred made him unreliable. Even if sorcery weren't illegal, she couldn't have used him. "I can't do that. I'm sorry."

"I'm not talking about anything official. Make me a consultant, like Rule. You need me." He moved closer. "I can help you Find it."

"I've a Finder on the team now."

His eyebrows went up. "Assuming she's any good—"

"Wait a minute. Why did you say 'she'?"

"Playing the odds. Almost all Finders are female." While she was still absorbing that, he went on persuasively, "Finders need something concrete to fix on, and you don't have a piece of that abomination of a staff for her to handle, do you? So she'll have to try for Harlowe, and he's protected."

"What do you mean?" she asked sharply.

"I've scried for him. He's shielded in some way, most likely by the staff itself."

If he was right, Cynna wasn't going to be the case-breaker Lily had been hoping for. "If a Finder can't locate him, how could you?"

His smile reminded her of Harry. Smug. "He isn't shielded one hundred percent of the time, and unlike Finding, scrying isn't tied to the moment."

"You've lost me."

"With scrying, the images come from elementals. Water's past, earth's present, air is future, and fire scrambles them all up. I scry with fire, which means fire elementals, which means I may get images from past, present, or future." He paused. "Two days ago, I saw Harlowe in the flames. *Without* the staff."

"Two days ago." Anger hit with a punch of renewed energy. She swung her feet to the floor and sat up straight. "It took you long enough to mention it."

"You're pissed," he observed. "But why am I obliged to keep you filled in, yet you don't have to tell me anything? And don't wave your badge at me. You can't compel me to divulge information the law doesn't recognize as valid."

"I can," Rule said evenly. "And will, if necessary. Lily was attacked tonight."

For a long moment the two men looked at each other without speaking. Some kind of complex message seemed to pass between them. Finally Cullen smiled. "Happily, you won't have to. Like I said, that's why I'm here. It took me two days because I needed to do a spot of research to be sure of my conclusions. Turns out my initial impression was correct. I saw Harlowe in hell."

Lily blinked. "I thought . . . when you said flames, I thought you meant your scrying flame. If he's in hell, he's beyond our reach."

"Purge your mind of theological cartoons." Cullen headed toward the door, where Harry waited, tail twitching.

"I did mean my scrying flame, not the brimstone sort. Hell isn't a travel destination for dead sinners. At least, this one isn't." He reached for the door. "I make no claims about the other sort."

This hell? The other sort? How many hells were there? Lily rubbed her temple. "Harry isn't supposed to go out this late."

"No?" Cullen quirked an eyebrow at the cat. "Sorry. Her door, her rules. At any rate, hell—or call it Dis, if you prefer," he said, coming back to sit on the coffee table beside her laptop. "That's what the natives call the place, according to a couple of my sources. I wonder whether they borrowed the name from Dante or inspired him? Anyway, Dis is the demon realm."

"And you say Harlowe is there?"

"Is, was, or will be, give or take a week or so. It ties in nicely with the demon attack, doesn't it?"

"It sure as hell . . ." Lily winced. That phrase was altogether too apt. "How could you tell where he was?"

"Demons, luv. I saw a couple of demons with him."

"We thought *She* might be there," Rule said. "It's the closest realm to ours, and we know She tried to open a gate to hell. Maybe She brought Harlowe to Her when that attempt failed."

Cullen's grin flashed. "Due to our brilliant heroics. I didn't get the idea Harlowe was Her devoted follower, though. More of an opportunist. It seems unlikely She'd exert herself much on his behalf. Could be he got his hands on the staff, and it reverted to Her when you"—he nodded at Lily—"killed Helen. He got taken along for the ride."

When you killed Helen . . . her hands gripping that blond head, pounding it against the cave's stony floor . . . The cold fingers of guilt or superstition crawled along Lily's insides, leaving a slimy trail in their wake. She shook her head. Dammit, she wasn't going to blame herself for doing what she'd had to do. "So you think Harlowe could have ended up in hell accidentally."

"Could be." He waved a hand dismissively. "Which doesn't tell us much, and we're getting off track."

"And you're a single-track kind of guy."

"I won't argue." He leaned forward. A shiny stone on a leather cord around his neck slipped out of his shirt.

"Is that a diamond?" Lily asked, surprised. Cullen wasn't exactly rolling in money. Rule said he spent almost everything on scraps of old spellbooks and such.

"Synthetic. Pretty thing, isn't it?" Cullen tucked it back inside his shirt, then stood and stretched, looking more like a cat than the part-time wolf he was. "I won't press you right now. It's late, you're tired, a bit battered—probably not sympathetic to my cause. But I leave you with this thought: How will you destroy the staff without me?"

"Ah." That was Rule. "So that's what you're thinking." He recited softly, *"Suus scipio scindidi—Id uri, uri, uri! In niger ignis incendi—Aduri vulnus ex mundus."*

"Exactly. And I must say I'm pleased that you're familiar with the *Indomitus*—so many aren't in these degenerate days."

"You used to quote it at me when you were drunk."

"I've always had a good memory," Cullen said complacently.

"What in the world are the two of you talking about? Briefly, please." Lily rubbed her temple and wondered when she'd be able to go to bed. "It sounded like some sort of poetry."

"Bingo," Cullen said. "The *Indomitus* is an epic poem, written in Latin—very old Latin, from before the clans finished mangling it into its current form. Not that we use it much today," he added with evident disapproval. "English is taking its place as our common tongue, just as it is with humans."

Rule spoke dryly. "I think Lily would prefer a translation to a linguistic debate. The events in the poem are part of the Great War," he told her. "The part I quoted refers to the staff of Gelsuid, who was an avatar of the goddess we don't name."

"Something tells me you aren't talking about World War I. Don't explain," she added hastily. "Clan legends later. Just tell me why you think that bit of old poetry has something to do with the staff we're hunting now."

Cullen shrugged. "It's the same staff, of course."

"Come on. You have no reason to think—"

"When we were in Helen's tender hands, you saw her holding a long, black piece of wood. That wasn't what I saw."

He hadn't had eyes at the time, but Lily knew he'd still "seen" the sorcéri. Apparently the staff had shown up on his sorcerous radar screen, too. "I'll bite. What did you see?"

"A wound, a rent, a tear in the fabric of the world. The wooden staff you saw may be a new construct, but the underlying truth of the staff is a very, very old rip in reality. That's why you need me—to close that hole. 'Cauterize the wound,' as the poem says." He was quite cheerful about it. "I'm good with fire."

"You are," Rule acknowledged. "But the *Indomitus* says to burn the staff with 'black fire.' I've never seen you use that. I'm not sure what it is."

"Mage fire. It's a bit dangerous. I'd no call to mess with it before, but I'm learning."

Considering that Cullen found it amusing to play with stray sorcéri in her living room, she didn't want to know what he considered "a bit dangerous." "I hope you're learning well away from populated areas."

He gave her a reproachful look. "But of course. It doesn't pay to alarm the neighbors with the occasional fire."

She opened her mouth to mention a few other hazards associated with fire—and yawned instead. "Sorry. You'd think a threat to the fabric of reality would keep me awake."

"To put it another way," Rule said, "good night, Cullen."

Cullen chuckled. "I can take a hint. I don't always, but I can." He came close enough to bend and drop a kiss on her cheek. "Get some sleep, luv. You can pester me with questions while I bedevil you with demands later."

"Leave your phone turned on for once, and I will."

"For you, I'll keep it turned on." He started for the door.

"Cullen . . ."

"Yes?" His eyebrows went up. "You've changed your mind? You'll accede to my every wish?"

"What do you know about possession?"

"Not much. The religious honchos are bloody close-mouthed about it, always have been. Jealous of their turf, I imagine. Still, my knowledge, patchy though it may be, would be difficult to cover before Rule grabbed me by the scruff of my neck and tossed me out. Is there a more specific question you'd like to ask?"

Lily squirmed mentally, but got it said. "Why would faith be a protection?"

"Damned if I know." He grinned. "Little joke there. I don't know that faith *is* a protection."

"Nettie believes it is. So does the FBI."

His eyebrows shot up. "Is that so? Interesting . . . maybe *The Exorcist* got one thing right." He turned his grin on Rule. "Remember when that came out? People thought it was for real. Bunch of idiots came crawling out of the woodwork, claiming to be experts. Lord, I remember this one ass on *Phil Donahue*—said he'd performed dozens of exorcisms. Dozens." He chuckled.

Lily snorted. "You're undercutting your credibility, Cullen. *The Exorcist* came out before I was born. You and Rule might have been out of diapers, but not by much."

Cullen slid Rule an enigmatic glance. "Ah, you caught me. I do love to make myself sound important, but that was a bit obvious, wasn't it?"

But he hadn't been trying to sound important. He'd

been chatting easily, conversationally, about something he expected Rule to remember—but that was absurd. Lily told herself she was being ridiculous, but the question came out anyway. "Just how old are you?"

"Persuaded you I'm a well-preserved centenarian, have I?" Cullen's smile was teasing. "Or maybe just sixty or seventy. I ought to be in the record books. I doubt there's another stripper my age still performing."

Rule's flat voice cut him off. "Don't."

Lily's stomach did the elevator thing—as if she'd plunged down so suddenly that gravity hadn't kept up.

Cullen sighed. "Didn't mean to put my foot in your mouth."

"I know. I've put off telling her, hoping for the right time . . . which this certainly isn't, but I won't lie to her about it. Or ask you to."

Lily found her voice. "Lie about what?"

He touched her hair. "I'm sorry, *nadia*. I should have told you."

Told her what? Not what he seemed to be saying. That was preposterous. She shoved to her feet. "You are not a hundred years old."

A smile touched his lips—young, firm lips. "No. Nothing so extreme. But I am older than I look. Older than I've allowed you to believe."

Her heart was pounding. "How old?"

"Fifty-four. Cullen is a bit older."

"Fifty-nine next June." Cullen's grimace was frankly apologetic. "I hope you noticed that I didn't lie to you. Quite."

She looked at the tall, beautiful young man claiming to be older than her mother and shook her head. "No, that isn't possible."

Neither of them answered. Cullen looked apologetic. Rule was wearing his inscrutable face, the one she couldn't read worth shit.

They meant it. She began to pace. "How could I never

have heard about this? How could you have fooled everyone all this time?" How could he have fooled *her*?

Rule rose. He moved so smoothly. He couldn't be fifty-four. "We've gone to some extremes to keep it secret. Until three years ago, it was still legal to shoot us on sight in five states. How much worse would it have been if humans knew we live twice as long as they do?"

Twice as long?

Lily's heart was pounding too hard, too fast. Her head felt stuffed with cotton. She'd known Rule was older than he looked—which was about her age. Twenty-eight. His assurance suggested a man beyond the mixed insecurity and infallibility of youth. *Mid-thirties,* she thought. That's what she'd guessed him to be the first time she saw him. "Your driver's license says you're thirty-five."

"Well." Cullen stood and headed for the door. "Never let it be said I'm not a sensitive guy, and I'm sensing that I'm not wanted right now." He reached for the knob.

"Wait," Rule said. "Can you set some kind of wards here? Otherwise we'll have to crate up Harry and head to my apartment."

"Sure, I could do something. Not true wards—they'd take too long—but a bit of 'don't see me' might do the trick. Tidy little spell. Doesn't use much power. Fuzzes the mind so people can't quite locate the spot I tie it to. I don't know if it works on demons, though."

"I'd prefer to keep demons out."

"I don't know of anything that will do that," Cullen said frankly. "Some believe holy symbols work, but I'm skeptical. In the old days . . . but we can't work with what was, can we? In any event, you've got an alarm system in place. Cats hate demons. Harry'll set up a howl if one comes near."

Lily looked for her cat, but Harry had apparently tired of watching the corner. He was nowhere in sight.

"Your call," Rule said quietly to her.

Her hands had made fists. She didn't notice until the

stinging in her palms grew too sharp. She forced herself to open them. "Here. They found me at my sister's wedding. They must know where your apartment is."

"Cullen?" Rule said.

"Will do. Do you have rosemary?"

"Will the dried stuff work?"

They didn't need her. Lily picked up her weapon. "I'm going to take a shower."

Cullen's eyebrows went up. "Armed?"

"Your spells may not work on demons, but I'm betting my bullets will."

EIGHT

~~~

IN the bathroom Lily turned on the tap, stripped off her bridesmaid's dress, wadded it up, and stuffed it in the trash. In spite of what she'd said to Cullen, her gun was on the bedside table, not in here with her. Her bathroom was too tiny for armed combat.

Panties and bra went on the floor as the tiny room filled with steam. She peeled off the gauze pad covering her wound.

Most of the damage didn't show. The doctors thought she'd been hit by a ricochet—there'd been no scorching around the entry, and the bullet had lodged instead of ripping a second hole in her back on its way out. But it had tumbled inside her flesh, tearing up muscle and chipping bone.

All she saw was a depressed, puckered circle, still an angry red. A crescent-shaped scab at one edge marked where it had torn open when she fell. They told her the scar would fade in time. She hoped so. She'd known since she was ten that she could be damaged, permanently and irreversibly—and that scars didn't have to stop her. But she was vain enough to dislike the way this one looked.

Rule thought the in-sleep thing might have speeded up healing on her shoulder as well as her head. Gingerly, Lily touched the small, puckered circle.

Orange.

There were drugs that crosswired the brain so you tasted a color or smelled a sound. Synesthesia, that's what it was called. LSD, peyote, mescaline . . . even marijuana had been known to blur the lines between the senses. But she wasn't on drugs, and her regular senses weren't crossing things up. Just the extra sense that let her touch magic.

Maybe this was normal. Her Gift was rare. She'd never met another touch sensitive, and there was precious little about them in folklore. She didn't have much to go on except her own experience, and she'd never run across a demon before. Maybe she experienced the magic from other realms differently.

But why had it stuck to her?

Frowning, she adjusted the water temperature, stepped into the tub, and pulled the shower curtain closed.

God, but that felt good. For a moment the sheer animal pleasure of hot water blanked her mind. She wanted to sleep right here, standing up, with hot water pouring over her . . . and not have to face Rule.

That was just lame. Disgusted with herself, Lily squirted shampoo into her hand. She could use her left hand enough to do that, but she couldn't raise that arm over her head. Washing her hair one-handed was awkward, but she'd be damned if she'd go to bed with dried blood sticking the strands together.

Rule had been washing her hair for her since she got hurt.

Guilt twinged. So he was older than she'd thought. Lots of women dated older men. What was the big deal?

She closed her eyes and let the water stream over her. He was fifty-four, she was twenty-eight, so he was twenty-six years older than her. Twenty-six years was pretty much a lifetime to her. Not to him. That was the problem.

She got out of the shower, dried off, and told the mother-voice in her head nattering on about taking care of her skin to shut up. Then reached for the lotion anyway.

Did he still argue with the mother-voice in his head? Or maybe it was a father-voice, because he was a guy . . . but surely at fifty-four he'd have found his own voice to listen to.

Lily pulled on a T-shirt and panties, tugged a wide-toothed comb through her hair, and gave serious thought to going to bed without drying it. The prospect of a wet pillow dissuaded her, though. She got out the blow drier and plugged it in.

Had they had blow driers when he was growing up? He would have been born about 1950. Blow driers came along a lot later than that, didn't they?

He looked maybe thirty. It hurt to find out he wasn't. That he had let her believe an untruth. She'd thought they stood on roughly the same cultural ground, and they didn't. When she was a kid, she'd listened to disco. He'd listened to . . . what? The Beatles? Elvis? She'd grown up watching *Cagney and Lacey*, *Cheers*, *Happy Days*. Rule had grown up in *Happy Days*.

She clicked off the blow drier, wound the cord around it, and shoved it in a drawer. She started to get out a fresh gauze pad and the tape, frowned, and decided she didn't need a bandage. Nettie's religious version of magic seemed to have worked on her—which was disconcerting, but she'd work out the ramifications of that later.

Then she took a deep breath and opened the door.

Rule was in bed, propped up against a couple pillows on the right side—she always slept on the left—with the sheet pulled up over his legs and hips. Beneath the sheet he was naked. He thought pajamas were one of the silliest things ever invented.

He was watching her closely. His eyes made her think

of water at night—full of mysteries and hints, revealing little.

She'd had it with mystery. "Why didn't you tell me?"

"Before you became clan, I couldn't. After that . . . fear, I suppose. Ignoble, but accurate."

"You were afraid I'd be upset?"

"Aren't you?"

Upset wasn't the right word. *Confused, disoriented, achingly aware of all the differences between them . . .*

"It isn't as if you haven't kept secrets, too. I've respected that."

"What are you talking about?"

"Grandmother."

She blinked. "But you know about her. I didn't tell you, but you saw her in action. Benedict even saw her Change."

His mouth turned down at one corner, a crooked not-smile. "I also know there aren't any, ah, were-beasts. Yet that's what she is. I haven't pressed you for an explanation."

"Bully for you. I don't have one."

"I wasn't asking you to explain."

She gritted her teeth. "You aren't listening. I didn't say I wouldn't explain. I can't, because I don't know. If there's anyone more secretive than your father, it's my grandmother."

He didn't say anything for a moment and then grimaced and rubbed his chest. "That does make my silence harder to explain."

"You're my mother's age. My father is only two years older than you are." A thought struck her. "You *do* age, don't you?"

His eyebrows lifted. "You've met my father, among others. Yes, we age. Just more slowly. Perhaps we heal the free radical damage scientists have begun touting as one cause of aging."

Lupi healed everything from colds to STDs to bullets.

Why wouldn't they be able to heal most of the damage that caused aging? "Copies," she muttered.

"What?"

"I've read about it. By the time we're seven or so, every cell in our bodies is a copy. By the time we're seventy, our DNA is running copies of copies of copies, and things start to wear out. Maybe the same thing about you that messes up lab tests keeps your copies clearer than mine."

"You do like things logical."

"Why not? Magic is a system, right? Figure out the rules and you know where you stand."

"You have more in common with Cullen than you'd like to think."

No, she didn't. "Is there anything else you haven't gotten around to telling me? Anything important?"

Two slow beats of silence were enough of an answer. Her stomach hurt. "We haven't been together long. I know that, but—"

"That isn't it. I . . . hell." He ran a hand over his hair. "I'm not supposed to tell you. It's . . . it falls within the Rhej's province."

The priestess or historian she was supposed to talk to in a couple days. "So this a clan secret. A lupus secret. It isn't just about you."

He didn't say anything. She turned away, padding over to her side of the bed. She could understand. She would probably have to keep secrets from him, too, sometimes. FBI secrets.

But they wouldn't be about *her*. Dammit. Maybe it was childish, but she wanted Rule to tell her, not this woman she'd never met. She yanked back the covers.

"Lily."

She scowled at him.

"I'm probably sterile."

Her mouth opened. Closed. She swallowed. "You have a son."

"A blessing. A miracle, perhaps. But I'm fifty-four years old, and Toby is my only child. Perhaps 'all but sterile' is more accurate."

His face was closed up, not letting her see what it had cost him to tell her. "But . . . you can't be sure. Unless you've been tested—"

"You aren't thinking. Laboratory tests don't yield useful results for one of the Blood."

Of course. Of course she knew that. "Still, you've been with a lot of women, and not always hung around long enough to know if . . . you can't be sure."

"It's given to us to know the moment our seed quickens."

They knew? Lupi always knew if a woman got pregnant? Rule would know if she . . . Lily rubbed her chest. There didn't seem to be enough air in her lungs.

She used birth control, of course. She'd started taking the pill as soon as she got her period, years before her first lover. Her mother had understood. Without, for once, the need for explanations or long discussion, her mother had known why Lily needed that protection.

She'd been eight when it happened, not yet fertile. She'd been abducted. Stuffed in a trunk and stolen . . . she and her best friend, Sarah. They'd played hookie and gone to the beach, where a nice, grandfatherly man grabbed them. Lily hadn't been raped because the police found her in time.

In time for her. Not for Sarah. So Lily knew in her blood, bones, and sinew that a woman's choices could be stolen, and she'd always made sure that choice—the decision to bear a child—rested with her.

Only now it didn't.

"I'm sorry," he said quietly.

"No." She took a deep breath, shoving confusion aside for now. "Don't apologize for what you can't help. I can see . . ." She could see him again with his son, swinging Toby in the air, filled with a clear, unfettered joy. Little though she would have believed it a month ago, Rule was a man made for fatherhood. "I'm sorry for your loss." The words she'd spoken to the families of victims seemed to fit.

"I've had time to grow accustomed. This is a blow for you. I don't know how you feel about having children."

She didn't, either. "There wasn't anyone on the horizon, so . . ." She gave a one-shoulder shrug. "I've put off thinking about it." Now she didn't know what to feel.

"You can still have children, if you choose."

Her mouth tightened. "By someone else, you mean."

"I understand that your upbringing tells you that would be wrong. My upbringing tells me it would be wrong to deprive you of such a fundamental joy as children out of a disinclination to share."

"It's more than upbringing." She didn't know how to explain to him why fidelity mattered, not when he saw it so differently. And . . . oh, God. She stiffened.

It falls within the Rhej's province. That's what he'd said about his secret. But what he'd told her wasn't a lupi secret . . . not unless what was true of him was true of other lupi, too.

They weren't completely sterile. That was obvious. But maybe the magic that healed them so very well messed with their fertility. Maybe that's why lupi had raised sex and seduction to a fine art, why they considered jealousy immoral. They'd die out if they didn't take every chance they could to try to make a baby.

Rule's face didn't tell her anything. And for once she wasn't going to ask. He'd broken some kind of law or custom by telling her as much as he had. She could wait to hear the rest.

Somehow. It helped that she was falling-down tired. She sat down on her side. "I guess Cullen did his little spell."

"Yes. The effect should wear off in about ten hours, or when the front door is opened."

"Weird."

He handed her a pillow and didn't comment on the fact that she wasn't sleeping naked as she usually did. That decision wasn't about him. Maybe the bad guys wouldn't be ready for a second assault this quickly. Maybe Cullen's spell would work like a dream, and maybe the demon had gone back to hell or Dis or whatever she was supposed to call the place.

And maybe not. If she had to fight bad guys, human or otherwise, she didn't want to do it naked. She turned off the light and lay down . . . and heard his sigh as his arms came around her.

A sigh of relief. He hadn't been sure she'd want to sleep with him, even if sleeping was all she could manage tonight.

It hadn't occurred to her to do otherwise. And what that meant she had no idea and was too tied to care. Gravity pressed down, squeezing out thoughts and worries, leaving her blessedly limp.

She yawned hugely. Rule tugged the covers up as he settled on his side, curling around her. Automatically she snuggled closer . . . and it felt good, it felt right, in spite of everything she'd learned tonight.

And all she hadn't learned. So many questions . . .

A heavy weight landed at the foot of the bed, then curled up against one of her feet. She could feel Harry purring, an inaudible rasp as soothing in its way as the male arm draped over her waist. Her eyes drifted closed as another yawn hit.

All unplanned, a question slipped out. "What kind of music did you listen to as a kid?"

"Hmm?" He sounded sleepy.

"When you were a kid, what music did you listen to?"

"Oh. Bach, Beethoven, Tchaikovsky. Anything with strings. Jazz."

Lord. He couldn't be normal or predictable about anything, could he? Lily gave up and let sleep have her.

NINE

EVERY now and then the crowd roared, a many-throated beast always muttering, muttering, when it wasn't screaming at itself. Far below, the ballplayers stood out vivid and tiny in their white uniforms against the light-flooded green.

It all looked so tidy down there. Safe. But she was up here, in the midst of the crowd-beast. And she wasn't safe.

Lily's heart pounded and pounded. She darted between the tall adult figures, looking for the way back. She'd gotten lost from her mother and sisters when she went looking for Grandmother.

Mother was going to be so angry. Lily's stomach clenched unhappily. *Don't wander off,* she always said. *Don't talk to strangers, don't whine, sit still and be a good girl, and don't wander off.*

Being a good girl was very, very boring. But maybe better than being lost.

The crowd beast roared again, many of its parts leaping to their feet. Popcorn spewed, fists waved, and loudspeakers pumped music into the tinny air. Lily gulped and tried to get around a re lly fat man who smelled bad, like bourbon. Lily hated the smell of bourbon. It made her think of when Uncle Chen got mean and started yelling. Mostly he yelled at his sons, not her, but she still didn't like it.

Mother hadn't even noticed that Grandmother was missing. Lily had tried to tell her, but she hadn't listened. She never listened. So it was up to Lily to find Grandmother, wasn't it?

She had to be here somewhere. That's why they came to the stupid ball games—because Grandmother liked them. So she was here. Lily just had to find her and then everything would be okay.

Maybe the crowd-beast had swallowed her. Grandmother wasn't very big. Not as little as Lily, but not big like the other grown-ups, either.

No, Lily told herself. No, that was stupid. Nothing could eat Grandmother. If the crowd-beast tried, she'd just tell it to back off. And it would. Grandmother was little, but only in her body. She was very big otherwise.

So was her secret. They weren't supposed to talk about it, not ever, not even to each other. It wasn't the same as Lily's secret, except sort of, because they were both about magic. People didn't like magic, so good girls didn't do it. And if they couldn't *help* doing it, like Lily couldn't help knowing when she touched something that had magic on it, then they weren't supposed to tell anyone.

Lily sniffed. Grown-ups were always making stupid rules. Especially her mother. Her mother was stuffed with rules, and most of them were dumb. Right now Lily wished she had a great big magic, one that would make everyone else go away so she could find Grandmother.

Unease stirred inside her. Something wasn't right. This whole setup wasn't right. Why was she thinking about adults as grown-ups? She was . . .

Suddenly the crowd-beast swelled up tight around her, like she was a splinter it meant to squeeze out. It was hard to breathe. Lily shoved with arms and body against all those legs and big, suffocating bodies. She managed to pop out, a tender little grape squeezed from its skin, into a small, clear space.

She stood there panting, looking for Grandmother. Or Mother. Looking for someone, anyone, who could—

"Do you need help, little girl?" The hand, coming from behind to rest on Lily's shoulder, made her jump. The voice, for all its friendly words, terrified her. It was high and sweet and cold, so cold . . . "Are you lost?"

The hand tightened, hurting-hard. Lily yelped and tried to wrench away, but another hand gripped her and slowly turned her around. Lily fought it. She didn't want to see, didn't want—

That face—that smiling, pretty woman's face framed by soft blond hair, and those eyes, empty like a doll's— Lily knew that face. Those eyes. "No!" she screamed. "No, you're dead, I know you are. I made you dead!"

"I'm going to eat you," the smiling woman said. "Then you'll be dead, too. We'll be together."

"No!"

"Together forever . . ." She was bending down, bending close.

"No, no, no! Be dead. I want you dead all the way— dead, dead, dead!" As the woman's hands dug in harder and her face came closer, Lily shut her eyes, wishing for the biggest magic ever, one that would kill the smiling woman forever.

And all of a sudden she was sitting on top of the other woman, who was on her back. She wasn't little anymore. And she was pounding the woman's head against the cold, stony floor, pounding it and pounding it. Blood and gray stuff leaked from the shattered skull she cupped in her two hands, and glistening white bone shards penetrated the hair. And that was wrong. That hadn't happened before. But it was happening now, and the woman wasn't smiling anymore, and her hair—it wasn't blond like it was supposed to be. It was . . . it was . . .

Lily stopped, horror welling up in her.

The woman's eyes blinked once. And it was her mother looking up at her, her mother's skull in her hands, her mother's black hair shiny with blood and sticky with brains.

"You killed me," she said.

Lily woke trying to scream.

"Shh . . . there, Lily, there, honey. It's okay. You're okay."

Rule. It was Rule looking down at her, and Rule's hand, warm and not hurting, on her right shoulder, while her bad shoulder throbbed as if Helen really had dug her fingers into it. She was an adult, not a child, and Helen was dead. Truly and forever dead.

Lily's breath shuddered in her chest. "That was a bad one," she whispered.

His voice was quiet, deep, the sheer masculinity of it soothing to her. "Maybe you should talk about it."

She shook her head, unable to put words to the horror. What good would talk do? She just wanted the smothering guilt to go away. It never troubled her in the daylight hours. When she was awake, she knew she'd done what she had to do.

So why the nightmares?

Go away, she told the lingering taint from the dream. And burrowed into Rule.

"Careful—your shoulder—"

"It doesn't matter." And it didn't, although it was throbbing like a bad tooth. But that meant nothing compared to the hard, physical reality of him. He closed himself around her, and his body was warm, warm enough to melt away fear and horror. She breathed in his scent and felt clean.

He was naked. She wasn't, but her legs were bare and tangled with his. His thighs were firm, slightly rough with hair . . . a roughness she needed. Craved. She rubbed her thigh up along his and found that his body was responding to their closeness, too.

A delicate heat sent tendrils winding out along her veins, down her thighs to her toes, tingling, making her hum from the inside out. She went still, cherishing the sensation. Then she drew her hand along his side, cherishing him.

He didn't ask her to put her desire into words. He didn't ask if she was sure, or remind her of her shoulder, or say anything at all. For that she blessed the years of experience she'd earlier resented.

Instead, he cupped her face in his hands and kissed her. Slowly. With a carnality as obvious and delicate as the heat stirring in her belly.

Yes, she thought. *Yes.* This was what she needed . . . the quiet turning to the other in the middle of the night, the wordless meeting of lips, skin, breath. The trust, unfurling one pale petal at a time, that he would be there.

He rolled her onto her back and came over her, touching softly, kissing her shoulder, pushing her T-shirt aside to nibble along her ribs, tickling her belly button with his tongue. He tugged her panties down her legs and off. She ran her hands over him, marveling, trying to say with touch all that she knew of him and treasured. And all that she still wondered over.

There were no crashing cymbals this time, no rising delirium of lust. Her shoulder ached, and she was riding a wave of exhaustion as surely as she rode the swell of desire.

Yet when he slipped inside her, her breath broke. As he stroked, smooth and easy, she found a quiet joy in meeting him one slow thrust at a time. And as she surrendered to the physical tide that carried her gently through pleasure to its peak, she surrendered her compulsion to name these feelings, to tag them as lust or love or mate bond. There was only the mystery, wordless, full, breaking over her in a soundless rush.

She fell back to Earth without ever having left it and was there to hold him when his breath broke, nearly soundless, as he reached the crest of his own wave. And after, he lay on top of her still, both of them smiling into the dark. She was asleep before ever he rolled off.

RULE stood in Lily's tub beneath the shower jets, yawning. Her apartment had its shortcomings, but did offer two boons: a windowless bedroom, easy to defend, and abundant hot water. This morning, hot water rated almost as high as defensible sleeping quarters.

After a night of sentry sleep, he'd woken early and completely. It had seemed best to leave the warmth of Lily's bed before he gave in to his body's urgings and woke her for another loving. She needed sleep. And she'd needed to sleep here, in her own space. He understood that. She'd had too many shocks yesterday.

Including those about him. Rule grimaced and grabbed the soap.

She'd turned to him, though. In the middle of the night, haunted by a nightmare she wouldn't discuss, she'd turned to him. Tension he hadn't noticed eased from his shoulders at the thought. The soapy scent mixed with steam, with the water's liquid massage, to pull him more fully into his senses. He closed his eyes and closed out thoughts, floating along the skin of the moment.

Another yawn took him. He shook his head. There had been a time when a single night of sentry sleep wouldn't have left him this drowsy. He was older now. Out of practice.

Out of training, Benedict would say.

Rule grinned as he worked up a lather, thinking of the older brother who'd trained him, along with so many other youngsters. Benedict wasn't easy on those he trained, but he never asked more of his cubs than they could give, and he had a knack for understanding each youngster's limits. Unlike some of the physically gifted, he didn't expect others to live up to his own standards.

Of course, that would have been unrealistic. Two-footed or four, Benedict was in a class of his own.

Those summers were years in the past, but Benedict's training stuck. His methods wouldn't suit human notions, but they weren't designed for humans, were they? Being woken out of a deep sleep by having a chunk ripped out of your shoulder by an enemy's teeth inspired a youngster to stay alert.

Grief pinched out his grin. He closed his eyes as memory arrived, sharp-clawed.

Mick.

For a moment he simply stood there, absorbing the pain, new and unblunted and tangled with so many other feelings. It had been Rule's other brother, Mick, whose teeth had ripped a chunk from his shoulder all those years ago. Mick was—*had* been—nearly Rule's age-mate, a rarity among his people. They'd met for the first time the summer Rule began formally training with Benedict.

There'd been rivalry between them, Rule thought, tilting his head back as the water washed away the soap. Of course there had been. But it had been friendly, not serious, back then.

Hadn't it? Did the lens of the present distort the past, or reveal it more clearly?

Let it be, Rule told himself, shutting off the water with an sharp twist of the faucet. Mick was dead. He'd died saving Rule's life—a hero's death. If he'd first endangered it, that was the mad Helen's doing, not Mick's. With the power from that accursed staff, she'd tipped Rule's brother into a sort of madness.

But she couldn't have gotten to Mick if the seed hadn't been there, the seed of jealousy of a particularly nasty sort. The clans had a word for it: *fratriodi.* Brother-hate.

Lily's cell phone rang while Rule was brushing his teeth. He heard her curse, fumble for the phone, and then answer. And he heard her snap fully awake, a change as distinct as the flipping of a light switch. So he finished quickly, shut off the water, and opened the door.

It was just after six A.M. The moon had set and the sun hadn't yet made an appearance, so she'd switched on the bedside lamp. She sat on the bed in a pool of that yellowish light scribbling on the pad she kept close, wearing pale yellow panties and a short black T-shirt that left a strip of her back and belly bare.

He'd removed those panties when she woke from a nightmare. She must have scrambled into them when the phone rang.

She glanced at him, exchanged some more police jargon with the person at the other end and disconnected. "I've got to go."

"I know. I missed the first part, though. Who was it?"

She shoved her hair out of her face, frowning at him. "I wish you'd quit listening to both sides of my phone conversations."

He shrugged. Even if he could stop his ears from hearing so much, he wouldn't. "You don't work homicide anymore. Why were you called about a murder in Temecula?"

"Possible homicide," she corrected. Maybe her frown hadn't been directed at him. It lingered as she stared into some mental space, totting up facts he lacked. "The call was from the FBI district office," she said, pushing to her feet. "They were contacted by local authorities in Temecula about a suspicious death."

"Why call you?" he repeated.

"There's a connection to Harlowe. A witness. The body was discovered two hours ago," she added abruptly and headed for the bathroom.

He stepped aside to let her pass, thinking.

This was hardly the first sighting of someone who might be Patrick Harlowe. Ten days ago, Rubén Brooks had succeeded in getting him put on the FBI's Ten Most Wanted list, his photo and description sent to law enforcement agencies all over the nation. But the man was relentlessly average—Anglo, five-ten, brown hair and eyes, one hundred sixty pounds. No scars, no distinctive features other than an unusually mellow voice. The kind of man, Lily had said in disgust, you could meet at a party and forget two minutes later. Rule didn't know how many reports of possible sightings had come in; Lily had only mentioned those few that seemed promising.

It was the first one connected to a possible homicide, though. She'd want to get to the scene quickly. He needed to get dressed.

He glanced at the closed bathroom door. First things first. If he didn't make coffee, she'd probably stop for the convenience store version along the way.

Rule returned from the kitchen just as Lily was emerging from the bathroom. "Why is it only a possible homicide?" he asked.

She pulled off her T-shirt as she padded up to the tall chest facing the bed. Her shoulder was much improved, he thought. Until now he'd had to help her with things that went over her head.

"Cause of death hasn't been determined," she told him and opened the top drawer, made a disgusted noise, and closed it again. He'd seen her do that several times. She'd automatically open that drawer, forgetting she'd emptied it to make room for some of his things.

She opened the second drawer and plucked out a scrap of black silk. "This is definitely not mine. Why would anyone wear a thong?" She tossed it to him. "It's got to feel like a permanent wedgie."

He pulled on his underwear and watched her step into hers—carnation pink this morning. He loved watching her get dressed. It was fun to see her cover what he would uncover later, yes, but there was a quiet intimacy involved that he treasured even more.

She always put on her panties first, then her bra. She preferred to shower at night and seldom wore pantyhose. She bought toothpaste in tubes, pickles in bulk, and panties in every color. Her wound interfered with the run on the beach she was used to, but she adhered religiously to her therapy program. When it was time to leave, she'd slip on her shoulder harness before her shoes.

Small details, perhaps, but he was learning her. "Why do you wear a bra?"

She looked down at her chest and shook her head. "God only knows."

He chuckled and moved closer. "I meant that a thong offers me some support. Keeps my dangly bits from bouncing around."

Her glance skimmed his body, eyebrows lifting. No doubt she noticed that there was more looking up than dangling at the moment.

He placed his hand beneath one of her pretty breasts, covered now in stretchy white lace, and dragged his thumb across the tip. "I like everything about these, you know—the size, shape, texture . . . and the taste. Especially that."

Her nipple ripened, and her eyes went smoky. That didn't keep her from batting his hand away. "I have to go."

"*We* have to go, you mean." Resigned, he went to the closet—which was organized by color, season, and type of garment. She'd managed to find a few inches of hanging space for him, but his selection was limited. He took out a pair of black slacks. "You're not wearing a bandage."

"The in-sleep thing seems to have helped. My shoulder isn't back to normal, but it's better." She joined him at the closet and took out one of the black T-shirts. "No need for you to get out this early."

"Try again," he said dryly, fastening his slacks. "Even if I were okay with you going without me when we know you're a target—"

"You're coming awfully close to the *allow* word."

"Yet skirting it deftly, I believe. Temecula is an hour away, if the traffic is kind."

"About sixty miles," she agreed.

"The mate bond might stretch that far, but this isn't a good time to test it."

"Oh. Right." She tossed her shirt on the bed, following it with a pair of tan slacks and a red jacket. "Why don't you make us some coffee? You'll bitch if you have to drink convenience store stuff."

"I already did." Surely even a human nose could smell it brewing. He looked at her in sudden, sharp suspicion. "Why don't you want me to go with you? What aren't you telling me?"

She sighed. "I was hoping to keep you from going all alpha and protective on me, but I guess it's a lost cause."

"Good guess. Keep talking."

"The witness was out with the deceased last night. He identified Harlowe as the one she'd left the club with."

"He knows Harlowe?"

"He made the ID from a photo they showed him."

"Then they already had some reason to think Harlowe was involved."

"Oh, yeah." Her eyes were as flat as her voice. "He wrote a little note on the victim's stomach with a felt-tip pen and signed it."

"What did it say?"

" 'This one's for Yu.' "

TEN

LILY was tired of being driven everywhere. It was hard to argue that she should get behind the wheel, though, even with the improvement in her shoulder. Rule was completely unimpaired. So she only grumbled a little about letting him drive.

No question he had a better ride than she did—a Mercedes convertible with buttery soft seats and a top-of-the-line sound system. She set her purse and laptop on the floorboard and put a mug of steaming coffee in the beverage holder. "Swing by the Holiday Inn on Harbor," she said, pulling her door closed. "The district office was going to call Weaver. We'll be picking her up."

He made a noncommittal sound and backed out of the parking space.

She glanced at him. "I don't have a problem with her, you know."

"That's good to hear."

"If I let myself get bent out of shape every time I run across one of your old lovers, I'd spend most of my time pretzeled."

"My reputation far exceeds the reality, you know. I haven't been with nearly as many women as the tabloids like to claim."

"I don't suppose that would be physically possible." Lily's finger tapped on her thigh. "I'm wondering if we should tell her about the mate bond."

"What?" He gave her a quick frown. "No."

"I know it's supposed to be a big secret, but we're asking her to operate without full information. That doesn't feel right."

"If it were up to me, I'd trust Cynna with that knowledge. But not even the Rho can decide to reveal some of the lore about our connection to the Lady. The Chosen are part of that lore."

"You mean no one can tell, ever?"

"Not exactly." He was silent a moment, frowning. "There's too much you don't know. You need to talk with the Rhej."

"I'm supposed to in a few days, but we need to clear this up ASAP."

"I'll have to go to Clanhome. She doesn't leave it, and she doesn't care for telephones."

"Sounds like Grandmother."

Lily shifted uncomfortably. Was she expected to worship the Lady now that she was clan? Not likely to happen, but she didn't want to get into that right now. "Tell me something. Weaver said you hadn't changed. People say that sort of thing all the time, but I guess it's pretty much true for you. How long ago did you know her?"

"Ten years. No, more like twelve."

"So maybe Weaver's more of a problem for you than for me. If she starts thinking about how little you've changed—"

"It's going to come out." He accelerated smoothly onto Harbor Drive. "Sooner or later, it will come out. Once enough of us stopped passing for human, it became inevitable that our longevity would be noticed. That's one reason some lupi objected to going public."

"How did it get settled that you would go public? Not by voting, I'm guessing."

He gave her one of those hard-to-read glances. "No, we didn't vote. The Rhos discussed, argued, formed alliances, and sometimes fought, but there was no consensus. Eventually my father decided to force the issue."

She considered what she knew of Isen Turner. "He had a hand in the *Borden* decision?"

"That, too, but I was referring to *Carr* v. *Texas*."

Lily's eyebrows rose. Since its founding, the U.S. government had mostly ignored "the lupi problem," leaving things up to the states to handle however they thought best. Until recently, the states had thought in terms of imprisonment, execution both formal and informal, even castration.

Carr v. *the State of Texas* had changed all that. The Supreme Court ruling had made lupi citizens when while in human form. Congress had promptly declared lycanthropy a public health hazard, ushering in more than a decade of forced registration and treatment. Now that, too, had been declared unconstitutional. Lupi's four-footed status remained murky, but there was a bill pending about that. "Was Carr Nokolai?"

"You underestimate Isen." His smile was tight. "William Carr was Etorri, one of our oldest and most revered clans. They have virtually no power. They're too tiny. But they have great *du*. Honor," he added, glancing at her. "Reputation, face, magic, history—*du* encompasses all that. Every lupus on the planet owes them, and will until the end of days."

That sounded like quite a story, but it would have to wait. "And . . . ?"

"Carr wasn't just Etorri. He was Rho. At that time, virtually any other lupus who did what he did would have been killed by those opposed to mainstreaming. Not the Etorri Rho."

"And this was somehow Isen's doing?"

"Yes."

That was all he offered, a flat "yes," no explanation. Lily's finger tapped faster. "The Carr decision took place, what—twelve years ago? More like fifteen," she corrected herself. "A few years before you and Weaver were cozy. You would have been thirty-six or so."

"Thirty-eight."

"Were you already your father's heir?"

"What are you getting at?"

"I'm trying to get things fixed in my mind, that's all."

His fingers flexed once on the steering wheel. "I was an adult fifteen years ago. You weren't. That continues to bother you."

"And that pisses you off."

"I am not pissed." He turned sharply into the drive that circled in front of the Holiday Inn.

She rolled her eyes. "Right. Do you see Weaver? She's supposed to wait down front for us."

"You're always telling me what I am. I'm pissed, I'm promiscuous—"

"I never said that!"

"It lies behind your comments like the seven-eighths of an iceberg that's submerged."

"I haven't called you promiscuous," she insisted.

"You don't have to call a black man a nigger to treat him like one."

"Oh, now I'm a racist."

"I didn't say that. Just as you didn't call me promiscuous."

"What are we arguing about? Can you tell me that much? Just what is it we're having this argument about?"

He stopped abruptly enough for her to lurch against her seatbelt. "I don't know. Nothing. There's Cynna."

"Great. Good." Lily stopped herself before she could blurt out something stupid like, "I guess *she* never called you promiscuous." For one thing, it was probably true. For another, it would have sounded entirely too petty and jealous. Which she wasn't. Not exactly.

But Rule had been promiscuous. Maybe not by his standards, whatever those might be, but by hers, he'd been quite the little honeybee, flitting from flower to flower . . . and he'd been flitting a lot longer than she'd realized. About twenty years longer.

His honeybee days were over, though. That's what counted. Maybe that's what had him on edge, too. Maybe trading every woman for one woman didn't seem like such a great deal this morning. He hadn't been given a choice, after all. The mate bond locked them both in this relationship, and however right it felt on the deepest level, there were all sorts of other levels that could play hell with happy-ever-after.

"Morning," Cynna Weaver said, opening the back door on the driver's side. She tossed in a scruffy black tote, slid inside, and glanced from one to the other of them. Her eyebrows lifted, rearranging the whorls on her forehead. "Whoa. You two arguing, or did someone die?"

Lily lifted her own eyebrows. "Kimberly Ann Curtis. Caucasian, brown and brown, five-seven, one-thirty. She turned twenty-two last March. Went by Kim."

"Okay, don't tell me. None of my business, I guess." Cynna settled back against the seat. "I'll admit the 'someone died' comment was stupid when we're headed to a murder scene—"

"Possible homicide," Lily corrected automatically.

"Whatever. It's godawful early yet. Don't expect clever from me for another couple hours."

"I can wait," Lily said dryly as Rule pulled away. "Fasten your seatbelt, please." The other woman muttered something about "seatbelt enforcer" but complied, so

Lily ignored the comment. Chances were that Weaver had never responded to vehicular crashes. She wouldn't know what a face looked like after impacting with a windshield. Or traveling through one.

"So what do we know about this possible homicide?"

"She was found about three-thirty this morning by Mike Sanderson, a coworker who says they dated sometimes but were not exclusive. Nonetheless, he was sufficiently bothered by it when she left the Cactus Corral last night with someone else that he went to her dwelling around three. He found her dead and called the police. No obvious signs of violence. No cause of death determined."

"Huh." Weaver unzipped her tote. "This Sanderson the one who ID'ed Harlowe? It was him she left with, right?"

"Right." Lily frowned at the tote. "I thought you didn't need any ingredients, that your spells were in your tattoos."

"You thought right." She took out a thermos. "Hot chocolate. Want some?"

"No, thanks. I've got coffee." Which was probably cold now. Lily picked up her mug, taking a sip to check. Yep. Cold.

"Don't know how anyone drinks that stuff." Cynna took a slug of her chocolate, which did smell good. "I'm wondering why Rule's driving. No offense, Rule—you're great eye candy, but you're a civilian. What are you along for?"

"Emergency sex," he said blandly.

She exploded into laughter. "Yu, you're getting some bennies I didn't think the bureau offered. I'm jealous."

Lily felt her cheeks heat and thanked God for thick skin. Blushing didn't show. "He's a civilian consultant."

Cynna snorted. "Never heard it called that before. I thought maybe he was bodyguarding you, what with Harlowe leaving you love notes now."

"That, too," Rule said. "You know about the note?"

"Yeah, I heard. Yu—" She grimaced. "If there's a way to say your last name so that it doesn't sound like a pronoun, it's beyond me."

There were three ways to say her last name in Chinese, two of which were beyond Lily, much to Grandmother's disgust. "I'm used to people having trouble with my surname."

"Let's use first names, then." She delved into her tote again, this time coming up with a foam takeout container.

"Okay." Though it wasn't, not really, but that just made Lily determined to get over it. "You should know that we acquired some new information last night."

"After you left the ER?"

"Yes. Seabourne paid me a visit."

"I have got to meet that dude. A sorcerer." She shook her head and opened the container, which turned out to hold a bagel. "Hard to believe, but reality's often a stretch. Some people find me hard to believe."

"He thinks you'll have trouble finding Harlowe, that the staff is shielding him."

"Won't know until I try, but I'm pretty good." She took a big bite.

Lily tried not to stare longingly at Cynna's bagel. She could have brought some food along . . . if she ever went to the store and bought stuff. "He also says he scried for Harlowe and found him in—ah, in hell."

That sent Cynna's eyebrows up. "No shit?"

"I don't think Seabourne was making it up. But he doesn't know if Harlowe is there now, was there recently, or will be there soon."

"Fire scrying, huh? Well, that is interesting." She licked a crumb off her thumb. "Ties right in with the demon who conked you on the head."

"So it seems. I have a question for you."

"Shoot." She took another bite.

"In order to Find something, you have to establish a connection with it, right?"

"That's how it works."

"I want you to hunt for Harlowe, then, not the staff. I've got some concerns about you connecting with it. It's . . . tainted." Lily was getting better at reading the expression beneath the tattoos. Cynna obviously didn't think much of Lily's caution. "Have you ever encountered death magic?"

Cynna frowned. "No. Nasty stuff."

Rule spoke. "The staff reeks of it."

"Yeah? What does it smell like?"

"Putrefaction."

Cynna made a face at her bagel. "You're killing my appetite."

Rule smiled. "You've grown more delicate. I can remember a time when it would take actual decay, not the mere mention of it, to have an effect."

Cynna grinned at the back of his head. "I've always had healthy appetites. Remember that night on the roof?"

"Weaver," Lily said, forgetting the first-name bit.

"Yeah?"

"Are you trying to annoy me, or is annoyance the usual by-product of your personality?"

The woman laughed. "Usual by-product, I guess. You two really do have an exclusive thing going?"

"We really do."

"Hmm." She looked at what was left of her bagel. For a moment there was no expression at all on that odd, striking face. "So what's this Seabourne like?"

"He's annoying, too. Also incredibly gorgeous."

"I really do need to meet him." She popped the last bite into her mouth, chewed, and then said, "You don't have to worry about me getting 'tainted' if I do sort something connected to the staff. I've got all sorts of protection written in. When I sort, I take the patterns I want to Find on my skin. The energy doesn't go any deeper."

That sounded a little like what Lily experienced when she touched magic. She felt its texture, but the magic itself slid off her as if she were greased. Still, unlike her, Cynna didn't remain entirely unaffected. "Your skin's part of you. I don't want you trying to find the staff."

She shrugged. "Harlowe's a better target, anyway."

Was she agreeing or evading? Lily gave one last warning. "Karonski has good protection, too. Helen went right through it. She couldn't get past Seabourne's shields to his mind, but she was still able to use the staff against him. It caused excruciating pain."

"You're going somewhere with this."

"She was also able to kill with it. She tried to use it on me that way. It had no effect."

"Because you're a sensitive. I get that."

"I hope you also get that standard arrest procedures won't work with Harlowe. I'm the only one the staff can't affect, so when we do find him, I go in alone."

Cynna snorted. "You may be immune to the staff, but there are plenty of other ways to get killed."

"She'll have backup," Rule said grimly.

"Thirty feet away and out of sight."

"That's too far. Cullen said Helen had to be within fifteen feet to affect him."

"Cullen's a sorcerer. What's safe for him may not be safe for others. Not that I'm convinced he knows the meaning of safety," she added, thinking of what he'd said about experimenting with mage fire.

"Why are you so bloody careful about everyone's safety but yours?"

"It's my safety at stake, too! I need to know that the people backing me up aren't being controlled by—"

"We've been over this. Harlowe can't read minds, so he can't take over minds."

"We don't know what all he can do. If you weren't so stubbornly sure—"

"Time out!" Cynna sang. "If the two of you can't play nice, you'll have to go to your rooms."

After a moment Rule said dryly, "Without our supper?"

"Only if you don't tell me what you're arguing about."

Lily took a deep breath. "Right." At least this time she knew what the argument was about. "The problem is that we've got more guesses than facts about what the staff can do."

"From what you've said, it can kill, hurt like hell, or take over your mind."

Rule spoke. "The first two, yes. Mind control— probably not, if it's in Harlowe's hands. Lily and I disagree about that," he added. "I believe the staff augments the user's natural Gift, if there is one. Helen was a telepath. Harlowe isn't."

"I'm not disputing that," Lily said impatiently. "But Helen didn't have a Gift that let her slice people up from a distance. That came purely from the staff. What else can it do that we don't know about?"

"Maybe it has no limits and the president and most of Congress are already under Harlowe's control. Lily, we can't guard against every 'maybe' you can conjure up."

"We'll take what precautions seem reasonable. Thirty feet is reasonable."

"To you."

"I'm in charge."

"We don't get to vote? And here I thought you were so enamored of democracy."

Lily tightened her lips on the hot response she wanted to make. They'd entertained Cynna enough with their squabbling.

How had they gotten so crosswise of each other so quickly after last night?

Those damned layers, she supposed. She yanked out a

CD at random and jammed it into the player. Then immediately turned down the volume.

She didn't have time to brood over the tangled layers of her love life. She turned to Cynna Weaver and asked to be filled in on how the woman's Gift worked. And did a pretty good job of not thinking about age differences, nightmares, or what had drawn Rule to the woman all those years ago.

ELEVEN

CYNNA hadn't expected to like Lily Yu. That was envy, of course, with a healthy dose of its kissing cousin, jealousy. But what could be more natural? She didn't fault herself for it. But somewhere along the line, a little worm of liking had surprised her by wiggling past all the other stuff.

Aside from that, though, she wasn't sure what to make of the woman. Lily seemed to know her business, but why had she brought Rule along? No doubt he could guard the hell out of her, but she wasn't exactly a fragile flower. Cynna couldn't see what he could contribute otherwise. The lupi weren't connected to the hunt for Harlowe ... unless there was something she hadn't been told?

It wouldn't be the first time she'd been left out of the loop. All too often, people thought of her as a handy sort of freak, like the spinner in a board game—toss her down, spin her around, see which way she pointed. The way they saw it, she didn't need a brain to find stuff. So they assumed she didn't have one.

Rule knew better, but he was just naturally secretive as hell. Still, she didn't think he'd out-and-out lie to her.

She'd watch for a chance to catch him alone, she decided, and ask him why he was really along.

Temecula lay about halfway between San Diego and L.A. on I-15. By the time they reached its fast-food and gas-station fringes, the sun had popped up over the horizon and Lily switched off the longhair music. She warned Cynna to be especially respectful of local authority.

Temecula, she said, used to be a small, sleepy town, but it had put on a real growth spurt in the past ten years. Like a gangly adolescent prone to tripping, it was jealous of its dignity. There was some rivalry between the newcomers and the oldtimers at the local cop shop. The ones who'd been around forever were outnumbered, but they had seniority and rank, and they didn't need outsiders telling them how to do things.

Kim had been doing okay for herself, Cynna thought as they pulled up near their goal. Up until someone killed her, that is. She'd lived in half of a little stucco duplex roofed with those red tiles Californians were crazy about. The yard was tiny but green. She counted four cops tramping around in it.

As soon as they parked and got out, one of those cops came over to tell them to move on. Lily showed him her badge. He wasn't impressed—said they'd have to wait until Detective Leung cleared them. He did manage to look apologetic when, in response to Lily's question, he told them the body had already been removed.

Lily looked furious.

So they waited. It felt good to be out of the car. Not that Cynna got carsick anymore—she had a dandy little anti-nausea spell—but she hated riding in the backseat. She always felt cramped and left out.

The air had that slick, cool feel she associated more with spring than fall. But this part of the country didn't really do fall, much less winter. She'd come here straight from another job in Kansas City with no time to pick up more clothes. She wasn't dressed right for the climate.

Actually, she just plain wasn't dressed right, but that was nothing new. She'd never gotten the hang of dressing like a fibbie. Cynna sighed as she looked at the China doll. Cynna was wearing tan slacks, too, but they didn't look like Lily's, and her jacket was not nearly as fashionable as the other woman's trim little red thing. Lily didn't carry an old black gym bag around, either. No, she had a big, flat leather envelope of a purse slung over her shoulder.

She and Rule were talking nearby, too low for Cynna to make out the words. They weren't arguing, but they weren't happy, either. That cheered Cynna up some. Call her petty, but she liked knowing the woman wasn't perfect.

Finally someone came out of the victim's front door. He was Asian and not in uniform, so Cynna allowed herself to jump to the conclusion that he was the guy they were waiting for.

Detective Leung was a small man, not much taller than Lily, and dressed just as pretty—pressed white shirt, navy suit, and narrow tie. He didn't have much in the way of lines to give away his age, but his hair was more salt than pepper. By the time he reached them, it was obvious he didn't plan to roll out the welcome mat.

He said his name and rank and then he got a good look at Rule. He went from chilly to frigid. "What is *he* doing here? And her?"

"Her" meant Cynna. She gave him an eat-shit-and-die smile.

Lily was crisp. "He's consulting, she's MCD, same as me . . . if it's any of your business. Who ordered the body removed?"

"I did. The techs were finished with it."

"I asked that the body not be moved."

"We don't always get what we want, do we? Guess I didn't get the message." His smile was tight—like his underwear, Cynna suspected. Just as she suspected he'd gotten the message and ignored it.

Lily's finger started tapping on her thigh. "I'd like to see your shield, Detective."

His eyes narrowed, but he took it out, flashed it, and then started to put it back in his inside jacket pocket.

Lily just stood there with her hand out. He paused, trying to look like he wasn't pissed. Finally she handed it over.

She dug into one of the pockets in that oversize envelope and pulled out a snazzy little leather folder with a notepad inside. There she jotted down his shield number before giving it back to him. "We'll look at the scene first. Where will I find the body?"

"The hospital morgue. We aren't a big city with a separate crime morgue. But, ah . . ." And here he started to feel a bit better. "I'm afraid I can't let you onto the scene."

Lily's eyebrows went up. "I'm at a loss to understand why you think you have a choice."

"Oh, I'll cooperate. If your district office wants to send someone else, I'd be glad to cooperate. But I can't very well let *you* onto the scene." He was enjoying himself now. "Not when you're implicated."

For a long moment, Lily didn't say a word. Cynna glanced at Rule, expecting him to say or do something. But he was just watching, wearing this little smile as if he expected to enjoy what came next.

"I'm sure it can be cleared up," Leung said, riding a good smug now. "But that note links you to the crime. I can't take any chance of the scene being . . . contaminated." He made it sound like the three of them contaminated the air by breathing it. "If you object, you can always go downtown and talk to the chief."

"You misunderstand," she said evenly. "Title 28, United States Code, Section 533 authorizes the attorney general to appoint officials to investigate crimes against the United States."

"What the hell does that—"

"Title 18, Chapter 51, Section 1111 makes it a federal crime to use magical means to commit murder. Chapter

19 makes it a federal crime to conspire to commit an act of violence, including violence by magical means. I am the duly constituted official investigating a conspiracy to attempt the murder of multiple persons, including law enforcement personnel, by magical means. My authority comes from the attorney general and supercedes that of your chief of police. My chief suspect was seen with your victim. He left me a goddamned signed note about it on the body. Title 18, Chapter 55—"

"I'm not disputing jurisdiction," he put in quickly. "I'm saying that you—"

"And I'm saying that you lack the authority to bar me from this scene. If you have concerns about my fitness or possible culpability in this crime, you may relate them to my superiors. Don't bother the district office—they lack the authority to interfere, too. You'd better go right to the head of MCD. Ruben Brooks. He's at FBI headquarters in Washington. Call him." She produced a cell phone from another of her bag's pockets and tossed it to him.

It spoke well for Leung's reflexes that he caught it in spite of his deer-in-the-headlights look.

Lily just kept rolling. "The number for his direct line is on speed dial. Hit seven."

"Wait a minute," he said. "I don't want—"

"If you're not prepared to challenge my fitness, then I request and require your cooperation." She turned and started for the duplex. The two closest uniformed cops were trying to look like they weren't enjoying the exchange. Maybe Leung wasn't popular with the rank-and-file.

Rule had caught his cue immediately and kept pace with her. Cynna dropped in behind.

"What was the victim wearing?" Lily asked without looking back.

"Nothing." Leung hurried to catch up and grabbed Lily's arm just as she reached the porch. "I'm not letting that *were* in. He's no federal agent."

He hadn't, Cynna noticed, tried grabbing Rule. Good call.

"You," Lily said, her voice as cold as her eyes were hot, "had better let go of me right now. Unless you are planning to make an arrest?"

He dropped his hand, looking like he wanted to hit her with it. She looked back at him, her gaze steady as the bead of a sniper. Finally he looked away.

She stepped onto the porch. "Turner won't be going inside right away. But that's my call, not yours." She opened her purse and pulled out a wad of plastic, which she separated into gloves and booties.

Cynna glanced at Leung's feet. He hadn't bothered with the booties. Now that she thought of it, he hadn't been wearing gloves when he came out of the house, either.

"Where was the body found?" Lily asked, bending to pull the plastic over one shoe.

"Bedroom at the back. In bed, arranged neatly—her hands were folded over her heart." He grudged it, but Cynna figured he was telling himself he'd won one battle, with the exclusion of Rule from the scene.

"Any signs of sexual assault?"

He shook his head. "No resistance wounds, no visible tearing, and I didn't see any traces of semen."

"The guy who found her—he's a friend or a boyfriend?"

"He claims they weren't steady, just dated now and then. But it bugged him enough when she went home with someone else that he came by later. Says he wanted to be sure she was okay." His expression announced how little he believed that.

"Did he have a key, or was the door unlocked?"

"Open, he says. Ajar, not wide open."

It was open now, too. Cynna could see an ordinary living room through the doorway—beige sofa and carpet, a television. No evidence techs in sight. Now that she thought of it, she didn't hear their little vacuums, either. Surely they hadn't done the whole place already?

Lily gave Rule a nod. He must have known what that meant, because he stepped up to the door, crouched down, and put his face next to the knob.

"What the hell—!" Leung exclaimed.

She waved him to silence. Rule got a good sniff, then faced into the beige living room. He did this thing with his head, like a dog scenting the air. Then he looked at Lily over his shoulder. Cynna got his profile—gorgeous, but grim. "I don't get anything distinctive from the door," he said. "But in there . . ." He jerked his head toward the living room. "Death magic."

Lily turned to Leung. "This is my investigation now, and this place is sealed. No one goes in without my say-so."

"You can't—"

"I just did."

LILY had to get her phone back from Leung. While he put in a call to his chief to complain about her, she punched seven—and prayed she hadn't just seriously exceeded her authority.

She glanced at her watch as the phone rang on the other end. Seven-thirty here meant eleven-thirty in D.C., so unless he was in a meeting . . .

"Hello, Lily," he said.

Unless he was in a meeting, he answered this phone himself. Only members of the Unit had the number. "I've got a murder by magical means. Harlowe's involved."

"Go on."

She filled him in, including her announcement about sealing the place. "So," she finished, "am I in trouble for exceeding my authority? And if not, can I get someone here to confirm manner of death in a way the courts will accept? Karonski would be best, but if not him, another

Wiccan. And I could use some evidence techs. Leung screwed up the scene, no telling how many big, dirty cop feet have already trampled through, but we still need to try. And who handles the door-to-door?"

There followed one painful second of silence, broken by Ruben's chuckle. "You seem to be dealing well with the loss of Karonski—whom you can't have back yet, I'm afraid, so we'll have to call in civilian experts. There's a coven in Los Angeles whose testimony has held up well. I'll send them down. Call the district office—no, I'll do it. They'll take over working the scene, but you'll need to solicit the cooperation of local authorities for the door-to-door."

"Yes, sir. Leung's an idiot, however." They would need a whole coven to do what Karonski normally did on his own? She had questions about that but filed them mentally for now. "He's the type who'd screw up the investigation just to make me look bad. Ah, I'm afraid we got off on the wrong foot."

"So I gathered," Ruben said dryly. "Cope. You'll take Weaver in to check out the scene?"

"Yes, sir. She's getting her feet covered now."

"Good. I have this feeling . . . well, keep her involved, just in case. Oh, about the staff. I've been asked to instruct you to preserve it for study, if at all possible."

Lily opened her mouth to protest—and closed it again. He hadn't actually told her not to destroy the staff, had he? Just that he'd been asked to tell her that. "Yes, sir," she said carefully.

"Call me this evening to update, unless events dictate otherwise."

She told him good-bye, disconnected, and put up her phone.

Cynna had been listening in with an interested expression on her face. Rule stood a little ways away, closer to Leung—probably eavesdropping on that conversation instead of hers.

Good. She knew what he'd think about any directive to preserve the staff instead of destroying it. She tended to agree with him, but needed to think it over.

"Come on," she said to Cynna. "Let's see what we can learn."

Lily knew she was locking the barn door after the proverbial horse had scooted. Leung had already botched the scene. But she'd preserve what she could, which meant Rule stayed out for now. He hadn't given her a hard time about that, proving he could be reasonable when he wanted.

The living room was small, beige, and spotless. She stopped in the middle of it, looking around. Kim Curtis had been a tidy person. The carpet was recently vacuumed, the room itself as tidy as Lily's apartment, if not as sparsely furnished. The matching armchairs looked new. The couch was slip-covered in ivory matelassé, with two pale green pillows that precisely matched the chairs. A couple of prints hung on the walls—nice frames, conventional landscapes. The entertainment unit held a large television, an old VCR, a new CD/DVD player, and five cloth-covered boxes.

No glasses or plates in sight. If Curtis had offered Harlowe a drink, they hadn't had it in here.

Lily went to the entertainment unit and opened one of the boxes.

"What are you looking for?" Cynna asked from behind her.

"I don't know." The boxes all held CDs and movies— tapes and DVDs. "She liked old musicals. And chick flicks."

"She was doing okay for herself, wasn't she? She was just twenty-two, but she had her own place, decent stuff."

"Yes." She straightened. "Maybe some of this wasn't paid for yet, but she was doing okay." Until she ran into Harlowe. Lily's jaw tightened. "Let's check out the bedroom."

"It was a real treat, watching you take that little pissant apart," Cynna said as she followed Lily down the hall. "Quite a lesson for me in respecting local authority."

Lily winced. "Is it too late for 'do as I say, not as I do'?"

Cynna chuckled. "Did you make up all that legal stuff you quoted at him?"

Lily stepped into the back bedroom and looked around. "I may have gotten some of the section numbers wrong. The gist was accurate."

"That's just scary. You really know all that code?"

"Bits and pieces. I've been trying to get up to speed." Kim hadn't done as much decorating in here. White walls, hand-me down furniture that didn't match, but it wasn't an interesting mismatch, either. "I don't know if Karonski told you, but I haven't been with the Unit long. I used to work homicide."

The unmade bed drooled white sheets and a faded pink-and-yellow comforter onto the floor. No blood, but the body had voided itself in death, so it didn't smell great in here.

"Gah." Cynna's nose wrinkled. "I'm glad I'm not Rule."

"He doesn't react to smells the way we do," Lily said absently. No pictures on the walls, but above the bed were three wooden crosses. Handmade, she thought. Pretty things, really. "Most of the time, scent is information to him. Like if we see a pile of dog shit on the ground, no big deal. We get the message to step around it. Smells are mostly like that for him."

"If you say so."

There was a Bible on the bedside table. Lily frowned at it, trying to fit the signs of religious devotion with someone who picked up a stranger in a bar. Some religious types strayed from the straight and narrow on a regular basis, yet that didn't seem to fit this time. Why?

Because the devotional items were in here, she realized.

In Kim's personal space, not out in her living area. Her faith hadn't been for show, yet she'd picked up a stranger in a bar. She turned to Cynna. "From what you told me, you can't look for traces of Harlowe yet because you don't have his pattern, but you can look for bits that don't match with the victim's."

"I'll need to sort some of her things first, pick up her pattern. Then . . ." She glanced at the bed. "Then I'll see what I can pick out that isn't hers."

"Have at it. I'll check things in my own way." Lily had only touched death magic once. It hadn't been pleasant. She tugged off one glove, steeling herself.

Cynna was removing her gloves, too. "I was thinking that we might be able to estimate the strength of the staff."

"How's that?"

"What's your I.M.P.?"

Lily paused. "My what?"

"I.M.P. You know—Innate Magic Potential." When Lily looked at her blankly, she asked incredulously, "You *have* been tested, haven't you?"

"Oh. Right." She remembered Karonski saying something about it. "The test wouldn't work on me because it uses a spell to gauge the strength of the subject's Gift. The spell would slide right off."

"Shit. I guess that makes sense. Maybe there's some other way to estimate the strength of your Gift. It was strong enough to keep the staff from affecting you, so—"

"It doesn't work that way. I don't . . ." Lily's voice drifted off as she placed her palm on the pillow, right where an impression remained from Kim Curtis's head.

"Hey, you okay?"

"I'm fine." That came out automatically. It was almost true. "I just hate the feel of this stuff."

"Death magic, huh? What does it feel like?"

"Ground glass and rotting flesh." Only worse. She didn't have words to describe the corruption of it. She'd hoped she could tell if there was some difference, some change in the magic with someone else using the staff, but the sheer foulness overwhelmed everything else.

Lily shook her hand to rid herself of the lingering sensation and pulled her glove back on. "As I was saying, being a sensitive isn't like other Gifts. I never used to think of it as a Gift at all, actually."

"Why not?"

Lily struggled for a way to explain. "You've got some kind of shields, right?"

"Sure." She looked around. "Um . . . I'm going to need to touch something of Kim's."

"We'll tag whatever you handle. Try not to leave fingerprints on anything else." She moved to the dresser, which held a mirror, jewelry box, and several bottles of perfume on a little tray. "Anyone with a Gift can learn to do spells, right?"

"Pretty much." Cynna elbowed open the closet door. "Some are better at spellcraft than others. Most of us are only really good at a few types of spells, the ones related most closely to our Gift." She sat on the floor and pulled out an athletic shoe, running her bare hand over it. "This will work," she said with satisfaction.

Apparently shoes absorbed more than sweat from their wearers. Lily opened the jewelry box. Kim Curtis had liked earrings and bracelets. No necklaces, though. "So shields would be stronger or weaker depending on how strong your Gift is and how good you are at that type of spell."

"Basically. There are ways to store power, but it helps to have a strong Gift."

"Well, I can't use magic," Lily said flatly, closing the jewelry box. "And I don't have shields. Being a sensitive is more like . . . like not being porous. Some substances won't soak up water, no matter how much you pour over them. Magic can't soak into me, no matter how much I'm hit with. Except . . ."

"Don't stop now. If there's an exception, I need to know about it."

"Last night Nettie was able to put me in sleep. I'm told she used some sort of religious energy, not magic. But it was still a spell. I don't see why it worked on me."

Cynna shrugged. "Can't help you much. I don't know what the difference is, either."

She put down the shoe and rose.

"I've got Kim's pattern. I don't know if I'll be able to pick up enough of Harlowe's to do any good, but I'll give it a shot."

"You *can* limit your scan to Harlowe, right? So you won't get anything from the staff."

"I don't scan. I sort."

"I'm not following you."

"They're two different operations. Scanning would be . . . oh, like looking for a red scarf you dropped on the floor. You'd see it from a distance. You wouldn't have to touch it or pick it up. Sorting is more like looking for a silk scarf in a tangled pile of scarves. You'd have to touch the scarves to find the one you wanted and work it loose from the others."

"Then be careful what you pick up."

She flashed Lily a grin and moved up to the bed. Gradually all expression bled out of her face, leaving only focus. She held her left hand at her waist, palm out as if deflecting something, and extended her right arm, elbow locked and fingers together, pointing down at the bed.

Slowly her arm swung to the left. Nothing else moved. She might have been a statue with a single moving part—the slowly swinging arm, moving now to the right. If she still breathed, it didn't show.

The arm hesitated and stopped. Gradually, her fingers spread out.

Her eyes rolled back in her head. As if every muscle in her body had simultaneously melted, she collapsed.

Lily leaped for her. She got there just before the woman's head smacked into the bed frame, but not with any grace. Off balance, Lily ended up going down with Cynna sprawled half on top of her.

She managed to sit up, shifting so Cynna's head rested on her thigh. She was checking her pulse when those whiskey-colored eyes blinked open and Cynna said, "Shit."

"Are you okay? What happened?"

"Turns out the sorcerer was right. That staff does not want to be found."

For a second Lily just stared at her. "You tried to find it. After everything I said—in defiance of a direct order—you tried to find the damned staff."

Now she looked sheepish. "I, uh, figured you didn't know what you were talking about."

Lily stood. Cynna's head hit the floor. "Hey!"

"Karonski was right when he called you a loose canon. How am I supposed to work with you when I can't trust you?" She wanted to punch something. "Did you bother looking for Harlowe's pattern at all?"

"Of course," She had the nerve to sound indignant. "What I found—I assume it's from Harlowe—was all tied up with the ugly stuff. Couldn't sort it out."

"That's no excuse."

"I wasn't excusing myself. Just letting you know." Gingerly Cynna got to her feet. "Whew. I feel as if I'm coming off a three-day drunk. Ah . . . I was wrong about one thing, so maybe you should, ah, check to see if . . . well, if something was done to me. It shouldn't be possible," she added hastily. "Not at a distance. But the impossible just keeps happening lately."

Lily was mad enough to let her stew a while. It was only after a severe struggle with her less professional side that she managed to say curtly, "I touched your skin when I checked your pulse. No trace of death magic, so I'd say the staff didn't do anything but knock you down."

"I guess you couldn't have missed it if there was just a teensy trace?"

"If death magic had a smell, it would be like that stuff they put in natural gas to make it smell bad—even the tiniest whiff and you know it's there. If I touch death magic, I know it."

"Good." There was no mistaking the relief in Cynna's voice. "Uh . . . there's one more thing I need to tell you. It's about Kim Curtis."

"Yes?"

"She isn't entirely gone."

TWELVE

RULE felt sick. "You're sure the residue you picked up isn't a ghost?"

They were waiting for the FBI's crime scene specialists to arrive. He and Cynna stood in one corner of the yard. Lily was on the porch, talking to the uniformed officer who'd been first on the scene. The rest of the police were gone. Leung had dismissed them in a temper fit when his chief told him to let the FBI have the scene.

At least the press hadn't showed up. Yet.

Cynna shook her head. "I don't know what I picked up, but with ghosts there's always a direction, you know? This time there wasn't."

"What made you try to find a dead woman?"

"I always check," she admitted. "When I'm called in, a lot of times someone has died violently. That's a good way to throw up a ghost. So I do a Find on the victim to make sure. If there is one, we call in a specialist."

He looked at her quizzically. "You've Found ghosts, then?"

"Sure. They're not that unusual. Most times they

aren't strong enough to manifest, so no one knows they're around."

"And when there isn't a ghost, you get . . . what?"

"Nothing. When people die, there shouldn't be anything for me to Find. This time there was . . . well, not all of her, but something of her. That's what a ghost feels like. Only this remnant wasn't tied to a place like a ghost would be. I don't know what it means."

"It means," Lily said grimly as she joined them, "that he didn't just kill her. He took her life—and fed it to the staff."

Cynna shook her head stubbornly. "I couldn't get a fix on the staff. How could I pick up on something inside it?"

"You connected with it, though. It knocked you on your ass. So where is it?"

"I couldn't tell, dammit! Something . . ." She stopped. Swallowed. "Something's blocking me."

"The staff, yes."

Cynna looked ill. Rule didn't feel too great himself. Was the remnant of Kim Curtis aware? Trapped, bodiless . . .

He turned to Lily. "Did you learn anything useful?"

"Maybe." There was strain around her eyes, a tightness he instinctively wanted to ease. "I heard a lot more about Mike Sanderson, the one who found her. I'm trying to get a handle on why she brought Harlowe home with her."

"You want to know if she was compelled."

"I know you don't think the staff can do that, but this isn't adding up. She had these crosses on her bedroom wall and a Bible by her bed. And the boyfriend thinks she was a virgin."

Rule's eyebrows went up.

"Makes you wonder, doesn't it? Of course, just because a guy thinks a woman's pure as the driven snow doesn't make it so, but according to Sanderson, she believed in chastity until marriage. That put him off—he isn't religious himself—but he was hooked. He kept hanging around. That's what he was doing last night. He knew she loved to dance, so he went to the Cactus Corral to see if she was there, and sure enough." She shook her head. "He's messed up now because he didn't try to stop her when she left with Harlowe."

"He blames himself. That's natural."

"He knew something was wrong. She danced with Harlowe one time and then she left with him."

Cynna shrugged. "Maybe Sanderson didn't know her as well as he thought. Or maybe Harlowe gave her some roofies or K."

"Maybe. We'll see if anyone noticed her acting sleepy or drunk. But I don't think Harlowe slipped the reluctant boyfriend a date rape drug."

"What do you mean?"

"When Sanderson saw her leaving with a man she didn't know, he went up to them. He asked her what was going on. And Harlowe just smiled at him and told him she'd be fine with him. And Sanderson completely bought it. That's what's eating him now. He thought it was just fine if she left with a stranger."

Rafe knew where she was heading. "This isn't the same as what Helen did to Abel. Harlowe didn't erase Sanderson's memories."

She hesitated, then said quietly, "It's more like what she did to your brother. Changed the way he thought about something."

His breath sucked in, quick and sharp. Memory's teeth only grew sharper when you turned your back on it. "Yes. She did do that."

"The effect seems to have worn off on Sanderson pretty quickly. A couple hours later he was here, checking up on Kim. He didn't buy the 'she'll be fine' bit for long."

Cynna looked skeptical. "You're drawing a lot of conclusions from very little evidence. Telepathy isn't the only explanation. For one thing, there are other Gifts."

Lily looked at her. "Such as?"

"Well, charisma. It's not as rare as telepathy, and if you put a good persuasion spell with a really strong Gift—"

"Shit, shit, shit!" Lily smacked her hand against her thigh. "I forgot. Karonski said something like that. That maybe Harlowe had a minor Gift of charisma."

"It's not in his report."

"It came up when we were talking. He was speculating, I think. I can't place the conversation, though. Can't get it in context."

That triggered Rule's memory. "After he and Croft had been tampered with, when we met them in their hotel room. He was describing their meeting. He said Harlowe might have a touch of a charisma Gift."

"It would explain a lot. Like why a devout young woman picked him up—"

"And why a man half in love with her didn't object."

"Whoa!" Cynna held up a hand. "I know I mentioned charisma as a possibility, but it would take one hell of a strong Gift plus an outstanding persuasion spell to alter people's normal behavior and morals that much. A touch of a Gift wouldn't cut it."

"The staff," Rule said grimly. "It changes the possibilities."

Cynna shook her head. "Did Sanderson say anything about Harlowe toting five feet of black wood? Did any of the witnesses? Doesn't seem like the sort of thing they'd let him bring into the club."

"He could have charmed them into allowing it."

"Or," Lily said quietly, "maybe he has a 'don't see me' on it."

"A what?" Cynna demanded.

"A spell that makes people not notice something."

Cynna thought about it and shook her head again. "Demons can do that, go unseen. But that's innate, like Rule's Change. Spells that duplicate the innate abilities of those of the Blood just don't exist. Too complex by far. It's like the difference between manipulating DNA and creating it."

"And yet Cullen cast a 'don't see me' on my apartment last night."

"I'm impressed . . . if it worked. But your apartment's stationary. A moving object would be a whole 'nother story. A 'don't see me' on a five-foot-length of wood carried around a crowded bar? Nuh-uh. I'm not buying it."

Rule and Lily exchanged glances. "I'll call him," she said, taking out her phone. "He said he'd answer if—damn." A white, American-made sedan pulled up, with a white, American-made van right behind it. The two vehicles parked, bracketing Rule's car. The men in the car wore gray suits.

Either the FBI or the IRS had arrived, and Rule didn't think the deceased was being audited.

"Weaver—"

Cynna grimaced. "Make it Cynna, okay?"

"Right. I forgot. Try to get hold of Karonski. Find out if he remembers why he thought Harlowe might have a charisma Gift. I need to brief our associates, see what kind of equipment they brought. Rule—"

"I'll call Cullen."

"Thanks. Use mine. He'll be more likely to pick up, since because he wants something from me." She handed him her phone and headed for the newcomers.

Rule watched Lily as he punched in Cullen's number. She'd told her once that a person her size either learned to move fast or got left behind. Not a bad metaphor for how she approached life in general, he thought. Her walk was brisk, efficient, utterly unself-conscious. And utterly female.

Then there was the way her hair swayed with her movement. He loved her hair. It was as black as a secret wish, shining in the clear light of the young sun, newly risen from its bed beyond the horizon. . . .

"You're really gone on her, aren't you?" Cynna said.

Rule glanced at her sharply. As the phone rang on the other end, he thought of all he hadn't told Lily. All he couldn't tell her. She suspected he'd kept some things from her about Cullen's search for the staff, and she was right. But that wasn't the worst of his omissions.

He hadn't lied to her last night. But when you slice truth too thin, you deceive.

The mate bond held them together, an inescapable gravity. But they had other ties—of affection, loyalty, duty. And sometimes gravity caused avalanches, mudslides, even earthquakes as opposing plates shifted, placing intolerable pressures on ground that wasn't as solid as it seemed. . . . "Yes," he said at last. "I am."

For once, Cynna's natural extravagance was dimmed enough to make a mask of the web of patterns over her face. "I see. Well, I need to get my phone. It's in your car, in my tote."

"Here." He gave her the keys, frowning as she walked away. After so many years, it shouldn't have mattered to Cynna that he wasn't available for fun and games. Apparently it did. He wasn't sure what to think about that, much less what to do.

Finally the ringing was cut off by Cullen's voice. "Changed your mind already, luv?"

"No," Rule said dryly. "I'm still of the same mind I was last night."

"Oh, it's you. If you're calling to pester me about the tracking spell—"

"I'm not, but I wouldn't mind knowing how it's working."

There was a moment's silence; then, grumpily: "It's not. Not properly, at least. I told you it was basically an earth spell, didn't I? Well, you wouldn't believe how many blasted churches source in part from earth—which would amaze their parishioners, I'm sure. The earth energy gets all tangled up with spiritual energies, which creates a bloody blast of interference every time you come within a few hundred feet. I *knew* that would happen, so I tried tying it to air, too, but air is chancy, and with all the pollution—"

"I get the idea." Three people had gotten out of the van. Lily broke away to talk to them. Cynna was talking on her phone. "You lost us."

"Twice," he admitted. "Picked you up again, but you were off the map for nearly a mile at one point."

"That's not good." Rule looked at his car, blocked now by two federal vehicles. He'd tucked the charm Cullen gave him last night under the driver's seat, where Lily was unlikely to see or touch it.

She was so bloody stubborn. Observant, too, unfortunately. Cullen's charm was supposed to allow her bodyguards to trail her, undetected—an excellent idea, if it could be made to work.

Rule slid his hand in the left pocket of his slacks and fingered the small gold button. It looked ordinary enough, though it was, in fact, truly gold—twenty karats, very soft and pure. "Perhaps we should test the panic button you gave me. If that doesn't work—"

"If you're not trying to insult me, then roll your tongue back up into your mouth so you don't keep stumbling over it. That thing is *simple*. Witches make them all the time. Now, if you didn't call to pester me about the tracking spell, what the hell do you want?"

"The answer to a question." Lily and the crime scene techs started for the house. Cynna had put away her phone and was following. Briefly he explained about Harlowe's victim and her reluctant boyfriend.

"You're right about one thing," Cullen said. "Helen could make people forget they'd seen the staff. Harlowe wouldn't be able to do that. At best, a charisma Gift might persuade them to lie about seeing him with it."

That could complicate things, Rule thought, when Lily talked to witnesses. "The boyfriend seems to have thrown off whatever effect Harlowe had on him pretty quickly."

"Charisma's a chancy Gift. Some are more susceptible to it than others, and if there's a lot of dissonance, the effects don't last. If that's all you needed to know, I need to get back—"

"Not so fast. If Harlowe needed the staff to get the effects he did on his victim and the boyfriend, then he had it with him, but no one mentioned seeing it. A 'don't see me' spell would explain that, but I'm told that's impossible with a moving object."

Cullen snorted. "It would present more problems than I'm up to handling, that's for damned sure. I can't even get this blasted tracking spell to work right. I need to talk to that Finder of yours. She might have some spells I could use. Or bits of them, anyway, once I take them apart to see how they work."

"She'd like to meet you, too. But right now, I need to know if the staff could be made invisible."

"Not true invisibility, I wouldn't think. That alters the physical properties of an object, which requires not only enormous power, but—"

"Cullen."

"Right. No theory, no explanations, just an answer." Rule could almost hear his friend shrug. "The staff is Hers. I wouldn't want to guess what all She can do that I can't."

"She's limited in how she can operate in this realm."

"But we don't know what those limits are, except in a very general way. We know she can't operate directly in our realm—she has to use an agent. Nor can she spy on us—on lupi, I mean."

That was both lore and, according to Cullen, common sense. He claimed that the supposed omniscience of the gods—or Old Ones, as he preferred to call them—was basically one hell of a good farseeing spell. And farseeing spells didn't work well on those of the Blood. "Or on Lily, as long as she wears the Lady's emblem."

"According to the Rhej, yes, and I'm inclined to think she knows what she's talking about. But otherwise . . . we know damn little about the staff. Don't know that much about demons, either," he added thoughtfully. "Except for the lower sort that idiots sometimes summon. *She* seems to have made some kind of alliance with one of the demon lords, though. Hard to say what that means."

"You're not cheering me up."

"You'll feel cheerier once I've destroyed that bloody staff."

Rule's gut clenched. "I'm moving up the time for the next circle to tonight."

There was a heartbeat's silence. "Something's happened."

All sorts of things. "I'll explain tonight."

"It will have to be late, or between shows. I'm dancing."

"Between shows, then. The same place—make sure Max saves it for us. Tell the others to arrive singly, as before."

"What am I, your bloody secretary?"

"I can't call," Rule said quietly. "I could be overheard."

"*Filius aper umbo.* All right. I'll play secretary this once."

Rule grinned in spite of himself. "You may be right, but I wouldn't mention the possibility to the Rho."

"We don't chat often, so I doubt it will come up. Ciao." Cullen disconnected.

Rule took a deep breath and did what he had to do, punching in a number he knew well. Why this felt like even more of a betrayal, he couldn't say. But it did.

His father answered the way he always did. "Yes?"

"I need Benedict."

"He won't be happy. He just got back to his mountain."

"It can't be helped. I'm calling another circle." Rule explained as briefly as possible. His father would know about the attack from Nettie, so it didn't take long to fill in the rest.

"All right. What time, then, and where?"

"Have him check with me. I'm not sure where we'll . . ." Rule's voice drifted off. Something he'd heard, though hadn't fully registered, had brought his senses on alert.

Lily. Speaking to someone inside. From this distance he couldn't make out the words, but the tone . . . He started for the duplex. "I'm needed."

"Go, then—*t'eius ven*. Call me after the circle." The Rho disconnected.

Rule reached the porch just as Lily came to stand in the doorway. Her quick glance his way told him little. "Baxter," she called.

One of the suits Cynna was talking to looked up. "Yeah?"

"We've found something."

Baxter started toward her, with Cynna right behind.

"What is it?" Rule asked. Lily looked at him and shook her head—and seeing her face clearly, he realized she wasn't upset or shaken, as he'd thought. She was in a cold rage.

"What have you got?" Baxter asked when he joined them. The agent from the district office was sixtyish and fit, with most of his remaining hair concentrated in a pair of gingery eyebrows. He wore rimless glasses and reeked of tobacco smoke. He glanced at Rule, giving off a faint whiff of *seru*—just enough to tell Rule that, age and appearances to the contrary, Baxter considered himself the dominant male in most situations.

After that single glance, he ignored Rule. "What have you got?"

"Harlowe left us another little present in the DVD player."

The bushy eyebrows lifted. "A bragger, is he?"

"You might say that." She inhaled, visibly reaching for

control. "He likes to take pictures, and Curtis wasn't his first kill."

GAN wasn't happy. Earth hadn't been as much fun as usual, not with it tied to *Her* tool. All Harlowe wanted to do was plan and kill, plan and kill. He wasn't interested in fucking anymore, since he couldn't do it.

And . . . well, all the killing was bothering it. It had hoped to see or *uth* a soul at the instant of death—that's when one ought show up, wasn't it? But that hadn't happened. To all its senses, humans died so very dead.

Gan knew humans were different. Their rules were all tied up with them having souls, and what demon could make sense of that? They even got together in groups to agree on the rules sometimes—that was called *democracy*—and they got really worked up about owning things. They had lots and lots of rules about ownership, even more than about sex. They fought wars over it, but ownership had nothing to do with who could eat who because they didn't eat each other. No, they ate dead things instead, and said *thou shalt not kill* but killed anyway.

But that was because they didn't have to do what their rules said. As long as they didn't get caught, they could break as many rules as they wanted, which was why Earth was usually such fun.

Not this time. It sighed and thumbed the remote again.

"Quit playing with that thing," Harlowe said testily. "You're distracting me."

It looked at the man in the other bed in what was called a *motel room*. Motel rooms were very boring, but Harlowe was being hunted, so he had to hide out. Gan could understand that—it had to sneak around, too, because the humans would hunt it if they knew it was here. But that could be fun, too.

Not in a motel room. When they stayed at the other

hiding place, with the Dozens, Gan had a pretty good time. It wasn't allowed to show itself, but it could play tricks, watch the others talk and fight and fuck, that sort of thing. Sometimes it got to steal stuff. The gang thought very highly of stealing, though of course they didn't know Gan was the one getting the money and guns. They thought Harlowe did everything.

But in a motel room, all it could do was watch TV. It sighed and pushed the channel change button again.

"Quit that," Harlowe snapped.

Harlowe sure wasn't any fun. The human wasn't killing right now, so he was planning. He had papers spread out all over the bed. "I can't find the fucking channel," it explained.

"Which fucking channel? There's a hundred of them!"

Gan brightened. "A hundred? That's a lot of fucking."

"Stupid little pervert. Not a hundred channels about fucking. A hundred fucking channels."

Gan's forehead wrinkled. "That doesn't make sense." One of the difficult things about Earth was that you couldn't hear meanings here, only words.

But Harlowe had lost interest and was studying his papers once more, muttering to himself. "Needs to be half again as big . . ."

Gan went back to *channel surfing*—cute turn of phrase, that. Humans were very inventive with language because they got all their meaning from words.

Still no fucking, but there was shooting. Was it a war? Gan's ears perked up. It was very curious about how humans conducted their wars. ". . . circle the wagons," the TV person cried. "Hurry! They're almost here!"

". . . still, if I got rid of the desk," Harlowe muttered, "the throne could go by the windows. What will I need with a desk, anyway?"

Gan tried to figure out what was happening on TV. Two groups of humans were shooting at each other. One group rode horses; the other didn't. The bunch on horses yelled a lot and seemed to be winning. Some of them had guns; some had bows and arrows.

Then two more people on horses rode up, guns blazing. Many of the other horse people fell off, dead, and the rest scattered. Then the other group was happy.

"Can't do it all overnight." Harlowe sounded crisp, satisfied. "The Oval Office will do for a throne room initially. Later, I can have the Capitol Building remodeled."

"Who was that masked man?" a TV woman asked one of the TV men.

The shooting was over, so Gan changed the channel. Things would get better soon, it reminded itself. Just last night Xitil had used Gan's hand to write some instructions for Harlowe—instructions that came from *Her.*

Gan had done its part. It had brought Lily Yu to Dis and drunk a little blood—and oh my, but that had been good! Fizzy and powerful . . . but not powerful enough to let it possess her. Not without help from Her, only She couldn't act directly. That would break the pact.

So She had to work through a tool. Once Harlowe did like he was supposed to do, Gan could get inside Lily Yu. Then it could have lots of fun.

But it wondered, as it watched a TV man cooking—that's what humans did to dead things before eating them—if Xitil knew that her new associate's tool was stark, staring crazy.

THIRTEEN

"**THERE** are three pictures he didn't send us. Three victims he didn't want us to know about."

"We can't be sure of that."

Lily cast an impatient glance over her shoulder. Baxter sat at his desk, a scuffed and scarred relic from the fifties that looked out of place in the modern building that housed the FBI's field office in San Diego. It held a jumble of file folders, a computer, five empty Dr. Pepper cans, and the one he'd just opened.

The man had a serious soda habit. "He killed on the twenty-fifth, the twenty-seventh, the twenty-ninth. No picture of a victim dated the thirty-first, but we've got one for the second and fourth of this month, then nothing on the sixth and eighth. Another victim on the tenth, and now Curtis on the twelfth. What does that say to you?"

"That we have a pattern. That doesn't mean he killed on the missing dates. Something could have interfered with him on those days. Maybe he didn't find the right type."

"He does have a type." She stopped in front of the murder board. There were seven prints pinned to it. Seven photos of women, all of them with light brown hair, all young, all naked. Five lay in beds, like Kim Curtis. One was in an alley, while one stared blindly up into the branches of a tree. None bore any marks of violence.

Seven tidy dead people, hands folded primly on their breasts.

"Why leave us pictures?" she asked. "Why make it easier for us to track him?"

"We haven't found him yet," Baxter pointed out. "But yeah, I know what you mean. He handed us a lot of information with those photos."

They'd been taken by a digital camera, which meant the images had data attached. He'd made the disk at Kinko's, for God's sake. "We know what camera he used and when he took each of the pictures. We've got names and places of death for three of them now—damn Leung's eyes."

"I can't blame him for not realizing the other vic in his territory was a homicide," Baxter said. "You get a dead hooker, no signs of violence, you don't say, 'Hey, I'll bet some dude with a magic staff sucked the life out of her.' "

"Once Curtis turned up in the same shape, arranged the same way, he knew he'd been wrong about Cynthia Porter. He held back on us until his chief leaned on him."

"You'll find that locals do that a lot."

She exchanged glances with the older man. Baxter knew she'd been one of the locals until very recently. "I didn't," she said evenly.

He shrugged.

She and Baxter hadn't exactly butted heads. MCD's jurisdiction was clear, and Baxter had put several people at her disposal without complaint. But he'd made it plain he thought her too young and inexperienced to have charge of an investigation of this size.

Lily tended to agree. She wanted Karonski back. She'd told Ruben that when she reported on the increased scope of the investigation. But the imp outbreak was getting worse. There's been a rash of fires, several accidents, and now a few fatalities. The governor of Virginia was talking about closing businesses, and the outbreak was being touted as the largest in a century. Ruben couldn't spare Karonski until they located and closed the leak.

They had made some progress. They had IDs now on three of the victims—one in Oceanside, another in Escondido, the third in Temecula, like Curtis. All three had been ruled death by natural causes and would have to be ritually examined. Lily felt a pang of sympathy for the coven from L.A. who'd been given that chore. They seemed competent, though—it had taken them about thirty minutes to confirm that Curtis had been killed by death magic.

Lily had spoken with the Temecula police chief and with three witnesses from the Cactus Corral, including the not-quite-boyfriend. She was waiting on another witness now—the bartender who'd apparently waited on Harlowe. It was his night off, and they hadn't tracked him down yet.

It was weird, hanging around waiting for others to turn up the witnesses and bring them to her. She was used to being out there hunting them herself, but someone had to coordinate the federal efforts with the local ones. Right now, that was her.

She'd be glad when Croft got here. "If he did have victims on the missing days"—and she believed in her gut that he had—"then he held back those photos for a reason. Why? Were there other victims we don't know about? The first one we have a picture of is from the twenty-fifth of last month."

"Eight days after you busted his operation with the Azá. Yeah, I'd like to know what he was doing for that week."

Maybe hiding out in hell. Lily hadn't mentioned that possibility to Baxter. Not only was it outlandish enough to make him doubt everything else she said, but it came from a source she couldn't reveal.

"We'll have another victim soon," Baxter was saying,

"if you're right about the staff and him having to feed it. I hope to God you're wrong, but I'm not counting on it."

She knew it. She knew it, and the certainty ate at her gut. "It keeps coming back to these pictures. Why take them? Why give them to us? Why did he want or need us to know so much?"

"He might not have known how much he was giving us. Lots of people aren't computer savvy. I'd never heard of that EXIT data before, myself."

"EXIF," Lily corrected absently, frowning at the map pinned to one end of the long bulletin board. They only had three vics identified so far, not enough to establish a definite pattern. But those three seemed to lead them north, away from San Diego. "Even if you didn't know the terminology, you'd have found out, wouldn't you? Before sharing your trophy photos with the FBI, you'd have made sure the images didn't give away more than you wanted them to."

Baxter smiled sourly. "Can't count on Harlowe being as bright as me."

"He's bright enough." Lily had spent enough hours learning about the man, getting to know him through the eyes of others, to be sure of that.

"The whizzes in profiling think he craves recognition. He was outwitting us, but that wasn't enough. He had to be sure we knew how clever he was."

"Maybe." Lily drummed her fingers once on the desk. "No, dammit, it doesn't fit. It just doesn't fit with the man he was before—ambitious, amoral, but not a serial killer, and damn good at taking care of his own hide. Something's changed, or we're reading this wrong."

The door opened. "Maybe he's decided he's invincible," Rule said. He held a flat cardboard box that gave off wonderful aromas—pepperoni and pizza sauce. "That he can't be caught or killed."

"What the hell," Baxter said. "You listening at the door?"

Lily frowned. Usually Rule took care not to make the humans around him uncomfortable. Maybe he was tired.

"I have good hearing." Rule walked up to the desk and put down the carton. "It's nearly eight o'clock, and I'm hungry. I thought you might like a couple of slices. I'm hoping," he said, glancing at Lily, "to share the rest with my lady."

My lady. Only Rule could say something like that and make it sound normal. "It would be handy if Harlowe cherished delusions of invincibility, but Cullen said that Helen was the one who took risks. Harlowe was more cautious."

"That was when Helen held the staff. Harlowe has it now."

"You think it changes the user's personality?"

"I think we've got lots of guesses and very little knowledge. I also think it's suppertime. There's a break room down the hall where we could take however much of this Baxter can spare us."

Baxter had already off-loaded three slices. "Go on, go on. The Bureau can survive without you for a few minutes."

The break room was only four doors away and deserted at this hour. "Where's Cynna?" Rule asked.

"There's nothing for her to use to Find Harlowe, so she's helping another team. Parental kidnapping. She was pretty sure she could Find the boy." Lily ripped off a few paper towels to serve as both plates and napkins. "What was that 'my lady' bit about?"

Rule was feeding coins into the vending machine. He smiled at her over his shoulder. "Aren't you?"

"It sounds . . ." Like the way he referred to his goddess, but Lily didn't want to go there. "Medieval. As if you're about to hop on your charger and go lance someone."

"I'll skip the charger. Horses don't tolerate us well." He brought two cans of soda to the table—Diet Coke for her, the straight stuff for himself. "Baxter's unusually comfortable with my presence."

"I explained that you're a civilian consult."

"It's more than that. Usually there's some sort of threat response, either fear or aggression or both. It's a visceral thing, not under conscious control. He mostly ignores me. That's rare."

She could believe that. Rule was hard to overlook. "He's got a touch of . . . well, otherness. It's too faint for me to identify, but there's something there. I'm guessing he's got a witch, maybe even someone of the Blood, in his ancestry. That might make him more tolerant than most." The smell was making her mouth water. She retrieved a slice and bit in.

"Perhaps." He sat and removed a slice, the warm cheese stretching in a long string. "Your sister had a civil ceremony, not a religious one."

She blinked. "Where did that come from?"

"Weren't you thinking that 'my lady' sounds a lot like the Lady?"

"Have you picked up a telepathy Gift?"

"No, you make me work for whatever insights I can come up with. Is it specifically my beliefs that bother you, or religion in general?"

She resisted the urge to squirm in her chair. "I just think that sort of thing is private. It makes me uncomfortable when people wear their beliefs out in public."

"Like underwear, you mean."

She grinned. "Maybe."

"I'm wondering if that's a personal opinion or one your family shares."

There were mushrooms on the pizza. Lily didn't exactly hate mushrooms, but she didn't exactly like them, either. She picked one off. "Family, I guess. The religious wars were mostly over by the time I was six, but we're talking an armed truce with occasional skirmishes, not real peace."

"They are of different faiths?"

"Mother's a twice-a-year Christian—Easter and Christmas. My father was raised Buddhist, but I'm not sure how much it really matters to him. You'd think they could have compromised, since they aren't especially devout, but . . ." She shrugged her good shoulder. Her pizza was getting cold, so she bit in.

"You would have gotten used to avoiding the whole subject, then, to avoid conflict in your family." He nodded. "Did you stop thinking about it, too?"

Pretty much. Lily picked off more mushrooms, not looking up. "I went through the usual questioning period in my teens. You know—why are we here, what does it all mean, that sort of thing. It seemed like everyone had a different answer, and no way to back it up."

"You wanted evidence. Proof."

"What's wrong with that? If we're talking about stuff as important as the meaning of life, shouldn't we want to something concrete to hang our theories on?"

"Nothing wrong living in a fact-based reality. But science, as good as it is with how, isn't equipped to deal with why."

As far as she could tell, no one was much good at dealing with the why, but that didn't stop them from thinking they'd locked truth up all nice and tidy. Lily frowned and took another bite, hoping he'd take the hint and drop the subject.

Rule laid his hand over hers. "I'm trying to understand you, not convert you."

Okay. She said that with a little nod because her mouth was full. He wanted to know where she stood, faith-wise, because that sort of thing mattered to him.

It must matter to her, too, or it wouldn't make her so uncomfortable.

That thought was disconcerting enough that she finished her slice in silence.

Rule seemed all right with that, not pushing for conversation while they ate. That was one of the great things about him, she thought. She wasn't entertainment for him. He didn't need her to make him laugh or bolster his ego or to figure him out so he wouldn't have to. A lot of men who said they were looking for a relationship really wanted a combination sex buddy, therapist, and mirror.

Maybe he'd looked for those things, too, when he was younger.

A little bump of discomfort poked her, like being elbowed in the side when there was no one around. She didn't like thinking about his age. *Tough,* she told herself. She might as well get over it. He wasn't going to grow younger.

One of the things bugging her, she realized, was that there was just plain more of him that she knew nothing about. About twenty years' worth. Maybe she should ask Cynna what he'd been like twelve years ago, when they were an item.

"What?" he said, wiping his hands on a paper towel.

"I didn't say anything."

"You were looking at me with big questions in your eyes."

She had a suspicion Rule wouldn't like her and Cynna comparing notes. "It's nice, being able to sit together without feeling that I need to jump your bones."

He grinned. "I'm crushed. But perhaps what you're feeling mostly is exhaustion. You had a rough day yesterday, and not enough sleep."

"I'm okay." For another couple of hours, anyway. "And you know what I mean. The mate bond has eased off, hasn't it? We can be farther apart now. A lot farther." There'd been a time when she couldn't let as much as a block separate them. "It feels good to be near you, but it's more of a half-a-beer buzz, not the whole six-pack."

"Did you chug six-packs in college? Somehow I can't picture it."

"I got drunk once. I didn't like it." Why people courted that complete loss of control she couldn't fathom. "What about you?"

"It's difficult for a lupus to get drunk. Our bodies regard alcohol as a toxin and clear it from our systems too quickly for us to become intoxicated."

"That could be handy . . . unless you really want to be drunk."

His grin flashed, quick and bright as a lightning stroke. "I did, yes, at that age. I wanted to see what it was like. I was as stupid as most boys, thinking ourselves adult once we pass a legal age marker."

She had a hard time picturing Rule in college. Had he gone out for sports? Been studious or wild? Had he had friends? Human friends, she supposed she meant. People not in the clans. "Does your father have pictures from when you were young? A kid or a teenager, I mean. I'd like to see them."

He tilted his head, surprised. "Henry has several albums. I'm sure he'd share them with you, if you asked."

Henry? Who . . . oh. "Your father's houseman or cook or whatever. He keeps the family pictures?"

"Henry has been part of my family for many years. He helped raised me."

Rule hadn't sprung from his father's seed alone, but she couldn't remember him ever referring to a second parent. That gaping absence warned her to go lightly. "You never mention your mother."

"You might say that I've had many mothers. Our people make much of children."

Okay, he wanted that door shut. She'd go along for now. This wasn't the best time for such personal stuff, anyway. "I guess Nettie was one of those motherly . . ." Her voice drifted off as realization struck. "Or not. She, uh, must be your age, or close to it. You probably played together."

"Ah . . . the gray hair is misleading. Nettie's only forty-four." He hesitated. "She's my niece."

"Your . . . niece?"

He nodded. "She was raised with her mother's people

but came to Clanhome to stay with Benedict most summers."

Nettie looked older than Rule. She looked older than her own father. What did it do to families when half of them—the female half—aged so much faster than the others? "How old is Benedict?"

"Sixty-four."

God. He did look older than Rule, but she'd have guessed him at about forty. Yet he had another eighty or more years ahead of him, while his daughter . . . "Damn," she said softly. "He'll watch her get old. And she'll never see him as an old man."

"It isn't easy for one of us to have a daughter when he's young."

A sudden thought struck her. "Is that why you don't marry—why lupi don't believe in marriage? You couldn't keep your secret from a wife. She'd age and you wouldn't, at least not as much. And she'd die. That would be hard."

Rule's face was all mask, no expression. "That's part of it."

"I'll get old and die before you will." There, she'd said it. Her heart beat unsteadily.

"Possibly."

Her eyebrows lifted. "If you live to twice the human lifespan, that's a hundred and fifty or more. I might get eighty-five or ninety years, if I stay healthy. So when I'm eighty and creaky, you'll be a lively one-oh-six."

"Sometimes a Chosen ages more like one of us. Not always. We don't know why."

He didn't know if he'd lose her while he still had years and years left. Not knowing . . . that could be as hard to handle as despair. She touched his hand.

He gripped hers suddenly, as if he knew her thoughts. As if he'd keep her young by force of will. After a moment his grip eased. He gave his head a little shake and released her hand. "I've enough to worry about in the present without tackling what-ifs that are years away. Most immediately, I'm afraid I've some clan business to take care of tonight."

"Okay. What's up?"

"The Rho has decided to call for an All-Clan." He began brushing the crumbs from the pizza into his palm and then dumped them in the box. "I'm needed to make some of the contacts."

"What's an All-Clan? Some kind of gathering of the clans?"

"Yes. It's held roughly every seven years. The last one was only two years ago, so we aren't due for one yet. But there are mechanisms for calling an All-Clan in an emergency. The Rho believes we're facing just that."

"Because of Her, you mean. The goddess. She has it in for lupi."

"That's right. We've already passed the word about Her, of course, but it's easy to disbelieve such a tale."

"So what does your father hope to accomplish? Does he think you'll be able to convince more of your people there's a real threat?"

"I never try to guess what Isen intends," Rule said dryly. "But one of his goals is certainly to persuade the doubters that the threat is real. That She is active in our realm again."

Lily frowned, tapping one finger against the table. Rule had said once that the lupi had been created to fight this goddess. Whether that was true or not, he believed it. So, apparently, did most lupi—even Cullen, who wasn't one to take much on faith. "What will it mean if the other clans believe you? What will they do?"

Rule hesitated, his dark eyes troubled. *"Thranga,"* he said at last. "Perhaps."

"Well, now I understand completely. If you . . ."

Rule's head turned, alerting her that he'd heard something. A second later she did, too—footsteps.

Baxter appeared in the doorway. "Hastings tracked

down the bartender at his girlfriend's place and is bringing him up. I told him we'd use my office. Might put the man more at ease than one of the interrogation rooms." He eyed the pizza box. "Any leftovers?"

"Nope." Lily pushed her chair back. "I'll be right there."

Baxter nodded and headed back down the hall. Lily took the empty pizza box to the trash can. They were out of time—again. There never seemed to be enough time for the questions that mattered.

Still, she could hit one of them. "What was your favorite TV show when you were a kid?"

"You ask the oddest things."

"I watched *Sesame Street*. Was that on when you were little?"

"No, I was a Mouseketeer."

"A Mouseketeer." A grin spread across her face. "Really? Did you have the hat?"

"I don't remember. No, I don't think I did." He came to her and put his hand on her good shoulder. "You'll be here awhile longer, I take it."

"Looks like. I tell you what. If it will make you feel better, I'll call you when I'm ready to leave." Lily was pleased with herself. Who said she couldn't compromise?

The twist to his mouth didn't look happy. "I expect my meeting to last awhile. I'm likely to be later than you will be."

"Okay. If you need to take your car, I'll get a ride."

"I can't leave unless you'll accept another guard in my place."

"Rule." *Don't overreact,* she told herself. Naturally he worried, with the way she'd been targeted. "I'm not claiming to be invulnerable, but I am a good shot. I can get myself home just fine."

"A gun is little defense if you're asleep when an attack comes."

She glanced at the hall. Was that the elevator? "You sleep, too."

"Sentry sleep is different."

"What's that? No, wait, I don't have time for explanations. I need to get back."

"Indulge me a moment first. I'll keep this brief." He took her face in his hands and bent to kiss her.

That was another great thing about him, she thought after he stepped back and she could think again. When he kissed, he gave it his complete attention. Maybe she'd been wrong about that "half-a-beer" analogy. "Remind me to ask you about sentry sleep."

"All right. Benedict's waiting in the parking lot to give you a ride when you're ready."

"What?"

"He thought it best to wait for you outside the building so he didn't have to disarm. He agrees about the value of bullets where demons are concerned."

"That's gratifying, but—"

"You might call downstairs and let the guard know so he doesn't think Benedict is lurking outside so he can bomb the building or something." He turned to go.

"Wait! Wait a minute! I didn't say I'd let him play bodyguard."

"Play?" Rule paused in the doorway, smiling. "You say that, yet you've met my brother."

She stared at him, unamused.

He sighed. "Lily, the Rho uses bodyguards. It doesn't diminish him."

"The Rho agrees to use them. I didn't agree to a damned thing."

"But you aren't stupid, so you will. Besides, you'll need a ride home. Why not use Benedict? He's here."

"He's here because you arranged it. You didn't ask me." She heard voices in the hall—the bartender, complaining about having his night off interrupted, and one of the agents soothing him.

"You've been busy. I took the liberty of entering Benedict's cell phone number on your phone's speed dial—number twelve. If you'll let him know when you're ready to leave, he'll be ready."

Which meant he'd planned this hours and hours ago, when she'd handed him her phone to call Cullen. Then sprung it on her at the last minute. "Dammit, I have to go. But we are going to talk about this."

He smiled. "Of course. Until later, *nadia.*"

FOURTEEN

~❦~

AT eight o'clock on Saturday night, Club Hell was packed and noisy. Rule felt the vibration from the music in the soles of his feet, even back in the cubbyhole Cullen used for a dressing room. He had no idea how the human patrons of the place could hear each other out there.

Of course, that was one of the reasons he'd chosen Club Hell for the circle. They needed to come together on neutral ground, and the club had supplied that many times over the years for less formal meetings than the one tonight. No one could eavesdrop on them physically. "Max said the others are already here."

"I saw a few of them." Cullen wiped his face with a towel. He was sweaty and as naked as the law allowed, having just finished his performance. "Including Leidolf."

That name jolted Rule. Max hadn't mentioned that, damn him. "Who did they send?"

"Dear Randy."

Randall Frey, the other clan's Lu Nuncio. Rule's counterpart. That was good, a sign they were taking this seriously . . . but he wouldn't turn his back on the man.

"I don't put much stock in Leidolf's decision to participate," Cullen said, tossing the towel on the shelf that served as his dressing table. "They want to know what you're up to, that's all."

Leidolf and Nokolai had a long, unhappy history. Most recently it included an attack on Rule's father that had left him badly injured and one Nokolai dead . . . along with three members of Leidolf. "That's true of others as well. We knew that once we convinced a certain number to come, others would decide they couldn't afford to be left out. Leidolf did send the heir."

"Status." Cullen grabbed his jeans. "Can't let their representative be outranked by you."

"Perhaps." Rule leaned against the wall, fighting an urge to fling open the door. Cullen was annoyingly impervious to the usual lupus distaste for small, enclosed spaces. "How many agreed to come tonight? Max was in a lather about something when he let me in the back door. He didn't hang around long enough to give me a head count."

Cullen grinned and stepped into his jeans. "I can imagine. Poor Max. He likes to be in the middle of things almost as much as he likes to play it safe."

Rule's eyebrows lifted. "You know something I don't?"

"Five more are attending this circle than came to the first one, in spite of the short notice—and they include a bumper crop of Lu Nuncios. Ought to make for a lively meeting. I can almost smell the *seru* now."

"What's changed?"

"Etorri is here."

Etorri . . . the most honored of them all. In the long centuries since the Great War, the clan had nearly winked out of existence more than once. The single Etorri who'd survived that conflict had been altered in ways that set him and his descendents apart; the magic was too wild in them, diminishing fertility. Somehow the clan had persisted, though. Equally amazing, perhaps, was their persistent integrity. They lived up to their *du*.

Etorri. The clutch of pride-blinded, self-righteous fools who had expelled Cullen from their ranks for practicing sorcery, dooming him to life as an outcast . . . if he lived. The clanless usually committed suicide or went insane.

For whatever reason, Cullen had done neither. Three weeks ago, his life as a lone wolf had ended when Nokolai claimed him with blood, earth, and fire. If Rule's feelings about the Etorri were mixed, Cullen's were volatile. "Who did they send?" he asked carefully.

"Who else?" Cullen's mouth twisted in what might have been meant for a smile. "My dear cousin. Oh, don't look so wary. No need to tiptoe around my tender feelings." Cullen yanked up his zipper and opened the door, not bothering with a shirt. Because he considered pants optional after a performance, that wasn't surprising. "I'll survive seeing Stephen again, and God knows he's too pure to be harmed by contact with us lesser beings."

"I'm glad you're not bitter."

Cullen gave a single bark of laughter.

Rule was glad to leave the closet-sized dressing room. The hall they entered wasn't a big improvement, though, being dim and narrow. One end opened onto the squalor Max called his office. They went the other way, into the scents and din of the club proper.

The cavernous room occupied both the basement and first floor of the building, with its upper reaches vanishing in the overhead gloom. Max took great delight in the décor. He'd borrowed from every hellish cliché he could find, creating a three-dimensional cartoon of the underworld complete with stony walls, fake fires, and a scent he insisted was brimstone.

Most of the club's patrons were human, of course. That lupi frequented the place made it a draw for thrill seekers, and for seekers of another sort. Several women tried to claim Rule's attention—some he knew, some he didn't. Several more tried to stop Cullen.

It must have been a good performance tonight. The

two of them made their way between the tables, managing to get by with a smile, a word, a nod, looking for the ones who weren't human.

There, at the bar. Rule caught the man's eye and gave a small nod. Across the room, another man saw them and gave the woman beside him a kiss and then stood. A pair of men at a table with several women created vast disappointment by taking their leave. All around the room, one and two at a time, men who resembled each other mainly by their unusual fitness began drifting toward the back of the room, where a spiral staircase wound up into a shadowed loft, invisible from below.

Rule and Cullen reached the stairs first. Rule started up, with Cullen behind him.

"Did you have any trouble getting away?" Cullen asked.

"No." He hadn't even had to lie. Not that he'd told her the truth, but he hadn't spoken a direct lie.

"Even if the tracking spell doesn't work—and I may have fixed it—Benedict's got the panic button, right?"

"Yes."

"My, but you're in a monosyllabic mood all of a sudden. I suppose you're feeling all squirmy with guilt. Bad habit, guilt."

"Shut up, Cullen."

"Right. You're making too much of this, you know. Lily's sensible. She'll be upset, but once she thinks about it—"

"Are we talking about the same woman?" Rule demanded. "The one who won't have bodyguards, so you have to invent a whole new spell so I can be sure she's protected? The one I had to trick into letting Benedict stay with her while I'm gone? She was attacked by a bloody demon last night, but oh, no, she doesn't need protection. That's sensible?"

They'd reached the loft, an open, unfurnished stretch that ran the length of the back wall. All the pillows had been chased to the edges of the carpeted floor to make room. There were no lights; the only illumination came from below.

With a glance, Cullen changed that. Twelve black candles set in a wide circle suddenly sported flames. Then he looked at Rule. "Maybe she doesn't like Benedict. I don't, myself."

Rule snorted.

Someone was coming up the stairs, making more noise than strictly necessary. That was courtesy. Rule took note and stuffed his regrets—and yes, dammit, his guilt—down where it wouldn't intrude on tonight's business.

Cullen took a white candle, still unlit, from a small tote and started for the head of the stairs. He stopped beside Rule and put a hand on his arm—a rare gesture. Lupi usually touched easily and often, but Cullen had spent most of his life apart. He'd stopped reaching out decades ago.

He spoke under the tongue now, so low that, even this close, Rule barely heard him. *"There's no point in punishing yourself, you know. Lily will do a fine job of that when the time comes."*

A smile ghosted across Rule's face. *"The funny thing is, you mean that as a comfort."*

Cullen's answering smile was swift and fleeting. He turned just as the first of the others reached the top of the stairs—Ben Larson of Ansgar, the largest of the Scandinavian clans. Ben was a fine fighter, but he could be overly deliberate, seeking certainty when none existed.

He frowned at the sight of Cullen. Perhaps he'd hoped Rule would have switched gatekeepers. Tough. They were all going to have to adjust to changes. The realms were shifting, and *She* was active once again.

"A moment," Cullen said to Ben. This time he waved his hand over the candle he held and murmured a few words to dance a flame onto the wick. That was theater, and Rule's idea. He wanted the others to get used to Cullen but saw no point in rubbing their noses in just how different his friend really was. Some of the Gifted could summon fire through ritual. Cullen called it by mind alone.

He held the candle out to Rule first. *"Accipisne alios in pace?"*

"Accipio in pace." Rule held his palm over the flame without quite touching it for a slow count of three—long enough to seal the pledge, briefly enough that by the time he left the burn would be healed. Then he moved to the nearest black candle and sat tailor-fashion, the candle at his back.

Cullen held the white candle out to Ben. *"Accipiaris in pace."*

"Advenio in pace." Ben held his hand over the flame as Rule had done and then took his place within the circle of candles.

One by one the rest entered, held one hand to the flame, and pledged peace. Con McGuire of Cynir. Stephen Andros, the Etorri Lu Nuncio, with the oddly pale eyes typical of his lineage and hair the color of dust. Ito Tsegaye of Mendoyo. Randall Frey of Leidolf—a smiling villain, that one. Ybirra's Javiero Mendozo, almost as dark-skinned as Ito. Rikard Demeny of Szós. The Kerberos heir, Jon Sebastian, who looked like an accountant and fought like a madman. Kyffin's Sean Masters.

Altogether, fifteen of the twenty-two dominant clans were directly represented, eight by their Lu Nuncios. One of the heirs and two of the *nonheris* sons had crossed an ocean to attend the first circle. For this one, Stephen Andros had traveled almost as far—the Etorri lands were in northern Canada.

Rule tried not to resent the fact that it had taken Etorri's lead to persuade many of them to attend. They were here. That's what mattered.

Once everyone was seated, Cullen extinguished his candle and sat apart, near the wall. He was responsible for guarding the circle from intrusions both physical and magical. *She* couldn't spy on them directly, but her agents might be able to.

Rule was responsible for what happened within the circle. No easy task, that. He began with silence, allowing them all a few moments to gather the inner stillness necessary for control.

Candles burned behind each man, leaving faces shadowed and laying their waxy scent heavily on the air. Music and voices washed up from below. And yes, beneath the heavy scent of the candles and the mingled personal scents of those present, Rule found more than a trace of *seru.*

Lu Nuncios were by definition dominant. Closing up so many together in a *pace* circle and getting them to listen, to cooperate, would be tricky. Outright violence was forbidden, as were challenges to later combat. But each of them would instinctively seek to dominate the others.

Including him, of course. Cullen was right. It should be a lively meeting. *"In pace convenio,"* he said formally. "Let us begin."

"You can start with an explanation," Rikard said. "Why is that one—" he jerked his head toward Cullen— "acting as gatekeeper?"

Rikard was the oldest of them, but age had never mellowed him. He remained fiery and prone to saying what others might leave unsaid out of caution or simple courtesy. "Because Nokolai's Rhej doesn't leave Clanhome. Because Cullen has the necessary skills. And because I chose him."

One of the *nonheris* muttered something Rule ignored. Rikard snorted. "Obviously you chose him. But—"

Stephen Andros interrupted. "We waste time arguing about what we've already accepted by sitting in circle. Nokolai called the circle. Nokolai therefore has the right to choose the gatekeeper."

Rule didn't thank him. That would be insult, implying that Stephen supported him—a subordinate position. But he met the Etorri heir's eyes for a moment in acknowledgment. Stephen Andros was built like a full-back, but he had the otherworldly eyes of a monk, a sage, . . . or a sorcerer.

Rule had wondered if it was that taint of otherness in Cullen's heritage that had made the impossible possible. There had never been a lupus sorcerer; their innate magic was said to crowd out any other type. He'd never asked. Cullen didn't speak of his life as Etorri.

"I would know more about why I am here." That was Ito Tsegaye of Mendoyo—dark, thin, and very tall. His English was heavily accented, tuned to melodies distant and strange. The Mendoyo had lived apart from the other clans for centuries while Africa was cut off from the European world; more than their accents were strange to Rule.

"You're here to take information back to your clan—and, I hope, some of you are here to join the fight against Her. Something has changed, and the realms aren't as distant as before. She's able to reach into our world once more, and She intends to destroy us."

Randall of Leidolf smiled. "That She would destroy us if She could, I don't doubt. But the rest of it . . . we've only your word about that."

Rule looked at him impassively. It took all his control to keep his own *seru* from spiking at the insult. "Yes, you have my word. All of you have heard of what happened—how Her followers were defeated and Her staff disappeared. But some of you have heard it only second- or third-hand. Do you wish to hear it from me?"

They did, though it took some discussion to reach agreement. Lily, Rule thought with a small smile, would have wanted him to take a vote.

"You are amused?" Ito asked.

"A private thought. My Chosen finds some of our ways strange, and for a moment I saw things through her eyes." Reminding the others of Lily wouldn't hurt. The Lady had never gifted a Lu Nuncio with a Chosen—not, at least, since the times of legend.

"Your Chosen . . . some say she's a sensitive."

Rule looked at the man who'd spoken. Con was a friend, but more, he was of the same mind as Rule. They had to organize now, while Her power in their realm was still limited. "Yes, she is."

That raised eyebrows. "Uncanny," Rikard announced.

"Not since Magya of Etorri—"

"Coincidence. It doesn't mean—"

"A Lu Nuncio with a sensitive Chosen—coincidence?" Con snorted. "Sure, and the Lady's just having a little joke on us."

Ben flushed angrily. "So you're an expert on the Lady's intentions now?"

"I'm saying it isn't coincidence. We don't call our mates 'Chosen' because the Lady hands them out at random."

"Very true," Randall said, "but we don't want to jump to conclusions, either." He turned to Rule, smiling his toothpaste ad smile. He was a handsome man, younger than Rule by a decade, with streaky blond hair, a pianist's long fingers, and more wiggles than a snake. "You aren't trying to make us think you're starring in a rerun of Senn and Magya, are you?"

"Randall." Rule smiled back gently. "I respect your character too much to try to make you think anything at all."

That brought grins and a couple of chuckles. Rule took advantage of the moment to begin his tale. It wasn't their way to shear a story of its personality, turning it into the kind of impersonal report Lily might submit, so this took a while.

There were a few glances at Randall when Rule spoke of the attack on his father—and later, more glances at Cullen, who'd played a heroic part at the end. And when he finished, the questions hit. The first few were easy, but inevitably someone asked about Lily.

"She's still a cop, yes, but with the FBI now."

"One of your federal police, you mean?" Ito asked.

"That's right." Rule took a deep breath. He couldn't put this off any longer—it was, after all, why he'd called the circle. "She's in charge of the hunt for the staff. That's how I learned today that the government doesn't intend to destroy it."

That brought outcries even from those who weren't wholly convinced the staff existed. Rule gave them a moment before continuing. "Lily has been told to preserve it for study. I don't know who wants the bloody thing, and it doesn't matter. We can't let them have it."

Even though "they" included Lily.

FIFTEEN

At ten-fifty-seven, Lily took the elevator down with her eyes closed, leaning against the wall. She was beyond tired, into the lightheaded stage when giggles or tears are equally easily come by.

Probably she should have left earlier. Okay, definitely she should have, but they had so little time—maybe a day. Then Harlowe would kill again.

The good news was that Rule wasn't around to nag. And the bad news . . . well, the bad news was that Rule wasn't around. She'd grown used to curling up with him at night. She'd miss that, at least for the few seconds between getting horizontal and falling asleep.

She got her eyes open and her back straight before the elevator door opened. The building had decent security, a mix of the old and the new—an electronically operated door plus a guard with a sign-in sheet. He teased her about having a "real patient date." She looked out the heavy glass doors and saw Benedict waiting.

It had been tempting to take a taxi home. Tempting, but stupid. If they made another try at her tonight, she'd lose precious seconds yawning. So she'd sucked it in and done the sensible thing, calling Benedict to let him know she was leaving. Just as she'd been told to do.

Her lips tightened. Rule thought she was being stubborn about needing protection. There was a pinch of that, she admitted as the guard hit the button that unlocked the door. But it was his high-handedness that infuriated her. He'd made a decision for her this morning and then waited all day to spring it on her.

She stepped out into air with barely enough snap to qualify as fall, air that smelled of concrete and car exhaust, yet it perked her up. It hadn't been groomed and filtered and pimped into a consumable product. It was just air being air.

Or maybe it was stepping from safety into possible danger that quickened her heartbeat. Whatever. She took a second to breathe in, feeling more awake than she had in hours.

"We're exposed here. It would be best to get to the car."

She glanced to her right at more than six solid feet of annoyed male. "Hello, Benedict. I'm pretty good, thanks. How are you?"

The smile that touched his mouth looked like an uncommon visitor. "It's good to see you again. Especially when you aren't bleeding. Can we go to the car now?"

She sighed. "Sure. Where . . . wait a minute. That's *my* car."

"I drive a Jeep. No doors, no protection."

"I suppose Rule gave you the keys."

"You're pissed."

"Good guess. Not at you, though." She fell into step beside him, feeling dwarfed. Rule was tall. His brother was just plain big—six-four and two-forty, at a guess, and every inch hard enough to bruise yourself on.

They didn't look alike. Benedict carried the human side of his ancestry on his skin—a coppery color that suggested native blood, as did his silver-shot black hair and dark eyes. He wore jeans with a black T-shirt and a denim jacket that hid his shoulder holster. And he was not, thank God, wearing the scabbard that sheathed the three feet of steel he favored at Clanhome. "What are you carrying?"

"This and that. Main weapon's a Sig Sauer."

"I use a Sig, too."

"Good choice. I wanted to bring my SAW, but there was a chance someone would check out the car. I wouldn't be much use to you if I got locked up."

"SAW . . . Squad Automatic Weapon. You're talking about a machine gun."

He nodded. "Good stopping power."

"I've more to be grateful for than I'd realized."

They reached her Toyota. He claimed the driver's side before she could, so Lily got in on the passenger side, frowning. "I could drive. My reflexes are almost as good as yours." She took after Grandmother that way.

"Almost as good a Rule's, maybe." He started the car. "Not mine."

She looked at him, wondering just how fast he was. Lily had seen him in action once, but he'd been a wolf at the time—one of several—and she'd been busy getting shot and shooting back. Aside from Rule, she hadn't known which wolf was which. So she felt a certain professional curiosity about Benedict's abilities. What would he be like in a fight in his human form?

Not that she wanted to find out tonight. She fastened her seatbelt. "Rule told me once you should have been Lu Nuncio. Not just because you're older than him, either. He thinks you're a better fighter."

Benedict made a small, impatient sound. "I thought he'd outgrown that."

"What do you mean?"

"I am a better fighter. That doesn't make me a better Lu Nuncio."

"The Lu Nuncio defends the Rho and answers any formal challenges, right? Fighting's a big part of the job description."

"He's also the heir. The one who will eventually be Rho. Rule will lead our people far better than I could."

"So you don't feel skipped over or slighted?"

He was silent for so long she wondered if she'd offended him. But when she glanced at him, he seemed to be thinking, though his eyes remained watchful, keeping track of the cars ahead, beside, and behind them. *Cop eyes,* she thought. It was odd to find them in someone who'd been on the other side of the law most of his life, until the law changed.

Finally, as he accelerated into the traffic on I-15, he said, "You're thinking about Mick. He wanted to be Rho. I never have. When our father named Rule heir, Mick was angry. I was relieved."

It was Lily's turn to fall silent. The twinned ribbons of taillights seemed to draw them along, just one more bead on a string. Her eyes grew heavy. She leaned her head against the headrest . . . then jerked it up again. She'd been close to drifting off.

I trust him, she thought, startled. Somewhere inside, she'd decided Benedict could be counted on to watch out for both of them. This wasn't like her, and she wasn't sure what to make of it.

Unlike Rule—or most of the other people she knew, for that matter—Benedict didn't have the radio on or a CD playing. Maybe he was listening for danger as well as watching. So they drove on through the crowded city night in silence, with only the glow of the dash lights to smudge the interior darkness, leaving more to be guessed at than revealed.

Why had she asked about his feelings? No doubt he had the usual assortment, but he kept them so far out of sight she wasn't sure he knew any more about them than she did. He wasn't likely to open up to her.

Yet instinct prompted her to believe him. There was something reassuring about Benedict, something oddly peaceful. He seemed so at rest within himself.

Not her. Now that she'd stopped doing, stopped talking, the discomforts of a healing body spoke all too loudly. She shifted, trying to find the best way to rest her shoulder, and then shifted again. And her mind was anything but quiet.

Finally, she broke the silence. "I'd like to ask you something, but it might be rude by your standards."

"Our standards aren't that different from yours."

"Maybe it's just plain rude, then. It's . . . about your daughter."

He gave her a quick glance. "Rule told you."

"Just tonight, yeah. And last night I learned about the, ah . . . the age thing. I'm still trying to get it sorted out."

"Shook you up." It was a simple observation, lacking either sympathy or judgment. "What did you want to know about Nettie?"

"Was her mother your Chosen?"

"No." The hitch between that flat answer and his next words was brief, a fraction of a breath. "I met Claire when Nettie was twelve. We didn't have children together."

A dozen more questions pressed at Lily. She was pretty sure Benedict's Chosen had died, but she didn't know how or how long ago. She wanted to know what happened when one partner in a mate bond died. How did it affect the one who remained?

She wanted to know more personal things, too. Had he loved Claire? Had they been friends as well as lovers? What had been the limits of their bond? Had they ever had their abilities cross over the way she and Rule had?

Lily was used to asking deeply personal questions, often at a time when feelings were raw. But this wasn't an investigation, and Benedict's reserve went deep. "Thank you for telling me," she said at last.

There was a hint of amusement in his voice. "That was all you wanted to know?"

"No, but—"

Her cell phone rang. She reached into her bag and thumbed it on. "Yes?"

"Lily Yu?" said an unfamiliar male voice.

She frowned. Very few people had this number. "Who is this?"

He chuckled, a pleasantly masculine sound. "I suppose we haven't spoken before. I'm Patrick Harlowe."

Exhaustion evaporated in a white-hot rush. She sat up straight. "Thoughtful of you to call. I've been looking for you."

"So I understand." He had one of those rich voices that invested everything he said with significance and a hint of intimacy. Like a televangelist, she thought, or someone selling kitchen gadgets on a late-night infomercial. "Haven't had much luck, have you?"

"Not so far." *Keep him talking.* She'd play whatever game he had in mind and keep him talking. People always gave up more than they realized if you could keep them talking. "How'd you get this number, anyway?"

"The same way I've learned so many interesting things recently—from One who is almost omniscient. I imagine you'd find that handy, in your job," he added. "Being able to watch or listen to anyone you wanted."

"That I would. But 'almost' means that She isn't omniscient, doesn't it? She can't watch lupi. Or me. And She can't talk to you directly." Could She? God, if the staff really had made Harlowe telepathic, able to get instructions and information directly from Her—

"Pretty sure of that, are you?" He might have been a favorite uncle indulging a pert niece. "But you're correct in this case. She isn't quite omniscient. As this call illustrates, however, we've found ways to work around those few limits She possesses. But the telephone is limiting, too, isn't it? So much more pleasant to become acquainted in person."

"You'd like to do lunch?" Lily kept her voice dry. "Gee, let me check my calendar."

"Lunch won't work for me." There was laughter in his voice now. He was enjoying himself. "How about right now? It's a bit late, but my schedule is so full these days."

Lily glanced at Benedict. His face was wiped clean of everything but focus.

Of course. He was listening to Harlowe, too. "I'm free tonight. Where shall we meet?"

"You'll have to come to me, I'm afraid. And I must insist that you don't tell anyone. No one at all, Lily—other than your driver, of course."

He knew someone was driving her? Lily looked at Benedict. She could still subvocalize, even if she couldn't hear it anymore: *"Are we being followed?"*

He shook his head.

"That goes for your driver, too. No phone calls. If anyone finds out about our little rendezvous I'll be hurt, and I'm afraid I don't react well when my feelings are hurt. And I *will* know, Lily." His voice dropped. "The One I serve may not be able to watch you directly, but She doesn't have to. She can observe the others—any and all the others—you might be tempted to call. Like your associates at the FBI, or the police . . . or even your family."

Lily's nape was suddenly clammy, as if someone had touched it with a cold, damp cloth. "So where do we meet?"

"I'll give you directions in a moment. First, there's someone here who'd like to speak with you."

"Wait—"

But he'd passed the phone to someone else. Someone whose voice struck Lily dumb and blind with fear.

"Lily?" Beth Yu spoke in her usual quick, lighthearted way. "Patrick wanted me to reassure you that I'm all right.

I'm not sure why. Really, I don't even know why he wanted to come here—this is *so* not my kind of place. But it's all right, you know. Patrick said so. He'll take care of me."

THE candles had burned halfway down. They'd discussed much and settled little, and it was almost time for Cullen to leave for his second performance.

Not that he had to dance anymore. Not for money, at least, and Rule had expected him to quit when the Rho put him on retainer for the clan—"like a damned lawyer," Cullen had said. But he continued to do two shows a night, two days a week. He'd told Rule he was hanging on to the part-time gig because the extra money helped.

Perhaps he believed that. Rule didn't. Cullen had never been much interested in money, seeing it mostly as a means to acquire the scraps of paper that were real treasure to him—bits of old spellbooks and such. No, Rule had to believe that dance gave Cullen something he needed.

At the moment, though, it was a confounded nuisance. "We'll need to wind this up soon," he said when he was able to get a word in. "Remember to be cautious about what you discuss after the circle is broken." There would be a number of meetings after this one, he was sure—less formal, but maybe more meaningful.

"I still don't know what you want." Ben was cranky. "What is it you want us to do? It's all very well to talk about doing battle with Her, but She's not here."

"Keep your eyes open," Rule said promptly, "and your noses to the ground. See if what I've said about the realms shifting, bringing changes, matches with what your clan is experiencing. I told you about the banshee sighting in Texas, for example."

"Possible sighting," Javiero corrected. "But I checked into it, and the stories of the witnesses hold up."

"What's happening in your own territories?" Rule asked. "Send word back about anything you learn that's unusual. Try to find out what others of the Blood might know or guess, too. You, Ben, might send word to the trolls, see if they're aware of any changes." Ben's clan was based in Scandinavia, which possessed the only remaining troll population of any size.

"Trolls." Ben snorted. "You ever tried talking to one? Might as well talk to a tree."

"Speaking of talking to trees," someone said, "I'll volunteer to check with the dryads."

That sally earned several grins and chuckles. Dryads were notoriously shy . . . and notoriously amorous, if you could overcome their timidity.

Ito shook his head. "I don't know dryads or trolls, but I know trees. With trees, you don't talk. You listen."

There was a moment's silence, all of them mildly embarrassed on Ito's behalf. He was well liked, but not well understood.

"We're getting off-track," Randall said. "Asking us to look for abnormalities is like telling us to pay attention to the letter *s*. Once your attention is called to it, you see it everywhere. Of course people will find oddities if they're looking for them."

"The letter *s* is common. Oddities are, by definition, uncommon. I'm not asking for news of, say, your sister's new hairstyle . . . however odd it may be." There were grins and a couple of chuckles. "But if you hear rumors of creatures or those of the Blood who shouldn't be in our realm, the rest of us need to know."

"So who do we tell? You?" Randall's upper lip lifted in scorn. "There's a plan. You can use everything you hear to further 'prove' your case, increasing your chances of being named war-leader if the clans fall into line with your father's megalomaniacal—"

"Best stop there." Rule held himself very still. "As I haven't spoken about your father's habit of killing from ambush, so you—"

"You may all tell me, if you like," Stephen said calmly.

"I'm willing to act as clearinghouse for such reports. Unless any of you doubt Etorri's ability to remain impartial?"

Randall didn't dare go that far, but he narrowed his eyes as his head swung toward Stephen. "You're buying into this absurd theory about the realms shifting?"

"Please," Ito said to the man beside him, "what is 'buying into'?"

Randall answered without taking his eyes off Stephen. "Believe. Agree with. Think it's more than cat box scrapings."

Stephen was unmoved. "Etorri was already considering the possibility that the realms were shifting when we received the invitation to a pax circle."

"Why?" Randall exploded. "For God's sake, what proof do you have?"

"First, it accords with the prophecy—"

That set everyone off. "What prophecy?"

"—Etorri loves all that mystical mumbo-jumbo—"

"If you've been sitting on a prophecy and haven't told anyone—"

"And second," Stephen said, "I have myself seen the Great Hunt in the northern forests."

Dead silence. Into that silence, Cullen's voice. "Rule."

Rule's head swung, his nostrils flared. "What?"

"We have to break circle *now*. Benedict's pushed the panic button."

SIXTEEN

RULE felt the hair lifting all over his body, as if he were a conduit for lightning. The edges of everything turned sharp. So did his mind. He didn't have to think about what to do—the necessary actions flowed, one from another, in crystal clarity.

"The circle is ended," he said, flowing to his feet. "Lily is in danger, perhaps under attack. I'm leaving. Cullen—"

He was on his feet, too. "The map's in my dressing room. So's your phone. Benedict may be trying to call."

Rule was already moving when one of the *nonheris* sons grabbed his arm. "Wait a minute." Rule backhanded him and kept moving.

There was a brief scuffle—the man he'd knocked down was angry, but Rikard and Con held him back. "Idiot," Rikard growled. "The man's mate is in danger. You're lucky he didn't break your neck."

Rule headed for the railing—the stairs would take too long—but Stephen was there. His lip lifted in a snarl.

"I'm not trying to stop you," Stephen said in that damned calm voice. "I'm coming with you."

"Come, then." Rule gripped the railing, flung himself over, and dropped.

The others followed.

The patrons of Club Hell were treated to an unexpected show that night. One, two, three, four at a time, men dropped out of the darkness overhead, landing on tables or the floor—and moving unbelievably fast. Like a river hitting the rapids, they flowed around or over any obstacles. Those who landed on tables simply leaped over anyone who'd been sitting there and hit the ground running.

THE Mercedes's tires squealed slightly as Benedict swung into the turn. Lily's tongue felt thick and clumsy, as if it were taking up too much space in her mouth. "We're on Fifty-ninth now," she told the man holding her sister hostage.

"Proceed to Barbara . . . I think that's what it says. Beth, dear, can you read those tiny letters? I don't know why they make maps so . . . yes? Oh, Bandera, not Barbara. Turn right on Bandera. Do try to hurry. You've only fifteen minutes left."

"Continue to Bandera and turn right," Lily repeated, looking at Benedict.

Harlowe knew someone was driving Lily. He didn't know who, or that Benedict could hear everything he said. Or that Benedict wore a headset attached to his own phone. Lily had dialed Rule's number for him so he could focus on driving.

Calling Rule was a calculated risk. Harlowe insisted on keeping her on the line, giving her a deadline, handing out directions one street at a time. They wouldn't know they'd arrived until they got there, so Benedict wouldn't know when to remove the headset. If Harlowe spotted it . . .

But they needed backup. Harlowe had Beth, and he was calling the shots—the time and place of their meeting were in his control, and he might not be in this alone.

Lily didn't dare call for official backup, but Rule would be able to hear Benedict speak subvocally. And Harlowe wouldn't.

If Rule ever answered his damned phone.

As if he were a magnet and she had a sliver of iron in her gut, she felt Rule's direction—and, roughly, his distance from her. He wasn't at Clanhome. Much closer. Somewhere in the city. She could have pointed toward him, but she couldn't reach across that distance and make him pick up his phone.

"This is a lousy neighborhood," she said, doing the one thing she could do: keeping Harlowe talking. "Come down in the world a bit, haven't you?"

"Temporary quarters, purely temporary. You should see the plans I've drawn up. Perhaps I'll show you before . . . Beth, don't bother me now. Where was I? Oh, yes, my plans. You come first, dear Lily. If it weren't for you I wouldn't be here, would I? I can't say I'm happy with you, not at all, but you'll get what's coming to you. And you'll . . . not *now,* Beth."

"So what are you planning?" she asked quickly, able to hear Beth's upset voice in the background. *Beth, please, play it cool. Don't make him angry.* "King of the world, maybe?"

"No, no." He was all good humor again. "They'll elect me. They'll all love me, you see."

Benedict tapped her arm. When she looked at him he tapped his headset and nodded.

Thank God. He'd finally reached Rule. "Funny," she said. "I'm not feeling much love for you right now."

"Yes, you're different, aren't you? That's your bad luck. But don't worry, dear—it's temporary. Or perhaps I should say *you* are." He chuckled over his little joke.

"You hold on to that thought, if it makes you feel better." Their biggest advantage was that Harlowe—or maybe his goddess—didn't seem to want Lily dead. He wanted to feed her to the staff or the demon or something, which took a lot more arranging than just killing her. This gave her a little maneuvering room.

Unless, of course, they were wrong about Harlowe's intentions.

"But you won't be a problem much longer. I'll take care of—now, now, didn't I tell you to leave her alone?"

The last was spoken to someone else. Lily heard a male voice, then Beth's, high-pitched and frightened.

"What's going on?" Lily demanded. "If you hurt her—"

"I do as I please. As long as I have her—"

"Alive and unharmed, or you'll make my job simple. I'll just kill you."

"Oh, but you can't. And even if you could, you wouldn't. You have to *arrest* me." He made it sound like the most amusing of impossibilities.

"I didn't arrest Helen."

That checked him briefly. "Well, well, you won't have the opportunity to kill me. But let's not be so grim. After all, your sister is alive and well. Not too happy at the moment, but that's her fault. She takes offense so easily."

Male laughter in the background. Lily's empty hand fisted, her nails digging in hard. "Maybe she finds you offensive."

"No, she's terribly in love with me. Although I—Beth, haven't I told you to be quiet?" Harlowe snapped.

Lily had to distract him. "Is this about vengeance, Harlowe? Is that why you want me—because I screwed up all your big plans?"

"I told Helen," he muttered. "I told her she was moving too quickly, but would she listen? And you . . . you think you're so clever, but it wasn't really your doing. It was Helen's stupidity that made things fall apart. Not that you're off the hook, oh, no, I'll—*what*?"

The voice she heard in the background this time was squeaky, high-pitched. "Oh, all right." Harlowe must have turned his head away. His voice was faint, the tone petulant. "Go ahead and tie her up, since she can't behave."

Lily heard her sister say his name—*Patrick*—clear and disbelieving. And the sound of a slap.

Then he was back, quite cheerful once more. "She'll learn. Perhaps I'll keep her. She is a pretty little thing, though not as loyal as she might be. She seems to think your safety is worth incurring my anger."

The staff might keep Beth hopelessly captivated, but it didn't change her basic nature or intelligence. She wouldn't understand what she was feeling . . . and had probably guessed by now that he'd used her to get to Lily.

Lily took a deep breath to steady her voice. "We're turning onto Bandera. Where next?"

RULE crouched down on the cool concrete of the parking lot beside Club Hell, his phone held to his ear. Cullen squatted beside him. They watched a moving dot of light on the map Cullen had unfolded as it crept along the line that represented Bandera Street.

So did the twelve men standing still and silent around them.

"All right," Rule told Benedict. "We've got your location. There are eight Lu Nuncios and seven *nonheris* here, plus myself and Cullen. I'm going to brief them now." A pause. "Yes. Call me back after you've reached them."

He disconnected and looked around at the silent men surrounding him. "Are you here from curiosity, or to help?"

"Is the staff involved?" Javiero asked.

"It is. Harlowe has taken my *nadia*'s sister and is using her to bring Lily to him. He has the staff."

"Then I'm in," Javiero said flatly, followed by a chorus of agreements, some vocalized, some simply nods.

"Understand this, then: We hunt, and I lead."

The single word *hunt* set the terms: instant obedience. No discussion, no questions. Rule was incapable of operating any other way at this point, and they understood that. Even Randall nodded reluctantly.

"Very well. Lily and Benedict are in her car. Benedict's driving. He'd assigned her guards, but he doesn't think they've been able to follow. He's calling them now." The guards had one of Cullen's charmed maps, but they didn't have Cullen to make it work when the signal got scrambled. "You can see from the map that Lily and Benedict are heading generally toward us at the moment. We don't have their destination yet—Harlowe's feeding her directions, keeping her on the phone. He claims he's getting real-time information from *Her* and will know if Lily contacts anyone."

That brought a few murmurs. Rikard scowled. "Is that possible?"

Cullen answered. "Possible? Yes. Likely?" He shrugged. "The legends make it clear She's able to observe our world, though She's blind to us."

"But no one can communicate between realms. Not even Her. Unless She has another pet telepath . . . ?"

"Unlikely." Instinct and need flowed hot inside Rule, a gathering force as compelling as blood or tides. For the moment, though, urgency was balanced by a mind washed cool and clear, as if by moonlight. *Thank you, Lady.* "Harlowe knew when she left the FBI building. He knew someone was driving her, but not who. Either he has someone physically following her and reporting her movements through conventional means, or *She* is somehow feeding him information." He paused to make his point. "Benedict says no one is following them. He would be difficult to fool."

Some nodded, some frowned. No one disagreed.

Stephen said thoughtfully, "Harlowe doesn't know that Benedict has contacted you, I take it. That suggests that his source of information is indeed our enemy. A human follower might see Benedict using his phone, but *She* wouldn't know, as long as he spoke to one of us."

Rule nodded absently, his attention on the map. He could feel Lily now—faintly, faintly, but her direction rested on the edges of his heightened senses like a feather just touching his skin. He'd never sensed her from this far away before—a Gift from the Lady, perhaps. He considered logistics.

"Why," one of the younger ones asked, "are we still standing here?"

Cullen nodded at the map. "We'll lose time if we take off in the wrong direction. Once she passes Garner Street, here—" he pointed at a line just ahead of the dot of light—"we'll know which direction we take."

Rule spoke. "We'll have to take multiple vehicles. Most of you don't know the city, so—"

His phone rang. He had it at his ear before it finished. "Yes." He heard his brother's voice, speaking too quietly for human ears, and answered, "They'll come. Hunt rules, my lead, Etorri as second."

After a few moments of listening, he rose smoothly. "Lily's guards were unable to follow, so it's up to us. She's heard from Harlowe. They'll be turning south on Garner. Toward us." He gathered the others with his gaze. "We go."

THE neighborhood sucked.

It was late enough that many of the houses were dark, and some of the streetlights had been shot out. But there was no full dark in a city this size. The dirty purple sky reflected the city's lights, providing a murky sort of illumination.

Lily knew how the area looked by day, anyway—the huddle of small houses slumping into decay, some vacant. The peeling paint and yards mostly dirt, with the occasional rusty car as lawn ornament. All too often, walls had been sprayed with graffiti in gang colors.

Cripps territory, back when she'd patrolled here for five memorable months. But the current graffiti told another story: the Dozens had taken over this turf.

They were a relatively new gang—part import, part home-grown. Many of their leaders were casualties of the brutal Central American wars that had raged for so long, teens and young adults who, as children, had witnessed atrocities up close and personal. A brother hacked to death. A mother gang-raped. A baby sister casually spitted by a soldier with a machete.

Children who had found their way to America, escaping with whichever relatives survived. Children who had grown up to commit atrocities.

As soon as Benedict made that last turn, she'd known they were about to arrive at Harlowe's hidey-hole. She'd motioned urgently for him to get rid of the headset. He had, thank God, ended the call and hidden the headset without argument or hesitation.

"I'm guessing our escort just pulled out in front of us," she told Harlowe now. "An old Chevy Impala, bright purple with orange flames on the sides. Lowrider. The driver and one passenger are Hispanic. The other one's African American."

"My, aren't you politically correct?" Harlowe was in high good humor now that she'd all but delivered herself into his hands. "You be sure to stay right behind Raul and his friends."

"I take it we're almost there." The front-seat passenger was talking on a cell phone, no doubt reporting that they'd picked up Lily and Benedict.

"Perhaps."

"I'm kicking myself for not thinking of the gangs earlier." Let him revel in how he'd outwitted her. Let him preen and strut and think himself invincible. "Where better for you to hide out? They'd respond well to a charismatic leader."

"The boys have been most helpful. They understand my message."

Benedict touched her shoulder. She glanced at him. "Why don't you tell me about that?"

"You want to hear my message?"

"Sure." Benedict made a pulling motion with one hand. She subvocalized: *"Drag it out? Stall?"* He nodded, and she returned it. It was good to know they were on the same page.

Harlowe was making mistakes. He was relying too much on his not-quite-omniscient goddess. He wasn't thinking straight, or he would have taken Her blind spot—the lupi—into account. Maybe he really did think he was invincible, as Rule had suggested earlier.

That didn't make him less than deadly. But it gave them a chance. Rule was on his way—with others, she hoped. How far he had to travel, she couldn't say, but she felt him more clearly all the time. "That is," she went on out loud, "I'd like to know if there's more to it than 'stick with me and you'll have all the money and women you want.'"

He chuckled. "Don't underestimate the Dozens. They want guns and booze and drugs as well. What about you, Lily Yu? What do you want?"

"I want my sister turned loose, alive and unhurt."

"So I assumed, or you wouldn't be following Raul. But what about yourself? Aren't you hoping to get out of this alive and unhurt, too?"

"I'm planning on it."

"My own plans fell through recently," he said, dreamy now. "I've made more, of course. Can't keep a good man down. But you might express some regret for having interfered in my plans. In fact, I feel sure you will. I'm predicting that you will soon be very, very sorry you presumed so much."

The Chevy stopped abruptly. Lily jolted as Benedict hit the brakes to keep from climbing up the other car's bumper. The passenger in the back seat of the purple car turned around, smiling at them. He rested the barrel of a sawed-off shotgun on the back of the seat, aimed straight at Lily.

"Predicting the future's an iffy business." Maybe she'd been wrong about Harlowe's goal. Maybe he'd brought her here because he wanted her killed where he could see it happen. "Even good precogs don't get it right all the time."

"We'll see. Pull over to the curb," he told her, almost purring. "Pull over and get out of the car. The boys will take you where you need to go."

There was one empty spot at the curb directly in front of a rundown stucco house, pale and colorless in the dark. The windows were boarded up, but light snaked out through cracks. A late model pickup, modified beyond recognition, occupied most of the front yard.

She glanced at Benedict. He looked bored. They might have been paying a visit to some tedious relatives.

But he would know just how scared she was. He'd smell it on her. Dammit, dammit . . . Lily took a breath and rolled the dice, staking her life, Beth's, and his on her best guess. "No."

"What? What did you say?"

"Once I put myself in your hands, I've lost all bargaining power. Send my sister out. Then we'll talk."

Benedict gave her a small nod.

Harlowe's laugh was less convincing than it had been. "You must be joking. Do as you're told, or Beth will regret it, even if you don't."

"My walking into that house won't make her safe. If you've got both of us, I've nothing left to bargain with."

"What about your safety?" Harlowe's voice lost its music as it rose. "Do you see the shotgun pointed at you? The others have guns, too. What makes you think you have a choice?"

"Shoot us, then." Her heart beat so hard and fast she

thought she'd be sick. "Tell them to blast away. Unless, of course, you think that might piss off your goddess."

"She doesn't control me. I'm in charge, you understand?"

"Yeah? So how come you keep killing the same woman over and over, Patrick? Do those brown-haired girls remind you of anyone?"

That tipped him over some edge. He cursed her—and Her. All women. While he ranted, Lily stole a glance at Benedict. "How long?" she whispered, meaning, *How long before we have backup?*

Looking sleepy, he spread both hands, closed them, and then spread the fingers of one hand again.

Fifteen minutes. Surely she could keep Harlowe from acting for fifteen minutes—though he was getting so wound up, she was afraid he'd have them shot to prove a point. She broke into his tirade. "Okay, okay, you're in charge. The big kahoona. I got that. But you still need to deal. You want me, you're going to have to deal."

Silence, except for his breath hitting the mouthpiece in windy bursts. He was panting as if he'd been running. "I'm not sending your sister out," he said at last. "That would be giving up my bargaining power, wouldn't it? Perhaps you need to be convinced. Felix," he said to someone else, "would you like to rape her for me? You can listen," he told Lily. "You can hear her beg."

Her hands went cold and numb. She flexed her hands, swallowed bile, and said, "We'll pull up to the curb, but I'm not getting out until I see Beth."

He giggled. "Tell you what—we'll take off her clothes while you're thinking things over."

Fourteen more minutes. She had to keep him talking for fourteen more minutes. "Don't know much about this hostage business, do you? You're not giving up enough to make me think I've got a chance. If I decide it's hopeless, I'm going to call in forty or fifty federal agents just to be sure you pay."

"And what do you think will happen to your sister if you do that?"

"I don't know. Will it be as bad as what happens to you if you don't deliver me to your goddess?"

Another long moment of silence. "Perhaps we can deal."

SEVENTEEN

BENEDICT ended the call with a single growled word: *Hurry.*

Force rose in Rule like an imminent explosion, hollowing him until all that remained was purpose, tipping him away from the rationality of the human toward the power of the beast. He found a new balance. Thought remained, but altered; words no longer led, but existed as small chips of focus for the gathering storm.

Cullen was in the Mercedes's back seat with his map spread out. Con was driving; Rule hadn't wanted to split his attention. They'd made good time while they had four lanes, but construction had sent them on a two-lane detour. They were practically crawling now due to some fender bender up ahead.

They were close, though. Rule felt Lily clearly now, like a separate pulse. He felt the moon, too, with her different call. But that call now fed rather than cooled the tide surging within him.

Soon, he told the rage in his blood. *Very soon.* "Stop the car," he told Con.

Con stopped the car. Rule hadn't said to pull over first, so he didn't. Three vehicles followed his, each riding the other's tail much too close for safety, had the drivers been human. Because they weren't, all three stopped immediately, as if they'd choreographed it.

Rule got out. So did those in the other cars—no questions, no debate.

Hunt rules.

"We're out of time," he told them, pitching his voice to be heard over the blaring horns of drivers behind them, speaking quickly because he couldn't hold off the Change much longer. "Lily has reached or is about to reach Harlowe. He's recruited a gang, a vicious bunch. I don't know how many are involved. They'll have guns." Rule stopped, his breathing ragged.

Just a few more minutes. "Cullen," he snapped, "stand back."

Map in hand, Cullen retreated several feet.

"We're very close," Rule continued. "Cars will only slow us now, so half of us go ahead, four-footed, at full speed. We'll approach from upwind—the humans won't scent us, but Benedict will. The sight of us will surprise them."

That brought a few grins. Very few humans had ever seen a lupus pack in full hunt. Those who had generally hadn't live to speak of it. "The other half stay with Cullen, led by Etorri. Stephen." He faced the other man. "Stay two-footed so you can give orders. Your job is to get Cullen close enough to destroy the staff. He can't Change or fight—he must retain all his power for the staff. Get him there quickly."

"Who goes with you?" Stephen asked quickly.

"Those nearest me, I ima—" But words shut off as the Change seized Rule. Earth stretched itself up inside him as if it would claw its way to the moon that called and called, using him as ladder.

As with birth or death, pain was part of the Change.

Sometimes it was a minor note in the song, like the ache of lungs and body during a race. Sometimes—when the Change had been held off too long, or took place away from Earth or at the dark of the moon—pain was a huge gong, belling its brassy note through every cell.

This time, the Change ripped him from human to wolf in a single, deafening blast.

One after another, those nearest him Changed, just as he'd expected. The sudden Change of an alpha leader sends a blast rippling out through the pack, dragging others along. As if reality were no more than a bubble waiting to be popped by some giant, mischievous finger, in eight places that bubble burst.

Clothing ripped. Horns ceased blaring as drivers stared, stunned. Somewhere a dog began to howl.

Seconds later, eight pairs of empty shoes stood where men had been. And eight huge wolves raced off into the night.

LILY'S breath felt harsh in her chest as she opened the car door. Her mind was a tight ball of focus.

Fourteen or fifteen young men—some in their teens, some in their early twenties—fanned out in a semi-circle in front of the concrete slab that served as a front porch. All were armed. She counted six rifles, two shotguns, and a wide array of handguns.

Barely visible behind them stood three people: Harlowe, Beth, and the gang member holding her motionless with one thick arm.

The darkness didn't hide everything. Harlowe's staff, for example. A dull black, it shouldn't have been visible, yet her eyes found it as easily as they picked out the man who gripped it. The gang member holding Beth was easy to spot, being more than a head taller than everyone else and built like a bull. Other than his size, only the pale do-rag and white T-shirt stood out clearly, but a fugitive glint of light caught the barrel of the gun he rested against Beth's head.

And Beth . . . Beth was fully dressed. Lily swallowed. Her sister hadn't been raped, and Harlowe had agreed to let her go.

At least Lily could put down the damned phone now. With her door cracked but not fully open, she turned to Benedict. "Stay here. Harlowe wants me alive. He has no reason to spare you."

"Can't do much from in here."

"Can't do much out there, either. Not with twenty or thirty bullets in you."

He just smiled that barely there smile of his and reached for the handle of his door.

She grabbed his arm. "I can't stop you. You're too damned big. But don't make yourself into a liability. With that staff, Harlowe can make you like him, believe him, want to follow him. Don't trust your reactions. Leave him to me."

He gave her a level look and a slow nod. "Understood. But his charisma won't matter much if he doesn't smell right."

"What does that mean?"

"Are you coming?" Harlowe called. "Beth, maybe you'd better ask your sister to hurry."

Lily heard Beth's cry of pain and flung open her door. "Okay, okay. Here I am. Now let Beth go." That was the deal—she and Benedict would get out, expose themselves to his little army of gangbangers, and he'd turn Beth loose.

She didn't expect him to keep it. *How much longer? Five minutes? More? Less?*

Rule was close now. Close and coming their way.

"I don't think so." Harlowe moved forward, the staff in his hand making him look like he belonged in a Christmas pageant playing one of the shepherds. But this staff didn't have a crook at the top. It was simply a long length of wood the color of coal.

From behind the wall of gangbangers Beth cried out, "Lily, I'm sorry. I'm so sorry."

"Not your fault," she said, standing in front of her car with her hands held out slightly at her sides—*see, I'm not drawing a weapon. No need to shoot anyone.* "Harlowe's staff has you hocus-pocused. You can't help—" She stopped, staring. "What the hell is *that*?"

That was pale, about as tall as Harlowe's hip, and looked like a cross between a kangaroo and a really weird nightmare.

"Hey, she sees me!" It jiggled on those oversize haunches, excited, its voice squeaky-high. "She can see me!"

"Of course she sees you, you cretin," Harlowe muttered. "She's a sensitive."

"I thought that was just for spells, but she can really see me, even though I'm *dshatu*."

"I can hear you, too," Lily said.

"Who or what are you talking to?" Benedict asked very low.

She started. It'd moved up on her right side so silently she hadn't known it was there. She answered softly. "The demon, I think. You can't hear it?" It, he, she . . . those were definitely breasts high on the naked chest, but the genitals, though small, were the dangly sort.

"No. Neither can anyone else, I think."

"Harlowe does." She raised her voice. "Are you a demon? Did you knock me out?"

"Yes, and I can hardly wait to—"

Harlowe rapped the demon on the head with his staff. "Try to be a little less stupid. And now," he said to Lily, "it's time to let my boys have your weapons."

She wrenched her attention away from the bizarre creature standing next to Harlowe. "Uh-uh. It's time for you to tell Mr. Muscles there to let Beth go."

Harlowe giggled. "Make me."

"All right," Benedict said.

She'd never seen anyone move so fast, not even Rule. She had the barest glimpse of something flashing out from his far hand—then a blow on her back knocked her to the ground.

Caught by surprise, she fell hard even as shots rang out, a rolling thunder that seemed to come from everywhere. She rolled onto her side, spitting out dirt, scrambling to get her weapon.

Screaming. More shots. The acrid bite of gunpowder in her nostrils and the feel of her gun in her hand.

And howling.

Huge, eerie, beautiful—howls bursting from the throats of enormous wolves. Two, three, half a dozen of them shot across the yard like streaks of moon-touched night in their mottled coats, straight at the gangbangers firing at them.

Those of the gang who remained, that is. Several were missing—fled or fallen, Lily couldn't tell in the darkness and confusion. And it was hard to see past the strong, furry body that had landed, legs spread, in a crouch over her.

"Rule!" Dammit, he was playing shield. She shoved at his belly—that's about all she could see—his belly, legs, and chest. "I can't see to fire. I can't see what happened to Beth." Or Benedict—was he down?

Harlowe yelled, "No, no! Stop it! Stop!"

Rule didn't budge. He faced out at the battle, growling.

Giving up, Lily flattened herself—prone position, arms out, weapon gripped in her right hand with her left to steady it.

The young giant was gone, but Beth wasn't free. Harlowe had her. She was fighting him, but she was so much smaller, untrained in any kind of combat. He pinned her with one arm. With the other, he used the staff. Where he pointed, agony followed.

He was indiscriminate. Wolves and men alike collapsed, screaming and writhing. Sometimes blood spattered. Sometimes it didn't. Harlowe kept yelling, "No, no" over and over, striking almost at random. And he was advancing toward Lily with that damned kangaroo-demon hopping along at his side.

She couldn't get a clear shot. "Beth, hold still!" she yelled over the screaming and gunshots.

"Grab her hand," Harlowe yelled. "Get her, grab her!"

"Get rid of the wolf! How'm I going to grab anything if he bites my hand off?"

"How?" It was a shriek. "It isn't working! He's supposed to love me, follow me—"

"You don't smell like a wolf, dummy! Careful—no, no!" The creature grabbed Harlowe's arm as he swung the staff toward Rule. "Don't hurt her body! I need that body! Get closer, get closer!"

The bizarre pair shifted, trying to come at her and Rule from the side. Rule shifted with them, his growl a steady thunder above Lily, and she squirmed around, trying desperately to get a bead on some critical part of Harlowe, terrified of hitting her sister.

A head shot. She'd have to try for a head shot. That should have been easy at this distance, but he kept moving and her own motion was limited by a damned stubborn hero of a wolf.

"Hurry!" the demon squealed. "The wolves are winning!"

"Shut up! And split up—he can't cover both of us!"

She wiggled to the right, tracking Harlowe as the demon went in the other direction. She bumped against Rule's leg, and there he was—*yes, hold still, you bastard, stay just like that.* She squeezed the trigger just as Harlowe darted aside again, damn him, damn him. Where—?

Faster than she could react, Rule spun—but the staff flashed down just as he whirled to face it.

It grazed his shoulder. His whole body spasmed and collapsed.

The world blanked out. There was only a sudden, vertiginous drop into terror and guilt. *My fault, it's my fault—first Beth, now Rule, hurt because of me. . . .*

Then rage flooded in, giving her the strength to shove him off her upper body so she could twist around, bring up her weapon—but a hot, dry hand clamped around her wrist, stopping her as surely as if it were made of iron.

It felt orange. Orange, like her shoulder.

"I've got her! Hurry, hurry!"

Harlowe flung Beth away. She fell to the ground and didn't move. Lily wrenched violently at her hand, but there was no budging the demon, so she tried to roll over, to get her weapon into her other hand, but her legs were still pinned by Rule's heavy body. She couldn't quite reach.

His face a mask of maniacal glee, Harlowe smacked the staff across her belly.

Foulness spurted over her like slime, breaking up into dozens of scrambling bits that hardened as they scuttled over her body, bits that clawed at her skin, ripping at her in ways indescribable while that hot orange hand held her and something pushed and pushed at her in a place nothing should have been able to reach—

She screamed.

A ball of black fire, eerie and terrible, erupted around Harlowe's head like an obscene halo and fled down his arm to the staff.

Pain struck, a sharp, clean knife sundering her world, sending her spinning, spinning . . . into nothing.

EIGHTEEN

WEARINESS. Pain. Sounds . . .

". . . except Rikard. Damned staff severed his neck. He was gone before he had a chance to heal."

"Hellfire. He went out in style, though. He'd be glad of that. He's the only other one?"

She knew the second voice, but memory was a slippery fish, freeing itself before she could claim it. She almost drifted away again, but the body's pain insisted on dragging her back from that beckoning dimness.

It felt as if a burning brand rested just below her belly button, throbbing along with her heartbeat. But there are worse pains than the physical. Floating between here and not-here, she was aware of loss so huge that her mind skittered away, refusing to close around the thought.

". . . got all the wounded away now, so I'll be going. The cops will be here any minute. You'd better clear out, too."

"And let her wake up to this?" The familiar voice was bitter.

"Her sister should wake up soon. She can . . ."

Her sister. Beth. Yes. She'd come to . . . to . . . all at once memory plopped in her lap, writhing and ugly. And incomplete.

She had to know.

When she forced her eyes open it was still dark. Dark and fuzzy, as if she'd forgotten how to make her eyes focus. The air stank of gunpowder, blood, and charred meat. Her mind flashed back to fire—uncanny fire, black at the center, flickering into blue at the fringes. Black fire haloing Harlowe, speeding down his staff . . . which had rested on her belly.

She'd been burned, then. Burned by mage fire. Maybe she would have fried along with Harlowe if not for her Gift . . . which wasn't quite the complete protection she'd always believed.

The dimly seen shapes resolved. Overhead, sky too smoggy for stars, glowing with the city's reflected light. And kneeling next to her, though he was looking away . . . that was Cullen, she realized, naked from the waist up. He was listening to someone standing beside him.

"If you aren't leaving, you might as well make yourself useful," the other man said. She had a vague impression of even features, pale skin, and light-colored hair, but darkness hid the details. "Her burn needs tending."

"I'm no healer."

"You never did pay attention to anything that couldn't be done sorcerously. Cold water will cool it so the flesh doesn't continue to cook."

"You have any?"

Enough of that. She didn't need to hear about herself. Lily licked her lips and found her voice. "Rule?"

The other man slipped away into the darkness so quickly and silently she might have imagined him. Slowly Cullen looked down at her. His eyes were weary beyond words. "I'm sorry, Lily. He's gone."

* * *

WEARINESS. Pain. Sounds . . .

Sounds without meaning, a babble of words she didn't know. Awareness flickered. Nothing in that babble drew her . . . yet something did.

Anger. Beneath the babble, powering it, lay anger. Someone was having a major hissy fit.

It might have been a sense of danger that kept her from slipping back into unknowing. It might have been curiosity. Once she'd lingered beyond that first heartbeat, though, she knew something was wrong. She hurt, and that was part of it . . . as if a fiery brand lay across her stomach, she hurt from some wounding. But there was more to the wrongness than that. Worse.

She had to know . . .

Confusion, vast and powerful as pain, startled her eyes open.

She saw sky—sky the color of tarnished brass, glowing like the embers of a dying fire. Glowing all over, with no sign of the sun. Beneath her the ground was stony. Pebbles dug into the skin of her back and butt . . . the bare skin of her back.

She was naked. That bothered her. She tried to think of what she should do about it, but her mind felt heavy, as if thoughts had weight and she lacked the strength to push and lift and arrange them. But she was lying naked on the ground beneath a brassy sky. That wasn't right, but . . . where was she supposed to be?

At least she wasn't cold. Neither cold nor hot, actually, except for her legs. They were very warm. Something heavy lay across her legs, warming them.

Oh . . .

An impulse stronger than pain or weakness moved her to stretch out one hand. She touched fur . . . fur that lifted slowly with a breath.

That was all right, then.

Her breath sighed out, her eyes closing once more.

DIZZINESS seized Lily, as if the world had tipped into some new, impossible angle. She stared up at Cullen's weary face, adrift.

No, she realized. The world wasn't askew. It was the gap that made it seem so—the gap between reality and what she'd been told. "No. He isn't."

"Lily . . ." Cullen's expression softened into something she'd never seen there before. Pity.

That irked her. "Not if you're using 'gone' as a euphemism for 'dead.' He isn't even that far away. Less than a mile." She'd tested the mate bond enough to be confident about the distance. "I can find him easily enough, though you might have to help me move."

He just shook his head, looking so wretched she didn't know if she should shake him or pat his hand. Her lips thinned, but she went on to her next question. "My sister. Harlowe knocked her down. Is she—"

"She's okay," he said quickly. "Knocked out, but Stephen said her breathing and heartbeat are fine, so she should come around soon. He moved her to the porch so she doesn't wake up next to what's left of Harlowe."

"Okay, that's good. Was Stephen the one you were . . . never mind." That could wait. They didn't have much time. "We need to find Rule."

He winced. "Lily—"

"Look, I don't know where he is, but he was hurt, not killed. Give me a hand. I need to sit up."

Cullen shook his head, bafflement mixing with his weariness. "No, you don't. You've been hurt."

"No kidding. But I lack authority when I'm flat on my back, and those sirens are getting close. You're going to need all the official weight I can muster to keep from being arrested and executed for using sorcery to fry Harlowe." And she had to find Rule.

He sighed. "Wait a minute. Let me try something. I don't have much juice left, but . . ." He pulled out the little diamond he'd taken to wearing around his neck.

"What's that for?"

"Think of it as a storage battery. Mage fire takes a lot of power, so I've been gathering it for a while."

At her apartment . . . when he'd been playing with the sorcéri, had he really been tucking them away for later? "I thought the how-to for that sort of thing was lost during the Purge."

"I'm fucking brilliant, aren't I?" His voice was as light as his face was bleak. He held the little diamond in one hand, held the other over her stomach, muttered something, and then pointed away.

A small flame burst where he'd pointed and then died. And a wave of wonderful cold sucked much of the heat from her stomach.

"I moved the heat around. Instant chill on your tummy. Better?"

"Yes. Thanks. Now help me up." She held out her hand.

Instead of taking it, he bent, slid an arm beneath her shoulders, and then lifted. It hurt, but the world didn't wink out. Once she caught her breath she did a quick scan of the area.

They were alone except for the dead.

There were a lot of them, dimly seen heaps crumpled here and there all over the small yard. And one mound near her feet—that would be Harlowe, or what was left of him. She wasn't eager for the police spots to reveal the details.

They'd be here soon. Sirens warbled their alarm from only blocks away. "Benedict?"

"Damned hero." He shook his head. "Timed things a little too close."

Something lurched in her chest. "He's dead, then."

"Hell, no. Full of holes, but he didn't even have the decency to pass out. Made us go get his knife back before he'd let himself be taken away. If he makes it through the night he'll be fine—though even he will take a while to heal."

"The others . . ." Whoever they were, and she had plenty of questions about that. "They took him away in spite of his injuries?"

"Can't leave anyone behind. Your compatriots would arrest them. The dead, though . . ." He hesitated. "Traditionally, they serve a final time by taking the blame for any dead humans. There are a number of them tonight."

"Not Rule," she said firmly. "You won't be pinning anything on him. He's not dead, and I can swear that he didn't kill anyone. He was with me."

"Lily." He looked haggard. "The staff exploded, then vanished. Rule went with it."

Two cop cars screeched around a corner, lights flashing, sirens howling.

"Argue with me later," she said quickly. "Here's the deal. Don't answer questions from anyone but me. Lawyer up if you have to. I'll say I think Harlowe burned himself up trying to kill me. I didn't see you, after all, so I can't testify about what you did or didn't do. And magic's dangerous stuff, right? Using the staff on a sensitive could have made it backfire on him."

"It's as good a story as any." He sounded indifferent.

He's grieving, she realized. *He doesn't believe me about Rule, and grief is making him numb to his own fate.* "Cullen," she said, and reached out to rest her hand on his bare arm . . . and froze.

Because it wasn't there. The buzz, the hum, the indefinable texture of magic she should have felt the second she touched his skin . . . it was gone.

* * *

SHE came awake all at once, jolted by fear. In her mind there lingered the echo of an eerie howl. Something about that sound . . .

She didn't hear it now, though—just the same angry, high-pitched babble as before. The same brassy sky glared down. No clouds, no sun. The same terrible pain throbbed on her stomach.

The weight on her legs was gone.

Her breath sucked in. Need gave her the strength to raise up on one elbow.

A huge wolf stood at her feet. He was beautiful—his coat black and silver, his proportions elegant. He was also angry, his lip lifted in a snarl that advertised the long, wicked teeth.

He was growling at the source of the babbling—a creature like nothing she could have imagined. It was a bright, greasy orange. And naked. And at least halfway male.

Aside from the small, soft genitals, the creature's lower half resembled a kangaroo or a child's toy dinosaur with its oversize haunches and spiked tail. Big feet. No belly button. The chest was muscular but decorated by a pair of very female breasts tipped by olive green nipples the size of half dollars. In contrast, the arms and shoulders looked almost human.

No hair. Neither around the genitals nor on the round head. A wide slit of a mouth crowded with teeth every bit as pointy as the wolf's, but not as long. The eyes were large and heavily lashed, absurdly pretty in that face. They were set too far apart above a pair of sphincters that she supposed were nostrils.

It stood about three feet tall. The size of a child.

"What are you?" she asked.

It jumped, its eyes widening. Then it rolled those eyes in a disconcertingly human way. "Great. That's just great. You didn't understand a word I've said, did you?"

"Were those words?"

"You're just lucky I know English," it grumbled.

The wolf glanced at her and stopped growling. He backed up, careful to keep the creature in sight, until he stood beside her.

She didn't like lying flat. She didn't like being naked, either, but there didn't seem to be an alternative at the moment.

Sitting up hurt, but she managed it. She pushed her hair out of her face and her fingers brushed something at her neck . . . a chain with a pendent. The feel of the pendent comforted her, both the shape and the faint buzz of magic from it. She clasped it in one hand and leaned against the wolf.

His fur wasn't as soft as it looked, but it felt good against her skin. He seemed content to serve as her support, so she laid an arm on his back and rested more of her weight against him. The contact felt good. Right.

He made a whining sound, almost like a question.

The creature spoke. "I suppose you didn't understand him, either."

"I suppose you did?"

It raised both hands to its head as if it wanted to rip out the hair it didn't have. "Could things be worse? Could it get any worse? I'm supposed to be *in* you, on Earth, but here I am, back in Dis—"

The ground rumbled. And *moved*.

Her fingers clenched in the wolf's fur. Earthquake? Her heart pounded. For the first time she looked around.

Rock. That's all she saw—big rocks, little rocks, pebbles. Orange, rust, gray, and yellow rocks. No trees, no grass, no weeds or water. Off in the distance she saw a single mountain, dull black and topped by what looked like a caldera. A dead volcano?

She hoped it was dead.

But she couldn't see far. They were in a small cul-de-sac, a low point bounded by the rock humped up around them. Rock that might be dislodged if the earth twitched again.

She didn't want to be here. She wasn't sure where she needed to go, but this was the wrong place for her, wrong in every way. She needed to move, to get out of here . . . but just sitting up drained her.

How could she travel? Where could she go?

The creature groaned. "She is *so* pissed. We've got to get out of here. There's a Zone real close. A Zone," it repeated impatiently when she looked blank. "You know. Where the regions overlap."

The wolf curled his lip in what looked more like scorn than temper.

"I know, I know. You don't trust me, but you should. As far as Lily's concerned, anyway—"

Lily?

"—because I can't let anything happen to her. I'm tied to her, by Xitil's great, glowing nipples! If she dies, I die! That stupid man was supposed to help me get into her, but I didn't get all the way in because your stupid sorcerer messed up the staff and now I'm tied to a stupid sensitive who shouldn't *be* here and Xitil is fighting it out with *Her* and—" its voice rose to a squeaky crescendo—"we've got to get out of here!"

The wolf turned his head to look directly at her with what she was sure was a question in his dark eyes.

"Don't ask me," she said in a voice dry as dust—dry as all the aching, empty places inside her. "I don't know what to believe, what to do. I don't know who you are, why we're here, where 'here' is, or . . ." She tried to swallow past the dryness, but her words came out raspy. "Or who I am."

The sky around the dull black cone of the volcano suddenly flared, shooting from dark brass to incandescent orange and gold—sunrise arriving with a bang. A second later, the ground shimmied beneath them, accompanied by a dull, distant rumble, like thunder below the ground.

"Remind me," the creature whispered, "not to ever, ever ask if things could get worse."

NINETEEN

THOUGH the man was always with the wolf, just as the wolf remained with the man, the form did make a difference. Instinct was closer to Rule when he was four-footed, words more distant. Which might have been just as well. Being more deeply of the moment than the man, the beast felt little fear for the future.

Not that there wasn't plenty in the present for alarm. Plenty that made him want to lift his nose and howl . . . but he'd already done that. The demon, damn its greasy orange hide, was right. It had been a stupid thing to do, but he couldn't have stopped that howl if his life had depended on it.

Which, of course, it might. Worse—so might Lily's. There was no saying who or what might have heard him. But in that first terrible second of discovery, wolf and man alike had lost control.

He'd tried to Change. And couldn't.

Now the beast wanted to act. Food, water, shelter—those needs the beast understood. The man agreed, but where to find any of that in hell?

Rule reined in his sense of urgency. There were no immediate threats. If the volcano was erupting, it was distant enough not to pose an urgent danger. What was it Benedict used to say? There's a time to act, a time to plan the next action, and a time to gather facts so you can plan.

A puff of sadness ghosted through him at the thought of his brother, who might well be dead. The wolf, more immediate than the man, paid it little heed. If he and Lily survived and managed to return home, then it would be time to worry about Benedict's fate.

Rule lifted his nose. The air was dry, windless. It carried little scent, and most of that was alien, useless to him.

He looked at the other two. Lily was fingering the nearly healed wound on her shoulder, perhaps wondering where that earlier hurt had come from. Her brows were knit. Her eyes looked lost.

How much was gone? Her personal memories were missing, obviously, but she hadn't lost everything. She retained language and basic motor skills. Did she remember Earth, even if she'd forgotten her family? Did she know he had another form, even if she couldn't remember his face? Some part of her knew him. He was convinced of that. Hadn't she accepted his support earlier?

But he couldn't ask her. He couldn't hold her or tend her wound. He couldn't even speak her name. Rule wanted to lift his nose to that ugly sky and howl again, but that would be entirely stupid.

She was so alone now, bereft even of memory. Unable to offer a man's comfort, he went to her and touched her arm gently with his nose. And recoiled.

Mixed with her own beloved scent was a whiff of cloves and exhaust. The scent of the demon.

She turned to him, her expression abstract. "Something wrong?"

Terribly wrong. But he couldn't tell her. Tentatively he sniffed again. The demon scent was faint, but it came from her skin. Yet the demon was obviously separate from her, so she couldn't be possessed. Could she?

The demon had said something about being tied to her. That tie was what he smelled, he supposed . . . but he hadn't realized it meant some part of the creature was actually *in* her. Part of her.

She'd sensed his turmoil or felt the need to ease her own. She reached for him, running her fingers through the thick fur of his ruff, scratching lightly. Relief flowed through him. The comfort of the mate bond was unchanged by whatever tie she had with the demon.

He turned his head to look at it. The demon was jiggling from foot to foot, looking all around anxiously . . . very much all around, because its head had the range of motion of an owl's. When it saw that Rule was watching, it said, "You'll have to take charge. We've got to get moving, and she's missing too many marbles to know what to do."

Rule bared his teeth.

"Speak English," Lily said, "not babble."

He'd hardly noticed that the demon had reverted to that other language. Somehow he understood the creature whether it spoke English or not . . . and it had seemed to understand him earlier.

Well, it was worth a try. He yipped at it.

"Ask questions later," the thing said, jiggling. "When we're in Akhanetton."

Rule lowered his rump and sat, staring pointedly at the demon. Lily glanced from him to the demon. "I don't think he's going anywhere. What did he ask?"

"All right, all right. He wants to know why I understand him." The demon rolled its eyes. "You people don't know *anything*. Meanings are one of the Rules."

"Is that supposed to mean something to me?"

"Not to you," the demon said morosely and plopped down on the ground. It sat rather like an ape or a gargoyle, though its thick tail caused it to tilt forward. The way its legs were jointed, they naturally splayed to the sides, with the knees pointed straight up—a position that put its genitals on prominent display.

"Then you'd better keep talking."

It heaved a sigh. "In the earth realm, you've got your laws of nature, gravity, and all that. Here we've got the Rules. One of them is that meanings are clear no matter where you are, so everyone always knows what you mean even if they don't know what you said. Unless you're really clever, that is—good at hiding one meaning behind another. I'm good," it added with simple pride. "Sometimes I can almost lie."

"I just hear your words. I can't tell what you mean. Or . . ." She looked at Rule, a small frown tucked between her eyebrows. "Or him."

The demon huffed out a breath. "It doesn't work with a sensitive. All sorts of things won't work right with a sensitive. And you're wearing Ishtar's token. Nobody told me about that. You'd think someone would have mentioned . . ." Its eyes widened. "Maybe Xitil didn't know! Maybe *She* didn't tell her! Oh, oh, oh!" It bounced to its feet. "Xitil must be *so* pissed! We've got to get out of here!"

"And go where?" Lily demanded. "Where's better than here? And who is Xitil?"

"Xitil's the prince of this region. My prince. We need to cross to Akhanetton—that's the closest region. It's scary." It shivered. "All that open sky . . . but there's no telling what will happen here. Xitil's fighting with *Her*."

"With who?"

"I'm not going to say Her name. Any of her names. She's a goddess. She might hear."

Rule growled a question.

"Okay, so it's Her avatar that's here, not the goddess Herself. That won't make much difference to us. Xitil won't be minding the store with the fight taking all her attention. Up could become down, or it might rain ashes, or—oh, you don't know anything, do you?" It looked hugely frustrated. "Dis is divided into regions. The regions, they aren't just ruled by their princes—they're *determined* by their rulers. Hot or cold, what grows or doesn't, all the little rules are set by the prince, who's *part* of all of it because she's eaten part of everyone. Do you see?"

"She's *eaten* part of everyone?" Lily said, revolted. "She ate part of you?"

"That's how it works! You people with your souls are used to death, so you kill too easy, but we preserve life."

"By eating each other alive?"

"Yes. Can we go now?"

"Not yet. You said my name is Lily."

It nodded. "Lily Yu."

"And his name? The wolf's?"

"He's called Rule Turner."

"Rule." She said it thoughtfully, as if searching for recognition, some snippet of memory. And looked disappointed. "I know him, though."

"Sure. You have sex with him a lot. Well, when he's not a wolf, you do. I don't know if you have sex when he's like this." It tipped its head to one side, eyes brightening—and penis beginning to harden. "I'd like to see that if you do."

Rule growled.

Lily ignored irrelevancies to focus on her questions. "What do you mean, 'when he's not a wolf'?"

"He's lupus. You're human. And I," it said, penis and expression drooping once more, "am in so much trouble. Neither of you is supposed to—yipes!"

Rule had heard it, too, and had spun to face the new threat before the demon stopped speaking.

Feet. Lots and lots of running feet, headed their way.

The demon bounded to a tall, nearly vertical rock face. "Get her over here!" it cried. "Get her flat against the rock, or they'll trample her!"

Some kind of stampede? Making up his mind quickly, Rule pushed at Lily with his nose.

"You want me to do like the creature says? I don't . . . what's that?"

Her ears must have picked it up now, too. Rule pushed at her urgently. Whatever was headed their way was coming fast.

She grimaced, but, by using his back to steady herself, managed to get to her feet.

He'd known she was hurt. Though he didn't remember those last moments on Earth, he'd smelled it when he awoke. But now he saw her wound clearly, and it worried him. Just below her navel was a puffy blister shaped like a fat cigar, but bigger. The skin around it was bright red and weepy.

Second-degree burn, he thought, alarmed. Were there bacteria in hell?

Stupid question. She'd have brought some in on her skin, and he could only hope her system was able to fight them off. The pain would be fierce, the healing slow. She needed medical treatment, dammit. He couldn't supply so much as a bandage. He had no shirt to tear into strips.

Neither did she.

That was odd, now that he thought of it. Why hadn't her clothes arrived with her? The Lady's token had made the crossing, but not Lily's clothing.

He had no answers, and damn little help to give. He could only pace anxiously alongside her as she stumbled toward the overhang, then place himself between her and the demon when she sank to the ground, her back against the rock. He heard the pounding of her heart—too fast—and her quick, short breaths.

Seconds later, the wave hit.

TWENTY

THEY cascaded over the edges of the cul-de-sac so fast
and in such numbers that Rule couldn't sort out what an
individual creature looked like. He had an impression of
endless gray bodies with too many legs, and a pungent
smell like mushrooms and grapefruit. They hurtled to the
floor of the cul-de-sac in the hundreds and kept running,
pouring up the other side in a steady stream.

It seemed to go on and on but probably lasted ten minutes or less. As suddenly as the flood had started it was
over, leaving a couple dozen bodies behind. Many had
been trampled into bloody pulp—red blood, so maybe
their metabolism was oxygen-based. A few still twitched.

The demon didn't move, so Rule didn't, either. Seconds later two huge shadows glided across the rocky
ground. Rule looked up.

Pterodactyls? Giant birds? They were too quickly
gone for him to pick up much detail, and his distance vision wasn't good in this form. They seemed to be trailing
the stampeding creatures. Hunting them, maybe.

The demon heaved a great sigh and, after giving the

sky a wary glance, wandered out into the open. Hoping that meant the coast was clear, Rule followed. He wanted to check out one of the creatures.

The body nearest him was almost intact. It looked rather like a roach without the carapace, only the size of a cat and with leathery gray skin. The six thin legs were hinged oddly, but were more animal than insect. He could see bone where the skin and sinew was missing. They ended in small, clawed feet. The head was pure bug, however—small, flattened, with faceted eyes and serrated mandibles.

Revolting to look at, he decided, but they didn't smell half bad. In a pinch, they would do. For him, anyway. His body would throw off any toxins. He didn't know if Lily could safely eat them—or if she'd be willing to try, short of starvation.

He hoped with everything in him they wouldn't have to find out.

"Might as well get to it," the demon said, resigned. It picked up one of the twitching creatures and bit its head off.

Lily made a choked sound. "You were saying something about how *we* kill too easily?"

It chewed and swallowed. "I didn't kill it. I ate it."

"Why am I not seeing the distinction?"

"It isn't dead now. It would have been if I hadn't eaten it, but now it's part of me. You people eat dead things and keep the physical stuff. We eat live things and keep the life. Not that *hirug* would be my first choice." It grimaced at the decapitated body it held and wrenched off one of the legs. "Stupid creatures. But they're here, and I'm going to need extra *ymu*."

When it opened that wide slit of a mouth completely, it looked like the whole lower half of its face was hinged. It crunched down on the leg. "You should have told me you were too weak to travel."

Lily sighed and leaned back against the rock. It

couldn't have been comfortable, but the burn on her stomach probably made leaning forward worse. "Your little snack won't help me travel. Unless you're planning to carry me, and I'm not—"

"Carry you? That would be stupid. Better if I give you a little boost and make your wound go away."

"You can't do that. You said I'm a sensitive, and that—that feels right. I can touch magic . . ." Her hand went to the Lady's talisman Rule had fastened around her throat when she became clan. "It can't touch me, though. Can't affect me."

"How do you think you got here?" it snapped. "By train?"

Her head jerked as if she'd been slapped, her eyebrows flying up.

"We're tied," it told her, impatient. "So I can affect you. I can't get inside you any more than I already am, but I'm partway there. I can give you . . . English doesn't have the words."

"Find some," she said tersely.

Its brow wrinkled. "Well, when I eat, I take *ymu* and *assig*. Ymu is the energy. Assig is the pattern, the memories and thinking. Not that hirug actually think, but you get the idea."

Rule did, and he didn't like it. He moved between Lily and the demon.

"I'm not going to hurt her! I'm going to help her."

Rule snarled.

"Wait."

He looked at Lily, startled.

The small frown tucked between her eyebrows reminded him of her mother. "I don't trust it, either, but he—it—she—" She stopped, frustrated. "What are you, anyway?"

"I'm called Gan. Your dumb language doesn't have a word for he-and-she, so you can call me it. We don't settle on a sex right away. Well, some demons never do, but most—"

"You're . . . a demon."

Gan rolled its eyes. "What did you think I was?"

"Then this place is . . ."

"Dis. Or hell, according to a lot of you people, but that's a misunderstanding."

Lily had already been pale. Now she looked shocky. When Gan started to speak Rule growled at it: *Shut up.*

She closed her eyes and then opened them as if she might be able to change what she saw that way. She looked at the stones, the bizarre sky, the dead and dying hirug, the demon. She drummed her fingers on her thigh. "Okay. You're a demon and we're in hell. How did we get here?"

"It was an accident. The sorcerer burned up the staff while I was trying to get into you."

Judging by the look on her face, the explanation didn't tell her much. She shook her head. "Never mind. We'll go into that later. You seem to be right about one thing—this area isn't safe."

And some other part of hell might be? Rule made a noise in his throat, frustrated by his inability to speak. And not at all sure they should budge from this spot.

He didn't know how they'd gotten here, but the staff had disappeared before when She called it to her. That times, Harlowe had been dragged along willy-nilly because he'd been holding it. Maybe that's what had happened this time. The burn on Lily's stomach suggested the staff had been touching her when it was hit with mage fire, and Rule had been touching her. So they'd been pulled into hell with it.

But what about the demon? Why would it have been pulled here? And where was the staff? If *She* had summoned it, wouldn't Rule and Lily have ended up wherever She was, too?

He glanced at the volcano. Not that he was complaining about Her absence. The farther away they were from

Her, the better. But if they'd been dragged here by the staff, they should have ended up with it.

The other possibility was that the destruction of the staff had somehow opened a gate. Cullen had called the thing a rent in reality, so that wasn't too far-fetched. If so, that gate might be their only way home.

But if Lily remembered the existence of gates, they weren't on her mind now. She had questions—that hadn't changed—and only one place to aim them. At the demon. "How do you do this whatever-it-is? And what will it do to me other than make me stronger?"

"I sort of get control of your body."

Rule growled.

Gan frowned at him. "If you want to say something, you have to think the words. Just making sounds doesn't work."

"I think I know what he meant," Lily said. "You are not taking over any part of me."

"I'm not talking about possession. If I could have done that, I would have. I was *trying*," it added, aggrieved. "I mean that I have to take charge of your body temporarily. So I can make it take ymu."

"This ymu is the energy you were talking about—that comes from living things?" She shook her head. "You're not stuffing me with death magic, either."

It rolled its eyes. "Ymu is not death magic! When you eat dead things, is that death magic? Ymu is just energy. You people have all kinds of energy in your world— bombs and electricity and gasoline—only you can't eat those energies, right? Your body would have to change to take gasoline energy instead of dead animal energy."

"Yes, but . . . I feel like you're pointing in one direction so I won't notice the card up your sleeve."

Its forehead wrinkled. "Card?"

"Never mind. How would this ymu help me?"

Its forehead wrinkled even more. "You could say that ymu makes things want to be in their proper form."

"Then a hirug's ymu would make my body want to be like a hirug."

"No, no, no! Ymu is the energy. The pattern is from the assig—which you can't do anything with. I can." It looked smug. "That's why I'm a demon. But you won't get any hirug assig and your body already knows its pattern, so I just have to get it to take the ymu and it will make itself strong and right again."

She chewed on her lip a moment. "How would you do that?"

"You could suck me off—"

This time it was Lily who growled.

"Okay, okay, it doesn't have to be sex. But you have to take something of my body into you. This is still eating. I can't put ymu in air."

"I have to *eat* part of you?"

"I'm not crazy about that, either, if you won't do sex, but . . ." It scowled, its brow wrinkling as if it was thinking fiercely. "Spit. Spit should work. I can push lots of ymu into it, then push some in your mouth."

Her face twisted in revulsion.

"What's that thing you say? Get over it. Yeah. Get over it. If you're picky about what you eat here, you starve. No McDonald's on the corner. No corner. Get it? No corner." It giggled, appreciating its own humor. "Before you can eat ymu, though, I have to tinker with your body. Make things more dense where they should be."

"Dense?"

"You don't have the words!" It rubbed its head with the hand not holding the dead hirug. Then it spat out a stream of what Lily called babble—and this time, Rule didn't know what it meant, either.

Words mixed with images and sensory impressions. He heard "hydrocarbon." Smelled blood. "Tender wheat" arrived with "liver" and the sound of water dripping. "Eggs" were part of an image of the glowing disc of the sun.

"See?" the demon finished in English. "He doesn't understand, either. You have to already have the ideas, or you can't get the meanings."

She nodded slowly. "One more question. Can this be undone later?"

"Sure." It looked at the hirug it still held and then tossed it to the ground. Apparently once something finished dying it became inedible. After another glance overhead, it began studying the remaining dead and dying hirug.

Lily rubbed her forehead. "I need to think about this."

In the distance, the mountain rumbled, though there was no accompanying trembling in the ground this time.

"Think fast," Gan said, bending to pick up another hirug.

Rule rubbed his head along Lily's arm, making a low, grumbling sound. *This is a bad idea. Don't do it.*

She ran a hand along his back. "You don't like it, do you? I don't, either. But what are my choices? I was barely able to make it out of the open before the hirug got here. I *hurt*. And I can't travel like this."

He poked her with his nose and pointedly sat down.

"You think we should stay put?"

For now, anyway. He nodded.

She shook her head. "I think we have to accept that the creature—the demon—that Gan knows how to survive here. And we don't. If it's giving it to me straight about needing to keep me alive, or it dies, too . . . what do you think?"

That he couldn't answer with a simple yes or no. He couldn't even write in the dirt. There wasn't enough of it. Rule made a frustrated sound.

"Never mind." She sank her fingers into his fur and scratched. "I don't know why I keep feeling like you ought to be able to answer . . . anyway, I think Gan's telling the truth about that part." She looked at the sky, where the fiery glow near the volcano was fading. "I wonder if you know anything about that goddess Gan says is duking it out with its prince."

Rule nodded again.

"You do, huh? I wish you could talk. She must be pretty tough if she can hold her own with a demon prince. You think she might help us?"

He shook his head vigorously.

"She's one of the bad guys?"

He nodded.

"Then it doesn't matter who wins the fight. Either one will be bad news for us."

Dammit, she was right—more right than she knew. And he wasn't thinking straight. If Her avatar survived the battle with the demon prince, She might come looking for Lily.

So yes, they might have to leave this spot, but not right this minute. Lily was letting the demon's urgency rush her to a decision. Slowly Rule shook his head. *Slow down. Give me time to look for any remnants of the staff, or some trace of a hellgate. To look for food and water, find out if it's possible for us to survive here.*

She titled her head to one side. "I can't tell if that means 'no, we can't stay,' or 'no, I don't agree.' I guess it doesn't matter. It's my decision."

He shook his head sharply. She didn't have enough information. She couldn't even consult her own memories, or she'd realize that he'd be bound by what she chose. If she stayed or if she moved on, that's what he would have to do, too.

But she wasn't paying attention. She'd raised one hand and leaned her head into it, looking strained and weary. And uncomfortable.

He could help a little there, at least. He moved up beside her so she could lean on him. She gave him a small smile and did just that, laying an arm over his back and resting against him. For several moments neither of them moved.

What would he do if she decided to take the demon up on its offer?

There wasn't much he could do, he realized. He might like the idea of attacking the demon, but it was their only guide in this world, however little he trusted it. And it claimed to be tied to Lily. He could try to interfere, not letting the demon approach, but that would do little other than make her angry. It wouldn't persuade her to rethink her decision, and he couldn't plant himself between them indefinitely.

"Damn," she said at last, straightening. "I wish I had clothes." She shook her head. "That's stupid. It's just stupid to be worrying about clothes right now, but I don't like this. I don't like being naked."

It wasn't stupid at all. He was, for having paid no attention to her nudity. Just because he didn't react to her body in this form the way he did as a man . . . but why hadn't her clothes come with her? The Lady's token had. So had he.

Later. He'd worry about that later. Right now he had to get her some protection. She was all-over skin, and her skin damaged easily. At the very least she needed shoes. He turned his head and yipped at the demon.

It snorted. "You see a Wal-Mart nearby? Here, clothes are for decorating high-status types. You can't just run out and buy them."

Rule yipped again.

"Feet that can be hurt by walking on them!" Gan snorted. "Humans are weird. If walking hurts her feet, she'll heal them. Once I give her some ymu, that is." It smiled slyly. "I bet I could get her some clothes in Akhanetton."

"All right," Lily said.

Rule's head swung back toward her.

"My body," she told him. "My choice. And I think I have to try Gan's way. This isn't a good place to be weak."

Gan hummed approvingly. "That's good thinking. Your brain's working better than I thought." It had found another twitching hirug. This one was more lively—three of the legs still functioned well enough that it tried to get away, which seemed to cheer up Gan. It smiled before it bit the thing's head off, chewed, and swallowed.

Then it started toward them. "Okay, all you have to do is hold still."

Lily put up a hand, palm out. "Hold it. You're not touching me with that in your hands."

"What?" Gan glanced at the remains of the hirug. "Oh. You don't like blood and stuff? A lot of humans do. And weren't you some kind of cop?"

"I don't know. Was I?"

It slapped its forehead. "Right. Missing marbles. I forgot." It gave its attention to polishing off the hirug, tossed aside a few bits that weren't sufficiently lively, and then lumbered toward Lily.

Rule's hackles lifted. This was wrong. It *had* to be wrong, but he didn't know how to stop her.

Gan stopped a couple of feet away, eyeing him warily. "I don't trust you. Go somewhere else."

The demon didn't trust *him*? Rule's mouth wasn't shaped right for laughter, ironic or otherwise.

Lily shoved at him. "Move. The sooner we get this over with, the better."

Apparently Lily didn't need her memory to be cussedly determined on independence. Grudgingly, he moved away a few feet—close enough to be on top of the demon in one leap, if necessary. It might be stronger than he was, but it was smaller and slower. If it hurt her . . .

Gan edged closer, staying as far away from Rule as it could. With Lily sitting, its head was roughly level with hers. It held out its hands. Its feet were large and flat, rather like a kangaroo's, but its hands were small. Child-size. Aside from the color, they looked quite human.

Lily stared at those small, orange hands, her face blank. Then she clasped them.

For several minutes nothing happened. Nothing he could see, anyway.

"You have to be still!" Gan said, frowning with that very wide mouth.

"I haven't moved."

"You're moving inside. Pushing back at me." It frowned harder. "Think about still things. Things that don't move at all. Think about them real hard."

She scowled and closed her eyes.

A few moments later, Gan leaned in close and opened its mouth over hers. She started to pull away, but it gripped her head and held her still. Rule stiffened, growling, but the kiss was over before he could be sure he should attack.

Gan stepped back, smiling.

Lily wasn't smiling. She swallowed. Swallowed again, as if she was having trouble keeping the demon spit down. Gradually her expression changed to puzzlement.

The redness around her burn was fading.

It went quickly then, faster by far than he could have healed that degree of damage. First the red, weepy skin turned creamy, then the blister-bubble began to shrink. Within five minutes, there was no sign she'd been burned. The wound on her shoulder was gone, too.

Was this, Rule wondered, how humans felt about his own ability to heal? Uneasy, unsettled, convinced that it wasn't supposed to be so easy? That such ease would have to be paid for at some point.

Lily touched her stomach and then rolled her shoulders as if testing the internal workings. Her eyebrows went up. "It worked. I feel . . ." She stretched out both arms. "I feel good."

"You ought to," Gan grumbled. "You've got enough

ymu in you for a Claw. Let's go." It started toward the other side of their cul-de-sac.

Lily stood easily, with no wincing, no need to balance herself on his back. She looked at him, and there was nothing in her face for him to latch onto—no softness, no apology, no doubt. Maybe an acknowledgment: he hadn't wanted this, and she'd done it anyway.

He was, he realized, thoroughly pissed. He looked away.

Gan was already scrambling up a ravine. Lily followed, so Rule did, too.

He took the rear. The cul-de-sac wasn't deep, and the ravine the demon had chosen for an exit made for an easy climb. He followed her as she followed the demon, and his anger didn't dissipate.

That was unfair. He knew it, though the knowledge didn't release him from the anger. Lily was sundered from her self in a way he could scarcely imagine, lost in hell with a wolf and a demon, unable to recall her own name. In pain, afraid, and lacking memory, why should she take his wordless counsel?

But anger isn't always logical, and his welled up from the deep places inside. For he was sundered, too, from a large part of himself—from his clan, his family, his world, and his other form. And he might never get any of that back. He might never speak in words again, or see his father or brother, or be there to help his son through his first Change. He might never pick something up with a hand instead of a mouth.

And if he stayed in this form too long, he would forget what it was to use his hands. He would cease thinking in words. The man would fade, and there would be only the wolf.

The part of him that was wolf didn't fear as the man did. He missed his clan, but he enjoyed his four feet, and his mate was near. And when was the future ever more than a mist? Yet the wolf's pain went deep, too.

Where there should have been the long, slow song, the pull and call that shaped his soul, there was silence. And for that there was no comfort.

There is no moon in hell.

TWENTY-ONE

LILY started awake, her heart pounding, her eyes wide with terror.

Scent seeped in through the fear-fog, a mix of antiseptic, flowers, and body fluids that said *hospital*. With that understanding, reason woke, too, and began sorting the sensory impressions into sense.

The sound she'd heard, the noise that had sprung her from sleep so abruptly . . . she backed up mentally, replayed it, and decided someone had dropped something on the hard hospital floor outside her room.

She'd been dreaming. Wisps of the dream clung to her despite the harsh awakening . . . thick fur beneath her hand, fur warmed by a strong body. There'd been a sense of physical well-being, too, and a goal, a place she needed to reach. She had to walk to get there. That's what she'd been doing when she was jerked awake. Walking.

In the dream she hadn't been alone. Here, she was.

It was early. Gray light from the room's single window barely smudged the outlines of things, but she could see that the space was empty of threats. Empty entirely, with a flat, lifeless feel, less real to her than a stage set.

As empty as she was with something nameless and necessary drained out.

Lily closed her eyes, riding out the backlash of unused adrenaline, waiting for her heartbeat to steady. She found herself alone with the numbness growing like a cancerous vine out of the dead place inside her. The place where her Gift used to be.

Grandmother, you said this couldn't happen. That it wasn't possible for me to stop being a sensitive. Suddenly she wanted her grandmother, wanted her with the intensity of a child waking from a nightmare, crying out in the dark. She needed to be held. She needed someone who could explain what had happened to her, even if she couldn't fix it.

She wasn't going to get what she wanted. Lily opened her eyes for the second time on a day she didn't want to face.

Rule was missing.

Missing, she reminded herself. Not dead.

Gradually the room took on context, substance, becoming real once more as the light subtly brightened outside. Just as her dream had suggested, she had a goal. She had to find Rule. She didn't know how—where to look, how to find out, who might have the pieces she needed to make sense of his vanishing. But she'd take her dream's advice there, too. She'd take one step at a time.

Her first step, she realized, would be literal. She had to get out of bed.

The skin's two main jobs were keeping contaminants out and fluids in. Large burns compromised its ability to do both tasks, so they'd given her antibiotics and kept her overnight to get her fluids replenished.

The IV had done a damned fine job. She was awash.

Sitting up wasn't too bad in a bed that answered her commands, but twisting around to slide off the bed hurt.

So did standing, breathing . . . she'd just have to put up with it. She began inching toward the bathroom, trailing her IV stand.

Maybe the nasty sense of unreality she'd woken up with had been an aftereffect of the painkiller they'd given her last night. She'd needed it. By the time they moved her to this room her mind had been so fuzzed by pain and emotion that she couldn't have reasoned her way through tic-tac-toe.

No more drugs, though. She had a lot of thinking to do.

They probably wouldn't offer her anything stronger than ibuprofen, anyway. She'd be leaving soon. There was no reason to keep her any longer.

Lily did what she could to make herself ready to face the day. She used the facilities, the hospital's toothbrush, and the hairbrush from her purse. She washed her face and hands and gave the shower a longing glance.

Even if she hadn't been warned against it, though, she wouldn't have taken a shower yet. She didn't have anything clean to put on. She'd have to call someone . . . someone other than her mother.

Lily stared at the shiny white sink, the forgotten hairbrush clutched tight in her hand. Words ran through her head, broken bits of actual dialogue tumbling around with all the things she might have said.

No doubt last night had been a take on every parent's nightmare—two children in the ER at the same time, both victims of violence. And her mother always handled anxiety by assigning blame, as if by fixing guilt she could fix the problem. So Lily supposed she was a fool for needing what Julia Yu was unable or unwilling to give . . . but understanding didn't stop the ache. Or the anger.

At first Lily had been too raw to comprehend her mother's tirade. So much of it was reruns, the same tired complaints about Lily's profession. Only so shrill. So full of blame. *Your fault,* her mother had said. *It's your fault your little sister is hurt, was nearly raped, nearly killed.*

What about me? Lily had said, or maybe she'd just thought that. *I'm so sorry Beth got hurt, but I'm hurt, too. I did my best. . . .*

When had her best ever been good enough? But her mother hadn't left it at that. *She's gone too far,* Lily thought. This time her mother had gone too far.

So had she. When Julia Yu had yoked Rule in with her daughter, needing more than one person to haul around the shitload of blame she was dumping—when she'd said it was just as well he was dead—Lily had slapped her.

Lily shook her head, throwing off thoughts that had nowhere to go but round and round. She put down the brush, shoved open the bathroom door—and her heartbeat went crazy.

The outer door had swung open at the same instant, leaving her and a dark-skinned man in baggy scrubs staring at each other in mutual surprise.

The doctor, she thought, feeling foolish as she took in the stethoscope and harried expression. She had to get over this business of jumping at every unexpected sound or sight.

Twenty minutes later she was back in bed scowling at the blank screen of the television. She'd pulled the tray-table in front of her. It held a steaming cup of coffee and the pen and pad from her purse.

They were keeping her another night "for observation."

There was no reason for it. The doctor had hemmed and hawed his way around an explanation, citing trauma and the danger of shock. Lily wasn't buying. There'd been some danger of shock last night, but that was over. The IV was gone.

The bastard with the stethoscope had actually patted her hand and told her she was lucky. HMOs and insurance companies were forever kicking people out too soon, and here she was being invited to stay an extra day. She should take advantage of it and rest.

Ruben had told her to rest, too. Damn him.

A paranoid type might think someone wanted to keep her where he could find her. Someone official, with plenty of pull. Someone who just might prefer that she be declared insane.

Of course, a paranoid type might be kept for observation in case she started seeing little green men conspiring against her.

Lily had reported to Ruben twice last night. First she'd called him from the scene, giving him a rough sketch of events. She'd followed up with a more detailed account while waiting to be moved from the ER to this room.

Something had changed between the first time she spoke with him and the second. Something or someone had convinced him Rule was dead, not missing.

He'd made noises about the lupi removing the body, just as they'd spirited away their wounded. She'd insisted they wouldn't do that without telling her. That's when he'd told her to rest.

Cullen hadn't believed her, either. No one did. And they should have.

There was no body.

Last night she hadn't liked where her thoughts were taking her. She'd hoped that sleep would clear her mind enough to come up with an explanation that didn't involve conspiracies. But today she found herself heading in the same direction.

Lily sipped at the coffee and started organizing her thoughts on paper.

Sequence, she wrote. Under that she began listing last night's events. She put asterisks next to the parts she'd heard secondhand.

According to Cullen, Benedict had scented the other lupi. Knowing help was almost there, he'd timed his play

to have the gang in a state of maximum confusion when
the wolves showed up, howling. He'd gotten Lily out
of the line of fire even as he'd taken care of the one holding Beth.

His knife had flown true. The gangbanger had died
fast with several inches of steel in his throat—too fast to
harm Beth. Then Benedict had opened fire on the rest of
the gang.

There'd been twenty of them, it turned out. Twenty
young men with weapons trained on him, ready to shoot.
He'd killed seven and wounded five before their return
fire took him down just as the pack arrived.

That had sent most of the remaining gang members
running. Most of those who hadn't run were dead—but
only one of them had been killed by the wolves. Harlowe
had been foaming-at-the-mouth crazy by then, fixated on
reaching Lily. He'd used the staff so erratically that he'd
done as much damage to his own people as to the lupi.

The staff, Lily wrote.

One. Harlowe had been holding it when Cullen hit him
with mage fire. He'd been toasted . . . but his body hadn't
gone missing.

Two. It had been touching Lily. She'd been burned, but
she hadn't vanished.

Three. It hadn't even been touching Rule, yet he was
gone.

Why? And why was she the only one who saw that his
death didn't explain anything?

She frowned at her list of events. *Make it complete,*
she told herself, and added: *Took patrol cop to Rule's
location. He wasn't there.*

Lily couldn't blame the local cops for thinking she
was nuts. She'd known where Rule was, been able to feel
his location precisely—on the west side of the dilapi-
dated house that had been the gang's headquarters. She'd
talked one of them into helping her get there . . . and
found nothing, no one, no sign of Rule.

Alternatives, she wrote. Under that went: *(1) The mate bond isn't working right* and *(2) The mate bond's working, but reality is screwed up.* She grimaced. Hard to see how she could prove or disprove either of those. Then she made herself write the last alternative: *(3) Rule's dead, and I'm delusional.*

But dammit, she felt him. Not nearby, no. He was at least ten miles away now, maybe more. But the sense of direction was as clear as it had ever been. If she was imagining this, then the mate bond had been a delusion all along.

She crossed out the last alternative.

Where did that leave her?

No one had seen him die. No one had seen his body carried away. Yet two groups, the lupi and the FBI, insisted that he was dead, not missing. One or both groups must have some compelling reason to want Rule declared dead, even if they suspected he was still alive.

That was where she hit a stumbling block. She couldn't come up with any scenario that would put Cullen in cahoots with the FBI . . . which left her either with two groups with different motives, or back at the delusional alternative. In which case she couldn't trust her perceptions or her logic and should meekly agree when they offered to tuck her away in a nice, safe place.

Fuck that.

Rule was alive. She was the only one who could find him, because no one else wanted to look.

How did she start looking?

With what she knew, of course. And she *knew* where he was—the direction, at least. She shoved back the table, bent and grabbed her purse from the floor, and pulled her city map out of the side pocket. She'd track him her way.

He'd moved, she realized, surprised. He was still moving . . . slowly, maybe at a walk. She made her best guess about the distance and noted her estimate of his location on the map. Every thirty minutes she'd check, she decided. And she wouldn't let herself wonder how she could find him, then bring him back, on her own.

Because it looked impossible, and if she let herself get bogged down in what was or wasn't possible, she'd never take the next step.

Whatever the hell that was.

THE sky in this place didn't change. That was hard to get used to. She had no idea how long she'd been walking, but it felt like a long time. Her feet hurt.

Otherwise, though, she was in good shape physically. That ymu was strong stuff. She felt as if she could keep walking for days if she had to . . . whatever "days" might mean in a place with no sun.

They'd left the barren heights behind and were walking along a narrow valley. Oddly, it had grown cooler as they descended, cool enough that she was beginning to envy the wolf his fur. So far, though, walking kept her reasonably warm.

Things grew here.

Nothing green. No sun meant no chlorophyll, she supposed. The most common plant looked like a succulent grass—thick, fleshy stuff the color of lemons that grew in patches that didn't reach the top of her foot. The other plants were mostly stem or stalk and didn't grow much higher than the "grass."

There was one exception—a rusty red vine that grew in great, looping piles to form thickets that dotted the valley like nests of enormous, vegetative snakes. She hadn't seen the vine up close. Gan wouldn't go anywhere near those thickets.

Occasionally the sky flared behind the mountains on her left. The volcano was out of sight, but signs of the battle continued.

Ahead was the Zone. Not far now—maybe thirty minutes, and they'd be there.

From a distance it had looked like a huge gray wall stretched from one side of the valley's mouth to the other, blocking the narrow egress. As they drew closer, it had lost definition rather than gaining it, growing almost misty and somehow hard to see. Unless she forced herself to stare at it her gaze would slide away.

That wasn't a spell, she knew. She didn't react to spells. Something about the nature of the barrier was simply hard to focus on. Whatever it was made of, though, it wasn't solid. At the top it faded into the sky like a shadow cast upward.

On the other side was their goal: Akhanetton. There they'd be out of reach of Gan's prince and the goddess Gan wouldn't name.

The Rules behaved oddly in a zone, according to Gan. And that was about all the demon had told her about zones. All she knew about Akhanetton was that it was another region. When she asked questions, Gan hushed her and looked scared.

She was pretty sure the demon was faking some of its fear to avoid answering questions.

Gan was especially jumpy now that they were in the open, but she hadn't seen any threats. Mostly bugs. Hell was big on bugs. Most of them were small and acted like regular insects, flying or scurrying about on their buggy business with the fearlessness only the lack of a brain could impart. The few larger ones had run away when the three of them came near.

More than bugs, though, more than plants, the valley had dust. Very fine dust in a funny color, sort of a dusky purple. Like desiccated twilight.

She remembered twilight. Also sunrise, the scent of the ocean, and the sound of a cat's purr. She had no idea how any of those sights and sounds related to her, but she remembered them now.

At first she hadn't had anything, not a single memory. But as she walked, from time to time a word would float in and make itself at home. Like when the whir of an insect's wings had made her think of a cat purring, and all of a sudden she had "cat" back—the size and shape of cats, their soft fur, and sharp claws. The way they moved, as if they owned whatever space they occupied.

She still couldn't relate to the name the demon said was hers, but maybe that, too, would return. Maybe at some point she'd know "Lily" again.

The dust, while kind to her feet, was hard on her nose and throat. It rose in puffs with every step. Her throat tickled, and she coughed.

"Shh," Gan said without looking back.

The demon led. She stayed a few paces behind, and the wolf roamed. She hadn't seen him for a while, yet she knew where he was.

That had come as a surprise. The first time he'd roved out of sight, casting around for dangers, she'd felt anxious until she realized she could sense him. Not his thoughts or feelings, nothing so specific, but she knew where he was.

He was on his way back to them now. The valley didn't offer much real cover, but between the few bushes and the dips and rises in the ground the wolf—Rule—managed to keep out of sight. He was silent, too, uncannily so. Even Gan couldn't hear him approach.

Rule could probably have survived here on his own, but he wouldn't desert her. Even though he was angry with her decision—and that had been obvious since they left the ravine—he'd stay with her. She knew that in a way she couldn't explain.

The demon would have done fine on its own, too. Not her. She wasn't a liability because of her wounds anymore. She was just useless.

Of course, if not for her the other two might have killed each other by now.

A great, dark shape melted up out of the ground in front of them. Gan yelped and jumped back and then shook its fist at the wolf. "Quit that!"

"Shh," Lily said.

Gan turned to glare at her.

The wolf—Rule—grinned. At least that's what his expression looked like to Lily. He rumbled at the demon.

"What did he say?"

Gan cast Rule a disparaging look. "Oh, the big puppy dog is tired and thirsty."

Rule growled louder.

"Come on, Gan. What did he really say?"

"He found some water," Gan said grudgingly. "He thinks we should take a break before crossing the Zone."

"Good." Yet she wasn't truly thirsty. She wanted to wash the dust from her throat, but she didn't actually need a drink. She wasn't hungry, either, and that was weird, now that she thought about it. A by-product of the ymu?

What else had that stuff done to her that she hadn't noticed? That maybe she wouldn't notice because she lacked the reference of memory to tell her something had changed?

Rule gave her a questioning look. She nodded, and he trotted off. She followed.

Gan did, too, grumbling about the detour, but she suspected the demon was ready for a break as well and only objected because it was the wolf's idea.

The ground here was easier to her feet than the rocks had been. The valley itself was monotonous, but the mountains on her right were rather pretty in their way. Vegetation softened and striated them into bands of color—yellow ochre, rust, and brown in shades from sand to coffee to grape.

Not much like the mountains on the other side of the valley.

She paused and looked back, trying to spot the place where they'd come down out of the rocks into this valley. Somewhere in that confusion of stone lay the ravine that was, in a sense, her birthplace. It held her first memories.

She couldn't find it.

"What?" Gan whispered. "Do you see something?"

The demon had stopped. The wolf had, too, and was looking at her over his shoulder. She shook her head, unable to put words to the feelings knotted up in her gut. It was too late to wonder if they'd be able to find their way back.

Forward was all she had. So she kept going.

TWENTY-TWO

THE waterhole was literally that—a hole in the rock where water bubbled up in what was more a large puddle than a pool. It was set in a depression like a small meteor crater. *Meteor,* she thought, surprised, as the word opened up an image of a starry sky. Space. The moon, and meteorite showers that looked like falling stars.

She paused, savoring space and falling stars. Gan made it to the little pond first and knelt, tipping forward on its short arms to dunk its head underwater. It came up sputtering and then bent and slurped at the water like a . . . well, a dog. Or a wolf.

She looked at Rule. He would have drunk his fill when he found the waterhole. Now he lay nearby, his eyes open but head drooping.

He's exhausted, she realized, and that troubled her. Had more time passed than she'd guessed? Or was something else affecting him? "How long have we been walking?" she asked abruptly.

Gan sat back on its haunches, having quenched

whatever thirst a demon feels. "According to whose clock? Time's more erratic here than you're used to."

"Time doesn't change. That just . . . it doesn't make sense."

"It does here. Though . . ." Its forehead wrinkled. "Around you it might operate more the way you're used to. I'm not sure how things work around a sensitive."

A dozen questions tempted her with side roads, but she held to her course. "Take a guess about how long we've been walking based on, uh, your own clock."

"Oh, maybe one of your days. I told you the Zone wasn't far."

Then Rule's exhaustion made sense, she thought, relieved. He'd probably covered twice as much territory as she had, and it had been a long time since he slept. Maybe he'd been awake for a long time before they arrived here, too.

That was a disconcerting thought, stretching as it did into a past she couldn't claim. She felt jealous, she realized. Jealous of Rule, for possessing what she'd lost. Jealous even of herself . . . the self who didn't exist anymore, except in the memories of others.

Of course, if Rule had been awake a long time, so had she. "I'm not sleepy."

"You're still charged up with ymu. It lasts a lot longer than the kind of meals you're used to. Once it runs low, you might get sleepy. Or mean. Or hungry. Or you might just keel over."

Great. "You don't know?"

It shrugged. "The only humans I know about who've taken ymu were possessed. It's probably different if you don't have a demon in you."

But she was tied to one—the one currently blocking her way. She stepped around it so she could wash the dust from her throat.

Gan shoved her back.

"Hey!"

"You've got to *look* first. See that?"

Now that it was pointed out, she did. A small vine thrust out of a fissure in the stone right where she'd been about to step. Pale and leafless, it looked more like an albino worm than a plant. "So?"

Gan rolled its eyes. "So why do you think we've been avoiding those things?"

This was one of the snaky vines? "I don't know. I asked, but you just hushed me." She tipped her head, studying it. "The mature ones are a different color."

"They've got a lot of blood in them."

Oh. She bent to take a good look, wanting to be sure she'd recognize one if she saw it. "I don't see any kind of mouth, but it's got fine hairs. Or maybe they're cilia."

"Whatever you call them, they're sticky. Real sticky. And they're the eating part."

"How? And why is it dangerous to me? It's too little to eat anything but bugs."

"You'd get away, yeah. But you'd have it stuck to you, and the sap would eat away your skin."

She was very careful about approaching the water-hole after that. When she knelt she saw a number of flying insects skimming the water—pretty things the size of her palm, almost colorless but with iridescent wings. They lit on the surface and took off again, making little ripples.

She wasn't crazy about drinking after them, so she just splashed her face. The water was cold, but her skin tingled with more than the chill. "It's everywhere in this place, isn't it?"

"What?" Gan plopped down on the bare rock next to the water, sitting in the tilted sprawl its tail necessitated.

"Magic. Not literally everywhere," she corrected herself, looking for a spot with some of the dust for cushioning. Bare rock wasn't as comfortable for her as it seemed to be for the demon. "But there are patches of it all over—the ground, the air, the water." Sometimes as she walked she'd felt it drift by, like a breeze, only the air wasn't moving. Just the magic.

That was different, wasn't it? She felt sure she wasn't used to having so much free magic floating around.

"You mean you can feel it? You're not even trying and you feel it?"

"Of course. There's nothing between my skin and everything else, and I'm a sensitive, remember?"

Gan snorted. "Better than you do, I bet. Unless you've found your missing marbles."

Her fists clenched. "Not exactly crammed with tact, are you?"

Rule stood and came over to her, rubbing his head along her hip. She dropped a hand to his shoulder, and just like that she felt better. Easier, as if she'd been holding an immaterial fist clenched around some thought or fear for a long time and could finally relax.

"I've gotten a little of it back," she said, speaking to him now, not the demon. "Nothing about me, but I remember . . . a place that isn't like this."

He made a low, rumbling sound. She looked to Gan for a translation.

"He says he'll remember for you. Could you try to be quiet now? Or do you just have to attract an *erkint* or two?"

"I think," she said, still talking to the wolf, "that Gan gets especially cautious about noise when it doesn't want to answer questions."

He nodded.

"I have a lot of questions, and you probably do, too. But maybe we'll save them until we've rested." Not that she was physically tired, though it would feel good to get off her feet. She was weary of questions, of the void inside her that gave back only silence. "I'll grill Gan later. I need to sit, and you need some sleep."

Rule hesitated but then agreed by moving to a spot slightly sheltered by the rise in the ground that made her think of the lip of a meteor crater. He lay down and looked at her. He had lovely eyes, warm and dark and capable of conveying quite a bit of meaning. Right now they seemed to offer an invitation.

She took him up on it, sitting down beside him. His body felt warm and furry and good. She stroked his back. "Go on, get some sleep. I'll keep watch."

Again he hesitated.

"Not used to letting someone else do the watching, are you? It's true, I won't be as good a sentry as you. I don't have your senses. But I don't need sleep right now, and you do."

He sighed and laid his head on her thigh. Within moments, he was asleep.

This, too, felt good. He'd been angry with her earlier, she knew. He hadn't wanted her to take the ymu, or for them to leave the ravine. But either he'd gotten over his anger, or he'd set it aside. He trusted her to keep watch while he slept, and that mattered. It mattered a lot.

If she hadn't had him with her here . . . well, she did, so there was no point in chasing that particular question. But even thinking it brought such a surge of feeling . . . like one of those ocean waves she remembered, it rolled up inside her, getting bigger and bigger.

Also like the waves she remembered, this one was salty. Her eyes filmed over with tears. He was the one good thing she had. "I'm so glad about you," she whispered—soft, soft, so she didn't wake him. "I'm so damned glad about you."

Gan giggled. She dashed a hand across her eyes and turned to it, angry—but the demon was paying no attention to her. It was preoccupied with the flying bugs with the shiny wings. Its hand shot out, closing around one of them.

She ought to appreciate Gan's presence, too. True, the demon acted from self-interest, but it had healed her wounds.

Gan popped the bug in its mouth.

Its habits weren't exactly appealing, but she and the wolf would find it much harder to survive here without the demon's guidance.

It grabbed another bug. This one it fed to the snake vine. It giggled again as the bug's wings thrashed.

There was a reason she hadn't bonded with Gan. She looked away.

Sitting still was hard. She'd wanted to rest, but now that she was resting, she wanted to move. She'd thought that the restlessness would go away once they left that ravine behind, but she'd brought it along with her.

She'd brought another feeling with her, too. One that fed the restlessness, though she sensed it wasn't the cause. An achy, needy feeling.

She wanted sex.

Now that she was sitting still, the ache was obvious. But she'd felt it for some time without paying it much notice—ever since Gan gave her the ymu, she realized. She remembered the startling rush of strength and energy, as if her blood had gone from flat to fizzy in an instant.

Maybe she always felt this way when her body was healthy and rested. But weren't demons supposed to be oversexed? Maybe these feelings came from Gan—she was tied to it, after all. Or from the ymu.

She glanced at Gan again. No way was she going to ask.

Gan had said that she and Rule used to have sex "when he wasn't a wolf." She frowned. It bothered her to think of him being different. Had he been a wolf a long time? What was he like when he wasn't a wolf?

She wished she could remember. Funny . . . she knew about sex, knew what her body wanted. She could imagine the way a man's hands would feel, but she couldn't remember being touched. She tried to call up a single, specific image—a face, a name, a place. And failed. What did her bed look like? Who had been it with her? Had she had many lovers? Or . . . another word arrived, but this one slammed into her mind with all the subtlety of a sledgehammer.

Marriage. What if she was married?

She looked at the wolf whose head was heavy and warm on her thigh, her brow wrinkling at the thoughts pinging through her mind. She wasn't wearing a ring . . . but she'd arrived here without clothes, so the lack of a ring didn't mean much.

She didn't realize she'd reached for the little charm hung around her neck until her fingers closed around it. The faint, familiar buzz of its magic made her shoulders loosen. Her necklace had arrived with her. Surely a wedding ring would have, too.

The demon sighed, stretched its short legs and leaned back on its tail. "This is boring."

Silence only mattered when the demon wasn't bored? She scowled at it. "What?" it said. "Aren't you bored just sitting there?"

It was like a child, she realized. A nasty little child who pulled the wings off flies—and fed them to carnivorous plants. But maybe demons didn't sleep, so Gan didn't realize it had to be quiet or it would wake up Rule. She shushed it.

Gan grimaced and pulled up a handful of the fleshy yellow grass.

She bet that once she started asking questions it would be hushing her and looking scared again. But they weren't budging until she knew more.

She'd rushed her decision, she admitted. Or allowed herself to be pushed into it, with pain arguing loudly on the side of the demon. She still thought she'd made the right choice, but she'd made it with very few facts. Before they crossed the Zone into the other region, she intended to get some answers.

She looked to her left at the murky barrier stretched across the mouth of the valley like a T-shirt that was fifty percent spandex, fifty percent mist.

Spandex. T-shirt. She smiled with pleasure as the words shifted all sorts of images and concepts into her mind. Gyms and working out. Department stores and malls. Socks and athletic shoes . . . and oh, but didn't she wish she had some of those right now!

Of course, she might as well wish for the whole mall so she could get a few other things, too. Panties, jeans, a shirt, a hairbrush . . . her hair must be a mess.

Her hair. She didn't know what it looked like. Or her face.

The surface of the water had been too ripply from the insects to give her back a reflection. She hadn't thought about it then. Now she needed to know.

The hand she raised trembled a little. She checked out her hair first. Not long, not short. Straight. Black, she saw when she pulled a strand in front of her face. And her face . . . she touched her cheeks, her chin, but didn't know how to assemble the messages from her fingertips into a picture. Were ears always this big? What about noses? Hers felt straight, but was it long or short? She didn't know how long a nose ought to feel. Or lips. Hers—

What was that?

She turned her head sharply and shook the wolf's shoulder. "Wake up. Quick. Gan, what are those?"

"What are . . . shit!" the demon cried even as the wolf lifted his head, shook it, and turned to see where she was pointing.

Four great, winged shapes were heading toward them, coming from the direction of the Zone.

"Shit, shit, shit!" Gan hopped from foot to foot, clutching its head as it looked around frantically. "I knew stopping here was a bad idea! I just knew it!"

The wolf was on his feet now, but he no more knew what to do than she did. There was no cover, nothing to shield them from overhead, and she lacked even the most rudimentary weapon . . . and those things were huge.

And coming fast. She could see them clearly now.

For a moment, awe outweighed everything else. Watching those four sinuous shapes the color of old copper winging straight at them, gliding across air with the sideways sway of a snake crossing sand, carried by wings whose tips would span a small house, all she could think was: *They exist. They really do exist.*

Dragons.

A cold nose poked her. "What—? Oh. Yes," she said as the wolf flattened himself as much as possible against the rim of the small depression. "Yes, I see."

There was nowhere to run, no way to defend themselves. Their only chance was to be hard to spot. She curled up against the rock.

She couldn't see the dragons anymore. The fear she hadn't felt a second ago struck. Her mouth went dry. Her heartbeat slammed into overdrive. She craned her head around, trying to spot them without moving. *This is how a rabbit feels, quivering in the grass while the eagle stoops, unable to see its death coming, but knowing. Knowing.*

She clenched her fingers in Rule's ruff. Maybe it was just coincidence that the dragons were flying this way. Maybe their vision was poor. Maybe . . .

The demon was still hopping in one place, halfway to hysterical. "They'll eat me! They're going to eat me, I know it!"

"Gan!" she called. "You're making yourself a target! Shut up and get down!"

It looked straight at her, its oddly lovely eyes wide with terror. "They'll eat me!" it shrilled. "I won't *be* anymore! You have a soul—you'll still be, but I won't! All of me will be gone!"

She stared at it, helpless. Should she tackle it, wrestle it to the ground? Could she? It was small, but so much heavier than it looked—

"*No!*" she screamed, grabbing at the wolf—too late.

He'd hurled himself up out of the depression. Had he

lost his mind? Did he think he could fight them, or outrun them, or—no. Oh, no.

"He's nuts!" The demon stared after the wolf, too, as he raced away—not dodging, but running flat out—fast, so fast. Not running directly away from the dragons, either, but at an angle. "He can't outrun them!"

No, he couldn't. He was trying to draw them away. Offering himself as easy prey.

She was on her feet. She didn't remember standing up. She watched as one of the greatest creatures of legend peeled away from the others, folded its wings, and dove, plummeting straight at Rule like an arrow loosed from a giant's bow. She was still watching that terrible dive when two of the remaining three folded their wings and dove.

The one stooping on Rule struck, skimmed the ground, lifted.

Four long seconds later, a shadow dimmed the glow from the sky. Then the talons closed around her.

TWENTY-THREE

CYNNA hated hospitals. So did everyone who didn't
work in one, she supposed, and maybe some who did.
Just the smell of this one made her want to turn around
and head the other way.

But there were things she hated worse, so she stepped
out of the elevator and scowled at the wall with arrows
pointing this way and that, depending on which room
number you wanted.

Okay, three-fourteen was to the left. She headed that
way at a good clip, her tote tucked under one arm, the
flowers she'd picked up at the grocery store gripped
firmly in her other hand. She hadn't been raised within
whiffing distance of any social graces, but she'd picked
up a few along the way. When you visited someone in the
hospital, you took flowers.

Cynna had never been one to dawdle, and with a good
head of anger steaming her brain, she chugged past the
nurse's station pretty quickly. A nurse with a bouncy ponytail called out something about stopping. She ignored that.

Damned bureaucrats. She'd thought Ruben was

different, but he'd caved, turned belly-up under the pressure. Well, she wasn't about to go along with it.

She was reaching for the door of three-fourteen when the nurse—persistent little shit—put a hand on her arm. "Miss! I've been trying to stop you. You can't go in there."

Cynna turned around slowly. "Don't touch."

It was the first good look the woman had gotten at Cynna's face. Her baby-blues opened wide.

There had been a time when Cynna enjoyed the stares—at least she wasn't invisible. There'd been a time when they annoyed her. These days she mostly didn't notice, but she was a little testy at the moment.

"What's the matter?" she asked. "Have I got dirt on my cheek? Is my lipstick smeared?"

"Uh . . ." The woman blinked. "You aren't wearing lipstick."

"No shit." Cynna grinned in a way she knew made people nervous. "So what're you staring at?"

Nurse Ponytail was made of stronger stuff than she looked. "Your tattoos. I shouldn't have. Excuse me for that, but you didn't stop. You can't go in there, miss. Visiting hours aren't for another two hours."

"You're full of assumptions, aren't you, Miss Nurse? How do you know I don't have three or four husbands scattered around? Here. Hold this." She thrust the flowers at the nurse so she could dig out her badge. "Happy?"

Damned if the woman didn't take the badge and examine it before handing it back. "It looks legitimate. Did you clear this visit with the head nurse?"

"No." Cynna stuffed her badge in her jacket pocket and took back the flowers. "Why don't you run along and tattle on me?" She turned away and shoved open the door. And stopped, letting her tote fall to the floor as she held her hands away from her sides.

The .38 aimed her way had an effect on her heart rate, too.

It was held by an aging Santa Claus in gold-rimmed

glasses, a cheap sports jacket, and ugly black shoes. Cop shoes. Cop eyes, too, behind those glasses.

She relaxed a bit. "Guess I should have knocked first."

"It's okay, T.J.," Lily said from the bed. "She's MCD."

"Knocking would be a good idea," he said, sliding his weapon back into a shoulder holster that was in a lot better shape than his shoes. "People keep trying to kill Yu. Makes me edgy."

"Understandable."

"They might miss and hit me," he explained.

She grinned and came farther into the room. It was typical hospital fare—semi-private, no window, two stiff, vinyl-covered chairs for visitors. No one was in the other bed. No flowers, Cynna noticed. Well, Lily hadn't been here long and would probably be turned loose soon.

If they didn't decide to lock her away somewhere else, that is. Someplace where she could be medicated and watched.

Lily didn't look bad. Pale, tired, and all-over tense, but otherwise okay. Not noticeably nutty . . . not grieving, either, from what Cynna could tell. But she had her face closed up tight, so Cynna might have been wrong about that.

Lily lifted a hand. "T.J., this is Agent Cynna Weaver. Cynna, this quivering mass of Jell-O is Detective Thomas James. I worked homicide with him."

"Make it T.J." He grinned, revealing a gold tooth and more charm than she'd expected from an old, fat white dude. "Only civilians call me Detective James."

"Sure, if you call me Cynna. When I hear 'Agent Weaver' I start looking for some suit with a briefcase."

"I hear you. Good to meet you, Cynna." He glanced at Lily. "Guess I'll be heading out."

"Uh . . . don't rush off on my account." Cynna knew she sounded insincere, probably because she was. Some things couldn't be said with an outsider around, even if he was a cop.

"I was ready to leave. Yu here has already heard all my stories, and the strain of trying to look interested is wearing her out."

"T.J." Lily gave him a long, level look. "Thanks."

He gave her a nod. "Still think you ought to come back, but I'll admit we can't offer you all the thrills you're getting with the feds. Shot, burned . . . think you could arrange to be stabbed next time, just for a little variety?"

"I'll see what I can do," she said dryly.

Cynna moved aside to let him by. On impulse she asked, "Did the ponytail nurse give you a hard time about showing up before visiting hours?"

"You mean Sally?" There was a knowing look in his eyes. "Nah, Sally likes me. Cute little thing, isn't she?"

She sighed. "Not my type."

"Never know, these days," he said vaguely. "Later."

Cynna wasn't sure what it was about her that gave people the idea she played on her own side of the fence, but this wasn't the first time she'd run up against that notion. Not just from men, either. She'd been hit on plenty by the DC-types of her own sex.

After the door closed behind T.J., Cynna sighed. "Maybe I need to wear a button. Something discreet like, 'No, I'm not lesbian.'"

The door opened again. "And I, for one, am pleased to hear it. Do you fool around?"

Cynna turned around. And fell in love.

"You must be Lily's Finder," said the most beautiful man in the world. "I've been wanting to meet you."

"I am so shallow," she muttered. Then, louder, "Listen, about fooling around . . . I've got some things to do first, but if you'd like to wait until after I've talked to Yu—to Lily, I mean—I'm up for a discussion of the subject."

"Should I tell you who he is before you jump him?' Lily asked from the bed. "Or would that detract from the mystery?"

"I've got this theory that it's classier to know a man's name before you get naked together, so shoot."

"Cullen Seabourne."

Shit. She should have known he was too good to be true. "The sorcerer." Her right hand was still full of flowers, so she used the left one to run a quick diagnostic, barely moving her fingers.

He noticed. It amused him. "Thank you. I'm afraid I haven't rediscovered the trick to creating a full, mobile illusion, however. Nor am I running any charm spells."

"He really does look like that." Lily didn't sound amused. More like weary. "As for charm, I haven't noticed any."

"Ouch." He came farther into the room, and oh, man, but he did know how to move. He had one of those lean bodies, all muscle and grace, like a Siamese cat. And knew how to display it—tight black jeans, a snug T-shirt the same startling blue as his eyes. His hair was a spicy brown.

She was pretty sure there were horses that color—rich and reddish, not quite auburn. He wore it too long, but Cynna wasn't complaining. And his face . . . God, what a face. She could have hung him on the wall and just looked at him all day. After they had sex, that is. Hot, sweaty sex for maybe five, six hours.

"Wait a minute," she said, scowling at a sudden thought. "You aren't gay, are you?"

His eyebrows lifted. "Didn't Lily tell you? I'm lupus."

And that, of course, was that. Lupi simply didn't produce homosexuals. The so-called experts coughed up all sorts of reasons, but Cynna considered it an argument in favor of a genetic link for sexual orientation. "And I'm very glad to meet you. Cynna Weaver." She held out her hand . . . and saw the flowers she was still clutching.

She turned to Lily. "Uh, these are for you."

"Thank you. I'm afraid I don't have a vase, but there should be a water pitcher around here somewhere."

"That'll do." God, how lame. Why hadn't she gotten a vase with the flowers? She looked around.

"Here." The love of her life handed her an ugly plastic pitcher.

"Great. I'll just fill this up with water."

The bathroom was tiny. Cynna turned on the water, but not too high. She didn't want to miss anything.

Lily said one word to Cullen—a name. "Benedict?"

"He's hanging in there. Beth was treated and released, I understand. She's okay?"

"As far as I know. Mother said . . ." Lily hesitated, as if she didn't want to repeat whatever her mother had said. "Beth will be staying with her and my father for a few days."

"What about you? Any change?"

Cynna returned, ugly plastic pitcher in hand, in time to see Lily shake her head.

The gorgeous Cullen didn't even notice her, intent on Lily and his questions. "Did they find the *toltoi*?"

"No."

"What's a *toltoi*?" Cynna asked, setting the improvised vase on the hospital table by the bed.

Cullen answered absently. "A charm. Her necklace got broken during the fight."

"Easy to see how that could happen." Harder to see why Cullen was so tense about a missing bauble. He was a sorcerer, though. Maybe he meant "charm" literally. "Change in what?"

"What do you mean?"

"You asked her if there was any change."

He was surprised. "I wanted to know if she felt better."

"Uh-uh." She shook her head. "You're good, but I'm not buying. I'm here because Lily is about to get dumped on, and I don't like that. But I don't like being kept in the dark, either. And that's happened right from the start."

The other two didn't exchange telling glances, but

their silence said plenty. Cullen broke it to ask, "Who's about to dump on Lily?"

"Have you seen the headlines?"

"Some of them."

"They aren't exactly good PR for any of us." The ones in the more respectable media ranged from "Gang Slaughtered in FBI Bust" to "Wolves on the Rampage?" Cynna's favorite tabloid had the FBI signing a demonic pact to wipe out all gangs, with the lupi acting as the demons' hit men. Talk radio was going with pretty much the same slant, only without the demonic middlemen.

"They were bound to be all over this one," Lily said. "Fourteen people killed, the lupi implicated, the FBI definitely involved . . . have they picked up on the death magic angle?"

"The *Times* mentions it. References an anonymous source on the San Diego PD."

Lily grimaced. "It's a reporter's wet dream, even if they don't yet know just what went down."

"They will soon," Cynna said grimly. "The Big Dick has scheduled a press conference for six P.M. Eastern. Just in time for the evening news." Dick Hayes was the FBI's acting director while the real boss recuperated from open heart surgery. The nickname given him by the rank-and-file was not a token of fondness. "He's going to throw you to the wolves."

Lily's sharp laugh surprised her. "No throwing required. I'm pretty much with the wolves already. Thanks for the warning, though."

"I don't think you get it. He's going to give them your name and tell them you're scheduled for psychiatric evaluation. They'll be all over you. Plus, he's got this idea you *faked* your Gift to get in the Unit. As if that . . ." She paused, frowning. "You aren't upset."

Lily shrugged one shoulder. "I'm not happy, but it was only a matter of time before the media got my name. It was my investigation. Besides, I'm an easy sacrifice, considering how short a time I've been with the Bureau. The psych evaluation is news," she admitted. "But not a big surprise."

"He ordered Ruben not to tell you." Cynna simmered over that a moment. "I can't believe Ruben agreed, but he did."

"I don't imagine he had much choice. He made sure I learned about it."

Cynna felt suddenly foolish. "I guess he figured I'd tell you."

"I guess he did."

Cynna decided to sit down. The chair was as uncomfortable as it looked. "Hayes wants you to be surprised so you'll look bad on camera."

"I'll have to talk to the press at some point, but maybe not yet. Maybe I should check out of here." She looked at Cullen. "Isen called a couple of hours ago."

"Oh?"

"He wants me to see the Rhej. Though it sounded more like he was passing on a summons from her."

Cullen's eyebrows lifted.

"Who or what is the Rhej?" Cynna asked.

"A holy woman. I wonder . . ." He shook his head, apparently unwilling to say more.

"He also wants me to come stay with him for a while. He was very gentle, very careful with me. Didn't believe me for a minute about Rule."

"You wouldn't be bothered by reporters at Clanhome."

"No." She chewed on her lip. "I'm going to tell Cynna."

"Lily—"

"About my Gift," she said, turning to Cynna. "It's gone."

Cynna blinked. "Can't be."

"That's conventional wisdom. It's impossible to lose a Gift, right? But I can't touch magic now."

Cynna couldn't think of anything to say. Losing her

own Gift . . . she couldn't get her mind around that. She was a Finder. She couldn't imagine who she'd be if that were suddenly not true. "The staff?" she said hesitantly. "You think it somehow zapped your Gift?"

"It felt . . . when Harlowe used it on me . . ." Her face wasn't closed anymore. More like haunted. "It felt as if something was clawing my skin off. I think it pried my Gift loose."

"Shit."

"Pretty much, yeah." She didn't say anything for a moment, looking down at the sheet drawn neatly over her legs. The head of the bed was raised, pillows propped behind her.

She looked so small in that bed. That shouldn't come as a surprise—she was a little bitty thing, after all. But something about the woman had made Cynna forget there just wasn't much of her, physically.

Lily looked up then and met her eyes. "Losing my Gift . . . that's one reason they think I'm nuts."

"Uh . . ."

"The way everyone sees it, either I really did lose my Gift and it sent me round the bend, or I'm blocking it as part of my denial." She glanced at Cullen. "That's what you think, isn't it?"

"I'm keeping an open mind," he said lightly.

Lily shook her head. "If you really thought there was a chance Rule was alive, you'd be looking for him."

His expression flattened. "Where? Your former compatriots searched the area, didn't they?"

"You've got ways of looking they lack."

"I'm no Finder."

"No," she said. And looked at Cynna.

"I wondered when you'd think of that. Rule . . ." Saying his name made her throat unhappy. She swallowed. "Ruben told me you're insisting that he's alive. I want to know why."

"If I tell you—"

"Lily," Cullen's voice was sharp.

She ignored him. "If I tell you what you want to know, will you try to Find him?"

"I already have."

TWENTY-FOUR

LILY'S head went light and dizzy. Big Dick's planned press conference hadn't come as a shock, but the whiff of hope hit her system like a double scotch on an empty stomach.

"Hey." That was Cullen, standing by her bed with a hand on her shoulder. "It helps if you keep breathing."

"Okay. I'm okay." She waved him away and got herself back under control. "Where? Where is he?"

Cynna held up both hands. "I did that wrong. Sorry. What I mean is that I *tried*, not that I Found him. What I did Find doesn't make sense. That's why I need to know why you're so sure he's alive."

Lily realized her nails were about to draw blood. She unclenched her fists. "All right. Then you'll tell me what you Found."

Cullen sighed. "As a clan member in good standing, this is where I'm supposed to threaten you with all manner of dire consequences."

"What can they do—kick me out?" She shook her

head. "Sorry. I know that's a big deal for you, but it doesn't mean as much to me."

"Let me help." As if she'd been still as long as she could, Cynna popped to her feet and began to pace. "I've got some of it figured out. I came up with three possible reasons for you to hold out on me. One, there's some kind of national security deal involved that I'm not cleared for. Except you'd tell me if that were the case, right? Or Ruben would have told me before I got here."

"That's not it."

"I didn't think so. Reason two. The stuff you've kept to yourself is personally embarrassing. People do that all the time, and cops aren't immune to the cover-up urge. But a good cop wouldn't do it, and Ruben has pretty high standards for the Unit. Rule's standards weren't so shabby, either. So that leaves me with reason number three." She glanced at Cullen. "Which you pretty much confirmed just now with that 'clan member in good standing' bit."

He raised his eyebrows politely. "Did I?"

"I'm wondering if that was on purpose."

Lily didn't wonder. She wasn't sure of his motives, but Cullen gave away very little by accident. "Go on."

"It's lupus secrets you're keeping, isn't it? And it has something to do with your relationship with Rule. Something that makes you think you've got the inside track on whether he's dead or alive. Something that makes him, well, *yours.*"

Lily nodded slowly. She'd underestimated Cynna Weaver. "You've got most of it. Rule and I are mate bound."

Cullen sighed and plopped down in one of the chairs, stretching out his legs and tilting his head back. "I wonder," he asked the ceiling, "if I'll be considered an accomplice for not stopping you?"

"You couldn't have."

"So what does mate bound mean, exactly?" Cynna asked.

"It's rare, I understand." And harder than she'd expected to put into words, especially with this woman she didn't know well . . . whom Rule had once known very well. "Lupi see the bond in religious terms. They say their goddess—they call her the Lady—occasionally chooses a life mate for one of them. And, uh, it's very physical. Sexual, but more than that. When it first hit, Rule and I couldn't be separated by more than a couple hundred yards. It's more relaxed now, thank God."

"What do you mean, you couldn't be separated?"

"If we put too much distance between us, we get dizzy. I'm told that if we get too far away we'd pass out, but we've never gone past the dizzy stage."

Cynna's lips pursed. She glanced at Cullen.

"Don't look at me," he said to the ceiling. "I'm an innocent bystander."

Lily continued doggedly. "Rule says the separation thing never goes away completely, but I don't know what our limit is now. I haven't tested it lately, but . . ." She paused, tensing.

The mate bond was like background music, she thought. If the radio was always playing, she didn't notice unless she stopped and paid attention. But let someone change the station or the volume . . .

"What is it?" Cynna asked.

"He's moving again. Moving fast."

"What do you mean, again?" Cullen asked sharply.

"He's been moving for some time, but slowly. Now . . ." She tried to estimate. "He might be in a car or something, because he's going a lot faster."

Cynna frowned. "Can you guess at the distance? Are you likely to pass out or something?"

"I don't know. He's farther away now than he has been since the bond happened, and the farther away he is, the fuzzier my estimate of distance. Direction, though—I get that right every time."

Cynna nodded. "It sounds a lot like Finding."

"What do you mean?"

"The farther away my target is, the less I can say about the distance. There's a limit, too. For me it's between a hundred and a hundred fifty miles. Within that limit I get direction. Beyond it . . ." She shrugged.

"You don't just Find physical objects, though. You said you turned up ghosts sometimes."

"Yeah." Her eyebrows twitched together. "That's sort of what it was like when I tried Finding Rule."

"He is not a ghost. The mate bond ties me to his body, which is very much alive." Somewhere. "What, exactly, did you Find?"

"I went to the scene this morning after I talked to Ruben, and I did a Find. I, uh, already had Rule's pattern, from when I used to know him. It's better to have the current pattern, but I thought I had enough that I'd be able to tell if he was still around."

"And?" Lily thought she might jump up and shake the woman.

"What I got was fuzzy. Real fuzzy. I didn't think it was a ghost, but it's hard to be sure when I had such a poor fix. But there was a direction, so I followed it. Right where my Gift told me he was, though . . ." She spread both hands. "A gas station. Lots of cars. No sign of Rule."

Her heart was pounding. Cynna had gotten the same results she had—a clear fix on a specific spot, yet no sign of Rule. That proved she wasn't crazy and that the mate bond was working right, didn't it? "Has that ever happened before?"

Cynna shook her head but then added, "Except with ghosts."

"Ghosts don't move around. Where was this gas station, and what time did you do the Find?"

"The corner of Middlebrook and Hessing. I got there about nine-thirty."

Lily leaned over and pulled her table closer, took the city map off it, and passed it to Cullen.

He raised his eyebrows as he took it.

"Check my notes," she said tersely. "I've been trying to track Rule. I had to guess at the distance, but the direction is right."

He unfolded it, studied it a moment, and then passed it to Cynna without a word.

"Where . . . oh, yeah, I see it." She looked at Lily. "Maybe you're better at guessing distance than you thought. The line connecting your estimates runs pretty close to my gas station. The times fit, too."

"Yes." She looked at Cullen—who was back to studying the ceiling. "Rule's people might expect me to be weird right now. I gather that the sudden breaking of the mate bond can have repercussions. But only if you start with the assumption that he's dead. And I can't see why you've done that."

That was one hell of a fascinating ceiling.

She kept going. "There's no body. The staff wasn't even touching Rule when you crisped Harlowe, so why assume he's dead? And now Cynna has confirmed that the mate bond is working. She and I both know where he is— only he isn't there. I only see one possibility. He's someplace that's tied to Earth geographically, but isn't Earth."

"I've tried," Cullen told the ceiling. "Haven't I tried? But she's determined, and maybe Isen is wrong. No, strike that—Isen is definitely wrong." Abruptly he pushed to his feet. "Being Rho isn't like being the pope, is it? No one granted him infallibility."

"What are you talking about?"

He began pacing. There wasn't much room for it. "Cast your mind back. I didn't say Rule was dead. At the time you weren't in any shape to consider nuances of speech, but what I said was that he was gone."

"So you *don't* think he's dead."

"He might be." Cullen shook his head. "I don't know. Isen wants me to lie to you about that, and I could. I'm an excellent liar, but my heart isn't in it. And I'm not good at blind obedience. Lost the knack, I suppose, in all those years I was clanless. . . ." Cullen stopped, tilting his head back and closing his eyes. "God, I'm tired."

"Tough. Keep talking."

He sighed. "You're right. Right about all of it, I'm afraid."

She closed her eyes. *Breathe,* she reminded herself. She did, and her muscles turned slippery, loosening up so suddenly it was a good thing she was propped up.

"So why would this Isen dude want you to lie about it?" Cynna demanded.

Cullen glanced at her. "Isen Turner. He's Rule's father and the Rho, the head of Nokolai . . . my clan. He wants to protect Lily."

"To *protect* me?" That sent a charge through her that brought her upright again, all but vibrating with anger. "By trying to convince me Rule's dead?"

"Think about it." Cullen's face could never be other than beautiful. Even when it had been butchered, the eyes gauged out, it had possessed a certain ravaged glory. But she'd never seen it look so naked—naked like an old, twisty tree. All bones, no softness.

He almost looked his age. "I spent a long time working out the possibilities last night. I'll give them to you the way I gave them to the Rho. One, Rule is dead. Wait." He held up his hand. "Hear me out."

He resumed his pacing, a two-legged panther caged in a modern hospital room. "Mage fire burns in places—call them dimensions—you can't see, and it burns very, very hot there. When my mage fire hit the staff, the hole in space that was its underlying reality imploded. It could have sucked Rule along somehow."

"Sucked him . . . where?"

"That's the question, isn't it?" He reached the wall and

turned. "Two. The staff was Hers. If She called it to Her the second the mage fire hit, she might have been able to recover part of it. I don't know why Rule would have been dragged with the staff. As you said, it was touching you, not him, so I didn't give this a very high probability. But it was just possible that the effect traveled along you without, ah, grabbing hold, because of your Gift. And Rule got taken instead."

To *Her*. The Old One or goddess or whatever. Lily's mouth was dry. "One problem with that. My Gift is gone."

He nodded without pausing in his restless motion. "Exactly. So I thought Rule probably was dead, only you were so damned sure he wasn't. I couldn't overlook the chance that you were right. I tried scrying for him."

"You didn't tell me." Anger burned still, but lower, retreating to a tight, sullen heat in her belly. "I take it you didn't find anything."

He grimaced. "I had to light the candle with a match. Didn't have enough juice left to raise a fever, much less start a fire. It's hard to get a salamander to notice a non-magical fire. I struck out."

"I didn't," Cynna said.

He gave her an unfriendly look. "No. So I've had to rethink some of my assumptions."

Lily drummed her fingers. "I don't see what any of this has to do with lying to me to *protect* me."

Cullen held out both hands, turning them palms up. "The way Isen saw it, either Rule was dead and you were delusional, and feeding that delusion wouldn't be healthy. Or else he was alive and we'd have to find a way of going after him. Of course, I don't know how to do that, but assuming we made it past that little road block, it was apt to be a suicide mission, so—"

"Wait a minute. You sound as if you know where he is."

His eyebrows lifted. "I thought you'd figured that out.

You said you knew he was in the realm most analogous to ours, physically."

She wanted smack him. "I don't know what that means!"

His mouth flattened. "Hell, luv. He's in hell."

A thousand feet up Lily discovered that ymu might keep her from sleeping, but she still needed oxygen. Or maybe it was fear, pure and simple, that made her pass out.

She came to as they descended. This would have struck her as lousy timing if she hadn't been so surprised to still be alive—and so busy trying not to throw up. From the ground, the dragons' flight had been grace itself. Experienced up close and personal, the ride was jerky as the great wings sculled through the air, tilting first one way, then the other.

Mountains again. These were green and gold, dust and rock—and hurtling toward her with stomach-wrenching speed. It was hard to breathe. The dragon's talons felt like hot steel bands clamped around her middle, leaving her head, arms, and legs dangling. Her hands and feet were numb. Cold air rushed passed, filling her ears with its ocean noise, making her eyes water and her nose run.

Rule was close.

The heart-song of his nearness hummed inside her as they spiraled down and down, giving her one clear note to hold onto amid the cacophony of fear and pain. He hadn't died. The dragon hadn't eaten him.

It looked like they'd die together in about thirty seconds though, when they smashed into the side of the mountain. No, wait, there was a crevice—it looked too narrow for the dragons' wings, but they tilted madly and sailed through, leveling off over the ocean.

Oh, God, the ocean. It was the first familiar thing she'd seen, though the colors weren't right. Blue. She remembered blue, a shifting symphony of blues. This

ocean shimmered through lichen colors—yellow ochre
with bands of rust and dusty olive, reflecting the odd sky.

No beach. The water rolled right up to the rocky cliff
face they flew along. Then the cliff fell back. They tilted,
turning into a wide inlet.

More cliffs—rocks meeting ocean, then a thin strip of
beach that widened—

They dove at it. As if the dragon had suddenly discovered gravity, they fell faster and faster. Her eyes watered
madly from the rush of air. She couldn't see.

She wanted to touch Rule, just to touch him once
more—

The dragon put on the brakes. Those huge wings
pulled sharply forward, cupping the air.

Her body tried to keep going. The talons didn't let it.
Too airless to scream, she blacked out again. Only for a
moment, though, this time. She was dizzily conscious
when, with the beach two stories beneath her, the bands
around her middle opened and she fell—

About five feet, into soft, warm sand. She hit awkwardly, catching a glimpse of the long tail passing overhead before the creature powered itself up again with a
windy flap of its wings.

She made it to her hands and knees and retched. With
nothing in her stomach, the process was both brief and
unproductive, but she missed seeing the second dragon
drop its burden, only catching a glimpse of its long tail as
it vanished upward again.

Dizzy and miserable, she sat back on her heels and
looked around.

She was in a giant sandbox. End to end, it stretched
about half the length of a football field. (*Football,* she
thought . . . men in uniforms chasing a funny-shaped
ball, fighting to possess it . . .) The sides were rocks—not
masonry, for although they were fitted, they hadn't been
shaped. She was twenty feet or so above the beach.

And twenty feet away, Rule was pushing to his feet.

"Rule!" She tried to stand, but pain shot through her left ankle and she plopped back down in the sand.

A moment later a furry head rubbed her arm.

She twisted and flung her arm over his back, wanting to bury her face in his fur. He yipped.

She pulled back. He was panting softly. "You're hurt." He touched his nose to his side.

The talons must have gripped too tight, or maybe he'd cracked something when the dragon dropped him. "Your ribs?"

He nodded and then touched her leg gently with one forepaw. The pad was rough and scratchy.

"I twisted my ankle when I landed. No biggie." She ran a careful hand over his side. Nothing protruded, anyway. If there was internal damage . . .

A squeal brought her head up. She watched as another dragon finished its kamikaze run at the ground, dropping a small, noisy orange demon in the sand about fifteen feet away.

So Gan was alive, too. Her relief surprised her.

Of course, relief might be premature. Maybe the three of them were carryout.

To her left were tall, rocky bluffs riddled with crevices. Next to their sandbox was a broad hollow in the cliff face, like a skinny kid pulling in his stomach—too shallow to be called a cave, but deep enough that half the sand was in shadow. She had the uneasy suspicion that bowl-shaped concavity wasn't natural, that something had dug out the rock.

Below the sandbox was beach, wide here, but tapering into nonexistence about fifty feet in one direction, seventy in the other. At the end of the beach farthest from the mouth of the inlet, grass grew.

Beach grass, she thought. *Ammophila arenaria.*

A damp tongue licked her cheek. She turned, startled . . . and realized both her cheeks were wet, and the salty taste in her mouth wasn't just from the sea. "I know the name of it," she murmured, threading her fingers into the wolf's ruff. "I know the name of the grass here."

The ocean drew her. The water was the wrong color, but it smelled right. It was quiet here, the waves small. As she watched a wave slid up the sand in a delicate froth, lost interest, and retreated.

"The dragons have a nice sandbox." She ran a hand through the sand, letting it dribble between her fingers. It was grainy and loose. It would be hard to walk on and all but impossible to run across. It was also warm. Nearly skin temperature, she thought, which was odd. The air was cool.

"We could climb out," she said, studying the rocks. "The cliff is high but rough enough to supply plenty of hand-and footholds."

The wolf poked her shoulder and pointed up with his nose. She tilted her head and saw half a dozen shapes silhouetted against the dull sheen of the sky. Guards?

If so, climbing out wasn't an option. For the moment, though, they weren't threatened. She drew a shaky breath and wished for clean water to wash the foul taste from her mouth.

Rule lay down beside her. He touched her ankle with his nose and looked at her with a questioning lift around his eyes.

"It doesn't hurt much." But it did hurt. Maybe the ymu was wearing off. She looked at Gan.

The demon sat in a small, orange huddle, rocking itself back and forth, moaning.

"Are you hurt?' she called.

"I'm going to die, I'm going to die," it moaned.

She didn't see any blood. Maybe it was short on optimism.

"What now?" she asked, mostly of herself. Absently she sifted one hand through the sand while hunting for options. There weren't many. "I'm going to see what happens if I climb down to the beach. Just so we know."

Rule sighed and pushed to his feet.

"I don't need an escort. You're hurt. If you . . . what's this?" She dug her hand deeper and pulled up . . . something. It was hard and sort of sand-colored, larger than her two hands put together, but thin, with a slight curve. A fragment of something, she thought. The edges were sharp. Could it be used as a weapon?

She dusted off some of the sand and her breath sucked in.

Pale colors seemed to run through it in a way that changed every time she tipped it to a new angle, colors with the subtle sheen of an opal.

Gan squealed. "Put it back! Put it back! We're all going to die!"

"What are you talking about?"

"You idiot! This is a dragon's nest! We're food for the babies! They hatch *hungry*!"

One of the rocks near the cliff blinked. And the earth moved.

Sand slipped and shifted as something beneath it rose, sending her rolling. She ended up on her back, both hands gripping futilely at sand as if she could hold it still, make it stop moving.

Up and up it rose—a head shaped like a snake's, but the size of a Volkswagen and with a scarlet frill at the back of the skull. A head long and flat and covered with iridescent scales whose colors ran one into the other—steel, blush, twilight. A head on a neck that seemed to stretch up forever, a Loch Ness Monster of a neck, the muscles taut and visible beneath the shimmer of scales—dawn, dusk, the tarnish of old mirrors.

The dragon's body humped up out of the sand like a football field–sized snake, sending sand slithering and flying, making her blink grit from her eyes. It was thickest in the middle between the pairs of legs, dwindling to a tail long enough to balance all that neck. It lay in a circle, the tail ending near the head, forming a living wall

around them. Along its back rested the origami folds of
its wings.

The dragon looked down at her out of eyes the size of
platters, eyes that were all silver and black with no whites.
Fear was a weight on her chest, a taste in her mouth, a
clamor in her brain and the noise in her ears from a pulse
gone wild. She knew only one clear thought: *That's no
baby.*

TWENTY-FIVE

CYNNA frowned at Cullen. "I don't buy it. Not as a sure thing, anyway. Too many assumptions."

Cullen gave his eyebrows a little lift. God, the man even had gorgeous eyebrows. Life wasn't fair. "Or else you don't know everything I do. That seems possible."

"Tie a knot in your ego for a minute, will you? Look at all the big, fat maybes you've stacked up. First we have to assume that hell actually is the closest physical analogue to Earth, but some say that's Faerie."

"They're wrong."

"I suppose you've checked that out personally?"

"No. I had it from ni'Aureni Aeith. I think you'll agree he ought to know."

"I might," Lily said. "If you tell me who Nee-orenee-aith is."

Cynna sighed. She could admit it when she was wrong. Not easily, but she could do it. "One of the lords of Faerie, if I've got the naming conventions right. You trust his information? I mean, the Fae are supposed to have a pretty playful attitude toward the truth."

"In this case I do. There was a debt."

"Okay. So, if Rule's in hell, how the hell did he get there?"

"I covered that. *She*'s in hell, and—"

"Not established."

Impatience flashed in those pretty blue eyes. "It's an assumption, but backed by fact—things that happened before you showed up. Somehow Rule must have been dragged along when She retrieved what was left of the staff."

She shook her head. "Too many maybes," she repeated. "Why not go for the simpler explanation?"

Cullen was all polite disbelief. "And that would be?"

"Demon transfer." She looked from one of them to the other. "Well, there was a demon, wasn't there, trying its damnedest to possess Lily? Not that anyone but her saw it, but—"

"I saw it," Cullen said. "Not with regular vision, but it was there."

"Okay, so that's confirmed. Now, I don't know why the demon would grab Rule when it had been targeting Lily, but it's still a simpler explanation, isn't it?"

"It might be," Lily said, "if I had any idea what demon transfer meant."

"Oh." She glanced at Cullen, her eyes widening—then narrowing as she grinned. "You don't know, either, do you? Ha. How about that. I know something the hotshot sorcerer doesn't."

He got even more polite. "Would you care to share your vast knowledge?"

"Put simply, demon transfer is when a demon takes something with it when it moves between realms."

He waved a hand dismissively. "Demons can't move freely between the realms any more than we can. That's why the hellgates were closed at the Purge—to keep the demons out. Seems to have worked."

"Yes, but—"

"I haven't noticed any demon hordes ravaging the countryside, have you?"

Cynna scowled. "Will you listen a minute? You may know all sorts of fancy spellcraft, but that's not demonology. Demons vary a lot more than people do."

"Six-year-olds who watch Saturday-morning cartoons know that much."

"Maybe they don't know that some demons can cross unsummoned and without a hellgate. Or maybe you should watch more Saturday-morning cartoons."

"You know this for a fact?" Cullen snapped.

"I do. They can carry stuff with them, too."

"Stuff?" Lily said. "Does that include people?"

Cynna grimaced. "I'd have to, ah, do a little research to find out for sure, but I think so." Research she was not eager to attempt.

"What kind of research?"

Cullen waved a hand dismissively. "Your explanation requires a few big, fat maybes as well. Maybe this particular demon can cross unsummoned. Maybe demon transfer works on people as well as objects. Maybe it decided to take Rule along instead of Lily. Maybe——"

"The demon was here, so obviously it *did* cross. If you'd get your big, fat ego out of the way——"

"This isn't about ego. We have to look at the facts, which you're confusing with opinions. The demon——"

Lily spoke. "Shut. Up."

Cynna turned to her, surprised.

The China doll looked like she was trying to stuff all sorts of messy emotions back down. "I don't care who knows more than who, I don't care who wins your little pissing contest, and I don't want to waste time finding out."

Shit. She was right. While Cynna made like the poor little misfit girl trying to get the cutest boy in class to notice her, Rule was trapped in hell. Maybe one of these days she'd grow up. "Sorry."

Lily drew a deep breath and let it out. "It does make a

difference how Rule ended up in hell. He's either with
what's-her-name or he's with the demon. But in the end,
it doesn't matter much. I might as well assume I'll be
dealing with a demon. There's no way to plan for an encounter with Her."

"Shit." That came from Cullen. He looked like he was
vibrating. "That's what I was afraid of. What Isen was
afraid of. That if you knew where Rule was you'd try to
go after him."

Lily looked at him as if he'd said something really stupid. She kept looking.

"All right. All right, I said!" He snapped that out as if
she'd been arguing with him instead of just turning that
flat, dark gaze on him. "I'll help. I'm a double-damned
idiot, but I'll help you. For whatever good it will do," he
added gloomily. "I don't know how to open a hellgate.
I don't know anyone who does."

Cynna really, really didn't want to say anything, but
her mouth made a decision without consulting her brain.
"I do."

Cullen's head swung toward her. "Who?"

In for a penny . . . She sighed. "Two people, actually.
One who does know, and one who might be able to figure
it out. That's Abel. You know him," she said to Cullen.
"Abel Karonski. He can close leaks, and wouldn't this be
like doing the same thing in reverse? We don't need a
great big gate."

His eyes narrowed as if he was totting things up mentally. Reluctantly he nodded. "It might work, if he's capable of creative thought. Spells don't reverse neatly."

"No duh."

Lily shook her head. "Karonski would be last-ditch.
Aside from the fact that he's in Virginia, he's not going
to agree. Opening a hellgate is illegal. Who's the other
person?"

"No one I want to talk to, if I can avoid it. She, ah,
probably wouldn't be happy about me tracking her down,

and she might not help, anyway. And if she did, it would come with a price."

For a few minutes, none of them spoke. Lily had herself back under control. Cynna couldn't read a thing on that pretty face as she sat there, one finger tapping against her thigh. Finally she said, "I need to get out of here. I guess the things I was wearing are around somewhere."

"I think your chums collected them as evidence," Cullen said. "Evidence of what, I'm not sure, but they have a passion for plastic baggies."

She grimaced. "There's a gift shop downstairs, isn't there? Would you see if—"

"No need," Cynna said. "I've got that covered. Only where . . . oh, yeah." She went to the door, where she'd dropped her tote upon being introduced to the cop with the Santa Claus face and the big gun. She snatched it, unzipped it, and pulled out a wrinkled T-shirt and the pants to her second-best gi. "They won't fit," she said apologetically, "but they're better than nothing."

For the first time, Lily smiled. It wasn't much, but it was a smile. "You came prepared to bust me out."

"Pretty much. Oh, here. You'll need this to hold them up." She pulled out her belt. Unlike the rest of the outfit, it was neatly folded.

Lily took it, a small V between her brows. "A brown belt. Judo? With those long legs, you'd be good at it."

"Judo's mostly defense. I've been told I'm offensive." She grinned. "Tae kwon do. I don't practice enough."

"Brown's nothing to apologize for." She swung her legs to the side of the bed, managing to keep it modest in spite of the hospital gown's shortcomings.

Cynna was hit with a nasty, rotten suspicion. "You do judo, don't you?"

Lily nodded. She was so short her feet didn't quite reach the floor, so she had to slide off the bed.

"What belt?" Cynna asked that even though she was sure she wouldn't like the answer.

"Black. Second *dan*. I'll be right back." She headed for the tiny bathroom, the mismatched clothes over her arm. She moved slowly, as if she hurt, but Cynna was pretty sure an offer of help would get her snapped at.

Second *dan*—that was like second-degree black. Impressive as hell, dammit.

"Jealous, *shetanni rakibu*?" Cullen's voice was lightly mocking.

Cold prickled up her spine, popping out in goose bumps on her arms. She wanted to rub them, but she wouldn't give him the satisfaction. "It's been a while since I heard that."

He nodded, satisfied. "Then you were a demon rider. I thought so."

What exactly did he think? How much did he know about *shetanni rakibu*? She asked very casually, "So where did you hear that title? It's not exactly common knowledge."

"I read a lot. Is it a demon you're hoping not to consult about opening a wee little hellgate?"

"Dumb question. Most of them wouldn't know how, either, or they'd do it. Seen any demon hordes ravaging the countryside lately?"

He surprised her by grinning. "Touché. If you're not consulting a demon about the gate, it must be someone in this realm. You know a master, don't you?"

"Everyone knows there aren't any real demon masters."

"Everyone knows there aren't any real sorcerers."

"You talk too much."

"It's part of my charm." He moved closer. "Are you going to help?"

She needed to say no. Lord, but she did not want to go looking for Jiri. She wasn't crazy about crossing into hell, either. "You didn't want to do it."

He snorted. "I'm a selfish sonofabitch. What's your excuse?"

"That the whole idea is nuts?"

"Consider that a drawback, do you?" He glanced at the

closed bathroom door. "She's going. With or without my help or yours, she'll find a way to go after him."

"Yeah." Cynna didn't think Lily was fooling herself about the odds. They just weren't a big factor in her decision.

What would it be like to have someone matter that much? To matter that much to someone?

Rule didn't matter to her that way. She'd had some hopes about him, yeah. She'd wanted to be with him again, and not just because of the mind-boggling sex. Lord, the things a lupus could do . . . but that hadn't been all of it. She'd wanted him to see who and what she'd become. To approve. It made her squirm to admit that, but it was true.

But Rule did matter. And she owed him.

Cullen moved closer. Close enough for her to see that he hadn't shaved that morning. Close enough to see the darker rims around his irises, and the way his pulse beat in the hollow of his throat. "Even aside from opening the hellgate, you know more about Dis and demons than I do. Our chances would be better with you along."

"That must have hurt, saying it out loud."

"I'm tough. I can take it." He ran his fingertips along the side of her neck. "What do you say?"

Her heart was pounding. He'd know it, too, dammit. "You offering me sex in exchange for tossing my career in the trash, maybe ending up in prison?"

He smiled into her eyes, and that was seduction more potent than the stroke of his fingers. "Think of it as a bonus. For both of us."

She stepped back. It was harder than it should have been. "Do I have 'idiot' stamped on my forehead?"

The bathroom door opened. Cynna glanced that way . . . and had to bite her lip.

"Did your mommy give you permission to play dress-up, little girl?" Cullen asked.

"Shut up, Cullen." Lily shuffled out.

Cynna's lips twitched. "Sorry. I should've stopped and picked up something in your size."

Lily flipped one hand, dismissing it. "Doesn't matter. Let's get me checked out."

"You could just leave." Cynna kind of liked the idea of smuggling her out.

"I need to get my prescription first. I don't have time to deal with an infection." She made it to the chair, lowered herself, and reached for the buzzer to call the nurse. Then she faced Cynna. "I need to make plans, and to do that, I need to know where you stand. The Bureau is not going to investigate Rule's disappearance. They aren't going to like it if we do."

"No duh." Cynna frowned. "It bugs me, though. Ruben made it sound certain-sure that Rule was dead, but he's not stupid. He had to realize that wasn't a sure thing. Well, when we tell him what we've figured out, he'll—"

"We won't be telling him."

"Huh? Wait a minute. Wait. I didn't agree to hold out on Ruben. I can see why you're suspicious, but you're wrong."

"You've worked for him a while."

"Long enough to be certain-sure he's righteous. Shit, if I had half his integrity I could count on a straight shot to heaven when the time comes."

"Ah . . . you believe in heaven?"

"Hey, I'm a good little Catholic girl now." A stab of honesty made her add, "Or at least I'm Catholic. Which reminds me." She reached for her tote again.

"Let's say Ruben's as straight as you think he is," Lily said as Cynna bent and rummaged in her tote. "That doesn't mean he can turn a blind eye to what I'm planning. Even if he were willing to do that, someone wants Rule declared dead and the case closed. Someone who can either persuade or order Ruben to go along."

"Sure. The Big Dick. Oh, here it is." Cynna grabbed the little paper sack and straightened.

Cullen nodded. "I see. The FBI has a master penis. That explains a lot."

Cynna grinned. "He'd like to think so. Dick Hayes is the acting director. I don't think he's bent, exactly. He's just an asshole. Here." She came up to Lily, dug into the sack, and held out a little cross on a gold chain.

Lily flinched.

Cynna drew it back, her forehead wrinkling. "I take it you aren't Christian."

"It's not that. I'm not sure what I am, but . . ." She blinked quickly, but Cynna had seen the sheen in her eyes. One hand went to her throat. "Rule's necklace is missing. I . . . it may not turn up, but I'm not going to wear another one in its place. Not yet."

"The *toltoi* isn't just from Rule," Cullen said in a low voice.

Lily gave a single nod and left her head down, her hair screening her face.

Better give her a minute, Cynna thought. The tied-down ones hated it when they came apart with someone watching. She turned to Cullen. "What about you? I've got an extra." The one she'd gotten for Rule. "It's been blessed and all."

His eyebrows sketched skepticism. "Doesn't the effectiveness of holy symbols depend on the faith of the wielder?"

"Partly, but not altogether. It makes a difference what kind of demon you're dealing with. Some don't respond to holy symbols at all. Ah . . . someone I know thinks it depends on what kind of pacts the demon's lord has with the various Powers. Demons are big on deals."

"Interesting theory." Cullen accepted the necklace and dribbled it from one hand to the other, frowning as if he were considering some weighty question. "When did you . . ." His voice drifted off as the door opened.

It was the ponytail nurse, and she was not happy about a patient checking out against doctor's orders. It was interesting to watch Lily handle her. She didn't get angry. Ponytail and the hospital weren't important enough to get angry over. She gave the facts: She was leaving. She wanted her prescription. They could bring her some papers to sign if they liked, but they had to do it quickly because she wasn't waiting.

It was amazing how well not arguing worked. Cynna resolved to try it sometime.

When the nurse huffed out the door, Lily leveled that steady gaze on Cynna. "If you're not going to Find this person yourself, I need the name."

Some people had such a clear grasp of right and wrong. Cynna envied them. Finding the moral highroad out of a welter of possible paths was always a struggle for her. It would be wrong to lie to Ruben. She was sure of that. And opening a hellgate—pretty much everyone would tell her that was wrong.

But it was wrong to leave Rule in hell. It was wrong to turn her back, pretend she couldn't do anything to help— and giving them Jiri's name and description wouldn't help. They'd never find her.

Another memory swam to the surface. The remembered voice was soft, male, and irritated. He'd been dying at the time. *"Stop talking of paying back. Is no back. Only now. Only on."*

That settled her. Paying it on couldn't mean turning away. "What the hell. I'm in."

TWENTY-SIX

THE huge eyes blinked.

She came back to herself with a jolt, knowing time had passed. How much? She didn't know. Seconds. A day.

Never mind. She scrambled to her feet, moving because she could. Because, whatever happened, she wanted to meet it on her feet. She put out a hand. Rule was there. Without having to look, she'd known that he'd come up beside her. She rested her hand on his back.

Had he been trapped by the dragon's gaze, too?

The lupus didn't look into my eyes. The demon knew better, but did it anyway.

The dragon hadn't spoken. Those great jaws hadn't opened or the mouth moved. The words had just appeared in her mind, sharp as glass—thoughts, but not her thoughts.

But that was impossible. She was a sensitive. Magic couldn't—

Yet I can. I am dragon.

With those words came a sense of something beyond arrogance. Power, perhaps. A vast, knowing power.

Vocalize. Your thoughts are mush. Forcing them into the sort of speech you are accustomed to gives them a small degree of clarity.

Her heart was trying to knock its way out of her chest. "Are we conversing, then?"

Rather than dining, you mean? Amusement, desert-dry, gusted through her mind. *When I hunger, I hunt. I don't have dinner fetched.*

"Why did you have us fetched?"

Utility. Politics. Curiosity. The great head lowered in a graceful arc.

She jumped back. Her bad ankle gave out, dumping her ingloriously on her butt. Rule didn't move, but his fur bristled. Gan squealed in terror.

But the movement didn't signal a change of mind about the dragon's dinner plans. It seemed to be settling in for a chat. It rested its head on its tail like a cat curling up for a nap, leaving the three of them entirely circled by dragon.

That long body gave off a lot of heat, she realized. That's why the sand was so warm. "That didn't really answer my question. Why did you bring us here?"

It has been many moons since I've seen a human. And never have I seen one linked to both a lupus and a demon. Most curious. How did you become half-souled?

"If you mean how did I lose my memory—I don't remember."

Those eyes blinked again. *Ah. You didn't know.* Its gaze shifted to the quivering lump of demon fifteen feet away. *Your demon didn't tell you.*

"Not my demon," she muttered. "A demon. Not mine."

Rule's head swung toward her, as if she'd surprised him. Then he looked at Gan, growling.

"Don't listen to the dragon," Gan said. Its attempt at

bravado was cancelled by the way it crouched with both arms over its head, as if that would protect it from the dragon's jaws. "He doesn't know anything about it. Besides, he can lie. I can't. Who are you going to believe?"

She snorted. "You lie all the time."

That annoyed it so much its arms fell away from its head. "No, I don't! I can't lie. Everyone knows what I mean even if I say something else. That's how it works."

"You may not tell out-and-out whoppers, but you lie by misdirection. Not all that well, actually, because you've never learned to manage your face. Maybe demons aren't used to reading expressions for clues because you all pick up each other's meanings. By picking your words carefully, though, you can mean what you say and still be lying."

Clever small bite. Demons prize the ability to deceive without lying. They do this by watching their words, as you say, and also by finding a self who means what they wish to say. This little one you call Gan doesn't have many selves, so it must rely primarily upon its choice of words.

She rubbed her temples. Not many selves?

Vocalize.

"Uh . . . what does 'many selves' mean?"

Demons consist of all the creatures they have eaten. Those eaten lose volition, not identity.

"So Gan isn't one demon? It's a whole bunch of them, but Gan's the one in charge?"

Gan is mostly imps, bugs, and other nonsentients— though I do hear at least one surprisingly old demon inside it. Gan is also Gan. Demon identity is not what you are used to. The dragon turned his gaze on the little demon. *You will now tell me why the human is half-souled.*

Gan cowered. "Oh, Great One, mighty of wing and mind, how would this feeble one know? I'm a demon, and such a small, insignificant demon, barely more than an imp. What do I know about souls?"

You are right, small bite. The demon does not deceive well, though the din of its mind makes it difficult to sort through what passes for its thoughts. The dragon's tail flicked out suddenly. It whizzed over Lily's head and thudded into Gan, sending the demon tumbling. *I have all your surface names and thirty-two of the deeper ones, Izhatipoibanolitofaidinbaravha—*

"All right, all right! Don't say it all!"

I can acquire the rest of your names if I choose. Or simply pull pieces of you off, but that would dirty my sand. Be truthful. What happened to the human?

If demons had been able to cry, Gan would have been sniffling. "I just wanted to get away—when that mage fire hit the staff, it *hurt!* I can cross all by myself," it added, puffing its chest a bit. "Hardly anyone can do that, but I can. But I was already tied to Lily Yu, so when I crossed, she came, too. And she's tied to the wolf in some weird way, so he got dragged along, and . . . and everything went wrong."

"You mean you did it?" she exclaimed. "You brought us here, not the staff?"

Gan heaved a windy sigh and nodded.

"Then you can take us back."

"No, I can't."

Rule lowered his head, growling.

Gan scowled. "I tried! You think I'd rather be eaten by dragons than go back to Earth? Well, they didn't eat us, but I thought they would, so I tried to cross. I tried and tried, but I couldn't."

Because Lily Yu did not come along completely. When you tried to possess her, you became partially lodged inside her. You brought that part with you, but left behind the named half. She is both here and there. The effect is rather as if you'd jammed something against a door. It won't open for you.

Horror squeezed the air from her lungs. "I'm—I'm missing more than memories? Are you sure?"

The dragon flicked her a glance. The black-and-silver eyes were too removed, too dispassionate, for anything as personal as contempt or compassion. *I do not say what I am not sure of. I wonder if your other half is a ghost? Neither of your sundered selves will live long, of course, but it would be interesting to—*

Rule howled and launched himself at Gan.

Ah, but he was fast! By the time Lily got to her feet he'd already hit once, bounced away before the demon's roundhouse swing could connect, and was circling for another leap.

The dragon's tail smashed into him in mid-air.

Lily cried out and stumbled over to him. He wasn't moving.

Foolish. I had expected better. He seemed to have some sense.

"Shut up," she said fiercely, kneeling. His heart was beating, she discovered when she pressed her hand to the bottom of his rib cage. But his ribs had already been cracked or broken. The lashing tail could have staved them in, punctured a lung.

"I guess you don't care that I'm bleeding over here," Gan said grumpily.

No, she didn't. The demon was alive and talking, while Rule . . . wait, his eyelids twitched. Then they blinked open.

Her breath shuddered out. "Where are you hurt?"

Slowly, as if it hurt, he lifted his head. With his nose he indicated his left foreleg.

Not his gut or his chest, then. Not a punctured lung.

A minor concussion as well, he thinks. But the leg is more of a problem. You will need to set it.

Okay. She drew in a breath and ran her hand along the leg. He jerked. "I'm sorry." She'd learned what she needed to know, though. Her fingertips glistened red. "There's a bit of bone sticking out through the skin. It needs to be set, splinted." Without anesthetic. She didn't want to think about how much that would hurt. "I . . . I don't know how to do it."

She looked at her hands. They were shaking. But that made sense. She was dying. She had memories of only a couple of days of life, and she was dying.

Such drama. You aren't dying yet.

"You said—"

I was interrupted. You'll die of your condition eventually, but the demon is keeping you alive for now.

She looked at Gan.

It sat in the sand, scowling. A chunk of flesh and muscle was missing where its shoulder met its neck. The wound seemed to have already stopped bleeding, but its orange skin was heavily splashed with blood. Red blood, like hers.

Rule really had meant to kill Gan. "You're keeping me alive?"

Its lower lip stuck out like a sulky child's. "Why do you think I made you take ymu? He needs me, too." Gan gave the dragon a wary glance. "To keep you alive. He probably plans to trade you to Xitil. If dragons aren't eating demons, they're trying to get more territory from us."

"Is that what you wanted me for?" she asked the dragon. "To trade?"

Perhaps. The demon is correct about my desire to keep you alive. If your wolf had been thinking, he would have realized that. Why else would I suffer having a demon brought here?

Rule lifted his head and looked straight at the dragon.

You would question me, wolf?

She couldn't tell if the trace of emotion coating that thought was amusement or irritation. She knew what she felt, though. Frustration. Everyone could understand Rule except her. "What did he say? Or think, or . . . whatever."

He wonders why I'm here at all. Why dragons are living with demons.

Gan snorted. "Living with us! Eating us, more like,

when you can. Trying to get more territory the rest of the time." It looked at Lily. "No one knows why the dragons left Earth. I was just an imp when some of them showed up here, but even imps heard about the battles. Dragons live by magic, see, but they can't be affected by it. That was their big advantage. Well, they're good fighters, too, but we outnumbered them thousands to one. But—"

But you did not unite to attack us, allowing us to prevail over the local lord and his court. Nor did you learn from this. When Xitil allowed Ishtar's enemy to guest with her, the other lords should have banded together and destroyed them both. They never even considered it. This was folly of a monstrous degree.

"Big wars are wasteful," Gan said. "Unpredictable. Xitil will destroy the avatar."

I am unsurprised by your attitude.

Ishtar's enemy? Hadn't Gan used that name, too? Lily shook her head. "Look, all that is interesting, but the timing's bad for history lessons. I need something straight to use for a splint, and something to fasten it with. Cloth, rope, leather . . . something I can tie around the leg and splint. And if you know anything about setting bones . . ." Her voice faltered. "I could use some help with that." She had no reason to think the dragon would offer it.

That great head turned, focusing on Gan. *The demon's kind are good with bodies.*

Gan sniffed. "I'm not going to help him. He tried to kill me."

You will do as I wish, Izhatipoibanolit—

"Right, right. But do you mean you want the wolf's leg fixed?" Gan was incredulous.

I do.

Gan heaved a huge, put-upon sigh and stood. "I can put his bone back in place, but it won't stay. He's no demon. He can't heal that quick."

"That's what the splint is for." Hope stirred, fragile and hard to trust. The dragon had broken Rule's leg, but now wanted it to heal straight. She didn't understand. Were dragons capable of compassion? "We have to stabilize the leg."

The dragon tilted his head up. After a moment, one of the circling shapes overhead broke from the rest, diving for the land at the top of the cliff.

We are well supplied with bones. One of my line-kin will bring you an assortment to choose from for the splint. There are coverings in your cave. Tear strips from one, or have the demon do so. It has good teeth.

"Uh—my cave?"

The place you will stay. The entrance is near the grass at the eastern end of the beach. With that, he stood.

The dragon's legs were short and thick in proportion to his body, bowed out like a lizard's. His haunches were house-high, his shoulders slightly lower. *There is food in the cave. You won't need it, but the lupus will. At the rear of the cave is a small freshwater spring.*

"I need food, too," Gan said. "I can't eat dead things."

You'll be fed. You'll continue to feed the human. Drop to the ground now.

The dragon moved.

A creature so large should have seemed ponderous. He wasn't. She had to flatten herself to avoid getting clipped by his tail when he started walking, but the wide-set legs carried him over the sand as agilely as one of his tiny kin.

"Wait!" Lily pushed to her feet. "Where are you going? When will you be back?"

The dragon flowed over the side of the sandbox, stepping down the twenty feet to the beach like a cat oozing off a couch.

"What's your name?" she called.

He just kept moving.

"How did you know we were in that other region? How did you know I'm a sensitive before you brought us here? *Why* did you bring us here?"

The great beast was a several dozen yards down the beach now.

"Dammit, I'm vocalizing at you!"

He stopped, his wings partially unfurled. They were doubled, those wings, like a moth's. Slowly the neck swung around until he was looking back at her. Faint, so faint she might have imagined it, she caught a wisp of amusement just before he straightened, rising up on his hind legs, the long body lifting up and up. The haunches bunched and he sprang for the sky like a cat leaping onto a windowsill.

Even from this distance, the wind from his wings stirred the sand, getting grit in her eyes. She was blinking them clean when she caught his last words: *Sam. I believe you may call me Sam.*

TWENTY-SEVEN

LILY needed clothes. Cynna's belt had to be snug to keep the pants from falling off, and snug hurt. She also had to do something about Dirty Harry.

So after checking herself out, she sat in the back seat of Cullen's old Bronco, fists clenched, trying not to think about what might be happening to Rule while she took care of her cat and her damned grooming. One of the officers had driven her car back to her place last night, and Rule's car had been impounded.

For a few blocks she leaned her head back and shut out the sound of Cynna and Cullen arguing. She needed to see Beth, talk to her. She didn't want to. Not when Beth was staying with their parents. But a phone call wasn't enough, not for this. She needed to know how badly Beth had been scarred by last night.

God, she was tired. She closed her eyes, but there was no rest inside her. Not with everything humming like an overloaded power line.

She was scared. All the way down scared. Not so much of dying, though she wasn't in denial about that.

Death was a strong possibility, but she knew how to keep going in the face of that sort of risk. As a cop, she'd usually had backup going into a dangerous situation. Barring that, she'd had training to fall back on. You identified your goal, made your plans, and did the best you could. Fear was normal, just one more factor to account for.

What was grinding at her wasn't as clean as the fear of death. The shaky feeling came from the fear that she wasn't enough. She didn't know enough, couldn't be enough or do enough to get Rule back. Her Gift was gone. She wasn't sure there was enough of her left to do what had to be done.

Maybe, even with her Gift, there wouldn't have been enough. What they were planning—or, so far, failing to plan—was nuts. One lupus sorcerer, one female Finder, and one damaged former homicide cop were going up against who knew how many demons on their home ground. How do you plan for that?

One step at a time, she told herself. If she couldn't tell if she was going in the right direction, tough. She still had to take that next step.

Up front, Cynna snorted. "You don't know what you're talking about. There's no technical difference between opening a big gate and opening a little one. It's just a matter of power."

They should have taken Cynna's rental. The Bronco's engine knocked so badly she wondered if Cullen kept it running with sorcery. But Cullen had insisted on driving, and Cynna wouldn't let him behind the wheel of her vehicle. Even one only temporarily hers.

"I don't imagine you've ever heard of McCallum's Theorem." Cullen sounded like an adult talking to a sweet but slow child.

"He's got a theory about hellgates?"

"No, it concerns the difference between relevance and resonance, but it suggests that—"

"There's only one kind of relevance that matters with gates. Now, if we were talking about voodoo—"

"Pretend you're more interested in figuring this out than one-upping me," Cullen said. "You won't embarrass yourself so much."

Lily wondered if she was going to have to kill them both, or if taping their mouths shut would be enough. "Bickering is one way of dealing with tension, but it isn't doing much for mine. Since neither one of you knows how to open a gate, can we talk about something more to the point? Make some plans?"

"Believe it or not," Cullen said, "our discussion is very much to the point. In a roundabout way."

"Sure. Right. Now I understand."

"We're trying to settle what kind of gate to open," Cynna said. "Single-relevance or multi-relevance. Only there isn't such a thing as a multi-relevance gate, so you're right. We're wasting time."

Cullen hissed. That's what it sounded like—a cat's hiss. "Lady save me from small-minded hedge witches. Just because you've never heard of something doesn't mean it's impossible."

Lily tried once more to get them back on track. "Because you don't know how to open a gate anyway, the discussion is moot."

Cullen was impatient. "We know the general principles behind it."

"Right," Cynna said. "That's like saying we don't know how to build a television, but we know the general idea behind how one works. Cullen thinks that once we get our TV we should tinker with it. I think that would be too dangerous. We've got no reason to think his idea is even possible."

"It's possible," Cullen insisted. "McCallum's Theorem—"

"Hold off on the theorem talk a minute," Lily said.

"What kind of risks are we talking about if you tinker with the spell? What advantages?"

"Ritual. Magic on this level requires a ritual, not just a spell."

"Whatever. Risks and advantages, Cullen."

"The major risk is that the ritual won't work. We don't get a gate. In which case we can back up and try again with the unaltered ritual."

"Maybe," Cynna said dryly. "If we all survive. We're talking about a major ritual here, involving forces we don't understand. There's no sure way to predict the outcome."

Lily frowned. "That's a big risk."

"And the advantage," Cullen said, "is that if it works we'd have full control of the gate and who and what passes through it."

She was silent a moment. Cynna and Cullen had needled each other about all the demons who weren't ravaging the countryside, but if they opened a gate they couldn't control . . . "That's a big advantage. Big enough to outweigh the risks—*if* this multi-relevance thing is possible."

He switched lanes with typical split-second timing. "Let's go back to the basics. You know gates are magical constructs, right? Located on or very near a node."

"Got that. The Azá were trying to open theirs right on top of a node. They needed the power from it."

"In part, yes. But nodes are also the places of greatest congruence. Think of them as spots where the realms almost touch. Now, magically speaking, congruence is one of the five fields of relevance. It's spatial. There's also physical, emotional, mental, and spiritual."

Lily shook her head. "I'm getting dizzy already. I thought spiritual stuff and magic were different. That's how Nettie was able to do some healing on me—because she wasn't using straight magic."

"Depends on who you talk to. Theories abound."

"Such as?"

"My early training was Wiccan. They consider spirit one of the five types of power—earth, air, fire, water, spirit. Chinese practitioners work with five energies, too, though they substitute metal for spirit and see the spiritual as entirely separate. So do many Protestant faiths. Catholicism is hopelessly muddled on the subject. Most shamans say there is a difference between spirit and magic but just smile mysteriously if you ask what it is."

"Like Nettie."

"Exactly. Houngans and mambos—"

"Who?"

"Male and female voodoo priests. Their magic is spirit-based, so naturally they don't distinguish between magic and spirit. And Buddhists . . ." He shrugged and added in a singsong, "Spiritual, nonspiritual—no difference. Duality is illusion."

Cynna chuckled. "I used to know someone who would have said just that."

Lily drummed her fingers on her thigh. "They can't all be right. What do sorcerers say?"

"Mostly we ignore the question. Spiritualism has that good and evil thing going on. Confuses things."

"And sorcerers hate to be confused," Cynna said. "They can't see spiritual stuff, so they treat it the way ungifted humans treat magic—as if it isn't real. And if it is, it shouldn't be."

Cullen gave a quick laugh. "Biased, but not completely inaccurate. Of course, the *Msaidizi* were faith based."

"The what?" Lily asked.

"Dizzies."

Oh. "What does this have to do with a hellgate?"

"The gates are magical constructs, like I said, but they were closed using a combination of spiritual and magical energies. To reopen a gate, we'd need spiritual energy as well as magic."

"That's what the Azá were doing, wasn't it? They believed in their goddess, and that belief was part of what

She needed to get that gate open." That plus a little bonus from death magic.

"Exactly. We can't supply a large faith-based community, so even if we knew how, we couldn't reopen a gate."

"But you're planning to open one."

"Open, not reopen. We'll have to build a new gate. Cynna and I have been arguing about how to, ah, tether it. She thinks congruence is the only criteria. I agree it's essential—we don't want to step out into thin air or the middle of a mountain, so the two spaces have to be congruent. But I think that with a small gate, other relevancies can be used, too."

Cynna spoke. "He means you."

"What?" She shook her head. "That's a joke, right?"

"Nope." Cullen slowed. They'd reached her apartment complex. "Five fields of relevance, remember? Spatial, physical, mental, emotional, and spiritual. The more fields we use, the more stable the gate and the greater our control."

"Theoretically," Cynna added darkly.

Cullen ignored that. "The mate bond gives us two more fields to use—physical and emotional."

"I . . . see. Sort of. Because Rule's there and I'm here, the mate bond is already sort of a gate. But once I'm there, too, that won't be true."

"That's why you need me," Cullen said cheerfully, pulling into the space next to Lily's car. "To figure out the hard parts. If I get it right, the gate will close behind us as soon as we cross. It will open again when you want it to, and nothing will be able to pass through it without your permission."

Whew. Lily ran a hand through her hair. "What happens if I'm killed?"

"Try to avoid that." He shut off the engine and opened his door. "It's a damned good way of keeping the other side from making use of our gate, though, isn't it?"

"Theoretically." She pushed her door open, too, and got

out. The burn throbbed, protesting the pressure from the belt. She eyed the stairs to her apartment grimly and started forward. "You've convinced me it's worth a try, though."

"I knew you'd see sense." She heard the click-click from the car's lock behind her. "If it's any consolation, I couldn't do it if you still had your Gift."

She acknowledged that with a nod. She wasn't ready to look on the bright side.

"If you were still Gifted, it might not have been a good idea for you to cross," Cynna added, coming around the car. "Considering what they say about sensitives in hell."

"What do they—hey!"

Cullen had swung her up into his arms. "Who says I'm not a thoughtful and considerate guy? You don't need to climb those stairs. All right," he added to Cynna as he headed for the stairs. "I'll bite. What *do* they say about sensitives in hell?"

" 'Feendly armies in foul affray dide fighte,' " she recited, " 'for who wolde holde the sixewitte hral. Bihood thes brutall beistis, who wolde their yvel powers incresen—and drinken of hir precious herte blood!' Here, give me your keys. I'll go ahead and open the door."

Lily dug them out of the side pocket of her purse. "I don't know what you said, but I didn't hear anything about sensitives."

"*Sixewitte* was the medieval term." Cullen started up the stairs behind Cynna. "The five senses were the five *wittes*. The way they saw it, sensitives had a sixth sense. Sixewitte."

"Ah . . . if I caught the gist, that's whose 'precious herte blood' the feendly hordes planned to drink."

"You got it," Cynna said, sticking Lily's key in the lock. "Feendly hordes being demons. Supposedly they get some special power from the blood of a sensitive."

Cullen reached the landing. He wasn't even breathing hard. Pretty good for someone pushing sixty. "I've never heard that verse. What's it from?"

" 'The Furiel Pyne of Helle.' It's pretty obscure. Fourteenth century, and it might be pure fiction, but the monk who—oh. Good grief. What are you doing here?"

FIVE minutes later, Lily sat in her one and only chair petting Dirty Harry, who had his motor going full-blast. The cat had claimed her lap when the man who'd been keeping him company stood up.

"I'd offer you a sandwich, but Harry and I ate the last of your ham," Abel Karonski said from her kitchen, where he was refilling his coffee cup. "Anyone want some coffee?"

"Why does everyone feel entitled to break into my place?" Lily asked the ceiling. "Sure, I'll take a cup, since it's my coffee and all."

Karonski rejoined them, carrying two steaming mugs and looking around vaguely as if her place might have sprouted another chair in his absence. His gaze paused on Cullen. "Seaborne," he said with a nod. "We met at your, ah, adoption ceremony. When you joined Nokolai, I mean."

Cullen was wearing his inscrutable face. "I remember."

"At the risk of repeating myself," Cynna said, "what are you doing here?" She was sitting on one of the floor cushions by Lily's big, square coffee table, the only other seating in the pocket-size living room. Cullen occupied the other cushion.

"I'm not really here. Think of me as a figment of your overheated imaginations."

"Nothing personal, Abel, but you've never figured high in my overheated imagination. Here." Cynna scooted off her cushion onto the floor. "Sit down and give those old bones a rest."

"Mouthy. Always mouthy. I'm only ten years older than you." He handed Lily a mug that read, *Don't Make Me Release the Flying Monkeys!* "You're not looking so great."

"Neither are you." The pouches under his eyes were looking more like duffel bags.

"Tired, that's all. We found the leak, and it's big. The biggest I've seen. I've called a Gathering to close it."

"A Gathering?"

"Multiple covens," Cullen said. "Anywhere from three to a dozen. That's a major working you're talking about."

"It's a major leak." He lowered himself awkwardly onto the cushion and then scowled at Lily. "I don't know why you don't own chairs. Everyone owns chairs."

"My figments have never complained about the seating before," she commented. "Or helped themselves to my ham. Maybe you'll explain why I'm imagining you're here."

"Officially I'm still in North Carolina. I'll be flying back as soon as we've talked." He sipped. "Good coffee."

"Rule's picky about coffee. He buys some fancy blend and grinds it fresh."

The silence that followed reeked of everything he didn't say. At last he sighed. "I'm sorry about Rule, Lily. Damned sorry."

She didn't respond. Just waited.

His eyebrows lifted. "You aren't going to insist that he isn't dead?"

"I'm pretty sure you know that. Just like I know you didn't fly twenty-five hundred miles to offer me your sympathy."

"No." He took another sip, heaved another sigh, and put the mug on the coffee table. "I'm here to tell you some things Ruben didn't want to go into over the phone. Also to be sure you aren't planning to do something stupid."

Lily kept her face stony. "Ruben's private line is as secure as any in the nation."

"So it is. I'm going to give you some background you aren't cleared for. Heavy duty stuff with lots of *top*s stamped in front of *secret*." He looked at Cullen. "I figure you see the advantage in continuing to fly under the official radar."

Cullen smiled pleasantly. "Just as you see the advantage in letting me hover there. Don't worry. I'm not going to run to the tabloids with the story."

"You won't tell anyone, or discuss it with anyone except those in this room. And you'll all be damned careful how you discuss it at all. You'll see why." He paused. "In the past year, two U.S. Congressmen and the under secretary of a major department have reported being contacted by a demon."

"What?" Lily's coffee jiggled, spilling a couple of drops on Harry. He gave her an indignant look and jumped down. "That . . . is certainly not what I was expecting." Demons didn't just dial up Congressmen and offer them deals. For one thing, they couldn't . . . or so everyone thought. "There hasn't been a confirmed case of demonic tampering with government in . . . well, not since Hitler."

Karonski nodded. "And that was a freak occurrence, the result of conditions unlikely to be duplicated in a thousand years. You can see why they're keeping the investigation quiet."

"They, not we?" Her eyebrows rose. "Who's investigating?"

"The Secret Service. They've needed some expert help, so Ruben's made a few of us in the Unit available to them on an informal basis. But it's their investigation, not ours."

"Are we talking about one demon?" Cynna asked. "Or more?"

He gave her a nod. "Good question. We'd like to know if we're looking at a widespread change in the relationship between the realms, which is what contact by multiple demons would suggest. Unfortunately, I can't tell you. The descriptions we've got don't match, but demons have a nasty habit of changing their body size and shape, so that isn't conclusive."

Cullen slid him an unreadable look. "And what does this have to do with Lily?"

"Think about it. If one appointee and three elected officials report unsolicited demonic contact, there's a damned good chance that others were contacted, too. And haven't reported it."

"Shit."

"The ones who reported it were taking a risk," Lily said slowly. "Supposedly demons can't initiate contact themselves, right? They have to be summoned. The Congressmen must have wondered if anyone would believe that it wasn't any of their doing."

Karonski gave her a nod. "They showed courage, all right. We're betting that others were contacted who didn't take the deal but didn't report it, either. Some would be afraid. Some probably persuaded themselves it never happened. Denial is a powerful force. But human nature being what it is, we have to assume there are people in powerful positions in the government who took the demon up on its offer."

"What kind of offer?" she asked.

"The usual. Fame, wealth, power. The power to do good can be a strong temptation for even the best of us."

Cynna shook her head. "Those pacts leave traces. It's not that hard to find out if someone has been sipping demon blood."

"Oh, yech," Lily said. "Is that how the pacts are sealed?"

"Blood is both the seal and the way power is transferred," Karonski said. "And yes, we can detect it. But it's not feasible to run blood tests on every member of Congress, their staffs and families, all the Secretaries and Under Secretaries, maybe a few dozen judges and—"

"Okay, okay," Cynna said. "But what is the Secret Service *doing* then? How do they investigate if they can't run tests?"

For a long moment Karonski didn't say anything.

"We'd hoped to bring in a sensitive," he said at last. "Someone who could tell who was clean with a single handshake."

Lily closed her eyes. *Shit, shit, shit . . .*

Cullen's voice was hard. "You also didn't fly twenty-five hundred miles to make Lily feel even worse about the loss of her Gift, I'm assuming."

Lily spoke without opening her eyes. "He's warning us. He thinks the acting director of the FBI may have been corrupted. That's why Ruben didn't say anything over the phone. Why Karonski is officially still in Virginia . . . and probably why the Secret Service is investigating, not us."

Karonski spread his hands. "We've got no evidence. None. No reason to think Hayes was contacted, except . . ."

"One of Ruben's feelings," she finished for him.

"Yeah." He picked up his coffee and took a drink. "Which was strengthened when Hayes put pressure on Ruben to close the investigation and declare Rule dead."

"I'm not getting the connection," Cynna said.

"You should. If Hayes is corrupted—" Karonksi interrupted himself. "That's a big if, of course. He might have done one of his damned cost-benefit analyses and decided it was cheaper to write off Rule. He could be clean himself but getting pressure from others who aren't. But if he is corrupted, he didn't make the decision. The demon did."

Lily's head hurt. She rubbed her temples. "And this hypothetical demon doesn't want anyone looking for Rule?"

"Either the demon . . . or the demon's master."

Cynna made a small sound.

Karonski looked at her, sympathy softening his eyes. "That makes the most sense, doesn't it? More than assuming the rules have changed. A true master could put a demon in contact with ordinary humans."

"You haven't brought me in on it." Her voice was

tight, her eyes turbulent. "I'm the one person who could Find her, and you haven't brought me in."

"Ruben wanted to. The Secret Service refused."

She looked away and then nodded.

"Which brings me to the other reason I'm here." He drained the last of his coffee and put the empty mug on the table. "Just in case any of you are thinking of doing something colossally dumb, like crossing into hell without official sanction, you should know that the Secret Service's chief suspect is Jiri Asmahani . . . Cynna's old teacher. This isn't a good time to renew that acquaintance."

There wasn't much to say after that. Karonski stood, told them all he'd see them later, and then paused in front of Lily. She didn't get up. Or speak. He stood in front of her for a long moment, looking tired and sad and like he wanted to say something. But in the end he shook his head, bent and patted her shoulder, and left.

He took about every last drop of hope with him.

Take the next step, she'd been telling herself. What did you do when you ran out of steps?

Even if she'd been willing to endanger an investigation into the demonic control of highly placed national officials, there was a chance Cynna's old teacher was behind the official ban on looking for Rule. She wasn't likely to change her mind just because Cynna said pretty please.

Karonski wasn't going to help them open a hellgate. Cullen didn't know how.

God, she was tired. She closed her eyes and thought about keeping them closed. Just not opening them ever again. She heard Cullen push to his feet and start pacing, muttering to himself. It sounded like Latin.

"Cynna," she asked without opening her eyes. "Is there any chance you could summon the demon who took Rule? Force it to take us to him, or bring him back?"

"No." She sounded miserable. "I don't have enough of its names."

"Okay." Cullen took a deep breath, let it out. "We've run out of other options."

That startled her eyes open. "Other options? As in, you have one I don't know about?"

"You know about it. Sort of." He stopped in front of her. "It's a long shot, but the only shot we've got left. You said the Rhej wanted to talk to you."

Baffled, she nodded.

"That's what you should do, then. Go talk to the Rhej."

TWENTY-EIGHT

CULLEN wouldn't explain. He wouldn't tell her why talking to the clan's historian or priestess or whatever might help. He wouldn't even tell her the woman's name. It was customary, he said, for the Rhej to choose who would receive her name, and she was never referred to outside her presence by anything but her title.

He had the jitters. He kept pacing, but when she asked why the idea of talking to the Rhej made him nervous he raised his brows, astonished, and told her he was a jumpy fellow. He'd thought she knew that.

So she took a shower.

She was careful. Getting her burn infected wouldn't help her or Rule or anyone, so she kept her bandages dry. But she *needed* the shower. She craved water, the feel and sound of it, and the notion, however foolish, that she could wash away some portion of last night.

She used Rule's shampoo. Standing there with her hair lathered and the water beating on her feet, she suddenly understood why she'd needed this shower.

The sobs hit fast, and they hit hard. She put her back to

the side of the shower stall and slid down until she was sitting on the hard tiles, head back, hands hanging limp between her knees, suds dripping on her shoulders. And wept.

No one, not even Cullen, would be able to hear her. She couldn't hear herself. It was safe to let go, let the pain and helplessness wash up through her in huge, terrible waves.

The weeping ended more gradually than it had begun. She was still leaking slightly when she stood and carefully rinsed her hair. She washed her face and underarms, looked at her razor, shook her head, and shut off the water without shaving.

She wasn't sure she felt any better, but maybe giving in to tears now would keep them from sneaking up on her later.

The mirror was fogged. She didn't bother to clean it, combing her hair out quickly. It could dry on its own this time. In the bedroom, she pulled on her bra and a pair of bikini panties and then grabbed a plain silk sheath she seldom wore. Her burn would be happier now, with nothing touching it. She folded up Cynna's things and took a breath.

Time to pull herself back together. Or fake it. She opened the door.

Cullen had stopped pacing. He stood at the window, frowning out the parking lot.

"Where's Cynna?" she asked.

"Went to pick up some lunch for us. Harry left with her. At least he went out. I doubt he's headed for Sub Express." He turned. His frown deepened. He started toward her.

Lunch. She'd eat, of course. However little she wanted to. "I don't suppose you've thought of anything else to try."

"No." He stopped, standing a little too close. "You've been crying."

"Shit. Couldn't you at least pretend to be tactful? I know it isn't your strong point, but at your age you should have some grasp of the basics."

"Crying's okay. I hear it reduces stress." He reached up and took one wet strand of hair between his fingers, rubbing it with his thumb. "There are other ways to destress."

"Tell me you didn't mean that the way it sounds."

His mouth kicked up at one side in a smile that didn't touch his eyes. "I'm making you an offer you're free to refuse."

She jerked her head away and stepped back. "God. I can't believe this. Rule's missing and you're—"

"Offering to help you feel better for a little while. No permanent cure, but physical ease benefits the mind, too."

"Is sex on demand your notion of comfort?"

"Yes."

She'd been sarcastic. He was serious.

"Rule wouldn't object, you know, or feel hurt. Not under the circumstances."

"I would."

He shrugged. "Okay. I'll admit I don't get the guilt thing. I assume that's what's put that look on your face? Rather as if you'd stepped in a pile of dog doo, which I must say is not the usual reaction. If you change your mind—"

"I won't."

"—just let me know. But if you think sex would make things worse for you, then we won't go there."

"Good."

"I'm not lusting after you, you know. Except in a general way, because you do have—"

"We aren't going there, remember?"

"Right." He turned back to the window. "Have you reached a decision?"

For a second she thought he was still talking about

having sex, which was stupid. He'd rattled her. "How do I
go about setting up a meeting with the Rhej?"

"You show up at her lair. She said she wants to talk to
you, so she'll probably be there."

He was looking out the window, so she couldn't see
his expression. And his voice sounded normal—lightly
mocking, though it wasn't obvious whether the mockery
was directed out or toward himself. Yet still she had the
sense that he was . . . not sad, exactly. Lost.

Rule had been his friend, perhaps his only real friend,
for many years. Years when he'd been clanless, leaving
him alone in a way no human could fully grasp.

Had he thought having sex with her would make him
feel closer to Rule?

Yech, she thought and tried to push the idea away. But it
clung the way a good hunch will, and gradually the disgust melted, leaving her a little disoriented. And hurting
for him. "Cynna might not mind the idea of comfort sex."

He smiled at her over his shoulder, his eyes blue and
sharp and somehow knowing. As if he'd guessed everything she'd been thinking . . . and maybe a few things she
hadn't quite wrapped her mind around yet. "There's a notion. She's annoying, but she smells good."

Lily blinked. At times she almost forgot Cullen was lupus. He was odd in so many ways that had little to do with
his wolfish part. "I hope you won't put it to her quite that
way."

"I speak fairly good western human when I have to,
but I don't think Cynna would require that."

"In other words, you'll say what women expect, but
you won't mean it."

He was amused. "I think of it as an imprecise translation. I don't lie. I don't have to."

No, he probably had more women making him offers
than he could properly attend to. "That," she said after a
moment, "is deeply annoying."

"It's all in your point of view. I find it convenient." His head turned. "Lunch is heading up the stairs."

"Already?" Funny. A few minutes ago she'd had no interest in food. She'd have eaten, just as she'd take care of her burn, because it was necessary. Now . . . it was weird, but she was hungry. Actually hungry. "I'll get the pickles. No one ever puts on enough pickles."

She had a next step again. And if the Rhej couldn't help, she'd think of something else. Lily headed for the kitchen, thinking about steps and friendship and what kind of ammo would be most likely to stop a demon.

CLANHOME. It rested in the mountains outside the city, sprawling over nearly two thousand acres. They weren't regal, these mountains, like their grander cousins to the north, nor garbed in towering pines. The slopes were steep but not terribly high; valleys were mostly narrow, cut by small, seasonal streams. This was chaparral country, with scrub oak, juniper, sage, and here and there the tough, ugly mountain mahogany tangled together on the rocky slopes.

It was cooler up here, downright nippy compared to sea level. The air smelled of dust and sage. At least that's what Lily smelled. She didn't know how much more the werewolf in front of her was smelling.

"So," Cynna said, "is this Rhej person a bit of a loner? She lives up here away from everyone else."

They were following a narrow path up one of those scrub-covered slopes. Cullen led; Cynna brought up the rear.

"Lots of people prefer to live slightly apart," he said. "They enjoy the contact with the wild. It doesn't make them loners."

Apart in this case meant away from the commons—a loose cluster of homes and small businesses along the only real road in Clanhome. The Rhej's home was less

distant than some, being only a couple of miles away
from the end of the gravel road.

But there was a great deal she didn't know about
Nokolai and Clanhome. She'd only been here three
times. Once when she was investigating a murder—the
investigation that brought her and Rule together. The second time she'd come to take part in her *gens amplexi,* the
ceremony when she was formally adopted into Nokolai.
On her third trip here a little over a week ago, she'd just
visited, trying to get to know some of the people she was
now bound to.

"You holding up okay?" Cullen asked as they struggled up the last, steepest part of the path.

"I'm fine." Utterly spent, actually, which was mortify-
ing but not unexpected. A wounded body turned tyrant,
insisting on channeling everything into healing. But her
burn wasn't hurting too badly. Looser clothing helped.
"Why didn't I meet the Rhej at the *gens amplexi?*"

Cullen stopped, though they weren't at the top of the
mountain. Maybe they didn't have to go all the way up.
He glanced over his shoulder at her, a small smile on his
mouth. "You did. You just didn't know it."

"More secrets," she muttered. "Your bunch is too
damned fond of secrets." She was breathing hard as she
came up beside him.

The ground leveled out here, forming a small clearing.
Not a natural clearing, though everything Lily saw was
native and looked like it had just happened to sprout
where it was. Bracken fern and spleenwort snuggled up
beneath a small pinyon pine. Mock parsley and wild cel-
ery grew in a tangle with yarrow and some species of
aster that still clung to a few small, bright blue blooms.
But many of the plants she saw wouldn't have grown on
this west-facing slope naturally. Someone had planted
them—after digging out the oak and juniper.

A huge job, that, without earth-moving equipment.
Maybe she'd had lupus muscles to help.

The house was set smack up against the mountain, a tiny adobe building almost the color of the dirt behind it, but with a shiny metal roof. As Lily's attention left the plants for the house, the front door opened. An old woman swept out a scatter of dust.

Lily stared. She recognized her, all right, though they hadn't spoken at the ceremony or the celebration that had followed. The woman stood maybe five feet high, which was enough to make her stick in Lily's memory. She was Anglo, over sixty, and fat—the roly-poly, happy-grandmother kind of fat. Her hair was white and straight and short. It looked like she cut it herself, maybe with hedge trimmers. Her eyes had once been blue.

Now they were milky. She was blind.

Those sightless eyes aimed right at them. "Well, come in," she said. "You didn't hike up here to watch me sweep my floor." And she turned around and went back inside.

Lily gave Cullen a hard look. "Secrets," she muttered, and headed for the little house.

Inside it was a single square room, its symmetry disturbed only by two bumped-out sections with doors that she guessed were the bathroom and a large closet. To her left was the kitchen area—open shelving above the single wooden counter with a tiny electric stove and a refrigerator straight out of the fifties. To her right was a round table and four wooden chairs. The bed, a double, was at the back, between the bumped-out portions. Two battered trunks lined up along one wall. Along the opposite wall was a cushy green recliner, a top-of-the-line stereo, and three large baskets. A gray tabby slept in the recliner.

No rugs. White plastered walls, dark wood floor . . . and an altar. Set smack in the center of the room, the rough-hewn stone held three white candle stubs, a scattering of sage, and a small silver saucer. Chiseled into the front of it was a symbol much like Lily's missing *toltoi*.

The Rhej stood at her stove with her back to the door. She wore jeans, an old flannel shirt, white socks, and no shoes. "You'll have tea," she informed them. "I made cookies, too. They're on the table."

"We didn't come here for cookies," Cullen said.

The old woman clucked her tongue. "Still angry, eh? It wasn't me said you were no Etorri all those years ago. Though as it turned out the Etorri Rhej was right, wasn't she? It just took Nokolai a while to realize you were ours."

"Ah . . ." Lily glanced from Cullen to their hostess. "Obviously you and Cullen know each other. He hasn't bothered to introduce us, so I will. The woman with me is Cynna Weaver, and I'm Lily Yu."

"I know that, child." She turned her head to smile at them. The smile fell away, wiped out by pure startlement.

Then she laughed. "Oh. Oh, my. I'm not half as clever as I'd like to think. Well, this will be interesting. You're Cynna?" She spoke to Cynna as directly as if she could see her.

Cynna agreed to that.

"You'll stay. Cullen, go run. It's been too long since you've Changed. Go enjoy your four feet instead of your brain for a while."

Cullen didn't look happy, but to Lily's surprise, he obeyed, giving the Rhej a single, stiff nod and leaving.

Nodding at someone who couldn't see? But then, Lily didn't understand how anyone could garden without sight. Unless . . . "Do you see the way Cullen does?" she blurted. "Second sight, or whatever it's called?"

She snorted. "I'm no sorcerer, and that is not what 'second sight' means. Sit down, sit down." She nodded at the table, already set with cups and saucers and dainty china plates. A larger plate held a dozen or more chocolate chip cookies.

Slowly Lily complied. Cynna sat, too, looking as clueless as Lily felt. The three cups had dried herbs in their bottoms. Cynna picked hers up and sniffed at it. "Are you a precog? You seem to have been expecting us."

"I wasn't expecting *you*." She shook her head. "Lady help me, I sure wasn't expecting you. I've spoken to Isen, of course, about last night, and the Lady said Lily would come. I figured Cullen would be bringing her."

"You talk to your goddess?" Cynna asked.

"Talk, argue . . . now and then I even listen. But the Lady is just the Lady. She's not into the god business anymore." She turned, teapot in hand, and waddled over to the table.

Lily didn't want to talk about goddesses, even if they weren't in the god business anymore. "You've created a beautiful garden." Though she couldn't see how. How did the woman know what seedlings to yank, which plant was which? How could she enjoy her garden when she couldn't see it?

The white eyebrows lifted. "Realized it wasn't wild growth, did you? Not many would."

"I like gardening, and I'm interested in native plants."

"Rule mentioned that you enjoy grubbing in the dirt." She found one cup with her fingers and then poured steaming water over the herbs in it, releasing their pungent scents. Rosemary, Lily thought, among others.

"The cookies are just those refrigerator things, but they're pretty good. Help yourselves. You probably won't like the tea, but drink it anyway. It's good for you." She located another cup and poured.

She found things by touch, Lily realized. She found people by . . . "You're an empath. A physical empath, I'd guess, because you aren't tuning into the plants' emotions. It's their physical state you sense." The Gift itself wasn't rare, but was usually considered one of the weak Gifts. The old woman obviously had a triple dose of it— which was probably why she lived apart. "You don't see me, but you feel me so clearly it's almost the same."

"Not the same," she said. "Better in some ways, not as good in others." She filled the last cup with water. "That'll need to steep a few minutes." She turned and padded back to the stove to deposit the teapot. "You going to tell me what you want?"

"You asked me to come."

"I know that. I may be eighty, but my memory's good." She chuckled as she came back to the table and pulled out a chair. "Damned good."

Lily looked at her dubiously. "Eighty?"

"Clan females don't age as slow as the males, but we do weather well."

"Ah . . ." Lily darted a glance at Cynna. "Are we going to talk about big, hairy secrets now?"

"That's why you're here. I'll tell you some of my big, hairy secrets, and you'll tell me yours. You're wondering why I'm letting Cynna listen in. I'll explain later." She bent over the steaming cup, sniffed, and nodded. "Good batch. It'll taste nasty, but it'll work. Drink up."

Cynna looked dubious. "What's in it?"

"Rosemary, rue, chamomile, a few others. All properly harvested." She "looked" at Lily. "It'll be good for Cynna and me, too, but it's mostly for you. Opens you up to the spell I'll add to help your body mend. Not that I'm a healer, but I've picked up a thing or two over the years. You'll need to sleep after."

Spells would work on her now. Lily's hands fisted in her lap.

The old woman leaned over and patted her arm. "I won't tell you it'll get better. It won't stop being a loss and a grief just because times passes. I went blind more than thirty years ago, and I still miss the sight of dew on the grass. Or a smile." She formed one of her own. "Lord, but I'd love to see a smile again. But the hurt changes over time, if you let it."

Lily started to nod and caught herself. "Okay." She took a breath and let it out. "I'm not here to talk about the loss of my Gift, though."

"You want to go after Rule."

She jerked slightly. "You *are* a precog. Or else Isen—"

"Isen's trying to keep you from doing that, yes. While hoping to do it himself or send some of his people, if he can come up with a way. He's a man and a father, not just the Rho. But you're Rule's Chosen. Of course you want to go after him." She picked up her teacup. "Drink your tea, child. I've a good deal to tell you, and I won't start until you've emptied the cup."

Was there something in the tea other than healing herbs? Lily picked it up, sniffed dubiously, and glanced at Cynna . . . who was holding her hand over her own cup, her face wearing that focused look.

After a second she shrugged, picked up her cup, and took a sip. "Oh, ugh. You weren't kidding about the taste. Rat turds."

"Not in this batch." The old woman downed her own tea in three big swallows, grimaced and then belched gently. "Before you tell me what you want from me, you need to know what a Rhej is. I'm the memory." She reached for a cookie. "You haven't drunk your tea."

If that's what it took to get her to talk . . . Lily tried to emulate the old woman. It took her five swallows, and she wasn't sure she'd keep the last one down. "The clan historian, you mean."

"I mean what I said. Eat." She pushed the cookies toward Lily, who took one and bit. "They get rid of the aftertaste." She finished her own cookie and dusted her hands. "You're thinking I memorize a bunch of songs and stories so I can pass on our oral history as it was passed on to me. You're half right. I do pass on what was passed to me, and I know and teach a lot of songs and stories. But I check their accuracy against the original sources."

"Ah . . . dead sources?"

She chuckled. "I'm no medium. The Etorri Rhej, now—but that's another story. A Rhej is always Gifted, though. There has to be a channel, but it doesn't seem to matter much what the Gift is. Speaking of Gifts . . . you guessed mine. I know yours was taken from you. What about you?" she said to Cynna abruptly. "You're Gifted, but I don't know what it is."

Cynna blinked. "I'm a Finder."

The white eyebrows lifted. "Interesting. As I was saying, a Rhej has to be Gifted so there'll be a channel, a way to receive what's been passed down. I hold memories going back more than five thousand years. Mostly Nokolai," she added casually, reaching for another cookie. "But some of the older memories are too important to trust to a single Rhej, so we all hold 'em."

"Five thousand years," Lily said blankly. "Five thousand *years*?"

"Give or take a few centuries." Her smile was a tad grim. "Makes for restless nights sometimes."

Cynna leaned forward. "Do they feel like your memories? I mean, is it all just crammed in there together, so that what someone experienced a thousand years ago is like what you lived through last year?"

The Rhej nodded. "Good question, but tricky to answer. You might think of the passed—that's how we refer to what's been passed to us—as computer files, being as how that's what your generation's used to. I like suitcases better, myself, but to each her own. If I need to check the details of a particular memory I open a suitcase, take out the one I want, and try it on. Once it's on, though . . . it isn't memory anymore. I'm there."

Either the woman was sincerely nuts, Lily decided, or she was sincerely . . . well, something completely outside Lily's experience. This was no put-on. She found herself tugged toward belief, maybe because she needed to believe. To think she'd found someone who could help.

But Cullen was the opposite of gullible, and he'd brought them here, to this woman. "You're saying that you experience what someone thousands of years dead lived through. You don't remember it. You experience it."

"That's right. But once we've finished our apprentice-ships, we don't open our suitcases often. We remember what's in them well enough for most things."

The sort of memories that would be saved wouldn't be pleasant, would they? They'd be from the big moments—the life-and-death struggles of the clan, not a baby's first steps or the beauty of a sunrise on a particular morning. Lily could see why the Rhej didn't open her "suitcases" often.

"I'd planned to tell you all of this anyway," the old woman said. "Along with a great deal more, including some of those songs and stories. You're Nokolai now. You need to know your clan. But you won't have time for that now. So." She slapped her palm on the table. "Time to spill your secrets. Tell me what you know or have guessed about Rule's disappearance."

It didn't take long. Lily knew how to boil a report down and present it dispassionately. She left out what Karonski had told them, of course, simply saying they'd had a lead on a possible source for opening a hellgate, but it hadn't panned out.

"So Rule's in the demon realm." The Rhej's voice was heavy. She was silent a moment. "It was Cullen's idea, I take it. To come to me."

"Yes. We need to open a gate, and we don't know how. Can you help us?"

She shook her head, but it looked more like "let me think" than a refusal, so Lily held her tongue. For several moments the old woman frowned at her thoughts.

"You've brought me a hard one," she said at last. "Normally I'd refuse and then grieve. There are things we're not allowed to reveal. That's another reason Cullen isn't fond of us," she added. "We know things that we won't tell him. Drives him crazy."

Lily smiled faintly. "It would."

"But now . . ." Her frown deepened. "I've been Rhej for forty-two years. I was apprenticed for twelve years before that. When I say I listen to the Lady, I'm not talking about hearing voices. If I get a feeling, a certain kind of feeling, I know it's from her. Oh, when it's clan business, I still use Tell-Me-Three-Times to confirm my feeling. That's how we're trained—check and double-check, using different rituals. But most of us only hear the Lady's voice once in our lives. It's enough." She gave a short nod.

"Do you have one of those feelings now?"

She snorted. "Got better than that. There's one time we don't use Tell-Me-Three-Times. If the Lady ups and speaks, well, that's it. Can't mistake her voice for anyone or anything else, not if you've ever heard it. And we all have, that once. Well, she woke me up last night. Three o'clock in the damned morning, and for the second time in my life I heard her voice."

Lily's heart was pounding. "What did she say?"

"Bring him back."

She closed her eyes, so dizzy with relief she swayed. "Then you'll do it."

"I'll do what I can. It may not be enough. The sort of memories you need . . . they were split hundreds of years ago. Too dangerous to rest just with one person. None of us holds the entire spell to open a gate."

"Then what?" she demanded. "What do we do? Will the other Rhejes help?"

"They should. When the Lady speaks . . . but you'd better hope the she's been shaking some other shoulders. The ban's been round for a long time, and we all remember why it was put in place. This is going to take time. Some of the others . . ." Her head turned toward the wall with the recliner. "Oh, for heaven's sake, Cullen. If you just have to hear what's going on, come on in."

A few seconds later a lean wolf trotted in the front door. He was smaller than Rule's wolf-form—his shoulders would hit below her waist—and his coat was a pale silver, not the black-and-silver of Rule's fur. And the sight of him hurt her heart.

Cynna made a small sound. Lily looked at her. "Knowing about it and seeing it are two different things, aren't they?"

"Yeah." Cynna's eyes never left the wolf, who came up to the table and fixed the Rhej with a pair of disconcertingly bright blue eyes.

"I guess you heard the most of it," the old woman said.

Cullen-wolf nodded.

"This is not going to be easy." She contemplated things for a moment and then pushed her chair back. "Or quick, so I'd best get started. You can take me to Isen's house. I'll use his phone. Someone bring the cookies. Isen's fond of chocolate chip." She stood. "I'm Hannah, by the way."

Cullen yipped and then pointed with his nose at Cynna.

"Wondering about that, are you? Why I let her learn so much?" Suddenly the old woman grinned and her face lit up, bright as a mischievous child. "I did say I'd explain. After all, she's not clan yet."

"Ah . . ." Cynna looked taken aback. "What do you mean, *yet*?"

Hannah's grin widened. "Just what it sounds like. You'll have to become Nokolai sooner or later. You're the next Rhej."

TWENTY-NINE

RULE woke from his first true, deep sleep in hell with a hard ache in his leg; the scents of earth, water, and smoke in his nostrils; and a clear head. He lay quietly, eyes closed, savoring the relief.

Most of his memories of the period immediately following the demon's bone-setting were a blur of pain punctuated by fitful sleep. Lily had woken him periodically, coaxing him to drink from her cupped hands. Sometimes he'd woken on his own. She'd always been near.

He did recall how he'd gotten to the cave. Lily had called down a dragon.

The agony of having his bone set had left him too weak and dizzy to stand. She'd been determined to get him in the cave, where there was water, since they lacked any kind of bowl or pot. The demon was strong enough to handle Rule's weight, but too small to manage his bulk. Lily had gotten one of the "coverings" the dragon had mentioned, a thick braided mat she could use as a stretcher. But there had been no way to lower him from the sandbox to the beach.

He'd tried to tell her to wait until he'd healed enough to do it on his own. Maybe his meaning lost something in the translation, or maybe she was just stubborn. She'd called for help.

One of the coppery-brown dragons had descended. Rule remembered the way Lily had ordered it to be careful of his ribs and gentle when it set him down. He remembered the miserable jerk of the takeoff, too, with the talons wrapped around his middle, but the flight had been brief. And the dragon had sent him down gently as ordered, right on the mat Lily had waiting outside the cave. Gan had dragged him in.

He'd been glad of the water, he admitted now. But his bladder was about to burst.

How long had he been sleeping?

Rule was familiar with injury and its aftermath. Lupi played hard, trained hard, and often fought hard, and their bodies cleansed themselves of pain killers and as efficiently as they disposed of alcohol and other toxins. So pain was no stranger. He knew to ride it, not fight it. But he'd never been cut off from the sweet song of the moon or away from Earth's rhythms.

He hadn't been sure he would heal.

Lupi drew from both earth and moon magic. The Change was wrought by their interplay, when the moon's call set the earth dancing in his blood and bones. Here there was no moon, and this earth wasn't Earth. Yet it was enough like his earth, it seemed. His sense of time was distorted, but he thought no more than a day or two had passed—a little slow, but close enough to his normal rate of healing.

His hunger fit that estimate. It had been much too long since he'd eaten.

He took a moment more to assess his situation. His head didn't hurt at all, so the concussion was healed. His ribs . . . well, he'd find out in a moment. Scents told him that Lily was near but not right beside him. He smelled demon and dragon, too, but more faintly—neither were present now. Good. But the smoke . . . what was that from?

He opened his eyes.

The cave was a single chamber about twenty feet deep, fairly regular, with a sandy floor. It was dim where he lay near the rear, but he saw well enough. The rough ceiling was less than five feet overhead—enough head room for him in this form, but Lily must have had to stoop to tend him.

The fire was near the cave's mouth. So was Lily. She was feeding it sticks. She was clothed, he noted with surprise. She'd wrapped a length of red fabric around her torso like a sarong. More of the dragon's coverings, he supposed. Like the one beneath him, the braided mat Gan had dragged him in here on.

Time to find out what shape he was in. Awkwardly he clambered to his feet, holding the splinted leg carefully.

Shit. That hurt. Just his leg, though. The ribs were tender, but not painful. Good. They'd be fully healed in another day or so. His leg would take longer. That had been a bad break. A week? Maybe a little more . . .

"What do you think you're doing?" Lily made a beeline for him. "You don't need to be standing, for God's sake. Lie down. Whatever you need, I'll get it."

He looked at her wryly and started for the mouth of the cave, clumsy but determined. Some things she couldn't do for him.

"Rule. You're not listening." She kept pace beside him, looking worried. "You do understand me, don't you?"

He nodded.

"Well, then, why . . . oh." She nodded. "Right. Uh, I've been using the grassy area for a privy, but that's too far for you. I guess . . . what's wrong?"

He'd paused in the mouth of the cave. Surely it had been lighter before. He looked up at the sky, where two dragons soared, high above. It was definitely darker than it had been. He looked at her.

"The light's fading," she agreed. "Looks like night does fall in hell, after all. Or in parts of it. Gan says there's no natural night and day here, but light and darkness get tugged around by the different demon lords. Xitil keeps her realm light most of the time, but the lord of the realm over there"—she waved out at the ocean—"goes for a more regular light-dark cycle. The dragons can't regulate their territory the way the demon lords do, so it trends along with its neighbors. This close to the ocean, we're in for bouts of darkness. That's one reason I wanted the fire."

He glanced over at it, nodded, and resumed his slow progress.

She kept pace beside him. "I sent Gan for some firewood. There wasn't much on the beach to burn. I hope it gets back soon—I'm almost out of sticks." She grinned. "At first Gan said starting a fire was easy, that demons can all do small magics like that. But he—it—took forever to get this one going. It blames the dragons, of course."

He glanced at her.

"Apparently they have sort of a dampening effect on magic. Gan says they soak it up."

The demon had said earlier that dragons were immune to magic. Apparently they weren't immune in the way Lily was, though, with it bouncing off them. They simply absorbed it.

That is, if the stupid little shit was telling the truth, or even knew what was true. Where was the demon, anyway? Rule looked up and down the beach. No sign of it—and that bright orange skin did stand out.

Well, he was far enough from the cave now. He'd have to squat and pee like a girl, though. He didn't think he could balance on two legs.

As soon as he started, his attentive nurse discovered a sudden need to attend to something in the cave.

He hobbled back. It was awkward as hell. He promised himself that the next time he saw a three-legged dog hopping around he'd have a better appreciation for the skill involved.

If he ever saw a dog again. Or anything else of Earth.

Lily was messing with the fire. She looked up, her expression almost shy. "Are you hungry? There's some fruit. A little meat, too . . . well, dead animals, really. There's two of them. There were three, but I tried to skin one and made a mess of it. I've been sharpening one of the bones the dragons brought when we splinted your leg," she added, "but it's not much of a knife."

He could smell the game—at least a day dead, but not spoiled. It would do. He gave her a nod and started for the back of the cave.

"No, I'll get it." She stood. "You've been rambling around enough."

He decided not to object, partly because that short walk had left him stupidly winded, partly because of the look on her face.

Happiness. He hadn't seen that in her eyes since her sister's wedding.

He lay down near the fire. The flames were small and gave off little heat, but a welter of emotions. Fire was a comfort for humans, bane to most beasts. He was uneasily aware of how little he enjoyed the flames. Surely the man hadn't slipped so far away in such a short time?

And yet he'd attacked without thought. When he learned what the demon had done, that his mate was dying because of it, there had been only the killing rage, the need to feel the demon's life bleed away beneath his teeth.

If the dragon hadn't stopped him, he would have been responsible for Lily's death.

He held no anger for the dragon over his injury. He'd earned his broken leg. It scraped against his raw places now for Lily to look so happy at the chance to do him a service, when he deserved it so little.

She needed the demon now. Needed it far more than she did him. And however ugly that thought was, he'd better get used to it. He had to get along with Gan somehow, or he'd make things harder for her.

But what, he wondered with a blind sort of agony, had happened to the part of her left behind? What became of such a strange remnant? *Lady,* he thought, and stopped, unsure what to ask. *Lady, she is yours. Care for her. All of her.*

Lilly brought back two creatures that looked like a cross between a rat and a naked jackrabbit. Nothing he'd seen here had fur. She glanced from the limp bodies to the fire. "I could cook them. Or try to."

He shook his head. Even in this form he enjoyed his meat cooked when it wasn't a fresh kill, but he was too hungry to wait.

Before he could take the game from her hand, though, he heard something approaching. He bristled to warn Lily. A few seconds later, he heard Gan muttering under its breath. A surge of loathing flattened his ears.

"Rule? What is it?"

The demon came into view. "This better be enough wood," it grumbled. It was carrying several branches under one arm. "I had to climb to the top to get it."

Lily frowned at Rule. "It's just Gan. You aren't going to attack it again, are you?"

It was harder than it should have been to remember the reasons he couldn't. The wolf wanted to, badly. And the man didn't disagree, but knew better.

His tail twitched in disgust, partly at himself. He took the two rat-rabbits from Lily's hand. He'd eat them outside. Less of a mess—and he wouldn't have to smell the demon while he ate.

He passed Gan on the threshold.

"Hey, look who's awake," it said. "It's old dark, mute, and crippled. Going to have a picnic, fur-face?"

Rule ignored it, carrying his meal several paces away and lying down. He glanced up. The sky was much darker now, more gray than copper, and the air had that near-shimmer of approaching twilight. And there were more dragons overhead than before—three, five . . . six now, and wasn't that another one headed this way?

Either they wanted extra guards at night, or the dragons were protection as well as jailers. Night often brought new dangers, and they didn't want Lily killed.

On that one point, he and the dragons agreed. He bit into a rat-rabbit and grimaced. Good thing he wasn't a picky eater.

"How far away do you think you were?" Lily asked the demon.

"How do I know?"

"Guess. I want to know the limits of this bond."

That jolted Rule. It echoed so precisely the way she'd reacted to the mate bond—test it, learn the parameters.

"Maybe three kilometers." There was a clatter as Gan dropped its load.

"Did you go to the limit of the bond?"

"I said I would, didn't I? It was like walking into a Zone that doesn't want you there. Everything turned thick and I couldn't breathe, so I backed up."

"I didn't feel anything." Lily crouched to feed one of the smaller branches into the fire. "Break a couple more in half, would you? They're too big."

"Of course you didn't feel anything." Gan cracked a three-inch thick branch over its knee. "I'm the one partly inside you, not the other way around."

The bond between Lily and the demon wasn't exactly like the mate bond, then. That didn't make Rule feel any better.

Rule finished off the first rat-rabbit methodically, glancing overhead every so often. The dragons were gathering along the top of the cliff. Odd. He'd stay out here a while, he decided. Keep watch.

"How did the dragons react to you climbing the cliff?" she asked.

"One of them kept track of me, but from a distance. They know I can't go far. You'll keep your end of our deal now, right?"

Rule stiffened, looking back at the cave. Lily had made a deal with the demon?

Lily had her fire going nicely now. She sat beside it. "Of course. One load of firewood equals five rounds of *I Spy*."

Gan grinned, showing its pointy teeth. "I get to go first." It plopped down on the dirt floor, stubby legs extended, and leaned back on its tail as it looked around, its gaze landing on Rule outside. "I spy something furry and stupid."

"Your turn will be over fast if you play that way," Lily said. "And you're supposed to use colors, remember?"

Rule shook his head and finished eating to the sound of "I spy something gray" and Lily's guesses. With the light nearly gone, almost everything in the cave was some shade of gray, so the game was likely to last a while.

How could she stand to be around the creature? She was playing kids games with it, for God's sake. If he . . .

A low, mournful sound drew his gaze up.

There were seven dragons now. Seven dragons lined up along the top of the cliff, silhouetted against the darkening sky, their long necks stretched up.

Again the sound came . . . longer, deeper. Haunting. A little like a didjeridu, he thought. And the dragons were making it.

He'd thought them mute. Not dumb, no—they had mindspeech, possibly true telepathy. But not once had he heard any of them make a sound, not a grunt or a cough, until now. Now, when they sang to the gathering dusk.

Inside the cave, Lily looked up. "What's that?"

Rule yipped: *Come out. Come out and hear this.* Another dragon had joined the first, and another.

"It's just the dragons," Gan said. "And it's still my turn."

"In a minute." Lily stood.

"We aren't finished!" Gan cried.

"Hush. I'll finish later. I want to hear this." She came out to stand beside Rule, looking up, as he was.

The dragons' long necks were their instruments. Lungs accustomed to charging those big bodies with enough oxygen to sustain flight powered their song, and they wrapped their voices together in harmonies like nothing he'd ever imagined—eerie, wordless, haunting.

He glanced at Lily. Everything he felt was on her face—awe, grief, a poignancy as vast as the growing darkness. She met his gaze and then sat beside him, their bodies touching. And for a timeless period, Rule forgot everything he'd lost, everything he stood to lose, in the glory of dragonsong.

It was full dark when it ended. Not pitch black; more like new-moon dark, Rule thought, once he could think again. Lily was leaning against him.

He turned to look at her, aching to put his arms around her. But even if he'd had the right-shaped mouth to speak, he didn't have words for what he'd just experienced.

Her face was damp. She met his eyes . . . and yawned. "Oh," she said, startled, and did it again. "I thought . . . but I'm sleepy. Really sleepy."

Everything inside Rule smiled. He'd worried about her sleeplessness. Her body might no longer want sleep, but the human mind needed to dream. He nudged her with his nose.

She gave a little laugh. "I guess I'd better get inside. I feel like I've been up for days . . . I have been, haven't I? But this hit so suddenly . . ." This time she yawned like she was going to crack her jaw.

He nudged her again. She smiled, pushed his muzzle away, and stood, blinking. "Straight to bed, I think." She looked a little unsteady as she headed for the cave.

Gan was inside, sulking, playing some game with a

few small pieces of bones. "Are you finally going to finish our game?"

"Sorry, Gan. I'm not going to be able to stay awake
long . . ." Another yawn. "Long enough. I'll give you an
extra round tomorrow to make up for waiting," she promised, heading for the back of the cave, wobbling a little.

"Shit." Gan stared after her. "It gets dark, and she
conks out."

Rule thought the darkness was coincidence, but maybe
not. He followed her.

Moments after lying down on the mat where he'd
slept, she was asleep. He sat beside her for a while, listening to Gan mutter. The demon seemed to be trying to
levitate the bones. It wasn't having much luck.

He was, he realized, extremely thirsty. But nature
called. He went outside to take care of that and then returned to drink from the small basin filled by the spring.
He was getting better at the three-legged bit, he thought.
But bending to drink was a bitch.

He emptied the basin and was waiting for it to refill
when he noticed an odd scent. Curious, he followed his
nose to a boulder. Dragon-scent, he realized. Faint enough
that he hadn't picked up on it from a distance. And not just
any dragon—this smelled of the one he thought of as Old
Black. The one who'd told Lily to call him Sam.

He looked up at the ceiling, puzzled. That huge beast
couldn't have fit back here. His tail, maybe . . . Rule
checked the ground around the spring and the boulder.
Only the boulder held the scent.

He'd moved it, Rule realize. The dragon had moved
the boulder. To hide something? Something like—a way
out? Excited, Rule yipped.

"Go chase your tail," Gan said, staring at its bone fragments. "I'm busy." One of the pieces lifted about an inch
at one end but then fell. "Stupid fucker!" Gan cried.
"Those dragons have eaten all the stupid magic here!"

Rule studied the boulder. He could have moved it

himself, if he had hands. As it was . . . he sighed and hob-bled to the front of the cave. He growled softly.

"Go away," Gan muttered, resting its chin in its hands "I'm not moving any stupid rocks for you."

Rule drew in the dirt with his paw—two horizontal lines crossed by two vertical lines. He put an X in one square and growled again.

Gan sat up straighter. Its expression was funny, as if it was trying not to look happy. "Tic-tac-toe? Well . . . it's not as good as *I Spy,* but you can't talk, can you? Okay, I guess I could do it. For twenty games, and you let me win every one."

Rule stared. The demon thought that would be fun? Knowing Rule was letting it win, it would still enjoy playing? He growled.

"Okay, okay. Ten games, but I win them all."

Why not? Rule nodded and then added a growl that meant: *If you can do it. You don't get anything for failing.*

"Ha. Of course I can do it." The little demon waddled to the back of the cave, and Rule showed it what he wanted moved. Gan and the boulder were the same height. It stud-ied the rock for a moment—then, as Rule watched in amazement, it grew smaller.

After a second he caught on. The demon had redistrib-uted its mass to make itself almost as inert as the boulder. It spread its newly shortened legs, pressed its tail into the ground, and began pushing.

The boulder rolled. And behind it . . . darkness. Stale air.

A tunnel.

Dread rose in Rule. He had a horror of small, closed spaces. If he went in there and Gan pushed the boulder back . . .

"I get to go first," Gan said, expanding back to its nor-mal size. "I'm exes, you're boos."

As promised, Rule let Gan win the first two games,

making it so easy he didn't see how the demon could get any pleasure from it. But Gan crowed over both staged victories as if it had won the sweepstakes.

Rule sighed and put a pawprint in one of the squares.

Gan studied the nine squares as intently as if there was some chance it could lose. And yawned. Its eyes widened. "Shit! Was that a yawn?"

Rule nodded.

"Demons don't sleep." Gan scowled. "I am not sleepy. I'm not going to start falling unconscious every so often like some stupid . . ." It yawned again. "Shit, shit, shit! She's making me sleepy! I've never felt this before. I don't like it." It looked like a sulky—and very ugly—child defying bedtime as it glared at Lily's sleeping figure. "This is all her fault."

Rule stood, growling.

"I'm not going to hurt her, stupid. Sit down. You still owe me eight games."

The demon was asleep before they finished the fourth game. Once Rule was sure it was sleeping soundly, he hobbled to the back of the cave. He stared into the tunnel for a long moment. It might be a dead end. But Rule didn't think dragons rolled boulders around for fun. The tunnel had been blocked for a reason.

Even if Gan pushed the boulder back, he told himself, he'd just have to bark. Lily would hear him and make the demon let him out. He could mark his route by scent. He wouldn't get lost. The lack of light wouldn't be a problem.

The tightness of the space would. And these rocks were mostly limestone. Good for forming caves, but also prone to shifting. To collapse.

He did not want to go in there.

He looked over his shoulder at Lily, sleeping for the first time in God knew how long. Gan thought the dragons meant to trade Lily to a demon lord. The big dragon hadn't denied it. If they had a chance of escape . . . he had no choice, really.

But he was shaking as he eased himself down onto his belly, his bad leg pushed in front of him, and inched under a mountain of stone.

THIRTY

ONE week later, Lily was at the airport, waiting for Cullen. Originally, Cynna had been supposed to pick him up, but she was upstate, looking for a missing child in one of the state parks. Lily could hardly argue for Cynna to ignore the needs of a lost child, but the other woman's absence made Lily feel as if her plan was unraveling.

Or maybe it was just her that was unraveling.

Cullen had flown to New Orleans yesterday. He called the trip research, though he'd refused to tell her what he hoped to accomplish—"you being an officer of the law and all, luv," he'd said with an irritating grin.

An officer of the law who was conspiring to open a portal to hell. She hitched her purse higher on her shoulder, scanning the faces of the disembarking passengers. She didn't have much room to criticize his methods.

It had been a long week.

Before Cynna left, she'd located three small nodes within a few miles of the spot both she and Lily felt Rule to be. He'd stopped moving around so much, which helped.

His current location corresponded to a point about two miles out to sea. Not so cool. That spot might be high and dry in Dis. She hoped so. But she was taking an inflatable raft, just in case.

Assuming they were able to cross, that is. There was a whole lot of nothing going on with the Rhejes. Hannah kept saying it took time to be sure of the Lady's will, but Rule might not have time. They didn't know . . . oh, there was Cullen. At last.

He had a carryon slung over one shoulder and his other arm slung over the shoulders of a dark-haired woman—fortyish, Caucasian, shapely, wearing a business suit that had probably started out crisp. Lily's lips tightened.

He saw Lily, turned to give the woman a murmured word and a kiss, and left her sighing.

"What kind of research were you doing in New Orleans, anyway?" she asked as soon as he reached her.

"Chill," he said. "Lorene and I were seatmates on the flight. I got what I went after." He patted his bag, looking smug.

"And what was that, exactly?" She started down the concourse.

He ignored her question and asked his own. "Where's Cynna?"

She told him, watching his face for signs of disappointment or relief. Despite all the sparks, he and Cynna hadn't fallen into bed together at the first opportunity. They probably couldn't stop arguing long enough, Lily thought.

"Anything else happen while I was gone? The scary old bats still conferring?"

"Hannah says they're doing the Tell-Me-Three-Times, checking out the Lady's will through rituals. But how long can that take? It's been seven days." The days weren't the worst, of course. It was the nights that made her crazy. She wasn't sleeping well. "They're trying to convince themselves the Lady doesn't want what she said she wanted. 'Bring him back.' That's what she told Hannah. How much clearer could she be?"

He gave a hard-to-read glance. "You beginning to accept that the Lady is real, are you?"

She shrugged impatiently. "Maybe. They think she is, so why won't they listen to Hannah?"

"Sweetheart, those women make the pope look like a screaming revolutionary. They aren't going to like any decision that wanders a hair outside tradition." He shrugged. "I guess when you carry that much of the past around inside you, you can't help getting hung up on the status quo."

"Yeah, well, if the status gets any more quo, we'll be moving backward."

"Is Hannah still convinced that Cynna's her replacement?" he asked as he got on the escalator.

"Yeah." She followed him. "And Cynna's getting annoyed. I don't blame her. Hannah keeps instructing her."

Cullen let out a laugh. Two women riding the up escalator stared at him, practically drooling. "I'd like to see that."

"You probably will. When Cynna objects, Hannah just smiles and says Cynna is Lady-touched, and she'll come around when it's time. As if Cynna could change religions just like that."

"It isn't a religion."

"What?" She stepped off the escalator after him.

"Serving the Lady. There's a spiritual aspect, or can be, but it isn't a religion. Cynna could go right on being a Catholic if she wants."

"You might not see a conflict, but I suspect the Church would." She frowned at him. "You sound like you want her to do it. To apprentice herself to Hannah."

He hesitated and then said slowly, "Hannah's eighty. That's old for a human, even one clan-born. There's been a buzz for years about her lack of an apprentice. She had one once. She was killed in the accident that blinded Hannah. That was more than thirty years ago." He looked at Lily. "Nokolai has to have a Rhej."

She was absurdly disappointed. She'd wanted him to share her anger, dammit. "That's not Cynna's problem. Anyway, I thought you didn't like the Rhejes."

Cullen stopped. He let his bag slip to the floor.

"What?" She looked around, barely resisting the urge to reach for her weapon. "What is it?"

"You." He moved behind her and put his hands on her shoulders.

She jolted and turned to face him. "Are you crazy? What are you doing?"

"I'm going to give you a massage." He moved behind her again. "You're wound so tight you're likely to plug someone for bumping into you. If you won't accept sex," he said, putting his hands on her shoulders again and kneading, "you'll have to make do with a back rub."

"Here?" But she didn't move. His fingers dug in just right, relaxing muscles she hadn't realized were so tight.

"Here. Where there are lots and lots of people around, and you won't worry about where I'm going to put my hands next. This is a strictly asexual massage."

She didn't think Cullen could do asexual if his life depended on it. But he wasn't trying to seduce her, she admitted. And . . . it felt good. His thumbs made circles on her neck, and it was like he'd poured warm oil along her muscles. Everything loosened.

"Damn, you're tight. I mean that in a strictly asexual way," he added. "Because I have no way of knowing—"

"Shut up, Cullen." But she smiled in spite of herself.

"Have you been working out? That's not as much fun as sex, but it can dissipate the tension."

"Sure. With an M16."

"Ah, I sense Benedict's strong hand. He's too banged up to train you himself, though."

"Jeff's put me and Cynna through our paces."

She'd gone to Benedict for tactical advice and firepower. Nokolai possessed a weapons cache that horrified the law enforcement officer in her, but was coming in damned handy now. She and Cynna would carry M16s; Cullen got Benedict's machine gun. He'd also carry the rocket launcher, and they'd each have grenades.

Benedict had helped with her lists, too.

They couldn't know how big their gate would be until Cullen had a chance to evaluate the ritual, maybe not until he worked it. Mass wasn't an issue, he'd told her, but size mattered. She didn't pretend to understand that, but she and Benedict had worked up lists of supplies and weapons based on various possibilities.

What should they take if it was just her, Cullen, and Cynna? If they could take either two extra people or one person and the rocket launcher, which should they leave out? Or if—oh, that's right. She hadn't told Cullen about that possibility. "He wanted me to ask Max to join us."

"Max?" His fingers paused. He chuckled. "I'd like to have seen his face when you invited him to go to hell."

"I didn't get to see it yet myself. He wasn't at the club."

Max was the owner of Club Hell, where Cullen danced. He was small, bad-tempered, foul-mouthed, and a gnome. Though no one was supposed to know the last bit.

"Why Max, anyway?" He began knuckling her spine. "He's no good with weapons."

"He can fight, though, and he's smaller than any of the lupi. Plus Benedict says gnomes are immune to demon magic. The compulsion type, at least."

Cullen made a scoffing noise. "Rumor. Tall tales."

"I don't think Benedict makes tactical judgments based on rumor. Will you ask him?"

"Sure. He'll turn me down, but I'll ask." He gave her shoulders a last squeeze. "Better?"

It was. She rolled her shoulders and nodded. "Thanks."

"I'm just looking after myself, you know." He picked up his bag.

"How's that?" she fell back into step beside him.

"You stay stretched this tight and you're going to screw up and get us all killed. Can't run things by committee once we cross, you know. You'll be in charge."

Uneasy and unsure why, she shook her head. "I'm the least knowledgeable of us. You or Cynna should be captain, or head wolf, or whatever you want to call it."

"Boss bitch?" He grinned at her scowl. "No, it needs to be you. Cynna's not used to running the show, and I'm not alpha enough."

She snorted. "Oh, yeah, I've noticed how submissive you are."

"I do like to be on top, but I try to be flexible. There are all sorts of other lovely positions. For example—"

"Cullen."

He flashed her a grin. "Right. Alpha isn't really a synonym for bossy, you know. I could handle that just fine. A true alpha . . . funny. I never tried to put it into words before, but I know I'm not one."

They'd reached the automatic doors leading outside. She went through first. "So is a true alpha different from a plain old alpha?"

"Yes," he said definitely. "What you mean by alpha isn't what a lupus means. You think of it as machismo— someone who dominates others. We mean someone who can't be dominated. A subtle but real difference. Bullies need to dominate, but can be cowed if you're tougher than they are."

She nodded, squinting against the sun. Where—? Oh, yeah. "I'm parked in Section C. So what's the rest of it?" she asked as they wove between the parked cabs waiting for a fare. "Because you've got the 'don't even try to dominate me' thing down pat, I'd say."

"Glad you noticed. The rest of it . . ." He shook his head, falling silent as they started across the parking area.

Lily let the subject drop. Why was she uncomfortable about being in charge after they crossed? It wasn't just her lack of knowledge. It was . . . guilt, she realized, feeling a little sick. She wasn't sure she should be trusted with their lives. She'd proven she was willing to risk them by roping them into doing this.

There was the way she was healing, too. Or not healing. The burn was better, but she still got so damned tired. She'd been taking naps in the middle of the day, for God's sake. That wasn't normal. If she couldn't—

"Rule has it."

"It?" He'd startled her. "What it?"

"The alpha thing. The part I don't have. So does Benedict. Mick didn't."

The brother who died. "I didn't really know Mick. He was already under Helen's control when we met, so I never had a chance to know the real person."

"The real Mick wasn't the sonofabitch you met, but he was no angel, either. He wanted to be Lu Nuncio. Helen didn't plant that desire. She just used it. Which way?" he asked as the reached Section C.

"Down here." She was almost sure this was the right aisle.

Cullen followed. "Mick convinced himself he'd be better for Nokolai than Rule, but his ambition was really all about what he wanted. Or what he didn't want. He hated the idea of submitting to his younger brother. Isen knew it. That's why he didn't name Mick heir.

"Isen's got it," he went on, seeming to speak to himself as much as her. "He's a ruthless bastard, but he's ruthless on behalf of the clan. Or sometimes for the good of all lupi, everywhere. A true alpha instinctively thinks of the clan first. I don't. I can," he added, with a twitch of a smile. "But it's an effort. With Rule, it's automatic."

Yes, it was. Lily's throat tightened. She nodded, concentrating on not letting her eyes fill. "Here's my car," she said unnecessarily, clicking her remote.

"You've got it, too."

"Me?" She shook her head. "The boss bitch part,

maybe. But I don't have the clan-first instinct. Half the time I forget I am clan."

"That's not what I mean. If you're in charge, you'll think of the group after we cross, not just what you want or need. You won't be able to stop yourself. Just like right now," he said, opening the door and tossing in his bag. "You're wanting to confess. You're afraid you might be willing to spend me to save Rule."

She stared. "And you think that qualifies me to lead?"

He smiled and patted her cheek. "You're proving my point, luv." He climbed in and shut the door.

Baffled, she shook her head went around to her side.

They were in the midst of heavy traffic on I-5 before he spoke again. "I didn't tell you what I went to New Orleans for."

"I noticed," she said dryly.

"I needed to confirm something about Dis I'd read in several references. Not good references, mind you. The only grimoires they didn't burn during the Purge were all but worthless—fiction mixed with fantasy and peppered with a few stray facts, probably by accident. I can't tell you how much nonsense got passed on from one medieval dabbler to another. One asshole would make up something to sound important, and half a dozen others dutifully recorded it."

"Actually, you have told me." Many times.

"Have I?" He glanced at her and then ahead. "That's why I needed to double-check this. The text I wanted is far more reliable than most. It, ah, wasn't available. But I was able to buy a photocopy of the pertinent pages. Cost a pretty penny just for that," he added. "Isen covered it, though."

"I take it this—" Her cell phone rang. "Pass me my phone, would you?"

He dug it out of her purse and handed it to her.

"Yes?" As she listened, her heart began to pound. "Yes. All right. Tell Cynna—no, I'll call her myself. Do you know when they . . . wait, let me get a pen."

But Cullen beat her to it. She repeated the information aloud, and he jotted down the flight numbers.

"Got it," she said. "We'll pick up the one from Canada. As Isen to send someone for the other one, so we can . . . Right. Later."

She disconnected and gave Cullen a tight grin. "You heard?"

His eyes sparked with the same excitement she felt. "The scary old bats are coming."

"Two of them are. Hannah says these are the two who matter. They've got the other pieces of the ritual. They've agreed to share those memories after they arrive, but they have to be present for the ritual."

It was going to happen. They were going to make it happen. "I'm heading for Club Hell. The first one will arrive in three hours. We can talk to Max and then come back to the airport for her."

"He's not going to agree."

"We have to try. Here." She handed him her phone. "See if you can reach Cynna. We need to know when she can return."

A few minutes later she breathed a sigh of relief when Cullen reported his brief conversation with Cynna. She Found the boy—still alive, thank God—and was at the Sacramento airport now, on standby for a flight back.

Her insides humming, Lily started going over her mental lists. What hadn't she done? What hadn't she thought of?

"Lily."

"Hmm?"

"I didn't finish telling you what I learned in New Orleans."

"Oh. Right." It must be important. "What was it, then?"

"There's no moon in Dis."

She waited a beat. When he didn't explain, she said, "And that means—?"

"Rule went there as a wolf. He won't have been able to Change."

She nodded, frowning, still not understanding why he was grave.

"Don't you know anything about us yet? By now he may not be thinking as a man, but as a wolf. He'll still know us, but he might not understand what we tell him." His breath gusted out. "He'll follow you, though. You're his mate, so he'll go through the gate with you."

That wasn't great, but still didn't seem enough to make the bones stand out so sharply in Cullen's too-beautiful face. "What's the rest of it?"

"If he's been in wolf-form too long, he'll have lost the man altogether. He won't be able to Change back."

Her mouth went dry. "It's only been a week. A week and part of a day."

"Here, yes. I've told you that time doesn't pass in other realms at the same rate as it does here. In Dis it's erratic. For Rule, a day may have passed. Or a week . . . or a month. A month," he said gently, "would be too long."

She opened her mouth to argue. She needed to argue. What he said was just stupid. Time didn't behave that way, jumping around all over the place. But when she looked at his grim expression, doubt hit, stealing her certainty and too much of her hope.

So she looked straight ahead. After a moment she repeated her mantra. "He's alive, though. Rule is still alive." This time she could add to it: "And we're going after him."

THIRTY-ONE

AFTER her first sleep in hell, Lily had woken up hungry. Very hungry.

Gan had woken up female.

The demon was less upset at having exchanged one set of genitals for another than at the prospect of suffering periodic bouts of unconsciousness. It—she—had shrugged and said fucking was fucking, and while cocks were great, didn't human females have multiple orgasms? And could Lily tell her how that worked?

Lily had slept twice more since then, each time waking with a terrible craving for ymu. Each time, Gan slept when she did and woke complaining. For each of her sleeps, Rule had slept four or five times. How many days did that make? She didn't know; she'd stopped thinking in those terms. But the light had faded three times now, dissolving slowly into darkness as if someone had the sky on a dimmer switch.

When it did, the dragons sang. And she and Rule sat together and listened. Those were the best times she'd known, when it was just her, Rule, the gathering darkness, and the unearthly beauty of dragonsong.

The light was beginning to fade again, and she was watching from her favorite spot, a flat rock that stuck out over the water. From here she had a view of the open ocean outside their inlet. An illusory freedom, maybe. But it soothed her.

Gan was with her, digging idly in the sand next to the rock. Rule wasn't.

She glanced overhead. It wouldn't be dark for some time. The dimming took a while. But she was worried. "The dragons haven't assembled yet for their song."

"Bunch of noise," Gan muttered.

The demon seemed to have no sense of what music was, much less any appreciation for it. It . . . she . . . had casually mentioned after the last dragonsong that the dragons put a lot of stock in their noisemaking. They called their leaders the Singers.

It was the first Lily had heard that the dragons had leaders. They didn't have anything as formal as a government, a king, or a council, but apparently these Singers had enough authority to negotiate pacts with their demonic neighbors. Gan hadn't known much more than that, though.

She looked at the other end of beach, at the grasses that marked the entrance to their cave. Worry put a pleat in her brow. Rule was in the tunnels again. He hated them. She'd seen him emerge shaking, but he kept going back.

"What?" she said distractedly. She hadn't heard half the demon's chatter.

"I asked what you think you're going to do with your stick. Poke a dragon, maybe? That'll scare them."

"Maybe." She went back to sharpening her spear, fashioned from the femur of a very large animal. Not much of a weapon, but it was all she had. "Or maybe I'll just poke rude little demons with it."

"No, you won't. You'd feel guilty." Gan looked smug. "Humans feel guilty about hurting things."

"Some do. Some don't."

"Well, you would. You're that kind. Besides, you like me."

Lily looked up, amused. "I do?"

"Sure. You won't let the wolf hurt me. He may have stopped trying to kill me, but he still wants to hurt me."

Lily's smile fell away. Twice since her last sleep she'd had to stop Rule from attacking the demon. Gan reveled in baiting him, true, but Rule had been able to ignore the demon's taunts before.

Something had changed, and it worried her.

"And it's not that you're afraid I won't feed you. I'd have to do that no matter how pissed I was, because I can't let you die. Besides," she added, "The dragon told me to keep feeding you. You know that. So you stopped the wolf because you like me."

"And you like me, too, of course."

"I'm a demon! I don't . . ." She frowned. "No, of course I don't. I've never liked anyone. It's like eating dead things. Demons don't do that."

"Demons don't sleep, either."

Gan scowled.

She shouldn't tease Gan. She might have to ask her for a favor. Lily looked down the beach again. This was Rule's first excursion without the splint. Over her objections, he'd chewed off the bindings after waking from his last sleep. And he'd been gone a long time, longer than usual.

She couldn't go looking for him. It was dead dark in those cramped passages, and she couldn't find her way by scent the way he did. The demon's sense of smell wasn't that keen, either, but Gan had an unerring sense of direction, or so she claimed. If Rule didn't show up soon, she'd have to bargain with Gan to . . .

A dark shape limped out of the cave. Her breath gusted out in relief.

The demon flung her piece of bone away. "It's boring here. I can't believe how long it's taking Xitil to finish off her guest."

"Maybe she already has. Would you know?"

"No, but they would." She waved up at the sky, where two of the smaller dragons circled—their guards and occasional waiters, making their breathtaking dives to drop food on the beach.

Living food. Gan ate hers that way. Rule chased and killed his.

She wished she could remember eating. She remembered all sorts of food—ice cream and rice, fried chicken and pickles. But she had no memory of how those things tasted.

"Have they been talking to you?" Lily asked. "They won't mindspeak me." Sam did, when he visited. He was curious about how Earth had changed in the years since his kind left. He and Rule had traded questions.

That is, they had at first. Not so much now. She looked at the dark, four-legged figure headed toward them.

"No," Gan said, "but things would be happening if Xitil had finished her fight. They wouldn't . . . hey, look who's here. Fur-face. Find any good escape routes lately?"

Rule didn't even look at the demon before jumping up on the rock to settle beside Lily. She breathed a sigh of relief. He was controlling himself. "You're limping."

He couldn't shrug, of course, but gave his shoulders a roll that had the same meaning.

He'd obviously understood her. Maybe she'd been imagining things. "Gan thinks it won't be long before Xitil finishes her battle with the goddess."

Rule gave the demon a glance and growled.

"What?" Gan snapped. "Think in words when you growl, stupid, or I don't get any meaning."

Rule yawned, showing how little he thought of the demon's opinion, then gave a few yips.

Gan snorted. "Dumb question. Xitil wouldn't eat a goddess."

Lily frowned. "But the goddess isn't really here, right? Xitil's fighting Her avatar."

"That's almost the same thing. Eating an avatar would be worse than eating a human. She'd go nuts."

Lily nodded. Demons ate almost anything except humans. By eating the flesh they consumed something of the person, and they couldn't absorb a human's substance properly. Gan thought it was the soul that drove them mad, but she was just guessing. Demons no more knew what a soul was than humans did.

But demons could drink human blood. It was the usual route to possession, as well as a potent delicacy or drug. And they wanted Lily's. The blood of a sensitive had some sort of special power here in hell.

Lily had questioned Gan enough to have some idea of what happened to her back on Earth. Gan had knocked her out and brought her to hell to sample her blood because it was more potent here. But then it had returned her to Earth. Blood alone wasn't enough to get past a sensitive's natural defenses. The demon had needed the goddess's help to finish the business. Lily wasn't clear about the details, but the goddess had invested some of Her power in a staff, and someone on Earth had used it to help Gan possess her. It had almost worked.

Rule growled a question at the demon.

Gan rolled her eyes. "I've told you and told you. I don't know why the goddess wanted me to possess Lily. You think we sat down and chatted about Her plans over tea?"

"You're still convinced that we're part of a deal between the dragons and Xitil, though," Lily said. "Sam keeps dodging that question."

"He hasn't denied it. And he could." Gan sighed wistfully. "Because he can lie and all. But what else would he

want us for? Well, he doesn't really want *us,* but he needs
me to feed you. I'm the only one who can do that, because of our bond." She smiled, pleased with her own importance. "And so far the wolf hasn't pissed him off
enough to get himself killed, I guess."

"Why not admit it, though?" Lily asked. "Sam doesn't
have anything to lose."

Rule growled something.

"What did he say?"

Gan shrugged. "I dunno."

"Gan—"

"I don't know! He doesn't trust the dragon. That's all I
picked up."

Forehead furrowed, she stroked Rule's head. Maybe
Gan was just getting tired of translating and was pretending not to understand. "What do you think?" she asked
him softly. *Understand me. Please, please, understand
me.* "Will Sam hand us over to Xitil?"

He looked at her with what she could swear was puzzlement. But then his eyes cleared and he yipped.

"He said there's a lot of demons," Gan said. "Not
many dragons."

"Their position is precarious, you mean."

He nodded.

Okay. It was okay. He'd understood and responded.
"What we really need to know is why my blood would be
so valuable to Xitil." They'd asked Gan about that several
times. The demon insisted she didn't know why the blood
of a sensitive was important, just that it was. "What am I?
One heck of a good bonbon, or does my blood have a
practical value?"

"You're more than a treat," Gan assured her. "You
don't have to worry about that. No one will kill you because then you wouldn't make more blood. But Sam *can't*
be planning to keep you. The others will hear about you,
and sooner or later they'll try to grab you so Xitil doesn't
get you. The dragons won't want that kind of trouble."

Lily was startled. "Are you talking about fighting? War?"

"No, no. Wars are for grabbing territory and giving the nobles a chance to gobble up the other guy's fighters. No one wants war with the dragons because they don't just eat, they kill, so the princes aren't going to . . . hey, look!" She jumped to her feet. "Mealtime!"

Lily looked up. One of their guards was diving at the beach the way they did when they delivered food, but its talons were empty. "That's no food run. Maybe they're playing tag. The second one's chasing the first one. Or is—what?"

Rule had pushed her, hard, with his nose. He whined and shoved at her again, urgently.

He thought they were being attacked. Her pulse rate jumped. Maybe the dragon diving at them was relieving the boredom of guard duty by playing scare-the-human. But if he wasn't . . .

They needed to get under something, quick. She jumped down. So did Rule.

No way could they make it to the cave. She sprinted for the cliff, Rule racing alongside her, Gan huffing a few paces behind. The dragons couldn't grab them from above if they were up against that wall of rock. She flattened her back against it, her heart pounding, her mouth dry, her brain silly with fear. She didn't want to look.

Stupid, she jeered at herself. *Think you can close your eyes and the bad dragon will go away?* She made herself look up and caught a glimpse of scarlet near the head of the pursuing dragon. There was only one of their guards with a frill that color, the same crimson as Sam's.

It was smaller than the one it chased, she realized. Younger?

Then the two collided.

Her breath caught. This was no game, but battle, real and bloody. The two grappled in mid-air, a confusion of flapping wings, snaky necks, and lashing tails. She couldn't see what was happening, who was winning. Then one broke away—the one who'd pursued, she realized, spotting the scarlet frill. Its wings worked desperately to carry it higher—for one wing was damaged. And pursuer had become pursued.

The smaller one tried to dodge, but its attacker caught up with it, seizing one great wing and shredding it viciously. The injured dragon fought free, but it was clumsy now, lumbering through the air. Its attacker closed again.

Slowly at first, then faster, the injured dragon fell, the long body tumbling, tangling with wings that no longer caught air. She caught glimpses of that scarlet frill as it plummeted. Her stomach clenched sickly. It hit up the beach near their cave, and she felt the impact in the soles of her feet.

The winner circled once, then dove again. Toward them.

"Oh, shit," she whispered. Maybe she'd poke a dragon with her big stick, after all.

"There's another one!" Gan piped. "Coming from behind the mountains!"

She squinted, trying to make out details. The sky had darkened enough that it was hard to see the dragons clearly against it, but— "It's Sam!"

Then the high, black shape folded his wings tight to his body and dropped, stooping like a giant hawk after a lesser bird. Aimed like an arrow at the dragon who had just killed.

It must have seen or sensed him, for it twisted, beating its wings frantically—but too late. Seconds later, Sam struck.

Dragons didn't all die silently. This one screamed as its back broke, a bass howl that ended in a great splay of blood as Sam slashed its throat open, both of them still dropping.

That body had little distance to fall. While Sam's wings beat hard, fighting to keep him from finishing his plummet, his victim made a huge splash some twenty feet from shore.

Go, that cool mental voice said as his wings prevailed and Sam began to climb. *Don't gawk. Get to the caves your lupus has been so determinedly exploring.*

"What's happening?" Lily cried.

The others will be here shortly, in case their tool failed. As it did. Satisfaction coated that thought. *I do not tolerate betrayal.*

Rule shoved at Lily. She staggered a few steps, then stopped. "What others? Why are they coming here?"

Sam was still climbing, but slowly, circling his way up. *The Singers. The fools dispute my possession of you. They come to kill you.*

"No!" Gan cried. "They can't kill her! That would be stupid! They need her!"

They have finally understood the folly of allowing a sensitive to fall into Xitil's hands. There will be no more negotiations.

"But the Singers—you were holding me for them!" Lily said. "They're your leaders—"

Not my *leaders. I took you and held you because I wished to. They wished to believe it was on their behalf. I allowed this until I learned that they planned to kill you without asking my permission. Go now.*

Rule shoved her, hard. She gave in and started down the beach at a trot, but called, "What changed? Why do the demons want my blood?"

You will ask questions of Death itself when it stoops for you! Remain underground until I summon you. It may be many sleeps before it is safe to emerge. The Singers will abandon their pique with me soon enough and cease challenging my possession of you. Xitil is coming. She has eaten god-flesh and is quite mad.

"Oh, no," Gan whispered. "Oh no, oh no, oh no . . ."

Mad or not, Sam's chill thoughts continued, growing distant as he rose, *she has too much power now to easily defeat. The others will need me.*

Who are you? Lily thought, stopping at the mouth of

the cave in spite of the insistent press of Rule's body. She knew that once inside, the dragon's mindspeech would be cut off by the earth. *What are you? Not a Singer . . .*

Not one of the little Singers, he agreed, the mental voice faint. *A Great Singer. Perhaps the last of the Great Singers . . .*

THIRTY-TWO

THE next day dawned cool and misty. Lily was sweating beneath her leather jacket anyway. Maybe it was the pack on her back, or the weight of the M-16 slung over her shoulder. Or maybe she was freaking, funked-out, bone-deep scared.

"They're taking forever," Cynna muttered, shifting from foot to foot.

Lily nodded. This was probably when she should say something heartening, but she was fresh out of heartening.

She wished Grandmother was here. Sharp and strong that wish rose in her, foolish as it was. Grandmother couldn't have gone with them. She couldn't have done anything but wait. But still, Lily wished she was here.

They'd assembled their odd crew on a low bluff near the ocean forty miles north of the city. It was private property, part of an estate, but the Rho had somehow arranged for them to be allowed on the grounds. Bribery, probably. It was the closest node to Rule—or where Rule would be, if he'd been on Earth.

Three women and a part-time male stripper held hands

in a circle atop the node. Behind each of them stood a tall black candle, unlit. Dead center in the circle was Hannah's stone altar. It held a silver bowl filled with water.

Lily hadn't been offered the names of the other two Rhejes. The youngest one, the Etorri Rhej, was a slim, ordinary-looking woman about Lily's age, with dirty blond hair and pale blue eyes. Cullen stood between her and the Mondoyo Rhej, a tall black woman with sleepy eyes who looked to be on the high side of forty. She'd arrived a scant few hours ago, having flown in from somewhere in northern Africa. Then there was Hannah—old, fat, sightless, and very much in charge.

Maiden, Mother, and Crone, Lily thought, looking at the three women. Weird. Hannah had said the Lady's workings often fell out that way, even when, as now, her human agents didn't plan it so.

The air was still and moist with ocean smells. Lily and Cynna waited on the ocean side of the node beneath a twisted oak, its trunk leaning perpetually away from the absent wind. On the other side of the node were twenty armed lupi, as many trained Nokolai as Benedict could call upon this quickly. If something did manage to get through the gate despite Cullen's precautions, it would be blasted.

On the other side of the armed lupi, Nettie waited beside a modified SUV that would serve as an ambulance if necessary. With luck, none of them would need Nettie's services, but Lily wasn't about to rely on luck.

Only Lily, Cullen, and Cynna were crossing. The gate would be too small, the power too little, to allow more to pass through. And, of course, they had to take a small enough party that there would be room for one more on their return.

Max could have come. He was small enough to ride through the gate piggyback, but when they finally tracked him down he'd cursed a lot, told them they were idiots, and kicked them out of the club. Max didn't deal well with grief, Cullen said. Lily wasn't sure if that was supposed to be a joke.

Lily stared at the circle, willing them to hurry. So far, all they'd done was hold hands. All that she could see, anyway.

" 'It is easy to go down into hell,' " Cynna murmured. " 'Night and day, the gates of dark Death stand wide . . . ' Guess old Virgil had that wrong, didn't he?"

"What?" Lily's turned to stare at the taller woman. "Virgil? Uh—is that poetry?"

Cynna shrugged the shoulder that didn't hold the strap of an M-16. "I like old poetry."

For an ex-Dizzy, Cynna knew the oddest things.

"Mir acculum," Hannah said suddenly. *"A dondredis mir requiem."*

"A dondredis mir requiem," the tall black woman repeated. The other woman and Cullen echoed the phrase in turn, then they joined voices in a quiet chant.

At last something was happening. This first part of the ritual required all four of them—grooming the energy, Cullen called it. The second stage would be up to him, however. That's when Lily . . .

"Is that a taxi cab?" Cynna asked incredulously.

It was. The cab bumped up the dirt road that led here from the highway, stopping in a flurry of dust where the ruts stopped on the other side of the armed Nokolai. Unable to see clearly past the men, Lily headed that way. Cynna fell into step beside her.

Cullen and the women continued chanting, oblivious. Just as Lily reached the guards, the back door of the taxi swung open. Four feet of bad-tempered ugly climbed out.

Cynna stopped. "What is *that*?"

"That," Lily said, feeling her mouth stretch in a wholly unexpected grin, "is what you'll be carrying through instead of your backpack."

Max possessed ugliness the way a few rare souls possess beauty, an ugliness that fascinated. His nose stretched toward his mouth like a cartoon witch's, as if it had melted, then reformed in mid-drip. He had no hair, not much in the way of chin or lips, and skin the color of mushrooms. He was skinny, with knobby joints and arms too long for his body.

Today he wore camouflage and army boots. God only knew where he'd gotten the outfit.

One of the lupi moved to intercept him. Lily gestured at him to let Max through.

Max was muttering under his breath as he stomped up to Lily. "I can't believe I'm here. I can't believe I'm this stupid. Well?" he demanded, coming to a stop. "What are you staring at?"

"A very welcome sight," she said softly. "Max, this is Cynna."

The tips of his ears turned red. He scowled and looked Cynna up and down. "Nice boobs. Too big, but they're shaped good."

Cynna shook her head and loosened the straps on her pack. "I hope you're worth giving up half our supplies."

"Lily," Cullen said.

She looked over Max's head at him.

He stood alone now, holding a silver athame—a ceremonial knife—in one hand. The three women sat in the grass a few feet away, still chanting softly. The candles were burning.

She took a deep breath and touched the canvas cases hung from her belt that carried extra clips. Show time.

Lily's part in the ritual was passive. From this point on she wasn't to speak, not until she crossed. He would tie the gate to her, as he'd suggested—he'd won that argument— but she need only stand there and let him do it.

That, and bleed a bit.

Lily walked over to him and felt nothing—not a trace, not a whisper of magic, though it must be thick in the air. She closed her mind to that loss and held out her left hand.

He murmured something, the words soft and

foreign. Then he took her hand in his, palm up, and ran the blade of his athame across the heel of her palm. It burned. Blood welled up quickly, and Cullen murmured more words. Then he turned her hand palm down and shook it, sprinkling the earth with her blood as he called out one word three times.

Vertigo seized her, a twisting, scraping otherness that slid inside, settling in her gut and turning her senses crazy. The world spun, and she staggered. Cullen's arm came around her waist, steadying her.

Gradually the world steadied, but the sense of otherness remained. She felt as if some bizarre geometry had been planted in her middle and was busily making itself at home.

She straightened and gave Cullen a nod.

He stepped back. Using the tip of his bloody knife, he began tracing the doorway that would surround the altar. Light followed the athame like the afterglow from a sparkler as he slit the fabric between the realms, and when he finished the air shimmered. It was like looking through heat waves.

Lily put a hand on her stomach. The shimmer somehow matched the shifting geometry in her gut. It wasn't painful, but it wasn't pleasant, either. She looked over her shoulder.

At her glance, Cynna bent her knees and Max climbed aboard. She'd have to duck to get through, but they'd fit. Cullen tucked his athame in his belt and slipped on the harness that held the rocket launcher, a huge tube almost as tall as he was. He picked up his machine gun and took his place at the rear.

They'd go through single-file. Lily gave them all a nod, unslung her M-16, and walked toward the shimmering air. Four paces, duck as she stepped over the alter—and into hell.

Where a battle already raged.

* * *

A small fire smoldered in the center of the rocky chamber Rule had led them to. It was a Swiss–cheese sort of a space, the walls holed in several places, with fissures in the ceiling. Some of the smoke from the fire escaped through those overhead cracks, but the fire still made the room smoky without providing much light.

Better than no light at all, though. Lily hugged her knees. Thank goodness Gan had been able to bring a load of firewood. She was small enough that she hadn't had to crawl the way Lily had in the worst of the passages. Things could be worse.

Who was she kidding? She hated this. Hated it. But not as much as Rule did.

How had he done it? How had he made himself keep coming back to these tunnels, over and over, hunting a way out? She'd known it took a toll on him, but she hadn't understood, not really. Not until she followed him into a darkness so heavy it had seemed to press the air from her lungs.

She had no idea how long it had taken them to reach this chamber, where the air was good and the ceiling was higher than her outstretched hands. Probably not the hours it had seemed. They'd trended more up than down, though. Were they anywhere near the top of the cliff where the dragons gathered to sing?

Gan spoke suddenly, her voice high and scratchy. "Xi-til's called Earth-Mover, you know."

"Does that mean what it sounds like?"

Gan nodded miserably. "She could bring it all down on us. It'd be easy for her."

"Good thing she wants me alive, then."

"But she's nuts," Gan whispered.

Rule lifted his head and snarled.

"I'm pretty sure that means 'shut up,'" Lily said. "Besides, didn't you say dragons damped magic or sucked it up or something?"

"Demon magic, yeah, but Xitil's got goddess stuff in her now! Who knows what that could do? She might be able to—"

"Shut up, Gan."

The demon swallowed and, for a wonder, fell silent.

Rule laid his head on his paws again, and Lily went back to passing the time the only way she could, by playing her memory game. Where was she?

Oh, yeah. Water beds. That had sprung to mind earlier, when she'd been sitting by the ocean. Before things went all to hell.

Waterbeds sounded wonderful. Imagine a bed filled with water . . . how soft would that be? You had to pump the water in. . . . Pumps, yes, she remembered pumps. Though the one she saw in her mind's eye wasn't for water, but for air. For filling up bicycle tires.

Had she ridden a bicycle? She felt a touch of excitement. It made sense that she'd remember the kind of pump she knew best, didn't it? She couldn't picture a pump for a waterbed at all. Maybe she'd never had a waterbed, but she had owned a bicycle.

What kind of bicycle? There were racers and . . .

Rule's head shot up. He almost quivered with sudden tension.

"What is it?" she whispered.

He got to his feet and paced a few steps, looking at the rock overhead, making a whining sound. He looked at her and then at the rocky ceiling. Then he shook his head hard, as if trying to clear it, and whined softly.

"What is it? Gan, what does he mean?"

"Nothing." Gan looked disgusted. "He's not making any sense."

"Rule?" Scared for more than one reason now, she went to kneel beside him. "Are you all right?"

He whined again, louder and longer, and then looked at the demon.

"He wants you to tell me!" she cried. "Try. Try hard."

Gan rolled her eyes. "It's nonsense. Something about you being out there and in here, too."

Rule yipped. Then he took her wrist between his teeth gently and tugged as he took a step away.

He wanted her to come with him. She drew a shaky breath and stood. "All right. Are you coming, Gan?"

Rule immediately trotted into one of the black, black holes. That one was a little roomier than some, at least. Though it probably wouldn't stay that way.

"Follow that idiot? He's lost it. You'd better stay here."

She just shook her head and, heart pounding, followed Rule into the darkness.

THEY wouldn't have survived their first five minutes in hell if the terrain where they came out had matched Earth's. They'd left a flat, low bluff. They came out into low, craggy mountains. Mountains where creatures were busy killing each other, while overhead, legend battled with nightmare.

"I'm running low on ammo," Cynna called. "I have to reload."

"I've got you covered," Lily said. She was hunkered down behind a rocky outcrop. They had no cover over-head, but the aerial battle was a mile behind them now. Just as well. Not only was it dangerous, it was distracting. She'd never thought dragons existed, and to see them fly-ing, fighting . . . she'd remember that always. And have nightmares about what they fought.

If she lived long enough to dream, that is.

Their progress had been halted in this rough pass be-tween two low peaks. *Trapped* might be the word to de-scribe their situation.

Crossing itself had been easy. The shimmer in the air had sort of shimmered through her as she stepped through the gate. Then she'd been elsewhere . . . a dark, nighttime elsewhere, with four man-sized demons standing fifteen feet away, staring at her in obvious shock.

That's what had saved her. That, and the training Benedict had insisted on. Two of the demons had recovered from their surprise fast enough to jump at her even as she swung her weapon at them.

She could testify that bullets did, indeed, work on demons. Especially when sprayed by a semi-automatic rifle. She'd gotten those two. Cynna, coming through right after her, had killed the other two.

After wiping out the small patrol or skirmishers or whatever the hell the first demons had been, they'd been able to advance steadily. Gradually the eerie, blank sky had grown lighter, until now it was about as bright as a stormy day. The visibility had still been lousy, though, when they first reached the pass. Cullen's nose had saved them.

There were more demons holding the pass than there had been in the first group. A lot more. A few were man-shaped, but most were four-legged, built like giant economy-size hyenas, but with small arms growing out of their chests. They had jaws that put Rule's to shame, teeth in rows like a shark's, and glowing red eyes.

She'd killed four of the red-eyes. It had taken Cullen's machine gun, though, to stop the big demon, the one who'd looked like a troll on steroids. He'd just kept coming and coming . . .

She shook her head, throwing off that memory. Later she could have nightmares about it. Right now she badly needed a plan.

The demons were hanging back for the moment, safe on the other side of the pass. The only way forward was single-file through a gap between two enormous boulders.

They had grenades but no way to get close enough to throw one. The same was true with the rocket launcher. They needed a line of sight to use it. Cullen couldn't throw fire at them. There was an odd dampening of magic here that both frustrated and intrigued him; nothing he or Cynna had learned about hell mentioned it. He could still call fire, but couldn't send it—his ability to affect anything with magic fizzled out above five feet from his body.

They didn't know how many demons were left. The red-eyes hadn't given up and wandered off, though. They liked to yell out ideas about what they'd do once they got their teeth on the humans. And she could understand them. Even though they weren't speaking anything she recognized as a language, she understood every nauseating detail.

Cullen was on her right, huddled behind the same rocky outcrop. Cynna was several yards off to her left and slightly ahead. She'd made it to a tall, sheered-off bit of mountain and was crouched behind a boulder.

Lily had known the general direction they had to go, but in this rough terrain there was no such thing as a straight route. Max had found the pass. He claimed he had an instinct for that sort of thing, and she supposed he must. But he'd disappeared after the fighting started.

She was trying not to think about that.

"I'm good to go," Cynna called.

"Right!" Lily barely resisted the urge to say, *Go where?* They were pinned down, unable to get past the red-eyed crowd. So far they'd been able to hold the demons back, but—

"Fire in the hole!" a voice called from above and up ahead.

Max? What —

Grenades were one hell of a lot louder in person than on a movie screen. Max threw three of them. Even after all the rocks stopped falling, Lily couldn't hear a thing.

Cullen rose to a crouch. She could see his lips moving. Nothing. She pointed at her ears and shook her head. He motioned ahead, patted his chest, and started forward.

Hard to command the troops when you can't hear them. But he wasn't stupid enough to march up to the demons if he didn't have a good reason to . . . ah. She heard Max herself now, faintly at first. Then louder.

"Got 'em all, the bloody boogers! Crash, smash, took 'em all out, rained those rocks down on them!"

He was jumping up and down on top of one of the enormous boulders. How in the world had he gotten up there?

Cullen called up to him. "I thought you didn't like guns?"

"Hate 'em! But I love explosions. Boom, crash, smash 'em all down!"

"It was a lovely boom," Cullen said politely. "But are you quite sure you got all of them?"

"Am I stupid? Do I dance around up here if there are some left? There's a couple legs sticking up out of the rubble that are still twitching, but you can shoot 'em as you go by. But, uh . . ." He stopped jumping. "The pass isn't exactly stable. More rocks came down than I expected. Maybe we should hurry."

Good idea. Lily rose, wary still. Cynna joined her. "Lily, I hate to say this, but if the pass is unstable . . . are we going to be able to get back if we cross it?"

Lily wiped the sweat off her forehead with the back of her hand. They'd been a trifle busy since it grew light enough to see their back trail. Lily wasn't surprised Cynna hadn't had a chance to check it out. "Look back," she said quietly.

"What do you . . . oh. Oh, hell."

They'd climbed quite a bit. Rocky slopes spread out behind them. And beyond those slopes—beginning to climb them—were demons. Uncountable numbers of demons. And toward the front of that mass, one very large demon. House-size, maybe . . . if you lived in a three-story house.

They were too far away for Lily to make out exactly

what that one, enormous demon looked like, but she could see enough to be glad she couldn't see more.

"Holy Mary, Mother of God," Cynna whispered. "Even if we turned back this second . . ."

"There's no going back," Cullen said grimly as he rejoined them. "They're already too close to the place we crossed. But the gate's with Lily. She can open it anywhere."

"But . . ." Cynna glanced at Lily and then set her shoulders. "Right. You've got the inflatable raft. If there's ocean on the other side of the gate, we'll be okay."

Lily felt sick. "You had the raft," she said quietly. "That's what was in the backpack I had you leave behind."

Cynna's mouth opened. Closed. She looked ahead, where the dust still hadn't settled from Max's grenades. "Well, the annoying little shit just saved our asses, so I guess you made the right decision. But I sure hope you can come up with a Plan B."

So did Lily. "Come on. Let's take the annoying little shit's advice and hurry." She started walking, going the only direction she could—forward, one step at a time.

THIRTY-THREE

THE widest part of the pass was filled with rubble and body parts. Lily tried not to look. Immediately beyond that it narrowed again and they skidded down a steep slope for about twenty feet. The land leveled abruptly, then, as they rounded a low shoulder of mountain, it opened up.

She stepped out onto a giant-size ledge maybe twelve blocks long and half a block wide. There was grass here, the first she'd seen. Otherwise it was flat, featureless. Beyond it the ground simply ended. Beyond that was the sea.

The ocean didn't look right, reflecting that ugly sky, but it smelled right. Lily paused, letting the breeze fill some of the empty places inside.

But she couldn't pause long. Rule was *close*. Only where—?

Her small troop spread out behind her, looking around as she was. "Where do we go from here?" Cullen asked.

"Maybe one of us should watch the pass," Cynna said. "Try to hold it."

"Ha! You volunteering?" Max shook his head. "Better if we get rid of it. Boom!" He rubbed his hands together, grinning.

"No," Lily said abruptly. "No, we can't go throwing grenades at the mountain. Rule is . . ." She started moving, scanning the blocks of stone that cradled the oversize ledge. "He's there. He's inside it."

The others followed. "Inside?" Cynna said dubiously.

"A cave or something." She was moving faster now, her heart pounding. He was so close, so horribly close. They hadn't brought earth-moving equipment, she thought, halfway to hysterical. They'd never once contemplated what they'd need to remove a few feet of rock. "But he's moving."

"Toward us?"

"No." That came out quick and frustrated. "That way." She gestured at the far end of the ledge, where a tumble of rock blocked them. And started running, as if her feet alone could bridge that last distance, carry her to him in spite of the rock between.

"Max," Cullen said, keeping pace beside her.

"What?" The gnome was huffing slightly as he ran.

"You're supposed to have an instinctive feel for rock. How do we get in, or get him out?"

"I'm working on it."

Lily barely heard them. *Here, he's here—*

And at the far end of the ledge, a huge, dark wolf stepped out from a crevice in the jumble of stone.

Maybe she cried his name. Maybe she just screamed it in her head. Her feet moved without her telling them to. She was running, stumbling over the rough ground—and then someone stepped out behind Rule.

She stepped out. Wearing a dark blue sarong and her token. Rule's necklace, the missing necklace.

Lily stopped dead. She reached out one hand—not to touch, but to push the impossible away. She looked into her own eyes from twenty feet away, saw her own face go pale, and heard herself say softly, "My lost parts. All my lost parts. You have them."

Then her knees buckled.

She didn't faint. Quite. But the next thing she knew was a rough, wet tongue on her face. "Rule." She touched his muzzle, his shoulder, ran her hand over his ribs. "Rule."

"This is beyond weird."

That was Cynna. Lily turned her head slowly, hoping not to see . . . but *she* still stood there, her face blank. A face not exactly like the one Lily had seen in the mirror a million times, because it wasn't reversed.

"Holy shit." That was a high, squeaky voice, vaguely familiar. And yet another person—creature—stepped out from that crevice. "There's two of you!"

A demon. The same small, orange-skinned demon who'd tried to possess her—the one who'd conspired with Harlowe, who'd grabbed her while Harlowe hit her with the staff.

Lily grabbed her weapon on her way back up.

Cynna and Cullen already had theirs aimed. But the other Lily moved fast, too. She stepped in front of the demon. "No! She's—this is Gan. She won't hurt you." She looked at Lily, then at the others, and licked her lips—a nervous gesture Lily had been trying for years to break herself of. "You'd like an explanation."

Cullen answered for all of them, without lowering his machine gun. "That would be good. Be sure to include what the hell you are."

"You know her!" Gan piped up. "She's Lily Yu!" Then, more subdued: "Of course, I guess the other one is, too."

The second Lily sighed. "This may take a while."

Lily glanced back at the pass. "Better make it the *Reader's Digest* version. We don't have much time. There's a war headed this way."

* * *

SHE felt more lost than ever. She'd followed Rule through darkness to find herself—her other self, the one that possessed everything she'd lost. The self who knew Rule in his other form. Knew him as a man.

She tried to keep her story short and coherent, but she was distracted by the sight of her face, her body, sitting on Rule's other side. That woman wasn't her. Maybe they'd started out as one person, but they weren't the same, not anymore.

They were sitting in a rough circle, all of them except the little one—Max—who'd taken a guard position in the rocks where he could watch the pass. At least the others had stopped pointing their guns at her . . . once Rule insisted. He'd gone up to the man—Cullen—and pawed at the muzzle of his machine gun, growling.

Gan had translated that time with no problem: *Put it down, you ass.*

They were all silent for a long moment when she finished. Finally, the other woman asked quietly, "How long do you think you've been here?"

"I don't know. We don't have regular days and nights here. After a while I didn't think about it that way anymore." She glanced at Rule. "He's slept about twenty times, I think. I don't know if that means it's been twenty days."

"Twenty." The other woman didn't sound happy. She kept stroking Rule, touching him. Lily wanted to push that intruding hand away, but . . . she swallowed. Rule wanted that touch. She could tell. He wanted both of them with him. To him, they were both Lily.

It was the other one who knew him from before, though. Who remembered whatever they'd shared on Earth. All he'd shared with her was . . . hell.

"We've got a problem," the other Lily said.

Cullen barked out a laugh. "Never let it be said you don't use understatement, luv."

"I'm talking about the gate. We've got too many people to go back through it."

"A gate." Her heartbeat picked up. Of course. They had to get here, didn't they? They hadn't all been dragged here by some realm-hopping demon, the way she had been. "You have a way back. We can go back."

"We have a small gate," Cullen said. "And, as Lily— one of you Lily's—pointed out, that's a problem. We planned this pretty tightly. If . . ." He stopped abruptly, looking up.

She looked up, too. And stood. "It's Sam!" That huge, winged shape could be no one else.

The others sprang to their feet, too. Cullen swung the long, hollow tube on his back around and onto his shoulder.

Do you shoot at everything you see?

That rocked them. Cullen recovered first. "Around here it seems like a good idea."

There are better targets. Sam began a slow, spiraling descent.

"Don't shoot at him. Sam's on our side . . . sort of." He'd saved her life, anyway, and killed one of his own kind to do it. She suspected that was mostly because of the insult of another dragon daring to dispose of his property, but still . . .

This is most curious. You seem to have connected with the missing half of your soul, but it is embodied.

"I noticed that," she said dryly.

The little demon didn't do that. I wonder . . . He was close now, the wind from his wings stirring her hair. *Yet you are the one with Ishtar's token.*

Cullen stared. "You know about the Lady's token?"

I know a great deal that you short-lives will never dream of. As gracefully as dandelion fluff, that great body drifted to the ground near the cliff's edge. The head swung around to look at them.

"Don't look at his eyes," Cullen said quickly.

An informed short-life. Sam was amused. *And . . . how interesting. You're a sorcerer of sorts.*

"Of sorts?" Cullen said indignantly.

And one of you has a gate. No, I misspoke. One of you is a gate. That is unusual. He settled his wings about him more comfortably. *And useful. I wish to make a deal.*

"Deal quick," the little one called down from his vantage point in the rocks. "They're coming. First wave should be here in fifteen minutes—and that's one fucking big demon coming along about thirty minutes behind it."

Yes. Xitil comes.

LILY couldn't stop glancing at her other self. Her, yet not her. The part with her Gift. The self who'd been with Rule all this time. You'd think she'd feel a tug, a sense of longing, something.

She wanted to knock the bitch's hand away from him.

Lily swallowed. Not now. She couldn't figure out how she could be bitterly jealous of herself—her other self—right now. Somehow she had to get them all out of here. "We'll have to hold the gate open longer."

Cullen shook his head. "Can't, luv. We're too far from a node for me to pull any energy, and there's precious little loose sorcéri around."

"The dragons soak it up," the other Lily said. "That's what Gan says, anyway."

Lily looked at the little demon, huddled unhappily against one of the larger rocks. It didn't say anything. It hardly seemed aware of them at all, tuned in to some private fear. "Plan B, then. Cullen, you'll carry, ah, the other Lily piggyback, and Max can ride Rule through."

There are two problems with that. First, you'll fall a great distance. The land is much higher here than in the earth realm.

She jumped. It was entirely too weird, having the dragon's thoughts just show up in her head. And how did he know what this area was like on Earth? "There will be ocean below us," she said tersely.

A long way below you. The main problem, however, is that your gate won't open.

"It will open." She just had to bleed again and say the word Cullen had taught her.

The dragon's gaze swung toward Cullen. *What happens, sorcerer, when you tie a spell to an object, and another object identical to the first is nearby?*

Cullen scowled. "They aren't identical. Well . . ." He looked from her to the other Lily. "Not entirely. They've had different experiences. They've . . . diverged."

They are one soul. I believe your gate won't open. The dragon's long tail twitched at the end. *But do try it and see for yourself. Unless, perhaps, you know how to check it without opening it?*

Lily pushed impatiently to her feet. Where was Max? "Max! Come down. We're going to get out of here."

The other Lily spoke suddenly. "What do you want, Sam? What deal are you offering?"

I can make the gate bigger. Much bigger. I can hold it open as long as is needed and fly you out. And I know how to solve the problem with the gate.

There was a second's silence, then the other one—the Lily wearing blue—cried, "No! No, there has to be another way!"

Cullen glanced at her and then back at the dragon. "Dragons *are* magic, but can't work it."

Most do not. I, however, am a Great Singer. I know more about gates than you've yet dreamed, sorcerer.

"Except how to open one, it seems. Or you wouldn't be talking about a deal. What do you want in return?"

The great tail lashed in obvious irritation. *Is it not obvious? I wish to leave. I wish to take those of my kind who still live and leave Dis.* Something like a mental sigh whispered along the edges of Lily's mind. *We are losing.*

"This is what you've wanted all along, isn't it?" the

other Lily demanded suddenly. "This is why you captured us. You wanted to leave hell. Only I don't see how you knew they'd come for us."

I didn't. I had . . . another way in mind.

Cullen shook his head. "I'm sorry for your people. But a gate large enough for you to fly through can't be tied to a person. It would destroy her."

For the first time the little demon spoke, its voice wobbly. "But you're a Great Singer. You said they couldn't win without you. How come you aren't winning?"

In her madness, Xitil has been quite clever. She—or the One she ate—made an alliance with the one you know as Tegelgor, lord of the realm to the south. In return for a large number of his lower demons, she has abandoned her region to him. She enters our land with every demon, every imp, every creature from her realm. We cannot fight such numbers.

"Tegelgor!" the demon squeaked. "Abandoned it? No, even crazy she wouldn't . . . *all* her demons? I didn't . . . I wasn't called to her. I felt a tug, but not a summons. She's got all my names. If she wanted me—"

You, too, have diverged, little demon.

What did that mean? Never mind. They were running out of time. "Where's Max, dammit?"

"Wait a minute, Lily." Cullen walked up to her. "I hate to admit it, but the dragon is right about one thing. I should check."

"How?"

He made a graceful gesture with one hand, murmuring something in that liquid language he'd used before, and frowned. Then he turned to the other one, the other her, and repeated it. He lost all of the color in his face. "Hell. The gate's jumping between the two of you. Oscillating."

"Then if we both do it—if we stand together and cut our palms—"

He was shaking his head. "When it's in her, it's stuck in the closed position. She's got your . . . she's a sensitive.

You're the only one who can open the gate, but when it's in her, you can't open it. Your—her—Gift won't let you."

"But if she's close enough to being me for the gate to jump between us, why wouldn't my Gift know me?" she cried. "It *is* me."

Because, as the sorcerer said, you have diverged. A spell, even one wrought by ritual, is a crude working compared to your Gift, Lily Yu. Your Gift recognizes differences between you that the gate cannot.

Her Gift didn't recognize her? She rubbed her forehead. "I'm out of ideas, here."

Then accept some of mine. I will do my best to shield you from—

He broke off in mid-thought. With unbelievable speed for so large a creature, he sprang for the sky. The wind from his wings knocked her down, so in that first second she didn't see what he was springing at.

Then she wished she hadn't.

It was long and red, the color of blood that's not quite dry. It had way too many short legs on the back two-thirds of its wormlike body, every one tipped in claws. And though its body was smaller than the dragon's, its wings were every bit as large, veined like a bat's.

The front third of its body was jaws. Jaws rimmed with teeth like the red-eyes', and when it opened those jaws and screamed, she saw all the way down its gullet.

It had the advantage on the dragon, swooping down at him from above, those jaws gaping. Sam flew straight at it. At the last second, he twisted. His jaws closed on one of those enormous wings and he twisted his neck, shredding the membrane. His wings beat hard, and he started to pull away.

Rule howled. Lily spun around even as he raced past her—raced to where the other Lily was even now turning, staring up at one of the red-eyes perched on a ledge above her, jaw gaping in evil imitation of the fanged worm battling the dragon overhead.

It leaped. And collided with Rule in mid-air.

They fell in a snarling, slashing tangle. Lily raised her weapon, but there was no chance to get a shot in without hitting Rule. She moved closer. Blood sprayed out, spattering her.

Rule's blood. Oh, God, his side—

"Get back!" Cynna shouted.

"You can't shoot! You'll kill him!"

"I'm not using a gun! Move, dammit!"

She looked over her shoulder—and moved quickly away.

Cynna stood just behind her with one arm straight up, the other straight out, pointed at the rolling mass of wolf and demon. Her lips were moving, but Lily couldn't hear her over the snarls and howls. And there was a bloody light streaming from her hand.

It didn't travel like light. The ugly red glow crossed the space between her and the battling animals sluggishly— too slow, too slow! Rule was down—he wasn't moving. Lily pulled her weapon to her shoulder again—

And the light hit. The demon stiffened and fell down dead.

"Sonofabitch," came Cynna's shocked voice. "It worked."

Lily raced to Rule.

So did Lily.

Blood covered his side, so much blood she couldn't see how bad it was. But it was bad. She knew it. His breathing was labored, his eyes closed. She looked up. A shock went through her as she met her own eyes.

"Leave now," the one in blue said. "You have to go right away and take him where he can heal. To a—a hospital." She said the word as if it was new to her. "He'll die here."

"The gate—"

"Sam told me how to fix it."

All at once she knew. Without knowing how, she knew

what the other woman meant. Her mouth went dry. "There has to be another way."

"Funny." Her lips quirked up, but her eyes shone with tears. "That's what I said." She reached up and ripped the chain with its dangling charm from her neck. "There isn't, though. You're the gate."

Slowly—knowing what she was doing, what she was accepting—Lily held out her hand.

And Lily dropped the *toltoi* into it. "Tell him . . ." She looked down and caressed Rule's head. "Tell him how glad I was about him. How very glad."

Lily's fingers closed around the necklace. She could only nod as her throat closed up.

And the other one—the other her—sprang to her feet. She tugged at the top of her sarong, and it came open. "Bind him with this. He's bleeding badly." She tossed it to Lily—and started running. Naked, barefoot, she ran full out.

For the cliff. Straight for the edge of the cliff.

It was the little demon who understood first. "No!" it howled, and started after her, short legs pumping. "No, Lily Yu! Lily Yu, I do like you! I do! Don't—"

She leaped.

Lily felt the air rushing past, air heavy with the scent of ocean. No, she was standing, standing on her feet, tears streaming down—down and down she fell, too far, so far from Rule—

A hammer smashed her, smashed her everywhere at once. And she died.

THIRTY-FOUR

AND blinked her eyes open.

It was Cullen's face she saw first. His arm supported her. "God," he whispered. "Lady above. Why? Why did she . . . and you. Are you—"

"Not . . . all right, no." Her tongue was thick. She swallowed. "The gate will work now."

Now would be good. They are in the pass, waiting for their lord to reach it and widen it. Xitil has grown somewhat stout recently. The dragon settled to the ground near the cliff's edge, but he didn't fully furl his wings.

Then came another voice, small, uncertain—Gan, standing at the edge of the cliff. "I'm alive. She died, and I'm alive. That's not right, is it?" Then, even more softly, "I did like her. I did."

Lily sat up. The *toltoi* was still clutched tight in her hand. She hadn't lost it when she . . . fainted. "Sam, we accept your deal. And I agree. Now is good."

Cynna finished tying the blue cloth around Rule's wounds. "Has anyone seen Max?"

Max turned out to be lying on the ground not far from

the ledge the red-eye had leaped from. He was unconscious, but alive—the red-eye had probably thought it
killed him when it flung him from the rocks. But gnomes
are notoriously difficult to kill.

Two dragons landed. Each took off with a rider and a
patient. First Cullen, who held Rule in front of him, his
blood soaking the indigo cloth that had been Lily's
sarong. Then Cynna, balancing Max's unconscious body
in front of her. Then . . .

"You have to take me!" Gan came running up. "I'll die.
Xitil will kill me slow. She'll pull out my eyeballs and—"
The demon stopped dead in front of her, eyes wide.
"You—you're- . . ." She looked down at her chest, rubbed
it, and looked up at Lily again. "You're Lily Yu," she whis-
pered. "I feel it. The bond. Only it's not the same."

She nodded. "Somehow I am. I'm . . . both. Yes," she
said suddenly. "I'll take you. God help me, if even death
isn't enough to get rid of you, what good would it do to
leave you behind?"

She and Gan climbed on Sam's neck, settling behind
his head. The frill that looked so delicate would serve as
a windbreak of sorts and give her something to grip. This
would be very different, she thought, from dangling from
the talons—and then the thought wisped away, and the
memory that went with it.

That kept happening. She wasn't equally both. One of
her had died . . . or mostly died.

But her Gift was back. Sam's magic thrummed against
her skin when she climbed onto his neck, powerful and
ancient. It should have been totally alien, nothing she'd
ever felt before, yet . . . that must be one of the other's
memories, she decided, holding tight to the bony frill.

They're here. With one huge leap, Sam plunged off the
cliff, stopping her heart—but he spread his wings. Instead of falling and falling, they soared.

Much smoother to ride here instead of in the talons.

Dragons circled in the air around them. A dozen? Two?

"How many of your kind are there, Sam?" she asked.

Twenty-three remain in Dis. The demons killed ten. Once . . . once we were a great deal more than that, but now we are now only twenty-three.

For the first time, real emotion came through with the mental voice. Sorrow, deep and untouchable—and old, very old.

Now, Lily Yu. Open your gate, and I will sing it wide.

She pulled a small pen knife from her pocket. No fancy ritual blades were needed this time. She grimaced and stroked the edge over the scab on her left palm, and she spoke the word of opening.

Those weird geometries shifted, coming awake inside her. The air shimmered in its small rectangle, hovering there, hundreds of feet over the ocean—and the dragon began his song.

Low and deep, the bass so strong she felt it much as she heard it, he sang. Like night had been given a voice, all that was dark and hidden thrummed through her—the cold between the stars and the stars themselves. The space inside her answered—growing, pushing out hard through her, a tumbled vertigo of space, so vast, too vast. The space inside her was bigger than the space outside, and that was impossible, it—

The song changed. Suddenly Sam was in it with her—in his song and in her head, but in her belly, too, where the geometries swelled ever larger, more complex, less real. But Sam's voice swam between her and the madness of inverted space, and Rule's necklace was in her pocket, and death was not quite the absolute she'd always thought.

Her hands held tight to Sam's frill as the first dragon folded its wings and arrowed into the shimmering air. And disappeared.

Rule had crossed. And Cullen. The one bearing Cynna and Max went next, as Sam sang. He sang still while the other dragons aimed themselves into the shimmer, one after another, and still he sang, coating the mad space inside her until all had crossed.

Then, at last, still singing, Sam aimed himself at that shimmer. He dove for it, and she rippled along with it . . .

And they were flying over another ocean, this one inky dark, with moonlight fracturing in silver glints on its waves. The moon—nearly full, and the stars—oh God, how she'd missed them!

Quickly, she said the other word Cullen had taught her. The space inside her popped like a soap bubble, and she was alone in her insides once more.

Mostly.

THERE is no inconspicuous way to land a dragon.

Sam did his best. He gathered his—flock? What do you call a swarm of dragons?—and took them to the bluff Lily and the others had set out from. But they were miles out to sea. Before they reached the shore, some bright soul had scrambled two Air Force fighter jets to pursue them.

They didn't fire, but it made for a tense welcome home.

They had to land one at a time. The bluff wasn't big enough for two dragons to land at once. The one bearing Cullen and Rule went first. As soon as he was down, Cullen passed Rule to one of the lupi—a brave soul, to come running up the way he had—calling out instructions as he jumped from his perch.

Lily couldn't hear him, of course, from so high up, but Sam relayed the gist of it. Cullen's first orders had most of the lupi holstering their weapons. The next brought Nettie running. The last one had someone fumbling for a cell phone so Cullen could call the Air Force and ask them not to fire on the nice dragons.

Sam seemed amused by that.

Cullen was talking on the phone when the second dragon landed, and Cynna and Max climbed down.

Apparently, Max had regained consciousness while several hundred feet in the air. It hadn't exactly sweetened his temper.

Then it was her turn. And Gan's.

What in the world was she going to do with a tame demon? She sure hoped Gan was tame. . . .

Send her to the gnomes. They'll understand her, since they are descended from demons themselves. When a demon catches a soul—

"What?" Gan cried. "What did you say about a soul?"

Lily could have sworn Sam laughed, quietly, in his mind.

They swooped down and down. She had to close her eyes as the ground rushed at them. It was too much like . . .

Lily Yu.

"What?" she shouted over the wind, as if that would make him hear her better.

Say hello to your grandmother for me.

Her grandmother? How did he . . . but they hit the ground then—not hard, but firmly. And all she could think about was getting to Rule. "We'll talk later," she said, swinging her leg over and sliding down. Gan plopped down beside her, and then stood there, scowling around at everyone. "I've got questions."

Why does that not surprise me? Duck.

With no more warning than that, Sam launched himself back into the sky.

Lily looked around quickly, spotted a Nokolai man she knew slightly, grabbed Gan, and thrust her toward him. "Keep an eye on her. She's mostly a demon, but not entirely. Don't shoot her unless you absolutely can't avoid it."

She took off running.

They'd loaded Rule on a stretcher and were carrying him toward Nettie's SUV. She reached him just as they opened the back of the vehicle and stopped, staring.

He was a man again. He'd Changed and was a man again. He was also naked and bloody, with a blood-soaked length of fabric that had once been blue wadded up against the deepest wound.

Of course, she thought. *He had to try. The moon is nearly full and he had to see if he would be able to Change at all—but what a risk, with him so weak from his wounds!*

She missed his fur, the lovely fur she's stroked so often . . . Lily blinked, disoriented, and the memory wisp fled.

He opened his eyes. "Lily?"

"Here," she said, coming up to take his hand. "I'm right here. We're back. We made it back." All the way back. He'd Changed. He hadn't lost himself to the wolf.

"I need to put him in sleep," Nettie said firmly. "And this time, he's going to the hospital. He's lost a lot of blood, and I am not performing surgery in the back of this SUV."

"No, he'll go to the hospital." That's what she'd asked. Get Rule back, get him to the hospital. . . .

"In a minute, Nettie," Rule said. His voice sounded wonderful. Not like he was dying, not at all. He searched her eyes. "I had the strangest dream. A terrible dream. I thought it was real. There were two of you, and one . . . one died."

He'd been unconscious. She'd been sure he was unconscious. "It wasn't a dream, but it wasn't entirely true, either."

"You're . . ."

"Both. I think."

"Enough," Nettie said, and laid her hand on his forehead.

Slowly his expression eased, his eyes drooping. "Yes," he murmured. "That's right. You're Lily."

His hand relaxed, releasing hers, as he slipped into the

healing sleep that was Nettie's Gift. Finally, the knots of tension in her shoulders began to relax.

Maybe it was just that simple. "Yeah," she whispered. "I am, aren't I?"

EPILOGUE

"**At** least think about it." Rule's throat was tight with frustration.

"No." Isen was blunt, as usual. "Not unless you give me some powerful reason to reconsider. Which you haven't."

Oh, but he had. Isen just wouldn't listen. Rule sat on the edge of his damned hospital bed and fought the urge to howl . . . though maybe he shouldn't suppress that particular urge. Maybe his father would believe him then. "The Lu Nuncio must have control." The words came out clipped. "I don't."

Isen waved that away. "It's temporary."

"I Changed!" The words burst out. "Here in the damned hospital, when the moon went full I Changed. I couldn't stop it."

"Hurt like hell, too, I imagine. Good thing you warned Glen ahead of time."

Glen was one of the guards keeping reporters out of Rule's room. Last night he'd had to keep the doctors and nurses out, too, until Rule mustered the will to Change back.

It had taken him a good half hour, and the ache to stay wolf, to feel and smell the world more fully, remained. "That makes it all right, I suppose," Rule said bitterly. "I can't control the Change anymore, but as long as I warn someone—"

"Son."

It was a rare word to hear from his father. Rule stilled.

Isen put his hand on Rule's shoulder. "This is pride speaking. Impatience. Your wolf is stronger than he used to be. So? You'll learn a new balance. It will take time, but I've no doubt you'll be able to do it. You've never disappointed me, not as a father or as a Rho."

Rule had never understood why his father had named him Lu Nuncio instead of Benedict. He understood even less now. He didn't know what to say.

Words didn't come as easily as they used to.

Isen squeezed Rule's shoulder once, then released it. "You'll have help. I hear some of that help coming now."

So did Rule. He turned his head, a smile starting.

The door opened. "How much of that welcome is for me, and how much for the fact that I'm busting you out of here?" Lily asked. But she was smiling, too, and she came to him without waiting for an answer.

As easily as breathing, his hand found hers.

Isen chuckled. "You two don't need me cluttering up the place. I'll see you at Clanhome," he told Rule. "We've a lot to do to get ready for the All-Clan."

"After Nettie releases him for light work, you mean," Lily said.

Isen waved that away. "He's one of the fastest healers in the clans. Nettie won't keep him in bed long—if you don't wear him out once you've got him home." He chuckled at Lily's expression and headed for the door.

But there he paused, looking back at her. "I don't know if I said it, but I'm damned glad to have my heir returned to me. You and Cullen and that other woman did that. I won't thank you. You didn't do it for me, but you should know you have Nokolai's gratitude. And mine. To have my son back . . ." His eyes sheened with sudden tears. He didn't blink them away, and he looked straight at Rule. "There are no words for that. No words."

Rule was too stunned to answer before the door closed behind his father. Slowly, the tightness in his throat eased.

It seemed he wasn't the only one having trouble with words.

"You ready?" Lily asked. "We decided to sneak you out through the kitchen."

"We?" He slid off the bed carefully. Various parts twinged, but those little hurts were drowned out by the protest put out by his side. He put a hand on the bandages there. The demon had ripped him up pretty thoroughly. Nettie had patched things while he was in sleep, but the patched bits hadn't finished growing together yet.

"Here." Lily pushed forward the wheelchair that had been delivered earlier. "The kitchen was Nettie's idea. Getting you away without the bloodsuckers of the press finding out has been a joint project. Your father will let them corner him in the lobby, where he's ostensibly waiting for you. He'll keep them busy while we escape."

Rule scowled at the wheelchair. "I don't need that."

"Humor me. If it was up to me, you'd stay in the hospital another couple days."

"If it was up to me," he started—then stopped, remembering.

He'd argued about remaining in the hospital once Nettie released him from sleep after the surgery. "She wanted you here," Lily had said, her face tense. "I promised her."

"Promised who?" he'd demanded.

"Myself. My other self."

The one he'd attacked a demon to save . . . the one who had then died to save him. Rule knew that in his gut, though Lily—this Lily, who both was and wasn't the one he'd known in hell—hadn't said so. She'd thrown herself away so they could open the gate, but she hadn't done it for the others. She'd done it for him.

This Lily smiled at him crookedly now. "I'm going to use it, you know," she said lightly. "Every chance I get. I'll guilt you right into behaving. Have a seat." She jiggled the wheelchair.

He sat.

But she didn't move right away. Instead he heard her suck in a breath and let it out slowly. "Not that you have anything to feel guilty about. You weren't even conscious. I was the one who let her do it."

Rule couldn't turn. His side wouldn't let him. But he could reach back and cover one of her hands with his. He knew she was carrying a lot of guilt. He didn't understand why, but he'd seen it on her face too often in the last three days.

She started the chair moving. "Did I tell you what Max said about Gan's tail?"

For now, the little demon was staying with Max, who'd accepted his houseguest quite cheerfully after she asked what he knew about multiple orgasms. Gan was supposed to be regrowing her body into a more human form, but so far had refused to give up her tail. "Do I want to know?"

"Probably not. It has to do with what she does with it during sex."

"You'd better tell me, then, or my imagination will drive me into a fever."

She chuckled. As she wheeled him to the staff elevator and they rode down, they talked comfortably enough.

Nettie met them in the basement. "Ready to tour the kitchen?"

Their elaborate maneuvers to avoid the press weren't just for Rule's sake. The reporters had been hounding Lily, making such pests of themselves that she'd given up, packed some clothes and her cat, and moved to Clanhome temporarily.

They weren't after her because she'd been to hell and back. They didn't know about that. Someone at the top of the bureaucratic food chain didn't want the public worrying about hellgates, and the FBI didn't want to lose its only sensitive. They needed Lily too much to prosecute her.

The realms were shifting. Sam had confirmed that when the two of them were trading questions. Earth was drawing closer to both Dis and Faerie, and the modern world was in for a bumpy ride. Lily's boss at the FBI realized this, and had persuaded at least one other person of the truth—the one at the very, very top of the governmental food chain.

So the reporters weren't interested in tales about hell. They wanted to know about the dragons . . . who'd disappeared.

Hard to see how the Air Force could lose twenty-three enormous beasts who, however powerful and beautiful their flight, couldn't outrace a jet. But they had.

Rule dozed most of the way to Clanhome. This tendency to nap at the drop of a hat was annoying, but normal at this stage of healing. He made it inside his father's house on his own two legs, however.

Two legs, not four. That ought to feel a lot more normal than it did.

But it pleased him that Lily had chosen to stay with his father. It was another step toward moving in with him permanently. He still wanted that, though not with the urgency he'd felt before. The fear behind that urgency was gone.

One Lily had risked everything to come after him. The other had died for him. How could he doubt her now?

He let her tuck him up in bed, then patted it. "Sit."

"I should—"

"Probably sleep. You haven't been doing enough of

that, I think." When she didn't answer he said gently, "Bad dreams?"

She nodded and, slowly, sat beside him. "Some. I almost lost you. I did lose you, but she didn't. And then she did."

"She?"

"She, I . . ." She managed a wry smile. "The demons have a point. Souls are confusing."

"It's not easy, being two-natured. It will take time to accustom yourself to it."

"Two-natured?" She was startled.

"It's something like that for you, isn't it? My wolf . . ." He touched his chest. "It's me, yet it isn't. Just as when I was the wolf, the man both was and wasn't me. The body matters."

"Yes! Yes, it does. We're one soul, but the memories aren't . . . it doesn't come out even. She—that part of me—doesn't get to have a turn at a body when the moon's full, like your wolf does. Only sometimes she peeks out of my eyes. On the way to the hospital I saw a bicycle and my eyes filled. I was so amazed by that bicycle, and by the memory of my old Schwinn. Then . . ." She shrugged. "It was gone. I had tears on my face, and I didn't know why."

"The memory game," he murmured. "I'll tell you about it, if you like."

She was silent a moment, looking down at her fingers picking nervously at the comforter she'd tucked around him. "Now I'm doubly jealous. Of you, for knowing her. Of her, for having you when I didn't. And if you think that sounds nuts"—she gave a short laugh—"I won't argue."

"Jealousy isn't rational. I was jealous of Gan."

"Yes, I . . ." Slowly the tension in her face softened into a smile. "I know. I remember." She rubbed her chest as if easing the memory physically into place. "I wish I understood. Even Sam didn't know the other me had a body. How could that happen?"

Rule thought he knew: the Lady. Somehow she'd preserved Lily's sundered self in two bodies—one with the *toltoi*, the other without.

Toward the end of his time in hell, Rule had been mostly instinct. The Lady had reached him through those instincts, prodding him, sending him again and again into those underground passages. When the time came, he'd been ready to lead them to the place the Lady needed them to be.

But not so she cold bring Rule back to Earth, as the others believed. It was Lily that Lady had needed rescued, Lily she had some purpose for. He was sure of that, sure in the same way he'd known he had to keep searching out those dark passages.

He was equally sure Lily wouldn't want to hear that. "Would you do something for me?"

"Yes."

Just that. Just *yes*. "Lie with me awhile. I'm not proposing to disturb Nettie's handiwork," he added quickly, seeing refusal on her face. "I just . . . I want to hold you. For so long I couldn't."

"Oh . . ." she said, her eyes closing. "Oh, I've wanted that."

And a few moments later, with her curled into him, her hair tickling his jaw, her body reminding him of pleasures he couldn't seek yet, and her scent filling him, he did the other thing he'd wanted so much to do while he was wolf. "I love you."

She went still. After a moment she said quietly, "I love you, too. And I . . ." She put her palm on his chest and a smile bloomed on her face. "I am so glad about. So very glad."

THE HAUNTED LANDS

Book I
Unclean

Book II
Undead
March 2008

Book III
Unholy
Early 2009

Anthology
Realms of the Dead
Early 2010

Also by Richard Lee Byers

R.A. Salvatore's War of the Spider Queen
Book I
Dissolution

The Year of Rogue Dragons

Book I
The Rage

Book II
The Rite

Book III
The Ruin

Sembia: Gateway to the Realms

The Halls of Stormweather

Shattered Mask

The Priests

Queen of the Depths

The Rogues

The Black Bouquet

FORGOTTEN REALMS®

The Haunted Lands | Book I

unclean

Richard Lee Byers

The Haunted Land, Book I

UNCLEAN

Cover art by Greg Ruth
Map by Rob Lazzaretti
First Printing: April 2007

9 8 7 6 5 4 3 2 1

ISBN: 978-0-7869-4258-9
620-95924740-001-EN

U.S., CANADA,
ASIA, PACIFIC, & LATIN AMERICA
Wizards of the Coast, Inc.
P.O. Box 707
Renton, WA 98057-0707
+1-800-324-6496

EUROPEAN HEADQUARTERS
Hasbro UK Ltd
Caswell Way
Newport, Gwent NP9 0YH
GREAT BRITAIN
Save this address for your records.

Visit our web site at www.wizards.com

For Janet

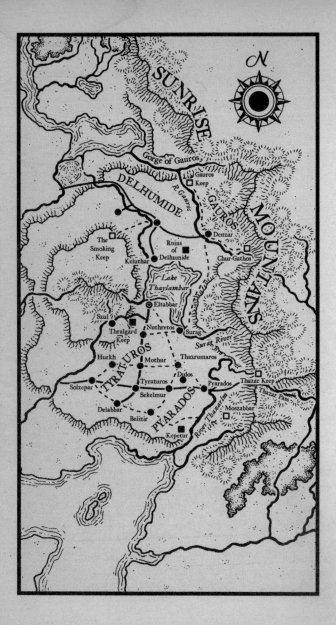

prologue

5 Mirtul, the Year of Risen Elfkin (1375 DR)

Like any wizard worthy of the title, Druxus Rhym could distinguish reality from dream and knew he was experiencing the latter. Thus, when people started screaming, the clamor in no way alarmed him.

It did, however, intrigue him. Perhaps an amusing spectacle lay in store. Maybe the dream even had something to teach him, some portent to reveal. Oneiromancy was a specialty of the Red Wizards of Divination, while he'd devoted the bulk of his studies to the art of Transmutation. But he was a zulkir, the head of his order and so one of the eight rulers of the land of Thay, and no one rose to such eminence without achieving mastery of many forms of magic.

He extricated himself from his tangled silk sheets and fur blanket and rose from his enormous octagonal bed with its velvet canopy and curtains. Magic had kept the air in his apartments warm just as it did in the real world, and when he murmured the proper command, it likewise lit the globular crystal lamps in their golden sconces.

The pulse of light splashed his reflection in the mirror, complete with weak chin and bulge of flab at the waistline of what was otherwise a skinny, stork-legged frame. Reflecting that it seemed unfair a fellow had to be homely even in his dreams, he ambled toward the door and the shrieking beyond. Some of the cries were taking on a choked or rasping quality.

He opened the door to behold eight sentries, four men-at-arms and four wizards, none of whom was any longer capable of guarding anything. Most had collapsed to their knees or onto their bellies, though a couple were still lurching around on their feet. All were melting, flesh, hair, clothing, and armor liquefying, blending, streaming, and dripping down to make multicolored puddles and splatters on the floor. Their screams grew increasingly tortured then fell silent, as mouths, throats, and lungs lost definition.

Her eyes and even their sockets gone, her nose sliding down her chin like molten candle wax, one young wizard extended a buckling arm in mute appeal for succor. Despite his comprehension that none of this was real, Druxus stepped back in reflexive distaste.

Once entirely melted, the puddles that had been the guards began to steam, dispersing their substance into the empty air. At the same time, the walls and ceiling started to dribble and flow. Druxus's forehead tingled and stung, and a viscous wetness slid down over his left eye.

Dream or no, the sensation was repugnant, and he decided to end it. Exerting the trained will of a mage, he told himself to wake, and at once he was back in his bed in his still-dark chamber where, heart thumping, he lay trying to slow his panting.

Strange, he thought, that he should have such a nightmare, and stranger still that it had been so vivid as to actually unsettle him in the end. It almost inclined him to think he ought to take it seriously as a portent or even a warning, but he didn't see how it could be, because he understood the subtext: He'd been dreaming about the book.

The book was nonsense. Or to give it its due, it was a bold and brilliant exercise in arcane theory but of no practical significance whatsoever. Why, then, should it trouble his unconscious mind?

He was still pondering the matter when invisible but powerful hands clamped around his throat.

The crushing grip instantly cut off his air. At the same time, a ghastly chill burned through his body, making his muscles clench and threatening to paralyze him.

He thrust shock aside to focus his will. Reckless foes had tried to assassinate him before, and even when surprised in his bed, he was never unarmed or helpless. The rings on his fingers, the silver-and-obsidian amulet around his neck, and the glyphs tattooed on his body were repositories of magic. He had only to concentrate and one or another of them would infuse his spindly frame with a giant's might, turn his attacker to stone, or whisk him across the realm to a place of safety. He decided on the latter course of action, and then the phantom heaved him up off the feather mattress and bashed his head against a bedpost.

The impact didn't kill him or even knock him unconscious, but it smashed his thoughts into a sort of numb, echoing confusion. The phantom ripped the talisman from around his neck then slammed his head against the obstruction once more.

Something banged. Druxus realized the door had flown open to hit the wall. Voices babbled and footsteps pounded. His guards had heard the sounds of the struggle and were rushing to save him.

Unfortunately, the phantom heard them coming as well. He threw Druxus onto the floor then rattled off an incantation.

Power crackled through the air, and a mote of light flew at the onrushing sentries. When it reached them, it boomed into a sphere of bright yellow fire, exploding with such violence as to tear some of its targets limb from burning limb.

The diversion gave Druxus a final opportunity to use his magic. He strained to focus, to command the proper tattoo to translate him through space, felt the power stir, then his assailant hit or booted him in the jaw. It jolted the stored spell out of his mental grasp.

The phantom continued to pound him until he was thoroughly dazed with agony, until he had no hope of using wizardry or doing anything else. He expected the beating to continue until he died.

After a while it stopped, and he felt a desperate pang of hope. Was it possible his assailant wasn't going to kill him after all?

"I'm sorry for this," the phantom said, his deep, cultured voice now sounding from several paces away, "but it's necessary."

He spoke the same words of power he'd employed before. Another spark flared into being then sprang at Druxus's face.

●● ●● ●● ●● ●● ●● ●● ●● ●● ●● ●● ●● ●●

Armored from head to toe in blue-enameled plate, mounted on a hairless, misshapen, slate gray war-horse infused with the blood and ferocity of some demon-beast from the Abyss, Azhir Kren, tharchion of Gauros, watched with mingled impatience and satisfaction as the combined armies of her province and Surthay waded the river. Impatience because fording a watercourse was always tedious and in theory dangerous: a force was divided and so vulnerable. Satisfaction because the army—a force made up of humans; towering, hyena-faced gnolls; blood orcs with their tusks and piggish features; scaly lizardfolk; and animated skeletons and zombies—made such a brave sight, and because she was confident they'd cross successfully.

Some might have considered her overconfident, for over the years, Thayan armies had often traversed this deep gorge with its maze of secondary canyons in order to invade Rashemen, their neighbor to the north. Thus, the Iron Lord, the witches, and their barbarous ilk surely expected another such incursion to come someday, but not this early in the year when, by rights, the spring thaws should have made the River Gauros too deep and swift to ford.

It wasn't, though. Azhir's wizards had tamed the torrent, though she didn't understand why, if they could do that much, they couldn't dry it up altogether. Still, the important thing was that the legions could cross and do so unmolested. Nobody was on the north side of the river to oppose them.

Laden like pack mules, gray-faced, empty-eyed zombies waded ashore. On the south side of the river, Homen Odesseiron, tharchion of Surthay and Azhir's co-commander, waved a company of blood orcs forward, and the officers relayed the order to their underlings. The bellowing carried easily above the murmur of the river and the babble of soldiers closer at hand and hinted at the terrifying war cries the creatures screamed in battle.

In truth, Azhir didn't particularly enjoy contemplating Homen with his wizard's robes, warrior's sword, lance, destrier, and perpetually dour expression. She didn't dislike him personally—since they were both governors of relatively poor and sparsely settled tharchs, denied a fair portion of the immense wealth and resources of southern Thay, she actually felt a certain kinship—but it vexed her to share command with him when this venture was entirely her idea. She'd had to talk him into it, and it had literally taken years, because the zulkirs didn't know about the expedition, would have forbidden it if they had, and Homen very sensibly feared their displeasure. The mage-lords wouldn't content themselves with discharging tharchions who so exceeded their authority. They'd punish the transgressors as only Red Wizards could.

But only, she was certain, if the invasion failed. If she presented her masters with a victory over the hated barbarians, with wagon-loads of plunder and hundreds of newly captured slaves, perhaps even with Rashemen itself conquered at last, they would surely reward her initiative.

She needed Homen's warriors to ensure such a triumph, so she had to treat him as an equal for the time being. She promised herself she'd find a way to claim the bulk of the credit and the highest honors when the time came.

He looked in her direction, and she dipped the tip of her lance to signal that all was well on her side of the river. Then voices started singing, the music intricate and contrapuntal, the sound high, sweet, and eerie as it resounded from the brown stone canyon walls. Azhir cast about, seeking the source, and arrows began falling from on high, thrumming through the air and thudding into the bodies of her troops.

At last she could see some of the archers, perched on ledges high above her. Perhaps it was no great marvel that they'd managed to conceal themselves until that moment. Rashemi were little better than beasts and possessed an animal's facility for hiding in the wild, but how could they possibly have known Azhir's army would come so early in the year, let alone seek to ford the Gauros at this particular spot?

An arrow slammed into the crest of her helm, jerking her head, and she realized her questions would have to wait. For now, she had a disaster to avert. She bellowed for her troops to shoot back, though her bowmen, loosing their shafts at targets much higher up, half hidden behind makeshift ramparts of piled stone, were going to have a difficult time of it. Meanwhile, Homen sent all the Thayans still on the south shore rushing forward to ford as rapidly as they could and join the fight.

Azhir realized her wizards had yet to join the fray. A few thunderbolts, conjured devils, and blasts of blighting shadow could do wonders to scour the foe from the escarpment overhead. She cast about and saw the warlocks scurrying to form the circles they used to perform rituals in concert.

Idiocy! They didn't need to waste precious moments coordinating to evoke hailstorms and the like. They could do that working individually. She spurred her steed in front of a scrambling wizard, cutting him off from the half-formed circle he was trying to reach. He was one of the scarlet-robed elite, and ordinarily even a tharchion would be well advised to show him a certain deference, but this wasn't an ordinary situation.

"Just hit them!" she shouted, brandishing her lance at the Rashemi.

"Listen!" he replied, his eyes wide. "Don't you hear it?"

Hear what? How was she supposed to hear anything in particular above the cacophony of the battle, the drone of arrows, wounded men screaming, the Rashemi women caterwauling, the blood orcs roaring, but then she did—a rumbling, roaring, crashing noise, growing louder by the moment and sounding from the east.

She realized it wasn't just Rashemi women singing. It was Rashemi *witches*, and chanting together, they'd broken the enchantment that had held the Gauros in check. Now the flood was reasserting itself, and the Thayan mages believed they had to combine forces to subdue the river once again.

Azhir permitted the Red Wizard to rush onward toward his fellows. She then faced the river and screamed, "Get out of the water *now!* Run for whatever shore is closer! Just get out!"

As far as she could tell, no one heeded her. In all likelihood, no one could hear.

That left the wizards as the army's only hope, which, she insisted to herself, should suffice. Thayan magic was the most potent and sophisticated in all Faerûn. Rashemi witches were merely savages with a certain knack for trafficking with petty spirits of forest and field.

But however insignificant their powers, they'd already accomplished their liberation of the flood. That allowed them to harry the Thayan wizards as the latter sought to chain it anew. Emerging from their hiding places on the heights, their faces and bare limbs painted, their hair barbarously long and unbound, the witches conjured enormous hawks and clouds of stinging flies to attack the spellcasters below or made brambles burst forth from the ground to twine around them like serpents. Meanwhile, the Rashemi archers sent many of their shafts streaking at the Thayan warlocks.

It all served to hinder the Red Wizards and their ilk. Some perished or suffered incapacitating wounds. Others felt obliged to forsake their nascent ritual at least long enough to wrap themselves in protective auras of light or scorch masses of swarming insects from existence. Meanwhile, the hiss and roar of the flood grew louder.

Crowned with driftwood and chunks of ice, the white towering wall that was the wave front seemed to burst into view all at once, as if it had leaped up from a hiding place of its own, not hurtled downstream. It was hurtling, though, so swiftly that many of the warriors likely didn't even perceive it until it swept over them, to drown and smash them and carry the corpses away.

It obliterated a significant portion of the Thayan host, split the remainder in two, and left Azhir's part trapped on the wrong side of the river, where the Rashemi were going to massacre them while their comrades watched helplessly.

A number of her wizards had manifestly made the same bleak assessment she had. Some vanished, translating themselves instantaneously through space. Others invested themselves with the power of flight then soared into the air.

Azhir realized she had to reach one of them before they all bolted, so she could compel him to take her with him as he fled. She spurred her hell-steed toward a figure in a red robe, and an arrow punched into the beast's neck, burying itself up to the fletchings. The charger stumbled then toppled sideways.

She kicked her feet out of the stirrups and flung herself clear. She landed hard, her armor clashing, but at least her leg wasn't caught or broken beneath her mount's carcass. She dragged herself to her feet and cast about, trying to locate the Red Wizard once more.

She couldn't find him or anyone else attired in telltale crimson. In fact, now that she was no longer astride a mount, she couldn't discern much of anything. Everything was too chaotic. Panicked Thayan warriors scrambled every which way, without order or rational purpose.

She could hear, though. Somewhere close at hand, Rashemi berserkers howled like wolves, working themselves into frenzy. In a heartbeat or two, they'd burst from hiding and throw themselves at the Thayans, completing the ruin the witches and archers had begun.

I truly am going to die here, Azhir thought. The realization frightened her, but she'd spent a lifetime denying fear and wouldn't go out a craven at the last. Promising herself she'd send at least a few Rashemi vermin to the Hells ahead of her, she pulled her sword from its scabbard.

Then the wind shrieked. Azhir could scarcely feel a breeze, but she perceived that the air must be profoundly agitated overhead, because the Rashemi arrows were veering and tumbling off course.

She caught a glimpse of the half-naked berserkers driving in on the Thayan flank. All at once, ice gathered on the ground beneath their feet and rose here and there in glittering spikes.

The Rashemi warriors slipped and fell, gashing themselves against the protrusions, which were evidently sharp as razors. More ice geysered upward from the central mass, forming itself into a crude, thick-bodied, faceless shape like a statue on which the sculptor had barely begun to work. The giant swung its hand, and the shattered bodies of two barbarians flew through the air.

Rain poured from the empty air to batter the canyon wall, and wherever it pounded one of the Rashemi, flesh blistered and smoked. The enemy made haste to shield themselves or scuttle for cover, which interrupted the witches' barrage of spells.

Then *he* appeared before Azhir, so suddenly she assumed he must have shifted himself through space, but without the ostentatious burst of light, crackle of power, or puff of displaced air that often accompanied such feats. Rather it was as if she'd simply blinked, and at that precise moment, he'd stepped in front of her. Though he could no doubt appear however he liked—and gossip whispered that his true form was ghastly indeed—Szass Tam, zulkir of Necromancy, looked as he always had whenever she'd met him. He was tall and dark of eye, with a wispy black beard and a vermilion robe trimmed with gems and gold. He was gaunt and pale even for a Thayan aristocrat, but even so, he seemed more alive than otherwise. Only his withered hands and the hint of dry rot that occasionally wafted from his person truly attested that he was a lich, a wizard who'd achieved immortality by transforming himself into one of the undead.

She started to kneel, and he caught hold of her arm and held her up. "No time for courtesies," he said. "My magic interrupted the attack, but it will resume in a moment. Get your people moving toward the river."

She stared at him in confusion. "We don't have a way to cross."

"I'm about to remedy that."

He produced a scroll, perhaps plucking it from the empty air, though it was also conceivable that, his shriveled fingers deft as a juggler's, he'd simply drawn it from his voluminous sleeve. He unrolled the vellum, turned to face the Gauros, and spoke the trigger phrase, releasing the magic stored in the parchment.

Three arches of crimson light shimmered into being above the river, spanning it from shore to shore. Bridges, Azhir realized, he built us bridges.

She grabbed the nearest warrior, held him and shouted at him until she made him understand that a means of escape was available. Then she released him to spread the word, even as she continued to do the same.

Perhaps her efforts did a little good, but it was primarily Szass Tam who goaded the Thayan warriors toward salvation. He multiplied himself to appear in a dozen places at once, each version bellowing to all in an amplified voice discernible even over the ambient din.

In less time than Azhir would have imagined possible, they were all scrambling for safety. The smooth, transparent curve of the bridge she chose looked as if it ought to be slippery as glass, but in fact, the surface was sufficiently rough that she had no difficulty negotiating it.

It was only when she was on the south shore, and Szass Tam was dissolving the bridges to forestall pursuit, that she remembered that a death beneath the blades of the Rashemi would have been a merciful fate compared to what the lich was likely to do to her.

•• •• •• •• •• •• •• •• •• •• •• ••

Homen Odesseiron had long ago learned that a battle doesn't end when the fighting stops. He and Azhir had to restore order to their battered and demoralized legions, make sure the healers tended the wounded, withdraw their force to a place of greater safety, and establish a defensible encampment.

It was hectic work, but even so, Homen stole the odd moment to savor the beauty of wisps of white cloud in the bright blue sky and the towering mountainsides with their subtle striations of dun and tan and their trim of fresh spring greenery. He made time because it might well be his final opportunity to enjoy anything.

Soon enough, Szass Tam led the two insubordinate tharchions into a tent—Homen's own green- and white-striped pavilion, as it happened, with his axe-and-boar standard planted before the entrance—to talk in private. Once inside, he kept the governors kneeling for a considerable time. The servants had spread carpets on the ground, but the exercise in humiliation made Homen's knees ache even so. Since Azhir was as old as he and wearing plate to boot, it was probably even more uncomfortable for her. He hoped so anyway.

"I confess," said Szass Tam at last, "I don't recall the council of zulkirs ordering a raid on Rashemen. Perhaps I missed a meeting."

There was a part of Homen that wanted to shout, It was all her idea, reckless, ambitious, hatchet-faced bitch that she is. She pressured me into it. But his pride wouldn't permit him to whine like a frightened child, and it wouldn't have done any good anyway. As governor of Surthay, he had to take responsibility for his own decisions.

"Your Omnipotence," he said, "I exceeded my authority and led my troops into a trap. I'm to blame and will accept whatever punishment you deem appropriate."

Szass Tam smiled. "Are you sure? You've seen the kind of punishments I'm wont to concoct. Get up, both of you. Do you have anything to drink stowed in these trunks? If so, perhaps you could pour us each a cup."

Feeling confused, Homen did as the necromancer had bade him. Szass Tam inhaled the bouquet of the Chessentan red, swished it around, then sipped from his golden goblet with every sign of a connoisseur's appreciation, though Homen wondered if the undead were truly capable of enjoying such pleasures. Perhaps the lich simply drank—and even, on occasion, ate—to appear more normal and so put folk at ease.

"Well," said Szass Tam, "it's clear what the two of you did, but kindly explain why."

"Master," Azhir said, "with respect, surely it's plain enough. I sought to perform great deeds for Thay, to fill her coffers with plunder and extend her borders."

"And to enrich and elevate yourself in the process." Szass Tam raised a shriveled finger. "Please, don't embarrass yourself by denying it. Kept within limits, self-interest is a virtue in a tharchion." His dark eyes shifted to Homen. "I take it you share your co-commander's sentiments?"

"Yes," Homen said. "Your Omnipotence knows that in my youth, I was a Red Wizard of Evocation. I could have remained with my order and enjoyed a privileged, luxurious existence, but the warrior's life called me. I aspired to win great victories on the battlefield."

Szass Tam nodded. "Yet for all your personal prowess and all the might of Thay's legions, you rarely prevailed in a campaign of any consequence."

Homen's face grew warm with emotion. Shame, perhaps. "That's true. Somehow, through the decades, Rashemen and Aglarond withstood us again and again, and now I'm an old man. I didn't want to go to the grave as the failed captain of a humbled realm."

"I understand." Szass Tam took another sip of wine. "But why not ask the zulkirs to authorize your expedition? We could have given you additional troops—"

"By the Black Hand!" Azhir exploded. She must have been utterly unable to contain herself to interrupt a zulkir. He arched an eyebrow, and realizing what she'd done, she blanched.

"It's all right," Szass Tam said. "Complete your thought."

"It's just—" Azhir took a breath. "Master, have I not asked for permission repeatedly over the course of the last several years, and have you not denied me every time? These days, the policy is *trade*"—her tone made the word an obscenity—"not war. All we want is our neighbors' gold, even though we already have plenty, even though the mountains of High Thay are full of it. I remember when we dreamed of ruling Faerûn!"

"As do I," Szass Tam replied.

Homen hesitated then decided that if the lich hadn't struck Azhir dead for her outburst, he might likewise tolerate a somewhat impertinent question. "Master, pardon me if I presume, but you almost sound as if . . . you agree with us? I thought you supported peace and the trade enclaves."

Szass Tam smiled. "There are only eight zulkirs, but our politics, our gambits and maneuverings, are more intricate than any sane outsider could imagine. You should be wary of assuming that all is as it appears, but we can talk more about that later." He shifted his narrow shoulders like a laborer about to set to work. "For now, we must determine how to turn today's debacle into a splendid achievement, a deed meriting a triumphal procession as opposed to pincers and thumbscrews."

Homen reflected that it was strange. By rights, conversation ought to produce enlightenment, but the longer the three of them talked, the more perplexed he felt. "You . . . mean to help us escape the consequences of our folly?"

"It should be easy enough," said the lich. "It's all in how one tells the story, isn't it? How about this: Because the two of you are astute commanders, with scouts and spies cunningly deployed, you discovered that a band of Rashemi intended to invade Thay via the Gorge of Gauros. You marched out to stop them and stop them you did, albeit at a heavy cost. Let all Thay applaud your heroism."

Homen studied Szass Tam's fine-boned, intellectual features, looking for some sign that the necromancer was toying with them, proffering hope only for the amusement of snatching it away once more. As far as he could tell, the undead warlock was in earnest.

"Your Omnipotence," Homen said, "if you show us such mercy, then for the rest of our days, we will serve you above all others."

"That seems fair." Szass Tam saluted them with his cup. "To better times."

chapter one

7–8 Mirtul, the Year of Risen Elfkin

It wouldn't take long for the crew, accomplished sailors all, to moor the cog and run out the gangplank, but Bareris Anskuld was too impatient to wait. He swung his long legs over the rail, and ignoring the shout of the mariner seeking to dissuade him, he jumped for the dock.

It was a fairly long drop and he landed hard, nearly falling before he managed a staggering step to catch himself. But he didn't break anything, and at last, after six long years abroad, he was home in Bezantur once more.

He gave his traveling companions on the ship a grin and a wave. Then he was off, striding up the dock and on through the crowds beyond, picking his way through stacks and cart-loads of goods the stevedores of the busy port were loading or unloading, sword swinging at his hip and silver-stringed yarting slung across his back.

Some folk eyed him speculatively as he tramped by, and

he realized with a flicker of amusement that they took him for some manner of peculiar outlander in a desperate hurry. They had the hurry part right, but he was as Thayan as they were. It was just that during his time abroad, seeking to make his way among folk who were seldom particularly fond of his country-men, he'd abandoned the habit of shaving the wheat blond hair from his head.

He supposed he'd have to take it up again, but not today. Today something infinitely more wonderful demanded his attention.

For all his eagerness, he stopped, stood, and waited respect-fully with everyone else while a pair of Red Wizards and their attendants passed by. Then he was off again and soon left the salt-water-and-fish odor of the harbor behind. Now home smelled as he remembered it, stinking of smoke, garbage, and waste like any great city, but laced with a hint of incense, for Bezantur was Thay's "City of a Thousand Temples," and it was a rare day when the priests of one god or another didn't parade through the streets, chanting their prayers and swinging their censers.

There were no great temples where Bareris was headed. A worshiper would be lucky to happen upon a mean little shrine. He passed through a gate in the high black wall and into the squalid shantytown beyond.

He took the back-alley shortcut he'd used as a boy. It could be dangerous if a fellow looked like he had anything worth steal-ing, and these days, carrying an expensive musical instrument, he supposed he did. But during his travels, he'd faced foes con-siderably more daunting than footpads, and perhaps it showed in the way he moved. At any rate, if there were thieves lurking anywhere around, they suffered him to past unmolested.

A final turn and his destination, just one nondescript shack in a row of equally wretched hovels, came into view. The sight froze him in place for a heartbeat, then he sprinted up the narrow mud street and pounded on the door.

"Open up!" he shouted. "It's Bareris. I'm back!"

After a time that seemed to stretch for a day, a tenday, an eternity, the rickety door creaked open on its leather hinges. On the other side stood Ral Iltazyarra. The simpleton, too, was as Bareris remembered him, doughy of body and face, with a slack mouth and acne studding his brow and neck.

Bareris threw his arms around him. "My friend," he said, "it's good to see you. Where's Tammith?"

Ral began to sob.

•• •• •• •• •• •• •• •• •• •• •• •• ••

The youth was nice-looking in a common sort of way, but he looked up at Dmitra Flass, often called "First Princess of Thay" for the sake of her sharp wits, iron will, and buxom, rose-and-alabaster comeliness, tharchion of Eltabbar and so mistress of the city in which he dwelled, with a mixture of fear and petulance that could scarcely have been less attractive.

"Maybe I did throw a rock," he whined, "but everyone else was throwing them, too."

"Bad luck for you, then, that you're the one who got caught," Dmitra replied. She shifted her gaze to the blood-orc warrior who'd dragged the prisoner before her throne. "Take him to your barracks and tie him to a post. You and your comrades can throw stones at him and see how he likes it. If there's anything left of him at sunset, turn him loose to crawl away."

The boy started to cry and plead. The orc backhanded him across the face then manhandled him out of her presence. Dmitra looked to see who the next prisoner was—in the wake of a riot, administering justice was a time-consuming, tedious business—and Szass Tam appeared in the back of the hall. She had a clear view of the doorway but hadn't seen him enter. Nor had she, Red Wizard of Illusion though she was, felt a pulse of magic. Yet there he was.

And about time, too, she thought. She rose, spread the skirt of her crimson brocade gown, and curtsied. As a mark of special favor, he'd decreed she need no longer kneel to him. Her courtiers and prisoners turned to see whom she was greeting, and they of course hastily abased themselves.

"Rise," said the lich, sauntering toward the dais, the ferule of his ebony staff clicking on the marble floor. "Dmitra, dear, it's obvious you're busy, but I'd appreciate a moment of your time."

"Certainly, Master." She turned to the blood-orc captain. "Lock up the remaining prisoners until—on second thought, no. I refuse to feed them or squander any more of my time on them. Give them ten lashes each and turn them loose." She smiled at Szass Tam. "Shall we talk in the garden?"

"An excellent suggestion." He'd always liked the garden, and the open-air setting made it difficult for anyone to eavesdrop.

Outside, it was a fine sunny afternoon, and the air smelled of verdure. Heedless of the thorns, which evidently couldn't pierce or pain his shriveled fingers, Szass Tam picked a yellow rose and carried it with him as they strolled, occasionally lifting it to his nostrils and inhaling deeply.

"I take it," he said, "that news of poor Druxus's assassination triggered a disturbance in the city."

"The orcs dealt with it."

He smiled. "I wonder if the mob was celebrating the welcome demise of a hated tyrant or expressing its horror at the foul murder of a beloved leader. Perhaps the commoners don't know themselves. Perhaps they simply enjoy throwing rocks and will seize on any excuse."

She shifted her flared skirt to avoid snagging it on a shrub. "I wondered if you were even aware of Druxus's murder. I assumed that if you were, you would have come immediately."

"Is that a hint of reproach I hear in your dulcet voice? I came as soon as it was practical. Believe it or not, matters of consequence sometimes do arise beyond the confines of the capital, and I trusted you to manage here, as you evidently have."

"I managed to keep order. It may take both of us to get to the bottom of Druxus Rhym's murder."

It galled her to admit it. She was proud of the network of spies and covert agents she operated on the lich's and her own behalf, but the affairs of the zulkirs were a difficult and perilous business for any lesser being to investigate.

"What have you learned so far?"

"Precious little. Not long after midnight on the morning of the fifth, someone or something managed to enter Druxus Rhym's apartments undetected. The intruder killed him and his bodyguards with blasts of fire."

"That's certainly enough to suggest a hypothesis. Druxus was well protected against both mundane and mystical threats. It would likely take a master wizard to slip into his bedchamber, a master who then employed evocation magic to accomplish his purpose. Surely the evidence points to Aznar Thrul or one of his particular protégés, acting at his behest."

Perhaps it did. Though relations among the zulkirs were mutable and complex, the council could be viewed as split into two factions, with Mythrellan, zulkir of Illusion, standing aloof from either, and tharchions like Dmitra either tacitly casting their lots with one mage-lord or another or striving assiduously to avoid taking sides. Szass Tam headed up one faction, Druxus Rhym had been his ally, and Aznar Thrul, zulkir of Evocation and tharchion of Priador, was the lich's bitterest rival among the opposition. Thus, it made sense that Aznar might murder Druxus. By so doing, he'd weaken Szass Tam's party and strengthen his own.

Still, it seemed to Dmitra that perhaps because he and Aznar so loathed one another, the usually judicious Szass Tam was jumping to conclusions. "One needn't specialize in evocation to conjure fire," she said. "Many wizards can do it."

"True," said the necromancer. "Still, I'm convinced my conjecture is the most plausible explanation."

"I suppose, and if we can prove it, perhaps we can rid ourselves of Thrul. Even his closest allies might forsake him rather than risk being implicated in his crime."

"The problem is, you won't be able to prove it. Aznar is too able an adept."

"Don't be so sure. With all respect, I don't care if he is a zulkir, with scores of potent spells at his command. Everyone makes mistakes. If he wrote anything down or let slip a careless word where a servant could overhear—"

Szass Tam shook his head. "I know the wretch and I can assure you, he didn't. He's too wily. If there's proof to be had, only magic will uncover it, and Yaphyll's the best person to attend to that." The woman to whom he referred was zulkir of Divination, and with Druxus Rhym slain, his staunchest remaining ally on the council. "I need you to focus your energies on another matter."

"Which is?"

"I've decided Samas Kul should be the new zulkir of Transmutation."

"May I ask why? He's a competent mage, but his order has others more learned."

"And I daresay we can trust them to advance the art of transmutation even if they aren't in charge. What's important is that the new zulkir side with us, and Samas will. Our faction is responsible for the new mercantile policy, and he's grown rich as Waukeen heading up the Guild of Foreign Trade. If we make him a zulkir, he'll have even more reason to support us."

"The election of a new zulkir is an internal matter for the order in question. It won't look well if folk realize we're trying to influence the outcome."

"Which is why the business requires your deft and subtle touch. Samas has the gold to buy support wherever it can be purchased. You and your minions will dig for information we can use to persuade electors not susceptible for bribery, and in general, do whatever you can to shape opinion among the transmuters. Make Samas seem a demigod and his opponents worms. Do you understand?"

She shrugged. "Of course. Bribery, blackmail, and slander, the same game we usually play."

"Excellent. I knew I could count on you." He raised the yellow rose, saw that it had already blackened and withered in his grasp, and with a sigh tossed it away.

•• •• •• •• •• •• •• •• •• •• •• •• ••

The ironbound door was below street level. Bareris bounded down the stone steps and pounded until the hatch set in the center of the panel opened. A bloodshot eye peered out, and its owner said, "What's the password?"

"Silver." Bareris lifted a coin for the doorkeeper to see.

The other man chuckled. "Close enough." A bar scraped as it slid in its mounts, then the door swung open. Bareris tossed the silver piece to the doorkeeper and advanced into the cellar.

The place had a low ceiling and a dirt floor. The flickering light of a scattering of tallow candles, stuck in wall sconces or empty wine bottles in the centers of the tables, sufficed to reveal the gamblers hunched over their cards and dice, the whores waiting to separate the winners from their profits, and the ruffians on hand to keep order and make sure the house received its cut of every wager. The tapers suffused the air with eye-stinging smoke and their stench, which mingled with the stinks of stale beer and vomit.

Bareris cast about until he spotted Borivik Iltazyarra. Tammith and Ral's father was a stocky fellow with a weak mouth and close-set eyes, which were currently squeezed shut as if in prayer. He shook a leather cup, clattering the dice inside, then threw them down on the table. They came up losers, and he cursed and flung the cup down. The croupier raked in the coins.

Bareris started forward then felt just how furious he was. He paused to take a long, deep breath.

It calmed him to a degree, but not enough to keep him from grabbing hold of Borivik's shoulders and tumbling him out of his chair and onto the floor.

The croupier jumped up and snatched for one of the daggers in his braided yellow belt. Another tough came running. Two of the gamblers started to rise.

Bareris sang a succession of rapidly ascending notes in a tone strident as a glaur horn. Power shimmered through the air. The croupier yelped and recoiled, wetness staining his crotch. His fellow ruffian balked, dropped his cudgel, and backed away trembling, empty hands raised to signal that he no longer intended any harm.

Bareris knew the two irate gamblers weren't experiencing any magical terror. He hadn't been able to cast the effect widely enough to engulf everyone, but the display of arcane power evidently made them think better of expressing their displeasure, because they froze then settled back down in their chairs.

Bareris raked the room with his gaze. "Does anyone else want to meddle in my business?" From the way they all refused to meet his eye, it seemed no one did. "Good." He pivoted back around toward Borivik, who was still sprawled on the floor.

"Bareris!" the older man stammered. "My boy! You . . . couldn't do that before."

In point of fact, he couldn't. For as long as Bareris could

remember, he'd possessed a knack for the magic implicit in music, but it was only during his wanderings that it had evolved into a genuinely formidable talent. The ventures he'd undertaken to make his fortune had required that he become a more powerful bard and a stronger swordsman, or else perish.

But he wasn't here to talk about such things. "I saw Ral," he said. "He tried to tell me what happened to Tammith, but he was too upset to make the details clear if he even understands them. You tell me."

Boravik swallowed. "It was all her own idea. I would never even have thought of such a thing."

"Damn you!" Bareris snarled. "Just tell it, or I'll sing the eyes out of your head."

"All right. We . . . owed coin. A lot. To bad people."

"You mean, you owed it."

It was maddening. Boravik was a skilled potter, or at least he had been once. There was no reason he shouldn't have lived a comfortable, prosperous life, but after his wife died bearing Ral, and it became clear the child was simple, he'd taken to drink, and when he drank, he gambled.

"Have it your way," Boravik said with a hint of sullenness. He made a tentative motion as if to rise, waited to see if Bareris would object, then drew himself clumsily to his feet. "I made the wagers, but the White Raven gang was going to hurt all three of us if I didn't pay. You remember what they're like."

"Go on."

"Well, you know Ral can't work. Maybe I could have, but no one will hire me anymore. Tammith did work, but earning a journeyman's wages, she couldn't make enough. Time was running out, and she decided that, to save us all, she needed to . . . sell herself."

"And you went along with it. You let your own daughter become a slave."

"How was I supposed to stop her, when neither of us could think of another answer? Maybe it won't be so bad for her. She's a fine potter. Good as a master, even if she hadn't worked long enough to claim her medallion. Whoever buys her, it will surely be to take advantage of her talents." Or her beauty, Bareris thought and struggled to suppress the images that rose in his imagination. "Maybe her owner will even let her keep a portion of the coin she earns for him. Maybe in time she can buy her free—"

"Stop prattling! Curse you, I promised I'd come home with enough wealth to give Tammith everything she could ever want."

"How were we supposed to know it would be this month or even this year? How were we supposed to know you were still alive, or that you still felt the same way about her?"

"I . . . don't know and it doesn't matter anyway. When did Tammith surrender herself?"

"A tenday ago."

A tenday! It was maddening to think that if Bareris had only bade farewell to his comrades and taken ship a little earlier, he might have arrived soon enough to prevent what had happened.

Yet a tenday was also reason for hope. Thay was a large and populous realm possessed of tens of thousands of slaves, but since Tammith had given up her liberty so recently, it should still be possible to trace her.

"I'm going to find Tammith and bring her home," Bareris said. "You get out of this place and don't come back. Use the coin your daughter gave you to pay the White Ravens and care for Ral, as she intended. If I come back to find you've drunk and gambled it all away, I swear by Milil's harp that I'll cut you to pieces."

The snores and slurred mumblings of the sleeping slaves weren't particularly loud, nor was the smell of their bodies intolerably foul. Lying in the midst of them, Tammith Iltazyarra suspected it was actually fear and sadness keeping her awake. In any case, awake she was, and so she stared up into the dark and wondered how things might have been if she'd spoken her heart six years before:

I don't care if we have coin. You're the only thing I need. Stay in Bezantur and marry me today.

Would Bareris have heeded her?

She'd never know, because she hadn't said it or anything like it. How could she, when she'd perceived what was in his heart? He'd said he needed to go for the sake of their future, and he meant it, but he also *wanted* to go, wanted to see foreign lands and marvels and prove himself a man capable of overcoming uncommon challenges and reaping uncommon rewards.

Maybe that had been because he was of Mulan descent, hence, at least in theory, a scion of the aristocracy. She, a member of the Rashemi underclass, had never had any particular feeling that she was entitled to a better life or that it would prove her unworthy if she failed to achieve it. He might have believed differently, knowing that at one time, his family had been rich and then lost everything.

Well, no, not everything. They'd still possessed their freedom, and with that reflection, dread clutched her even tighter, and sorrow sharpened into abject misery.

She lay helpless in their grip until someone off to her left started to cry. Then, despite her own wretchedness, she rose from her thin, scratchy pallet. The barracoon had high little windows seemingly intended for ventilation more than illumination but enough moonlight leaked in to enable her to pick her way through the gloom without stepping on anyone.

The weeping girl lay on her side, legs drawn up and hands hiding her face. Tammith knelt down beside her, gently but insistently lifted her into a sitting position, and took her in her arms. Her fingers sank into the adolescent's mane of long, oily, unwashed hair.

In Thay, folk of Mulan descent removed all the hair from their heads and often their entire bodies. Rashemi freemen didn't invariably go to the same extremes, but if they chose to retain any growth on their scalps at all, they clipped it short to distinguish themselves from slaves, who were forbidden to cut it.

Soon, Tammith thought, I'll have a hot, heavy, filthy mass of hair just like this, and though that was the least of the trials and humiliations the future likely held in store, for some reason, the realization nearly started her sobbing as well.

Instead she held her sister slave and rubbed her back. "It's all right," she crooned, "it's all right."

"It's not!" the adolescent snarled. She sounded angry but didn't try to extricate herself from Tammith's embrace. "You're new, so you don't know!"

"Someone has been cruel to you," Tammith said, "but perhaps your new master will be kind and wealthy too. Maybe you'll live in a grand house, wear silk, and eat the finest food. Maybe life will be better than it's ever been before."

Even as she spoke them, Tammith knew her words were ridiculous. Few slaves ended up in the sort of circumstances she was describing, and even if you did, how contemptible you'd be if mere creature comforts could console you for the loss of your liberty, but she didn't know what else to say.

Light wavered through the air, and something cracked. Tammith looked around and saw the slave trader standing in the doorway. An older man with a dark-lipped, crooked mouth, he looked odd in his nightclothes and slippers with a blacksnake whip in one hand and a lantern in the other.

She wondered why he'd bothered to come check on his merchandise in the dead of night when he already employed watchmen for the purpose. Then a different sort of man came through the door behind him, and she caught her breath.

chapter two

10 Mirtul, the Year of Risen Elfkin

Despite its minute and deliberate imperfections, the sigil branded on Tsagoth's brow stung and itched, nor could his body's resiliency, which shed most wounds in a matter of moments, ease the discomfort. The blood fiend wished he could raise one of his four clawed hands and rip the mark to shreds, but he knew he must bear it until his mission was complete.

Perhaps it was the displeasure manifest in his red-eyed glare and fang-baring snarl that made all the puny little humans cringe from him—not just the wretches scurrying in the streets of Bezantur, but the youthful, newly minted Red Wizards of Conjuration guarding the gate as well. Tsagoth supposed that in the latter case it must have been. With his huge frame, lupine muzzle, and purple-black scaly hide, he was a monstrosity in the eyes of the average mortal, but no conjuror could earn a crimson robe without trafficking with dozens of entities equally alien to the base material world.

In any case, the doorkeepers were used to watching demons, devils, and elementals, all wearing brands or collars of servitude, come and go on various errands, and they made no effort to bar Tsagoth's entry into their order's chapter house, a castle of sorts with battlements on the roof and four tiled tetrahedral spires jutting from the corners. A good thing, too. He could dimly sense the wards emplaced to smite any spirit reckless enough to try to break or sneak in, and they were potent.

Inside the structure he found high, arched ceilings supported by rows of red marble columns, faded, flaking frescos decorating the walls, and a trace of the brimstone smell that clung to many infernal beings. He tried to look as if he knew where he was going and was engaged in some licit task as he explored.

No one questioned him as he prowled around, and after a time he peered into yet another hall and beheld a prison of sorts, a pentacle defined in red, white, and black mosaic on the floor. The design caged two devils, both displaying the ire of spirits newly snared and enslaved. The kyton with its shroud of crawling bladed chains snarled threats of vengeance. The bezekira, an entity like a lion made of glare and sparks, hurled itself repeatedly at the perimeter of the pentacle, rebounding each time as if it had collided with a solid wall. Judging from their chatter, the two Red Wizards minding the prisoners had made a wager on how many times the hellcat would subject itself to such indignity before giving up.

It wouldn't do for either the warlocks or the devils to spy Tsagoth, not yet, so he dissolved into vapor. Even in that form, he wasn't invisible, but when he put his mind to it, he could be singularly inconspicuous. He floated to the ceiling then over the shiny shaven heads of the Red Wizards. Neither they nor their captives noticed.

Beyond the hall with the mosaic pentacle was a row of conjuration chambers adjacent to a corridor. Three of the rooms were in use, the occupants chanting intricate rhymes to summon additional spirits. One of those chambers was several round-arched doorways removed from the other two, and Tsagoth hoped its relative isolation would keep the warlocks in the other rooms from overhearing anything they shouldn't. Still in mist form, he flowed toward it.

Beyond the arch, a Red Wizard chanted and brandished a ritual dagger in front of another magic circle, this one currently empty and drawn in colored chalk on the floor. Though intent on his magic as any spellcaster needed to be, he had a glowering cast to his expression that suggested he was no happier to be practicing his art than Tsagoth was with his own assignment.

In the wake of Druxus Rhym's assassination, Nevron, zulkir of Conjuration, had directed his underlings to summon spirits to buttress the defenses of himself, Aznar Thrul, and Lauzoril, the third member of their faction. If, as many people believed, Thrul himself had engineered Rhym's death, then it followed that the effort was merely a ruse to divert suspicion, and maybe the fellow flourishing the knife resented being forced to exert himself to no genuine purpose.

Perhaps, Tsagoth thought with a flicker of amusement, he'll thank me for helping him complete his chore quickly. He floated through the arch, over the mage and along the ceiling, then, fast as he could, he streamed down into the center of the pentacle. There he took on solid form once more. His forehead immediately throbbed.

The conjuror stared. A demon was supposed to materialize in the chalk figure, and to superficial appearances, that was exactly what had happened, but it wasn't supposed to manifest until the Red Wizard finished the spell.

"Eenonguk?" he asked.

Tsagoth surmised that was the name of the spirit the warlock had tried to summon, and he was willing to play the part if it would help him complete this phase of his task more easily. "Yes, Master," he replied.

"No," the wizard said. "You're not Eenonguk. Eenonguk is a babau demon." He dropped the athame to clank on the floor and snatched for the wand sheathed on his hip.

Tsagoth hurled himself forward. As he crossed the boundary of the pentacle, his muscles spasmed, and he staggered. But since the warlock hadn't drawn the figure to imprison creatures of his precise nature, it couldn't contain him.

It had delayed him, though. The wand, a length of polished carnelian, had cleared the sheath, and the Red Wizard nearly had it aimed in his direction. The blood fiend sprinted fast as ever in his long existence, closed the distance, and chopped at the conjuror's wrist with the edge of his lower left hand. The blow jolted the rod from the wizard's grasp.

Tsagoth grappled the Red Wizard, bore him down, and crouched on top of him. He gave the wretch a moment to struggle and feel how helpless he was then bared his fangs.

The display made him feel a pang of genuine thirst, for all that the blood of humans was thin and tasteless stuff. Resisting the impulse to feed, he stared into his captive's eyes and stabbed with all his force of will, stabbed into a mind that, he hoped, terror had disordered and rendered vulnerable.

The Red Wizard stopped squirming.

"You will do what I tell you," Tsagoth said. "You will believe what I tell you."

"Yes."

"You meant to summon me here and you did. Afterward, you bound me without incident."

". . . without incident," the mage echoed.

"And now you'll see to it that I'm assigned to the house of Aznar Thrul."

His broad, tattooed hand numbed by all the alcohol he'd already consumed, Aoth Fezim carefully picked up the white ceramic cup and tossed back the clear liquor contained therein. The first few measures had burned going down, but now it was just like drinking water. He supposed his mouth, throat, and guts were numb as well.

His opponent across the table lifted his own cup, then set it down again. He twisted in his chair, doubled over and retched.

Some of the onlookers—those who'd bet on Fezim to win the drinking contest—cheered. Those who'd wagered on his opponent cursed and groaned.

Aoth murmured a charm, and with a tingle, sensation returned to his hands, even as his mind sharpened. It wasn't that he minded being drunk, to the contrary, but it was still relatively early, and he feared passing out and missing all the revelry still to come. Better to sober up now and have the pleasure of drinking himself stupid all over again.

He waved to attract a serving girl's attention and pointed at the length of sausage a fellow soldier was wolfing down. The lass smiled and nodded her understanding, then gave a start when a screech cut through the ambient din. Indeed, the entire tavern fell quiet, even though the cry was nowhere near as frightening as it could be when a person heard it close at hand or could see the creature giving voice to it.

At the same moment, Aoth felt a pang of . . . something. Discomfort? Disquiet?

Whatever it was, nothing could be terribly wrong, could it? After an uneventful flight up the Pass of Thazar, he and Brightwing were properly billeted in the safety of Thazar Keep. He'd seen to his familiar's needs before setting forth in search of his own amusements, and in the unlikely event that anyone was idiot enough to bother her, she was more than capable of scaring the dolt away without any help from her master.

Thus, Aoth was tempted to ignore her cry and the uneasiness that bled across their psychic link, but that wasn't the way to treat one's staunchest friend, especially when she was apt to complain about it for days afterward. Consoling himself with the reflection that even if there was a problem, it would likely only take a moment to sort out, he rose, strapped his falchion across his back, and picked up the long spear that served him as both warrior's lance and wizard's staff. Then, pausing to exchange pleasantries with various acquaintances along the way, he headed for the door.

Outside, the night was clear and chilly, the stars brilliant. The buildings comprising the castle—massive donjons and battlements erected in the days of Thay's wars of independence against Mulhorand, when the vale was still of strategic importance—rose black around him, while the peaks of the Sunrise Mountains loomed over those. He headed for the south bailey, where Brightwing was quartered, well away from the stables. Otherwise, her proximity would have driven the horses mad and put a strain on her discipline as well.

A soldier—tall, lanky, plainly Mulan—came around a corner, and an awkward moment followed as he stared down, waiting for Aoth to give way. The problem, Aoth knew, was that while he claimed Mulan ancestry himself, with his short, blocky frame, he didn't look it, particularly in the dark.

He was easygoing by nature, and there was a time when he might simply have stepped aside, but he'd learned that, looking as he did, he sometimes had to insist on niggling matters of precedence lest he forfeit respect. He summoned a flare of silvery light from the head of his lance to reveal the badges of a rider of the elite Griffon Legion and the intricate tattooing and manifest power of a wizard.

Not a Red Wizard. Probably because the purity of his blood-line was suspect, none of the orders had ever sought to recruit him, but in Thay, any true scholar of magic commanded respect, and the other warrior stammered an apology and scurried out of the way. Aoth gave him a nod and tramped onward.

The masters of Thazar Keep housed visiting griffons in an airy, doorless stone hall that was a vague approximation of the caverns in which the species often laired in the wild. At present, Brightwing—so named because, even as a cub, her feathers had been a lighter shade of gold than average—was the only one in residence. Her tack hung from pegs on the wall, and fragments of broken bone and flecks of bloody flesh and fat—all that remained of the side of beef Aoth had requisitioned for her supper—befouled a shallow trough.

Brightwing herself was nine feet long, with a lion's body and the pinions, forelegs, and head of an eagle. Her tail switched restlessly, and her round scarlet eyes opened wide when her master came into view.

"It's about time," she said.

Her beak and throat weren't made for articulating human speech, and most people wouldn't have understood the clacks and squawks. But thanks to the bond they shared, Aoth had no difficulty.

"It's scarcely been any time at all," he replied. "What ails you?"

"I have a feeling," the griffon said. "Something's moving in the night."

He grinned. "Could you be a little less specific?"

"It's not a joke."

"If you say so." He respected her instincts. Heeding them had saved his life on more than one occasion. Still, at the moment, he suspected, she was simply in a mood. Maybe the beef hadn't been as fresh as it looked. "Is 'something' inside the walls or outside?"

Brightwing cocked her head and took a moment to answer. "Outside, I believe."

"Then who cares? The Sunrise Mountains are full of unpleasant beasts. That's why Tharchion Focar still keeps troops here, to keep them from wandering down the pass and harming folk at the bottom. But if something dangerous is prowling around outside the fortress, that's not an emergency. Somebody can hunt it down in the morning."

"Morning may be too late."

"We aren't even part of the garrison here. We just deliver dispatches, remember? Besides which, there are sentries walking the battlements."

"We can see more than they can and see it sooner. I mean, if you'll consent to move your lazy arse."

"What if I find you more meat? Maybe even horseflesh."

"That would be nice. Later."

Aoth sighed and moved to lift her saddle off the wall. "I could have chosen an ordinary familiar. A nice tabby, toad, or owl that would never have given me a moment's trouble, but no, not me. I wanted something special."

Despite his grumbling and near-certainty that Brightwing was dragging him away from his pleasures on a fool's errand, he had to admit, if only to himself, that once the griffon lashed her wings and carried him into the air, he didn't mind so very much. He loved to fly. Indeed, even though the slight still rankled sometimes, in his secret heart, he was glad the Red Wizards had never come for him. He wasn't made for their viciousness and intrigues. He was born for this, which didn't make the high mountain air any less frigid. He focused his attention on one of the tattoos on his chest, activating its magic. Warmth flowed through his limbs, making him more comfortable.

"Which way?" he asked. "Up the pass?"

"Yes," Brightwing answered. She climbed higher then

wheeled eastward. Below them, quick and swollen with the spring thaw, the Thazarim River hissed and gurgled, reflecting the stars like an obsidian mirror.

The griffon's avian head shifted back and forth, looking for movement on the ground. Aoth peered as well, though his night vision was inferior to hers. He might have enhanced it with an enchantment, except that having no notion this excursion was in the offing, he hadn't prepared that particular spell.

Not that it mattered, for there was nothing to see. "I humored you," he said. "Now let's turn back before all the tavern maids choose other companions for the night."

Brightwing hissed in annoyance. "I know all humans have dull senses, but this is pathetic. Use mine instead."

Employing their psychic link, he did as she'd suggested, and the night brightened around him. Nonetheless, at first he didn't see anything so very different. He certainly smelled it, though, a putrid reek that churned his belly.

"Carrion," he said. "Something big died. Or a lot of little things."

"Maybe." She beat her way onward. He considered pointing out that rotting carcasses didn't constitute a threat to Thazar Keep, then decided that particular sensible observation was no more likely to sway her than any of the others had.

At which point the undead came shambling out of the dark, appearing so suddenly that it was as if a charm of concealment had shrouded them until the griffon and her rider were almost directly over their heads. Hunched, withered ghouls, sunken eyes shining like foxfire in their sockets, loped in the lead. Skeletons with spears and bows came after, and shuffling, lurching corpses bearing axes. Inconstant, translucent figures drifted among the horde as well, some shining like mist in moonlight, others inky shadows all but indistinguishable in the gloom.

Aoth stared in astonishment. Like goblins and kobolds, undead creatures sometimes ventured down from the mountains into the pass, but at worst, five or six of them at a time. There were scores, maybe hundreds, of the vile things advancing below, manifestly united by a common purpose. Just like an army on the march.

"Turn around," the wizard said. "We have to warn the keep."

"Do you really think so," Brightwing answered, "or are you just humoring me?" She dipped one wing, raised the other, and began to wheel. Then something flickered, a blink of blackness against the lesser murk of the night.

Aoth intuited more than truly saw the threat streaking up at them. "Dodge!" he said, and Brightwing veered.

The attack, a jagged streak of shadow erupting from somewhere on the ground, grazed the griffon anyway. Perhaps she'd have fared even worse had it hit her dead on, but as it was, she shrieked and convulsed, plummeting down through the sky for a heart-stopping moment before she spread her wings and arrested her fall.

"Are you all right?" asked Aoth.

"What do you think? It hurt, but I can still fly. What happened?"

"I assume one of those creatures was a sorcerer in life and still remembers some of its magic. Move out before it takes another shot at you."

"Right."

Brightwing turned then cursed. Ragged, mottled sheets of some flexible material floated against the sky like kites carried aloft by the wind. Still relying in part on the griffon's senses, Aoth caught their stink of decay and noticed the subtle, serpentine manner in which they writhed. Though he'd never encountered anything like them before, he assumed they must be undead as well, animated pieces of skin that had taken advantage of Brightwing's momentary incapacity to soar up into the air and bar the way back to the castle.

The skin kites shot forward like a school of predatory fish. Brightwing veered, seeking to keep them from all converging on her at once. Aoth brandished his spear and rattled off an incantation.

A floating wall of violet flame shimmered and hissed into existence. The onrushing skin kites couldn't stop or maneuver quickly enough to avoid it, and the heat seared them as they hurtled through. They emerged burning like paper and floundered spastically as they charred to ash.

Aoth hadn't been able to conjure a barrier large enough to catch them all, and the survivors streaked after him. He destroyed more with a fan-shaped flare of amber flame then impaled one with a thrust of his lance. Meanwhile, twisting, climbing, diving, Brightwing snapped with her beak and slashed with her talons. Another rider might have worried that his mount's natural weapons would prove of little use against an exotic form of undead. Aoth, however, had long ago gifted the griffon with the ability to rend most any foe, even as he'd enhanced her stamina and intelligence.

The kite on the point of his lance stopped writhing, then Brightwing shrieked and lurched in flight. Aoth cast about and saw one of the membranous creatures adhering to her just below the place where her feathers ended. The kite grew larger. Tufts of hair the same color as the griffon's fur sprouted from its surface.

Aoth recited another spell. Darts of emerald light leaped from his fingertips to pierce the leech-like creature, tearing it to bits. Precise as a healer's lancet, the magic didn't harm Brightwing any further, though it couldn't do anything about the raw, bloody patch the kite left in its wake.

Aoth peered and saw other foes rising into the air. By the dark flame, how many of the filthy things could fly? "Go!' he said. "Before they cut us off again!"

Brightwing shot forward. Aoth plucked a scrap of licorice root from one of his pockets, brandished it, recited words of power, and stroked the griffon's neck. Her wings started beating twice as fast as before, and the pursuing phantoms and bat-winged shadows fell behind. He took a last glance at the force on the ground before the darkness swallowed it anew. The undead foot soldiers started to trot as if something—their officers?—were exhorting them to greater speed.

During the skirmish, Aoth had been too hard-pressed to feel much of anything. Now that it was over, he yielded to a shudder of fear and disgust. Like any legionnaire, he was somewhat accustomed to tame or civilized undead. The zulkris' armies incorporated skeleton warriors and even a vampire general or two, but encountering those hadn't prepared him for the palpable malevolence, the sickening sense of the unnatural, emanating from the host now streaming down the pass.

But dread and revulsion were of no practical use, so he shoved them to the back of his mind, the better to monitor Brightwing. As soon as the enchantment of speed wore off, he renewed it. The griffon grunted as power burned through her sinews and nerves once more.

The ramparts of Thazar Keep emerged from the gloom. Using Brightwing's eyes, Aoth cast about until he spotted a gnoll on the wall-walk. The sentry with its hyena head and bristling mane sat on a merlon picking at its fur, its long legs dangling.

"Set down there," said Aoth.

"It isn't big enough," Brightwing answered, but she furled her pinions, swooped, and contrived to land on the wall-walk anyway, albeit with a jolt. More intent on grooming itself than keeping watch, the gnoll hadn't noticed their approach. Startled, it yipped, recoiled, lost its balance, and for a moment looked in danger of falling off the merlon and down the wall. Brightwing caught hold of it with her beak and steadied it.

"Easy!" said Aoth. "I'm a legionnaire, too, but there is trouble coming. Sound your horn."

The gnoll blinked. "What?"

"Sound the alarm! Now! The castle is about to come under attack!"

The gnoll scrambled to its feet and blew a bleating call on its ram's-horn bugle, then repeated it over and over. One or two at a time, warriors stumbled from the various towers and barracks. To Aoth, their response seemed sluggish, as if they couldn't imagine that their quiet posting might experience a genuine emergency. He spotted one fellow carrying a bucket instead of a weapon. The fool evidently assumed that if something was genuinely amiss, it could only be a fire, not an assault.

"Find the castellan," said Aoth, and Brightwing leaped into the air. They discovered the captain, an old man whose tattoos had started to fade and blur, in front of the entrance to his quarters, adjusting the targe on his arm and peering around. Brightwing plunged down in front of him, and he jumped just as the gnoll had.

"Sir!" Aoth saluted with his spear. "There are dozens, maybe hundreds, of undead advancing down the pass. I've seen them. You've got to get your men moving, get them into position on the wall. Priests, too, however many you have in residence."

Bellowing orders, the castellan strode toward a barracks and the soldiers forming up outside. After that, things moved faster. Still, to Aoth, it seemed to take an eternity for everyone to reach his battle station.

But maybe the garrison had made more haste than he credited, for when he next looked up the vale, the undead had yet to appear. He realized the flying entities that had pursued him would certainly have arrived already if they'd continued advancing at maximum speed, but evidently, when it became obvious they couldn't catch him, they'd slowed down so the entire force could move as a unit.

Standing beside him on the wall-walk, squinting against the dark, the castellan growled, "I hope for your sake that this isn't just some drunken . . ." The words caught in his throat as, creeping, gliding, or shuffling silently, the undead emerged from the dark.

"The things in the air are the immediate threat," said Aoth, not because he believed the captain incapable of this elementary tactical insight but to nudge him into action.

"Right you are," the officer rapped. He shouted, "Kill the flyers!"

Bows creaked, and arrows whistled through the air. A priest of Bane shook his fist in its black-enameled gauntlet, and a flare of greenish phosphorescence seared several luminous phantoms from the air. Aoth conjured darting, disembodied sets of shark-like jaws that snapped at wraiths and shadows with their fangs.

Archery and magic both took their toll, but some of the flying undead reached the top of the wall anyway. A gnoll staggered backward and fell to a bone-shattering death with a skin kite plastered to its muzzle. A smallish wraith—the ghost of a little boy, its soft, swollen features rippling as if still resting beneath the water that had drowned the child—reached for a cowering warrior. Brightwing pounced and slashed it to flecks of luminescence with her talons. Aoth felt a chill at his side and pivoted frantically. Almost invisible, just dark against dark, a shadow stood poised to swipe at him. He thrust with his spear and shouted a word of command, expending a measure of the magic stored in the lance to make the attack more potent. His point plunged through the shade's intangible body without resistance, and the thing vanished.

"We're holding them!" someone shouted, his voice shrill with mingled terror and defiance, and so far, he was right.

But charging unopposed while the defenders were intent on their flying comrades, the undead on the ground had reached the foot of the wall. Ghouls climbed upward, their claws finding purchase in the granite. The gate boomed as something strong as a giant sought to batter it down. Walking corpses dug, starting a tunnel, each scoop of a withered, filth-encrusted hand somehow gouging away a prodigious quantity of earth.

Aoth hurled spell after spell. The warriors on the battlements fought like madmen, alternately striking at the phantoms flitting through the air and the snarling, hissing rotten things swarming up from below.

This time it wasn't enough. A dozen ghouls surged up onto the wall-walk all at once. They clawed, bit, and four warriors dropped, either slain or paralyzed by the virulence of their touch. Their courage faltering at last, blundering into one another, nearly knocking one another from the wall in their frantic haste, other soldiers recoiled from the creatures.

Then green light blazed through the air, shining from the Banite cleric's upraised fist. It was a fiercer radiance than he'd conjured before, and though it didn't feel hot to Aoth, it seared the ghouls and the phantoms hovering above the wall from existence.

Indeed, peering around, Aoth saw it had balked the entire assault. Creatures endeavoring to scale the wall lost their grips, fell, and thudded to the ground. Beyond them, other undead cowered, averting their faces from the light. Here and there, one of the mindless lesser ones, a zombie or skeleton, collapsed entirely or crumbled into powder.

Aoth smiled and shook his head. It was astonishing that a cleric in an insignificant outpost like Thazar Keep could exert so much power. Maybe the Banite had been hoarding a talisman of extraordinary potency, or perhaps he had in desperation called out to his deity, and the Black Hand had seen fit to answer with a miracle.

Trembling, his features taut with a mixture of concentration and exultation, the priest stretched his fist even higher. Aoth inferred that he was about to attempt a feat even more difficult than he'd accomplished already. He meant to scour the entire undead horde from existence.

Then his eyes and most of his features shredded into tattered flesh and gore. One of his foes, perhaps the same spellcasting specter or ghoul that had injured Brightwing, had somehow resisted his god-granted power and struck back. The Banite reeled, screamed, and the light of the gauntlet guttered out. The undead hurled themselves forward once more.

At least the priest hurt them, thought Aoth. Maybe I can finish what he started. He started to shout an incantation, and darkness swirled around him like smoke from some filthy confla-gration. Crimson eyes shone toward the top of the thing amid a protrusion of vapor that might conceivably serve it as a head.

He tried to threaten it with his spear and complete his recita-tion simultaneously, but even though he was a battle wizard and had trained himself to articulate his spells with the necessary precision even in adverse circumstances, he stumbled over the next syllables, botching and wasting the magic. Suddenly, he had no air to articulate anything. The spirit had somehow leeched it from the space around him and even his very lungs.

His chest burning, an unaccustomed panic yammering through his mind, he endeavored to hold his breath, or what little he had left of it, and thrust repeatedly with his spear. If the jabs were hurting his attacker—an undead air elemental, did such entities exist?—he couldn't tell. Darkness seethed at the edges of his vision, and he lost his balance and fell to his knees.

Pinions spread for balance, rearing on her hind legs,

Brightwing raked the spirit with her claws and tore at it with her beak. The entity whirled to face her, a movement mainly perceptible by virtue of the rotation of the gleaming eyes in the all but shapeless cloud that was its body, but before it could try stealing her breath, it broke apart into harmless fumes.

Aoth's one desire was to lie where he'd fallen and gasp in breath after breath of air, but his comrades needed the few spells he had left for the casting, so he struggled to his feet and peered around, trying to determine how to exert his powers to their best effect.

To his dismay, he couldn't tell. It didn't appear there was anything anyone could do to turn the tide. There were more undead than live soldiers on the battlements. The diggers had finished their tunnel under the wall, and ghouls and skeletons were streaming though. Everywhere he looked, shriveled, fungus-spotted jaws tore flesh and guzzled spurting blood, and the gossamer-soft but poisonous touch of shadows and ghosts withered all who suffered it. The air was icy cold and stank of rot and gore.

"Go," someone croaked.

Aoth turned then winced to see the castellan swaying and tottering in place. Moments before, the officer had been an aged man but still vital and hardy. Now he looked as senescent and infirm as anyone Aoth had ever seen. His face had dissolved into countless sagging wrinkles, and a milky cataract sealed one eye. His muscles had wasted away, and his clothes and armor hung loose on his spindly frame. His targe was gone, perhaps because he was no longer strong enough to carry it. Aoth could only assume that one of the ghosts had blighted the poor wretch with a strike or grab.

"Go," the captain repeated. "We've lost here. You have to warn the tharchion."

"Yes, sir. Brightwing! We're flying!"

The griffon hissed. Like her master, she didn't relish the idea of running from a fight, even a hopeless one. Still, she crouched, making it easier for him to scramble onto her back, and as soon as he had, she sprang into the air.

As her wings hammered, carrying them higher, another flyer glided in on their flank. With its outstretched bat wings, talons, and curling horns, it somewhat resembled a gargoyle, but it had a whipping serpentine tail and looked as if its body were formed of the same shadowstuff as the night itself. It had no face as such, just a flat triangular space set with a pair of pale eyes blank and round as pearls.

After all that he'd experienced already, Aoth might have believed himself inured to fear, but when he looked into the entity's eyes, his mouth went dry as sand.

He swallowed and drew breath to recite the most potent attack spell he had left, but the apparition waved a contemptuous hand, signaling that he was free to go, then beat its wings and wheeled away.

chapter three

12 Mirtul, the Year of Risen Elfkin

Dmitra believed she possessed a larger and more effective network of spies than anyone else in Thay. Still, she'd found that when one wished to gauge the mood of the mob—and every person of consequence, even a zulkir, was well-advised to keep track of it if he or she wished to remain in power—there was no substitute for doing some spying oneself.

Happily, for a Red Wizard of Illusion, the task was simple. She merely cloaked herself in the appearance of a commoner, slipped out of the palace via one of the secret exits, and wandered the taverns and markets of Eltabbar eavesdropping.

She generally wore the guise of a pretty Rashemi lass. It was less complicated to maintain an effective disguise if appearance didn't differ too radically from the underlying reality. It was easier to carry oneself as the semblance ought to move and speak as it ought to speak. The illusion had an additional advantage as well. When she cared to join a conversation, most men were happy to allow it.

But by the same token, a comely girl roaming around unescorted sometimes attracted male attention of a type she didn't want. It was happening now, as she stood jammed in with the rest of the crowd. A hand brushed her bottom—it *could* have been inadvertent, so she waited—then returned to give her a pinch.

She didn't jerk or whirl around. She turned without haste. It gave her time to whisper a charm.

The leer would have made it easy to identify the lout who'd touched her even if he hadn't been standing directly behind her. He was tall for a commoner, and his overshot chin and protruding lower canines betrayed orcish blood. She stared into his eyes and breathed the final word of her incantation.

The half-orc screamed and blundered backward, flailing at the illusion of nightmarish assailants she'd planted in his mind. The press was such that he inevitably collided with other rough characters, who took exception to the jostling. A burly man carrying a wooden box of carpenter's tools booted the half-orc's legs out from under him then went on kicking and stamping when the oaf hit the ground. Other men clustered around and joined in.

Smiling, hoping they'd cripple or kill the half-orc, Dmitra turned back around to watch the play unfolding atop a stage built of crates at the center of the plaza. The theme was Thay's recent triumph in the Gorge of Gauros. A clash of armies seemed a difficult subject for a dozen ragtag actors to address, but changing their rudimentary costumes quickly and repeatedly as they assumed various roles, they managed to limn the story in broad strokes.

It was no surprise that a troupe of players had turned the battle into a melodrama. Such folk often mined contemporary events for story material, sometimes risking arrest when the results mocked or criticized their betters. What impressed Dmitra was the enthusiasm this particular play engendered.

The audience cheered on the heroic tharchions and legion-naires, booed and hissed the bestial Rashemi, and groaned whenever the latter seemed to gain the upper hand.

Dmitra supposed it was understandable. Thayans had craved a victory over Rashemen for a long time, and perhaps Druxus Rhym's murder made them appreciate it all the more. Even folk who claimed to loathe the zulkirs—and the Black Lord knew, there were many—might secretly welcome a sign that the estab-lished order was still strong and unlikely to dissolve into anarchy anytime soon.

Still, something about the mob's reaction troubled her, even if she couldn't say why.

One of the lead actors ducked behind a curtain. He sprang back out just a moment later, but that had been enough time to doff the bear-claw necklace and long, tangled wig that had marked him as a Rashemi chieftain and don a pink—he couldn't dress in actual red under penalty of law—skull-emblazoned tabard in their place. He flourished his hands as if casting a spell, and the audience cheered even louder than before to see Szass Tam magically materialize on the scene just when it seemed the day was lost.

Dmitra knew the reaction ought to please her, for after all, the lich was her patron. If the rabble loved him, it could only strengthen her own position. Still, her nagging disquiet persisted.

She decided not to linger until the end of the play. She'd assimilated what it had to teach her, and to say the least, the quality of the performance was insufficient to detain her. She made her way through Eltabbar's tangled streets to what appeared to be a derelict cobbler's shop, glanced around to make sure no one was watching, unlocked the door with a word of command, and slipped inside. A concealed trapdoor at the rear of the shop granted access to the tunnels below.

Dmitra reflected that she'd traversed the maze so often, she could probably do it blind. It might even be amusing to try some-time, but not today. Too many matters demanded her attention. She conjured a floating orb of silvery glow to light her way then climbed down the ladder.

In no time at all, she was back in her study, a cozy, unas-suming room enlivened by fragrant, fresh-cut tulips and lilies and the preserved heads of two of her old rivals gazing morosely down from the wall. She dissolved her disguise with a thought, cleaned the muck from her shoes and the hem of her gown with a murmured charm, then waved her hand. The sonorous note of a gong shivered through the air, and a page scurried in to find out what she wanted.

"Get me Malark Springhill," she said.

By marriage, Dmitra was the princess of Mulmaster, even if she didn't spend much time there, or in the company of her husband, for that matter, and she'd imported some of her most useful servants from that distant city-state. Her hope was that their lack of ties to anyone else in Thay would help ensure their loyalty. Despite the fact that he now shaved his head and sported tattoos like a Mulan born, Malark was one of these expatriates. Compactly built with a small wine red birthmark on his chin, he didn't look particularly impressive, certainly not unusually dangerous, until one noticed the deft economy of his movements or the cool calculation in his pale green eyes.

"Tharchion," he said, kneeling.

"Rise," she said, "and tell me how you're getting along."

"We're making progress. One of Samas Kul's opponents has withdrawn from the election. Another is being made to appear petty and inept."

"So Kul will be the next zulkir of Transmutation."

Malark hesitated. "I'm not prepared to promise that as yet. It's not easy manipulating a brotherhood of wizards. Something could still go wrong."

She sighed. "I would have preferred a guarantee. Still, we'll have to trust your agents to complete the work successfully. I have another task for you, one you must undertake unassisted." She told him what it was.

Her orders brought a frown to his face. "May I speak candidly?"

"If you must," she said, her tone grudging.

Actually, she valued his counsel. It had spared her a costly misstep, or provided the solution to a thorny problem, on more than one occasion, but it wouldn't do to permit him or any of her servants to develop an inflated sense of his importance.

"This could be dangerous, not just for me but for both of us."

"I'm sending you because I trust you not to get caught."

"The tharchion knows I'm willing to take risks in pursuit of sensible ends—"

She laughed. "Are you saying I've lost my sense?"

He peered at her as if trying to gauge whether he had in fact given offense. Good. Let him wonder.

"Of course not, High Lady," he said at length, "but I don't understand what you're trying to achieve. Whatever I learn, what will it gain you?"

"I can't say, but knowledge is strength. I became 'First Princess of Thay' by understanding all sorts of things, and I mean to comprehend this as well."

"Then, if I have your leave to withdraw, I'll go and pack my saddlebags."

•• •• •• •• •• •• •• •• •• •• ••

Bareris doggedly jerked the rope, and the brass bell mounted beside the door clanged over and over again. Eventually the door opened partway, revealing a stout man with a coiled whip and a ring of iron keys hanging from his belt. For a moment, his expression seemed welcoming enough, but when he saw who was seeking admittance, it hardened into a glare.

"Go away," he growled, "we're closed."

"I'm sorry to disturb the household," Bareris answered, "but my business can't wait."

It was less than two hundred miles from Bezantur to the city of Tyraturos, but the road snaked up the First Escarpment, an ascending series of sheer cliffs dividing the Thayan lowlands from the central plateau. Bareris had nearly killed a fine horse making as good a time as he had then spent a long, frustrating day trying to locate one particular slave trader in a teeming commercial center he'd never visited before. Having reached his destination at last, he had no intention of meekly going away and returning in the morning. He'd shove his way in if he had to.

But perhaps softer methods would suffice. "How would you like to earn a gold piece?"

"Doing what?"

"The same thing you do during the day. Show me the slaves."

The watchman hesitated. "That's all?"

"Yes."

"Give me the coin."

Bareris handed over the coin. The guard bit it, pocketed it, then led him into the barracoon, a shadowy, echoing place that smelled of unwashed bodies. The bard felt as if he were all but vibrating with impatience. It took an effort to keep from demanding that his guide quicken the pace.

In fact, they reached the long open room where the slaves slept soon enough. The wan yellow light of a single lantern just barely alleviated the gloom. The watchman called for his charges to wake and stand, kicking those who were slow to obey.

Confident of his ability to recognize Tammith even after six years, even in the dark, Bareris scrutinized the women.

Then his guts twisted, because she wasn't here. Tracking her, he'd discovered that since becoming a slave, she'd passed in and out of the custody of multiple owners. The merchant who'd bought her originally had passed her on to a caravan master, a middleman who made his living moving goods inland from the port. He then handed her off to one of the many slave traders of Tyraturos.

Who had obviously sold her in his turn, with Bareris once again arriving too late to buy her out of bondage. He closed his eyes, took a deep breath, and reminded himself he hadn't failed. He simply had to follow the trail a little farther.

He turned toward the watchman. "I'm looking for a particular woman. Her name is Tammith Iltazyarra, and I know you had her here within the past several days, maybe even earlier today. She's young, small, and slim, with bright blue eyes. She hasn't been a slave for very long: Her black hair is still short, and she doesn't have old whip scars on her back. You almost certainly sold her to a buyer who wanted a skilled potter. Or . . . or to someone looking to purchase an uncommonly pretty girl."

The watchman sneered. Maybe he discerned how frantic Bareris was to find Tammith, and as was often the case with bullies, another person's need stirred his contempt.

"Sorry, friend. The wench was never here. I wish she had been. Sounds like I could have had a good time with her before we moved her out."

Bareris felt as if someone had dumped a bucket of icy water over his head. "This is the house of Kanithar Chergoba?"

"Yes," said the guard, "and now that you see your trollop isn't here, I'll show you the way out of it."

Indeed, Bareris could see no reason to linger. He'd evidently deviated from Tammith's trail at some point, though he didn't understand how that was possible. Had someone lied to him along the way, and if so, why? What possible reason could there be?

All he knew was his only option was to backtrack. Too sick at heart to speak, he waved his hand, signaling his willingness for the watchman to conduct him to the exit, and then a realization struck him.

"Wait," he said.

"Why? You've had your look."

"I paid gold for your time. You can spare me a few more moments. I've heard your master is one of the busiest slave traders in the city, and it must be true. This room can house hundreds of slaves, yet I only see a handful."

The watchman shrugged. "Sometimes we sell them off faster than they come in."

"I believe you," Bareris said, "and I suspect your stock is depleted because someone bought a great many slaves at once. That could be why you don't remember Tammith. You never had a reason or a chance to give her any individual attention."

The watchman shook his head. "You're wrong. It's been months since we sold more than two or three at a time."

Bareris studied his face and was somehow certain he was lying, but what did *he* have to gain by dissembling? By the silver harp, had they sold Tammith to a festhall or into some other circumstance so foul that he feared to admit it to a man who obviously cared about her?

The bard struggled to erase any trace of rancor from his features. "Friend, I know I don't look it in these worn, dusty clothes with my hair grown out like an outlander's, but I'm a wealthy man. I have plenty more gold to exchange for the truth, and I give you my word that however much it upsets me, I won't take my anger out on you."

The guard screwed up his features in an almost comical expression of deliberation, then said, "Sorry. The girl wasn't here.

We didn't sell off a bunch of slaves all at once. You're just wrong about everything."

"I doubt it. You paused to consider before you spoke. If you don't have anything to tell me, what was there to think about? You were weighing greed against caution, and caution came out the winner. Well, that's all right. I can appeal to your sense of self-preservation if necessary." With one smooth, sudden, practiced motion intended to demonstrate his facility with a blade, Bareris whipped his sword from its scabbard. The guard jumped back, and a couple of the slaves gasped.

"Are you crazy?" stammered the guard, his hand easing toward the whip on his belt. "You can't murder me just because I didn't tell you what you want to hear!"

"I admit," Bareris replied, advancing with a duelist's catlike steps, "my conscience will trouble me later, but you're standing between me and everything I've wanted for the past six years. Or since I was eight, really. That's enough to make me set aside my scruples. Oh, and snatch for the whip if you must, but in all my wanderings, I never once saw rawhide prevail against steel."

"If you hurt me, the watch will hang you."

"I'll be out of the city before anyone knows you're dead, except these slaves, and I doubt they love you well enough to raise the alarm."

"I'll shout for help."

"It won't arrive in time. I'm almost within sword's reach already."

The watchman whirled and lunged for the door. Bareris sang a quick phrase, sketched an arcane figure in the air with his off hand, and expelled the air from his lungs. Engulfed in a plume of noxious vapor, the guard stumbled and doubled over retching. Holding his breath to avoid a similar reaction, Bareris grabbed the man and pulled him out of the invisible but malodorous fumes. He then dumped the guard on his back, poised his sword at his breast, and waited for his nausea to subside.

When it did, he said, "This is your last chance. Tell me now, or I'll kill you and look for someone else to question. You're not the only lout on the premises."

"All right," said the slaver, "but please, you can't tell anyone who told you. They said we weren't to talk about their business."

"I swear by the Binder and his Hand," Bareris said. "Now who in the name of the Abyss are you talking about?"

"Red Wizards."

At last Bareris understood the watchman's reluctance to divulge the truth. Everyone with even a shred of prudence feared offending members of the scarlet orders. "Tell me exactly what happened."

"They—the mages and their servants—came in the middle of the night, just like you. They bought all the stock we had, just the way you figured. They told Chergoba that if we kept our mouths shut, they'd be back to buy more, but if we prattled about them, they'd know, and return to punish us."

"What were the wizards' names?"

"They didn't say."

"Where did they mean to take the slaves?"

"I don't know."

"Why did they want them?"

"I don't know! They didn't say and we had better sense than to ask. We took their gold and thought ourselves lucky they paid the asking price. But if they'd offered only a pittance, or nothing at all, what could we have done about it?"

Bareris stepped away from the watchman and tossed him another gold piece. "I'll let myself out. Don't tell anyone I was here, or that you told me what you have, and you'll be all right." He started to slide his sword back into its worn leather scabbard then realized there was one more question he should ask. "To which order did the wizards belong?"

"Necromancy, I think. They had black trim on their robes and jewelry in the shapes of skulls and things."

Red Wizards of Necromancy! Bareris pondered the matter as he prowled onward through the dark, for Milil knew, he couldn't make any sense of it.

It was the most ordinary thing in the world for wealthy folk to buy slaves, but why in the middle of the night? Why the secrecy?

It suggested there was something illicit about the transaction or the purchasers' intent, but how could there be? By law, slaves were property, with no rights whatsoever. Even commoners could buy, sell, exploit, and abuse them however they chose, and Red Wizards were Thay's ruling elite, answerable to no one but their superiors.

Bareris sighed. Maybe the watchman was right; maybe it was something ordinary folk were better off not understanding. After all, his objective hadn't changed. He simply wanted to find Tammith.

Evidently hoping to avoid notice, the necromancers had marched her and the other slaves away under cover of darkness, but someone had seen where they went. A whore. A drunk. A beggar. A cutpurse. One of the night people who dwell in every city.

Exhausted as he was, eyes burning, an acid taste searing his mouth, Bareris cringed at the prospect of commencing yet another search, this one through squalid stews and taverns, yet he could no more have slept than he could have sung Selûne down from the sky. He arranged his features into a smile and headed for a painted, half-clad woman lounging in a doorway.

•• •• •• •• •• •• •• •• •• •• •• •• ••

The fighter was beaten but too stubborn to admit it, as he demonstrated by struggling back onto his feet.

Calmevik grinned. If the smaller pugilist wanted more punishment, he was happy to oblige. He lowered his guard and stepped in, inviting his opponent to swing. Dazed, the other fighter responded with slow, clumsy haymakers, easily dodged. The spectators laughed when Calmevik ducked and twisted out of the way.

It was amusing to make his adversary reel and stumble uselessly around, but Calmevik couldn't continue the game for long. The urge to beat and break the other man was too powerful. He froze him with a punch to the solar plexus, shifted in, and drove an elbow strike into his jaw. Bone crunched. Calmevik then hooked his opponent's leg with his own, grabbed the back of his head, and smashed him face first to the plank floor where he lay inert, blood seeping out from around his head like the petals of a flower.

The onlookers cheered. Calmevik laughed and raised his fists, acknowledging their acclaim, feeling strong, dauntless, invincible—

Then he spotted the child, if that was the right word for it, peeking in the tavern doorway, one puffy, pasty hand pushing the bead curtain aside, the hood of its shabby cloak shadowing its features. The creature had the frame of a little girl and he was the biggest man in the tavern, indeed, one of the biggest in all Tyraturos, and he had no reason to believe the newcomer meant him any harm. Still, when it crooked its finger, his elation gave way to a pang of trepidation.

Had he known what it would involve, he never would have taken the job, no matter how good the pay, but he hadn't, and now he was stuck taking orders from the ghastly representative his client had left behind. There was nothing to do but finish the chore, pocket the coin, and hope that in time he'd stop dreaming about the child's face.

Striving to make sure no one could tell he was rattled, he made his excuses to his sycophants, pulled on his tunic, belted on his broadsword and dirks, and departed the tavern. Presumably because it was the way in which an adult and little girl might be expected to walk the benighted streets, the child intertwined its soft, clammy fingers with his. He had to fight to keep himself from wrenching his hand away.

"He's here," she said in a high, lisping voice.

Calmevik wondered who "he" was and what he'd done to deserve the fate that was about to overtake him, but no one had volunteered the information, and he suspected he was safer not knowing. "Just one man?"

"Yes."

"I won't need help, then." Which meant he wouldn't have to share the gold.

"Are you sure? My master doesn't want any mistakes."

She might be a horror loathsome enough to turn his bowels to water, but even so, professional pride demanded that he respond to her doubts with the hauteur they deserved. "Of course I'm sure! Aren't I the deadliest assassin in the city?"

She giggled. "You say so, and I am what I am, so I suppose we can kill one bard by ourselves."

•• •• •• •• •• •• •• •• •• •• •• •• •• ••

Tired as he was, for a moment Bareris wasn't certain he was actually hearing the crying or only imagining it. But it was real. Somewhere down the crooked alleyway, someone—a little girl, perhaps, by the sound of it—was sobbing.

He thought of simply walking on. After all, it was none of his affair. He had his own problems, but he'd feel callous and mean if he ignored a child's distress.

Besides, if he helped someone else in need, maybe help would come to him in turn. He realized it was scarcely a Thayan way to think. His countrymen believed the gods sent luck to the strong and resolute, not the gentle and compassionate, but some of the friends he'd found on his travels believed such superstitions.

He started down the alley. By the harp, it was dark, without a trace of candlelight leaking through doors or windows, and the high, peaked rooftops blocking all but a few of the stars. He sang a floating orb of silvery glow into being to light his way.

Even then, it was difficult to make out the little girl. Slumped in her dark cloak at the end of the cul-de-sac, she was just one small shadow amid the gloom. Her shoulders shook as she wept.

"Little girl," Bareris said, "are you lost? Whatever's wrong, I'll help you."

The child didn't respond, just kept on crying.

She must be utterly distraught. He walked to her, dropped to one knee, and laid a hand on one of her heaving shoulders.

Even through the wool of her cloak, her body felt cold, and more than that, wrong in some indefinable but noisome way. Moreover, a stink hung in the air around her.

Surprise made him falter, and in that instant, she—or rather, it—whirled to face him. Its puffy face was ashen, its eyes, black and sunken. Pus and foam oozed around the stained, crooked teeth in their rotting gums.

Its grip tight as a full-grown man's, the creature grabbed hold of Bareris's extended arm, snapped its teeth shut on his wrist, and then, when the leather sleeve of his brigandine failed to yield immediately, began to gnaw, snarling like a hound.

Bareris flailed his arm and succeeded in shaking the child-thing loose. It hissed and rushed in again, and he whipped out a dagger and poised it to rip the creature's belly.

At that moment, he would have vowed that every iota of his attention was on the implike thing in front of him, but during his time as a mercenary, fighting dragon worshipers, hobgoblins, and reavers of every stripe, he'd learned to register any flicker of motion in his field of vision. For as often as not, it wasn't the foe you were actually trying to fight who killed you. It was his comrade, slipping in a strike from the flank or rear.

Thus, he noticed a shift in the shadows cast by his floating light. It seemed impossible—the alley had been empty except for the child-thing, hadn't it?—but somehow, someone or something had crept up behind him while the creature kept his attention riveted on it.

Still on one knee, Bareris jerked himself around to confront the new threat. The lower half of his face masked by a scarf, a huge man in dark clothing stood poised to cut down at him with a broadsword. The weapon had a slimy look, as if its owner had smeared it with something other than the usual rust-resisting oil. Poison, like as not.

With only a knife in his hand, and his new assailant manifestly a man of exceptional strength, Bareris very much doubted his ability to parry the heavier blade. The stroke flashed at him, and he twisted aside, simultaneously thrusting with the dagger.

He was aiming for the big man's groin. He missed, but at least the knife drove into his adversary's thigh, and the masked man froze with the shock of it. The bard pulled the weapon free for a second attack, then something slammed into his back. Arms and legs wrapped around him. Teeth tore at the high collar of his brigandine, and cold white fingers groped for his eyes.

The child-thing had jumped onto his shoulders. He reared halfway up then immediately threw himself on his back. The jolt loosened the little horror's grip. He wrenched partially free of it and pounded elbow strikes into its torso, snapping ribs. The punishment made it falter, and he heaved himself entirely clear.

By then, though blood soaked the leg of his breeches, the big man was rushing in again. Bareris bellowed a battle cry infused with the magic of his voice. Vitality surged through his limbs, and his mind grew calm and clear. Even more importantly, the masked ruffian hesitated, giving him time to spring to his feet, switch his dagger to his left hand, and draw his sword.

"I'm not the easy mark you expected, am I?" he panted. "Why don't you go waylay someone else?"

He thought they might heed him. He'd hurt them, after all, but instead, apparently confident that the advantages conferred by superior numbers and a poisoned blade would prevail, they spread out to flank him. The masked man whispered words of power and sketched a mystic figure with his off hand. For a moment, an acrid smell stung Bareris's nose, and a prickling danced across his skin, warning signs of some magical effect coming into being.

Wonderful. On top of everything else, the whoreson was a spellcaster. That explained how he'd concealed himself until he was ready to strike.

For all Bareris knew, the masked man's next effort might kill or incapacitate him. He had to disrupt the casting if possible, and so, even though it meant turning his back on the child-thing, he screamed and sprang at the larger of his adversaries.

He thought he had a good chance of scoring. He was using an indirect attack that, in his experience, few adversaries could parry, and with a wounded leg, the masked man ought not to be able to defend by retreating out of the distance.

Yet that was exactly what he did. Bareris's attack fell short by a finger length. The masked man beat his blade aside and lunged in his turn.

The riposte streaked at Bareris's torso, driving in with dazzling speed. Evidently the big man had cast an enchantment to quicken his next attack, and with Bareris still in the lunge, it only had a short distance to travel. The bard was sure, with that bleak certainty every fencer knows, that the stroke was going to hit him.

Yet even if his intellect had resigned itself, his reflexes, honed in countless battles and skirmishes, had not. He recovered out of the lunge. It didn't carry him beyond the range of the big man's weapon, but it obliged it to travel a little farther, buying him the time and space at least to attempt a parry. He swept his blade across his body and somehow intercepted his adversary's sword. Steel rang, and the impact almost broke his grip on his hilt, but he kept the poisoned edge from slashing his flesh.

Eyes glaring above the scarf, the big man bulled forward, rendering both their swords useless at such close quarters, evidently intending to use his superior strength and size to shove Bareris down onto his back. Perhaps frustration or the pain of his leg wound had clouded his judgment, for the move was a blunder. He'd forgotten the dagger in the bard's left hand.

Bareris reminded him of its existence by plunging it into his kidney and intestines. Then the child-thing grabbed his legs from behind. Its teeth tore at his leg.

Grateful that his breeches were made of the same sturdy reinforced leather as his brigandine, Bareris wrenched himself around, breaking the creature's hold and turning the masked man with him like a dance partner. He flung the ruffian down on top of his hideous little accomplice then hacked relentlessly with his sword. Both his foes stopped moving before either could disentangle him- or itself from the other.

His sword abruptly heavy in his hand, Bareris stood over the corpses gasping for breath. The fear he couldn't permit himself while the fight was in progress welled up in him, and he shuddered, because the fracas had come far too close to killing him and left too many disquieting questions in its wake.

Who was the masked ruffian, and what manner of creature was his companion? Even more importantly, why had they sought to kill Bareris?

Perhaps it wasn't all that difficult to figure out. As Bareris wandered the night asking his questions, he'd mentioned repeatedly that he could pay for the answers. Small wonder, then, if a thief targeted him for a robbery attempt. The masked man had been such a scoundrel, and as for the child-thing . . . well, Thay was full of peculiar monstrosities. The Red Wizards created them in the course of their experiments. Perhaps one had escaped from its master's laboratory then allied itself with an outlaw as a means of surviving on the street.

Surely that was all there was to it. In Bareris's experience, the simplest explanation for an occurrence was generally the correct one.

In any case, the affair was over, and puzzling over it wasn't bringing him any closer to locating Tammith. He cleaned his weapons on his adversaries' garments, sheathed them, and headed out of the alley.

As he did so, his neck began to smart. He lifted his hand to his collar and felt the gnawed, perforated leather and the raw bloody flesh beneath. The girl-thing had managed to bite him after all. Just a nip, really, but he remembered the creature's filthy mouth, winced, and washed the wound with spirits at the first opportunity. Then it was back to the hunt.

It was nearly cock's crow when a pimp in a high plumed hat and gaudy parti-colored finery told him what he needed to know, though it was scarcely what he'd hoped to hear.

He'd prayed that Tammith was still in Tyraturos. Instead, the necromancers had marched the slaves they'd purchased out of the city. They'd headed north on the High Road, the same major artery of trade he'd followed up from Bezantur.

He reassured himself that the news wasn't really too bad. At least he knew what direction to take, and a procession of slaves on foot couldn't journey as fast as a horseman traveling hard.

He doubted the horse he'd ridden up from the coast could endure another such journey so soon. He'd have to buy anoth—

Weakness overwhelmed him and he reeled off balance, bumping his shoulder against a wall. His body suddenly felt icy cold, cold enough to make his teeth chatter, and he realized he was sick.

chapter four

19–20 Mirtul, the Year of Risen Elfkin

Tsagoth heard the slaves when he and his fellow demons and devils were still some distance from the door. The mortals were banging on the other side of it and wailing, pleading for someone to let them out.

Their agitation was understandable, for in one respect at least, Aznar Thrul was a considerate master to the infernal guards the Red Wizards of Conjuration had given him. He'd ordered his human servants to determine the dietary preferences of each of the newcomers and to provide for each according to his desires.

Some of the nether spirits were happy to subsist on the same fare as the mortal contingent of the household. Others craved the raw flesh or blood of a fresh kill, preferably one they'd slaughtered themselves. A number even required the meat or gore of a human or other sentient being. Tsagoth currently stalked among the latter group as they headed in to supper.

Yes, he thought bitterly, everyone had exactly what he needed.

Everyone but him, as the nagging hollowness in his belly, grown wearisome as the smarting, itching mark on his brow, attested.

The abyssal realms were vast, and the entities that populated them almost infinite in their diversity. Even demons couldn't identify every other type of demon, nor devils every other sort of devil, thus no one had figured out precisely what manner of being Tsagoth truly was. But had he explained or demonstrated what he actually wanted in the way of a meal, that would almost certainly have given the game away.

A hezrou—a demon like a man-sized toad with spikes running down its back and arms and hands in place of forelegs—turned the handle and threw open the door. The slaves screamed and recoiled.

The hezrou sprang on a man, drove its claws into his chest, and carried him down beneath it. Other spirits seized their prey with the same brutal efficiency. Some, however, possessed a more refined sense of cruelty, and savoring their victims' terror, slowly backed them up against the walls. An erinyes, a devil resembling a beautiful woman with feathered wings, alabaster skin, and radiant crimson eyes, cast a charm of fascination on the man she'd chosen. Afterward, he stood paralyzed, trembling, desire and dread warring in his face, as she glided toward him.

Tsagoth didn't want to reveal his own psychic abilities, and in his present foul humor, tormenting the humans was a sport that held no interest for him. Like the toad demon and its ilk, he simply snatched up a woman and bit open her neck.

The slave's bland, thin blood eased the dryness in his throat and the ache in his belly, but only to a degree. He contemplated the erinyes, now crouching over the body of her prey, tearing chunks of his flesh away and stuffing them in her mouth. How easy it would be to leap onto her back—

Yes, easy and suicidal. With an effort, he averted his gaze.

After their meal, the demons and devils dispersed, most

returning to their duties, the rest wandering off in search of rest or amusement. Tsagoth prowled the chambers and corridors of the castle and tried to formulate a strategy that would carry him to his goal.

The dark powers knew, he needed a clever idea, because Aznar Thrul's palace had proved to be full of secrets, hidden passages, magical wards, and servants who neither knew nor desired to know anything of the zulkir's business except as it pertained to their own circumscribed responsibilities. How, then, was Tsagoth to ferret out the one particular secret that would allow him to satisfy his geas?

Somebody could tell him, of that he had no doubt, but he didn't dare just go around questioning lackeys at random. His hypnotic powers, though formidable, occasionally met their match in a will of exceptional strength, and if he interrogated enough people, it was all but inevitable that someone would recall the experience afterward.

Thus, he at least needed to concentrate his efforts on those most likely to know, but what group was that exactly? It was hard to be certain when the intricacies of life in the palace were so strange to him. He'd rarely visited the mortal plane before, and even in his own domain, he was a solitary haunter of the wastelands, not a creature of castles and communities.

Perhaps because he'd just come from his own meager and unsatisfying repast, it occurred to him that he did comprehend one thing: Everyone, demon or human, required nourishment.

Accordingly, Tsagoth made his way to the kitchen, or complex of kitchens, an extensive open area warm with the heat of its enormous ovens and brick hearths. There sweating cooks peeled onions and chopped up chickens with cleavers. Bakers rolled out dough. Pigs roasted on spits, pots steamed and bubbled, and scullions scrubbed trays.

Tsagoth had an immediate sense that the activity in this

precinct of the palace never stopped. It faltered, though, when a woman noticed him peering through the doorway. She squawked, jumped, and dropped a saucepan, which fell to the floor with a clank. Her coworkers turned to see what had startled her, and they blanched too.

The blood fiend realized he could scarcely question one of them with the others looking on. He stalked off but didn't go far. Just a few paces away was a cold, drafty pantry with a marble counter and shelves climbing the walls. He slipped inside, deepened the ambient shadows to help conceal himself, and squatted down to wait.

Soon enough, a lone cook with a stained white apron and a dusting of flour on her face and hands scurried past, plainly in a hurry to accomplish some errand or other. It was the work of an instant to lunge out after her, clap one of his hands over her mouth and immobilize her with the other three, and haul her into the cupboard.

He stared into her wide, rolling eyes and stabbed with his will. She stopped struggling.

"I'm your master, and you'll do as I command." He uncovered her mouth. "Tell me you understand."

"I understand." She didn't display a dazed, somnolent demeanor like that of the Red Wizard of Conjuration he'd controlled. Rather, she was alert and composed, as if performing a routine part of her duties for a superior who had no reason to feel displeased with her.

Tsagoth set her on the floor and let go of her. "Tell me how to find Mari Agneh."

In her time, Mari Agneh had been tharchion of Priador, until Aznar Thrul decided to depose her and take the office for himself. Mari desperately wanted to retain her authority, and that, coupled with the fact that it was an unprecedented breach of custom for any one individual to be zulkir and tharchion both, impelled her to a profoundly reckless act: She'd appealed to Szass Tam and his allies among the mage-lords to help her keep her position.

But the lich saw no advantage to be gained by involving himself in her struggle, or perhaps he found it outrageous that any tharchion should seek to defy the will of any zulkir, even his principal rival. Either way, he declined to help her, and when Thrul learned of her petition, he was no longer content merely to usurp her office. He made her disappear.

Rumor had it that he'd taken her prisoner to abuse as his slave and sexual plaything, that she was still alive somewhere within the walls of this very citadel. Tsagoth fervently hoped that it was so. Otherwise, it would be impossible for him to fulfill his instructions, which meant he'd be trapped here forever.

The cook spread her hands. "I'm sorry, Master. I've heard the stories. Everyone has, but I don't know anything."

"If she's here," Tsagoth said, "she has to eat. Someone in the kitchen has to prepare her meals, and someone has to carry them to her."

The cook frowned thoughtfully. "I suppose that's true, but we fix so much food and send it all over the palace, day and night—"

"This is one meal," Tsagoth said. "It's prepared on a regular basis, and it goes somewhere no other meal goes. It's likely the man who prepares it has never been told who ultimately receives it. If he does know, he hasn't shared the secret with anyone else in the kitchen. Does that suggest anything to you?"

She shook her head. "I'm sorry, Master, no."

Frustrated, he felt a sudden wayward urge to grab her again and yank the head off her shoulders, but tame demon that he supposedly was, he couldn't just slaughter whomever he wanted and leave the corpses lying around. Besides, she might still be useful.

"It's all right," he said, "but now that you know what to look for, you'll watch. You won't realize you're watching or remember talking to me, but you'll spy anyway, and if you discover anything, you'll find me and tell me."

"Yes, Master, anything you say."

He sent her on her way, then crouched down and waited for the next lone kitchen worker to bustle by.

•• •• •• •• •• •• •• •• •• •• •• •• •• ••

Aoth swung himself down off Brightwing and took a final glance around, making sure there were no horses in the immediate vicinity.

Divining his concern, the griffon snorted. "I can control myself."

"Maybe, but the horses don't know that." He ruffled the feathers on her neck then tramped toward the big tent at the center of the camp. Cast in the stylized shape of a griffon, his shiny new gold medallion gleamed as it caught the light of the cook fires. The badge proclaimed him a newly minted officer, promoted for surviving the fall of Thazar Keep and carrying word of the disaster to his superiors.

The same accomplishment, if one was generous enough to call it that, made him the man of choice to scout the enemy's movements, and he'd spent some time doing precisely that. Now it was time to report to the tharchion. Aware of his business, the sentry standing watch in front of the tent admitted him without a challenge.

Currently clad in the sort of quilted tunic warriors employed to keep their own metal armor from bruising their limbs, Nymia Focar, governor of Pyarados, was a handsome woman with a wide, sensuous mouth, several silver rings in each ear, and a stud in the left side of her nose. As he saluted, she said, "Griffon rider!

After your errand, you must be hungry, or thirsty at the least. Please, refresh yourself." She waved her hand at a folding camp table laden with bottles of wine, a loaf of bread, green grapes, white and yellow cheeses, and ham.

Her cordiality didn't surprise him. She was often friendly and informal with her underlings, even to the point of taking them into her bed, though Aoth had never received such a summons. Perhaps his blunt features and short, thick frame were to blame. In any case, he was just as happy to be excused. Nymia had a way of turning into a ferocious disciplinarian when she encountered a setback, sometimes even flogging soldiers who'd played no part in whatever had gone amiss. He'd noticed that in such instances, it was often her former lovers who wound up tied to the whipping post.

"Thank you, Tharchion." He was hungry, but not enough to essay the awkwardness of reporting and shoving food into his mouth at the same time. A drink seemed manageable, however, certainly safer than the risk of giving offense by spurning her hospitality, and he poured wine into one of the pewter goblets provided for the purpose. In the lamp-lit tent, the red vintage looked black. "I scouted the pass as ordered. Hundreds of undead are marching down the valley, in good order and on our side of the river."

It was what she'd expected to hear, and she nodded. "Why in the name of the all-devouring flame is this happening?"

"I can only repeat what others have speculated already. There are old Raumviran strongholds, and the ruins of a kingdom even older up in the mountains. Both peoples apparently trafficked with abyssal powers, and such realms leave ghosts behind when they pass away."

As Thay with its hosts of wizards conducting esoteric experiments would leave its stain when it passed, he reflected, then wondered where the morbid thought had come from.

"Once in a while," he continued, "something skulks down from the ancient forts and tombs to trouble us, but we've never seen a horde the size of this, and I have no idea why it's occurring now. Perhaps a true scholar might, but I'm just a battle mage."

She smiled. "I wouldn't trade you. Destroying the foul things is more important than understanding precisely where they came from or what agitated them. Is it your opinion that they intend to march straight through to engage us?"

"Yes, Tharchion." He took a sip of his wine. It was sweeter than he liked but still drinkable. Probably it was costly and exquisite, if only he possessed the refined palate to appreciate it.

"Even though they can't reach us before dawn?"

"Yes."

"Good. In that case, we'll have the advantages of a well-established position, daylight, and the Thazarim protecting our right flank. Perhaps the creatures aren't as intelligent as we first thought."

Aoth hesitated. Wizard and griffon rider though he was, he was wary of seeming to contradict his capricious commander, but it was his duty to share his perspective. It was why they were talking, after all.

"They seemed intelligent when they took Thazar Keep."

"Essentially," Nymia said, "they had the advantage of surprise. Your warning came too late to do any good. Besides, the warriors of the garrison were the least able in the tharch. I sent them to that posting because no one expected anything to happen there."

He didn't much like hearing her disparage men who had, for the most part, fought bravely and died horrific deaths in her service, but he was prudent enough not to say so. "I understand what you're saying, Tharchion. I just think it's important we remember that the enemy has organization and leadership. I told you about the nighthaunt."

"The faceless thing with the horns and wings."

"Yes." Though he hadn't known what to call it until a mage more learned than himself had told him. "A form of powerful undead generally believed extinct. I had the feeling it was the leader, or an officer at least."

"If it impressed a griffon rider, I'm sure it's nasty, but I have all the warriors I could gather on short notice and every priest I could haul out of his shrine. We'll smash this foe, never doubt it."

"I don't, Tharchion." Truly he didn't, or at least he knew he shouldn't. Her analysis of the tactical situation appeared sound, and he trusted in the valor and competence of his comrades. Maybe it was simply fatigue or his memories of the massacre at Thazar Keep that had afflicted him with this edgy, uncharacteristic sense of foreboding. "What will you do if the undead decide to stop short of engaging us?"

"Then we'll advance and attack them. With any luck at all, we should be able to do it before sunset. I want this matter finished quickly, the pass cleared and Thazar Keep retaken. Until they are, no gems or ores can come down from the mines, and there won't be any treasure hunters heading up into the peaks for us to tax."

Nor safety or fresh provisions for any miners, trappers, and crofters who yet survive in the vale, Aoth thought. She's right; it is important to crush this enemy quickly.

"Do you have anything else to report?" Nymia asked.

He took a moment to consider. "No, Tharchion."

"Go and rest then. I want you fresh when it's time to fight."

He saw to Brightwing's needs, then wrapped himself in his bedroll and attempted to do as his commander had suggested. After a time, he did doze, but he woke with the jangled nerves of one who'd dreamed unpleasant dreams.

It was the bustle of the camp that had roused him to a morning so thoroughly overcast as to mask any trace of the sun in the eastern sky. Sergeants tramped about shouting. Warriors pulled and strapped on their armor, lined up before the cooks' cauldrons for a ladle full of porridge, kneeled to receive a cleric's blessing, or honed their swords and spears with whetstones. A blood orc, eager for the fight to come, howled its war cry, and donkeys hee-hawed, shied, and pulled at their tethers. A young human soldier attempting to tend the animals wheeled and cursed the orc, and it laughed and made a lewd gesture in response.

Aoth wondered whether an undead spellcaster had sealed away the sun and why no one on his side, a druid or warlock adept at weather-craft, had broken up the cloud cover. If no one could, it seemed a bad omen for the conflict to come.

He spat. He was no great hand at divination and wouldn't know a portent if it crawled up his nose. He was simply nervous, that was all, and the best cure for that was activity.

Accordingly, he procured his breakfast and Brightwing's, performed his meditations and prepared the day's allotment of spells, made sure his weapons and talismans were in perfect order, then roamed in search of the scouts who had flown out subsequent to his return. He wanted to find out what they'd observed.

As it turned out, nothing of consequence, but the effort kept him occupied until someone shouted that the undead were coming. Then it was time to hurry back to Brightwing, saddle her, and wait for his captain to order him and his comrades aloft.

When the command came, the griffons sprang into the air with a thunderous snapping and clattering of wings. As Brightwing climbed, Aoth studied the enemy. The light of morning, blighted though it was, afforded him a better look than he'd enjoyed hitherto, even when availing himself of his familiar's senses.

It didn't look as if the undead had the Thayan defenders

outnumbered. That at least was a relief. Aoth just wished he weren't seeing so many creatures that he, a reasonably well-trained warlock even if no one had ever seen fit to offer him a red robe, couldn't identify. It was easier to fight an adversary if you knew its weaknesses and capabilities.

A hulking, gray-skinned corpse-thing like a monstrously obese ghoul waddled in the front ranks of the undead host. From time to time, its jaw dropped halfway to its navel. It looked like, should it care to, it could stuff a whole human body into its mouth. Aoth scrutinized it, trying to associate it with something, any bit of lore, from his arcane studies, then realized he could no longer see it as clearly as he had a moment before.

The morning was growing darker instead of lighter. The clouds had already crippled the sunlight, and now some power was leeching away what remained. He thought of the night-haunt, a being seemingly made of darkness, and was somehow certain it was responsible. He tried not to shiver.

Every Thayan warrior was accustomed to sorcery and had at least some familiarity with the undead. Still, a murmur of dismay rose from the battle formation below. Officers and sergeants shouted, reassuring the common soldiers and commanding them to stand fast. Then the enemies on the ground began to lope, and dangerously difficult to discern against the darkened sky, the flying undead hurtled forward.

Its rotten wings so full of holes it was a wonder it could stay aloft, the animated corpse of a giant bat flew at Aoth and Brightwing. He decided not to waste a spell on it. He was likely to need every bit of his magic to deal with more formidable foes. Availing himself of their empathic link, he silently told Brightwing to destroy the bat. As the two closed, and at the last possible moment, the griffon lashed her wings, rose above the undead creature, and ripped it with her talons. The bat tumbled down the sky in pieces.

Meanwhile, Aoth cast about for other foes. They were easy enough to find. Brandishing his lance, shouting words of power, he conjured blasts of flame to burn wraiths and shadows from existence until he'd cleansed the air in his immediate vicinity. That afforded him a moment to look and see how the battle as a whole was progressing.

It appeared to him that he and his fellow griffon riders were at least holding their own in the air, while their comrades on the ground might even be gaining the upper hand. Archery had inflicted considerable harm on the advancing undead, and the efforts of the clerics were even more efficacious. Standing in relative safety behind ranks of soldiers, each in his or her own way invoking the power faith afforded, priests of Bane shook their black-gauntleted fists, priestesses of Loviatar scourged their naked shoulders or tore their cheeks with their nails, and servants of Kelemvor in somber gray vestments brandished their hand-and-a-half swords. As a result, some of the undead cringed, unable to advance any further, while others simply crumbled or melted away. Several even turned and attacked their own allies.

It's going to be all right, Aoth thought, smiling. I was a craven to imagine otherwise. But Brightwing, plainly sensing the tenor of his thought, rapped, "No. Something is about to happen."

She was right. In the midst of the Thayan formation, wherever a group of priests stood assembled, patches of air seethed and rippled, then new figures exploded into view. They were diverse in their appearance, and in that first chaotic moment, Aoth couldn't sort them all out, but a number were mere shadows. Others appeared similarly spectral but with blazing emerald eyes, a murky suggestion of swirling robes, and bizarrely, luminous glyphs floating in the air around them. Swarms of insects—undead insects, the griffon rider supposed—hovered among them, along with clouds of sparks that wheeled and surged as if guided by a single will. Figures in hooded cloaks, evidently the ones who'd magically transported their fellow creatures into the center of their enemies, immediately vanished again, perhaps to ferry a second batch.

Aoth had reported that the undead host included at least a few spellcasters, but even so, no one had expected any of their foes to possess the ability to teleport themselves and a group of allies through space, because, as a rule, the undead didn't, and they hadn't revealed it at Thazar Keep. Thus, the maneuver caught the Thayans by surprise.

Yet it didn't panic them. The priests wheeled and rattled off incantations or invoked the pure, simple power of belief to smite the newcomers.

Nothing happened. Nothing at all.

Shadows pounced at the priests, sparks and insects swarmed on them, and they went down. Warriors struggled to come to their aid, but there were stinging, burning clouds to engulf them as well, and phantoms to sear them with their touch, and in most cases, they failed even to save themselves. Meanwhile, the bulk of the undead host charged with renewed energy to crash into the shield wall of the living, which immediately began to deform before the pressure.

Perhaps, Aoth thought, he could aid the clerics. He bade Brightwing swoop lower, but instead of obeying, the griffon lashed her wings and flung herself straight ahead. A moment later, something huge as a dragon plunged through the space they'd just vacated. Aoth hadn't sensed the creature diving at them. He was grateful his familiar had.

The thing leveled out, turned, and climbed to attack again. It was yet another grotesquerie the likes of which Aoth had never encountered before, a creature resembling a giant minotaur with bat wings, fangs, and clawed feet instead of hooves, its whole body shrouded in mummy wrappings.

Brightwing proved more agile in the air and kept away from

the enormous thing while Aoth blasted it with bright, booming thunderbolts and darts of light. The punishment stabbed holes in it and burned patches of its body black, but it wouldn't stop coming.

Then Brightwing screeched and lurched in flight. Aoth cast about and couldn't see what ailed her. "My belly!" she cried.

He leaned far to the side, relying on the safety straps to keep him from slipping from the saddle. From that position, he could just make out the greenish misty form clinging to her like a leech, its insubstantial hands buried to the wrists in her body, her flesh blistering and suppurating around them.

The angle was as awkward as could be, and Aoth was afraid of striking her instead of his target, but he saw no choice except to try. He triggered the enchantment of accuracy bound in one of his tattoos, and his forearm stung as the glyph gave up its power. He charged his lance with power and thrust.

The point caught the phantom in the flank, and it shriveled from existence. Freed from its crippling, excruciating embrace, Brightwing instantly furled her wings and dived, seeking to evade as she had before.

She failed. The bandaged horror missed the killing strike to the body it had probably intended, but one of its claws pierced her wing.

The undead creature scrabbled at her, trying to achieve a better grip and rend her in the process. Beak snapping, she bit at it. Shouting in fury and terror, Aoth stabbed with his lance.

Finally the huge thing stopped moving. Unfortunately, that meant it fell with its talon still transfixing the griffon's wing, and she and her rider plummeted along with it. For a moment, they were all in danger of crashing to the ground together, but then Brightwing bit completely through the claw, freeing herself. Wings hammering, shaking the severed tip of the talon out of her wound in the process, she leveled off.

Aoth peered about. It was too late to help the priests. They were gone, yet the Thayans on the ground had at least succeeded in eliminating the undead from the midst of their formation, and mages and warriors, all battling furiously, had thus far held back the rest of the undead host. For the next little while, as he and his injured mount did their best to avoid danger, he dared to hope the legions might still carry the day.

Then the surface of the Thazarim churned, and hunched, gaunt shapes waded ashore. They charged the Thayan flank.

Aoth cursed. He knew of lacedons, as the aquatic ghouls were called. They were relatively common, but so far as he'd ever heard, they were sea creatures. It made no sense for them to come swimming down from the Sunrise Mountains.

Yet they had, without him or any of the other scouts spotting them in the water, and swarms of undead rats had swum along with them. Like a tide of filthy fur, rotting flesh, exposed bone, and gnashing teeth, the vermin streamed in among the legionnaires, and men who might have stood bravely against any one foe, or even a pair of them, panicked at the onslaught of five or ten or twenty small, scurrying horrors assailing them all at once.

It was the end. The formation began to disintegrate. Warriors turned to run, sometimes throwing away their weapons and shields. Their leaders bellowed commands, trying to make them retreat with some semblance of order. Slashing with his scimitar, a blood-orc sergeant cut down two members of his squad to frighten the rest sufficiently to heed him.

"Set me down," said Aoth.

"Don't be stupid," Brightwing replied.

"I won't take you back into the middle of that, hurt as you are, but none of the men on the ground is going to escape unless every wizard we have left does all he can to cover the retreat."

"We haven't fallen out of the sky, have we? I can still fly and fight. We'll do it together."

He discerned he had no hope of talking her out of it. "All right, have it your way."

Brightwing maneuvered, and when necessary, she battled with talon and beak to keep them both alive. He used every spell in his head and every trace of magic he carried bound in an amulet, scroll, or tattoo to hold the enemy back. To no avail, he suspected, because below him, moment by moment, men were dying anyway.

Then, however, the morning brightened. The clouds turned from slate to a milder gray, a luminous white spot appeared in the east, and at last the undead faltered in their harrying pursuit.

•• •• •• •• •• •• •• •• •• •• •• •• ••

Ysval could bear the touch of daylight without actual harm, yet it made his skin crawl, and soaring above his host, the better to survey the battle, he stiffened in repugnance.

Some of his warriors froze or flinched, their reaction akin to his own. Specters faded to invisibility, to mere impotent memories of pain and hate. Still other creatures began to smolder and steam and hastily shrouded themselves in their graveclothes or scrambled for shade.

Ysval closed his pallid eyes and took stock of himself. His assessment, though it came as no surprise, was disappointing. For the moment, he lacked the mystical strength to darken the day a second time.

The nighthaunt called in his silent voice. He'd made a point of establishing a psychic bond with each of his lieutenants and so was confident they'd hear. Sure enough, the ones who were still functional immediately moved to call back those undead so avid to kill that they'd continued to chase Tharchion Focar's fleeing troops even when their comrades faltered.

Once Ysval was certain his minions were enacting his will, he swooped lower, the better to provide the direction the host would require in the aftermath of battle. Several of his officers saw him descending and hurried to meet him where, with a final snap of his wings, he set down on the ground.

He gazed at Shex, inviting her to speak first, in part because he respected her. In fact, though blessedly incapable of affection in any weak mortal sense, he privately regarded her as something of a kindred spirit, but not because they particularly resembled one another.

Like himself, she had wings and claws, but she was taller, tall as an ogre in fact, and her entire body was a mass of peeling and deliquescent corruption. Slime oozed perpetually down her frame to pool at her feet, and even other undead were careful to stand clear of the corrosive filth.

No, Ysval felt a certain bond with her because each of them was more than just a formidable and genuinely sentient undead creature. Each was the avatar, the embodiment, of a cosmic principle. As he *was* darkness, so she was decay.

At the moment, she was also unhappy. "Many of our warriors can function in the light," she said in her slurred, muddy voice. "Let those who are capable continue the pursuit. Why not? The legionnaires won't turn and fight."

They might, he replied, *if they think it's the only alternative to being struck down from behind.* He'd noticed that even many undead winced and shuddered when he shared his thoughts with them, but she bore the psychic intrusion without any sign of distress. *We've won enough for one day. We've dealt a heavy blow to the enemy, and the pass, our highway onto the central plateau, lies open from end to end.*

Which meant that for a time at least, the host would disperse to facilitate the process of laying waste to as much of eastern Thay as possible. In a way, it was a pity. It had been millennia since he'd commanded an army, and he realized now that he'd missed it.

Still, raiding, slaughtering helpless humans and putting their farms and villages to the torch, was satisfying in its own right, and he had reason for optimism that the army would join together again by and by. It was just that the decision didn't rest with him but with the master who'd summoned him back to the mortal realm after a sojourn of ages on the Plane of Shadow.

Shex inclined her head. Viscous matter dripped from her face as if she were weeping over his decision. "As you command," she said.

Her sullen tone amused him. *I promise,* he said, *there's plenty more killing to come. Now, see to the corpses of the tharchion's soldiers. The ghouls and such can feed on half of them, but I want the rest intact for reanimation.*

chapter five

25 Mirtul, the Year of Risen Elfkin

Surthay, capital of the tharch of the same name, was a crude sort of place compared to Eltabbar, and since the town lay outside the enchantments that managed the climate in central Thay, the weather was colder and rainier. Even murky Lake Mulsantir, the body of water on which it sat, suffered by comparison with the blue depths of Lake Thaylambar.

Yet Malark Springhill liked the place. At times the luxuries, splendors, and intricacies of life at Dmitra Flass's court grew wearisome for a man who'd spent much of his life in the rough-and-tumble settlements of the Moonsea. When he was in such a mood, the dirt streets, simple wooden houses, and thatch-roofed shacks of a town like Surthay felt more like home than Eltabbar ever could.

That didn't mean he could dawdle here. He didn't understand the urgency of his errand, but his mistress seemed to think it important and he didn't intend to keep her waiting any longer than necessary. He'd finish his business and ride out tonight, and with luck he could complete the wearisome "Long Portage" back up the First Escarpment before the end of tomorrow.

He headed down the rutted, dung-littered street. This particular thoroughfare, a center for carnal entertainments, was busy even after dark, and he made way repeatedly for soldiers, hunters, fishermen, pimps, and tough-looking locals of every stripe—for anyone who looked more dangerous and intimidating than a smallish, neatly dressed, clerkish fellow armed only with a knife.

Only once did he resent stepping aside, and that was when everyone else did it too, clearing the way for a legionnaire marching a dozen skeleton warriors along. Malark detested the undead, which he supposed made it ironic that he owed his allegiance to a princess who in turn had pledged her fealty to a lich, but serving Dmitra Flass afforded him a pleasant life and plenty of opportunity to pursue his own preoccupations.

He stepped inside a crowded tavern, raucous with noise and stinking of beer and sweaty bodies. A legionnaire turned and gave him a sneer.

"This is a soldier's tavern," he said.

"I know," Malark replied. "I came to show my admiration for the heroes who saved Surthay from the Rashemi." He lifted a fat purse and shook it to make it clink. "I think this is enough to stand the house a few rounds."

He was welcome enough after that, and the soldiers were eager to spin tales of their valor. As he'd expected, much of what they told him was nonsense. They couldn't *all* have slain Rashemi chieftains or butchered half a dozen berserkers all by themselves, and he was reasonably certain no one had raped one of the infamous witches.

Yet it should be possible to sift through all the boasts and lies and discern the essence of what had happened buried beneath.

Malark listened, drew his inferences, and decided further inquiries were in order, inquiries best conducted elsewhere and by different methods.

Stiffening and swallowing, he feigned a sudden attack of nausea and stumbled outside, ostensibly to vomit. Since he left his pigskin pouch of silver and copper coins behind on the table, he was reasonably certain no one would bother to come looking for him when he failed to return.

He found a shadowy recessed doorway and settled himself to wait, placing himself in a light trance that would help him remain motionless. Warriors passed by his hiding place, sometimes in groups, sometimes in the company of painted whores, sometimes young, sometimes staggering drunk. He let them all drift on unmolested.

Finally a lone legionnaire came limping down the street. By the looks of it, an old wound or fracture in his leg had never healed properly. Though he was past his prime, with a frame that had once been athletic and was now running to fat, he wore no medallion, plume, or other insignia of rank, and was evidently still a common man-at-arms.

He didn't look intoxicated, either. Perhaps he'd just come off duty and was heading for the same soldier's tavern Malark had visited.

In any case, whatever his business, he appeared perfect for Malark's purposes. The spy waited until the legionnaire was just a few paces away, then stepped forth from the shadows.

Startled, the legionnaire jumped back, and his hand darted to the hilt of his broadsword. Then he hesitated, confused, perhaps, by the contradiction between the menace implicit in Malark's sudden emergence and the innocuous appearance of his empty hands and general demeanor. It gave the spy the opportunity to step closer.

"What do you want?" the soldier demanded.

"Answers," Malark replied.

That was apparently enough to convince the warrior he was in trouble. He started to snatch the sword out, but he'd waited too long. Before it could clear the scabbard, Malark sprang in and slammed the heel of his hand into the center of the other man's forehead. The legionnaire's leather helmet thudded, no doubt absorbing part of the force of the impact. Not enough of it, though, and his knees buckled. Malark caught him and dragged him into the narrow, lightless space between two houses.

When he judged he'd gone far enough from the street that he and his prisoner would remain unobserved, he set the legionnaire down on the ground, relieved him of his sword and dirk, and held a vial of smelling salts under his nose. Rousing, the warrior twisted away from the vapors.

"Are you all right?" Malark asked, straightening up. "It can be tricky to hit a man hard enough to stun him, but not so hard that you do any real harm. I like to think I have the knack, but armor makes it more difficult."

"I'll kill you," the soldier growled.

"Try if you like," Malark said and waited to see if the prisoner would dive for the sword or dagger now resting on the ground beyond his reach or attack with his bare hands.

He opted for the latter. Wishing the space between the buildings weren't quite so narrow, Malark nonetheless managed to shift to the side when the captive surged up and hurled himself forward. He tripped the legionnaire then, while the other man was floundering off balance, caught hold of his arm and twisted, applying pressure to the shoulder socket. The warrior gasped at the pain.

"We're going to have a civil conversation," said Malark. "The only question is, do I need to dislocate your arm to make it happen, or are you ready to cooperate now?"

As best he was able, the legionnaire struggled, trying to break free. Malark applied more pressure, enough to paralyze the man.

"I really will do it," said the spy, "and then I'll go on damaging you until you see reason."

"All right!" the soldier gasped.

Malark released him. "Sit or stand as you prefer."

The bigger man chose to stand and rub his shoulder. "Who in the Nine Hells are you?"

"My name is Malark Springhill. I do chores of various sorts for Tharchion Flass."

The legionnaire hesitated, his eyes narrowing. Perhaps he'd never risen in the ranks, but he was evidently more intelligent than that fact would seem to imply. "You . . . are you supposed to tell me that?"

"Ordinarily, no," Malark replied. Out on the street, a woman laughed, the sound strident as a raptor's screech. "I'm a spy among other things, and generally I have to lie to people all the time, about . . . well, everything, really. It's something of a luxury that I can be honest with you."

"Because you mean to kill me."

"Yes. I'm going to ask you what truly happened in the Gorge of Gauros, and I couldn't let you survive to report that anyone was interested in that even if you didn't know who sent me to inquire. But you get to decide how pleasant the next little while will be, and how you'll die at the end of it.

"You can try withholding the information I want," Malark continued, "in which case, I'll torture it out of you. Afterwards, your body will be broken, incapable of resistance when I snap your neck.

"Or you can answer me freely, and I'll have no reason to hurt you. Once you've given me what I need, I'll return your blades, permit you to unsheathe them, and we'll fight. You're a legionnaire. Surely you'd prefer the honor of a warrior's death, and I'd like to give it to you."

The legionnaire stared at him. "You're crazy."

"People often say that, but they're mistaken." Malark decided to confide in the warrior. It was one technique for building trust between interrogator and prisoner, and besides, he rarely had the chance to tell his story. "I just see existence in a way others can't.

"A long, long while ago, I learned of a treasure. The sole surviving dose of a philter to keep a man from aging forever after.

"I coveted it. So did others. In those days, I scarcely knew the rudiments of fighting, but I had a friend who was proficient, and together we bested our rivals and seized the prize. We'd agreed we'd each drink half the potion, and thus, though neither of us would become immortal, we'd both live a long time."

"But you betrayed him," said the legionnaire, "and drank it all yourself."

Malark smiled. "Are you saying that because you're a good judge of character, or because it's what you would have done? Either way, you're right. That's exactly what I did, and later on, I started to regret it.

"First, I watched everyone I loved, everyone I even knew, pass away. That's hard. I wept when my former friend died a feeble old man, and he'd spent the past fifty years trying to revenge himself on me.

"I attempted to move forward. I told myself there was a new generation of people to care about. The problem, of course, was that before long, in the wink of an eye, or so it seemed, they died, too.

"When I grew tired of enduring that, I tried living with dwarves and later, elves, but it wasn't the same as living with my own kind, and in time, they passed away just like humans. It simply took a little longer."

The soldier gaped at him. "How old are you?"

"Older than Thay. I recall hearing the tidings that the Red Wizards had fomented a rebellion against Mulhorand, though I wasn't in these parts to witness it myself. Anyway, over time, I pretty much lost the ability to feel an attachment to individual people, for what was the point? Instead, I tried to embrace causes and places, only to discover those die too. I lost count of the times I gave my affection to one or another town along the Moonsea, only to see the place sacked and the inhabitants massacred. I learned that as the centuries roll by, even gods change, or at least our conception of them does, which amounts to the same thing if you're looking for some constancy to cling to.

"But eventually I realized there was one constant, and that was death. In its countless variations, it was happening all around me, all the time. It befell everyone, or at least, everyone but me, and that made it fascinating."

"If you're saying you wanted to die, why didn't you just stick a dagger into your heart or jump off a tower? Staying young forever isn't the same thing as being unkillable, is it?"

"No, it isn't, and I've considered ending my life on many occasions, but something has always held me back. Early on, it was the same dread of death that prompted me to strive for the elixir and betray my poor friend in the first place. After I made a study of extinction, I shed the fear, but with enlightenment, suicide came to seem like cheating, or at the very least, bad manners. Death is a gift, and we aren't meant to reach out and snatch it. We're supposed to wait until the universe is generous enough to bestow it on us."

"I don't understand."

"Don't worry about it. Most people don't, but the Monks of the Long Death do, and there came a day when I was fortunate enough to stumble across one of their hidden enclaves and gain admission as a novice."

The legionnaire blanched. "You're one of *those* madmen?"

"It depends on your point of view. After a decade or two, paladins descended on the monastery and slaughtered my brothers and sisters. Only I escaped, and afterward, I didn't feel the need to search for another such stronghold. I'd already learned what I'd hoped to, and the rigors and abstentions of the ascetic life had begun to wear on me.

"According to the rules of the order, I'm an apostate, and if they ever realize it, they'll likely try to kill me. But though I no longer hold a place in the hierarchy, I still adhere to the teachings. I still believe that while all deaths are desirable, some are better than others. The really good ones take a form appropriate to the victim's life and come to him in the proper season. I believe it's both a duty and the highest form of art to arrange such passings as opportunity allows.

"That's why I permitted younger, healthier, more successful men to pass by and accosted you instead. It's why I hope to give you a fighter's death."

"What are you talking about? It's not my 'season' to die!"

"Are you sure? Isn't it plain your best days are past? Doesn't your leg ache constantly? Don't you feel old age working its claws into you? Aren't you disappointed with the way your life has turned out? Why not let it go then? The priests and philosophers assure us that something better waits beyond."

"Shut up! You can't talk me into wanting to die."

"I'm not trying. Not exactly. I told you, I want you to go down fighting. I just don't want you to be afraid."

"I'm not! Or at least I won't be if you keep your promise and give back my sword."

"I will. I'll return your blades and fight you empty-handed."

"Ask your cursed questions, then, and I'll answer honestly. Why shouldn't I, when you'll never have a chance to repeat what I say to Dmitra Flass or anybody else?"

"Thank you." The inquisition didn't take long. At the end, though Malark had learned a good deal he hadn't comprehended before, he still wasn't sure why it was truly important, but he realized he'd come to share his mistress's suspicion that it was.

Now, however, was not the time to ponder the matter. He needed to focus on the duel to come. He backed up until the sword and dagger lay between the legionnaire and himself.

"Pick them up," he said.

The soldier sprang forward, crouched, and grabbed the weapons without taking his eyes off Malark. He then scuttled backward as he drew the blades, making it more difficult for his adversary to spring and prevent him had he cared to do so, and opening enough distance to use a sword to best effect.

Malark noticed the limp was no longer apparent. Evidently excitement, or the single-minded focus of a veteran combatant, masked the pain, and when the bigger man came on guard, his stance was as impeccable as a woodcut in a manual of arms.

Given his level of skill, he deserved to be a drill instructor at the very least. Malark wondered whether it was a defect in his character or simple bad luck that had kept him in the ranks. He'd never know, of course, for the time for inquiry was past.

The legionnaire sidled left, hugging the wall on that side. He obviously remembered how Malark had shifted past him before and was positioning himself in such a way that, if his adversary attempted such a maneuver again, he could only dart in one direction. That would make it easier to defend against the move.

Then the warrior edged forward. Malark stood and waited. As soon as the distance was to the legionnaire's liking, when a sword stroke would span it but not a punch or a kick, he cut at Malark's head.

Or rather, he appeared to. He executed the feint with all the necessary aggression, yet even so, Malark perceived that a false attack was all it was. He couldn't have said exactly how. Over the centuries, he'd simply developed an instinct for such things.

He lifted an arm as if to block the cut, in reality to convince the legionnaire his trick was working. The blade spun low to chop at his flank.

Malark shifted inside the arc of the blow, a move that robbed the stroke of much of its force. When he swept his arm down to defend, the forte of the blade connected with his forearm but failed to shear through the sturdy leather bracer hidden under his sleeve.

At the same moment, he stiffened his other hand and drove his fingertips into the hard bulge of cartilage at the front of the warrior's throat. The legionnaire reeled backward. Malark took up the distance and hit him again, this time with a chop to the side of the neck. Bone cracked and, his head flopping, the soldier collapsed.

Malark regarded the body with the same mix of satisfaction and wistful envy he usually felt at such moments. Then he closed the legionnaire's eyes and walked away.

•• •• •• •• •• •• •• •• •• •• •• •• •• ••

North of the Surag River, the road threaded its way up the narrow strip of land between Lake Thaylambar to the west and the Surague Escarpment, the cliffs at the base of the Sunrise Mountains, to the east. The land was wilder, heath interspersed with stands of pine and dotted with crumbling ruined towers, and sparsely settled. The slaves and their keepers marched an entire morning without seeing anyone, and when someone finally did appear, it was just a lone goatherd, who, wary of strangers, immediately scurried into a thicket. Even tax stations, the ubiquitous fortresses built to collect tolls and help preserve order throughout the realm, were few and far between.

Tammith had never before ventured farther than a day's walk from Bezantur, but she'd heard that the northern half of Thay was almost all alike, empty, undeveloped land where even freemen found it difficult to eke out a living. How much more difficult, then, must it be to endure as a slave, particularly one accustomed to the teeming cities of the south?

Thus she understood why so many of her fellow thralls grew more sullen and despondent with each unwilling step they took, and why Yuldra, the girl she'd sought to comfort just before the Red Wizards came and bought the lot of them, kept sniffling and knuckling her reddened eyes. In her heart, Tammith felt just as dismayed and demoralized as they did.

But she also believed that if one surrendered to such emotions, they would only grow stronger, so she squeezed Yuldra's shoulder and said, "Come on, don't cry. It's not so bad."

Yuldra's face twisted. "It is."

"This country is strange to me, too, but I'm sure they have towns somewhere in the north, and remember, the men who bought us are Red Wizards. You don't think they live in a tent out in the wilderness, do you?"

"You don't know that they're taking us where they live," the adolescent retorted, "because they haven't said. I've had other masters, and they weren't so close-mouthed. I'm scared we're going somewhere horrible."

"I'm sure that isn't so." In reality, of course, Tammith had no way of being certain of any such thing, but it seemed the right thing to say. "Let's not allow our imaginings to get the best of us. Let's play another game."

Yuldra sighed. "All right."

The next phase of their journey began soon after, when they finally left the northernmost reaches of Lake Thaylambar behind, and rolling plains opened before them. To Tammith's surprise, the procession then left the road where, though she eventually spotted signs that others had passed this way before them, there was no actual trail of any sort.

Nor did there appear to be anything ahead but rolling grassland, and beyond that, visible as a blurry line on the horizon, High Thay, the mountainous tharch that jutted upward from the central plateau as it in turn rose abruptly from the lowlands. From what she understood, many a Red Wizard maintained a private citadel or estate among the peaks, no doubt with hordes of slaves to do his bidding, but her sense of geography, hazy though it was, suggested the procession wasn't heading there. If it was, the warlocks had taken about the most circuitous route imaginable.

Suddenly three slaves burst from among their fellows and ran, scattering as they fled. Tammith's immediate reflexive thought was that, unlike Yuldra and herself, the trio had figured out where they all were going.

Unfortunately, they had no hope of escaping that fate. The Red Wizards could have stopped them easily with spells, but they didn't bother. Like their masters, some of the guards were mounted, and they pounded after the fugitives. One warrior flung a net as deftly as any fisherman she'd ever watched plying his trade in the waters off Bezantur, and a fugitive fell tangled in the mesh. Another guard reached out and down with his lance, slipped it between a thrall's legs, and tripped him. A third horseman leaned out of the saddle, snatched a handful of his target's streaming, bouncing mane of hair and simply jerked the runaway off his feet.

Once the guards herded the fugitives back to the procession, every slave had to suffer his masters' displeasure. The overseers screamed and spat in their faces, slapped, cuffed, and shoved them, and threatened savage punishments for all if anyone else misbehaved. Yuldra broke down sobbing the moment a warrior approached her. The Red Wizards looked vexed and impatient with the delay the exercise in discipline required.

The abuse was still in progress when Tammith caught sight of a horseman galloping steadily nearer. His wheat-blond hair gleamed dully in the late afternoon sunlight, and something about the set of his shoulders and the way he carried himself—

Yes! Perhaps she shouldn't jump to conclusions when he was still so far away, but in her heart she knew. It was Bareris, after she'd abandoned all hope of ever seeing him again.

She wanted to cry his name, run to meet him, until she realized, with a cold and sudden certainty, that what she really ought to do was warn him off.

.. ..

Outside in the streets of Eltabbar, the celebration had an edge to it. The mob was happy enough to gobble free food, guzzle free ale and wine, and watch the parades, dancers, mummers, displays of transmutation, and other forms of entertainment, all of it provided to celebrate the election of Samas Kul to the office of zulkir. Yet Aoth had felt the underlying displeasure and dismay at the tidings that in the east, a Thayan army had met defeat, and in consequence, undead marauders were laying waste to the countryside. He suspected the festival would erupt into rioting after nightfall.

Still, he would rather have been outside in the gathering storm than tramping at Nymia Focar's side through the immense basalt ziggurat called the Flaming Brazier, reputedly the largest temple of Kossuth the Firelord in all the world. That was because it was entirely possible that the potentate who'd summoned the tharchion had done so with the intention of placing the blame for the recent debacle in Pyarados. Since she, the commander who'd lost to the undead, was the obvious candidate, perhaps she'd dragged Aoth along to be scapegoat in her place.

Maybe, he thought, he even deserved it. If only he'd spotted the lacedons—

He scowled the thought away. He hadn't been the only scout in the air, and nobody else had seen the creatures either. Nor could you justly condemn anyone for failing to anticipate an event that had never happened before.

Not that justice was a concept that automatically sprang to mind where zulkirs and Red Wizards were concerned.

Aoth and his superior strode in dour silence through yellow and orange high-ceilinged chambers lit by countless devotional fires. The heat of the flames became oppressive, and the wizard evoked the magic of a tattoo to cool himself. Nymia lacked the ability to do the same, and perspiration gleamed on her upper lip.

Eventually they arrived at high double doors adorned with a scene inlaid in jewels and precious metals: Kossuth, spiked chain in hand, smiting his great enemy Istishia, King of the Water Elementals. A pair of warrior monks stood guard at the sides of the portal and swung the leaves open to permit the new arrivals to enter the room beyond.

It was a chamber plainly intended for discussion and disputation, though it too had its whispering altar flames glinting on golden icons. Seated around a table in the center of the room was a more imposing gathering of dignitaries than Aoth had ever seen before even at a distance, let alone close up. Let alone taking any notice of his own humble existence. In fact, four of the five were zulkirs.

Gaunt, dark-eyed Szass Tam, his withered fingers folded, looked calm and composed.

Yaphyll, zulkir of Divination and by all accounts the lich's most reliable ally, was a slender woman, somewhat short for a Mulan, with, rather to Aoth's surprise, a humorous, impish cast of expression manifest even on this grave occasion. She looked just a little older than he was, thirty or so, but she had actually held her office since before he was born with magic maintaining her youth.

In contrast, Lallara, zulkir of Abjuration, though still seemingly hale and vital, evidently disdained the cosmetic measures which might have kept time from etching lines at the corners of her eyes and mouth and softening the flesh beneath her chin. Scowling, she toyed with one of her several rings, twisting it around and around her forefinger.

Astonishingly obese, his begemmed robes the gaudiest and plainly the costliest of the all the princely raiment on display, Samas Kul likewise appeared restless. Perhaps he disliked being called away from the celebration of his rise to a zulkir's preeminence, or maybe the newly minted mage-lord was worried he wouldn't make a good impression here at the onset of his new responsibilities and so lose the respect of his peers.

Rounding out the assembly was Iphegor Nath. Few indeed were the folk who could treat with zulkirs on anything even approximating an equal footing, but the High Flamelord, primate of Kossuth's church, was one of them. Craggy and burly, he wore bright orange vestments, the predominant hue close enough to forbidden red that no man of humbler rank would have dared to put it on. His eyes were orange as well, with a fiery light inside them, and from moment to moment tiny flames crawled on his shoulders, arms, and shaven scalp without burning his garments or blistering his skin. His air of sardonic composure was a match for Szass Tam's.

Nymia and Aoth dropped to their knees and lowered their gazes.

"Rise," said Szass Tam, "and seat yourselves at the table."

"Is that necessary?" Lallara rapped. "I'm not pleased with the tharchion, and her lieutenant doesn't even wear red. By the looks of him, he isn't even Mulan."

"It will make it easier for us all to converse," the lich replied, "and if we see fit to punish them later, I doubt that the fact that we allowed them to sit down first will dilute the effect." His black eyes shifted back to Nymia and Aoth, and he waved a shriveled hand at two vacant chairs. "Please."

Aoth didn't want to sit or do anything else that might elicit Lallara's displeasure, but neither, of course, could he disobey Szass Tam. Feeling trapped, he pulled the chair out and winced inwardly when the legs grated on the floor.

"Now, then," said Szass Tam, "with the gracious permission of His Omniscience"—he inclined his head to Iphegor Nath—"I called you all here to address the situation in Tharchion Focar's dominions. It's serious, or so I've been given to understand."

"Yet evidently not serious enough," the High Flamelord drawled, "to warrant an assembly of all eight zulkirs. To some, it might even appear that you, Your Omnipotence, wanted to meet here in the temple instead of your own citadel to avoid the notice of those you chose to exclude."

Yaphyll smiled a mischievous smile. "Perhaps it was purely out of respect for you, Your Omniscience. We came to you rather than put you to the inconvenience of coming to us."

Iphegor snorted. Blue flame oozed from his hand onto the tabletop, and he squashed it out with a fingertip before it could char the finish.

"You're correct, of course," Szass Tam told the priest. "Regrettably, we zulkirs fall into two camps, divided by our differing perspectives on trade and other issues, and of late, our squabbles have grown particularly contentious, perhaps even to the point of assassination. That makes it slow going to accomplish anything when we all attempt to work together, and since this particular problem is urgent, I thought a more efficient approach was required."

"Besides which," Iphegor said, "if you resolve the problem

without involving your peers, you'll reap all the benefits of success. The nobles and such will be that much more inclined to give their support to you in preference to Aznar Thrul's cabal."

"Just so," said Samas Kul in a plummy, unctuous voice. "You've demonstrated you're a shrewd man, Your Omniscience, not that any of us ever imagined otherwise. The question is, if we score a hit in the game we're playing with our rivals, will that trouble or displease you?"

"It might," the primate said. "By convening here in the Flaming Brazier and including me among your company, you've made me your collaborator. Now it's possible I'll have to contend with the rancor of your opponents."

"Yet you agreed to meet with us," Lallara said.

Iphegor shrugged. "I was curious, I hoped something would come of it to benefit the faith, and I too understand that Pyarados needs immediate attention."

"Masters!" Nymia said. All eyes shifted to her, and she faltered as if abruptly doubting the wisdom of speaking unbidden, but now that she'd started, she had no choice but to continue. "With all respect, you speak as if Pyarados is lost, and that isn't so. The undead seized one minor fortress and won one additional battle."

"With the result," snapped Lallara, "that they're now devastating your tharch and could easily range farther west to trouble the entire plateau."

"The ghouls have overrun a few farms," Nymia insisted, the sweat on her face gleaming in the firelight. "I still hold Pyarados,"—Aoth realized she was referring specifically to the capital city of her province—"and I've sent to Tharchion Daramos for assistance. He's bringing fresh troops from Thazalhar."

Yaphyll smiled. "Milsantos Daramos is a fine soldier, a winning soldier, and Thazalhar is too small and sparsely populated for a proper tharch. I wonder if it might not be a good idea to merge it and Pyarados into a single territory and give the old fellow authority over both."

Nymia blanched. "I beg you for one more chance—"

Szass Tam silenced her by holding up his hand. "Let's not rush ahead of ourselves. I'd like to hear a full account of the events in the east before we decide what to do about them."

"Aoth Fezim," Nymia said, "is the only man to survive the fall of Thazar Keep. For that reason, I brought him to tell the first part of the story."

Aoth related it as best he could, without trying to inflate his own valor or importance. He made sure, though, that the others understood he'd fled only when the castellan had ordered it and not out of cowardice.

Then Nymia told of the battle at the west end of the pass, justifying her defeat as best she could. That involved explaining that forms of undead had appeared whose existence Aoth had not reported and that neither he nor the other scouts had noticed the creatures swimming beneath the surface of the river. The griffon rider wasn't sure if she was actually implying that he was responsible for everything that had gone wrong or if it was simply his trepidation that made it seem that way.

When she finished, Szass Tam studied Aoth's face. "Do you have anything to add to your commander's account?" he asked.

Partly out of pride, partly because he was all but certain it would only move the zulkirs to scorn, Aoth resisted the urge to offer excuses. "No, Your Omnipotence. That's the way it happened."

The lich nodded. "Well, obviously, victorious soldiers inspire more trust than defeated ones, yet I wouldn't call either of you incompetent, and I don't see a benefit to replacing you with warriors who lack experience fighting this particular incursion. I'm inclined to keep you in your positions for the time being at least, provided, of course, that everyone else is in accord." He glanced about at the other zulkirs.

As Aoth expected, none of the others took exception to their faction leader's opinion, though Lallara's assent had a sullen quality to it. Rumor had it that, willful, erratic, and unpredictable, she was less firmly of the lich's party than the faithful Yaphyll and was something of a creative artist in the field of torture as well. Perhaps she'd been looking forward to inflicting some ingeniously gruesome chastisement on Nymia, her subordinate, or both.

"Now that I've heard Tharchion Focar's report," Iphegor said, "I understand what's happening but not why. I'd appreciate it if someone could enlighten me on that point." He turned his smoldering gaze on Yaphyll. "Perhaps you, Your Omnipotence, possess some useful insights."

Aoth understood why the high priest had singled her out. She was, after all, the zulkir of Divination. Uncovering secrets was her particular art.

She gave the High Flamelord a rueful, crooked smile. "You shame me, Your Omniscience. I can repeat the same speculations we've already passed back and forth until our tongues are numb: We're facing an unpleasantness that one of the vanished kingdoms of the Sunrise Mountains left behind. Despite the best efforts of my order, I can't tell you precisely where the undead horde originated or why it decided to strike at this particular time. You're probably aware that, for better or worse, it's difficult to use divination to find out about anything occurring in central Thay. Jealous of their privacy, too many wizards have cast enchantments to deflect such efforts. When my subordinates and I try to investigate the undead raiders, we meet with the same sort of resistance, as if they have similar wards in place."

Lallara sneered. "So far, this has all been wonderfully productive. Even a zulkir has nothing to offer beyond excuses for ineptitude."

If the barb stung Yaphyll, she opted not to show it. "I will say

I'm not astonished that ancient spirits are stirring. The omens indicate we live in an age of change and turmoil. The great Rage of Dragons two years ago was but one manifestation of a sort of universal ferment likely to continue for a while."

Iphegor nodded. "On that point, Your Omnipotence, your seers and mine agree." He smiled like a beast baring its fangs. "Let us give thanks that so much is to burn and likewise embrace our task, which is to make sure it's the corrupt and unworthy aspects of our existence which go to feed the purifying flames."

"Can we stay focused on killing this nighthaunt and its followers?" Lallara asked. "I assume they qualify as 'corrupt and unworthy.'"

"I would imagine so," said Szass Tam, "and that's our purpose here today: to formulate a strategy. Tharchion Focar has made a beginning by sending to Thazalhar for reinforcements. How can we augment her efforts?"

Samas Kul shrugged his blubbery shoulders. The motion made the tentlike expanse of his gorgeous robes glitter and flash with reflected firelight. "Give her some more troops, I suppose."

"Yes," said the lich, "we can provide some, but we must also recognize our limitations. We reduced the size of our armies after the new policy of trade and peace proved successful. The legions of the north just fought a costly engagement against the Rashemi. Tharchions Kren and Odesseiron need to rebuild their forces and to hold their positions in case of another incursion. I don't think it prudent to pull warriors away from the border we share with Aglarond either. For all we know, our neighbors to the north and west have conspired to unite against us."

"Then what do you suggest?" asked Iphegor Nath.

"We already use our own undead soldiers to fight for us," the lich replied. "The dread warriors, Skeleton Legion, and such. . . . I propose we manufacture more of them. We can disinter folk who died recently enough that the remains are still usable and lay claim to the corpse of any commoner or thrall who dies from this point forward. I mean, of course, until such time as the crisis is resolved."

"People won't like that," Lallara said. "We Thayans put the dead to use in a way that less sophisticated peoples don't, but that doesn't mean the average person *likes* the things or wants to see his sweet old granny shuffling around as a zombie." She gave the lich a mocking smile. "No offense."

"None taken," Szass Tam replied blandly. "There are two answers to your objection. The first is that commoners have little choice but to do as we tell them, whether they like it or not. The second is that we'll pay for the cadavers we appropriate. Thanks to the Guild of Foreign Trade, we have plenty of gold."

Samas Kul smirked and preened.

"That may be," said Iphegor, "but it isn't just squeamish commoners who'll object to your scheme. I object. The Firelord objects. It's his will that the bodies of his worshipers be cremated."

"I'm not averse to granting your followers an exemption," said Szass Tam, "provided you're willing to help me in return."

The priest snorted. "At last we come to it. The reason you included me in your conclave."

"Yes," Szass Tam replied. "I intend to put the order of Necromancy in the forefront of the fight against the marauders. My subordinates won't just supply zombies and skeletons to Tharchion Focar. They'll stand in the battle lines themselves and use their magic to smite the foe. Dealing with the undead is their specialty, after all, so they should acquit themselves admirably, but our forces will prove more formidable still if the church of Kossuth commits itself to the struggle. Pyarados needs warrior priests to exert their special powers versus this sort of threat, and none are more capable than your Burning Braziers."

"According to Tharchion Focar," Iphegor said, "some of the

menace in Pyarados, new worshipers will flock to your altars.

"Surely that's sufficient incentive," Szass Tam continued. "Surely it's more important than anything else we could offer, so must you really haggle like a fishwife for additional concessions?"

Iphegor grinned. "It seemed worth a try, but perhaps it is beneath our dignity. All right, I agree to your terms. When the tharchions and your zombies and necromancers march out, the Burning Braziers, Black Flame Zealots, Brothers and Sisters of the Pure Flame, and the Order of the Salamander will march with them."

Szass Tam returned the smile. "I'm glad to hear it."

The council of war broke up a short time later, and left Aoth feeling both relieved and a little dazed. As he and Nymia retraced their steps through the temple, he murmured, "They spoke so freely."

"Because the High Flamelord insisted on candor," the tharchion replied.

"Yes, but they did it in front of us. They could have sent us out of the room when they started talking about their rivalries and politics and all the rest of it, and I wish they had." He chuckled without mirth. "A man who 'doesn't even wear red' doesn't need to know about such things."

"They didn't bother," Nymia said, her sweaty face set and hard, "because we're insignificant to them. You'd do well to remember it."

.. ..

The slaves, guards, and masters were just ahead. The setting [su]n stretched their shadows in Bareris's direction like dark fin[ger]s reaching to gather him in.

Though why that ominous simile flickered through his mind,

undead apparently possess the ability to strip clerics of their magic. You can understand my reluctance to send my followers into such a situation."

"Ah, yes," said Szass Tam, "the quells. Even the most learned necromancers believed that, like nighthaunts, the last of them perished eons ago, but now that we know of the threat, we can employ countermeasures. We'll guard the priests better—perhaps your orders of militant monks should undertake the task—and arm them better as well, so they're capable of defending themselves even under adverse circumstances."

"Arm them with what?" Iphegor asked.

"With this."

Suddenly a baton of crimson metal reposed in Szass Tam's withered fingers. Though Aoth was looking straight at the zulkir of Necromancy, he had the odd feeling that somehow he'd just missed seeing the rod materialize. Startled, Samas Kul gave a little jerk that set his layers of flab jiggling. Yaphyll smiled at his discomfiture.

"Take it, please," Szass Tam said.

Iphegor accepted the baton which, Aoth now observed, had stylized tongues of flame etched on its surface. As soon as the primate gripped it, the small flames dancing about his person poured hissing down his arm and over the weapon. The tip of it blazed up as if someone had soaked it in oil. Now it resembled a brightly burning torch, and despite the cooling enchantment of his tattoo, Aoth shrank back slightly from the fierce radiant heat.

"I feel the power in it." The primate rose and brandished the torch in an experimental manner. "What exactly does it do?"

"I'll show you," said Szass Tam, rising, "using these targets."

He waved his hand to indicate the entities now occupying one corner of the room. Aoth hadn't noticed them materializing either, nor had he sensed any telltale fluctuation of magical forces in his vicinity. Nymia caught her breath in surprise, or alarm.

One of the creatures was a zombielike "dread warrior," an undead soldier still possessed of the martial skills it had mastered in life, its eyes aglow with yellow phosphorescence. The other was some sort of ghost, a bluish transparent shape that flowed and warped from one moment to the next. Its face flickered repeatedly from wholeness to raw, bleeding ruin, as if an invisible knife were cutting away the nose, lips, and eyes in turn. Aoth assumed the display reprised agonies the spirit had suffered while alive.

After his recent experiences, he felt an unreasoning urge to lash out at the undead things with his spells before they could strike at him, but in point of fact, they weren't moving to menace anyone. Szass Tam's magic evidently caged them where they were.

Iphegor gave the lich a glower. "People aren't supposed to be able to translate anything in or out of the temple without my consent."

"I apologize if it seemed disrespectful," said Szass Tam. "Perhaps later on Lallara can help you improve your wards." As zulkir of Abjuration, as protective magic was called, she was presumably well suited to the task. "For now, though, shall we proceed with our demonstration?"

"All right." The high priest extended his arm, aiming the baton as if it were a wizard's wand or a handheld crossbow. "I assume I point the fiery end at the object of my displeasure."

"Yes. Now focus. Place yourself in the proper frame of mind to cast a spell or chastise undead through sheer force of faith, but you aren't actually going to expend any of your own power. You're simply going to release a measure of what's stored in the rod."

Iphegor snorted. "I do know how to employ a talisman."

"Of course. When you're ready, the trigger word is 'Burn.'"

"Burn," Iphegor repeated.

Dazzling flame exploded from the end of the torch the captive undead. When the flare died a heartbeat were gone as well. The burst had reduced the drea to wisps of ash, while the phantom left no tangibl whatsoever.

"Impressive," Iphegor conceded.

"Thank you," Szass Tam replied. "The discharge is a of fire and that pure essence of light and life which is po undead creatures, and I guarantee you, the Burning Brazi be able to invoke it as required, even if other magic fails."

"There will still be a significant element of danger, an still need to give me an adequate reason to put Kossuth's ser in harm's way."

"Concern for the common folk who need your help?" Ya suggested, grinning.

Judging from her scowl, Lallara found the high priest's recalcitrance less amusing. "Szass Tam already offered to exempt your followers from the mandate to surrender their dead."

"True, that's something," the fire priest said, "and are these torches, which, I assume, the Braziers will keep eve the threat is past. Still, if I'm to throw in with you and enmity of Thrul and his party, I need more."

"It seems to me," said Szass Tam, "that you're getting seek ascendancy over our fellow zulkirs, don't you aspi the worship of Kossuth the primary faith in the realn

"It already is," said Iphegor.

"Granted," said the lich, "but the churches of and Shar are also strong, and in time, one of ther supplant you. As you and Yaphyll agreed, this is a 'change and turmoil.' We're offering you a chanc your continued dominance. If your faith receive ment from the zulkirs and plays a heroic part in he couldn't imagine, because this was a joyous if not miraculous moment. He'd lost precious days to the virulent fever the child-thing's bite had induced. It had been only by the grace of Lady Luck that he'd spotted the tracks that told him the thralls and their captors had left the road. Yet he hadn't fallen so far behind he could never catch up, nor lost the trail either, and his search had come to an end. He kicked his weary horse into a gallop.

A small woman, her dark hair just beginning to grow out, scrambled forth from the ranks of the slaves. It was Tammith. Even at a distance, even after six years, he knew her instantly, as it was plain she'd recognized him despite his outlander's clothing and the sweaty unshaven locks flopping around his head. Crisscrossing her arms, she waved her hands over her head until an orc grabbed her and shoved her back in among the other thralls.

Seeing her subjected to rough treatment made Bareris all the more frantic to close the distance. Still, he forced himself to rein in his mare, because it had looked as if she was waving him off, and some of the guards were maneuvering to intercept him if he came any closer.

It was the final inexplicable oddity in a whole string of them. First he'd learned that necromancers had purchased Tammith and the other slaves in the middle of the night and marched them out of Tyraturos under cover of darkness. Then, bribing and questioning folk along the way, he'd gradually realized that over the course of the last several tendays, people—some recognizably Red Wizards, others possibly their agents—had marched a considerable number of slaves into the sparsely popu-lated north, where the demand for such chattels was ordinarily limited. After that came the discovery that Tammith's owners didn't appear to be taking her to a town, fief, or farm but rather into open country.

Bareris didn't need to know what it all meant. He only wanted to extricate Tammith from the middle of it, but it came to him that, eager as he was to be reunited with the woman he loved, it might be prudent to approach the caravan with caution.

He reviewed the list of all the spells he knew, imagining how he might use them if things went awry, then sang a charm to augment his force of personality. While the enchantment endured, people would see him a shade taller and handsomer than he actually was. They'd find themselves more inclined to like, trust, and oblige him.

That accomplished, he walked his horse forward, sang, and accompanied himself on the yarting, like any wandering minstrel seeking a cordial welcome. On the surface, the song was simply the familiar ditty "The Eagle and the Mouse," but he wove magic through the lines. Enough, he hoped, to beguile the guards and keep them from loosing arrows at him before he drew close enough for conversation.

He paced the tune to conclude just as he reached the mass of people clustered in front of him. By then, charmed, perhaps, by his music, two Red Wizards had stepped forth to meet him. Both were young, which he supposed made sense: Their seniors were surely above the mundane chore of transporting slaves across country. It likewise gave him reason for hope. Older Red Wizards were wealthy almost without exception, but neophytes might still be striving to make their fortunes, hence that much more susceptible to bribery.

Bareris crooned words that would keep his steed from wandering or getting into mischief, swung himself down from the saddle, and dropped to one knee in front of the Red Wizards. The show of respect was arguably excessive. By custom, a bow would have sufficed, but he wanted to flatter them.

"You can stand up," said the one on the right. He had jam stains on his robe and a bulge of paunch beneath it, though his spindly Mulan frame was still lean elsewhere. In time, that was likely to change if he didn't master his love of sweets. "That was a fine song."

" 'That was a fine song,' " mimicked the other mage, his face tattooed in black and white to make it resemble a naked skull, and the fellow with the soiled robe winced at the sneer in his voice. "Who are you, sirrah?"

As a Mulan, Bareris was entitled to a more respectful mode of address, even from a Red Wizard, but he chose not to make an issue of it. "Bareris Anskuld, sir."

"Apparently," said the skull-faced wizard, "you've been following us."

"Yes, sir, all the way from Tyraturos."

The leaner mage sneered at his partner. "So much for your promise to cover our tracks. Have you ever done *anything* right?"

The jam lover flinched. "I reanimated the child just the way our master taught us, and Calmevik was supposed to be one of the best assassins in the city. Everybody said so."

Bareris's mouth turned dry as dust, and a chill oozed up his back. The trap in the alley hadn't been an essentially random misfortune after all. The Red Wizards were so determined on secrecy that they'd left minions behind to kill anyone inquiring into their business, and now he, idiot that he was, had delivered himself into their murderous clutches.

Yet he still had his enchantment heightening his powers of persuasion and other tricks held in reserve. Perhaps, unlikely as it seemed, he could still steer this confrontation where he wanted it to go. It was either that or try to run, and with Tammith's desperate, yearning eyes on him, the latter was a choice he simply couldn't make.

Feigning perplexity, he said, "Are you joking with me, Masters? I didn't meet this Calmevik or anyone who tried to hurt me. I'm just . . . do you see that pretty lass over there?" He pointed.

The skull-faced necromancer nodded. "The one who's been staring at you. Of course."

"Well, just as I followed you all the way north from Tyraturos, I tracked her all the way from Bezantur, where she sold herself into slavery just tendays ago as the result of a tragic misunderstanding. She thought her family needed the gold, but they didn't. She had no way of knowing I was already bound for home after years abroad, coming back to marry her with enough gold in my purse to support her and her kin forever after."

The black- and bone-colored face sneered. "How terribly sad, but it's no concern of ours."

"I understand that," Bareris said, "but I'm begging for your help." He couldn't break into actual song, or the Red Wizards would likely realize he was casting a spell, but he pitched and cadenced his voice in such a way as to imply melody in an effort to render himself still more charismatic and persuasive. "I've loved Tammith ever since we were children growing up in the gutters of Bezantur. It wasn't an easy life for a Mulan child whose family had fallen in poverty. Older boys bullied and beat me, and one day, even though she was of Rashemi descent herself, Tammith came to my aid. We both wound up with bruises and black eyes, on that day and others subsequent, but she never once regretted befriending me. That's the kind of loyal, courageous spirit she possesses. The spirit of someone who deserves a better life that slavery."

The wizard with the flabby belly looked caught up in the story, perhaps even touched by it. Bareris wasn't surprised. The mage had the air or someone who'd likewise been bullied in his time, but if his partner was mellowing, it wasn't apparent from his demeanor.

Still, if a tale of love couldn't move him, maybe baser considerations would. "So I've come to buy her out of bondage," Bareris continued, "and I'll pay well, more than she can possibly be worth to anyone but the man who loves her." He opened one of the hidden pockets in his sword belt, extracted three of the diamonds he and his former comrades had found cached in a dragon-worshiper stronghold, and proffered them in his palm for everyone to see. Even in the failing light, the stones gleamed, and impressed, warriors cursed or murmured to one another. "One jewel for each of you wizards, another for your retainers."

The pudgy mage swallowed as if greed had dried his throat. "Perhaps we could make some sort of arrangement," he said, then stiffened as if expecting his colleague to rebuke him.

But the other necromancer simply smirked and said, "Yes, why not? As the troubadour said, it's a great deal of coin, and what's a single slave one way or the other?" He stretched out his hand, and Bareris gave him the diamonds. "It's a bargain then. The wench is yours. Take her and ride away."

Tammith cried Bareris's name and ran toward him. He turned to catch her in his arms. It should have been a moment of supreme exultation, but he realized that all he felt was fear.

Because it was too easy. Yes, he'd cast glamours that predisposed others to indulge him, sometimes even in defiance of their own best interests or common sense, and had offered treasure in addition, but the mage with the tattooed face had never appeared to fall under the influence of the spells, and the grim truth was he and his fellow necromancer were obviously supposed to keep their mission a secret, which would seem to preclude permitting Bareris and Tammith to depart to talk of what they'd seen.

Had Bareris been in the necromancer's position, and had he, like so many Red Wizards, felt scant obligation to honor a pledge given to an inferior, he might well have pretended to accede to his petitioner's pleas just to put him off his guard. Then he'd attack as soon as a good opportunity presented itself.

Yet Bareris couldn't simply assume treachery and strike first. He didn't dare start an unnecessary fight when, outnumbered as he was, he had so little hope of winning it. Weeping, Tammith flung herself into his embrace, kissed him, and babbled endearments. He hugged her but couldn't reply in kind. He was busy listening.

Yet even so, the necromancer with the tattooed face whispered so softly that for a moment, Bareris wasn't sure if he was actually hearing his voice or only imagining it. Then he felt a subtle prickling on his skin that warned of magic coming into being.

He whirled, dragging the startled Tammith around with him, and shouted. Bardic power amplified the cry into a thunderous boom capable of bruising flesh and cracking bone. The sound smashed the Red Wizard off his feet, and for an instant, Bareris dared to hope he'd killed him, but no, for he started to get up again.

Still, at least Bareris had disrupted the other man's spellcasting, and in so doing, he bought himself a moment he hoped to use to good effect. He beckoned to his horse. Ordinarily, the mare wouldn't have responded to such a gesture, but steed and rider still shared the empathic bond he'd sung into being just before he'd dismounted, and she came running.

He poised himself to leap onto the horse's back and haul Tammith up behind him, but having drawn himself to one knee, his black-and-white skull face now streaked with blood, the lean necromancer brandished a talisman. A bolt of crackling darkness leaped from the charm to spear the mare from behind. She shriveled as though starving past the point of emaciation in a single heartbeat, and her legs gave way beneath her. She crashed to the ground, shuddered, and lay still.

The injured wizard lurched to his feet but evidently couldn't stand straight. Rather, he held himself doubled over as if his midsection was particularly painful. He looked about, no doubt taking in the fact that neither his fellow necromancer nor any of their servants had yet moved to attack or otherwise hinder Bareris. Perhaps the enchantments the bard had cast still influenced them even now, or maybe hostilities had simply erupted too suddenly.

"Get him!" the Red Wizard screamed. "Get him, and we'll divide up *all* his jewels! But take him alive! A true bard will be useful!"

The guards readied their weapons and closed in from all sides. Bareris whipped out his sword and struggled to hold back panic and think. If they hoped to take him alive, that would hamper them a little. If he could somehow seize another horse—

Why then, he thought, the wizards would simply blast the animal out from under Tammith and him as they tried to ride away, or else the guards would shoot it full of arrows. Before the enemy readied themselves for battle, there had existed a slim chance of fleeing successfully on horseback, but it was gone now.

"Give me a knife," Tammith said. He could hear the fear in her voice, but only because he knew her so well. He handed her a blade and she positioned herself so they could protect one another's backs. "I'm sorry you came for me, sorry this is happening, but glad I got to kiss you one last time."

"It wasn't the last time."

In fact, he knew it very likely had been, but he wouldn't abandon hope even in his private thoughts, wouldn't defeat himself and save the enemy the trouble. Maybe he and Tammith could at least kill a few of the bastards before the remainder overwhelmed them.

Blood orcs shrieked their harrowing cry and charged. Bareris chanted, and power stung and shivered down his limbs. Tammith gasped as she experienced the same sensation.

The world, including the onrushing orcs, slowed down, or at least that was how it appeared. In reality, Bareris knew, he and

Tammith were moving more quickly. The enchantment had given him a critical advantage in other combats, and he could only pray it would again.

A whip whirled at his calves. Had it connected, it would have wrapped around his legs and bound them together, but he leaped over the arc of the stroke and slashed the eyes of an orc armed with a cudgel. That put another guard behind him, in position to bash his head with the pommel of its scimitar. It was too sluggish, though, compared to his unnatural celerity. He pivoted, sliced its belly, turned, stepped, and hacked open the throat of the brute with the whip while it was still drawing the rawhide lash back for a second stroke.

That finished all the foes immediately in front of him, and it was then that he heard Tammith half cry, half gasp his name. It was possible she'd been screaming for a moment or two, and he'd been too intent on the blood orcs to hear.

He turned. Another guard, a human on horseback, had looped a whip around Tammith's neck and was lifting her off her feet, essentially garroting her in the process. She flailed with her knife but couldn't connect. Neither her bravery nor the charm of speed sufficed to counter the warrior's advantages of superior strength and skill.

Bareris sprang in and cut at the guard's left wrist, and his blade bit to the bone. The horseman dropped the whip and Tammith with it. Blood spurting from his gashed extremity, features as bestial with rage and pain as the tusked, piggish face of any of the orcs, he prompted his mount—a trained war-horse, evidently—to rear and try to batter Bareris with its front hooves.

Bareris sidestepped and thrust his point into the animal's side. The destrier fell sideways, carrying its rider with it. They hit the ground hard and lay motionless thereafter.

Bareris cast about and found Tammith, a raw red welt now

striping her neck, standing just behind him. "I'm sorry," she said.

He realized she meant she was sorry she hadn't managed to kill the rider with the whip, sorry Bareris had needed to save her. "It's all right." It occurred to him that the two dead horses sprawled on the ground constituted obstacles of sorts. If he and Tammith stood between them, it would make it difficult for very many of their foes to come at them at once. "Come on." He scrambled to the proper position, and she followed.

There he began another song. It would strengthen and steady them, and he could weave specific spells through the melody as needed. Pivoting, he peered to see who meant to attack him next.

A rider with a net spurred his mount into a canter. Crouching, blood orcs circled as if they hoped to clamber over the top of one of the dead horses and take their adversaries by surprise.

Then the wizard with the tattooed face shouted, "Stop! You imbeciles are next to useless, but I can't afford to lose all of you. Forget about taking the minstrel alive, and don't go within reach of his sword, either. Shoot him and his whore, and So-Kehur and I will smite them with spells." He gave Bareris a vicious smile. "Unless, of course, you prefer to surrender."

"Don't," Tammith whispered. "I don't know what they'll do to us if we give up, but I'm sure it will be terrible."

Bareris suspected she was right, yet what was the alternative? To condemn her to die here and now? For while the two of them had evaded capture and injury thus far, it was obvious they no longer had any chance of getting away. It was only the Red Wizard's order to take them alive that had provided even the illusion of hope, and that was no longer in effect.

"We have to surrender," he said, "and hope we can escape later on. Set the knife on the ground." He stooped to do the same with his sword, and then someone gave a startled yell.

Bareris looked around to see slaves scrambling in all directions. Evidently they shared Tammith's conviction that some ghastly fate awaited them at the end of their trek, and they'd decided to take advantage of their keepers' distraction to make a break for freedom.

"Stop them!" the necromancer with the flabby midsection—evidently his name was So-Kehur—wailed.

Some of the guards obeyed. Horsemen galloped and wheeled to cut the thralls off. A blood orc dashed after a group of fleeing men and started slashing them down from behind, evidently on the assumption that if it killed enough of them, the slaughter would cow the rest into giving up.

Of course, not every warrior turned his back on Tammith and Bareris, but as best the bard could judge, even those who hadn't seemed momentarily flummoxed. So, for that matter, did the necromancers. Perhaps he had a hope left after all.

"Follow me!" he said to Tammith. He bellowed a battle cry and charged.

For an instant, he considered running at So-Kehur. Evidently worthless in a crisis, the round-bellied mage had yet to cast a spell and was surely an easier mark than the skull-faced warlock. He must possess an extraordinary aptitude for some aspect of sorcery, or else exceptionally good family connections, to account for his induction into an order of Red Wizards despite the lack of iron in his soul.

The problem was that even if they were of equivalent rank, it was plainly the necromancer with the tattooed face who'd taken charge of the caravan. Should they find themselves at odds, he was the one the warriors would obey, and just to make matters worse, he obviously held his fellow mage in contempt. Bareris could easily imagine himself grabbing So-Kehur, using him as a shield, threatening him with his sword, and having the tattooed wizard laugh and order his underlings to go ahead and shoot them both.

No, if Bareris was going to take a hostage, it had to be the skull-faced mage himself, and so he ran straight at him. He prayed Tammith was still following close behind him but didn't dare waste the instant it would take to glance back and find out.

An arrow whistled past his head. An orc scrambled to block his path, and he split its skull. For a moment, his sword stuck in the wound, but then he managed to yank it free, flinging drops of blood through the air in the process.

Realizing his peril, the skull-faced necromancer brandished the talisman that had killed Bareris's horse, a round medallion, the bard now observed, fashioned of ebony and bone. He wrenched himself to the side, and the jagged blaze of shadow missed him by a finger length.

He raced onward. Just a few more strides would carry him within striking distance of his foe, and with enchantment quickening his actions, he had reason for hope that his adversary didn't have time to attempt any more magic.

But the necromancer had a trick in reserve. Even as his body backed away, his face seemed to spring forward like a striking snake. In reality, Bareris perceived, it was the tattooed skull mask that had torn free of his skin, and as it did, it rounded itself into a snarling head, and a gaunt, decaying body materialized beneath it. It had, in fact, become a ghoul, a slave creature or familiar the Red Wizard had carried inside his own body to evoke in a moment of ultimate need.

Startled by the vile-smelling thing's unexpected materialization, Bareris faltered. The ghoul leaped, its jagged, filthy nails ripping at his face. They nearly snagged him, but then trained reflex twisted him out of the way. He hacked at the bumpy ridge of spine in the corpse eater's withered back, and the undead's legs buckled beneath it.

Bareris sprinted on. Looking unexpectedly soft-featured and callow with his macabre mask stripped away, the Red Wizard

Published by Wizards of the Coast, Inc. FORGOTTEN REALMS, WIZARDS OF THE COAST, and their respective logos are trademarks of Wizards of the Coast, Inc., in the U.S.A. and other countries.

U.S., CANADA,   EUROPEAN HEADQUARTERS
ASIA, PACIFIC, & LATIN AMERICA   Hasbro UK Ltd
Wizards of the Coast, Inc.   Caswell Way
P.O. Box 707   Newport, Gwent NP9 0YH
Renton, WA 98057-0707   GREAT BRITAIN
+1-800-324-6496   Save this address for your records.

Dazzling flame exploded from the end of the torch to engulf the captive undead. When the flare died a heartbeat later, they were gone as well. The burst had reduced the dread warrior to wisps of ash, while the phantom left no tangible residue whatsoever.

"Granted," said the lich, "but the churches of Bane, Cyric, and Shar are also strong, and in time, one of them could well supplant you. As you and Yaphyll agreed, this is a generation of 'change and turmoil.' We're offering you a chance to guarantee your continued dominance. If your faith receives special treatment from the zulkirs and plays a heroic part in destroying the

menace in Pyarados, new worshipers will flock to your altars.

"Surely that's sufficient incentive," Szass Tam continued. "Surely it's more important than anything else we could offer, so must you really haggle like a fishwife for additional concessions?"

Iphegor grinned. "It seemed worth a try, but perhaps it is beneath our dignity. All right, I agree to your terms. When the tharchions and your zombies and necromancers march out, the Burning Braziers, Black Flame Zealots, Brothers and Sisters of the Pure Flame, and the Order of the Salamander will march with them."

Szass Tam returned the smile. "I'm glad to hear it."

The council of war broke up a short time later, and left Aoth feeling both relieved and a little dazed. As he and Nymia retraced their steps through the temple, he murmured, "They spoke so freely."

"Because the High Flamelord insisted on candor," the tharchion replied.

"Yes, but they did it in front of us. They could have sent us out of the room when they started talking about their rivalries and politics and all the rest of it, and I wish they had." He chuckled without mirth. "A man who 'doesn't even wear red' doesn't need to know about such things."

"They didn't bother," Nymia said, her sweaty face set and hard, "because we're insignificant to them. You'd do well to remember it."

The slaves, guards, and masters were just ahead. The setting sun stretched their shadows in Bareris's direction like dark fingers reaching to gather him in.

Though why that ominous simile flickered through his mind,

lifted his talisman for another blast. Bareris had believed he was already running his fastest, but somehow he achieved an extra iota of speed to close the distance. He cut at the necromancer's hand, and the medallion and severed fingers tumbled through the air.

At that instant, Bareris hated the wizard, relished hurting him, and had to remind himself that he needed him alive. He shoved the necromancer down onto the grass, lifted his sword to threaten him—

A voice chanted rhyming words, and the ambient temperature fluctuated wildly. Bareris realized So-Kehur wasn't entirely useless after all. He'd finally found the presence of mind to cast a spell.

Something stabbed into the middle of Bareris's back. It didn't hurt, precisely, but weakness streamed outward from the site like ink diffusing through water. His sword suddenly felt too heavy to support. The blade dropped, and the hilt nearly pulled itself from his grasp. He collapsed to his knees.

He told himself he didn't need his stolen strength. He could hold a hostage down with his weight, and menace him with the lethal sharpness of his blade. He floundered after the necromancer with the maimed hand, but now the mage was the quicker and stayed beyond his reach.

Until a mesh of sticky cable abruptly materialized on top of Bareris, binding and gluing him to the ground. "I did it!" So-Kehur crowed. "I took him alive, just like you wanted."

"So you did," the other wizard gasped, rising unsteadily, "and now I'm going to kill the wretch." Using his intact hand, he fumbled in one of his scarlet robe's many pockets, no doubt seeking the talisman required to facilitate some sort of death magic.

Enfeebled as he was, it was difficult for Bareris even to turn his head. Still, praying she could help him somehow, he peered around for Tammith, only to see her slumped on the ground clutching at a bloody wound in her leg. An orc stood over her, spear aimed to stab her again if she attempted further resistance. Elsewhere, the creature's fellow guards had all but completed the task of catching and subduing the rest of the slaves.

Bareris would have taken any risk to rescue or protect Tammith, but those things were no longer even remotely possible. He had to escape alone now in the hope of returning for her later, if, indeed, he could even manage that.

Rapidly as he dared—too much haste and he might botch the casting—he started singing. Weak as he was, he felt short of breath and had to struggle to achieve the precise intonation and cadence the magic required.

His would-be killer seemed clumsy with his off hand and was possibly on the verge of sinking into shock from the amputation of his fingers. He was slow producing his talisman, but when he realized Bareris was attempting magic, he managed to snatch it forth, flourish it, and jabber hissing, clacking syllables in some foul abyssal tongue.

A thing of tattered darkness, with a vague, twisted face and elongated fingers, swirled into existence between the necromancer and the prisoner caught beneath the sticky net. The wizard pointed, and the shadow pounced.

At the same instant, Bareris completed his spell-song. The world seemed to shatter into motes of light and remake itself an instant later.

The greatest spellcasters could work magic to whisk themselves and a band of comrades hundreds of miles in a heartbeat. Bareris had seen it done. He himself had no such abilities, or he would have employed them to carry Tammith to safety as soon as he clasped her in his arms, but he had mastered a song to translate a single person several yards in a random direction. A desperation ploy that could, with luck, save a man's life after other measures failed.

Thus, he now sprawled on his belly a short distance away from his enemies and the slaves. As best he could judge, no one had spotted him yet, but somebody unquestionably would if he couldn't conceal himself within the next few moments. He tried to crawl, and with the curse of weakness still afflicting him, the effort was so difficult it made him sob.

Crouching low, the shadow-thing started to pivot in his direction. Then something grabbed him by the sword belt and yanked him backward.

chapter six

26 Mirtul, the Year of Risen Elfkin

Mari Agneh rarely had much of an appetite, and this morning was no exception. She scraped the eggs, fried bread, and peach slices off her dish into the chamber pot then performed what had come to be a ritual.

First, she slid the edge of the knife that had arrived with breakfast across her forearm. The blade appeared sharp but failed to slice her skin. In fact, the length of steel deformed with the pressure, as if forged of a material soft as wax.

Next she gripped the spoon. It too was made of metal and had an edge of sorts. A trained warrior, striking in fury and desperation, should be able to hurt someone with it, but when she thrust it at her outstretched limb, she felt only a painless prod, and the utensil bent double.

That left the pewter plate. She slammed it against her arm, and it didn't even sting. It was like swiping herself with a sheet of parchment.

It was always thus. Every item that entered her prison immediately fell under the same enchantment, a charm that made it impossible for her to use it to hurt anyone, herself included. Strips of bed sheet and portions of the skimpy whorish costumes that were all she was given to wear unraveled as soon as she twisted them around her neck and pulled. Even the walls turned soft as eiderdown when she bashed her head against them.

She wondered how many more times she could perform her tests before accepting the obvious truth that her captor's precautions would never ever fail, before abandoning hope.

What would happen to her then? Would she let go of the last shreds of her pride? Of sanity itself? The prospect was terrifying yet perversely tempting too, for if she broke or went mad, perhaps the torments would be easier to bear. Perhaps Aznar Thrul would even grow bored with her. Maybe he'd kill her or simply forget about her.

She struggled to quash the weak, craven urge to yield and be done with it, then noticed the vapor seething through the crack beneath the door.

Mari's first thought was that some malevolent god had seen fit to grant the prayer implicit in her moment of despair, that Thrul, or one of his servants, was blowing a poisonous mist into the room to murder her. She didn't actually believe it. The zulkir hadn't shown any sign of growing tired of his toy, and she was certain that if he ever did decide to dispose of her, he'd at least want to watch her die. No, this was something else, which didn't make it any less alarming.

The vapor swirled together and congealed into a towering creature with purple-black hide, four arms, a vaguely lupine countenance, and a brand on its brow. Mari retreated and picked up a chair. Like every other article in her prison, the seat would fall to useless pieces if she tried to strike a blow with it, but perhaps the demon, if that was what the thing was, didn't know that.

Of course, it was ludicrous to imagine that such a horror might fear a nearly naked woman brandishing a chair in any case, but it was all she could think of to do.

The demon either smiled or snarled at her. The shape of its jaws was sufficiently unlike the structure of a human mouth that she couldn't tell which.

"Greetings, Tharchion," it rumbled. "My name is Tsagoth, and I've been hunting you for a while."

"I don't believe Aznar Thrul sent you," she said, struggling to keep her voice steady. "If he wanted you to molest me, he'd also want to be here when you did it. If I were you, I'd think twice about bothering me without his consent."

Tsagoth snorted. "You're right. I am here without the zulkir's permission, so scream for help if you think anyone will come. Let's get that out of the way."

It—or rather, *he*, for the hulking creature was plainly male—was right. She could try calling for help, but she wouldn't.

"No. No matter how bad it gets, I never beg the swine for anything."

Tsagoth's hideous grin stretched wider. "I like that."

His attitude didn't actually seem threatening. Rather, it was . . . well, something else, something anomalous.

Still wary, but increasingly puzzled as well, she asked, "You like what?"

"Your toughness. I know something of what you've endured, and I expected to find you ruined, but you're not. That will make our task easier."

"What task?"

"Killing Thrul, of course. Attaining your revenge."

She shook her head. "You don't look like you need help to kill anybody you take a mind to kill."

"You flatter me, Tharchion. I'm more than a match for most prey, but I'm not capable of destroying one of the most powerful wizards of your world. Nor, perhaps, is anyone, so long as he's on his guard and armored with his talismans, enchanted robes, and whatnot. But what about those occasions when he lays aside his staff, divests himself of his garments, and is enflamed and heedless with passion? Don't you think he might be vulnerable then?"

"You mean, you want to hide here and attack while he's . . . busy with me?"

"No, we can't do it that way, not when we don't know how many days or tendays it will be before he next visits you. I'm supposedly a slave here in the palace. If I go missing, people will search for me, and even if they didn't, I imagine Thrul would sense a third party—a denizen of the Abyss, no less—lurking in your chamber. You'll have to be the one to kill him, and though I know little of humans, I suspect you'll prefer it that way."

"I would if it would work," Mari said, "but I don't see how it can. His magic prevents any object that enters the room from serving me as a weapon and limits me in other ways as well. If he gives me a direct order, I have no choice but to follow it." No matter how degrading. She felt nauseated at the memory of the laughter of the sycophants he'd brought to watch her perform.

"You won't need a weapon if you are the weapon," Tsagoth said, "and your puppet strings will break if you cease to be the sort of creature they were fashioned to control."

"You want to . . . change me?"

"Yes." Evidently the mark on his forehead itched, for he scratched at it with the claws on his upper left hand. "I'm a blood fiend. An undead. As vampires prey on humans, so does my kind prey on demons, and like vampires, we can, when we see fit, share our gifts and essential nature with others."

"But you normally transform other creatures from the nether-world, don't you?"

"Yes," Tsagoth said, "and to be honest, I don't know if it

will work the same on you. You mortals are fragile vessels to contain the power I hope to give you. I can only tell you that he who summoned me cast spells to increase the likelihood of our success."

"Who are you talking about?"

"I'm forbidden to say. Someone who wants to help you avenge yourself. Does anything else truly matter?"

Mari frowned. "It may. I'm willing to risk my life. As a warrior, I did it more times than I can remember, but if I change into something like you, will I still be the same person inside? Will I keep my soul?"

The blood fiend shrugged. The gesture looked peculiar with four arms performing it. "I can't say. I'm a hunter, not a scholar of such esoterica, but ask yourself if this spark you mortals prize so highly is truly of any use to you. Does it make your punishments and humiliations any less excruciating? If not, what good is it compared to a chance for retribution?"

Maybe he was right, and even if not, it abruptly came to her that in all probability, he was going to transform her whether she consented or not. Ultimately, he was as much a slave as she was and had no choice but to carry out his master's commands. He was offering her the opportunity to agree because . . . she wasn't sure why. It seemed preposterous to imagine that such a being could like her or consider her a kindred spirit, but perhaps her initial defiance had elicited a measure of respect.

If so, she was glad to have it. It had been a long while since anyone, even the servant who brought her meals, had shown her anything but contempt. She didn't want to forfeit that regard by showing fear, by obliging him to treat her as victim and pawn instead of accomplice, and perhaps that was what ultimately tipped the balance in her mind.

"Yes," she said. "Make me strong again."

Tsagoth grinned. "You were never truly strong, human, but

you will be." He clawed a gash into the palm of his lower left hand and held it out to her. "Drink."

His blood was like fire in her mouth, but she forced herself to suck and lap it anyway.

•• •• •• •• •• •• •• •• •• •• •• •• •• ••

Bareris wasn't sure if he was a guest or a prisoner of the gnolls, and at first he was nearly too sick to care. So-Kehur's curse of weakness was to blame. Ordinarily such afflictions passed quickly, but the effects of arcane magic, partaking as it did of primordial chaos, were never entirely predictable, and maybe some lingering vestige of the illness from which Bareris had only recently recovered rendered him particularly susceptible. In any event, it had taken him well into the next day to start feeling any stronger at all.

Thus, when, guards shouting and cracking their whips, the caravan resumed its trek, he'd had no choice but to simply lie and watch, not that he could have prevented it in any case. Lie and watch as Tammith's captors marched her away into the gathering darkness.

Once the procession vanished, the gnoll who'd dragged him back into the low place in the earth, thus hiding him from the Red Wizards and their minions, rose, hoisted him onto its back, and headed north. A head taller than even a lanky Mulan, the creature with its hyenalike head, coarse mane, and rank-smelling spotted fur manifestly possessed remarkable strength and stamina, for its long stride ate up the miles without flagging, until it reached the rude camp—three lean-tos and a shallow pit for a fire—it had established with several others of its kind.

Evidently they were all out hunting and foraging, for as the night wore on, they returned one or two at a time with rabbit, edible roots, and the like, which they grilled all together in an iron skillet. Bareris's rescuer—or was it captor?—insisted that he receive a share of the meal, and while some of its comrades snarled and bared their fangs, none was as big or powerful-looking, and their display of displeasure stopped short of actual resistance.

When the sun rose, they mostly lay down to sleep, though one stood watch. When Bareris's strength started to trickle back, he wondered if he could take the sentry by surprise, kill it or club it unconscious, and flee while the other gnolls slumbered on oblivious.

If so, it might be prudent to try. Gnolls had a savage reputation, and it was by no means ridiculous to conjecture that eventually the hyenafolk meant to fry some bard meat in their skillet.

Yet he was reluctant to strike out at anyone who, thus far at least, had done him more good than harm, and his lingering weakness, coupled with his frustration over his failure to liberate Tammith, nurtured a bleak passivity. He simply lay and rested until sunset, when the sleeping gnolls began to rouse.

The big one walked over and peered down at him. "You better," he said. As his form was half man and half hyena, so was his speech half voice and half growl. If he hadn't possessed the trained ear of a bard, Bareris doubted he would have understood.

"I am better," he agreed, rising. "The curse is finally fading. My name is Bareris Anskuld."

The gnoll slapped his chest. "Wesk Backbreaker, me."

"Thank you for hiding me from my enemies."

"Hide easy. Sneak around humans and stinking blood orcs all the time. They never see." Wesk laughed, and though it sounded different, sharper and more bestial than human laughter, Bareris heard the bitterness in it. "Or else they kill. Not enough gnolls to fight them. Not enough singer, either. Crazy to bother them like you did."

Bareris sighed. "Probably."

"But brave. And fight good. Like gnoll."

"That's high praise. I've seen your people fight." No need to mention that he'd witnessed it during his wanderings and had been fighting on the opposing side. "Was that the reason you rescued me?"

"Help you because you chop fingers of Red Wizard."

"Did he wrong you somehow?"

Wesk snorted. "Not just that one. All Red Wizards. Gnoll clan fight in legion. Wesk's father. Father's father. Always. Until Red Wizards say, no more war. Trade now. Then they make blood orcs and say blood orcs better than gnolls."

Bareris thought he understood: "To save coin, someone decided to reduce the size of the army, and you and your clan brothers were discharged."

"Yes. Just hunters now. Robbers when we can. Not fair!"

"On the ride north, I heard that Thay's at war with Rashemen again. The legions of Gauros and Surthay are looking for recruits."

"Recruits?" Wesk snarled. "Crawl back to take orders from blood orcs? No!"

"I understand. It's a matter of pride." A mad thought came to him. "If you won't serve a tharchion, what about working for me?"

Wesk cocked his head. "You?"

"Why not? I can pay." In theory, anyway. In fact, most of his wealth was in his sword belt and purse, which the gnolls had already confiscated, but he'd worry about that detail when the time came.

"To kill Red Wizards? Want to, but no. Told you, gnolls too few."

"I understand we can't wage all-out war on them, but we can make fools of them, and maybe it will involve bleeding an orc or two along the way."

Wesk grunted. "Everyone needs to hear, but some not talk your talk. I . . . " He hesitated, evidently groping for the proper word.

"Translate? No need." Bareris sang softly, and the growling, yipping conversations of the other gnolls abruptly became intelligible to him. While the enchantment lasted, he would likewise be able to speak to them in their own language. *"Let's gather everyone up."*

The impromptu assembly convened around the ashes of last night's cook fire, and Bareris found that the unwashed-dog smell of gnoll was markedly worse when several of the creatures gathered together. Some of the hyenafolk glared at him with overt scorn and hostility, some seemed merely curious, but with the possible exception of Wesk, none appeared cordial or sympathetic.

But a bard had the power to make good will flower where none had existed before, and as he introduced himself and spun his tale, he infused his voice with subtle magic to accomplish that very purpose.

Yet even so, he wondered if a story of a loved one in peril could possibly move them. If gnolls were even capable of love, they'd never, so far as he knew, permitted a member of another race to glimpse any evidence of it. On the other hand, they were tribal by nature. That suggested something approximating a capacity for affection, didn't it?

In the end, perhaps the person he moved the most was himself. Spinning the story made everything he'd experienced acutely, painfully real, and when he told of seeing and touching Tammith only to lose her again immediately thereafter, it was all he could do to keep from weeping, but he couldn't allow the gnolls to think him a weakling.

He ended on a note of bitter anger akin to their own: *"So you see how it's been for me. I undertook what should have been a simple task, especially considering that I was willing, nay, eager, to reward anyone able to help me, but I met contempt, betrayal, and bared blades every step of the way. Now I'm done with the mild and reasonable approach. I'm going to recover Tammith by force, and I want you lads to help me."*

The gnolls stared at him for another moment, and then one, with a ruddy tinge to his fur and longer ears than the rest, laughed his piercing, crazy-sounding cackle. *"Sorry, human. It can't be done."*

"Why not?" Bareris demanded.

"Because the slaves go to Delhumide."

For a moment, Bareris didn't understand. They were all in Delhumide, and what of it? Then he realized the gnoll wasn't speaking of the tharch but of the abandoned city of the same name.

Twenty-three centuries before, when Thay had been a Mulhorandi colony, Delhumide had been one of its greatest cities and bastions of power, and when the Red Wizards rebelled, they'd deemed it necessary to destroy the place. They'd evidently used the darkest sort of sorcery to accomplish their purpose, for by all accounts, the ground was still unclean today. Demons walked there, and a man could contract madness or leprosy just by venturing down the wrong street. No one visited Delhumide except the most reckless sort of treasure hunter, and few of those ever returned.

"Are you sure?" Bareris asked. It was, of course, a stupid question, born of surprise, and he didn't wait for an answer. *"Why?"*

"We don't know," said the gnoll. *"We have better sense than to go into Delhumide ourselves."*

"Even if we could," said Wesk. After listening to his broken Mulhorandi, Bareris found it odd to hear him speak fluently,

but he naturally had no difficulty conversing in his own racial language. *"Soldiers guard the place by day, and at night, the things come out. I don't know if they're the fiends that have always haunted the place or pets of the Red Wizards—maybe some of both—and it doesn't matter anyway. They're there, and they're nasty."*

"I understand," Bareris said, *"but you fellows are experts at going unseen. You told me so yourself, and I witnessed your skill firsthand when you hid the both of us. I'll wager your legion used you as expert scouts and skirmishers."*

"Sometimes," said Wesk.

"Well, I'm a fair hand at creeping and skulking myself, so long as I'm not crippled. With luck, we could sneak in and out of Delhumide without having to fight every warrior or lurking horror in the ruins."

"To steal back your mate," said the gnoll who'd jeered at him before.

"Yes. I've never seen Delhumide, but you've scouted it from the outside anyway. You can figure out the safest path in. Together, we can rescue Tammith, and in gratitude for your help, I'll make you rich enough to live in luxury in Eltabbar or Bezantur until the end of your days. Just give me back my pouch and sword belt."

The gnolls exchanged looks, then one of them fetched the articles he'd requested from the shade beneath one of the lean-tos. As he'd expected, the gnoll removed his sword from its scabbard first, and when he looked inside the pigskin bag, the coins were gone.

•But the gnolls hadn't discovered the secret pocket in the bottom of the purse. He lifted the bag to his mouth and exhaled into it. His breath activated a petty enchantment, and the hidden seam separated. He removed the sheets of parchment, unfolded them, and held them up for the gnolls to see. *"Letters of credit from the merchant houses of Turmish and Impiltur. A little the worse for wear, but still valid."*

Wesk snorted. *"None of us can read, singer, nor has any idea how such papers are supposed to look. Maybe you guessed that and decided to try and fool us."*

"No, but I can offer you a different form of wealth if that's what you prefer." He started opening the concealed pockets in the sword belt and was relieved to find that the gnolls hadn't found those either.

He brought out rubies, sapphires, and clear, smooth tapered king's tears. It was an absurd amount of wealth to purchase the services of half a dozen gnolls, yet for this moment anyway, he felt a sudden, unexpected spasm of loathing for the stones. If he'd never departed Bezantur to win them, he could have prevented Tammith from selling herself into slavery, and what good had they done him since? He had to resist a wild impulse to empty the belt entirely.

He spread the jewels on the ground with a flourish, like a juggler performing a trick. *"Here. Take them if you're willing to help me."*

The gnoll with the prominent ears laughed. *"What's to stop us from taking them without helping you, then cutting up that pouch and belt and all your belongings to see if anything else is stashed inside? Wesk liked seeing you lop a Red Wizard's fingers off. It made him curious enough to haul you back here and find out who you are, but we're not your friends, or friends to any human. We rob and eat hairless runts like you."*

Bareris wondered if Wesk would take exception to his clan brother's assertion. He didn't, though, and perhaps it wasn't surprising. Bareris had claimed he was capable of leading the gnolls in a dangerous enterprise. If so, he should be competent to stand up for himself when a member of the band sought to intimidate him.

Or maybe the whim that had moved Wesk to rescue him originally had simply been a transient aberration, and now the towering creature was all gnoll again, feral and murderous as the foulest of his kin.

Either way, it scarcely mattered. Bareris had known that displaying the jewels was likely to provoke a crisis, and now he had to cope as best he could. *"Take the stones and give nothing in return?"* he sneered. *"Strange, that's just what the Red Wizards and blood orcs tried to do, and I thought you deemed yourselves better than they are."*

The gnoll with the long ears bared his fangs. *"We are better. They couldn't kill you and take your treasure, but we can."*

"No," said Bareris, *"you can't. It doesn't matter that you withheld my sword or that you outnumber me."* In reality, it almost certainly would, but he did his best to project utter self-confidence. *"I'm a bard, a spellcaster, and my powers are what will enable us to make jackasses of the Red Wizards. I'll show you."*

He picked up one of the king's tears and sang words of power. Tiny sparks flared and died within the crystal, and a sweet smell like incense suffused the air. Alarmed, some of the gnolls jumped up and snatched for their weapons or else lunged and grabbed for Bareris with their empty hands.

None of them acted in time, and light burned from within the jewel. It had no power to injure the gnolls. That would inevitably have resulted in a genuine battle, which was the last thing he wanted, but the hyenafolk were essentially nocturnal by nature, and the sudden flare dazzled and balked them. Coupled with the charms of influence Bareris had already spun, it might, with luck, even impress them more than it actually deserved to.

At once, while they were still recoiling, the bard sprang to his feet and punched as hard as ever in his life. The uppercut caught the gnoll with the long ears under the jaw. His teeth clicked together, and he stumbled backward.

"That," Bareris rapped, *"was for impudence. Threaten me again and I'll tear you apart."*

He then brandished the luminous king's tear as if it were a talisman of extraordinary power, and as he spoke on, he infused his words with additional magic—not a spell of coercion, precisely, but an enchantment to bolster the courage and confidence of all who heard it.

"It comes down to this," he said. *"Even if you could kill me and steal the gems, it wouldn't matter. You'd still be a legion's castoffs, worthless in everyone's eyes including your own, but I'm offering you a chance to take revenge on the sort of folk who shamed you, and more than that, to regain your honor. Don't you see, if you join me in this venture, then you're not mere contemptible scavengers anymore. You're mercenaries, soldiers once again.*

"Or perhaps you don't care about honor," he continued. *"Maybe you never had it in the first place. That's what people say about gnolls, that in their hearts and minds, they're vile as rats. You tell me if it's true."*

Pupils shrunk small by the magical glare, Wesk glowered for a moment. Then he growled, *"Put out the light and we'll talk some more."*

Bareris's muscles went limp with relief, because while he still had little confidence that the gnolls would prove reliable if things became difficult, he discerned that, for the present at least, they meant to follow him.

chapter seven

29 Mirtul, the Year of Risen Elfkin

Aoth and Brightwing studied Dulos, the hamlet far below. For a moment, the place looked ordinary enough, the usual collection of sod-roofed huts and barns, but then the griffon rider observed that no one was working the fields and that sheep, pigs, and oxen lay torn and rotting in their pens. Then, his senses linked to his familiar's, he caught the carrion stink.

"The undead have been here," he said.

"No, really?" Brightwing replied.

Aoth was too intent on the work at hand, and perhaps too full of memories of the massacres at Thazar Keep and beside the river, to respond to the sarcasm in kind. "The question is, are they still here, or have they moved on?"

"I can't tell from up here."

"Neither can I. Perhaps the Burning Braziers can. Or the necromancers. Let's return to the company."

The griffon wheeled, and her wings, shining gold in the

sunlight, swept up and down. Soon Aoth's patrol appeared below.

The force was considerably smaller than the army that had met disaster in the mouth of the Pass of Thazar. Supposedly, once the undead horde gained access to the central plateau, they'd dispersed into smaller bands. Thus, Nymia Focar's host had no choice but to do the same if they hoped to eradicate the creatures as rapidly as possible.

When Brightwing landed, Aoth's lieutenants were waiting to confer with him, or at least they were supposed to be his lieutenants. Nymia had declared him in charge, but Red Wizards had little inclination to recognize the authority of anyone not robed in scarlet, while the militant priests of Kossuth had somehow acquired the notion that Szass Tam and the other zulkirs had all but begged Iphegor Nath to dispatch them on this mission and accordingly believed everyone ought to defer to them.

Aoth tried to diminish the potential for dissension by making sure to solicit everyone's opinions before making a decision and by pretending to weigh them seriously even when they betrayed complete ignorance of the craft of war. It seemed to be working so far.

"The enemy," he said, swinging himself off Brightwing's back, "attacked the village."

Her red metal torch weapon dangling in her hand, the scent of smoke clinging to her, Chathi Oandem frowned. The hazel-eyed priestess of Kossuth had old burn scars stippling her left cheek, the result, perhaps, of some devotion gone awry, but Aoth found her rather comely nonetheless, partly because of her air of energy and quick intelligence.

"They've come this far west then, this close to Eltabbar."

"Yes," said Aoth. "It makes me wonder if they might even have been bold enough to attack Surag and Thazrumaros." They were larger towns that might have had some hope of fending off an assault. "But for the time being, our concern is here. Can someone cast a divination to see if the settlement is still infested?"

Chathi opened her mouth, no doubt to say that she'd do it, but Urhur Hahpet jumped in ahead of her. Evidently not content with a single garment denoting his status, the sallow, pinch-faced necromancer wore a robe, cape, and shoulder-length overcape, all dyed and lined with various shades of red, as well as a clinking necklace of human vertebrae and finger bones.

"If it will help," he said, with the air of a lord granting a boon to a petitioner, "but we need to move up within sight of the place."

So they did, and Aoth made sure everyone advanced in formation, weapons at the ready, despite the fact that he and Brightwing had just surveyed the approach to the hamlet from the air and hadn't observed any potential threats. After seeing the lacedons rise from the river, he didn't intend to leave anything to chance.

Nothing molested them, and when he was ready, Urhur whispered a sibilant incantation and spun his staff, a rod of femurs fused end to end, through a mystic pass. The air darkened around him as if a cloud had drifted in front of the sun, reminding Aoth unpleasantly of the nighthaunt's ability to smother light.

"There are undead," the wizard said. "A fair number of them."

"Then we'll have to root them out," said Aoth.

Urhur smiled a condescending smile. "I think you mean burn them out. Surely that's the safest, easiest course, and it will give our cleric friends a chance to play with their new toys."

The Burning Braziers bristled. Aoth, however, did his best to mask his own annoyance. "Safest and easiest, perhaps, but it's possible there are still people alive in there."

"Unlikely, and in any case, you're talking about peasants."

"Destroying the village would also make it impossible to gather additional intelligence about our foes."

"What do you think there is to learn?"

"We'll know when we find it." Aoth remembered his resolve to lead by consensus, or at least to give the appearance, and looked around at the other officers in the circle. "What do the rest of you think?"

As expected, the other necromancers sided with Urhur, but rather to Aoth's relief, the Burning Braziers stood with him, perhaps because Urhur so plainly considered himself their superior as well. It gave the griffon rider the leeway to choose as he wanted to choose without unduly provoking the Red Wizards, or at least he hoped it did.

"Much as I respect your opinions," he said to Urhur, "I think that this time we need to do it the hard way. We'll divide the company into squads who will search house to house. We need at least one necromancer or priest in every group, and we want the monks and Black Flame Zealots sticking close to the Burning Braziers in case a quell or something similar appears. Clear?"

Apparently it was. Though after he turned away, he heard Urhur murmur to one of his fellows that it was a crime that a jumped-up little toad of a Rashemi should be permitted to risk Mulan lives merely to pursue a forlorn hope of rescuing others of his kind.

The nature of the battle to come required fighting on the ground, and as the company advanced, Aoth and Brightwing strode side by side.

"You should have punished Urhur Hahpet for his disrespect," the griffon said.

"And wound up chained in a dungeon for my temerity," Aoth replied, "if not now, then when the campaign is over."

"Not if you frightened him properly."

"His specialty is manipulating the forces of undeath. How easily do you think he scares?"

Still, maybe Brightwing was right. The Firelord knew, Aoth

had never aspired to be a leader of men—he only needed good food, strong drink, women, magic, and flying to make him happy—and he still found it ironic that he'd ascended to a position of authority essentially by surviving a pair of military disasters. Contributing to a victory or two struck him as a far more legitimate qualification.

Which was to say, he was certain of his competence as a griffon rider and battle mage but less so of his ability as a captain. Still, here he was, with no option but to try his best.

"Maybe Urhur won't survive the battle," Brightwing said. "Maybe that would be better all around." It was one of those moments when the griffon revealed that, for all her augmented intelligence and immersion in the human world, she remained a beast of prey at heart.

"No," Aoth said. "It would be too risky, and wasteful besides, to murder one of our most valuable allies when we still have a war to fight. Anyway, it wouldn't sit right with me."

The griffon gave her wings a shake, a gesture denoting impatience. Her plumage rattled. "This squeamishness is why they never gave you a red robe."

"And here I thought I was just too short."

As the company neared the village, Aoth heard the flies buzzing over the carcasses in the corral, and the stink of spilled gore and decay grew thicker and fouler. The sound and smell clashed with the warmth and clear blue sky of a fine late-spring day, a day when lurking undead constituted a preposterous incongruity.

It occurred to him that if he could only expose them to the light of the sun shining brightly overhead, they might not lurk for long. He pointed his spear at the barn he and his squad were approaching, a structure sufficiently large that it seemed likely two or more families had owned it in common.

"Can you tear holes in the roof?"

Brightwing didn't ask why. She was intelligent enough to

comprehend and might well have discerned the reason through their psychic link even if she weren't. "Yes." She unfurled her wings.

He stepped away to give her room to flap them. "Just be careful."

She screeched—derisively, he thought—and leaped into the air.

Aoth led his remaining companions to the door. He started through then hesitated. Should a captain take the lead going into danger or send common and presumably more expendable warriors in ahead? After a moment's hesitation, he proceeded. He'd rather be thought reckless than timid.

Inside, the mangled bodies of plow horses and goats lay where they'd dropped. The buzzing of the flies seemed louder and the stench more nauseating, as if the stale, hot, trapped air amplified them. Overhead, the roof cracked and crunched, and a first sunbeam stabbed down into the shadowy interior. Particles of dust floated in the light.

For a moment, nothing stirred except the swarming flies and the drifting motes. Then a thing that had once been a man floundered up from underneath a pile of hay. Clutching a saw as if it hoped to use the tool as a makeshift sword, it shuffled forward.

The zombie wore homespun peasant garb and showed little sign of decay, but no one who observed the glassy eyes and slack features could have mistaken it for a living thing. It made a wordless croaking sound, and its fellows reared up from their places of concealment.

Aoth leveled his spear to thrust at any foe that came within reach and considered the spells he carried ready for the casting. Before he could select one, however, Chathi stepped to the front line. Not bothering with her torch, she simply glared at the zombies and rattled off an invocation to her god. Blue and yellow fire danced on her upper body, and Aoth stepped back from the sudden heat. All but one of the zombies burst into flame and burned to ash in an instant. His face contorted with rage and loathing, a soldier armed with a battle-axe confronted the one remaining, first sidestepping the clumsy stroke of a cudgel and lopping off the gray hand that gripped it then smashing the undead creature's skull.

Was that it? Aoth wondered. Had they cleared the barn? Then Brightwing screeched, "Watch out! Above you!"

A hayloft hung over the earthen, straw-strewn floor, and now darkness poured over the edge of it like a waterfall. In that first instant, it looked like a single undifferentiated torrent of shadow. It was only when it splashed down and the entities comprising it sprang apart, launching themselves at one foe or another, that Aoth could make out the vague, inconstant semblances of men and hounds. Even then, the phantoms were difficult to see.

Brightwing's cry had no doubt served as a warning of sorts even to those who couldn't understand her voice. Still, the dark things were fast, and some of Aoth's men failed to orient on them quickly enough. The shadows snatched and bit, and though their touch shed no blood and left no visible marks, warriors gasped and staggered or collapsed entirely. The soldier who'd destroyed the zombie bellowed and swept his axe through the spindly waist of the creature facing him. By rights, the stroke should have cut the spirit entirely in two, but manifestly unharmed, the phantom drove its insubstantial fingers into its opponent's face. He fell backward with the undead entity clinging like a leech on top of him.

"You need some form of magic to hurt them!" Aoth shouted. "If you don't have it, stay behind those who do!" He pivoted to tell Chathi to use her torch.

Unfortunately, she'd dropped it, probably when one of the ghostly hounds charged in and bit her. The same murky shape was lunging and snapping at her now. She might have destroyed or repelled it with a spell or by the simple exertion of faith that had annihilated the zombies, but perhaps the debilitating effect of her invisible wound or simple agitation was hampering her concentration. Meanwhile, the monk assigned as her bodyguard was busy with two shadows, one man-shaped and one canine, of his own.

Aoth charged the point of his lance with additional power and drove it down at the shadow-beast assailing Chathi. The thrust drove into the center of the phantom's back and on through into the floor. The spirit withered away to nothing.

"Thank you," the priestess stammered, teeth chattering as if she'd taken a chill.

"Pick up the torch and use it," Aoth snapped then glimpsed motion from the corner of his eye. He pivoted toward it.

The shadow gripped the semblance of a battle-axe in its fists, and despite its vagueness, Aoth could make out hints of a legionnaire's trappings in its silhouetted form. The warrior who'd slain the zombie had risen as a shadow to menace his former comrades, and the transformation had occurred mere moments after his own demise.

Aoth tried to swing his spear into position to pierce his foe, but he'd driven it too deep into the earth. It took an instant too long to jerk it free, and the phantom warrior rushed into the distance and swung its axe.

Had the axe been a weapon of steel and wood and not, in effect, simply the ghost of one, the blow would have sheared off his right arm at the shoulder. As it was, the limb went numb. Cold and weakness stabbed through his entire body, and his knees buckled. He stumbled, and the shade lifted the axe for another blow.

Before it could strike, a flare of flame engulfed it, and it burned away to nothing. As close as they'd been, the blast could easily have burned Aoth as well, but he wasn't inclined to complain.

"Thanks," he gasped to Chathi.

"Now we're even," she replied, grinning. Torch extended, she turned to seek another target.

Striving to control his breathing, Aoth invoked the magic bound in his tattoos to alleviate his weakness and the chill still searing his insides. He then rattled off a spell. Darts of blue light hurtled from his fingertips, diverging to streak at shadows at various points around the barn. Some saw the attack coming and sought to dodge, but the missiles veered to compensate. It was one of the virtues of this particular spell that in most situations it simply couldn't miss.

Next he conjured a crackling, forking flare of lightning. Like his previous effort and Chathi's attacks, it blasted more shades out of existence, but plenty remained, or so it seemed to him, reinforced by the tainted essences of those they'd already managed to slay, and he wondered if he and the Burning Brazier could eradicate them in time to keep them from annihilating the squad.

Then a crash sounded overhead. Scraps of wood and shingle showered down, and Brightwing plunged after them through the breach she'd created into the midst of several shadows. Her talons and snapping beak flashed right and left.

Her entry into the battle helped considerably. It only took a few more breaths to clear the remaining shades away.

The griffon tossed her head. "Stick me on the roof to punch holes. What a clever idea."

"It would have been useful," said Aoth, "if it had been a different sort of undead, vampires maybe, or certain types of wraith, hiding inside here." Something about his own words nagged at him, but he wasn't sure what and didn't have time to puzzle it out. He turned to Chathi. "Can you tend to those who are hurt?"

"You're first," she said.

She murmured a prayer, and a corona of blue flame rippled across her hand. She lifted her fingers to his face, and this time he, who'd experienced the healing touch of a cleric of the Firelord on previous occasions, had little difficulty resisting the natural urge to flinch away.

As he'd anticipated, the heat of the flames was mild enough to be pleasant as it flowed through him to melt chill and debility away. Her caress was pleasurable in a different way. Her fingers were hard with callus like his own, the digits of a woman who'd trained to fight the enemies of her faith with mundane weapons as well as magic, but there was softness in the way they stroked his cheek, and they lingered for a moment after the healing was done.

It gave him something else to think about, but not now, not when he didn't know what else was lying in wait in the hamlet or how the other squads were faring. He waited for her to minister to anyone else who'd suffered but survived the shadows' touch, then formed up his troops and moved on.

As it turned out, the undead had congregated in four sites altogether, whether for mutual defense or simply out of some instinct to flock, Aoth wasn't knowledgeable enough to guess. It wasn't easy to clean out any of the three remaining locations, but none proved as difficult as the barn. The Thayans purged the village with acceptable losses on their own side, or so Nymia Focar would certainly have said.

As he glumly surveyed the several dead men laid out on the ground, Aoth found he had difficulty achieving a similar perspective. Over the years, he'd grown accustomed to watching fellow legionnaires die, but never before had it been because he himself had ordered them into peril.

Necklace rattling, bony staff sweating a greenish film, perhaps the residual effect of some spell he'd cast with it in the heat of battle, Urhur Hahpet sauntered up to view the corpses.

"Well," he said, "it appears there were no survivors for you to rescue."

"No," Aoth said.

"I assume, then, that you gleaned some critical piece of information to justify our casualties."

Aoth hesitated, fishing inside himself for the insight that had nearly come to him after Chathi burned the zombies. It continued to elude him. "I don't know. Probably not."

Urhur sneered. "By the Dark Sun! If you claim to be a wizard, act like it. Stop moping. You blundered, but you're lucky. You have necromancers to shield you from the consequences of your poor judgment. Just stand back and let me work."

Aoth did as the Red Wizard wished. Urhur cast handfuls of black powder over the bodies then whirled his staff through complex figures. He chanted in a grating language that even his fellow mage couldn't comprehend, though the mere sound of it made his stomach queasy. The ground rumbled.

Aoth felt a sudden urge to stop the ritual, but of course he didn't act on it. Szass Tam himself had decreed that his minions were to exploit the fallen in this manner. Besides, Aoth had served with zombies and such since his stint in the legions began. Indeed, thanks to the Red Wizards who'd brought them along, he already included a fair number in the company he currently commanded, so above and beyond any normal person's instinctive distaste for necromancy and its products, he didn't understand his own reaction.

The dead rose, not with the lethargic awkwardness of common zombies, but with the same agility they'd exhibited in life. The amber eyes of dread warriors gleaming from their sockets, they came to attention and saluted Urhur.

"You see?" the Red Wizard asked. "Here they stand to serve once more, only now stronger, more difficult to destroy, and incapable of cowardice or disobedience. Improved in every way."

Responsive to Xingax's will, the hill-giant zombie fumbled with the array of lenses on their swiveling steel arms. The hulking creature was trying to give its shortsighted master with his mismatched eyes a clear, close view of the work in progress on the floor below the balcony, but it couldn't align the glasses properly no matter how it tried. Finally Xingax waved it back, shifted forward on his seat, and pulled at the rods with the small, rotting fingers at the ends of his twisted, stubby arms.

There, that was better. The activity below flowed into focus just as the two scarlet-robed wizards completed their intricate contrapuntal incantation.

Clinking, the heap of bones in the center of the pentacle stirred and shifted. It was, of course, no feat to animate the intact skeleton of a single man or beast. A spellcaster didn't even need to be a true necromancer to master the technique. But if the ritual worked, the bones below, the jumbled remains of several creatures, would become something new and considerably more interesting.

Despite the presumed protection of the pentacle boundary separating them from Xingax's creation, each of the Red Wizards took a cautious step backward. The bone pile lifted a portion of itself—a temporary limb, if one chose to see it that way—and groped toward the mage on the left. Then, however, it collapsed with a rattle, and Xingax felt the power inside it dissipate. The wizard it had sought to menace cursed.

Xingax didn't share his assistant's vexation. The entity's failure to thrive simply meant he hadn't solved the puzzle yet, but he would. It just took patience.

Perhaps the problem lay in the third and fourth stanzas of the incantation. He'd had a feeling they weren't entirely right. He twisted around to his writing desk with its litter of parchments, took up his quill, and dipped it in the inkwell. Meanwhile, below him, zombies shuffled and stooped, picking up bones and carrying them away, while the Red Wizards began the task of purifying the chamber. Everything had to be fresh, unsullied by the lingering taint of the ritual just concluded, if the next one was to have any hope of success.

Xingax lost himself in his ponderings, until the wooden stairs ascending to his perch creaked and groaned, and the undead giant grunted for his attention.

Now Xingax felt a pang of irritation. Unsuccessful trials didn't bother him, but interruptions did. Glowering, he heaved himself around toward the top of the steps.

A pair of wizards climbed into view. They knew enough to ward themselves against the aura of malign energy emanating from Xingax's body and had surely done so, but potbellied So-Kehur with his food-spotted robe appeared queasy and ill at ease even so.

The mage's nervousness stirred Xingax's contempt. He knew what he looked like to human eyes: an oversized, freakishly deformed stillborn or aborted fetus. Pure ugliness, and never mind that, if his mother had carried him to term, he would have been a demigod, but a necromancer should be inured to phenomena that filled ordinary folk with horror.

At least Muthoth didn't show any overt signs of revulsion, which was not to suggest that he looked well. Bandages shrouded his right hand, and bloodstains dappled his robe; even dry, they had an enticing, unmistakable coppery smell. The ghoul familiar he'd worn like a mask of ink was gone.

Muthoth regarded Xingax with a blend of arrogance and wariness. The undead entity supposed it was understandable. Muthoth and So-Kehur were Red Wizards, schooled to hold themselves above everyone except their superiors in the hierarchy, yet they were also young, little more than apprentices, and

Xingax manifestly occupied a position of authority in the current endeavor. Thus, they weren't sure if they needed to defer to him or could get away with ordering him around.

One day, Xingax supposed, he'd likely have to settle the question of who was subordinate to whom, but for now, he just wanted to deal with the interruption quickly and return to his computations.

"What happened to the two of you?" he asked.

"We had some trouble on the trail," Muthoth said. "A man attacked us."

Xingax cocked his head. "A man? As in, one?"

Muthoth colored. "He was a bard, with magic of his own."

"And here I thought it was an article of faith with you Red Wizards that your arts are superior to all others," Xingax drawled. "At any rate, I assume you made him pay for his audacity."

Muthoth hesitated. "No. He translated himself elsewhere."

"By Velsharoon's staff! You couriers have one simple task, to acquire and transport slaves without attracting undue attention— never mind. Just tell me exactly what happened."

Muthoth did, while So-Kehur stood and fidgeted. Impatient as Xingax was to return to his experiments, he had to admit it was a tale worth hearing if only because it seemed so peculiar. He was incapable of love in both the spiritual and anatomical senses, but in the course of dealing with beings less rational than himself, he'd acquired some abstract understanding of what those conditions entailed. Still, it was ultimately unfathomable that a man could so crave the society of one particular woman that he'd risk near-certain destruction on her behalf.

Of course, from a practical perspective, the enigmas of human psychology were beside the point, and Xingax supposed he ought to focus on what was pertinent. "You didn't tell this Bareris Anskuld you were heading into Delhumide, did you?" he asked.

"Of course not!" Muthoth snapped.

"It's conceivable," said Xingax, "that he's inferred it, but even if he has, I don't see what he can do about it. Follow? If so, our sentinels will kill him. Tell others what he's discovered? We'd prefer that he not, and we'll try to find and silence him, but really, he doesn't know enough to pose a problem. He may not dare to confide in anyone anyway. After all, the will of a Red Wizard is law, and by running afoul of the two of you, he automatically made himself a felon."

Muthoth nodded. "That's the way I see it."

"We're just sorry," said So-Kehur, "that the bard killed some of our warriors, and the orcs had to kill a few of the slaves."

Muthoth shot his partner a glare, and Xingax understood why. While telling their story, Muthoth had opted to omit that particular detail.

"Did you reanimate the dead?" Xingax asked.

"Yes," Muthoth said.

"Then I suppose that in all likelihood, it didn't do any extraordinary harm." Xingax started to turn back to his papers then realized the wizards were still regarding him expectantly. "Was there more?"

"We assumed," said Muthoth, "that you'd want to divide up the shipment, or would you rather I do it?"

Xingax screwed up his asymmetrical features, pondering. He didn't want to forsake his creative work for a mundane chore. He could feel the answer to the puzzle teasing him, promising to reveal itself if he pushed just a little longer. On the other hand, the slaves were a precious resource, one he'd occasionally come near to exhausting despite the best efforts of the couriers to keep him supplied, and he wasn't certain he could trust anyone but himself to determine how to exploit them to best effect.

"I'll do it," he sighed.

He beckoned to the giant zombie, and the creature picked

him up to ride on its shoulders as if he were a toddler, and the mindless brute with its low forehead and gnarled apish arms, his father. His frayed, greasy length of umbilicus dangled over the zombie's chest.

In reality, it wasn't necessary that anyone or anything carry Xingax. If he chose, he could move about quite adequately on his own, but it suited him that folk should think him as physically helpless as his ravaged fetal form appeared. For the time being, he and his associates were all on the same side, but an existence spent primarily in the Abyss had taught him just how quickly such situations could alter, and a time might come when he'd want to give one of his compatriots a lethal surprise.

His balcony was one of a number of such vantage points overlooking the warren of catacombs below. Despite the extensive labor required, he'd ordered the construction of a system of catwalks to connect one perch to the next and only descended to mingle with his living associates when necessary. Even necromancers couldn't maintain their mystical defenses against his proximity every moment of every day, nor could they work efficiently if vomiting, suffering blinding headaches, or collapsing in convulsions.

As his undead giant lumbered along with Muthoth and So-Kehur trailing at its heels, it pleased Xingax to see the complex bustling with activity, each of his minions busy at his—or its—job. That was as it must be, if he was to make progress in his investigations and earn his ultimate reward.

One of the Red Wizards had conjured a perpetual gloom to shroud the platform overlooking the enormous vault where the couriers caged newly arrived slaves. The prisoners' eyes couldn't penetrate the shadows, but an observer experienced no difficulty looking out of them. Thus, Xingax could study the thralls without agitating them.

He didn't scrutinize any one individual for long. He trusted his first impressions, his myopia notwithstanding. "Food," he said, pointing. "Basic. Basic. Advanced. Food. Basic." Then he noticed the wizards simply standing and listening. "Why aren't you writing this down?"

"No need," said Muthoth. "So-Kehur will remember."

"He'd better," Xingax said. He continued assigning the slaves to their respective categories until only two remained.

They were young women who'd found a corner in which to settle. Likely aghast at what she'd glimpsed on the walk to her current place of confinement, the one with long hair appeared to have withdrawn deep inside herself. Her companion was coaxing her to sample the porridge their captors had provided.

"Food and food," Xingax concluded, feeling a renewed eagerness to return to the problem of the defective ritual. "Is there anything else?"

Maddeningly, it appeared there was. "My hand," said Muthoth, lifting the bandaged one. "I've heard about your skill with grafts, and I was hoping you could do something to repair it."

"Why, of course," Xingax said. "I have a thousand vital tasks to occupy me, but I'll *gladly* defer them to help a mage so incompetent that he couldn't defend himself against a lone madman even with a second wizard and bodyguards to help. Because that's *exactly* the sort of ally I want owing me a favor."

Muthoth glared, looking so furious that Xingax wondered if he was in danger of losing control. So-Kehur evidently thought so. He took a step backward, lest a sorcerous attack strike him by accident.

Xingax called on the poisonous power inside him. He stared into Muthoth's eyes and released an iota of it, hoping to suggest its full devastating potential in the same way that a mere flick of a whip reminds a slave of the shearing, smashing force of which the lash is capable.

Muthoth flinched and averted his eyes. "All right! If you're too busy, I understand."

"Good," Xingax rapped. He started to direct his servant to carry him away then noticed that the confrontation had delayed him long enough for another little drama to start playing itself out in the hall below.

Specifically, one of the blood orcs had entered the makeshift barracoon. The warrior was somewhat reckless to enter alone. It must assume the slaves were too cowed to try to hurt it, and to all appearances, it was right. They shrank from it as it prowled about.

The orc's gaze fell on the two women sitting on the floor in the corner. It leered at them, started unfastening its leather breeches, and waved for the slave with the short hair to move away from her companion.

The orc's actions were neither unusual nor illicit. The wizards and guards had permission to amuse themselves with the slaves provided they didn't damage them to any significant degree. Still, despite the lure of his work, Xingax lingered to watch for another moment. Though he would never have admitted it to another, he sometimes found the alien matter of sexuality intriguing as well as repugnant.

To his astonishment, the short-haired slave stood up and positioned herself between the orc and her friend. "Find someone else," she said.

The orc grabbed her, perhaps with the intention of flinging her out of its way. She hit it in the face with the bowl of gruel. The earthenware vessel shattered, and the warrior stumbled backward. The slave lunged after it, trying to land a second attack, but the guard recovered its balance and knocked her staggering with a backhand blow to the face. Her momentary incapacity gave it time to draw its scimitar.

It stalked after the thrall, and she retreated. "Help me!" she called. "If we all try, we can kill at least one of them before the end! That's better than nothing!"

Apparently the other slaves were too demoralized to agree, because none of them moved to help her. Knowing then that she stood alone, pale with fright but resolute, the short-haired woman shifted her grip on the shard of bowl remaining in her hand to make it easier to slash with the broken edge.

"She has courage," Xingax said.

"That's the one the bard wanted to buy," So-Kehur said.

"Really? Well, perhaps his obsession does make at least a tiny bit of sense. In any case, I was wrong about her." Xingax waved his hand, dissolving the unnatural gloom so the orc could see him. "Leave her alone!"

Surprised, the warrior looked up to find out who was shouting at it. It hesitated for a moment, seemingly torn between the prudence of unquestioning obedience and the urgency of anger, then howled, "But she hit me!"

"And she'll suffer for it, never fear." Xingax turned to So-Kehur. "The woman comes to me."

.. ..

After Aoth's company destroyed the creatures occupying Dulos, he opted to stop there for the night. His weary warriors could use the rest.

So could he, for that matter, but he proved incapable of sitting or lying still. Eventually he abandoned the effort, left the house he'd commandeered, and started prowling along the perimeter of the settlement.

It was a pointless thing to do. Shortly before dusk, he and Brightwing had flown over the immediate area and found it clear of potential threats. On top of that, he already had sentries posted.

Yet he couldn't shake a nagging unease. Maybe it was simply because the undead were more powerful in the dark. If any remained in the region and aspired to avenge their fellows, this was the time when they would strike.

Abruptly a shape appeared in the pool of shadow beneath an elm, and though Aoth could barely see it, its tilted, knock-kneed stance revealed it to be undead. No living man would choose to assume such an awkward position, but a zombie, incapable of discomfort, its range of motion altered by its death wounds, very well might.

Aoth leveled his spear and drew breath to raise the alarm, then noticed the gleam of yellow eyes in the creature's head. The thing was a dread warrior, one of his own command. As it still possessed sufficient intelligence to fight as it had in life, so too could it stand watch, and apparently Urhur Hahpct or one of his fellow Red Wizards had stationed it here to do so. Maybe the whoreson believed Aoth's security arrangements were inadequate, or perhaps it was simply that the necromancer, too, felt ill at ease.

"Don't blast it," said a feminine voice. "It's one of ours."

Startled, heart banging in his chest, Aoth jerked around to see Chathi Oandem smiling at him from several paces away. He tried to compose himself and smile back.

"I wasn't going to," he said. "I recognized it just in time to avoid making a fool of myself."

The priestess strolled nearer. Though she still carried her torch weapon, she wasn't wearing her mail and helmet anymore, just flame-patterned vestments that molded themselves to her willowy form at those moments when the cool breeze gusted.

"I thought all wizards had owl eyes and could see in the dark."

Aoth shrugged. "I know the spell, but I haven't been preparing it lately. I'd rather concentrate on combat magic, especially considering that I can look through Brightwing's eyes when I need to."

"Except that the poor tired creature is asleep at the moment."

If Chathi had observed that, it meant she'd passed by his quarters. He felt a rush of excitement at the thought that perhaps she'd gone there intentionally, looking for him, and kept on seeking him after.

"Good. She's earned her rest."

"So have you and I, yet here we are, up wandering the night. Is something troubling you?"

He wondered if a captain ought to confide any sort of anxiety or misgivings to someone at least theoretically under his command, then decided he didn't care. "There shouldn't be, should there? We won our battle and received word this afternoon that other companies are winning theirs. Everything's quiet, yet . . . " He snorted. "Maybe I'm just timid."

"Then we both are. I've trained since I was a little girl to fight the enemies of Kossuth, and I've destroyed my share, but these things! Is it the mere fact they're undead or that we have no idea why they came down from the mountains that makes them so troubling we can't relax and celebrate even after a victory?"

"A bit of both, I suppose." And something more as well, though he still wasn't sure what.

She smiled and touched his cheek as she had to heal him. Even without a corona of flame, her hardened fingertips felt feverishly warm. "I wonder—if you and I tried very hard, do you think we could manage a celebration despite our trepidations?"

He wanted her as urgently as he could recall ever wanting a woman, but he also wondered if he'd be crossing a line he shouldn't, for all that Nymia did it constantly. She was a tharchion and he but a newly minted captain.

"If this is about my having saved your life," he said, playing for time until he was sure of his own mind, "remember you saved mine, too. You said it yourself, we're even."

"It's not about gratitude but about discovering a fire inside me, and when a priestess of Kossuth finds such a flame, she doesn't seek to dowse it." Chathi grinned. "That would be blasphemy. She stokes it and lets it burn what it will, so shall we walk back to your quarters?"

He swallowed. "I imagine one of these huts right in front of us is empty."

"Good thinking. No wonder you're the leader."

When she unpinned her vestments and dropped them to pool around her feet, he saw that her god had scarred portions of her body as well as her face, but those marks didn't repel him either. In fact, he kissed them with a special fervor.

•• •• •• •• •• •• •• •• •• •• •• •• •• ••

Each gripping one of her arms, the two blood orcs marched Tammith toward the doorway, and she offered no resistance. Perhaps she'd used up her capacity for defiance seeking to protect Yuldra, or maybe it was simply that she realized the two gray-skinned warriors with their swinish tusks were on their guard. She had little hope of breaking away and wouldn't know which way to run if she did.

The spacious vault beyond the door proved to be a necromancer's conjuring chamber lit, like the rest of the catacombs, by everburning torches burning with cold greenish flame. Though Tammith had never seen such a place before, the complex designs chalked on the floor, the shelves of bottled liquids and jars of powders, the racks of staves and wands, and the scent of bitter incense overlying the stink of decay were familiar to her from stories.

Two Red Wizards currently occupied the room, along with half a dozen zombies. A couple of the latter shuffled forward and reached out to collect Tammith.

The gods had been cruel to make her believe that she might still have Bareris and freedom only to snatch them away. Her spirit had nearly shattered then, and she still didn't understand why it hadn't. Perhaps it was the knowledge that her love had escaped. He could still have a life even if she couldn't.

In any case, she hadn't yet succumbed to utter crippling terror and had vowed to meet her end, whatever it proved to be, with as much bravery as she could muster. Still, the prospect of the enduring the touch of the zombies' cold, slimy fingers, of inhaling the fetor of their rotten bodies close up, filled her with revulsion.

"Please!" she said. "You don't need those creatures to hold me. I know I can't get away."

The Red Wizards ignored her plea, and the zombies, with their slack mouths and empty eyes, trudged a step closer, but then a voice spoke from overhead.

"That sounds all right. Just position a couple of the zombies to block the exit, in case she's not as sensible as she seems."

Tammith looked up and observed the loft above the chamber for the first time. The giant zombie was there and its master, too. A number of round lenses attached to a branching metal framework hung before the fetus-thing like apples on a tree. From her vantage point, the effect was to break his body into distorted sections and make it even more hideous, if such a thing was possible.

Since the creature had decreed that she was to come to him, she'd expected to encounter him wherever she ended up. Still, the actual sight of him dried her mouth and made her shudder. How could anything so resemble a baby yet look so ghastly and radiate such a palpable feeling of malevolence? She struggled again to cling to what remained of her courage.

She didn't hear either of the Red Wizards give a verbal command or notice a hand signal either, but the zombies stopped advancing as the fetus-thing had indicated they should. The orcs looked to one of the necromancers, and he waved a hairless, tattooed hand in dismissal. The guards wasted no time departing, as if even they found the chamber a disturbing place.

Tammith forced herself to gaze up at the baby-thing without flinching. "Thank you for that anyway. I'm tired of being manhandled."

"And corpse-handled is even worse, I imagine." The creature smirked at its own feeble play on words. "Think nothing of it. This could be the beginning of a long and fruitful association, and we might as well start off in a friendly sort of way. My name is Xingax. What's yours?"

She told him. " 'A long and fruitful association?' Then . . . you don't mean to kill me?"

"Actually, I do, but death needn't be the end of an entity's existence. Lucky for me! Otherwise I wouldn't have fared very well after my mother's cuckold husband tore me from the womb."

"I . . . I won't be one of those." She gestured to indicate the zombies. "I'll make your servants tear me to pieces first."

Xingax chuckled. "Do you imagine I'd have no use for the fragments? If so, you're mistaken, but please, calm yourself. I don't intend to turn you into a zombie. You have a much more interesting opportunity in store.

"You've seen enough," continued the fetus-thing, "to discern what this place is: an undead manufactory. Given sufficient resources, we'd create only powerful, sentient specimens, since those are the most useful for our purposes. Alas, the reality is that it takes considerably more magic to evoke a ghost or something similar than it does to make a mindless automaton like my giant or my helpers' helpers.

"So we function as we best we can, given our limitations. Many of the slaves who come here end up as zombies or at best ghouls. Others go to feed newly created undead in need of such sustenance, and afterward we animate their skeletons. Only a relative few have the chance to attain a more advanced state of being."

Tammith shook her head. "I can tell you think that's a boon. Why would you offer it to me when I've raised my hand to your servants more than once?"

"For that very reason. You have a boldness we can put to good use. Assuming the transformation takes. That's the other thing I should explain. I recreate types of undead that became extinct long ago and breed others altogether new. It's a part of my mandate, and more than that, my passion. My art. The closest I'll ever come to fatherhood. The problem is that we have to refine the magic by trial and error, and well, obviously, it isn't right until it's right."

She imagined what might befall a captive when the magic was still wrong. She pictured herself shrieking in endless anguish, her body mangled like an apprentice potter's first botched attempt at shaping a vessel on the wheel. Hard on that image came the realization that she'd been a fool to cringe from the prospect of becoming a zombie. It was the best fate that could befall her. Her body would remain a thrall but her soul would fly free to await Bareris in the afterlife.

She lunged at the nearer of the Red Wizards. He had a dagger with a curved blade sheathed on his belt. She'd snatch it, slash the artery in the side of her neck, and all fear and misery would spurt away with her blood.

The necromancer had obviously been waiting for her to attempt some sort of violence. He barked a word she didn't understand, swept his left hand through a mystic figure, and black motes swirled around it to form a spiral.

The flecks of darkness didn't hurt her, but they fascinated her. She had no choice but to pause and stare at them, even though a part of her, now disconnected from her will, screamed that she mustn't.

The wizard stepped back and the zombies shambled forward, closing in on her. Their clammy hands grabbed her and held tight. The spiral faded, allowing her to struggle, but writhe as she might, she couldn't break free, and when she stamped on her captors' feet, snapped her head backward to bash a zombie's jaw, and even sank her teeth into spongy, putrid flesh, it didn't matter. Since the creatures didn't feel pain, the punishment couldn't make them fumble their grips.

"I rather expected that," said Xingax, "but it's still a shame. You were doing so well."

"Shall I subdue her?" asked the mage with the dagger.

"I suppose it would be best," Xingax replied.

The Red Wizard extracted a pewter vial from a hidden pocket in his robe, and holding it at arm's length, he uncorked it. He then moved to stick it under Tammith's nose. She strained to twist her face away, but with the zombies immobilizing her, it was futile.

The fumes had a nasty metallic tang she tasted as well as smelled. Her limbs went slack, and wouldn't so much as twitch no matter how she struggled. She might as well have been asleep.

"Put her in the pentacle," Xingax said.

The zombies laid her on her back, spread her arms wide, and crossed her legs at the ankle. Then, for a considerable time, the Red Wizards chanted rhymes in an unknown tongue while brandishing smoking censers; slender, gleaming swords; and a black chalice carved from a single piece of jet.

At first it was sinister but ultimately incomprehensible. Eventually, however, the necromancer with the dagger—she had the impression he was the senior of the pair—crouched down beside her and dipped his forefinger in the black cup. It came out red. He rubbed her lips with it, then her gums, then worked it past her teeth to dab at her tongue. She tasted the salty, coppery tang of blood.

After that, she could somehow perceive the power gathering in the air and conceived the crazy, terrifying notion that the chanted incantations were a thing unto themselves, a living malignancy that was simply employing the mages to further the purposes implicit in the tercets and quatrains. She still couldn't comprehend them, but she felt the meaning was on the very brink of revealing itself to her and that when it did, she wouldn't be able to bear it.

A mass of shadow seethed into existence above her, thickening until she could barely see the ceiling or Xingax peering avidly down at her through a pair of lenses positioned one before the other. The clot of darkness took on a suggestion of texture, of bulges, hollows, and edges, as if it had become a solid object. Then it shattered.

Into an explosion of enormous bats. The rustling of their countless wings echoing from the stone walls, they flew in all directions. Xingax cried out in excitement. The Red Wizards, for all that they'd conjured the flock and were presumably in control of it, retreated to stand with their backs against a wall.

A bat lit on a zombie's shoulder and plunged its fangs into its throat. The animated corpse showed no reaction to the bite, but despite its passivity, the bat fluttered its wings and took flight again only a heartbeat later.

Three bats settled on a second zombie, bit it, and abandoned it immediately thereafter. Because they crave the blood of a living person, Tammith thought, her heart hammering. Because they want me.

She made a supreme effort to roll over onto her belly. If she could only move a little, she could crawl away from the middle of the floor, then . . . why, then nothing, she supposed. The part of her that was still rational realized it wasn't likely to matter, but she needed to try. It was better than simply accepting her fate, no matter how inescapable it was.

Her limbs trembled. The effect of the vapor was wearing off. She felt a thrill of excitement, of lunatic hope, and then the first bat found her. Cold as the zombies' fingers, its claws dug into her chest for purchase as its fangs sought her throat.

As it sucked the wounds it had inflicted, the rest of the flock descended on her, covering her like a shifting, frigid blanket, the bats that couldn't reach her shoving at the ones who had like piglets jostling for their mother's teats. Scores of icy needles pierced her flesh.

Had she ever imagined such a fate, she might have assumed that so much cold would numb her. Somehow, it didn't. The assault was agony.

The bats tore at her lips, nose, cheeks, and forehead. Not my eyes, she silently begged, not my eyes, but they ripped those too, and then she finally passed out.

•• •• •• •• •• •• •• •• •• •• •• •• •• ••

Tammith woke to pain, weakness, searing thirst, and utter darkness. At first she couldn't remember what had happened to her, but then the memory leaped at her like a cat pouncing on a mouse.

When it did, she decided Xingax couldn't possibly have intended to create the crippled, sightless creature she'd become. The experiment had failed as he'd warned it might.

"So kill me!" she croaked. "I'm no use to you!"

No one answered. She wondered if she actually was alone or if Xingax and the Red Wizards were still present, silently studying her, preparing to put her out of her misery, or—gods forbid!—readying a new torment.

Suddenly she was frantic to know, which made her blindness intolerable. She felt a flowing, a budding, in the raw orbits of her skull, and then smears of light and shadow wavered into existence before her. Over the course of several moments, the world sharpened into focus. She realized she'd healed her ruined eyes, or if the bats had destroyed them entirely, grown new ones.

It suggested that Xingax's experiment hadn't been a *complete* failure after all, but she appeared to be alone nonetheless. Her captors had deposited her in a different chamber, a bare little room with a matchboarded door. Up near the ceiling, someone had cut a hole, probably connecting to the ubiquitous system of catwalks, but if the aborted monstrosity was up there peeping at her, she couldn't see it.

Which, she recalled, didn't necessarily mean he wasn't. He'd concealed himself easily enough when taking stock of the new supply of slaves. She wheezed his name but received no reply.

She supposed that if she did constitute some sort of glorious success, and he wasn't here to witness it, the joke was on him. But in fact, she doubted it. The Red Wizards had managed to stuff a little magic into her, enough to preserve her existence and restore her vision, but accomplishing the latter had left her even weaker and more parched than before. She stared at the myriad puncture wounds on her hands and forearms, willing them to close, and nothing happened.

At that point, misery overwhelmed her. She curled up into a ball and wept, though her new eyes seemed incapable of shedding actual tears, until a key grated in the lock of the door. It creaked open, and an orc shoved Yuldra through and slammed it after her. The lock clacked once again.

Tammith extended a trembling hand. She knew the other captive couldn't do anything substantive to ease her distress, but Yuldra could at least talk to her, clasp her fingers, or cradle her, perhaps. Any crumb of comfort, of simple human contact with someone who wasn't a pitiless torturer, would be better than nothing.

Yuldra flinched from the sight of her ravaged body, let out a sob of her own, wheeled, and scrambled into a corner. There she crouched down and held her face averted, attempting to shut out the world as she had before.

"How many times did I take care of you?" Tammith cried. "And now you turn your back on me?"

Nor was Yuldra the only person who'd so betrayed her. She'd spent her life looking after other people. Her father the drunkard and gambler. Her brother the imbecile. And what had anyone ever done for her in return? Even Bareris, who claimed to love her with all his heart, had abandoned her to chase his dreams of gold and excitement in foreign lands.

She realized she was on her feet. She was still thirsty, it was a fire burning in her throat, but she'd shaken off weakness for the moment, anyway. Anger lent her strength.

"Look at me," she snapped.

Her voice was sharp as the crack of a whip, and like a whip, it tangled something inside of Yuldra and tugged at her. The slave started to turn around but then shook off the coercion.

"Fine," Tammith said, stalking forward, "we'll do it the hard way."

She didn't know precisely what *it* was. Everything was happening too quickly, with impulse and fury sweeping her along, but when her upper canines stung and lengthened into fangs, their points pressing into her lower lip, she understood.

The realization brought a horror that somewhat dampened her rage if not her thirst. I can't do this, she thought. I can't be this. Yuldra is my friend.

She stood and fought against her need. It seemed to her that she was winning. Then her body burst apart into a cloud of bats much like the conjured entities that had attacked her, and that made the world a different place. The sense of sight she'd so missed became secondary to her ability to hear and comprehend the import of her own echoing cries, but the fragmentation of her consciousness was an even more fundamental change. She retained her ultimate sense of self and managed her dozens of bodies as easily as she had one, yet something was lost in the diffusion: conscience, perhaps, or the capacities for empathy and self-denial. She was purely a predator now, and her bats hurtled at Yuldra like a flight of arrows.

Rather to Tammith's surprise, given Yuldra's usual habit of cringing helplessness, the other slave fought back. She flailed at the bats, sought to grab them, and when successful, squeezed them hard enough to crush an ordinary animal, wrung them like washcloths, or pounded them against the wall. The punishment stung, but only for an instant, and without doing any real harm.

Meanwhile, Tammith clung to the other thrall and jabbed her various sets of fangs into her veins and arteries. When the hot blood gushed into her mouths, she felt a pleasure intense as the fulfillment of passion, and as it assuaged her thirst, the relief was a keener ecstasy still.

Before long, Yuldra weakened and then stopped struggling altogether. Once Tammith drank the last of her, the bats took flight. They swirled around one another, dissolved, and instantly reformed into a single body, now cleansed of all the wounds that had disfigured it before.

That didn't make the remorse that came with the restoration of her original form any easier to bear. The guilt fell on her like a hammer stroke, and she felt a howl of anguish welling up inside.

"Excellent," Xingax said.

She looked up. The fetus-thing had been watching through the hole high in the wall, just as she'd suspected, and had now dissolved the charm that had hidden him from view.

"I believe that with practice," he continued, "you'll find you can remain divided for extended periods of time. I'm confident you'll discover other uncommon abilities as well, talents that set you above the common sort of vampire."

"Why didn't you answer me when I called to you before? Why didn't you warn me?"

"I wanted to see how far instinct would carry you. It's quite a promising sign that you managed to manifest a number of your abilities and take down your first prey without any mentoring at all."

"I'm going to kill you," she told him, and with the resolve came the abrupt instinctive realization that she didn't even need to shapeshift to do it. His elevated position afforded no protection. She dashed to the wall and scrambled upward like a fly. It was as easy as negotiating a horizontal surface.

Partway up, dizziness and nausea assailed her. Her feet and hands lost their ability to adhere to the wall, and she plunged back to the floor. She landed awkwardly, with a jolt that might well have broken the old Tammith's bones, though the new version wasn't even stunned.

As the sick feeling began to pass, Xingax said, "You didn't really think we'd give you so much power without insuring that you'd use it as we intend, did you? I'm afraid, my daughter, that you're still a thrall, or at best, a vassal. If it's any comfort to you, so am I, and so are the Red Wizards you've encountered here, but so long as we behave ourselves, our service is congenial, and we can hope for splendid rewards in the decades to come."

chapter eight

30 Mirtul, the Year of Risen Elfkin

Delhumide gleamed like a broken skeleton in the moonlight. The siege engines and battle sorceries of the ancient rebels had shattered battlements and toppled towers, and time had chipped and scraped at all that had survived the initial onslaught. Yet the Mulhorandi had built their provincial capital to last, and much remained essentially intact. Bareris found it easy to imagine the proud, teeming city of yore, which only served to make the present desolation all the more forbidding.

He wondered if it was simply his imagination, or if he truly could sense a miasma of sickness and menace infusing the place. Either way, the gnolls plainly felt something too. They growled and muttered. One clasped a copper medallion stamped with the image of an axe and prayed for the favor of his god.

Having cajoled them this far, Bareris didn't want to give them a final chance to lose their nerve. As before, enchantment lent him the ability to speak to them in their own snarling, yipping language, and he used it to say, *"Let's move."* He skulked forward, and they followed.

He prayed they weren't already too late, that something horrible hadn't already befallen Tammith. It was maddening to reflect on just how much time had passed since he'd watched the Red Wizards and their cohorts march her away. It had taken him and the hyenafolk a while to reach Delhumide. Then, for all that the gnolls had scouted the general area before, Wesk Backbreaker insisted on observing the perimeter of the city before venturing inside. He maintained it would increase their chances of success, and much as Bareris chafed at the delay, he had to admit the gnoll chieftain was probably right.

As they'd gleaned all they could, so too had they begun to plan. After some deliberation, they decided to sneak into Delhumide by night. True, it was when the demons and such came out, but even if the horrors were in fact charged with guarding the borders of the ruined city, it didn't appear they did as diligent a job as the warriors keeping watch by day. Bareris hoped he and the gnolls had a reasonable chance of slipping past them unmolested, especially considering that though creatures like devils and the hyenafolk themselves could see in the dark, they couldn't see as far as a man could by daylight.

He and his companions picked their way through the collapsed and decaying houses outside the city wall then over the field of rubble that was all that remained of the barrier at that point. The bard wondered what particular mode of attack had shattered it. The chunks of granite had a blackened, pitted look, but that was as much as he could tell.

The gnolls slinking silently as mist for all their size, the intruders reached the end of the litter of smashed stones fairly quickly. Now they'd truly entered Delhumide, venturing deeper than any of their scouts had dared to go before. A cool breeze moaned down the empty street, and one of the hyenafolk jumped as if a ghost had ruffled his fur and crooned in its ear.

Wesk waved, signaling for everyone to follow him to the left. Their observations had revealed that shadowy figures flitted through the streets on the right in the dark. Occasionally, one of the things shrieked out peals of laughter that inspired a sudden self-loathing and the urge to self-mutilate in all who heard it. Bareris had no idea what the entities were, but he was certain they'd do well to avoid them.

The intruders turned again to avoid a trio of spires that, groaning and shedding scraps of masonry, sometimes flexed like the fingers of a palsied hand. The facades of crumbling houses seemed to watch them go by, the black empty windows following like eyes. For a moment, a sort of faint clamor like the final fading echo of a hundred screams sounded somewhere to the north.

The noise made Bareris shiver, but he told himself it had nothing to do with him or his comrades. Delhumide was replete with perils and eerie phenomena; they'd known that coming in. It wasn't a problem if you could keep away from them, and so far their reconnaissance had enabled them to do so.

That luck held for another twenty heartbeats. Then one of the gnolls deviated from their course by just a long, loping stride or two, just far enough to stick his head into a courtyard with a rusty wrought-iron gate hanging askew and a cracked, dry fountain in the center. Something had evidently snagged the warrior's attention, some hint of danger, perhaps, that demanded closer scrutiny.

The gnoll suddenly snarled and staggered, tearing at himself with his thick canine nails. At first Bareris couldn't make out what was wrong, but when he saw the swelling black dots scurrying through the creature's spotted fur, he understood.

The gnolls had fleas, a fact he'd discovered when he started scratching as well, and the parasites on the outlaw in the courtyard were growing to prodigious size. Big as mice, they swarmed over him, burying their proboscises and heads in his flesh to drain his blood. Bulges shifted under the gnoll's brigandine as insects crawled and feasted there as well.

A second gnoll rushed to help his fellow, but as soon as he entered the courtyard, he suffered the same affliction. The two hyenafolk flailed and rolled and shrieked together. Their fellows hovered outside the gate, too frightened or canny to risk the same consequence.

Bareris sang. Magic warmed the air, and he felt a sort of tickling as his own assortment of normal-sized fleas jumped off him. He then charged into the courtyard, and the enchantment radiating outward from his skin drove the giant parasites off the bodies of their hosts just as easily. With a rustling, seething sound, they scuttled and bounded into the shadows at the rear of the space.

He still had no desire to linger inside the crooked gate. For all he knew, the influence haunting the courtyard had other tricks to play. Fast as he could, he dragged the dazed, bloody gnolls back out onto the street, where the spirit, or whatever it was, couldn't hurt them any further. At least he hoped it couldn't, because they needed a healer's attention immediately if they were to escape infirmity or worse, and in the absence of a priest, he'd have to do.

He chanted charms of mending and vitality. The other gnolls looked on curiously until Wesk started grabbing them and wrenching them around. *"Keep watch!"* the chieftain snarled. *"Something else could have heard the ruckus or hear the singer singing."*

Gradually, one gnoll's wounds stopped bleeding and scabbed over, a partial healing that was as much as Bareris could manage for the time being. The other, however, appeared beyond help. He shuddered, a rattle issued from his throat, then he slumped motionless. Meanwhile, the survivor sat up and, hand trembling, groped for the leather water bottle strapped to his belt.

"How are you?" Bareris asked him.

The gnoll snorted as if the question were an insult.

"Then when you're ready, we'll press on."

"Are you crazy?"

Bareris turned and saw that the speaker was Thovarr Keentooth, the long-eared gnoll he'd punched during their first palaver.

"You said you knew how to get us in and out without the spooks bothering us," the creature snarled, spit flying from his jaws. He apparently meant to continue in the same vein for a while, but Wesk interrupted by backhanding him across the muzzle and tumbling him to the ground.

"We said," the chieftain growled, *"we'd do our best to avoid the threats we knew about, but there might be some we hadn't spotted. This was one such, and you can't blame the human or anyone else for missing it, seeing as how it was invisible till someone stepped in the snare."*

"I'm not talking about 'blame,'" Thovarr replied, picking himself up. *"I'm talking about what's sensible and what isn't. There's a reason no one comes here, and—"*

"Blood orcs do," Bareris said. *"Are they braver than you?"*

Thovarr bared his fangs like an angry hound. *"The pig-faces have Red Wizards to guide them. We only have you, and you talk big but don't keep us out of trouble."*

"Enough!" snapped Wesk. *"We're soldiers again, and soldiers expect to risk their lives earning their pay. If you don't have the belly for it, turn back now, but know it means the rest of us cast you out for a coward."*

That left Thovarr with three options: obey, leave his little pack forever, or fight Wesk then and there for his chieftaincy. Apparently the first choice was the most palatable, the perils of

Delhumide notwithstanding, because the long-eared gnoll bent his head in submission. *"I'll stick,"* he growled.

They dragged the dead warrior's corpse into a shadowy recessed doorway, where, they hoped, it was less likely anyone or anything would notice it. There they abandoned it without ceremony. Bareris had dealt just as callously with the mortal remains of other fallen comrades when a battle, pursuit, or flight required immediate action, and he had no idea whether gnolls even practiced any sort of funerary observances. It wouldn't have astonished him to learn that they ate their dead as readily as they devoured any other sort of meat or carrion that came their way. Still, he found it gave him a pang of remorse to leave the creature unburied and unburned, without even a hymn or prayer to speed its soul on its way.

Maybe it bothered him because Thovarr was essentially correct. If Bareris hadn't used magic to undermine the gnolls' better judgment, they would never have ventured into Delhumide. His friends from more squeamish—or as they might have put it, more ethical—lands might well have deemed it an abuse of his gifts.

But his present comrades were hyenafolk, who boasted themselves that their kind lived only for war and slaughter, and Bareris was paying them a duke's ransom to put themselves in harm's way. If he'd sinned, then the Lord of Song could take him to task for it when his spirit knelt before the deity's silver throne. For now, he'd sacrifice the gnolls and a thousand more like them to rescue Tammith.

Wesk lifted a hand to halt the procession. On the other side of an arched gateway rose a cylindrical tower. Constructed of dark stone, vague in the darkness, it reminded Bareris of some titan's drum.

He peeked around the edge of the gate and squinted at the flat roof, but he couldn't spot anything on top of it. He'd considered singing a charm to sharpen his eyes before entering the city but had opted not to. He could only cast so many spells before exhausting his powers. Better, then, to trust the night vision of his companions and conserve his magic for other purposes.

"Is it up there?" he whispered, referring to the blood-orc sentry that usually kept watch on the roof.

Wesk bobbed his head up above the low wall ringing the tower to check. *"Yes."*

"Can you really hit it from down here?" Bareris asked.

He knew Wesk was a skillful archer, maybe even as adept as he claimed. He'd watched the gnoll shoot game on the trek to Delhumide, and only once had the creature missed. Still, Bareris was enough of a bowman in his own right to know just how difficult a shot it was. The orc was four stories up and partly shielded by a ring of merlons.

Wesk grinned. *"I can hit it. I'm not some feeble runt of a human."*

He caressed the curves of his yew bow and growled a spell of his own, evidently some charm known to master archers and hunters. The longbow glinted as though catching Selûne's light in a way it hadn't before, despite the fact that nothing had changed in the sky. Wesk nocked an arrow, stepped into the center of the gate, drew the fletchings to his ear, and let the missile fly.

To Bareris's eyes, the shaft simply vanished into the dark, but from Wesk's grunt of satisfaction, and the fact that he didn't bother reaching for a second arrow, it was evident the first one had found its mark. Bareris imagined the orc collapsing, killed before it even had an inkling it was in peril.

He and the gnolls skulked across the open ground between the wall and the tower. They had no reason to think anyone else was looking—it seemed likely the rest of the folk inside were happy to shut themselves away from the terrors infesting the night—but they couldn't be sure.

Stone steps rose to a four-paneled door. As Bareris climbed

toward it, he hoped to find only a handful of warriors waiting on the other side. Whoever was garrisoning this particular outpost, though, he and the hyenafolk had no choice but to deal with them.

That was because one could only see so far into a ruined city while scouting it from the outside, and thus the intruders had little idea what lay beyond this point. If they were to avoid lurking demons and locate Tammith, someone would have to enlighten them.

Bareris tried the door and found that, as expected, it was locked or barred. He motioned for the gnolls to stay behind him then bellowed.

The magic infusing his voice cracked the door and jolted it on its hinges but failed to break it open. He threw himself against it and bounced back with a bruised shoulder, but then Wesk and Thovarr charged past him and hit the barrier together. They smashed it out of its frame to slam down on the floor of the hall beyond. Orcs, three kneeling in a circle around their dice and piles of coppers, and two more wrapped in their blankets, goggled at them in amazement.

As it turned out, there were no mages on hand, and with the orcs caught unprepared, the fight that followed was less a battle than a massacre. In fact, that was the problem. Caught up in the frenzy of the moment, the gnolls appeared to have forgotten that the point of their incursion was to take at least one of the enemy alive.

Bareris cast about. For a moment, he could see only gory, motionless, gray-skinned bodies and the hyenafolk still hacking at them. Then he spotted an orc that was down on its back but still moving, albeit in a dazed manner, groping for the dirk in its boot. Thovarr swung his axe over his head to finish the creature off.

"*No!*" Bareris shouted. He lunged and shoved Thovarr away

from the orc, swiped the latter's hand with the flat of his sword to stop its reaching for the knife, and aimed his point at its throat. *"We have to talk to one of them, and this appears to be the only one left."*

He proceeded with the interrogation as soon as the gnolls verified that the rest of the tower was empty. *"You can answer my questions and live,"* he told the orc in its own language, *"or I can give you to my friends to kill in whatever fashion amuses them. It's up to you."*

"I can't tell you anything!" the orc pleaded. *"I'll die!"*

"Nonsense. Perhaps your masters will punish you for talking if they get their hands on you, but you can run away."

"That's not it," said the orc. *"The Red Wizards put a spell on me, on all of us. If we talk about their business, we die."*

From the manner in which he attended to the conversation, it was apparent Wesk understood the orcish tongue, and now he and Bareris exchanged puzzled glances. The bard wondered again what endeavor merited such extraordinary attempts at secrecy.

"Listen to me," Bareris said, infusing his voice with the magic of persuasion, *"you don't* know *that your masters truly laid a spell on you. It would have been a lot less work simply to lie and claim they did. Even if the enchantment is real, you can't be sure it took you in its grip. It's the nature of such charms that they can always fail to affect a particular target. On the other hand, you know my sword is real. You see it with your own eyes, and you can be absolutely certain of dying if I cut your throat with it. Bearing all that in mind, whom do you choose to obey, the wizards or me?"*

The orc took a deep breath. *"I'll answer."*

"Good. Where in the city do the slaves end up?"

The prisoner sucked in another breath. Bareris realized the orc was panting with fear. *"They—"*

A single word was all it took. The orc's back arched, and

surprised, Bareris failed to yank his sword back in time to avoid piercing the orc's neck. But the point didn't go in deep, and he doubted the orc even noticed the wound. The orc was suffering far more grievous hurts.

The orc's back continued to bend like a bow, and his extremities flailed up and down, pounding the floor. His eyes rolled up in their sockets, and bloody froth foamed from his mouth. Hoping the creature might survive if he could only keep him from swallowing his tongue, Bareris cast about for an implement he could wedge in his mouth, but before he could find one, the orc thrashed a final time and lay still. A foul smell suffused the air. The warrior had soiled himself in his death throes.

"Well," said Wesk, *"it wasn't lying about the geas."*

"No," Bareris answered.

He felt a twinge of shame for compelling the orc to such a death, and scowling, he tried to quash the feeling. He'd had no choice but to force the creature to speak.

"So what do all of us 'soldiers' do now?" Thovarr asked. *"Just wander around and look for the slave? Delhumide's big, and it's got a spook hiding in every shadow."*

Bareris prayed it hadn't come to that. *"We search this place,"* he said. *"Maybe we'll find something useful."*

They began by searching the orcs' bodies then moved on to ransacking their possessions. Wesk dumped out the contents of a haversack, picked up a parchment, unfolded it, and then brought it to Bareris.

"Is this anything?" asked the gnoll.

Bareris studied the scrawled diagram. It didn't have any words written on it, just lines, circles, rectangles, and dots, and for a moment, he couldn't decipher it. Then he noticed certain correspondences, or at least he hoped he did. He rotated the paper a quarter turn, and the proper orientation made the similitude unmistakable.

"It's a map of this part of the city."

Wesk eyed it dubiously. *"Are you sure?"*

"Yes. It's difficult to tell because it's crudely drawn and the orc left so much off, but this is the breach in the wall we came through, here are the laughing shadows, and here the towers that squirm of their own accord. The mapmaker used the black dots to indicate areas best avoided. This is the building we're in now, and this box near the top must be the place where the Red Wizards themselves have taken up residence. Why else would anyone take the trouble to indicate the best path from here to there?"

The gnoll chieftain leered like a wolf spying a lost lamb. *"Nice of the pig-faces to go to so much trouble just to help us out."*

With the map to guide them, they skulked nearly to the center of Delhumide without running afoul of any more malevolent spirits or mortal foes, but as Bareris peered expectantly, waiting for the structure indicated on the sketch to come into view, he felt a sudden difference and froze. The gnolls sensed something as well, and growling, they peered around.

It took Bareris a breath or two to puzzle out precisely what they'd all registered. Probably because it was the last thing he would have expected. *"It's . . . more pleasant here. The feeling of evil has lifted."*

"Why?" asked Wesk.

Bareris shook his head. *"I don't know. Just enjoy the relief while you can. I doubt it will last."*

It did, though, and when they finally beheld their goal, he knew why. It was a square-built, flat-roofed hall notable for high columns covered in carvings and towering statues of a manlike figure with the crowned head of a hawk. Thayans no longer worshiped Horus-Re, but bards picked up a miscellany of lore in the course of acquiring new songs and stories, and Bareris had no difficulty identifying the Mulhorandi god. The structure was a temple, built on hallowed ground and still exerting a benign influence on the immediate area centuries after.

Bareris shook his head. *"I don't understand. I'm sure it's the right place, but why would the Red Wizards set up shop in a shrine like that?"*

"The god's power keeps the bogeys away," suggested Wesk. *"The bogeys the warlocks didn't whistle up themselves, I mean."*

"Maybe, but wouldn't the influence also make it more difficult to practice necromancy? It's inherently—"

"What's the difference?" Thovarr snapped.

Bareris blinked, then smiled. *"Good point. We don't care what they're doing, how, or why. We just want to rescue Tammith and disappear into the night. We'll keep our minds on that."*

Employing buildings, shadows, and piles of rubble for cover, they crept partway around the temple to look for sentries. It didn't take Wesk long to spot a pair of gaunt figures with gleaming yellow eyes crouched atop the roof.

"Undead," he said. *"I can hit them, but zombies and the like are hard to kill. I don't know if I can put them down before they sound the alarm."*

"Give me one of the arrows you mean to shoot," Bareris said.

The gnoll handed it over, and Bareris crooned to it, the charm a steady diminuendo from the first note to the last. At its end, the whisper of the wind, the skritch-skritch-skritch of one of the gnolls scratching his mane, and indeed, the entire world fell silent.

Bareris handed the arrow back and waved his arm, signaling for Wesk to shoot when he was ready. The gnoll chieftain laid it on the string, jumped up from behind the remains of a broken wall, and sent it streaking upward. Sound popped back into the world as soon as the shaft carried its invisible bubble of quietude away.

Wesk's followers shot their own arrows, and at least half found their mark, but as the gnoll had warned, the undead proved difficult to slay. Shafts jutting from their bodies like porcupine quills, they picked up bells from the rooftop and flailed them up and down. Fortunately, though, the sphere of silence now enshrouded them. The bells refused to clang, and after another moment, the amber-eyed creatures collapsed, first one and then the other.

Wesk balled up his fist and gave Bareris a stinging punch to the shoulder. *"For a human,"* said the gnoll, *"you have your uses."*

"I like to think so," Bareris replied. *"Let's go."*

Keeping low, they ran toward the temple. Their path carried them near a weathered statue of Horus-Re. In its youth, the figure had brandished an ankh to the heavens, but its upraised arm had broken off in the millennia since and now lay in fragments at its feet.

The temple proved to consist primarily of long, open, high-ceilinged galleries, with a relative scarcity of interior walls to separate one section from the next and no doors to seal any of the entrances and exits. To Bareris's war-trained sensibilities, that made it a poor choice for a stronghold, but perhaps in Delhumide, the site's aura of sanctity seemed a more important defense than any barrier of wood or stone.

In any case, he was far more concerned about something else. The temple was occupied. From time to time, they slipped past chambers where folk lay sleeping. But there were fewer than Bareris had expected, nor did he observe any indication that Red Wizards were practicing their arts here on a regular basis.

Eventually Wesk whispered the obvious, *"If all those slaves were ever here, they aren't anymore."*

"They must be," Bareris said, not because he truly disagreed, but because he couldn't bear to endorse the gnoll's conclusion.

"Do you want to wake somebody and ask him?"

The bard shook his head. *"Not unless he's a mage. Any soldier would likely just go into convulsions like our orc. It's not worth the* risk of rousing the lot of them, at least not until we've searched the entire place."

They prowled onward, looking for something, anything, to suggest an answer to the riddle of the missing thralls' whereabouts. In time they found their way to a large and shadowy chamber at the center of the temple. Once, judging from the raised altar, the colossal statue of Horus-Re enthroned behind it, and faded paintings depicting his birth and deeds adoring the walls, the chamber had been the hawk god's sanctum sanctorum. More recently, someone had erected a freestanding basket arch in the middle of the floor, its pale smooth curves a contrast to the brown, crumbling stonework on every side. When Bareris spotted it, he caught his breath in surprise.

"What?" whispered Wesk, twisting his head this way and that, looking for danger.

"The arch is a portal," Bareris said, *"a magical doorway linking this place to some other far away. I saw one during my travels and recognize the rune carved on the keystone."*

"Then we know what became of your female," said Wesk.

"Apparently, but what sense does it make? If the Red Wizards want to do something in private, what haven is more private than Delhumide? No one comes here. Conversely, why bother with this dangerous place at all, if you're only using it as a stepping stone to somewhere else?"

Wesk shrugged. *"Maybe we'll find out on the other side."*

"Hold on," Thovarr said.

Bareris assumed he meant to point out the recklessness of walking through the gate when they had no idea where it led or what waited beyond, but before the gnoll could get going, a scarlet-robed figure stepped into view through a doorway midway up the left wall. At first, the wizard didn't notice the intruders, and Thovarr had the presence of mind to fall silent. Wesk laid an arrow on his bow.

But as he drew it to his ear, the mage glimpsed the intruders from the corner of his eye, or sensed their presence somehow. He was wise enough not to waste breath and time crying for help that would surely arrive too late to save him, nor did he attempt to scramble back through the doorway as Bareris might have done. Perhaps the space he'd just vacated had only the one exit, and he didn't want to trap himself.

Instead he flourished his hand, and the black ring on his thumb left a streak of shadow on the air. Each gripping a greatsword, four pairs of skeletal arms erupted from the band. They emerged tiny but swelled to full size in a heartbeat.

They were an uncanny sight to behold, and even Wesk faltered for an instant. The Red Wizard snarled words of power, and the bony arms flew at the gnoll and his companions. Ignoring the imminent threat of the greatswords, Wesk shot an arrow at the mage, unfortunately not quickly enough to keep the warlock from finishing his incantation. A floating disk of blue phosphorescence shimmered into being in front of him, and the arrow stuck in that instead, just as if it were a tangible wooden shield.

Then the disembodied arms hurtled into the distance and started cutting with their long, heavy blades. The intruders had the advantage of numbers, but even so, Bareris realized the wizard's protectors would be difficult to defeat. The only way to stop them or even slow them down was to hit hard and square enough to cleave a length of bone entirely in two, and they flitted through the air so nimbly that it was a challenge to land a stroke at all.

But the necromancer was an even greater threat, and Bareris didn't dare leave him to conjure unmolested. He stepped between a set of skeletal arms and Wesk, ducked a cut, and riposted, buying the gnoll chieftain the moment he needed to drop his bow and ready his axe. After that, though, the bard extricated himself from the whirl of blades and charged the mage who, the translucent, arrow-pierced disk still hovering between him and his foes, the skirt of his robe flapping around his legs, was himself sprinting toward the white stone archway. Apparently he believed safety, or at least help, awaited him on the other side.

Bareris was too far away to cut him off. He sang a charm so rapidly that he feared botching the precise rhythm and pitch required, but he didn't have the option of taking his time.

Magic groaned through the air, and the section of floor under the Red Wizard's feet bucked as though an earthquake had begun. The vibration knocked the mage staggering then dumped him on his rump. Bareris dashed on, closing in on the warlock while likewise interposing himself between his foe and the portal.

The Red Wizard thrust out his arm. A glyph tattooed on the back of his hand leaped free of his skin and became a hand itself, levitating and seemingly formed of shadow. It bobbed over the top of the floating shield, then streaked at Bareris.

The bard tried to dodge, but the hand grabbed him by the shoulder anyway. Agony stabbed outward from the point of contact to afflict his entire body.

It was the fiercest pain he'd ever experienced, severe enough to blind and paralyze, which was no doubt the object. Evidently still intent on reaching the gate, but looking to finish off his adversary as well, the necromancer simultaneously circled in the appropriate direction and hissed sibilant rhyming phrases.

The pain is in my mind, Bareris insisted to himself, and I can push it out. He struggled to straighten up, turn in the mage's direction, and lift his sword once more. For a heartbeat, it was impossible, and then the bonds of torment constraining him ripped like a sheet of parchment tearing in two.

He spun around. His eyes widening, the necromancer appeared startled, but the floating shield automatically shifted to defend its creator as thoroughly as possible. Bareris poised himself as if he meant to dart to the right then dodged left instead. That fooled the shield and brought him within striking distance of the wizard. He drove his point into the other man's chest. The enchanter fell back with his final incantation uncompleted.

Bareris studied the mage for another moment, making sure their duel was truly over, then pivoted to survey the rest of the battle. Two of the gnolls were down, but with a final chop of his axe, Thovarr was reducing the last of the disembodied arms to inert splinters of bone.

His allies' success gave Bareris the opportunity to contemplate the enormity of what he'd done, or the seeming enormity. He'd earned a death by torture the moment he'd lifted his hand to So-Kehur and his skull-masked partner, so in practical terms, it shouldn't matter that he'd now killed a Red Wizard outright.

Yet it gave him pause. The eight orders taught every person and certainly every pauper in Thay to think of their members as superior, invincible beings, and though Bareris's experiences abroad had given him ample reason to feel confident of his own prowess, perhaps a part of him still believed the myth and was accordingly appalled at his temerity, but then a surge of satisfaction washed his trepidation away. After all, these were the bastards who'd taken Tammith away from him, and this particular specimen didn't look so exalted or omnipotent anymore, did he?

Wesk trotted up to him, bow in hand once more. He had a cut on his forearm where a greatsword must have grazed him, but he wasn't paying it any mind.

"I don't hear anyone coming," he said, *"do you?"*

Bareris listened. *"No."* Evidently the fight hadn't made a great deal of noise. He was glad he hadn't needed to produce any of the prodigious booms or roars of which his magic was capable. He pointed to the gnolls still lying on the floor. *"How are they?"*

"Dead." If Wesk felt bad about it, no human could have told it from his manner. *"So what now?"*

"We hide the bodies and what's left of the skeleton arms. With luck, that will buy us more time before anyone else realizes we were here."

"And then we go through the gate?"

Bareris opened his mouth to say yes, then thought better of it. *"No. Thovarr's right. We don't know where it leads or what's waiting beyond, but we do know the necromancer believed that if he could reach the other side, it would save him. That means he could have had a lot of allies there. More than we, with half our band already lost, can hope to overcome."*

Wesk cocked his head. *"You didn't come this far just to give up."*

"No, but I'm going on alone, clad in the dead wizard's robe, in the hope that trickery will succeed where force would likely fail."

"Did you notice that the robe has a bloody hole in it? You put it there."

Bareris shrugged. *"It's not a big hole and not too bloody. Bodies don't bleed much after the heart stops. If I throw a cloak on over the robe, perhaps no one will notice."*

He'd also sing a song to make himself seem more likable and trustworthy, the very antithesis of a person meriting suspicion, but saw no point in mentioning that. He was still leery of allowing the gnolls to guess the extent to which he'd used magic to manipulate them.

Wesk grunted. *"Better, maybe, to disguise yourself with an illusion or be invisible."*

"Perhaps, but I don't know those particular songs. Somehow I never had the chance to learn them. Now let's get moving. We need don't anybody else blundering in on us while we stand around talking."

They dragged the bodies to the room from which the Red

Wizard had emerged. It turned out to be a small, bare, rectangular space the clergy of Horus-Re might have used to store votive candles, incense, and similar supplies. Bareris wondered what the mage had been doing in here and realized he'd never know.

He was stripping his fellow human's corpse when Wesk exclaimed, *"Your hair."*

Bareris reflexively raised a hand to touch his tangled, sweaty locks. *"Curse it!"* Like any Mulan who hadn't spent the last several years in foreign lands, the Red Wizards uniformly employed razors, depilatories, or magic to keep themselves bald as stones.

Wesk pulled his knife from its sheath. *"I don't suppose you can truly shave without lather and such, but I can shear your hair very short, and the robe has a cowl. Keep it pulled up and maybe you'll pass."*

The gnoll proved to be about as gentle a barber as Bareris had expected. He yanked hard on the strands of hair, and the knife stung as it sawed them away. Bareris had no doubt it was nicking him.

"Gnolls take scalps for trophies sometimes," said Wesk. *"You make the first cut like this."* He laid the edge of his knife against Bareris's forehead just below the hairline.

"I had a hunch that was what you were doing," Bareris replied, and Wesk laughed his crazy, bestial laugh.

When the gnoll finished, Bareris brushed shorn hair off his shoulders and chest, put on the scarlet robe over his brigandine and breeches, then donned his cloak and sword belt. He hoped he could get away with wearing a sword. Though it wasn't common, he'd seen other Red Wizards do the same. But he realized with regret that he'd have to leave his yarting behind. The musical instrument would simply be too unusual and distinctive.

He handed it to Wesk. *"Take this. It's not a ruby, but it'll fetch a good price."*

The gnoll archer grinned. *"Maybe I'll keep it and learn to play."*

"Thank you all for your help. Now clear out of here. Try to be far away by daybreak."

"Good hunting, human. It was good to be a soldier again, even if our army was very small."

The gnolls stalked toward the exit. Singing softly, Bareris headed for the arch.

chapter nine

30 Mirtul–1 Kythorn, the Year of Risen Elfkin

For the briefest of instants, the universe shattered into meaningless sparks and smears of light, and Bareris felt as if he were plummeting. Then his stride carried him clear of the portal, and his lead foot landed on a surface just as solid and level as the floor in Horus-Re's holy of holies. But because his body had believed it was falling, he lurched off balance and had to take a quick step to catch himself.

Seeking to orient himself as rapidly as possible, he peered around. He was in another stone chamber, this one lit by the wavering greenish light of the sort of enchanted torch that burned forever without the heatless flames consuming the wood. It didn't look as though Mulhorandi had built this room. Its trapezoidal shape, the square doorways, and the odd zigzag carvings framing them were markedly different than the architecture of his ancestors or any other culture he knew of.

The portal was a white stone arch on this side too, identical to its counterpart. Armed with spears and scimitars, wearing cyclopean-skull-and-four-pointed-star badges that likely proclaimed their fealty to one Red Wizard or another, a pair of blood orcs were standing guard over it. They eyed Bareris curiously.

Their scrutiny gave the bard a twinge of fear. Indeed, it inspired a witless urge to whip his sword from its scabbard and try to strike the sentries down before they could raise an alarm. He raked them with a haughty stare instead.

They straightened up as much as their stooped race ever did, thrust out their lances with the shafts perpendicular to their extended arms, drew them back, and pounded the butts on the floor. It was a salute, and Bareris breathed a sigh of relief that he'd deceived the first creatures he'd encountered anyway.

One guard, afflicted with a runny walleye that rendered it even homelier than the common run of orc, looked back at the portal expectantly. When no one else emerged, it asked, "No slaves this time, Master?"

"No," Bareris said. "I traveled on ahead carrying word of how many you're getting and when. It should help with the planning." He hoped his improvisation made at least a little sense.

The orc's mouth twisted. "You need to see the whelp, then."

The whelp? What in the name of the Binder's quill did that mean? "The one in charge," he said warily.

The orc nodded. "That Xingax thing. The whelp is what we call it." It hesitated. "Maybe we shouldn't, but it's not one of you masters. It's . . . what it is."

"I understand," Bareris said, wishing it were true. "Where is it?"

"Somewhere up top. That'll take you up." The orc used its spear to point to a staircase behind one of the square doorways.

Bareris started to say thank you, until it occurred to him that the average Red Wizard probably didn't bother showing courtesy to orcs. "Got it." He turned away.

"Master?"

Breathing more quickly, fearful he'd betrayed himself some-how, the bard pivoted back around. "What?"

"I don't mean to bother you. I wouldn't, except you haven't been here before, have you? I understand you're a wizard, and ten times wiser than the likes of me, but you know to protect yourself before you go close to Xingax, don't you?"

"Of course," Bareris lied, wondering what sort of protection would serve and hoping he wouldn't need it. Given the choice, he'd steer well clear of "the whelp," whatever it was.

He discovered that the room above the arch connected to a series of catwalks that apparently allowed one to make a full circuit of the various lofts and balconies without ever descend-ing to the more extensive and contiguous system of chambers and corridors comprising the primary level below. Unlike the rest of the stronghold, the walkways appeared to be of recent construction, and it seemed plain the Red Wizards—or rather, their servants—had expended a fair amount of effort building them, which was odd, considering that Bareris didn't see anyone else moving around up here.

Peculiar or not, their vacancy was a blessing. It allowed him to explore without venturing near to anyone who might penetrate his disguise, and in time he came to suspect the advantage was essential. Viewed up close, his face might have betrayed horror and disgust no matter how he tried to conceal them.

He soon concluded from the complete absence of windows that he was underground. Stinking of incense and carrion, the chilly vaults felt old, perhaps even older than Delhumide, and like the haunted city, breathed an aura of perversity and danger. Unlike Delhumide, however, the catacombs bustled with activ-ity. Necromancers chanted over corpses and skeletons, which then clambered to their feet, the newly made zombies clumsily, the bone men with clinking agility. Warriors drilled the undead in the use of mace and spear, just as if the creatures were youths newly recruited into the legions. Ghouls practiced charging on command to shred straw dummies with fang and claw. A half dozen shadows listened as, its face a carnival of oozing, eyeless rot beneath its raised visor, a corpse armored in plate expounded on strategy and tactics.

Anyone but a necromancer would likely have found it ghastly, but it was inexplicable as well. The Red Wizards were free to turn their slaves into undead men-at-arms if they so desired. They created such monstrosities all the time. Thus, Bareris wondered anew: Why the secrecy?

Though he still didn't care. Not really. All that mattered was spiriting Tammith away from this nightmarish place before her captors could alter her.

He refused to entertain the notion that perhaps they already had until he found his way to a platform overlooking a crypt housing dozens of listless, skinny, ragged folk with the whip scars and unshorn hair of thralls. Bareris scrutinized them all in turn, then peered into every empty shadow and corner, and none of the prisoners was Tammith.

His nerves taut, he marched onward, striding faster, no longer concerned that his boots would make too much noise on the planking beneath them or that haste would make him appear suspicious to anyone looking up from below. He gazed down into chamber after chamber and felt grateful the catacombs were so extensive. Until he ran out of spaces to check, he could still hope. But at the same time, he hated that the warren was big and labyrinthine enough to so delay his determination of the truth.

He passed through yet another newly cut doorway then at last he saw her, lying on her back on the floor of an otherwise empty room with a scatter of earth around and beneath her. Sleeping, surely, for she displayed no marks to prove otherwise. No wounds, and none of the bloat or lividity of a corpse.

"Tammith!" he called, trying to make his voice loud enough to wake her but not so loud as to be overheard outside the chamber.

She didn't stir. He called again, louder, and still she didn't respond.

He trembled and swallowed, refusing to believe someone had killed her with a poison or spell that didn't leave a mark, recently enough that her body hadn't yet started to deteriorate. It simply couldn't be so.

Except that he knew it very well could.

There were no stairs in this particular room. He swung himself over the guardrail and dropped, as, in what had come to seem a different life and a brighter world, he'd once leaped from the deck of a ship onto a dock in Bezantur.

The landing jarred but didn't injure him. He rushed to Tammith, knelt, and touched her cheek. Her skin was as cool as he'd feared it would be. His voice breaking, he spoke her name once more.

Her eyes flew open. He felt an incredulous, overpowering joy, and then she reached up and seized him by the throat.

•• •• •• •• •• •• •• •• •• •• •• •• •• ••

In one respect at least, the temple of Kossuth in Escalant was like most other human households: Nearly everyone slept away the time just before dawn. That was why Hezass Nymia, tharchion of Lapendrar and Eternal Flame of the god's house, chose that time to lead his four golems on a circuit of the principal altars. Carved of deep brown Thayan oak to resemble men-at-arms, the glow of the myriad sacred fires reflecting from their polished surfaces, the automata had been fashioned first and foremost to fight as archers, and their longbows were a part of their bodies. Hezass had them carrying sacks in their free hands.

Lifeless and mindless, the golems were tireless as well. Yawning, Hezass envied them that and wondered if this surreptitious transit was truly necessary. He was, after all, the high priest of the pyramidal temple and so entitled to his pick of the offerings the faithful gave to the Firelord.

It was the accepted custom, but custom likewise decreed that the hierophant should exercise restraint. One could argue that such self-control was particularly desirable if the previous Eternal Flame, proving not so eternal after all, had fallen to his death under mysterious circumstances, and the current one had somehow managed to secure his appointment even though several other priests were further advanced in the mysteries of the faith.

Yes, all in all, it was best to avoid the appearance of greed, Hezass thought with a wry smile, but the truth was, he had little hope of avoiding the reality. He coveted as much as he coveted, and he meant to have it. Better then to do some of his skimming when no censorious eyes were watching.

The golems' wooden feet clacking faintly on the marble floor, the little procession arrived at another altar, where women often prayed to conceive, or if they had, for an easy delivery and a healthy baby. Hezass picked up a string of pearls, scrutinized it, and put it back. He liked to think he had as good an eye as any jeweler, and he could see the necklace was second-rate. The delicate platinum tiara, on the other hand, was exquisite.

Responsive to his unspoken will, one of the golems proffered its sack, but since it only had the one functional hand, Hezass had to pull open the mouth of the bag and drop the headdress in himself. As porters, the constructs had their limitations, but their inability to speak made up for them.

"That is a nice piece," drawled a masculine voice.

Startled, Hezass nearly whirled around but caught himself in time. Better to move in a leisurely fashion, with a dignity befitting an Eternal Flame and tharchion, like a man who hadn't gotten caught doing anything illicit. He turned to meet the dark-eyed, sardonic gaze of a gaunt figure whose capacious scarlet sleeves currently concealed his withered fingers.

Hezass dropped to his knees. "Your Omnipotence."

"It looks Impilturan," Szass Tam continued. "Brides from wealthy families often wear such ornaments on their wedding days. Please, stand up."

Hezass did so, meanwhile wondering what this unexpected intrusion portended. "I haven't had the honor of meeting with Your Omnipotence in some time."

"We've both been busy," said the lich, sauntering closer, the hem of his red robe whispering along the floor, "but you're awake, I'm always awake, most of the rest of the world is asleep, so this seems a convenient moment for us to talk."

Hezass wondered how Szass Tam had known he was awake and precisely where to find him. "I'm at your service, of course."

"Thank you." The necromancer casually pulled a crystal-pointed enchanted arrow from a golem's quiver, examined it, and dropped it back in. "I admit, it concerns me a little to find you out of bed. If you're suffering from insomnia, I know a potion that will help."

"I'm fine," said Hezass. "I'm just getting a head start on my duties."

The wizard nodded. "I can see that, though technically, it's arguable whether pilfering from the offerings constitutes a duty."

Hezass forced a smile. "Your Omnipotence always did have a keen sense of humor. You know, surely, that I'm entitled to my share."

"Oh, absolutely, but if you start claiming it while the coins and other valuables still lie on display atop the altars, before the clerks make their tally, doesn't that mean you underreport the take to the Flaming Brazier and send Eltabbar less than its fair share? If so, isn't that the equivalent of robbing the Firelord himself? I'm afraid Iphegor Nath would think so. He might try to punish you even if you are a tharchion, and who's to say he wouldn't succeed? He's made a considerable contribution to the campaign against the undead horde in the east, and we zulkirs are accordingly grateful."

Hezass drew a long, steadying breath. "Master, you know that even if there's anything . . . irregular about my conduct as Eternal Flame, it's no worse than the way other folk in authority behave every day across the length and breadth of the realm. You also knew what sort of man I am when you helped me rise in the church and later gave me Lapendrar to govern."

"That's true," said Szass Tam, "and I'll tell you a secret: It doesn't bother me if you dare to rob a god. Do the gods deal with us so kindly or even justly as to merit abject devotion?" He waved his hand at the offerings on the altar. "Look at all this—not the gold and gems that usually catch your eye, but the copper, bread, and fruit. Needy women have given what they could ill afford, perhaps all they possessed, to bribe your god, yet he won't answer all their prayers. Some petitioners will remain barren or perish in childbirth even so. Why is that, and what's the sense of a world where it's possible for women to miscarry and infants to die in their cribs in the first place?"

Hezass had no idea what the necromancer was talking about or how to respond. "Master, you understand I share a true bond with Kossuth even if I do pocket a few too many of the trinkets the faithful offer him. He forgives me my foibles, I believe. Anyway, the world is what it is. Isn't it?"

Szass Tam smiled. His expression had a hint of wistfulness about it, the look, just conceivably, of someone who'd briefly hoped to find a kindred spirit and been disappointed. "Indeed it is, and I didn't mean to cast aspersions on your creed or bore you with philosophy either. Let's focus on practical concerns."

"With respect, Your Omnipotence, your 'practical concern' seems to be to blackmail me, but why? I have no choice but to do whatever a zulkir commands, and beyond that, I'm grateful for everything you've done for me. I'm happy to aid you in return."

"Your loyalty shames me," the lich replied, and if he was speaking ironically, neither his voice nor his lean, intellectual features betrayed it. "If only everyone were as faithful, but 'the world is what it is,' and with the council of zulkirs divided against itself, even I sometimes find it expedient to make it clear to folk that, just as I reward those who cooperate with me, so too do I have ways of rebuking those who refuse."

Hezass smiled. "You've covered the rebuking part. Now I'd like to hear about the reward."

The dead man laughed. A whiff of decay escaped his open mouth, and Hezass made sure his features didn't twist in repugnance.

"As one of your peers recently reminded me," Szass Tam said, "the miners dig prodigious quantities of gold out of the mountains of High Thay."

"So I understand," Hezass said.

"At present, most of it comes down to the Plateau via the road that runs east. That's natural, since it's really the only highway worthy of the name, but I see no fundamental reason why more gold couldn't move west and south, following the courses of the rivers, perhaps with magical aid to see the caravans safely over the difficult patches, and obviously, if it does, it will descend into Lapendrar. You can tax it as it passes from hand to hand and turn a nice profit thereby."

"A nice profit" was an understatement. Hezass suspected that over the course of several years, he might amass a fortune to rival Samas Kul's. "You truly could arrange it?"

"Why not? Pyras Autorian is my friend, no less than you."

More, actually, Hezass thought. He was Szass Tam's confederate, or to be honest about it, his underling. Pyras Autorian was purely and simply the lich's puppet, a docile dunce who did exactly and only what his master told him to do, which suddenly seemed like quite an admirable quality, since it meant there was no doubt Szass Tam could deliver on his offer.

"What must I do," Hezass asked, "to start all this gold cascading down from the heights?"

"Quite possibly nothing, but here's what I'll require if it turns out I need anything at all . . . "

•• •• •• •• • •• •• •• •• •• •• •• •• ••

Tammith's fingers dug into Bareris's neck as if she'd acquired an ogre's strength. Her mouth opened to reveal canine teeth lengthening into fangs. She started to drag him down.

He tried to plead with her, but her fingers cut off his wind and denied him his voice. He punched her in the face, but the blow just made her snarl. It didn't stun her or loosen her grip on him.

At last he recalled a trick one of his former comrades, a warrior monk of Ilmater and an expert wrestler, had taught him. Supposedly a man could use it to break free of any stranglehold, no matter how strong his opponent.

He swept his arm in the requisite circular motion and just managed to knock her hand away, though a flash of pain told him it had taken some of his skin along with it, lodged beneath her nails. She immediately grabbed for him again, but he threw himself back beyond her reach.

He scrambled to his feet and so did she. "Don't you know me?" he wheezed. "It's Bareris."

She glided forward, but not straight toward him. She was maneuvering to interpose herself between him and the door.

He drew his sword. "Stop. I don't want to hurt you, but you have to keep away."

Rather to his surprise, she did stop. A master sword smith had forged and enchanted the blade, giving it the ability to cut foes largely impervious to common weapons, and perhaps the creature Tammith had become could sense the threat of the magic bound in the steel.

"That's good," Bareris said. "Now look at me. I know you recognize me. You and I—"

Her body exploded into smaller, darker shapes. Astonished, he froze for an instant as the bats hurtled at him.

His fear screamed at him to cut at the flying creatures. He yanked off his cloak and flailed at them with it instead, fighting to fend them off while he sang.

Something jabbed his arm and then the top of his head. Bats were lighting on him and biting him despite his efforts to keep them away. He struggled to ignore the pain and horror of it lest they disrupt the precise articulation the spell required.

The bats abruptly spun away from him as if a whirlwind had caught them. In fact, they were suffering the effects of the same charm that had repelled the enormous fleas. It was supposed to work on any sort of vermin, and apparently even creatures like these were susceptible.

The bats swirled together and became Tammith once more. Her fangs shortened into normal-looking teeth, and her face twisted in anguish. "I'm sorry!" she whispered. "I'm sorry."

He inferred that his magic had done what his punch could not: Shock her out of her predatory frenzy and restore her to something approximating sanity. He sheathed his blade, put his cloak back on, extended his hand, and stepped toward her.

"It's all right," he said.

She recoiled. "Stay away! I don't want to hurt you."

"Then you won't."

"I will. Even though I . . . fed on poor Yuldra already. Something about who you are, what we are to each other, makes it worse. Don't you understand what's happened to me?"

He realized he was reluctant to say the word "vampire," as if speaking it aloud would seal the curse for eternity. "I have some idea, but what magic can do, it can undo. People say the holiest priests even know rituals to . . . restore the dead to life. We just have to get you away from here, and then we'll find the help you need."

She shook her head. "No one can help me, and even if somebody could, I'm not able to go to him. I'm more of a slave now than I was before Xingax changed me. He chained my mind, bound me to serve the wizards and their cause."

"Maybe I can at least do something about that. It wouldn't be the first enchantment I've broken with a song."

"You can't break this one. Get away from here while you still can."

"No. I won't leave without you."

She glared at him. "Why not? You abandoned me before."

Her sudden anger shocked him. "That's not true. I left Bezantur to make us a future."

"Well, this is the one you made for me."

"That isn't so. I'm going to save you. Just trust—"

A voice sounded from overhead: "What are you doing in here?"

Bareris looked up to behold the most grotesque creature he'd ever seen. Riding on the back of what appeared to be a zombie hill giant, the thing looked like a man-sized, festering, and grossly malformed infant or fetus. He surmised that it could only be Xingax, "the whelp."

Bareris reminded himself that he was still wearing a red robe and still cloaked in an enchantment devised to quell suspicion and inspire good will in others. In addition to that, Xingax was squinting down at him as if the mismatched eyes in his lopsided face didn't see particularly well. Perhaps this encounter needn't be disastrous.

The bard lowered his gaze once more. He hoped Xingax would take it for a gesture of respect, or a natural human response to profound ugliness, and not an attempt to keep the creature from getting a better look at an unfamiliar face.

"I was just curious to see what you'd made of the slave."

"Do I know you?"

A bead of sweat oozed down Bareris's brow. He wished he knew the proper attitude to assume. Was Xingax a servant, something a supposed Red Wizard should treat with the same arrogance he showed to most creatures, or did the abomination expect a degree of deference?

"I'm new. So far, I'm just performing routine tasks. Creating zombies and the like."

"I see. What's your name?"

"Toriak Kakanos."

"Well, Toriak, let's have a decent look at your face, so I'll know you in the future."

Bareris reluctantly complied. When his eyes met Xingax's, a malignant power stabbed into the core of him, searing and shaking him with spasms of debilitating pain. He crumpled to the floor.

"It was a good try," Xingax said, "but I meet all the wizards as soon as they come through the portal. Is it possible this is . . . what was the name? . . . never mind. The bard who tried to rescue you before."

"Yes," Tammith groaned.

"Drink from him and try to change him as the ritual changed you. It's another good test of your new abilities."

Bareris fought to control his breathing then started singing under his breath.

"Please," Tammith said, "don't make me do it."

"Why not?" Xingax replied. "Don't you love him? Wouldn't you rather he continue on still able to think, feel, and remember? Isn't that better than making him a mindless husk?"

"No!"

The whelp snorted. "I'll never understand the human perspective. It's so perverse. Even so, it grieves me to deny my daughter's request, but the truth of the matter is, if this fellow wields bardic magic, survived a battle with Muthoth, So-Kehur, and their guards, and found his way to our secret home, then, like yours, his courage and talents are too valuable to waste. I must insist you transform him. You'll thank me later."

Haltingly, as though still struggling against the compulsion, Tammith advanced on Bareris.

Her resistance gave him time to complete his song, and its power washed the pain and weakness from his body. The question was, what to do next?

He was sure he had no hope of defending himself against Tammith and Xingax simultaneously. He had to neutralize one of them fast, before either realized he'd shaken off the effect of the fetus-thing's poison gaze, and unfortunately, Tammith was both the more immediate threat and the one within reach of his sword.

Despite what she'd become, striking the blow was the hardest thing he'd ever done, but he wanted to survive and do so as a living man, not an undead monstrosity, so he leaped to his feet and drove his sword into her stomach.

The stroke would have killed any ordinary human, if not instantly, then after a period of crippling agony, but if the tales he'd heard were true, a vampire would survive it. He prayed it was so, and he prayed too that the wound would incapacitate her long enough to make a difference.

He yanked his sword free of her flesh, and she doubled over

clutching at the gash. Making sure he didn't look up and meet Xingax's gaze again, he dashed for the doorway. The catwalk banged as the giant zombie lumbered after him.

The huge corpse had longer legs than he did. Aware that he was running short of spells, he nonetheless sang a charm to quicken his stride. It might be the only hope he had of keeping ahead of his pursuers.

Of course, it likely wouldn't be long before he blundered into some of Xingax's allies, at which point the fetus-thing would yell for them to stop him. Then, with new foes in front of him and his current ones pounding up behind, it would make no difference how fast he could run.

He halted, lifted his head, and shouted. The blast of sound jolted and splintered the section of catwalk immediately in front of the huge zombie. Its next heavy stride stamped a hole in the weakened planks, and then it crashed through altogether, carrying its rider along with it.

The two creatures slammed down hard in a clattering shower of broken wood. Bareris didn't expect the fall to destroy the zombie outright, but he dared to hope he'd damaged it and maybe slain the feeble-looking Xingax.

The zombie tried to rise and the whelp slipped from its shoulders. Evidently he couldn't hold on anymore. The undead giant fell back on top of him when one of its legs buckled beneath it.

Bareris could scarcely believe how well the trick had worked. How lucky he'd been. He sprinted on, found a staircase, climbed to the catwalks, and headed for the portal. He'd just promised Tammith he wouldn't leave her here, but the plain truth was now he had to get away or die, quite possibly when she murdered him herself. He vowed to himself that he'd return and next time rescue her. Somehow. Somehow.

His guts churned, his vision blurred, and a pang of headache jabbed through his skull. Something was making him ill. He cast about for the source of his distress and saw nothing.

He recalled his orc informant warning him that a person needed protection merely to come into proximity with Xingax. Could that possibly be what ailed him? If so, where was the whelp? A sudden blast of cold coated the right side of his body with frost and chilled him to the core. He'd seen battle mages conjure such attacks. Shaking, he looked for cover and found none within reach. He turned to see where the magic had originated.

Visible now, Xingax floated in empty air a few yards away from the catwalk. Obviously, the fall hadn't killed him, and he didn't actually need the zombie to carry him around. He certainly hadn't had any difficulty catching up to Bareris.

Stricken as he was, the bard almost looked into the abomination's eyes before recalling he mustn't. At the last possible instant, he averted his gaze.

Not that it was likely to matter. He'd drained his reserves of magic nearly dry, and his twisted little infant's mouth leering, Xingax was hovering out of reach of his blade. From that position, the fetus-creature could throw spell after spell without fear of effective reprisal.

Bareris could only think of one ploy to attempt, and it was nowhere near as clever as breaking the catwalk had been. In fact, it was as old as any trick in the world, but it would have to serve. He allowed himself to collapse onto the walkway and lay motionless thereafter.

A wary foe might suspect he was merely feigning death or unconsciousness and continue smiting him at range. If Xingax took that tactic, he was finished.

But maybe the abomination wouldn't be that cautious. He seemed smugly confident of his own powers and likewise devoted to his work. He might be reluctant to kill Bareris here and now and settle for reanimating him as a zombie when it could still be possible to turn him into a more powerful undead.

I'm helpless, Bareris thought. Sick. Frozen. Dead. Just come closer and you'll see.

As if heeding his silent entreaties, Xingax floated over to hang directly over him. One larger and set higher than the other, his dark eyes squinted.

Striving to deny sickness and injury their grip of him, bellowing a war cry to infuse himself with vigor and resolve, Bareris sprang to his feet. Still doing his best to avoid looking into Xingax's eyes, he cut open the creature's chest.

Xingax gave an ear-splitting screech like the cry of the baby he so resembled. Bareris slashed away a flap of flesh from one of the creature's cheeks.

The fetus-thing started to fly away from the catwalk. Bareris lunged and caught the dangling length of cold, slimy umbilicus. It threatened to slide out of his fingers, but he clamped down tight, twisted it around his wrist, and held Xingax in place as if the latter were a dog straining at a leash.

He kept on cutting and thrusting. Xingax hurled another blaze of chill from his small, decaying hands, but Bareris discerned his intent, twisted aside and evaded the worst of it then retaliated by lopping off one of the outthrust extremities at the wrist. His next cut sliced the smaller of the creature's eyes.

The whelp screamed and vanished, leaving a segment of gray rotting birth cord behind in Bareris's fingers. His final wail echoed.

Fearful that his foe had simply become invisible once more, Bareris pivoted and slashed at the air all around him. His blade failed to find a target, and in another moment, he realized he felt better. Xingax truly had departed, evidently translating himself instantaneously through space and taking his aura of sickness along with him.

Unfortunately, that didn't fix the chill burns on Bareris's skin. With luck, his healing songs would keep the injured patches from turning into genuine frostbite and gangrene, but he didn't have the magic or time to spare to attempt it now. He cast away the section of umbilicus, brushed rime from his garments, and strode in the direction of the portal, until he heard a commotion up ahead.

Then he realized that Xingax, surmising his foe would make for the magical gate, had transported himself there when he fled, where he'd no doubt arranged for some of his minions to guard the portal with special care while the rest scoured the catacombs for the man who'd maimed him.

Bareris struggled to suppress a surge of panic, telling himself there had to be another way out of here, wherever here was. He just had to find it.

He threw away his cloak. At a distance, the brown mantle was probably more conspicuous than the bloody rent in his robe. He hid his sword and sword belt beneath the voluminous crimson garment. Then he hurried away from the sound of the searchers and toward a portion of the maze of vaults and tunnels he had yet to explore.

Eventually he spotted a subtle change in the ambient illumination up ahead. He rounded a corner and saw a trapezoidal opening with a ray of wan light shining through. Puzzling as it seemed, given his near-certainty that he was underground, the wizards' lair possessed a window after all.

He lowered himself from the catwalk by his hands, dropped, stuck his head out the opening, and then he understood. The vaults were adjacent to a wide cylindrical shaft plunging deep into bedrock. He'd heard stories of an ancient people who'd excavated well-like fortresses in the Sunrise Mountains. Apparently they'd dug out at least one city as well, constructed on a grander scale, and he was standing in it. The morning sun hadn't yet risen high enough to shine straight down into the central vacancy, but even so, the light reflecting down from the gray clouds revealed other windows, as well as doorways connecting to chiseled balconies and staircases.

Intending to locate one of those doors, he turned, then heard his pursuers once more. They were manifestly closing in. Before, the noise they'd made had simply been a drone. Now he could make out some of the words that one orc was growling to another.

Bareris realized he didn't dare spend any more time in the tunnels looking for anything. He had to get out now, so he clambered out the window feet first.

He was no expert climber, and fatigue and the flare of cold had stolen a measure of his strength, but fortunately, the ancient builders hadn't polished the walls of the shaft smooth, or if they had, time had come along behind them and roughened them again. There were hand- and footholds to be had, and refusing to look down at the gulf yawning beneath him, the bard hauled himself upward.

Finally he reached one of the spiraling staircases. He dragged himself onto the steps, lay on his belly for a moment panting and trembling, then forced himself to rise and skulk onward.

In time he spotted a pair of human guards at the top of the steps. As best he could judge, no one had alerted them that an intruder had penetrated the catacombs below, for they appeared more bored than vigilant and were looking outward, not down the stairs.

Trying to be silent, Bareris drew his sword from beneath his robe and held it behind his back. Then he crept on.

Despite his efforts at stealth, one of the sentries apparently heard him coming. The warrior turned, and reacting to the sight of a red robe, he began to salute with his spear as the orcs at the portal had.

Then, his eyes widening, he exclaimed, "What's this?" and leveled the weapon.

Bareris charged, knocked the lance out of line with his sword, and drove the blade into the warrior's chest. Where it stuck fast as the other spearman attacked. Bareris let go of the hilt, twisted to avoid his adversary's thrust, grabbed him, and shoved him off the edge of the landing. Shrieking, the warrior plummeted down the well.

His pulse hammering in his neck, Bareris peered about. He was on top of a mountain, with brown, jagged peaks rising on every side to stab the overcast sky, and except for the subterranean city he'd just exited and a well-trodden trail running down the rocky slopes from the lip of the shaft, no sign of human habitation anywhere. He still suspected he was in the Sunrise Mountains, but he'd never even seen them before, and he knew that in fact, he could be anywhere.

At least he had the dawn to give him his directions. He'd head west, south, and/or downward, depending on which was most practical at a given moment, and hope to find his way to the Pass of Thazar or one of the eastern tharchs. He saw little choice but to try. By all accounts, a lone man couldn't survive in these mountains for long.

To his disappointment, the dead warrior at his feet wasn't carrying any food, but he did have a leather water bottle. Bareris appropriated that, his spear, and his cloak. Spring had come to the lowlands, but up here the wind whistling out of the north was cold, and the night would be colder still.

Once he'd outfitted himself as well as he was able, he trotted down the trail. It was the best way to distance himself from the wizards' stronghold, the fastest, easiest way to travel, but he'd need to forsake the path in just a little while, because his foes would come after him, and his only hope of evading them was to vanish into the trackless crags and gorges.

chapter ten

4–5 Kythorn, the Year of Risen Elfkin

Aoth looked around the table at Nymia Focar, his fellow captains, and an assortment of high-ranking Burning Braziers and Red Wizards. Many of his comrades looked tired, and tight mouths and clenched jaws revealed the determination to participate in the council of war despite the ache of one's wounds. Yet everyone seemed happy as well, whether expansively or quietly, and the singing and whooping outside the hall mirrored the mood of satisfaction within.

It was the satisfaction that came with victory. Upon learning the undead had in fact assaulted the sizable town of Thazrumaros and overrun the eastern half of it, Nymia had hastily reunited the greater part of her army to attack the creatures in their turn, and though the battle had claimed the lives of a number of Thayan warriors, in the end, she'd prevailed.

Now the common soldiers were celebrating, drinking the town dry and bedding every woman who felt moved to so reward its saviors. Aoth wished he were reveling with them.

Leaning on a crutch, his leg splinted, an officer hobbled in and took the last available chair. The yellow lamplight gleaming on the rings in her ears and the stud in her nose, Nymia sat up straighter, tacitly signaling that she was ready to begin. The drone of casual conversation died.

"My good friends," Nymia said, "you scarcely need me to tell you what your valor has accomplished over the course of the past several days. I've just received a message from Milsantos Daramos, and he and his troops have been similarly successful, cleansing the southern part of Pyarados as we've cleansed the north."

Everyone exclaimed and applauded, and Aoth supposed he might as well clap with them. It was good news, as far as it went.

When they'd all had their fill of self-congratulation, Nymia continued. "It's plain that when we combine Thayan arms, Thayan wizardry, and Kossuth's holy fire, these ghouls and specters are no match for us, so I propose to finish destroying them as expeditiously as possible. It's time to join forces with Tharchion Daramos, drive up the Pass of Thazar, and retake the keep. I only need to know how soon your companies can be ready to march."

The war leaders began to discuss how many casualties they'd sustained, how much flour and salt pork and how many crossbow bolts remained in the supply wagons, and all the other factors that determined an army's ability to travel and fight. Maybe, thought Aoth, he should leave it at that.

For after all, every other face at the table was a long, fair-complexioned, indisputably Mulan visage. Every other captain had more experience as an officer. Every other wizard was a Red Wizard. Thus, it was unlikely that his opinion would weigh very heavily with anyone.

Still, he felt it was his duty to voice it.

He raised his hand to attract Nymia's attention. "Yes," she said, smiling, "Aoth, what is it?"

He found he needed to clear his throat before proceeding. "I'm concerned that when we talk about rushing up the pass as fast as we can, or of the enemy as if their final defeat were a certainty, that we aren't taking the threat seriously enough."

Nymia cocked her head. "I take it very seriously. That's why, after our initial setbacks, I recruited the help required to deal with it."

"I know, but there's still a lot we don't understand."

"Of course—exactly where the undead came from, and why they decided to descend on us now. Perhaps we'll find out in due course, but do we actually need to know to defeat them? Judging from our recent successes, I'd say no."

"With respect, Tharchion, it's more than that. I told you about the fall of Thazar Keep, and the priest who wielded so much power against the undead. None of the creatures should have been able to stand against him, yet something struck him down."

One of the senior Burning Braziers, a burly, middle-aged man with tattooed orange and yellow flames crawling up his neck, snorted. "Are you well-versed in the mysteries of faith, Captain?"

"No," said Aoth, "but I know overwhelming mystical force when I see it, whether the source is arcane or divine."

"What, specifically, was the source in this instance?" asked the fire priest. "Which god did this paragon serve?"

"Bane."

"Oh, well, Bane." The Burning Brazier's tone suggested that all deities other than his own were insignificant, and his fellow clerics chuckled.

Nymia looked at Aoth. She was still smiling, but with less warmth than before. "I understand why you're concerned, but we already knew the enemy has special ways of striking at our priests, and we've already taken special measures to protect them. Is there anything else?"

Just let it go, thought Aoth, but what he said was, "Yes. Have you noticed the particular nature of the creatures we've been fighting of late?"

Idly fingering one of the bones comprising his necklace, Urhur Hahpet grinned and shook his head. "Unless I'm mistaken, they were undead, the very entities we set out to fight."

"At one point," Aoth replied, "you, my lord, asked me what could be learned by confronting our foes at close quarters instead of simply burning them from a distance. After pondering the matter, I'm now able to tell you. For the most part, the creatures we've been destroying were zombies, ghouls, and shadows. Nasty foes but familiar ones, and often plainly the reanimated remains of farmers, villagers, and even animals the marauders slaughtered, not members of the original horde."

Nymia frowned. "Meaning what?"

"That the work we've done so far was necessary, but we've yet to inflict much harm on our true foe. The marauders' strength is still essentially intact. They still have their nighthaunt, most of their skin kites, diggers, and quells, and the rest of the strange creatures we don't really know how to fight."

Nymia looked to the necromancers. "You're the authorities on these horrors. Is it possible Aoth is right?"

Urhur shrugged. "I agree, we've destroyed relatively few of the exotic specimens, but it's conceivable that Tharchion Daramos has encountered more of them and also that we overestimated their numbers to begin with." He gave Aoth a condescending smile. "If so, you're not to blame. It can be difficult for anyone not an expert to tell the various species of undead apart, and the terror and chaos of a massacre would impair almost anybody's ability to make an accurate count."

"My orcs fished some water ghouls out of the river," a captain said. "They count as 'exotic,' don't they?"

"I'd say so," Urhur replied. "At any rate, the essential point is this: Yes, we're facing a few rare and formidable creatures, but as Tharchion Focar said, we're prepared to deal with them. In the final analysis, no undead can withstand the magic specially devised to command or destroy its kind, or to give credit where it's due, Kossuth's fire, either."

"All I'm suggesting," said Aoth, "is that we proceed cautiously."

"We will," Nymia said briskly, "but proceed we must, and never stop until we've purged Pyarados of this plague, which brings us back around to the question of just how soon we can head into the pass."

Realizing it would be fruitless to argue any further, Aoth at last managed to hold his tongue.

After the council of war broke up, he tried to join the merry-making in the streets, only to make the depressing discovery that it failed to divert him as in days of yore. Wondering why anyone ever aspired to become an officer, nipping from a bottle of sour white wine, he prowled aimlessly and watched other folk wallowing in their pleasures.

Finally, his meandering steps led him back to the home in which and Brightwing were billeted. The griffon perched atop the gabled roof. When she caught sight of him, she spread her wings and half-leaped, half-glided down to the street. A stray mongrel that evidently hadn't discerned her presence hitherto yipped and ran.

"How did it go?" Brightwing asked.

Aoth grinned a mirthless grin. "About as well as I expected. Nymia's desperate to prove her competence and avert the zulkirs' displeasure. Everybody else is proud of himself for besting a terrible foe. Accordingly, no one was in the mood to hear that we've only won a few petty skirmishes, with all the battles that matter still to come."

Brightwing gave her head a scornful toss. "I don't understand how humans can ignore the truth just because it's unwelcome."

Aoth sighed. "Maybe the others are right and I'm wrong. What do I know anyway?"

"Usually, not much, but this time, you're the one with his eyes open. What will you do now?"

Aoth blinked in surprise at the question. "Follow orders and hope for the best. What else can a soldier do?"

"If he serves in the Griffon Legion, he can fly south and speak his mind to this Milsantos Daramos."

Aoth realized it could conceivably work. Pyarados was Nymia's domain to govern, but as tharchion of Thazalhar, Milsantos was her equal in rank, and since she herself had asked him to participate in the current campaign, they shared authority in the muddled fashion that, the war mage abruptly realized, had hampered Thayan military endeavors for as long as he could remember.

In this case, however, it might prove beneficial. If he could convince Tharchion Daramos of the validity of his concerns, the old warrior could then pressure his fellow governor to adjust her strategy, and it seemed possible if not probable that Nymia actually would heed him. Aoth had never met the man, but of all the tharchions, he had the reputation for being the canniest commander, and the most sensible in general.

Yet . . .

"I can't," he said. "Nymia Focar is my tharchion. It would be an act of disloyalty for me to run to another commander with my concerns. To the Abyss with it. This is a strong army and we'll win. We may pay a heavier price for our victory than Nymia anticipates, but we'll have it in the end."

Brightwing grunted, an ambiguous sound that might signify

acquiescence, disapproval, or both at once.

Aoth resolved to put his misgivings out of his mind. "I wish I knew where Chathi's gone," he said.

"Why, nowhere," she replied.

He turned. The priestess stood in the house's doorway with a pewter goblet in either hand. She wore only a robe, open all the way down the front, though the night obscured all but a tantalizing suggestion of what the gap would otherwise reveal.

Aoth felt a grin stretch across his face. "I thought you'd be off somewhere celebrating with everybody else."

"I hoped that if I waited for you, we could have a sweeter time together. Was I wrong?"

"No," said Aoth, "you were right as blue skies and green grass." He strode to her, and enfolded in her arms, he did indeed succeed in forgetting all about the undead. At least for a while.

•• •• •• •• •• •• •• •• •• •• •• •• •• ••

Though he'd known her for twenty years, Aznar Thrul had never beheld the face of Shabella, high priestess of Mask, god of larceny and shadow, and mistress of the thieves' guild of Bezantur. Every time he'd seen her, she'd worn a black silk mask and hooded gray woolen cloak over the rainbow-colored tunic beneath.

That, of course, was simply the way of the Maskarran, and it had never bothered him before. Now it did. What, he wondered, if this isn't the same woman with whom I've conspired for all these years? What if someone else, some agent of my enemies, killed her and took her place? Even if I unmasked her, I wouldn't know.

Trying to push such groundless fancies out of his mind, he scowled at her across the length of the small room he used for private audiences, and as a servant closed the door behind her, she bowed deeply, spreading the wings of her cape.

He left her in that position for several heartbeats, rather hoping it pained her middle-aged back muscles but knowing it probably didn't. Though she likely hadn't committed a robbery with her own hands in a long while, her position required her to train to maintain the skills and athleticism of an all-around master thief, and he had little doubt that she could still scale sheer walls and lift latches with the ablest burglars and stalk and club a victim like the most accomplished muggers.

"Get up," Aznar said at last. "Tell me what's happening in the streets." He already knew, but the question was a way of starting the conversation.

"The common folk," she said, "are celebrating the good news from Pyarados." As always, her soft soprano voice sounded gentle and wistful, belying the iron resolve and ferocity she displayed when circumstances warranted.

" 'The good news,' " he parroted. "Meaning what, precisely?"

"That the legions are pushing back the undead."

"In the opinion of the mob, who deserves the credit for their success?"

Most people hesitated before telling Aznar Thrul something he didn't want to hear. Shabella never did, and that was one of the things that made him if not like at least respect her.

"Szass Tam," she said, "who committed the order of Necromancy to the struggle, convinced Iphegor Nath to send the Burning Braziers, and armed the priests with their torch weapons."

"And who just recently saved the northern tharchs from a Rashemi invasion."

"Yes."

"Curse it!" Aznar exploded. "I don't care what the whoreson's done. How can they make a hero of a lich?"

"We Thayans aren't a squeamish people," Shabella replied. "You Red Wizards made sure of that when you recruited orcs, zombies, and even demons to serve you. The commoners had little choice but to get used to them."

"Spare me your gloss on the history of the realm. Tell me who spreads these tidings through the alehouses and markets in a way that lionizes Szass Tam at the expense of everyone else who contributed to the victory."

"Agents employed by Dmitra Flass and Malark Springhill, most likely."

"If you know that, why haven't your cutthroats silenced them?"

"Because I don't really know, I simply infer. The taletellers are wily and my followers haven't yet identified them.

"Too busy skirmishing with the Shadowmasters?" he asked, referring to the one cartel of thieves that sought to supplant her and her organization.

"I have to address the problem," Shabella said. "I'm no use to you dead."

"Are you of any use currently? Perhaps your rivals wouldn't be so foolish as to give their business priority over mine."

"The local Shadowmasters are only one chapter of a greater network based in Thesk. Would it truly suit Your Omnipotence to have foreigners controlling all thievery south of the First Escarpment?"

"It might at least suit me to see someone else officiating in front of Mask's high altar, so get out of here and do what needs doing."

She bowed and withdrew.

The unsatisfactory interview left Aznar feeling as restless and edgy as before, but perhaps he knew a way to lift his spirits. It had been a month since he'd visited Mari Agneh.

Though he didn't play with her as frequently—or, often, as elaborately—as in the first years of her captivity, she still amused him on occasion, which made her a rarity. Generally, the torment of a particular victim eventually came to seem repetitive and stale, at which point he consigned that prisoner to his or her final agonies and moved on to the next.

He supposed it was Mari's austere good looks and defiant spirit that he still found piquant, combined with the fact that she was nearly the first person of significance he'd punished after assuming the mantle of a zulkir. In her way, she was a memento of his ascension.

Smiling now, he rose, took up his staff of luminous congealed flame, and exited the private chamber into a larger hall where bodyguards, clerks, and other functionaries awaited his pleasure. He waved them off and tramped on alone, through one magnificently appointed space after another. His passage was a like a ripple in a pond, agitating everyone. Sentries came to attention and saluted, while everybody else groveled in the manner appropriate to his station.

Such displays became less frequent once he made his way to corridors that, while no less handsomely decorated, were smaller and less well travelled. From there, a concealed door admitted him to his private prison.

Mari gave him a level stare as he entered her cell. "I'm going to kill you tonight," she said.

It surprised him a little. She hadn't made that particular threat in quite a while, not since they'd proved her helplessness time and again.

"By all means, try," he answered. "It always made our times together that much more entertaining, but first, take off your clothes, and keep your eyes on me as you do it. I want you to see me seeing you."

She obeyed, as of course she had to. His magic left her no choice.

"Now crawl to me on your belly and clean my shoes with your tongue."

She did that, too.

"Now hug the whipping post." He wouldn't need to tie or shackle her to keep her there. His spoken will sufficed even for that.

He laid down his staff, took down the whip from its hook on the wall, and cut her back into a tidy crosshatch of bloody welts. Though it was the least of his accomplishments, he'd always taken a certain satisfaction in his skill with a lash. He fancied that if he hadn't been born with a talent for magic, he could have been one of Thay's more successful slavers. Perhaps it would have been a less stressful and demanding existence than the life of a zulkir.

Mari invariably struggled against the need to cry out. Perhaps what remained of her warrior's pride demanded it, whereas he found pleasure in overcoming that resistance, striking for as long as it took to get her squealing like an animal.

Perhaps the day's worries and frustrations had wearied him more than he knew, for tonight, it seemed to take an unusually long time. He grew hot and sweaty, peeled off his crimson robe, and then the garments underneath, all the way down to his smallclothes.

Eventually Mari gave him a reaction, though not precisely the one he was expecting. Her shoulders began to shake, and she made a breathy, rhythmic sound. For a moment, he assumed she was sobbing then he realized that in reality, the noise was laughter.

He shook his head. He'd just been imagining she was the one plaything that would never break, and here was the first sign her sanity was crumbling at last. Life could be so drearily perverse.

"Turn around," he said, and she did. "Tell me what's so funny."

"The flogging doesn't hurt," she said, "not really, and you don't have any pockets anymore." She charged him.

Though she hadn't lifted her hand to him in quite some time, he was always watchful for it, always prepared, even in the deepest throes of lust, and it was no different now. "Stop!" he snapped.

She didn't stop. She raked her nails across his eye and punched him in the throat.

Half blind, half choking, he reeled back, then reflex took over. She was right, he'd divested himself of his protective talismans and the physical components required to cast many of his most powerful spells. He was the greatest master of Evocation in all Thay, though, and capable of creating many other effects by word and gesture alone. He croaked a word of power, jabbed out his hand, and bright globes of light burst in rapid succession from his fingertips. Swelling larger, they hurtled at Mari, each engulfing her in its turn, and with a deafening crackle, discharging the lightning that constituted its essence into her body.

Startled, hurt, Aznar had lashed out with one of the most potent attacks available to him, and he immediately realized the response was excessive. Such an abundance of magic he might have used to kill a giant or wyvern. In all likelihood, there wouldn't even be anything left of her body and not much left of the furniture either.

When he caught his breath, wiped the tears from his stinging eye, and blinked the blurriness out of the world, he saw that he was half right. The spell had blasted the whipping post and bed frame into smoking scraps of kindling. The blankets, pillows, and mattress were on fire, but Mari stood where she'd stood before, seemingly unscathed.

Unscathed but not unchanged. She had four arms, not two, and her smooth ivory skin had darkened and roughened into purple scales. Her eyes glowed red, and the bottom half of her face had lengthened into a muzzle complete with fangs.

It occurred to him that, except for her merely human stature and the fact that she was still manifestly female, she now resembled one of the demon guards stationed elsewhere in the palace. What did that mean? The order of Conjuration had supplied those demons. Was it possible Nevron had turned against him?

Mari gathered herself to spring, and Aznar realized he'd better put such speculations aside. He'd unravel the mystery of his captive's transformation in due course, but for now, what mattered was defending himself against her. It was obvious that in her altered condition, she no longer felt constrained to obey his commands.

Lightning hadn't harmed her, but maybe fire would. She lunged at him, and with a simple exertion of his will, he released the power bound in a tattooed glyph on his left forearm. It pained him like a bee sting, and Mari's entire body exploded into flame.

Plainly hurt, she staggered, and looking forward to watching her flounder, shriek, and burn, he stepped out of her blundering way.

She caught her balance and pivoted to threaten him anew. Two of her hands swiped at him with their talons. One grazed his shoulder and drew blood.

The blaze enshrouding her hand didn't sear him. He'd long since forged unshakable alliances with fire, acid, lightning, and cold, and Mari's claws scarcely broke his skin. Even so, he suffered a shock of weakness and dizziness. He swayed, and she nearly succeeded in catching him by the throat when she snatched for him again.

Retreating, he chanted while miming the making of a snowball and then the act of throwing it. Hurtling chunks of ice sprang into existence to batter Mari and knock her back a step, but they didn't put her down any more than the lightning and fire had. In fact, her corona of punishing flame was guttering out faster than it was supposed to, revealing only superficial burns that were already starting to heal.

Damn it, he needed the items cached in his robe. They were the keys to unlocking his most devastating spells, and apparently nothing less would serve to neutralize his foe. Unfortunately, Mari stood between the garment and himself. He had to get past her somehow and likewise obtain the additional moment he'd need to retrieve the garment and pull out one of the appropriate talismans.

With a wave of his hand, he filled the air with what was, to him, merely a tinge of gray. To any other eyes, though, it would seem impenetrable darkness. Mari snarled and rushed him, plainly seeking to catch him before he could shift away from the spot where she'd seen him last.

He whispered a word of power and whisked himself through space. Now that he was outside the clot of shadow, it was opaque to him as well, though he could hear Mari flailing around inside.

He picked up his robe. It was on fire from collar to hem, but not yet so badly burned that it would disintegrate if he tried to put it on, and he lifted it to do so. His hands would find his spell triggers far more easily if his pockets were hanging in their accustomed places about his body.

Mari sprang from the cloud of darkness. Obviously, she'd figured out Aznar was no longer inside. If only she could have stayed fooled for one more heartbeat! Then everything would have been all right.

She snatched, caught the robe in her claws, and for an instant, the two of them pulled on it like children playing tug of war. Alas, she was the stronger, and when the burning, weakened cloth ripped in two, the piece in her talons was by far the larger. Laughing, she shredded it, and crystals, medallions, and vials tumbled to the floor. Then she reached for Aznar, who, backing up until his shoulders banged against a wall, perceived that his paltry piece of the robe possessed at least a few pockets, though which ones, he couldn't tell. He stuck his hand in one at random and brought out a folded paper packet of powdered ruby.

It made him want to laugh, but there was scarcely time for that. He jabbered a rhyme and lashed the particles of red glittering dust through the air to explode into tiny sparks.

A cube with transparent crimson walls sprang into existence around the onrushing Mari. She slammed into the side of it and rebounded.

She'd charged so close to Aznar that when it popped into existence, the magical cage nearly trapped him as well by pinning him between itself and the wall behind him, but he sucked in his breath and managed to sidle free. Meanwhile, Mari attacked the enclosure with the frenzy of a rabid animal, repeatedly breaking and regrowing her talons.

"Strike at it all you like," Aznar Thrul panted. "It will hold. It will hold for days." Plenty of time for him to decide how best to chastise her and solve the puzzle of her metamorphosis.

For now, he required the aid of a healer to take away the sick feeling her claws had slashed into his flesh and strong drink to quiet his jangled nerves. He snapped his fingers to extinguish all the various fires then turned and exited the cell.

He was several paces down the corridor when four strong hands gripped him by the shoulders and forearms. He just had time to realize that, like many a true tanar'ri, Mari must also possess the ability to translate herself through space, then she yanked him close and plunged her fangs into his neck.

•• •• •• •• •• •• •• •• •• •• •• •• •• ••

Tsagoth had tried to finagle a guard station close to Mari Agneh's hidden cell, so he'd have some hope of knowing when Aznar Thrul went to torture her. Unfortunately, though, he'd been unsuccessful, and when screams started echoing from that general direction, he had no idea whether they meant the former tharchion had struck at her captor at last or portended something else entirely.

He dissolved his body and reshaped it into the guise of a gigantic bat. Flight was often a faster, more reliable means of travel than blinking through space when he didn't know precisely where he was going. Wings beating, he raced through imposing chambers and hallways, over the heads of humans, orcs, and other folk who were, in many cases, either running toward or away from the source of the noise.

He rounded another corner, and free of her prison at last, Mari Agneh came into view. Tsagoth felt a strange, unexpected stirring of pride at the marvel he'd created. Painted with fragrant human gore—Aznar Thrul's, no doubt—from mouth to navel, she was a pitiful runt compared to any true blood fiend, but in every other respect, he'd succeeded in transforming a feeble, insignificant mortal into an entity like himself.

She was confronting four warriors, a trio of spearmen, and one swordsman clad in the more ornate trappings and superior armor of an officer. Dissolving his bat guise, Tsagoth started the shift to his more customary form. Generally speaking, it was more useful for combat.

Before he could enter the fray, Mari sprang and raked the guts out of a spearman. In so doing, she perforce turned her back on some of his allies, and another warrior drove his lance deep into her back. She scarcely seemed to notice. She whirled with such force that she jerked the weapon from his hands, grabbed hold of his head, and slammed him to the floor. Part of his face came away in her talons, and he didn't move thereafter.

The remaining spearman dropped his weapon and bolted. The officer, however, raised his sword to cut at Mari's head, and Tsagoth sensed potent enchantment seething in the gleaming gray blade. Perhaps Mari did too, for though she'd essentially ignored the spears, she now retreated and lifted a hand to ward herself.

The officer instantly spun his sword lower, extended the point, and exploded into a running attack. The move was all offense and no defense, arguably reckless in any situation and certainly so against an opponent as formidable as Mari, but it caught her by surprise, and the enchanted sword punched all the way through her torso.

Shouting, the warrior jerked his weapon free and raised it to cut. As it streaked down, she caught it in her two upper hands. The keen edge cut deep enough to sever one of her thumbs, but at least she kept it from cleaving her skull and brain.

She shifted closer to the swordsman and used her two remaining hands to gather him in. Then she plunged her fangs into his throat and sucked at the gushing wound.

All this, before Tsagoth could even complete his transformation and come to her aid. It made him feel even more gratified. He started toward her, and the mark on his brow gave him another twinge. He clawed it from existence, and his hide tickled as it immediately started to heal.

"I assume Aznar Thrul is dead," he said.

To his surprise, she failed to reply or acknowledge him in any fashion. She just kept guzzling blood. The prey in her grasp trembled, and his extremities twitched.

"Other people are coming," he said. "We can escape, but we should go now." She still didn't answer, so he laid his hand on her shoulder.

Snarling, she turned and knocked his arm away, and when he gazed into her glaring crimson eyes, he saw nothing of reason or comprehension there. It was as if she were a famished dog and he a stranger trying to drag her away from a side of beef.

As he'd warned her, humans were frail vessels to receive the power of a blood fiend, and her metamorphosis had driven her crazy. The only question was whether the insanity was permanent or temporary. If the latter, it might be worthwhile to try and see her safely through it.

Or not. When he heard shrill, excited voices and looked around, he saw a veritable phalanx of foes approaching, with men-at-arms around the edges of the formation and scarlet-robed wizards in the center.

It was possible that two blood fiends could defeat such a band, but Tsagoth saw little reason to make the experiment. His bemused interest in the odd hybrid entity he'd created and his casual notion that perhaps he ought to school her as his sire had mentored him lost their cogency when his own well-being was at issue. Now he only cared about extricating himself from this situation as expeditiously as possible.

The spear still embedded in her back, Mari helped him by whisking herself through space and ripping into the warriors in the front of the formation. The imminent threat riveted every foe's attention on her, and Tsagoth had no difficulty translating himself in a different direction without any of the warlocks casting a charm to hinder him.

He didn't shift as far as prudence alone might have dictated. At the last possible instant, he decided that, even if he was unwilling to stand with the savage, demented creature he'd created, he was curious to see how she would fare, so he contented himself with a doorway some distance away.

She fought well, slaughtering most of the warriors and two of the Red Wizards before one of the other mages showered her with a downpour of conjured acid. Her scales smoking and blistering, she fell, and eyes seared away, face dissolving, struggled futilely to rise. The warlock chanted and created a floating sword made of emerald light. The blade chopped and slashed repeatedly until she stopped moving.

Her destruction gave Tsagoth a slight twinge of melancholy, but only enough to season rather than diminish his satisfaction at the completion of what had proved an onerous chore. Glad that the system of wards protecting the fortress was better suited to keeping intruders out than holding would-be escapees in, he slipped through the net and into the night beyond.

chapter eleven

7 Kythorn, the Year of Risen Elfkin

Bareris crept down the trail, a narrow, crumbling path that ran along a sheer drop, and then the moonlight dimmed. Heart hammering, he crouched low and cast about until he discerned that it was only a cloud veiling Selûne's face.

Flying with wings or without, as bats or insubstantial wraiths, the hunters prowled by night, and as often as not, Bareris found that required him to flee through the dark as well. At first he'd hoped he could simply find good hiding places and lie up until dawn, but close calls two nights in succession convinced him no refuge was safe enough. Perhaps, wearing the forms of wolves or rats, his foes could track him by scent. In any case, it seemed the better option was to keep moving and try to stay ahead of them.

Even with magic sharpening his vision, it was exhausting, dangerous work to negotiate mountain terrain in the dark. It made foraging more difficult as well. His throat seemed perpetually dry, and his belly, hollow.

Often, he wondered why he was even bothering with this forlorn, foredoomed attempt to escape. He'd promised to save Tammith, but truly, what were the chances? In all the lore he'd collected, from the soberest historical annals to the most fanciful tales, there was nothing even to hint that a vampire could recover her humanity.

And what was the point of going on without her? How could he endure the knowledge that she blamed him for what had befallen her or the suspicion that she was right to do so? He'd failed her at least twice, hadn't he, once when he'd left her behind in Bezantur, and again when he'd bungled his attempt to rescue her.

If the future held nothing but misery, wouldn't it be better to put an end to the ordeal of running? A shout or two would draw the undead to him, then he could fight them as they arrived. With luck, he might have the satisfaction of destroying a couple before they slew him in his turn.

He felt the urge repeatedly, but as of yet he hadn't acted on it. Maybe, in defiance of all reason, a part of him hadn't abandoned hope that Tammith could still be saved, or perhaps the raw animal instinct to survive was stronger even than despair.

He skulked onward and came to a saddleback connecting one peak with the next, a wide, flat ridge that promised easier, faster trekking for a while. Hoping to find water as well, he quickened his stride, and then he felt a coldness, or perhaps simply an inde-finable but sickening wrongness, above his head.

He threw himself onto his stomach, and hands outstretched to grab, rend, or both, the misty form of his attacker streaked over him. He rolled to his feet and drew his sword. The phantom lit on the rocky ground, or nearly so. Its form flickered and jumped so as to suspend its feet slightly above the earth one instant and sink them partly into it the next. Blighted by the entity's mere proximity, the little gnarled trees and bushes in the immediate area dropped their leaves and withered.

Bareris took his first good look at the spirit then gasped. He never would have expected to encounter a creature uglier than Xingax, yet here it was. Indeed, despite their vague, flowing inconstancy, its features somehow embodied the *idea*, the very essence, of hideousness in a way that even their twisted, hook-nosed, pop-eyed asymmetry couldn't wholly explain. The mere sight of them ripped at something inside of him.

For an instant, he was afraid his heart would stop, his mind would shatter, and he'd collapse retching helplessly, or faint. But then he bellowed a war cry, and though the spirit remained as ghastly looking as before, its ugliness no longer had claws sunk in his spirit—a fact that wasn't likely to matter in the long run. Now that he could think more clearly, he recognized the undead as a banshee, an entity so powerful he had little hope of defeating it.

The banshee began to moan, and like the sight of its face, the noise pierced him to chill and stab something essential at his core. Steeling himself against the pain, he drew breath and sang, and the magic in his voice countered the lethal malignancy in the phantom's.

Still wailing, the banshee stretched out its long fingers and flew at him. He started chanting his charm of haste, waited until his foe was nearly upon him, then sidestepped. The undead hurtled past, and he cut at it. Though it passed through the banshee's wavering form, his sword encountered no tangible resistance, and he had no way of telling if he'd actually hurt the spirit. Since he was wielding an enchanted blade, it was possible but by no means a certainty.

His muscles jumped as the spell of quickness infused him. The banshee wheeled and rushed him anew, and his accelerated condition made it seem to fly more slowly. He bellowed, a blast of noise that might well have broken a tangible adversary's bones. Maybe it wounded the spirit as well, but as before, he could see no indication of it. The attack certainly didn't slow the banshee down, not even for a heartbeat.

Grimly aware his brigandine was no protection against the entity's ghostly touch, he dodged and cut, sang and shrouded himself in a field of blur that might make it more difficult for the banshee to target him. He kept himself alive for a few more heartbeats.

Then the banshee sprang backward. For a moment, he imagined that he'd wounded it badly enough that it feared to continue fighting him. Then he felt the chilling scrutiny of a new presence, whose advent the banshee had evidently perceived a moment before he had.

It could easily be a fatal error to take his eyes off his original foe, but he needed to understand what was happening, so he risked a glance around. At first, he saw nothing, but then phosphorescence oozed through the air like a brush stroke flowing downward.

The streak of glow gradually assumed a manlike shape. Bareris gasped, because though it was like looking into a poorly made mirror in a dark room, he could tell the murky form was supposed to mimic his own.

Only for a moment, though. Then the thing rejected or was unable to sustain the resemblance. It softened until it was simply a luminous shadow with the hint of some form of armor in its shape and a length of sheen extending from its hand.

Bareris didn't know what the newcomer was, nor could he see a point to its brief impersonation of him, but he could only assume it was another of Xingax's hunters. Against all probability, he'd seemed to be holding his own against the banshee, and now his achievement didn't matter a jot. Fighting in concert, the two spirits were certainly capable of slaying him, and he felt a crazy impulse to laugh at his dismal luck and the ongoing ruination of all his hopes.

Instead, he faced the newcomer, the nearer of his foes, and came on guard. He'd at least make the vile creatures work for their kill.

The phantom came on guard in its turn, hesitated, then turned to face the banshee, to all appearances taking Bareris for its ally and making plain its opposition to its fellow undead.

The banshee screamed, and Bareris sang to leech the poison from the sound. Then, even though it was apparently leery of the phantom, it raced forward to attack with its hands once more. Perhaps the will of its necromancer masters compelled it.

In the moments that followed, Bareris discerned that his new comrade, whatever else it might be, was a master swordsman, landing cunning strokes, retreating to avoid the banshee's snatching, clawing attacks, and scoring anew with stop cuts when the moaning ghost lunged after it. The newcomer likewise understood how best to exploit a numerical advantage and consistently maneuvered to insure that it and Bareris remained on opposite sides of their opponent.

The banshee pounced at the spectral swordsman. Bareris leaped after it and spun his blade through its head. The banshee frayed into tatters of glow, which then winked out of existence.

That left Bareris gasping for breath and peering at the remaining phantom through the empty space their foe had occupied a moment before. The entity shifted its sword to threaten him.

Wonderful, thought the bard. It didn't oppose the banshee because it wanted to help me. It just wanted to make sure it got to kill me itself. Probably I'm to be its supper in one fashion or another.

Yet the spirit didn't follow through and attack. It hesitated as though uncertain of what to do.

Doubtful that he could defeat the phantom in any case, Bareris decided to lower his sword. "Thank you for helping me," he said. "Unfortunately, I'm still in danger. Other enemies are seeking me, and the banshee and I made more than enough noise to draw them here. If you see fit to stand with me a second time, I'll be forever in your debt, or if you have a way we can hide or escape, that would be better still."

The spirit stared at him, then turned and started walking away. Bareris followed.

As the phantom strode, the sword melted from its hand, and its outline softened until it was just a luminous haze. Then that too faded away, though Bareris could still somehow sense it as an aching emptiness drifting on before him.

It led him into thick brush, and he had to shove and scramble to keep up. Then he took another step and found only empty air beneath his foot. He plummeted into darkness.

•• •• •• •• •• •• •• •• • •• •• •• •• ••

Samas Kul hadn't been sure he wanted to leave the banquet even temporarily. He'd eaten and drunk a considerable amount, enough to make even a fat man sluggish, enough to incline him to stay on his couch and sample all the courses and vintages still to come, no matter how enticing the reason to arise.

But he found the enclosed garden at the center of the mansion refreshing. The fountain gushed, the water glimmered in the moonlight, and the scent of jasmine filled the air. Best of all, the breeze cooled his hot, sweaty face. It made him hopeful that he'd be able to perform without recourse to magic, and that was always a relief.

"Girls!" he called. "Where are you?"

The women in question were gorgeous twin courtesans provided by his hostess. People exerted themselves mightily to entertain a man who was both zulkir of Transmutation and Master of the Guild of Foreign Trade, but perhaps not mightily enough, because the twins didn't answer.

He wondered if they'd thought a game of hide and seek amongst the flowerbeds and arbors would arouse him. If so, they'd mistaken their man. He'd abandoned such callow amusements many years and many pounds ago. These days, he preferred passion without an excess of exertion.

"Girls!" he repeated, this time putting the snap of command into his voice. "Show yourselves."

Still, no one replied, and abruptly he remembered that Druxus Rhym and Aznar Thrul were dead. Someone or something had caught them alone and murdered them. By all accounts, Thrul had even been preparing for coition, or a perverse alternative to it, when destruction overtook him.

But neither Rhym nor Thrul had anticipated trouble, nor had either had his talismans and spell triggers ready to hand. Samas invoked the power pent in a ring, and a protective aura, invisible as air but strong as steel, radiated from his body. He gave his left arm a shake and a wand of congealed quicksilver dropped from his voluminous sleeve into his pudgy fingers. He whispered a word of power and the darkness seemed to brighten. Now he could see as clearly as an owl.

That made it possible to spot the figure slipping through a doorway on the far side of the garden. Samas pointed the wand at the newcomer. A single flare of power should suffice to turn the wretch into a snail, after which it would be simplicity itself to capture him, change him back, and put him to the question.

But the man didn't move to attack, nor believing himself unobserved, did he continue skulking either. Instead, he dropped to his knees.

"Your Omnipotence," he said. "Thank you for coming. I realize I'm not as appealing a sight as the whores who delivered my invitation, but you can dally with them later if you're still so inclined. They understand they're to await your pleasure."

"How is it they answer to you? Duma Zan is paying them."

"You assumed that, and Lady Zan believes you invited the twins to attend the feast as your guests. In reality, I hired them to serve as my go-betweens."

"Who in the name of the Abyss are you?"

"Malark Springhill. We've never met, but perhaps you've heard of me."

"Dmitra Flass's man."

"Yes. May I rise?"

Samas hesitated. "I suppose so. What's this all about?"

"As you've surely heard by now, Szass Tam is convening the council of zulkirs. Tharchion Flass requests the honor of a private conversation with you, Yaphyll, and Lallara prior to the conclave."

Samas blinked. "You mean, with the three of us alone? And Szass Tam none the wiser?"

"Yes."

"Everyone knows Dmitra is the lich's creature. Is he trying to test our loyalty?"

"If you believe so, Your Omnipotence, then may I suggest that you attend the meeting, then hurry to Szass Tam and tell him what was said."

Samas realized he'd been standing too long. His back was beginning to ache, and he felt a little short of breath. He cast about, spotted a marble bench, and lowered himself onto it. "What does Dmitra want to talk about?"

"I have no idea."

Oh, you know, Samas thought, it's just that the "First Princess of Thay" wants to tell us herself. "At least explain why you found it necessary to contact me in this melodramatic fashion."

Malark grinned. "If I may say so, Master, you don't know the half of it. To make it possible for me to reach all three of you zulkirs in time, my mistress conjured me a flying horse, and as I understand it, when an illusionist manufactures such a creature, it isn't altogether real. Recognizing its ephemeral nature yet still riding it high above the ground makes a man feel rather bold.

"But to answer the question," the outlander continued, "you are watched. I should know. Some of the watchers report to me, but there may be others who report directly to Szass Tam, and if so, I'd rather they not tell him you and I have spoken.

"Now then: What answer should I deliver to Tharchion Flass?"

Frowning, Samas pondered the question. Like any sane person, he had no desire to run afoul of Szass Tam, yet as Malark himself had pointed out, he could always claim afterward that he attended the secret meeting as the lich's loyal ally, to make sure no one was plotting against him. Meanwhile, his truest fealty was to himself, and he hadn't prospered to the extent he had by ignoring any opportunity to find out what the other grandees of the realm were scheming or to accrue every conceivable advantage.

"Where and when does she want to see us?"

•• •• •• •• •• •• •• •• •• •• •• •• •• ••

Bareris saw that he'd stepped into an overgrown but open stone well. It was like the shaft he'd climbed out of days before, only narrower. Falling, he dropped his sword and grabbed at the curved wall beside him but failed to find a handhold.

Below him, metal rang, and an instant later he slammed down on a hard, uneven surface. Once the shock of the impact passed, and it was clear the short drop had merely bruised him, he discerned that he and his weapon had landed on a portion of a staircase spiraling into the depths. The disquieting vacancy that was his phantom guide hovered farther down.

He wondered if the spirit had just attempted to lure him into a fatal fall. If so, it would be crazy to continue following it.

But if it wanted him dead, it could have just attacked him with its sword, or let the banshee kill him. It seemed more likely that it had simply expected him to spot the shaft before blundering over the edge.

In any case, Bareris might have nowhere to go but down. By now, more of Xingax's hunters could easily have reached the ridge.

He rose, picked up his sword, and grumbled, "Warn me next time." The entity drifted onward, and he stalked after it.

Before long they came to the first of the vaults opening onto the well. The chamber was a sort of crypt, with supine, somewhat withered-looking figures of pale stone, their arms crossed, laid out in rows on the floor. They could have been sculptures, but Bareris' intuition told him they were corpses, coated with rock or ceramic or somehow petrified entirely. That suggested the ancients hadn't excavated this place to serve as a village or fortress either. It was a warren of tombs.

The dead bodies brought the phantom wavering in and out of visibility as it took on the semblance of first one and then another, but it didn't cling to any of them for long.

The crypts grew larger as Bareris and his guide descended. Stone sarcophagi, in some cases carved with the images of the dead, hid their occupants from view. Faded, flaking murals on the walls proclaimed their achievements and their adoration of their gods. The phantom borrowed faces from some of the carved and painted images as well, only to relinquish them just as quickly.

The bottom of the well was in view when the phantom led Bareris off the steps and into one of the vaults. A moment later, a gray, plump, segmented creature half as long as the bard was tall crawled from behind a bier. It raised its hairless, eyeless, but nonetheless manlike head and swiveled it in his direction.

Bareris's body clenched into rigidity, and pain burned

through his limbs. He struggled to fill his lungs then chanted a charm of vitality.

The agony and near-paralysis faded. Intending to dispatch the sluglike creature before it could afflict him a second time, he lifted his sword and took an initial stride, but the spirit stepped to block the way, and a shadow blade extended from its murky hand.

Meanwhile, the crawling thing turned, retreated deeper into the crypt, and called out in a language Bareris had never heard before.

He hesitated. Despite the unpleasantness he'd suffered a moment before, it now seemed as if the worm-creature wanted to talk, not fight, and he certainly didn't want to battle it and the wraith at the same time if it wasn't necessary.

He sang to grant himself the gift of tongues then called, *"I couldn't understand you before, but I will now."*

"I said to keep your distance," the eyeless being replied. *"I don't want to turn you to stone—not unless you mean me harm—but I can't stop the force emanating from my body any more than you can stop the flow of blood through your veins."*

"I didn't come to hurt you," Bareris said. *"I asked your . . . companion here to take me somewhere safe because other undead creatures are hunting me. I should warn you, they might track me into the well. They've sniffed out some of my other hiding places."*

"I doubt they'll find this one," the creature said. *"Those who built it had a fear of necromancers tampering with their remains, so they took precautions to prevent such indignities. They laid their dead to rest in a secret place far from their habitations and also arranged for me to dwell here, to petrify the corpses and make them impossible to reanimate. Most importantly from your perspective, they laid down wards to keep a wizard's undead servants from locating the tombs."*

Bareris felt the tension flow out of him, leaving a profound weariness in its place. *"That's good to hear."*

"Sit. Mirror and I can offer no other comforts fit for a mortal man, but you can at least rest."

The bard flopped down with his back against a wall. *"Mirror is an apt name for your friend, I suppose. Mine is Bareris Anskuld."*

"I'm Quickstrike. A gravecrawler, as you can see."

Bareris shook his head. *"I have to take your word for it. I've never met or even heard of a creature like you before."*

"Truly? I wonder if the rest of my kind have vanished from the world." Quickstrike sounded more intrigued than dismayed by the possibility. *"Men also called us ancestor worms."*

"Interesting," Bareris said, and it was, a little. Despite the despair that had consumed him of late, he couldn't help feeling somewhat curious about his new companions. Curiosity was a fundamental aspect of the character of any bard. *"Are gravecrawlers undead?"*

"Of a sort, but not the sort that was ever human or preys on humans, not as long as they behave themselves."

"I assure you, I intend to. And Mirror is a ghost?"

"Of a particularly brave and accomplished warrior, I believe. As you will have guessed, Mirror is simply the nickname I gave him, based on his habit of filching an appearance. He doesn't remember his true name or face any longer, or much of anything really."

"Why not?"

Quickstrike's body rippled from head to tail in a manner that suggested a man stretching. *"He fell victim to the power that destroyed his entire people. It's a sad story, but one I can relate if you want to hear."*

Bareris had the feeling that, after centuries with only the mute, nearly mindless Mirror for company, Quickstrike enjoyed having someone to talk to, while for his part, he had nothing better to do than listen.

"Please do. I've spent much of my life collecting tales and songs."

"Well, then. In its time, not so very long after the fall of Netheril, a splendid kingdom ruled these mountains. It owed much of its greatness to a single man, Fastrin the Delver, a wizard as clever and powerful as any who ever lived.

"For much of his life, Fastrin worked wonders to benefit his people and gave sage counsel to their lords. Eventually, however, he withdrew from the world, and those few who saw him thereafter said he was troubled but couldn't or wouldn't explain why, which kept anyone from realizing just how dire the situation was. Fastrin wasn't just morose, he was going mad.

"One sunny summer morning," Quickstrike continued, "he emerged from his seclusion and started methodically slaughtering people, laying waste to one community after another, but he wasn't content with simply ending the lives of his victims. His magic mangled their minds and souls. In many cases, it may have obliterated their spirits entirely. Even when it didn't, it stripped them of memory and reason."

"Like Mirror," Bareris said.

"Yes. He was one of many who tried to stand against Fastrin. Sadly, their valor accomplished nothing. I suppose a few people must have escaped by taking flight, but at the end of the wizard's rampage, the kingdom he'd done so much to build no longer existed. He then turned that same lethal, psyche-rending power on himself."

"What was it all about? Even lunatics have reasons, though they may not make sense to the rest of us. Did anyone try to parley with him?"

"Yes," said the ancestor worm. "Fastrin said he'd been robbed, and since he was unable to identify the thief, everyone must die. It was the only way to be safe."

Bareris shook his head. "I don't understand."

"No one did, and Fastrin refused to elaborate."

"May I ask how you learned all this?"

"When I was buried in this place? Well, even Fastrin couldn't kill an entire realm in a day, or a tenday, and as the massacre continued, folk sought my counsel. Ancestor worms were accounted wise, you see. When I ate the flesh of the dead, before I grew beyond the need of such provender, I absorbed their wisdom. Alas, nothing I'd ever learned offered any remedy to the disaster.

"Later, when people stopped coming here, I ventured forth to discover if anyone remained alive. I didn't find any humans, but by good fortune, I encountered a hunting party of orcs, who then attacked me."

Bareris smiled crookedly. " 'Good fortune,' you say."

"Very much so, because they didn't all turn to stone. One simply bled out after I pierced it with my fangs, and when I ate some of it, it turned out that it had witnessed Fastrin's suicide from a safe distance. Either the wizard didn't notice, or since the orc hadn't been a subject of the kingdom, it didn't figure in his delusions and he saw no reason to attack it. Either way, at least I now knew what had happened, grim though it was, so I returned home.

"Now tell me your tale."

Bareris winced. For a moment, Quickstrike's story had distracted him from his sorrows, and he had no desire to return to them. "It's not worth telling."

"When it involves you fleeing the undead? Don't be ridiculous."

Bareris reflected that the gravecrawler was, in fact, his host, so he owed the creature some accounting of himself. "As you wish. I don't know how much you know about the kingdoms of men as they exist today. I hail from a realm called Thay . . . "

He tried to relate the tale as tersely as possible, without any of the embellishments he would have employed if he'd been enjoying himself or striving to tease applause and coins from an audience. Still, it took a while. Long enough to dry his throat.

He drank the last swig from one of his water bottles. "And

that's it," he concluded. *"I warned you it wasn't much of a story. A good one has a shape to it. Even if it makes you feel sadness or pity, it somehow lifts you up as well, but mine's just bungling, futility, and horror."*

Quickstrike cocked his eyeless head. *"You speak as if the story's over."*

"It is. It doesn't matter if I make it out of these mountains and live another hundred years. I've already lost everything I cherished and the only fight worth fighting."

"My existence and mind are different from yours. I don't love, and long solitude that no human could endure suits me. All my knowledge of mortal thoughts and feelings is secondhand, and it's possible that on the deepest level, I cannot understand, but I think you still have a path to walk, and Mirror will help you on your way."

"What do you mean?"

"He wanders, and despite the damage to his mind, he knows these peaks and valleys, these Sunrise Mountains, as your people name them. He can keep you hidden from your pursuers while he guides you back to your own country."

"Does he want to? Why?"

"Because he's empty. He needs something to reflect, to fill and define him, and you, the first live man we've seen since he manifested in these vaults centuries ago, can do so in a way that lifeless paintings and carvings and I, an undead, inhuman creature, cannot."

"You make it sound as if he'll drain sustenance from me like a leech."

"No more than your reflection in any other glass."

Bareris still didn't like the sound of it. *"Won't you miss him?"*

"No. I wish him well, but I told you, my needs and feelings aren't like yours."

Bareris decided it wasn't worth further argument. The truth was, if he meant to go on living, he did need help, besides which, if Mirror insisted on accompanying him, he probably couldn't stop him anyway. But if they were to be companions, he ought to stop talking about the ghost as if he weren't there, even though he barely was.

He cast about and found a streak of blur hanging in the air. *"Thank you,"* he said. *"I'm grateful for your aid."*

As he'd expected, Mirror made no reply.

chapter twelve

9–11 Kythorn, the Year of Risen Elfkin

Yaphyll looked around the shabby, cluttered parlor, a room in a nondescript house that Dmitra Flass probably owned under another name. It was easy to imagine a goodwife shooing her children out of the chamber so she could dust the cheap ceramic knickknacks and scrub the floor, or her husband drinking ale and swapping ribald jokes with his cronies from the coopers' guild. Today, however, the occupants were rather more august.

Voluptuous by Mulan standards, the "First Princess of Thay" was as annoyingly ravishing as ever. Samas Kul was as obese, ruddy-faced, sweaty, and ostentatiously dressed, while, as was so often the case, Lallara looked vexed and ready to vent her spleen on the first person who gave her an excuse.

Though Yaphyll remained dubious that attending Dmitra's secret meeting was actually a wise idea, she found it marginally reassuring that the tharchion seemed as ill at ease as everyone else. Oh, she masked it well, but every Red Wizard of Divination mastered the art of reading faces and body language, and Yaphyll could tell nonetheless. Dmitra likely would have manifested a different sort of nervous tension had she been engaged in a plot to harm or undermine her superiors.

On the other hand, Dmitra was a Red Wizard of Illusion, so how could anyone be certain whether to trust appearances where she was concerned?

At least, now that Samas had finally waddled in and collapsed onto a couch substantial enough to support his bulk, Dmitra appeared ready to commence.

"Masters," she said, "thank you for indulging me. Ordinarily, I wouldn't presume to take the lead in a meeting with my superiors, but since—"

"Since you're the only one who knows what in the name of the Dark Sun we're here to talk about," Lallara snapped, "it only makes sense. We understand, and you have our permission to get on with it."

"Thank you, Your Omnipotence. I'm concerned about the welfare of the realm, worried and suspicious because I have information you lack and have thus been able to draw inferences you haven't."

"What are they?" Samas asked, fanning his face with a plump, tattooed hand.

"That Szass Tam murdered both Druxus Rhym and Aznar Thrul, that he betrayed a Thayan army to its foes, and that he disseminated a false report of a Rashemi invasion."

Lallara laughed. "This is ludicrous."

"If we consider the evidence, Your Omnipotence, perhaps I can persuade you otherwise. May we start with the assassination of Druxus Rhym?"

"By all means," Samas said. "It seems like the quickest way to lay your suspicions to rest. As I understand it, the murderer used evocation magic to make the kill."

"As could any of us," Dmitra replied. "We all tend to rely on spells deriving from our particular specialties, but in fact, each of us possesses a more comprehensive knowledge of magic. Certainly that's true of Szass Tam, universally recognized as the most accomplished wizard in the land. My conjecture is that he used the spells he did precisely to throw suspicion on the order of Evocation, Aznar Thrul being one of his enemies."

"But Druxus wasn't," Yaphyll said. "He was Szass Tam's ally, no less than any of us. Szass had no motive to kill him."

"He had one," Dmitra replied, "to which we'll return again: to create a climate of fear. I'll grant you, that by itself isn't sufficient motive to turn on a supporter, and as yet I can't resolve the discrepancy, but I can demonstrate that Szass Tam hasn't sought the identity of the murderer with the zeal one would expect of a compatriot with nothing to hide."

"How so?" Lallara asked.

"I have the most competent spy network in the realm, and Szass Tam knows it. Over the years, it's served him well, yet he virtually forbade me to use my agents to seek the identity of the assassin. He said that you, Mistress Yaphyll, would attend to it."

Yaphyll blinked. "I tried for a while. In fact, Szass and I tried together. Then when our divinations failed to reveal anything, he suggested I turn my attention to other concerns and said he would continue to hunt for the killer by other means. I assumed he was referring to your spies."

"None of that proves anything," Samas said.

He looked about, spotted the drink and viands laid out on a table by the wall, and made a mystic gesture in their direction. A bottle floated into the air and poured red wine into a goblet. A knife smeared honey on a sweet roll.

"No," said Lallara, eyes narrowed, "it doesn't, but I'll concede it's curious, and I also agree that Szass Tam is one of the few people who might have been able to slip into Druxus's bedchamber undetected or sneak an agent in. He's also one of the few capable of thwarting Yaphyll's divinations, especially if he was actually present to undermine the efficacy of the rituals in some subtle fashion."

"There's also this," Dmitra said. "Szass Tam made sure that you, Master Kul, would be elected Druxus Rhym's successor. I don't doubt you were a suitable candidate for the post, but still, why was he so concerned that it be you in particular? Could it have been partly because he knew you felt no great fondness for Rhym, and—forgive me for presuming to comment on your character—weren't the kind of man who would exert himself unduly to investigate a murder that worked to his benefit, even if the crime did constitute an affront against the order of Transmutation?"

Lallara snorted. "You have that right. All this hog cares about is stuffing his coffers and stuffing his mouth."

Samas glared at her. "I understand I'm your junior and that you have a shrewish disposition. Still, have a care how you speak to me."

"Masters, please," Dmitra said. "I beg you not to quarrel among yourselves. If my suspicions are correct, that's the last thing you should do."

"Is there more to say about Druxus's death?" Yaphyll asked.

"Unfortunately no," Dmitra replied, "so let's consider the battle in the Gorge of Gauros." She smiled. "I myself have a spy's nose for truth and falsehood, and from the start, something about the tale that came down from the north smelled wrong. Since Szass Tam figured prominently in the story, and he'd just piqued my curiosity by terminating my inquiries into Druxus Rhym's murder, I decided to look into the matter of the 'Rashemi invasion' instead.

"I found out there wasn't any. The barbarians weren't on their way south to attack us. Tharchions Kren and Odesseiron were marching north to invade Rashemen, but after a near-disastrous battle forced them to abandon their ambitions, Szass Tam supported them when, to avert the anger of the rest of you zulkirs, they claimed the Rashemi were the aggressors."

"And you think," Lallara said, "it was because, coming so soon after Druxus's murder, that story added to the 'climate of fear' Szass Tam hoped to create."

"Yes," Dmitra said, "but if we look deeper, we'll discern even more. Allow me to describe the battle in detail." She did so with the concise clarity of a woman who, though she wore the crimson robes of a wizard, also possessed the requisite skills to command troops in the field. "Now several questions suggest themselves: How did the Rashemi know our legions were coming and where best to intercept them? How were the witches able to counter the Thayan wizardry holding the river in check so easily? How was it that Szass Tam discerned the army's peril from wherever he was and translated himself onto the scene just in time to avert calamity?"

Yaphyll chuckled. "Perhaps the greatest mage in Thay perceives all manner of signs and portents invisible to lesser beings like ourselves." At the moment, she didn't actually feel like jesting, but they all had their masks to wear, and hers was the cute lass with the light heart and irrepressible sense of humor. Even after she rose through high in the hierarchy of her order, and any person of sense should have realized she possessed a ruthless heart and adamantine will, it had caused foes and rivals to underestimate her. "But you're positing that his spies reported Kren and Odesseiron's plans before they ever marched and he then somehow conveyed critical military and arcane intelligence to the Rashemi, providing them with the means to smash the Thayan host, and finally, he rushed to the tharchions' rescue."

"Exactly," Dmitra said, "because it isn't enough to frighten everyone. He also wants to convince the nobles, legions, and commons that he's the one champion who can end our woes. Obviously, the recent trouble in Pyarados must have seemed like a boon from the gods. It's given him the chance to play the savior not just once but twice."

Samas swallowed the food in his mouth, and then, his full lips glazed with honey, asked, "Why would he suddenly care so much about the opinion of his inferiors?"

"With your permission, Your Omnipotence," Dmitra replied, "before we ponder that, perhaps it would be well to finish our review of recent events, to consider the death of Aznar Thrul."

Yaphyll grinned. "Must we? I'd hoped that was one matter we understood already. In the wake of Druxus's murder, Nevron loaned the other members of his faction demons bodyguards. One of the spirits slipped its tether and surprised Thrul when he was amusing himself with a female slave and ill prepared to defend himself. It tore them apart and afterward some of Thrul's followers killed it in its turn."

"I suspect," Dmitra said, "the truth is more complex. From what my spies have managed to determine, it's not clear that the thrall's body has been recovered. We do know the creature that ran amok liked to kill by biting its victims in the throat and that some people remember it as originally being huge and male, whereas the entity the conjurors ultimately slew possessed the same four arms, scales, and what have you, but was no taller than a human being and female.

"I believe the original creature was a blood drinker and transformed the slave into an entity like itself so she would kill Aznar Thrul. In other words, it wasn't a demon in the truest sense, but rather some exotic form of vampire."

"Which suggests," Lallara said, "that it wasn't really a conjuror who summoned and bound it but rather a necromancer like Szass Tam, who then slipped it into Thrul's palace amid a troupe of Nevron's demons."

Samas nodded, his multiple chins wobbling. "Figuring that the murder of a second zulkir would spread that much more terror throughout the land. I understand, but we should also recognize that at least this death benefits us as well. Thrul was our enemy. With him gone, our faction controls the council, at least until the conjurors elect a new leader, and if he turns out to be sympathetic to our views, we can run things as we like for the foreseeable future."

"That assumes," Dmitra answered, "your faction remains intact, that you still view yourselves and Szass Tam as sharing common interests."

"Why wouldn't we?" Samas asked.

"I see it," Yaphyll said, and though she still wasn't certain Dmitra was correct, the mere possibility made her feel queasy. "Supposedly, Thay is in jeopardy. The Rashemi threaten from the north and undead marauders from the east. An unknown foe strikes down the zulkirs one by one. Fortunately, a hero has demonstrated the will and capacity to save the realm—if given a free hand to do so. You think that's the object of convening the council, don't you, Tharchion? Szass Tam is going to ask us to elect him supreme ruler of Thay."

Lallara grinned a sardonic grin. "Only temporarily, no doubt. Just until the crisis is resolved."

"He can't believe we would ever consent to such a thing!" Samas cried. "It's one thing to acknowledge him as the eldest and most accomplished of the zulkirs and the leader of our faction—first among equals, so to speak—but none of us fought all the way up to the loftiest rank in the land just to enthrone an overlord to command us as his vassals."

"I understand that," Dmitra said, "but I still felt it incumbent on me to warn you. Imagine if I hadn't. You've pledged your loyalty to Szass Tam, and knowing just how shrewd and powerful he is, you have no inclination to cross him. You take your seat in council worried over threats to the realm and your own personal safety as well. It appears the lich is the only person who's enjoyed any success confronting any of the various problems. Certainly that's what the populace at large believes.

"Now then: In the situation I've described, when Szass Tam requests his regency, or however he intends to put it, who among you, without knowing how the others feel, is bold enough to be the first to denounce the proposal?"

Yaphyll wished she could claim that she would find the courage, but she wondered if it was so. No zulkir could show weakness by confessing to fear of anyone or anything. But the truth was, even though he'd supported her in all her endeavors, she was afraid of Szass Tam, and she could tell that Samas and even Lallara, with her bitter, thorny nature, felt the same.

Lallara laughed. "Hear the silence! It appears, Tharchion, that none of us would dare."

"That means four votes in favor," Dmitra said, "and with Evocation's seat empty, at best three against. The measure passes. To forestall that, I hope the three of you will pledge here and now to stand firm against it."

"No," said Samas Kul, "or at least, not yet."

Dmitra inclined her head. "May I ask what more you require to persuade you, Master?"

"Yes, illusionist," the fat man replied, "you may. You've whistled up a host of phantoms to affright us, but I'd be more inclined to cower if I understood why you of all people would want to warn us. You're one of Szass Tam's favorites. If he crowned himself king, you'd benefit."

"You forget," Yaphyll said, "Tharchion Flass has sworn to serve all of us zulkirs, and I'm sure that, like all of us, she's concerned first and foremost with the welfare of the realm."

Lallara shot her a poisonous glance. "Your little drolleries are growing even more tiresome than usual." She shifted her glare to Dmitra. "The hog raises a valid point. If this is all a charade, it's hard to imagine what you could possibly be trying to achieve, but still: Why should we trust you?"

"Because Szass Tam no longer does," Dmitra replied. "In times past, he would have confided in me. Involved me in any scheme to which I might prove useful, even the assassination of a fellow zulkir, yet now, suddenly, he dissembles with me and only asks me to advance his schemes in a limited fashion, even though I've given him no reason to question my loyalty.

"Why? I can't imagine, any more than I know what he gained by murdering Druxus Rhym, or why, after contenting himself with being senior zulkir for so long, he's decided to strike for even greater authority. Not understanding alarms me.

"What I do know is that life in Thay as it's currently governed has been good to me. I have a nasty suspicion that, for whatever reason, I wouldn't find existence so congenial under Szass Tam's new regime."

She smiled. "So I'm trying to keep things as they are, and hope to manage to do so with minimal risk to myself. I've taken pains to keep Szass Tam from learning of this meeting, and if none of you tattles that I sought to rally you against him, I shouldn't suffer for it."

Lallara grunted. "What you say makes a certain amount of sense, Tharchion, which isn't to imply I embrace it as complete and utter truth. And perhaps your motives don't matter so very much, because Samas was right about one thing: He, Yaphyll, and I are all averse to installing the lich in a new office higher than our own. It's clear from our manner even if we haven't declared it outright, so I say, yes, let's seal a secret pact of resistance, just in case."

Yaphyll nodded. "Agreed. No kingship or regency for anyone, ever, under any circumstances." Unless, of course, she could somehow, someday win such a prize for herself.

Samas Kul heaved a sigh. "I agree, too, I suppose."

It was as eloquent an oration as Szass Tam had ever given. He enumerated the dire menaces facing Thay in general and the zulkirs personally. He reminded the other mage lords of his accomplishments, recent and otherwise, and pointed out how divided leadership could prevent even the greatest realm in Faerûn from achieving its goals or coping in an emergency. The failed military endeavors of recent decades were obvious examples.

He also promised he'd step down as soon as he eliminated the threats to the common weal. He omitted, however, any mention of the hideous punishments he'd meted out to folk who had, at one time or another, balked or angered the oldest and most powerful wizard in the land. He was certain the other zulkirs recalled those without his needing to allude to them.

Yet when he saw the glances that passed among Yaphyll, Lallara, and Samas Kul, he realized that somehow the other members of his faction had already known what he was going to propose. Known, palavered in secret, and resolved to oppose him as staunchly as the remaining zulkirs, and that was staunchly indeed. The other three were his long-time enemies: Nevron with his perpetual sneer and the brimstone stink of his demon servitors clinging to his person; Lauzoril, deceptively bland and clerkish; and Mythrellan, who affected to despise everyone else on the council, who changed her face as often as other great noblewomen changed their gowns, frequently to something with an element of the bizarre but always exquisite nonetheless. Today her eyes were gold and her skin sky blue. A haze of unformed illusion ready for the shaping made her image soft and blurry.

Even though he recognized early on that he was almost certainly speaking in vain, Szass Tam carried on to the end then called for a vote. It seemed possible that, now that the moment for support or defiance had arrived, his supposed allies might lose their nerve.

Alas, they remained resolute. Only Szass raised his hand in support of the proposal he himself had introduced. Nevron leered to see his foe so humiliated. Even prim Lauzoril managed a smirk.

Though he hadn't expected to find Yaphyll, Samas, and Lallara united against him, Szass had thought himself prepared for the possibility that his ploy would fail. Still, the mockery inspired an unexpected paroxysm of rage. He yearned to lash out at every adversary, old and newly revealed, seated around the gleaming red maple table.

He didn't, of course. Attacking six other zulkirs at once might well prove suicidal, even for a mage more powerful than any one of them. Instead, making sure his mask of affability didn't slip, he inclined his head in seeming acceptance.

"So be it," he said. "We'll continue on as we always have, deciding all matters by consensus. Be assured, I don't resent it that you rejected my plan, prudent though I believe it was, and I'll keep working diligently to solve the problems that plague us."

At the same time, simply by thinking, he sent a signal. He'd prepared the magic beforehand, with sufficient concern for subtlety to ensure that even the extraordinarily perceptive Yaphyll wouldn't notice it thrilling through the aether.

After that, everyone blathered on for a while longer, and though he felt a seething impatience to depart, he supposed that really it was fine. His minions needed time to do their work.

As soon as the meeting broke up, he spurned Samas, Yaphyll, and Lallara with their slinking excuses and attempts at reconciliation and translated himself back to his study in the citadel of the order of Necromancy. It took the warlock waiting there an instant to notice his arrival, and then the fellow flung himself to his knees. Tsagoth knelt as well, albeit with a glower. Apparently the blood fiend had expected his master to liberate him once he accomplished the death of Aznar Thrul, but as demonstrated by that success, he was too useful an agent to relinquish when so many challenging tasks remained.

"Get up," Szass Tam said. "Tell me what's happening."

"Yes, Master," said the younger necromancer, rising. Szass had the conceit that if he peered deep into his subordinate's eyes, he could glimpse an indefinable wrongness there, a hint of the psychic shackles binding the live wizard to silence and obedience, but perhaps it was only his imagination. "Our agents are spreading the tidings that, in their arrogance, folly, and ingratitude, the other zulkirs denied you the authority you need to preserve the realm."

"With the proper enchantments in play to make the news seem as infuriating as possible."

"Yes, Master, just as you directed."

"Good." Szass Tam turned to Tsagoth. "You know what to do from here. Go tell your partners."

•• •• •• •• •• •• •• •• •• •• •• •• ••

Nular Tabar glanced back at the shuttered three-story brick house behind him. It wasn't the primary stronghold of the order of Conjuration in Eltabbar. That imposing citadel was on the other side of town, but despite a lack of banners, overt supernatural manifestations, and the like, everyone in the neighborhood knew this was some sort of chapter house. People saw the mages and their retainers passing in and out.

They weren't coming out now. They were leaving the protection of the property to Nular and the dozen legionnaires in his patrol, and at that point, it remained to be seen just how hard the job would be. Though in normal times, no commoner dared annoy Red Wizards, scores of people had gathered to glare, mill about, and shout slogans and insults at the house. Apparently, they all wanted Szass Tam for their king, were angry they weren't going to get him, and had decided to hold Nevron, notoriously one of the lich's enemies, responsible for their disappointment. The zulkir of Conjuration wasn't here to bear the brunt of their anger, but a structure belonging to his order was.

Nular had formed his patrol into a line to block the approach to the house as best they could. The problem was that a dozen soldiers couldn't form a very long line without standing so far apart as to give up the ability to protect one another's flanks. He wasn't about to order that, which meant that a fool hell-bent on getting at the building could dart around the end of the formation.

Sure enough, a wiry, dark-haired youth with a sack clutched under his arm lunged at the gap on the southern end. The warrior last in line pivoted and swung his cudgel but was too slow. The lad sprinted on unbashed.

"Hold your positions!" Nular shouted then raced after the youth himself.

The adolescent was quick, but so was he, and he possessed the advantage of long Mulan legs. He caught up, lifted his baton to bash the lad over the head, then thought how the brutal sight might further enflame the mob. He dropped the cudgel to dangle from the strap around his wrist and grabbed the youth with his empty hands instead.

The boy dropped the bag to wrestle and turned out to have some notion of what he was doing. He tried to jam his knee into Nular's groin, and the guard twisted and caught the attack on his thigh. Next came grubby fingers gouging for his eyes. He protected them by ducking his head then butted the adolescent in the face. The lad faltered, and Nular threw him down on his back. That seemed to knock the fight out of him.

Clad in rags, the lad was plainly a pauper. The stained sack gave off a fecal stink. Most likely he'd meant to use the contents to deface the Red Wizards' door.

"Stay down," Nular panted, "or I swear, next time I'll use my sword on you."

The boy glowered but didn't move.

"What in the name of the Kossuth's fire is the matter with you?" Nular continued. "Would you throw away your life on an idiot prank? You know the wizards punish disrespect."

"Szass Tam has to be regent!" the youth replied.

"Why do you care? What difference do you think it will make to the likes of you?"

And as long as Nular was posing questions, how had the boy and his fellows learned the outcome of the zulkirs' deliberations so quickly? As often as not, lesser folk never even heard the council had met, let alone what it decided.

It was a mystery, but someone shrewder than Nular would have to puzzle it out. His job was simply to keep order in one section of Eltabbar's labyrinthine streets.

"Get up," he said, "and pick up your bag of filth. Now go home! If you're still here in forty breaths, or if I catch you out of doors again tonight, I'll gut you." He prodded the youth with the tip of his club to start him moving.

Once he'd herded the lad to the other side of the line, Nular scrutinized all the others like him. Feeding off one another's outrage, they were growing more agitated by the moment. It was only a matter of time before the stones started flying.

He was no orator, but he had to say something to try and calm them. He was still trying to frame the words in his mind when some of them cried out, and they all flinched back.

He turned to see what had alarmed them. Standing behind the line was a towering four-armed creature with dark scales and gleaming scarlet eyes.

Nular felt a strange blend of fear and relief, the former because every sane person was leery of demons, and the latter because it was plain the conjurors in the house had sent the creature to help him.

He gazed up at its wolfish face. "Do you understand me?" he asked.

The entity chuckled. "Yes."

"Good. That will make things easier. The sight of you has frightened the mob. We need to keep them intimidated. With luck, scare them into going elsewhere."

"No, warrior. We need to slaughter them. Don't worry, fighting in concert, we'll manage easily."

Nular frowned. "Maybe we would, but I'm hoping it won't be necessary."

"It already is. The rabble's impudence is an affront to my masters and must be punished accordingly."

"Do your masters understand that the unrest isn't just happening here? The 'rabble' have taken to the streets across the city. If we kill people, the violence could spread and spread. We could end up with a riot far worse than those we've endured already."

The demon shrugged. "That's nothing to me. My masters command, and I obey. Are you not obliged to obey Red Wizards, also?"

Nular hesitated. "Yes, but you're not one. If we're going to do this, I at least need to hear the order from one of the conjurors." He started to walk around the creature toward the house.

The spirit shifted so as to remain directly in front of him. "That isn't necessary," it said, and its crimson eyes flared brighter.

Nular rocked backward as though something had struck him a blow. He felt bewildered, as if he'd just awakened from a dream so vivid that he couldn't be certain what was real.

Then he caught his balance, and his confusion passed. Or partly so. "What . . . what were we saying?" he asked.

"That we're going to kill the rebels."

"Yes." That sounded right, or at least familiar. "Swords!"

A couple of his men—the clever ones, who might rise from the ranks one day—eyed him dubiously, but they were all well trained and exchanged their truncheons for their blades without protest. He did the same.

"Now forward!" Nular shouted. "Keep the line and cut the bastards down."

The mob might have had the stomach for a fight with a dozen legionnaires, but legionnaires and an ogre-sized demon were a more daunting prospect. They screamed and tried to run, but their numbers were such that they got in each other's way. The ones closest to their attackers couldn't evade the soldiers' swords and the creature's fangs and talons, and thus they had no choice but to turn again and fight.

It was all right though. The soldiers' training, armor, and superior weapons aided them, of course, but it was the demon's ferocity that truly rendered the mob's numerical advantage inconsequential. Striking quickly as a cat, ripping men to pieces with every blow, the spirit butchered more foes than all its human allies put together, until a rioter charged it from behind and buried an axe in its back. Whereupon the demon screamed, collapsed to its knees, then melted away to nothing at all. Nular could scarcely believe that a creature, which had seemed the very embodiment of inhuman might, could perish so easily, but evidently it was so.

"I killed it!" yelled the axeman, brandishing his gory weapon. "I killed it!" His comrades roared in triumph then hurled themselves at the legionnaires with renewed savagery.

With the fiend gone and rioters circling to get behind their remaining adversaries, the advancing line wasn't viable anymore.

The legionnaires needed a formation that would enable them to guard each other's backs.

"Square!" Nular bellowed. "Square!"

But they couldn't form one. The enemies swarming on them from every side, grabbing and beating at them, made it impossible to maneuver. Pivoting, fighting with his sword in one hand and his cudgel in the other, Nular realized the press had suddenly grown so thick that he couldn't even see his men anymore, just hear the clangor of their opponents' blows pounding on their shields.

That clashing noise diminished as, no doubt, the legionnaires fell one by one. Something smashed or cut into Nular's knee, and he dropped too. His injured leg ablaze with pain, he glimpsed men running toward the conjurors' chapter house, then a burly laborer lifted a shovel high and plunged the edge down at his throat.

•• •• •• •• •• •• •• •• •• •• •• •• •• ••

At first, Faurgar Stayanoga thought, it had made sense. They'd take to the streets as the priest in the alehouse had urged, and when the zulkirs saw how many they were, and how displeased, they'd have to rethink their decision.

More than that, it had been fun. Intoxicating. His whole life, Faurgar had walked warily in the presence of Red Wizards, legionnaires, or any Mulan really, but tonight, roaming the streets with hundreds like himself, he hadn't been afraid of anyone. They'd all said whatever they wanted as loud as they wanted. Defaced, smashed, and torched whatever they wanted. Broken into shops and taverns and taken whatever they wanted.

But he was scared, because the legions had turned out in force to deal with the disturbance, and he and his friends were trapped, with blood orcs advancing from one side and human warriors from the other. The orcs leered and howled their piercing battle cries. The men strode quietly, with faces like stone, but despite their differing attitudes, both companies looked entirely ready to kill.

Faurgar looked up and down the street and found nowhere to run. Some of his companions pounded on doors, but no one would open to them. Evidently hoping the legionnaires would spare the lives of any who surrendered, others raised their hands or dropped to their knees. The rest, defiant still, brandished the knives and tools that were all they possessed in the way of weapons.

Faurgar simply stood, mouth dry, heart pounding, uncertain of what he ought to do. It didn't look to him as if the guards intended to spare anyone, and if so, it seemed better to go down fighting. But if he was wrong, if there was even the slightest chance of surviving . . .

By the Great Flame, how had he come to this? He was the son of respectable parents and a journeyman mason. He didn't belong in the middle of this nightmare.

The orcs reached the first kneeling man. Steel flashed, blood spurted, and the penitent collapsed to flop and twitch like a fish out of water. Soldiers trampled him as they continued to advance.

All right, thought Faurgar, now we know for certain that they mean to kill us all. So fight! But he didn't know if he could. Tears were blurring his vision, and even if they hadn't been, the urge to cringe was so strong that he could hardly bear even to look at the warriors. How, then, could he possibly strike a blow?

As if too full of bloodlust to permit their human comrades an equal share in the killing, the orcs abruptly screamed and charged. One ran straight at Faurgar.

Fight! he told himself, but when he tried to raise his trowel, his hand shook so badly that he dropped it. Knowing it was craven and useless, but powerless to control himself, he crouched and shielded his torso and face with his arms.

And as if the Storm Lord were responding to the spectacle of his wretchedness, the night burned white. Prodigious booms shook the earth, and torrents of frigid rain hammered down, ringing on the legionnaires' armor and drumming on everything else.

The legionnaires faltered in shock. Barely audible over the thunder and the downpour, the commander of the orcs bellowed at his troops. Faurgar couldn't speak their language, but he had a fair idea of what the gray-skinned creature was saying: It's only rain! Go on and kill the rabble as I ordered you to!

The orcs moved to obey, then a flare of lightning struck a peaked rooftop on the right-hand side of the street. The flash was blinding, the crash loud enough to jab pain into Faurgar's ears, and everyone froze once more.

One of the human soldiers shouted and pointed. Blinking, Faurgar reflexively glanced to see what had caught the legionnaire's attention. He expected to observe that the thunderbolt had set the shingled roof on fire, but it wasn't so. Rather, a tall, thin man in a red robe stood in the middle of the charred and blackened place where the lightning had struck, as if he'd ridden the bolt down from the sky.

"That's Szass Tam!" someone exclaimed, and certainly the guards were coming to attention and saluting. Faurgar and his fellows knelt.

The lich's dark gaze raked over them all, warrior and cornered troublemaker alike. "This won't do," he said. He seemed to speak without raising his voice, yet despite the din of the storm, Faurgar could hear him clearly from yards away.

"Unlike some," Szass Tam continued, "I'm not eager to see Thayan soldiers slaughtering Thayan citizens, not as long as there's any hope of avoiding it. Accordingly, you legionnaires will give these people one last chance to disperse and retire to their homes in peace."

"Yes, Your Omnipotence!" the commander of the human guards shouted.

"And you citizens," the necromancer said, "will do precisely that. I understand that you've behaved as you have out of concern for the realm, and to that degree, your patriotism does you credit, but you can't accomplish anything by damaging your own city and compelling the guards to take harsh action against you. I promise a better outlet for your energies in the days to come.

"Now go," he concluded, and a heartbeat later, inexplicably, he was gone. Faurgar had been looking straight at him, yet had a muddled sense that he hadn't actually seen the wizard vanish.

The human officer barked orders. His company divided in the middle, clearing a corridor for Faurgar and his companions to scurry along. The orcs scowled but offered no protest. Szass Tam was their zulkir too.

Their zulkir, and the greatest person in the world. Thanks to him, Faurgar was going to live.

•• •• •• •• •• •• •• •• •• •• •• •• •• ••

Malark stood at the casement watching the lightning dance above the city. The peaceful city. Even those folk who hadn't had the opportunity to hear Szass Tam speak had discovered that cold, blinding, stinging rain washed the fun out of looting, vandalism, and assault, or in the case of the legionnaires, it dissolved their zeal to chase those guilty of such offenses.

The door clicked open behind him, and he smelled the perfume Dmitra was wearing tonight. He turned and knelt.

"Rise," she said, crossing his darkened, austerely furnished room, a silver goblet in her hand. "I've received a message from Szass Tam. He's retiring to his estate in High Thay for the time being. I can contact him there, but the implication is that I should refrain except in case of an emergency."

"Do you think he knows you warned the other zulkirs of his intentions?"

"By the Black Hand, I hope not. I also hope it was the right thing to do. My instincts told me it was, and they've rarely played me false, but still . . . " She shook her head.

"If I may say so, Tharchion, you look tired. If you don't feel ready to sleep, shall we sit and watch the storm together?"

"Why not?" He moved a pair of chairs up to the window and she sank down into one of them. "Do you have anything to drink, or must I call for a servant?"

"No wine." Now that she'd come closer, he knew what she'd been drinking. He could smell it on her breath despite the overlay of perfume. "But some of that Hillsfar brandy you like."

"That will do."

As he passed behind her to fetch clean cups and the decanter, he automatically thought of how to kill her where she sat. One sudden blow or stranglehold, and no magic would save her, but he didn't actually feel the urge to strike. Aside from the inconvenience to himself, obliged to give up a congenial position and flee Thay just when life here was becoming truly interesting, there wouldn't be anything profoundly appropriate or exceptionally beautiful about the death. Dmitra was his benefactor, perhaps even in a certain sense his friend, and she deserved better.

She sipped brandy and gazed out at the tempest. "You have to give Szass Tam credit," she said after a time. "First he incites what could have been the worst riot in the history of Eltabbar. He even tricks the mob into believing Nevron and the conjurors sent demons to kill them. Then he ends the crisis in the gentlest way possible, making himself a hero to every person who feared for his life and chattels, every rioter who escaped punishment, and any legionnaire who was squeamish about killing other Thayans."

Malark smiled. "While simultaneously demonstrating just how powerful he is. I assume it's difficult to spark a storm in a clear sky."

"Yes, though we Thayans have been the masters of our weather for a long while. I'm actually more impressed by the way he appeared in dozens of places around the city all at the same moment. Obviously, people were actually seeing projected images, yet by all accounts, the phantasms didn't behave identically. They oriented on the folk they were addressing, and if anyone dared to speak to them in turn, they deviated from the standard declaration to answer back. I'm a Red Wizard of Illusion, and I have no idea how one would go about managing that." She laughed. "And this is the creature I opted to betray."

"But with considerable circumspection, so instead of fretting over what can't be undone, perhaps it would be more productive to contemplate what's just occurred. What game is Szass Tam playing now?"

"I don't know, but you're right, he is still playing. Otherwise, what's the point of the riot?"

"He must realize now that the other zulkirs will never proclaim him regent no matter how much he makes lesser folk adore him."

A gust of wind rattled the casement in its frame.

"I wonder," Dmitra said. "Suppose he murders another zulkir or two. Suppose he tempts one or more of those who remain with the office of vice-regent, subordinate to himself but superior to all others. Sounds better than death, doesn't it?"

It didn't to Malark, but he didn't bother saying so. "Now that I think about it, the various orders must be full of Red Wizards who'd love to move up to be zulkir, even if the rank was no longer a position of ultimate authority. It's easy to imagine one or more of them collaborating with Szass Tam. They work together to assassinate Nevron, Samas Kul, or whomever, get the traitor elected to replace him, and afterward the fellow acts as the lich's dutiful supporter."

Dmitra nodded. "It could happen just that way, but not easily, not when Szass Tam needs a majority on the council, and not with all the other zulkirs now striving assiduously to keep themselves safe. I actually think the game has entered a new phase."

"Which is?"

"I wish I knew." She laughed. "I must seem like a pathetic coward. It's one zulkir against six, who now enjoy my support, yet I'm frightened of the outcome. I have an ugly feeling none of us has ever truly taken Szass Tam's measure, whereas he knows our every strength and weakness. I can likewise imagine our very abundance of archmages proving a hindrance. The lich is a single genius with a coherent strategy maneuvering against a band of keen but lesser minds bickering and working at cross purposes."

"Then you'll have to make sure that, no matter what the zulkirs imagine, it's actually you calling the tune."

"A good trick if I can manage it, whereas your task is to figure out what Szass Tam means to do next."

Malark grinned. "Even though I've never met him, and you tell me he's a genius. It should prove an interesting challenge."

chapter thirteen

13–14 Kythorn, the Year of Risen Elfkin

Borrowing Brightwing's eyes to combat the darkness, Aoth rode the griffon above the mountainsides on the northern edge of the valley. It was a necessary chore. As far as the Thayans could tell, after they'd chased the undead up the pass, the creatures had retreated into the Keep of Thazar, but it was possible they hadn't all done so. Even if they had, with flying wraiths and ghouls possessing a preternatural ability to dig tunnels among their company, it was by no means a certainty that they'd all remain inside the walls. Ergo, someone had to make sure no enemy was slinking through the night.

"It didn't have to be you," Brightwing said, catching the tenor of his thoughts. "You're an officer now, remember? You could have sent a common soldier and stayed in camp to guzzle beer and rut with your female."

"I know." Maybe he hadn't been a captain long enough to delegate such tasks as he ought. He'd so often served as a scout, advance guard, or outrider that he still felt a need to observe things for himself whenever possible. "But you're getting fat. We need to work some of the lard off your furry arse."

Brightwing clashed her beak shut in feigned irritation at the jibe then exclaimed, "Look there!"

Two beings were descending a slope. One was a living man—a Mulan, to judge from his lanky physique, though his head and chin weren't properly shaved—wearing a sword. Evidently he was a refugee who'd somehow avoided death at the hands of the undead infesting the valley. Gliding along behind him, perceptible primarily as a mote of cold, aching wrongness, was some sort of ghost. No doubt it was stalking him and would attack when ready, though Aoth couldn't imagine what it was waiting on.

Lady Luck must love you, the war mage silently told the refugee, to keep you alive until Brightwing and I arrived. With a thought, he sent the griffon swooping lower then flourished his spear and rattled off an incantation.

Darts of blue light hurtled from the head of the lance to pierce the phantom through. The punishment made it more visible, though it was just a pale shadow with a hint of armor in its shape and the suggestion of a blade extending from its hand. It rose into the air as Aoth had hoped it would. He wanted to draw it away from the man on the ground.

"Run!" Aoth shouted.

Instead, the stranger called, "Don't attack him! He's my guide! Mirror, don't fight! Come back to me!"

Aoth hesitated. Was the man a necromancer and "Mirror" his familiar?

Maybe not, because the ghost kept on flying at Aoth and his mount, and after his recent experiences with the undead, he had no intention of giving it the benefit of the doubt. He wheeled Brightwing in an attempt of keep away from the spirit and chanted words of power. For a moment, Mirror wavered into a short, broad, better-defined figure not unlike himself, then melted into blur once more.

"Stop!" the refugee roared, and his voice echoed from the mountainsides like thunder.

A palpable jolt made Brightwing screech and spoiled the mystic gesture necessary for the completion of Aoth's spell. Mirror's misty substance rippled like water, and then it—or he—floated back down toward the stranger like a hound called to heel.

With their psyches linked, Aoth could taste Brightwing's anger almost as if it were his own. She believed the man they'd been seeking to rescue had treacherously attacked them, but striving for clarity of thought despite the flare of emotion, Aoth discerned that the magical cry hadn't actually injured her, and the stranger had targeted both her and Mirror. Maybe he'd just been trying to halt the confrontation without harm to any of the parties involved.

"Calm yourself," he told the griffon. "Let's land and talk to him."

"I'd rather land and tear him apart," Brightwing snarled, but once she'd furled her wings and glided to the ground, she held her position several paces away from Mirror and the stranger.

Not so sure of the peculiar duo's benign intentions that he cared to dismount, Aoth remained in the saddle. "I'm Aoth Fezim, captain and battle wizard in the Griffon Legion of Pyarados. Who are you, and what are you doing wandering in this region?"

"My name is Bareris Anskuld," the stranger replied, and when Aoth viewed him up close, his haggard weariness was apparent. Weariness and something more. He had a bleakness about him, as if something of vital importance to him had gone horribly, irreparably awry. "A bard and sellsword. I've been lost in the mountains and trying to find my way out. I met Mirror, and he chose to lead me. Is that the Pass of Thazar below us?"

"Yes."

"Good. Thank you for the information and for trying to help when you thought I was in danger. Mirror and I will move on now, if it's all right with you."

Aoth snorted. "No, musician, it's not 'all right.' You need to give a better account of yourself than that, considering that my comrades and I are fighting a war of sorts in the vale."

"A war? With whom?"

"Undead that came out of the mountains to the north, the same as you and your ghost friend."

The bard's eyes narrowed, and though he seemed no less despondent than before, his taut expression now bespoke a bitter resolve. "In that case, Captain, you should hear my tale in its entirety."

•• •• •• •• •• •• •• •• •• •• •• •• •• ••

It had taken most of the night to put the little meeting together while making sure none of the necromancers learned of it, and eyes smarting, nerves raw with tension and lack of sleep, Nymia Focar looked around the shadowy tent at the other three folk in attendance and found something to dislike in each of them.

Though evidently a Mulan of sorts and gifted with a facility for one of the lesser forms of magic, Bareris Anskuld was essentially a filthy, ragged vagabond. It was preposterous to imagine he had anything of importance to relate.

Despite his advanced years and the forfeiture of his rest, Milsantos Daramos, Tharchion of Thazalhar, looked fresh and alert and stood straight as a spear shaft. He'd even taken the trouble to put on his armor. That was reason enough to dislike the old man with his seamed face and shaggy white brows even if she hadn't resented the necessity of begging his aid to salvage her province and the fact that everyone considered him a better commander than herself.

She found, however, that Aoth vexed her most of all. The half-breed had his uses, but she never should have promoted him. The pressures of command had evidently disposed him to absurd apprehensions and fancies. Rather to her embarrassment, he'd already blathered about them in one council of war, and here he was, making a fool of himself again, and dressing her in motley and bells as well.

For he'd somehow managed to persuade her to give Bareris a hearing in the covert manner he desired, and she winced to think what might happen if the Red Wizards learned she'd gone behind their backs.

She supposed that meant it behooved her to get this nonsense over with as rapidly as possible, to minimize the possibility of anyone else finding out about it. "Let's hear it," she rapped.

Aoth had already given her the gist of the story in terse summation, but Bareris told it in detail and was more persuasive than she'd expected. Perhaps the very strangeness of the tale made it seem more credible, for how—to say nothing of why—would anyone make such things up?

But she wanted the story to be false. Since her audience with the zulkirs and Iphegor Nath, everything had gone splendidly, until she was ready to retake the Keep of Thazar itself. The lack of siege equipment shouldn't prove an insurmountable obstacle if the Burning Braziers performed as promised. She didn't need complications arising at the last moment.

So she did her best to pick holes in Bareris's story. "If you wanted to take slaves into the mountains, why not just march them there directly? Why bother with Delhumide and a portal?"

"Because they didn't want anyone to see the thralls going east," Bareris answered, "lest he draw a connection between them and the raiders."

"Also," said Milsantos, idly fingering a raised gilded rune on his breastplate, "it would be easier. The Sunrise Mountains are difficult terrain to negotiate and swarming with wild goblin and kobold tribes to boot."

"Still," she said, "where's the proof this story is true?"

"The proof," Aoth said, "is that Bareris's report illuminates matters we couldn't understand before. The enemy was able to overcome the priest in Thazar Keep, send lacedons swimming downriver, and reanimate the folk they slaughtered in such quantities because they aren't all undead. Some are living necromancers."

"That isn't proof," she snapped, "it's speculation."

She realized she craved a drink, and despite a suspicion that, tired and upset as she was, it would do her more harm than good, she picked up a half-finished bottle of wine. The cork made a popping sound as she pulled it out.

"Tharchion," Bareris said, "if my word isn't good enough, let me tell my story to one of the Burning Braziers. He can use clerical magic to verify that I'm speaking the truth."

Nymia had no desire to involve another person in their deliberations. Besides, she abruptly discerned that, much as she'd struggled to deny the perception, her instincts told her the bard was being honest.

She looked around for a clean cup, couldn't find one—she'd allowed her orderly to retire earlier—and swigged sweet white wine from the neck of the bottle. The stuff immediately roiled her stomach.

"For purposes of argument," she said, "let's say you are telling the truth as best you understand it. Your story suggests we're facing a cartel of rogue necromancers, traitors to their order."

"Maybe," said Milsantos, "and maybe not. I have informants in Eltabbar. I'm sure you do too, but have you heard from yours in the past couple days? Mine got a letter to me."

"And they said something pertinent to our situation here on the eastern border of the realm?"

"Perhaps. Two days ago, Szass Tam tried and failed to persuade the other zulkirs to proclaim him regent. In light of that, let's consider recent events."

"To have any hope of winning the council to his way of thinking," said Aoth, "the lich had to seem a successful if not triumphant figure, so he manufactured a threat to the eastern tharchs then played a crucial role in combating it. That means it isn't 'rogue' mages standing against us. It's conceivable the entire order of Necromancy is involved, including the Red Wizards in our own army."

"Impossible," Nymia said. "No one could keep such a huge conspiracy secret."

"He could," Bareris said, "if he silenced his underlings with enchantment. I told you about the guard who died when I tried to question it."

"That was an orc. No one would dare to lay such a binding on a Red Wizard."

"A higher-ranking and more powerful Red Wizard would."

"Curse it!" she exclaimed. "Even if all these crazy guesses are correct, don't you see, it's none of our business what games the zulkirs play with one another. All we need to know is that an undead host threatens Pyarados, and the council, Szass Tam included, wants us to destroy it."

"What," said Milsantos, "if Szass Tam has stopped wanting it? He desired our victories to advance a particular strategy, which has now failed. In the aftermath, what remains? A siege in which his followers and creatures are fighting on both sides. Can we be absolutely certain he's still backing us?"

"Why would he stop?" she demanded.

"To create the impression that when Szass Tam is honored as is his due, things go well, but when the other zulkirs deny him, they go disastrously awry? Truly, Nymia, I can't guess, but I shrink from the thought of what will happen if the necromancers and zombies in our own ranks suddenly turn on us in the midst of battle. Better, I think, to try our luck without them."

"So we send them away? Restrain them? Insult Szass Tam and the entire order of Necromancy?"

The old warrior smiled a crooked smile. "When you put it like that, it's not an appealing prospect, is it? We'd certainly need to win and hope our success would motivate the other zulkirs to shield us from the lich's displeasure."

"I don't know if we even have the authority to deal with Red Wizards in such a manner."

"You're tharchions," said Aoth. "This is an army in the field. The Burning Braziers will support you. They hate the necromancers condescending to them. *Take* the authority."

She considered it for several heartbeats then shook her head. "No. Not without proof, and I mean something I can see with my own eyes, not just a wanderer's tale, even should a cleric vouch for him."

"Then I'll interrogate one of your Red Wizards," Bareris said. "He'll tell the truth or die in a fit like the orc. Either way, you can be certain."

Nymia hesitated. "Neither Tharchion Daramos nor I could consent to such an outrage. You'd have to act alone, without our aid or intercession, and if you failed to extort the proof you promise, we'd order your execution. It would be the only way to make sure the stink of your treason didn't attach itself to us."

Bareris shrugged as if the prospect of a slow death under torture was of no concern. "Fine."

"Except," said Aoth, "that you won't have to do it alone. I'll help, and I know a fire priestess who will too." He grinned. "Now that I think of it, I can steer you to the perfect Red Wizard as well."

••   ••   ••   ••   ••   ••   ••   ••   ••   ••   ••   ••   ••   ••   ••

Bareris crooned his charm of silence, each note softer than the one before. He centered the charm on the sword sheathed at this side. It seemed as good an anchor point as any.

With the final note, the camp, quiet already here in the dregs of the night, fell absolutely silent. He, Aoth, Chathi, and Mirror, only perceptible as the vaguest hint of visual distortion, sneaked up to the rear of Urhur Hahpet's spacious, sigil-embroidered tent a few breaths later.

Aoth gave Chathi an inquiring look. Even without benefit of words, his meaning was plain. He was asking if she was certain she wanted to risk this particular venture. She responded with an expression that expressed assurance, impatience, and affection all at once.

The lovers' interplay gave Bareris a fresh pang of heartache. He turned away and peered about to make certain no one was looking in their direction. Nobody was, so he drew his dagger, cut a peephole in the tent, and looked inside.

No lamps or candles burned within. Evidently even necromancers, who worked so much of their wizardry at night, had to sleep sometime. But Bareris had sharpened his sight with magic, and he could make out a figure wrapped in blankets lying on the cot.

He gave his comrades a nod, then reinserted his dagger in the hole and pulled it downward, cutting a slit large enough for a man to squirm through, as he proceeded to do.

With the tent now enveloped in silence, he had no need to tiptoe, so he simply strode toward the man in the camp bed. But before he could cross the intervening space, something small and gray leaped onto Urhur Hahpet's chest, then, eyes burning with greenish phosphorescence, immediately launched itself at Bareris's face.

It was a zombie or mummified cat, evidently reanimated to watch over its master as he slept. Bareris swung his arm and batted it out of the air. It scrambled up and charged him.

Though the shriveled, stinking thing wasn't large enough to seem all that dire a threat, Bareris suspected its darkened fangs and claws might well be poisonous, either innately or because Urhur painted them with venom. Accordingly, he felt he had to deal with the cat at once. He shifted the knife to his off hand, whipped out his sword, and drove the point into the undead animal's back, nailing it to the earth. It made a final frenzied scrabbling attempt to reach his foot then stopped moving. The sheen in its eyes faded.

By then, though, Urhur had cast off his covers and was rearing up from the bed. The silence would keep him from reciting incantations, and since he didn't sleep in his clothes, he didn't have his spell foci ready to hand, but he was wearing a presumably enchanted necklace of small bones and grasping a crooked blackwood wand he'd apparently stashed beneath his blankets or pillow. He extended the arcane weapon in the intruders' direction.

Bareris yanked his sword out of the feline carcass, sprang forward, and poised the weapon to strike at the wand. At the same instant, a gout of dark fire, or something like it, leaped from the end of the wand to chill him. Refusing to let the freezing anguish stop him, he delivered the beat, and the wand flew from Urhur's grasp.

Bareris and his comrades had observed two withered, yellow-eyed dread warriors standing guard in front of the tent, and now the sentries pushed through the flap of cloth covering the doorway. He'd hoped the magical silence would keep them from discerning that their master needed them, but perhaps they were responding to a psychic summons.

Though Bareris hadn't taken his eyes off his foes to glance around and check, he assumed Aoth, Mirror, and Chathi were likewise inside the tent by now, and he'd depend on them to deal with the dread warriors. He had to stay focused on Urhur, because the Red Wizard merely needed to scurry into the open air, dart beyond the confines of the zone of silence, and scream for help to ruin his plan.

He tried to lame Urhur with a slash to the leg. The necromancer flung himself backward into the taut canvas wall of the tent, rebounded, and landed on the ground behind the cot. Fearful that Urhur would squirm out under the bottom of the cloth barrier, Bareris dropped his dagger, grabbed the camp bed, and jerked it out of his way.

Meanwhile, Urhur gripped one of the bones strung around his neck, and a seething dimness shrouded his form. Still aiming for the leg, Bareris thrust. Urhur tried to snatch his limb out of the way, but the blade grazed him even so.

Malignancy burned up the sword and into Bareris's hand, chilling and stinging him like the blast from the wand. Urhur scrambled up and reached for him. A tattoo on the back of the necromancer's hand gleamed, releasing its power, whereupon his nails grew long and jagged as the claws of a ghoul.

By the time Bareris recovered from the shock of the hurt he'd just sustained, Urhur had already lunged near enough to rend and grab, too close for the sword to be of use. Bareris dropped the weapon and caught the mage by the wrists.

They wrestled, shoving and staggering back and forth, and as they did so, the bard caught glimpses of the rest of the fight. Aoth swung his falchion, its heavy blade shining blue with enchantment, and buried it in a dread warrior's chest. The creature stumbled, and Mirror, somewhat more visible now, his shadow weapon currently shaped like Aoth's, struck it as well. Meanwhile, Chathi brandished a hand wreathed in fire, and the other undead guard collapsed before her, breaking and crumbling in the process.

Bareris thought he should be faring as well or better than his comrades. He was stronger than Urhur and a superior brawler, but he didn't dare risk even a single scratch from the wizard's nails for fear it would incapacitate him, and every time he landed a head butt or stamp to the toes, his adversary's protective aura caused the impact to pain him as well.

Urhur abruptly opened his mouth wide, revealing that his teeth, too, had grown long and pointed. He yanked Bareris close and bit at his neck. Caught by surprise, the bard just barely managed to jerk his upper body backward in time. Drops of saliva spattered him as the crooked fangs gnashed shut.

Then, however, Urhur lurched forward, and his legs buckled beneath him. Employing the pommel of his falchion as a bludgeon, Aoth clubbed the necromancer's head a second time. Urhur slumped entirely limp. Sore and weak from the punishment he'd endured, Bareris tore away the necklace of bones, depriving the Red Wizard of his defensive aura, then threw him to the ground.

Aoth's falchion glowed brighter as he released the counterspell he'd stored in the steel. Bareris abruptly heard the rasp of his own labored breathing as the spell of silence dissolved. Meanwhile, Urhur's claws and fangs melted away.

"Are you all right?" Aoth whispered.

"When this is over," Bareris replied, "I'll want the aid of a healer, but I can manage for now."

Chathi moved to the door of the tent, shifted the flap, and peeked out. "I don't think anyone's noticed anything amiss."

"Good," said Aoth. "Can you restore Urhur to his senses?"

"Most likely." She rooted in her belt pouch, produced a pewter vial, uncorked it, and held it under the Red Wizard's nose.

Urhur's eyes fluttered open, then he flailed, but to little effect. Bareris, Aoth, and Chathi were crouching all around him to hold him down and menace him with their daggers.

"Calm down," said Aoth. "You probably realize I don't like you, but my friends and I won't kill you if you answer our questions."

"You're insane," Urhur said. "You'll all die for this outrage."

Aoth smiled. "Yes, if it doesn't work out, which means we have nothing to lose. If I were you, I'd think about the implications of that."

Perhaps seeking to calm himself, Urhur took a deep breath. "Very well, I'll answer your questions. In all likelihood, I would have done so in any case. I have no secrets."

"If so," said Aoth, "you must be the only Red Wizard who can make that claim, but before we proceed, I want you to think about something. I just cast a counterspell. Bareris and Chathi are each going to do the same. I hope that if anyone has laid a magical binding on you, it will turn out that one of us has succeeded in breaking your fetters, and you can give us what we require without suffering for it."

"I have no idea what you're babbling about."

"I admit," Aoth continued, "if you do tell the truth, you'll be running a risk. We'll have no way of knowing in advance whether we've actually freed you, but I guarantee that if your responses fail to satisfy us, we'll kill you. Bareris, Chathi, do what you need to do."

Bareris sang his charm, and the priestess chanted her invocation to the Firelord.

"Now," said Aoth to the prisoner, "tell us who created the undead horde."

Urhur's eyes shifted left, then right, as if he was looking for succor. "How should I know? All anyone knows is that they came down out of the mountains."

"You're lying," said Aoth.

He clamped a hand over the necromancer's mouth, and Bareris and Chathi exerted their strength to hold him motionless. Mirror glided forward, bent down, and slid his shadowy fingertips into Urhur's torso.

It wasn't the sort of violation that broke the skin, shed blood, or made any sort of visible wound, but Urhur bucked and thrashed in agony. His body grew thinner, and new lines incised themselves on his face.

"Enough," Bareris said, and Mirror pulled his hand away.

"I'll wager," said Aoth to Urhur, "that you've unleashed ghosts and such on a good many victims in your time, but I wonder if you'd ever felt a phantom's touch yourself. It looked painful, and you look older. I wouldn't be surprised if Mirror has leeched years from your natural span. Now shall we have him tickle your guts again, or will you cooperate?"

"I don't deserve this," Urhur whimpered. "Szass Tam didn't give me a choice. When I tried to keep you from discovering too much or warning Tharchion Focar and the other captains, I didn't even understand what I was doing. I mean, not entirely. My memory's funny. It's like I'm split in two."

"Just tell us," said Aoth. "Where did the marauders come from?"

"Why do I have to say? It's plain you already know."

"We need to hear," the war mage said.

"All right, curse you. My peers made them."

"And helped them to their victories?"

"Yes!"

"What are your orders now that you and the other Red Wizards in this army are supposed to fight the nighthaunt and its primary host yourselves?"

"I—" Urhur's eyes rolled up in his head.

His back arched and his limbs jerked as the dying orc's had done. He jerked in a final great spasm that broke Chathi's grip on his arm then lay motionless with bloody foam oozing from the corner of his mouth.

The fire priestess placed her hand in front of Urhur's contorted features, feeling for his breath. After a moment, she said, "He's dead."

"Damn it," said Aoth. "I'd hoped we'd forestalled that. Obviously, we only delayed it. Still, he admitted some things. Enough, I hope, to spare us a meeting with the headsman." He looked back at the slit in the rear of the tent.

Clad in long, plain, hooded cloaks like many a common legionnaire, two figures pushed through the opening then threw back their cowls to reveal themselves as Nymia and Milsantos. The tharchions had trailed Bareris and his comrades up to the tent, then skulked outside to listen to the interrogation.

"You've done well," Milsantos said.

"They've made a filthy mess," Nymia growled. "They attacked and killed a Red Wizard, and we still don't know that the necromancers mean to betray us."

"If they don't," Bareris asked, "then why couldn't Urhur say so? Why was that the question that finally triggered the seizure?"

"I don't know," the female commander answered. "I don't pretend to comprehend all the ins and outs of wizardry, but if Szass Tam only changed his plans after the other zulkirs rebuffed him, how could he already have sent new orders to minions hundreds of miles away from Eltabbar?"

"The same way," said Milsantos, "my informants passed a message to me: magic."

"I suppose," Nymia said. "Still—"

"Still," Milsantos said, "you don't like it that we have, in effect, colluded in the murder of a Red Wizard, and you shrink from the thought of making a whole troupe of them our prisoners. So do I. I didn't come to be an old man, let alone retain my office for lo these many decades, by indulging in such practices. But we now have genuine reason to suspect the necromancers of treachery, and I won't send legionnaires into battle with such folk positioned to strike at their backs. They deserve better, and so do we. Remember, if we lose, the enemy is apt to kill us, too, and if they don't, the zulkirs might."

"Yet if we anger Szass Tam and the order of Necromancy . . . " Nymia threw up her hands. "Yes, all right, we'll do it your way, assuming we even have followers stupid enough to lay hands on Red Wizards."

Chathi smiled. "The Braziers will help you, Tharchion."

"And I," said Aoth, "know griffon riders who'll do the same."

.. ..

Malark jumped, caught the top of the high wrought-iron fence with its row of sharp points, and swung himself over without cutting himself or even snagging his clothing. He then dropped to the grass on the other side, his knees flexing to absorb the jolt.

As one of Dmitra Flass's lieutenants, he actually had no need to enter in such a fashion. He could have presented himself at the gate and waited for the watchman to appear and admit him or procured his own key, but why bother? For a man trained as a Monk of the Long Death, hopping the fence was easy as climbing a flight of stairs.

Alert and silent by habit, not because he expected trouble, he strolled onward through Eltabbar's largest cemetery. The meadows with their stone and wooden markers were peaceful after dark.

He often came here where no one could find and interrupt him to mull over one problem or another.

But tonight he found the place less soothing than formerly. The air was pleasant, neither too hot nor too cool, and perfumed with the scent of flowers. A night bird sang, and the stars shone, but the sight of so many open graves, yawning like raw wounds in the earth, offended him. Death was supposed to be an ending, but for the poor wretches interred here, it had only been a brief respite. They'd toil and struggle on through the mortal world as zombie soldiers.

Yet much as Malark deplored Thay's practice of employing such warriors, he could do nothing about it. So he scowled and resolved to put the matter out of his mind and focus instead on the puzzle he needed to unravel.

Szass Tam had manipulated events to persuade the council of zulkirs to elect him regent. His efforts had failed, yet it was plain he was still maneuvering. To what end?

Malark had reviewed all the intelligence available to him, all the secrets his agents daily risked their lives to gather, and he still had no idea. It was almost enough to discourage him, to persuade him that Szass Tam was as transcendently brilliant as everyone maintained, so cunning and devious that no other being could hope to fathom his schemes.

But Malark refused to concede that. Though he was no wizard nor, thank the gods, a lich, he was as old as Szass Tam, and his extended span had afforded him the opportunity to develop a comparable subtlety of mind. No doubt the undead necromancer possessed the power to obliterate a mere excommunicant monk with a flick of his shriveled fingers, but that didn't mean he could outthink him.

The spymaster wandered by another pair of gaping graves, which still stank of carrion even though their former occupants were gone. He'd passed quite a few such cavities in just a short while, and he suddenly wondered if anyone except Szass Tam and his followers knew how many had been opened altogether or whether all the corpses really had gone to serve Tharchions Focar and Daramos, the commanders who'd marched up the Pass of Thazar to counter a threat in the east.

He whirled and dashed back the way he'd come, meanwhile wondering if Dmitra was already asleep or amusing herself with a lover. If so, she wouldn't appreciate being disturbed, but Malark needed another flying horse, and he needed it now.

●● ●● ●● ●● ●● ●● ● ●● ●● ●● ●● ●● ●● ●●

The sky above the mountains was blue, but as one pivoted toward the Keep of Thazar, it darkened by degrees, so that the castle seemed to stand in a private pocket of night.

As yet, Aoth hadn't seen the nighthaunt or any of the undead except for a few ghouls and skeletons on the battlements, but he had little doubt the winged creature was responsible for the shroud of darkness. He recalled the boundless malevolence of the nighthaunt's blank pearly eyes, the contemptuous way it had allowed him to escape—because Szass Tam wanted news of the attack to travel, evidently—and all the horrors he'd witnessed on the night the fortress fell, and despite himself, he shivered.

His reaction annoyed him and made him wish the battle would begin. Once the waiting ended, his jitters should end with it. They always had.

Unfortunately, it wasn't time yet. First, the Burning Braziers had to complete their ritual, and unless it succeeded, the legionnaires had no hope of a successful assault.

To better survey the castle and the army arrayed before it, Aoth had ascended a hillock with Brightwing and Bareris—and Mirror too, presumably, though the spirit was entirely imperceptible at present—and so he turned to the singer.

Though bards were generally garrulous to a fault, following their interrogation of Urhur Hahpet, Bareris had lapsed into sullen taciturnity. But perhaps Aoth could draw him into a conversation. He was still curious about the man, and it would be something to occupy his mind.

"It will be a tough fight," said Aoth, "but we can win. Even without our zombies, we have a sizable army, and even without the necromancers, we have wizardry. I'm not the only war mage in the host."

Bareris grunted.

"Of course," Aoth persisted, "we wouldn't have a chance if not for you. Makes me glad you asked to fight in my company."

"Don't be. My luck is bad."

Aoth snorted. "I'd say you were damn lucky to make it out of the mountains alive, and we were lucky you turned up here when you did."

Bareris shrugged. "The gravecrawler said I still had a path to walk, and maybe this is it. Revenge. As much as I can take, for as long as I'm able."

Aoth was still trying to decide how to answer that when the ground began to shake. The Burning Braziers had warned their comrades of what to expect, but some of the soldiers standing in formation in front of the castle cried out anyway.

"This is it," Aoth said.

He swung himself onto Brightwing's back, and the griffon beat her wings and soared into the air. Bareris trotted to join the axemen he intended to fight among.

The tremors intensified, and men-at-arms on the ground crouched to avoid being knocked down. Riders and grooms struggled to control frightened horses. Trees lashed back and forth, and stones rolled clattering down the mountainsides, until something huge and bright burst from the empty stretch of ground between the Keep of Thazar and the besieging army.

At first an observer could have mistaken it for a simple eruption of lava. Then, however, it heaved itself higher, and the contours of a lump of a head; a thick, flailing arm; and a hand with four stubby fingers became apparent.

Tall and massive as one of the castle towers, the searing heat of it perceptible even from far away, the colossal elemental finished dragging itself up out of the ground then clambered unsteadily onto its broad, toeless feet. Some of the legionnaires shrank from the terrifying spectacle. Others, remembering that this was supposed to happen, cheered.

Aoth thought the mystical feat deserved acclamation. Had the Burning Braziers summoned and bound a fire elemental big as a spire, that would have been impressive enough. But such an entity, formidable as it was, lacked the solidity required for the task at hand, so the clerics had opted for a spirit whose nature blended the hunger of flame with the weight of stone. That almost certainly made the magic more difficult for them, given that they lacked any special affinity for the element of earth, yet they'd managed nonetheless.

Its tread shaking the earth, the giant advanced to the castle wall, took hold of a row of merlons at the top, and ripped away a chunk of the battlements. It tossed the fragment of stone and masonry inside the fortress—to crush some of the enemy, Aoth hoped—and gripped the wall once more.

Ghouls came running and skin kites soared, to leap and plaster themselves onto the elemental like fleas and mosquitoes attaching themselves to a man. The colossus didn't even seem to notice, and the heat of its luminous body charred them to nothing.

Unfortunately, that didn't mean the behemoth would prove impervious to the efforts of ghosts and spellcasters. The former might be able to leech the life from it, and the latter to break the priests' control over it or send it back to its native level of existence. The Thayan archers and crossbowmen on the ground shot their missiles at any such foe that showed itself on the battlements. Aoth's fellow war mages hurled thunderbolts and fire.

No one with sense would position himself in front of such a barrage or anywhere close, but somebody needed to peer down inside the castle courtyards and counter whatever mischief was happening there. Aoth urged Brightwing higher, and other griffon riders followed his lead. He hoped that if they flew high enough, no stray attack from their own side would hit them.

"If I do catch an arrow in the guts," said Brightwing, discerning the essence of his thoughts, "you'll know when we both plummet to our deaths."

"Put your mind at ease," Aoth replied. "I have a spell of slow falling ready for the casting. Whatever awfulness happens to you, your beloved master will fare all right."

Brightwing laughed.

They raced into the pocket of darkness. Zombies shot crossbows at them, but the bolts flew wild. Brightwing streaked over the curtain wall, and as Aoth had anticipated, live wizards, gathered in circles, were chanting on the ground below. They'd forsaken red robes for nondescript garments, but they no doubt belonged to the order of Necromancy nonetheless.

Aoth prepared a blast of fire to keep them from interfering with the elemental, but wraiths flew up at him, and he had to use the magic to incinerate them instead. Fortunately, his fellow griffon riders, adept at hitting a mark even from the back of a flying steed, harried the necromancers with arrows. Meanwhile, stone crunched and crashed as the magma giant continued to demolish the exterior wall.

Aoth cast spell after spell, more than he liked with so much fighting still to come, but if he and his allies failed to protect the elemental until it completed its work, it wouldn't matter how much magic remained to him. Phantoms and necromancers perished, or abandoning their efforts to stop the giant, bolted for cover.

Brightwing wheeled and dived. Arrows loosed by their own allies streaked past her and Aoth, but he saw that she was right to risk that particular hazard in order to respond to a greater one. Possibly cloaked in enchantments that armored them against common missiles, two necromancers had ascended the battlements. Chanting and whirling their hands in mystic passes, they were glaring not at the elemental but at the war mage and his familiar.

Aoth doubted that he could have cast any of his own attack magic before they completed their incantations, but Brightwing reached them in time. Her outstretched talons punched into the torso of the necromancer on the left, while her wing knocked the one on the right off the wall-walk to drop, thud, and lay motionless on the ground below.

The griffon beat her wings, gaining altitude once more. "I guess he didn't have a charm of slow falling."

"Apparently not," Aoth said.

Then Brightwing lifted one wing, dipped the other, and turned, affording him a fresh view of the fortress, and he felt a reflexive pang of dread.

The nighthaunt had appeared atop the flat, rectangular roof of the central citadel, and despite its apparent lack of a mouth, was attempting magic of its own. Aoth couldn't understand the words of the incantation, but he could hear them inside his mind. Indeed, they pained him like throbs of headache. His fellow griffon riders, those who were still alive, assailed the creature with arrows, but the shafts glanced off its dead black form.

Meanwhile, the elemental was moving more slowly, as if in pain. Glowing chunks of it flaked and sheared away to shatter on the ground.

Aoth hurled lightning at the nighthaunt, but that didn't seem to bother it any more than the arrows. For a moment, he was grimly certain the demonic entity would succeed in destroying the elemental before the latter could break down enough wall to do any good.

But enraged by its agonies, perhaps, the disintegrating giant balled its hands into fists and hammered the stonework repeatedly, then flung its entire body at the barrier as if it were a battering ram. The entity and a broad section of wall smashed into fragments together.

Aoth scrutinized the breach then smiled. He and his allies had hoped the elemental would demolish the entire wall. Due to the nighthaunt's interference, that hadn't happened, but the opening was wide enough for an attacking army to enter in strength, not just a vulnerable few at a time.

The Thayan force cheered. Aoth and the other griffon riders wheeled their mounts and retreated to join their comrades. There was no longer any need to linger in a highly exposed and dangerous position directly above the castle.

It was Aoth's duty to return to his command, but he detoured to set down among the Burning Braziers and the monks who were their bodyguards. He cast about, spied Chathi sitting on the ground, slid off Brightwing, and strode to the fire priestess.

She rose to meet him. Her fire-scarred face was sweaty, with a gray cast to the skin.

"Are you all right?" he asked.

"Fine," she said. "It's just that the ritual was taxing, particularly once the nighthaunt tried to oppose us."

"If you aren't fit to fight, you've done plenty already." Even as the words left his mouth, he knew how she'd respond.

"I'm a Burning Brazier. I still have magic to cast, and there's a battle to be won. Of course I'm going to fight!"

"Of course. Just be careful." He wished she still served as a member of his company, where he could better keep an eye on her, but now that the army had reunited, the servants of Kossuth constituted their own unit.

Chathi rolled her eyes. "Yes, Mother. Now go do your job and I'll do mine."

He wanted to kiss her, but it would be inappropriate with others looking on. He touched her forearm in its covering of mail then returned to Brightwing.

As the griffon sprang into the air, she asked, "Are you worried about the priestess for any special reason?"

Aoth sighed. "I suppose not."

"Then that makes it all the more pathetic."

It didn't take Aoth, or any of the officers, long to arrange their companies to their satisfaction. The common legionnaires already knew their parts in the battle plan. Wizards conjured blasts of frost and showers of hail to cool the red-hot scatter of debris that would otherwise obstruct the way, and then the army advanced. Aoth and Brightwing took to the sky once more.

The Thayans proceeded warily. Archers shot at any foe that showed itself on the remaining battlements. Mages cast flares of fire and clerics, pulses of divine power through the breach, in hopes of smiting any creature lying in wait just out of sight on the other side.

Aoth and Brightwing flew over the wall, and spears leveled and shields locked, the first warriors passed through the breach. Rather to the mage's surprise, at first nothing appeared to oppose their progress, but once a substantial portion of their force had entered, undead exploded from the doors and windows of nearby buildings. Others came racing down the unnaturally benighted lanes leading to the central redoubt or rose over the rooftops. The invaders raised their weapons against the threat.

Surrounded by their floating, luminous runes, quells suddenly materialized among the largest formation of fire priests, but the guardian monks assailed the creatures with glowing batons and blazing swords and hammered, slashed, and burned the apparitions out of existence. With that threat eliminated, the senior cleric barked a command, and moving as one, the Braziers extended their scarlet metal torches.

Weapons, Aoth suddenly recalled, that Szass Tam had supplied. If the Red Wizards in their company had been poised to betray them, could they rely on these particular devices?

He shouted for the priests not to discharge the torches, but the cacophony of battle was already deafening. Bows groaned and flights of arrows thrummed. Shields crashed as animate corpses hurled themselves against them. Officers bellowed orders, and legionnaires yelled war cries, called for help, or screamed in agony. Nobody noticed one more voice clamoring from overhead.

The red rods exploded in their wielders' hands, flowering into orbs of flame big and hot enough to incinerate the clerics, the monks hovering protectively around them, and any legionnaire unlucky enough to be standing adjacent to the servants of Kossuth. Aoth picked out Chathi an instant before she attempted to use her weapon. She vanished in a flare of yellow, and when that faded a heartbeat later, nothing at all remained.

My fault, thought Aoth, abruptly sick to his stomach. I knew where the torches came from. Why didn't I think to suspect them before?

Startled, warriors pivoted in the direction of the bursts of flame, then stared aghast as they realized that the majority of the priests, invaluable allies against the undead and an integral part of the tharchions' strategy, were gone. The shadows and skeletons hurled themselves at the living with renewed fury.

•• •• •• •• •• •• •• •• •• •• •• ••

Singing, the war chant audible even over the ambient din, Bareris sidestepped a blow from a zombie's flail, riposted with a thrust to the torso, and the gray, rot-speckled creature collapsed. Around him, Mirror—still just a gleaming shadow but more clearly visible than the bard had seen him hitherto—and Aoth's axemen hacked down their own opponents. Bareris knew his battle anthem was feeding vigor and courage to his mortal allies. Perhaps even the ghost derived some benefit.

The Binder knew, they could use all the magical help they could get. Half their troops were still outside the wall, and those who'd already entered were jammed together in a space too small for them to deploy to best advantage. Assuming they survived this initial counterattack, they'd need to battle their way up the relatively narrow streets before assaulting the actual keep at the center of the fortress. As Bareris knew from past experience, that sort of combat was always arduous and apt to exact a heavy toll in lives.

Still, he judged the tharchions were correct. Their plan could work, and the knowledge of that didn't so much assuage as counterbalance the guilt and despair that engulfed him whenever he thought of Tammith. Accordingly, he fought hard, thankful for those moments when the exigencies of combat focused his entire mind on the next cut or parry, more than willing to die to help wreck the necromancers' schemes.

Then yellow light flared behind him, painting the curtain wall and buildings with its glow. He glanced back and saw the empty space a good many of the Firelord's servants had occupied only a moment before. Nothing remained of them but scraps of hot, twisted metal and wisps of floating ash.

Farther away, another contingent of Burning Braziers aimed their torches at the phantoms flying down at them like owls diving at mice. Perhaps, their attention locked on the imminent threat, they hadn't even noticed what had just happened to their fellows. The red metal rods exploded and they perished instantly, slain by the same force to which they'd consecrated their existences.

Bareris suspected that with the priests lost, the battle was almost certainly lost. All he and his comrades could do was attempt to destroy as many of the enemy as possible before the creatures slaughtered them in their turn.

So he struck blow after blow, splintering skeletons and hacking shambling cadavers to pieces, until Aoth and Brightwing plunged to earth in front of him. The griffon's talons impaled the ghoul Bareris had been about to attack, and her weight crushed the false life out of it.

When he saw the war mage, Bareris realized that in all probability, he wasn't the only one who'd lost a woman he loved. "Chathi?" he asked.

Aoth scowled. "Never mind that. Get on."

"What—"

"Do it!"

Bareris clambered up behind the legionnaire. Brightwing instantly leaped back into the air, nearly unseating him. Mirror floated upward to soar alongside his living comrades.

"After the priests burned to death," said Aoth, "Tharchion Daramos waved me down. I'm a galloper now, a messenger. Nobody on the ground could push through this press, but Brightwing can carry me over it."

"What's that got to do with me?"

"I can reach the folk I need to reach, but it's hard to make them hear me over all the noise unless I waste time setting down, but you're a bard with magic in your voice. They'll hear you."

"Fine. Just tell me what to say."

Bareris soon discovered that hurtling back and forth above the battle was no less perilous than fighting on the ground. Skeletal archers loosed shafts at them, and necromancers hurled chilling blasts of shadow. Wraiths soared to intercept them. Brightwing veered, swooped, and climbed, dodging the attacks. Aoth struck back with darts of amber light evoked from the head of his lance. Bareris and Mirror slashed at any foe that flew within reach of their blades.

Meanwhile, they delivered the tharchion's orders: The legionnaires must protect the surviving priests—servants of gods other than Kossuth, mostly, who'd served with the armies of Pyarados and Thazalhar since before the Burning Braziers arrived to lend their strength—and wizards at all costs. Difficult though it would be, the soldiers also needed to push forward to make room for the rest of their comrades to enter the fortress. Archers were to find their way to upper-story windows and rooftops, where they could target the enemy without the ranks of their own comrades obscuring their lines of sight. Thayans with mystical capabilities, be they arcane, deity-granted, or arising simply from the possession of an enchanted weapon, must concentrate their efforts on the specters and any other enemy essentially immune to common steel.

To Bareris's surprise, their efforts made a difference. The startling destruction of the fire priests had thrown the army into confusion, if not to the brink of panic and collapse, but Milsantos's commands were sound. By degrees, they reestablished order and valid tactics. Even more importantly, perhaps, they rallied the legionnaires by reminding them that a highly competent war leader was still directing the assault. The battle wasn't over yet.

Bareris, though, still believed it was nearly over. His comrades, humans and screaming blood orcs alike, were fighting like devils, but they were also steadily dying, in some cases to rise mere moments later and join the enemy host.

The gallopers finished delivering Milsantos's current list of orders and flew back for a new one. Broadsword in hand, the gilt runes on his plate armor and kite shield glowing, affording him the benefit of their enchantments, the aged warrior had stationed himself atop a portion of the surviving walls, the better to oversee the battle. Nymia had joined him on his perch. Bareris winced to see both commanders occupying the same exposed position, but at least they had a fair number of guards and spellcasters clustered around to protect them, and there was little safety to be had anywhere in any case.

Brightwing furled her pinions and lit on the wall-walk, while Mirror simply hovered off to the side. Aoth saluted with a flourish of his lance and rattled off the messages from the officers on the ground.

His features grim inside his open helm, Milsantos acknowledged them with a brusque nod. "Based on what you've seen flying over the battle, what's your impression?"

"We're losing," said Aoth.

"Yes," said Milsantos, "I think so too."

"We could handle the ghouls and dread warriors," Nymia said. Slime caked her mace and weapon arm, proof that at some point, she'd needed to fight her way to the battlements. "It's the ghosts and such that are killing us, and they'd be powerless if the sun were shining." She gave one of the mages a glare.

The warlock spread hands stained and gritty with the liquids and powders he used to cast his spells. "Tharchion, we've tried our best to dispel the gloom."

"But the nighthaunt's magic is too strong," Bareris said. "What if we kill the thing? Would that weaken the enchantment?"

"It might," said the mage.

"Let's do it then."

Nymia sneered. "Obviously, we'd kill it if we could. It's what we came to do, but we lost sight of it just after the elemental broke the wall. It isn't fighting in the thick of the battle any more than Tharchion Daramos and I are."

"Then we draw it out," Milsantos said, "using ourselves as bait. You and I descend from these battlements, forsaking the wards the mages cast to protect us. We mount our horses, and with a relatively small band of followers, break through the ranks of the enemy. Then we charge toward the central keep as though in a final desperate, defiant attempt to challenge the power that holds it." He smiled crookedly. "You know, chivalry. The kind of idiocy that loses battles and gets warriors killed."

"As it would this time," Nymia said.

"Maybe yes, maybe no. We'll ride with our best fighters and battle mages. The wizards will enhance our capabilities with enchantment, and we'll hope that when the nighthaunt spies us looking vulnerable, cut off by virtue of our own stupidity from most of our followers, it will come to fight us itself. It's a demon, isn't it, or near enough. It must *like* killing with its own hands, and it must particularly hanker to slay us. Once it does, it's won.

"Of course," the old man continued, "even if it does reveal itself, it won't be alone, but we'll use every trick we know and every scroll and talisman we've hoarded over the years, and whatever else threatens us, we'll all do our utmost to strike it down."

Nymia shook her head. "Commit suicide if you like, but I won't join you."

"It needs to be both of us," Milsantos said, "to bait the trap as enticingly as possible. Consider that we're not likely to leave this place alive in any case. Would you rather stand before your god as victor or vanquished? Imagine, too, your fate if you did escape but abandoned the zulkirs' legions to perish. The council would punish you in ways that would make you wish a nighthaunt had merely torn you apart."

"All right," Nymia sighed. "We'll do it, with Aoth and a goodly number of the other griffon riders flying overhead to fend off threats from the air."

"I'm coming," said Bareris, and to his relief, neither of the tharchions objected.

He then had to scramble to commandeer a destrier. He knew how to fight on horseback and assumed he'd be of more use doing so than clinging to Brightwing's rump.

Once in the saddle, he crooned to his new mount, a chestnut gelding, establishing a rapport and buttressing its courage. Meanwhile, Aoth delivered orders. Soldiers and spellcasters shifted about, positioning themselves for the action to come.

Milsantos nodded to the aide riding beside him, and the young knight blew a signal on his horn. As one, bowmen shot whistling volleys of arrows into the mass of undead clogging one particular street. Wizards assailed the same creatures with blazes of flame and lightning, while the remaining priests hammered them with the palpable force of their faith.

The trumpeter sounded another call. The barrage ended. The men-at-arms holding the mouth of the street drew apart, clearing a path. Astride a black charger, its barding aglow with some of the same golden sigils adorning his plate, Milsantos dropped his lance into fighting position. Others in the company he'd assembled did the same, then they all charged up the corridor.

The barrage just concluded had thinned out the undead blocking the way and left the survivors reeling. The charge slammed into the creatures, and spears punched through their bodies. The horses knocked zombies and skeletons down, and their pounding hooves pulped and shattered them.

Still, foes remained, and undaunted by the annihilation of so many of their fellows, they attempted to drag the riders and their mounts down. No lancer—despite his career as a mercenary, he'd never had the opportunity to master that particular weapon— Bareris slashed at his decaying, skull-faced assailants with his sword and urged his horse onward. The riders had to keep moving or their plan would fail almost before it had begun.

A ghoul slashed Bareris's horse's shoulder with its long, dirty claws, and the animal lurched off balance. Fearful that the virulence of the undead creature's touch had paralyzed his steed, the bard riposted with a head cut. The ghoul fell, and not crippled after all, the destrier regained its footing and raced onward.

Overhead, griffons screeched, men shouted, and magic boomed and crackled. Plastered with writhing skin kites, a winged steed and its master crashed on a roof, tumbled down the pitch, and dropped in a heap in the street. Bareris looked to see if it was Aoth and Brightwing who'd fallen—it wasn't—but otherwise didn't even glance at the portion of the fight raging in the air. He didn't dare divert his attention from his own assailants.

He hacked a skeleton's skull off the top of its spine, felt more than saw a lunging shadow, and obliterated it with a thrust. Then, suddenly, no foes remained within reach of his blade. He peered about and saw that he and his companions had fought their way clear.

They galloped onward. Skillful enough to sound his instrument even astride a running horse, Milsantos's trumpeter blew more calls on his horn. His efforts were supposed to create the impression that the riders were signaling the bulk of the army they'd just left behind to enable the two forces to act in concert, to make the nighthaunt worry that the tharchions were well on the way to the culmination of some cunning strategy, even if it wasn't apparent what it was, and that their adversaries had better act swiftly to balk them.

In Bareris's judgment, it wasn't an entirely preposterous notion. Plainly their company could do *some* damage if left unopposed to maneuver and strike at the rear of the undead host, and even if the nighthaunt wasn't concerned about that, they could still hope their manifest vulnerability would draw it out into the open.

One of the griffon riders yelled, "There!"

Bareris looked up, saw the nighthaunt staring down at him from the battlements atop the gate of the central keep, and immediately comprehended why even a veteran war mage like Aoth feared the dead black, pale-eyed monstrosity. Though its mere presence didn't poison a man like Xingax's could—at least not at this distance—it nonetheless seemed the very embodiment of boundless power wed to unrelenting, all-encompassing hatred. A man could scarcely bear to look at it, and at the same time, transfixed with dread, he found it all but impossible to tear his gaze away. Wings ragged and peeling, body oozing slime, a larger and even more hideous creature stood beside the leader of the undead marauders, while luminous shades hovered in the air behind it, but in that first terrible moment, Bareris scarcely even registered their existence.

"Halt!" shouted Milsantos, and for the most part, the Thayan horsemen obeyed. They had no need to ride farther now that the nighthaunt had appeared, but two men, their nerve breaking, wheeled and fled back the way they'd come.

Tharchions, the nighthaunt said, his silent psychic voice beating at Bareris's mind like a bludgeon. *My name is Ysval. You fight well but have no hope of winning. Yield and I'll spare you, not to continue precisely as you are, but you and your captains at least will retain your essential identities.*

"No," Milsantos said. "The council of zulkirs ordered us to destroy you, and that's what we intend to do."

I hoped you'd answer thusly, Ysval said.

He lashed his wings and hurtled down into the midst of his foes. Trained war-horses screamed and shied. The nighthaunt tore one animal's head off with a swipe of his talons. Blood sprayed from the end of the shredded neck. The wraiths followed their captain toward their mortal foes.

In response, some of the battle mages aimed wands or rattled off incantations. Priests brandished the symbols of their faiths and cried the names of their gods. Flares of power, some visible, some not, flung some specters backward like leaves in a gale and seared others from existence.

Other spellcasters read the trigger phrases from scrolls. Walls of roaring fire and shimmering light sprang up around the horsemen, some at ground level, others floating in midair. Unfortunately, they weren't large and numerous enough to overlap and enclose the riders completely. Wraiths could and no doubt would slip through the gaps between barriers, but at least they'd no longer find it possible to overwhelm their opponents in a single onrushing, irresistible swarm.

In theory, that should leave the majority of the Thayans free to focus on Ysval and the relatively small number of lesser undead that had succeeded in closing before the magical barriers sprang into existence. No doubt recognizing that he'd blundered into a snare, the nighthaunt stopped lashing out with claw and tail and simply stood for a moment. Bareris surmised the creature was trying to shift himself to the safety of another level of existence, but nothing happened. Studying ancient texts, the enchanters had discovered that nighthaunts possessed that particular ability, and one of them had already cast a spell to keep him from exploiting it.

Ysval laughed. *Well done, but it won't save you. I could kill the lot of you all by myself if necessary.* He shook his fist and enormous hailstones hammered from the air, ringing on the armor of the foes in front of him.

Bareris sang a charm and urged his reluctant mount closer to Ysval. Then the horse thrashed and toppled. Bareris kicked his feet from the stirrups, flung himself out of the saddle, and though he landed hard, just managed to keep the animal's weight from smashing down on top of his leg.

He scrambled to his feet and found himself facing Tammith across the steed's still-shuddering carcass.

Tammith felt as if she'd been split into two creatures. One had struggled with all her strength to turn away from Bareris, and if she couldn't flee the battle altogether at least kill other people instead. But the other, demonic and perverse, lusted to destroy him precisely because she'd loved him her whole life long, and that Tammith proved the stronger. Reveling in her newly acquired strength, she leaped from the rooftop where she'd been lurking, hoping to drop on a horseman as he rode by, rushed Bareris's mount, and bit a chunk of flesh from the underside of its neck, all before he even realized she was there. The charger fell, and she hoped he'd wind up stuck underneath it. If so, he'd be helpless. Easy prey.

But he threw himself clear, rose, and his eyes widened at the sight of her. She spat out the wad of gory horseflesh in her mouth, and that made his dear, handsome features twist. To her, with her divided psyche, his horror and grief were simultaneously excruciating and the funniest thing she'd ever seen.

"Are you still going to rescue me?" she asked, grinning.

"Yes," he said. "If it can be done, I'll do it. Just give me the chance. Don't make me hurt you."

"You're right," she said, "we mustn't fight. No matter what happens or what I've become, we mustn't hurt one another." She turned away from him, then instantly spun back around and leaped over the body of the horse.

Though she'd believed her deception persuasive, he was ready to receive her attack. Even so, her outstretched hands nearly grabbed him, but with a quickness that suggested he was employing his charm of speed, he sidestepped and slashed open her belly in almost the same place where he'd wounded her before.

It hurt. Her guts started to slide through the rent, and doubling over, she clutched at herself to hold them in. She swayed and fell onto her side.

This time, her pretense was evidently more convincing, for with a seasoned warrior's caution, Bareris then looked about, checking for any foes that might have crept up on him while he was busy with her. He believed her incapacitated, and why shouldn't he? The same sort of injury had neutralized her before.

But as Xingax had promised, she grew stronger every day, and as a result, she healed more rapidly. As soon as Bareris turned his head, she flowed to her feet and pounced at him.

Darts of golden light streaked down from overhead to stab into her body and make her falter. A deep male voice bellowed, "Behind you!" Bareris pivoted, and as she lunged, he extended his sword. She stopped just short of the point, sprang back, and started shifting back and forth, trying to confuse him and create an opening. Her predatory instincts instructed her in the proper way to feint and glide.

She wasn't fooling Bareris. He was too canny. She stood still, stared into his eyes, and tried to catch and crush his will, but that didn't work either. In fact, as soon as she made herself a stationary target, he ran at her and slashed her leg out from underneath her.

She fell. He stopped, turned, and hesitated. When he cut at her spine, she understood that he'd been trying to calculate how best to incapacitate her without destroying her. The slight pause gave her time to explode into a flock of bats.

With her consciousness divided among her various bodies, her humanity, or what remained of it, diffused along with it, and her need to kill Bareris became as pure as it was profound. She nearly succumbed to the urge to attack.

Nearly, but not quite, because though conscience and mercy were gone, memory remained, and she recalled that he knew a song to repel her in this guise. The bats flew several yards beyond his reach, swirled around one another, and coalesced into her womanly form once more. Her gashed leg throbbed as it took her weight but didn't give way. It was mostly healed already.

She hobbled toward him, trying to make it appear that her damaged limb was weaker than it was. He swung his sword into a low guard, and she noticed he wasn't singing. Just as he was too averse to fighting her to attempt a killing blow, so too was he neglecting to exploit his magic to best advantage.

In effect, that meant he'd already surrendered, for half measures couldn't save him. He was forcing her to murder him, to carry the resulting anguish through all the years of her endless undead existence, and his weakness and selfishness enraged her. She rushed him, his sword whirled up to threaten her, and she sprang at him anyway. The blade sheared into her side, but not enough to balk her. She slammed into him and carried him to the ground beneath her.

He gasped at the grip of her hands, cold and poisonous as any specter's touch. She could have leeched the life from him through that contact, but it wouldn't be as satisfying as draining his blood. Grappling, seeking to immobilize him, she opened her mouth to bite.

Bareris bellowed up into her face, and the thunderous sound seared her like a blast of fire. The world went black, and the sudden pain made her fumble her grip on her prey. Bareris shoved her and heaved himself out from underneath her.

Her sight began to restore itself after a moment, but the world remained a blurry, murky place. Still, she could make out Bareris scrambling to his feet, and her ruined face hanging in tatters from her skull, she jumped up to attack him once again.

He started chanting, and she laughed to hear it. Good, she thought, you understand now. I'm not your beloved anymore.

I'm unclean, foul, and a slave to creatures fouler still. Please, please, destroy me if you can.

Meanwhile, she strove to strike, seize, and bite him as relentlessly as ever. Her throat burned with thirst.

His magic shrouded him in a misty vagueness that made it even more difficult for her half-blind eyes to pick him out. Still, she thought she'd judged where he was and sprang to grab hold of him.

He twisted away, avoiding her touch and leaving her floundering off balance for just an instant, time enough for his sword to leap at her neck. He bellowed a war cry as it sheared into her flesh and the bone underneath.

The world seemed to jump, and then she was on the ground, her right profile pressed against the dirt. She tried to rise but couldn't move. A long shape sprawled in front of her, and after a moment she recognized her own decapitated body.

The realization stunned her. It was so quick, she thought. After she and Bareris had fought so hard, so intimately, it didn't seem real that a single sudden cut had ended everything.

Looming over her like a giant, weeping, Bareris stepped between her and her body. He raised his sword over his head.

•• •• •• • •• •• •• •• •• •• •• •• •• ••

Mirror had a sense that he was supposed to engage Ysval if possible. Had someone so instructed him? He couldn't recall, but it seemed right. He strode toward the ink-black creature and the legionnaires who were fighting the thing already. A different warrior called out to him, but like so many things, the words simply failed to convey any meaning.

In another moment, however, a second voice, a soft, insinuating baritone, snagged him and pulled him around to face a man wrapped in a hooded gray mantle. The speaker was alive, but even so, Mirror discerned without knowing or wondering how he knew that he was one of the enemy, likely a warlock who'd employed magic to avoid detection hitherto.

The mage swirled his hands through mystic passes. "You're undead," he crooned. "You belong on our side."

Mirror felt something changing inside him. Like any sensation, it was seductive, simply because it filled the emptiness, but even so, it seemed to him that he shouldn't allow it to continue. He sprang at the wizard, closing the distance with one prodigious leap, and drove his sword into the man's chest. To his vague disappointment, the weapon didn't cleave flesh or spill blood like a proper blade, but it did stop the mage's heart.

Mirror pivoted back toward Ysval and observed another horror battling its way toward the nighthaunt. Tall as an ogre, approximately female in form, the winged, leprous entity ravaged men and horses with her talons, shredding them and rotting their flesh with gangrene all in an instant. Even the liquid filth streaming from her open sores was dangerous, blistering any living creature it touched.

Mirror abruptly recalled that such abominations were known as angels of decay. He thought he might have encountered one on a different battleground but couldn't actually remember.

In any case, the sight of her sharpened his awareness of the battle as a whole, and he recognized what a mistake it would be to allow her and Ysval to stand together. The nighthaunt was already holding his own against the men-at-arms and battle mages assailing him from all sides. If such a formidable comrade came to his aid, the mortals would have no chance at all.

Fortunately, Mirror thought he could prevent that. Though he dimly recalled someone calling him "undead" at some point in the past, he didn't know if he truly was or not, but instinct whispered that neither the angel's infectious touch nor her slather of corrosive muck had any power to harm him.

He flew at her and cut at her flank. Lightning-quick, she twisted out of the way and slashed with her talons. The first blow somehow streaked harmlessly through him, but he sensed that the next one would smash and tear, and he raised his arm to intercept it. As he started the motion, he wore no shield, but by the time he finished, there it was, round and affixed to his forearm by three sturdy straps. He knew it should have a coat-of-arms painted on the front and momentarily longed to view it.

He couldn't, of course, not while he was fighting. The angel's talons slammed into the targe and knocked him backward. Seeking to deny him time to recover, the creature lunged after him. Flinging spatters of slime, her flaking wing swatted him and sent him reeling farther.

He thought that would likely prove the end of him, but strangely, a simple exertion of will served to halt his flailing stagger and restore his equilibrium, as if he had no weight at all. He thrust at the angel, caught her by surprise, and his shadowy blade slid deep into her cankerous torso.

She cried out in her rasping voice, stumbled, but she didn't fall. He pulled his sword back, and they traded blows. Sometimes she evaded his strokes and sometimes they sheared into her, albeit without leaving a mark thereafter. At certain moments, her talons whizzed harmlessly through him, at others, his shield or plate defected them, and occasionally, they slashed him. Then he experienced a shock that was less pain than an upheaval of the elements of his being. The aching hollow at his core yawned wide, threatening to swallow everything else.

It was difficult to tell how many times the angel needed to wound him before that would actually happen, just as it was hard to judge how badly he was hurting her. He truly had no idea who was winning until she suddenly pitched forward. Her corpse liquefied completely almost before it splashed facedown in the street.

Victory over such a formidable foe filled him with triumph, and intense emotion sharpened and deepened his thoughts. He sensed that he'd fought many times, and war remained his proper occupation. It might not ever make him remember, but at least while embroiled in the midst of it he comprehended there was something he'd forgotten.

He flew at Ysval.

•• •• •• •• •• •• •• •• •• •• •• •• •• ••

Bareris's hand was steady as he hacked open Tammith's severed head to cut the brain within, then he slid his enchanted blade into her heart. He felt as numb and empty of feeling as any of the zombies he'd faced this day.

As soon as he finished, however, he started to shake, and anguish and self-loathing welled up inside him.

At the end, he'd had no choice but to slay Tammith. Otherwise, she would certainly have killed him, and as it turned out, it simply hadn't been in him to surrender to that.

He'd likewise deemed it necessary to desecrate Tammith's remains, lest she rise to fight anew. Yet he now understood that such an act, however essential, could be unbearable and unforgivable as well.

It would be the easiest thing in the world to run his sword into his own heart.

But that would mean abandoning the fight to defeat Xingax, Ysval, and the necromancers, and that was unacceptable. The wretches had to be punished. They had to lose and suffer and die.

Singing a pledge of vengeance, he cast about to see where Ysval was.

•• •• •• •• •• •• •• •• •• •• •• •• •• ••

Aoth thrust the point of his lance into a shadow. The phantom frayed into tatters of darkness.

The ghosts were coming faster now, more and more of them finding their way through the gaps in the sheets of flame and planes of radiance the wizards had conjured to hold them back. Aoth and his fellow griffon riders fought doggedly to keep the spirits in the air from flying down to aid their commander.

He looked around and realized that at last the battle had granted him and Brightwing a moment to catch their breaths. No new foes had yet appeared in their immediate vicinity. It gave him a chance to peer down and assess what was happening on the ground.

Ysval clawed. Milsantos caught the blow on his shield, but the impact knocked him out of the saddle. The nighthaunt virtually tore the old man's war-horse out of his way as if it were a curtain and lunged after him, but in so doing, the undead captain exposed his flank to Bareris, who, chanting, slashed the creature's night black body with his sword. As did Mirror, flitting around to attack from behind. Ysval faltered, and Milsantos clambered to his feet.

Ysval pivoted and drove his talons into Mirror's chest. The ghost's misty form writhed and boiled. Ysval raised his other hand for a follow-up blow. Bareris cut at him but failed to divert the nighthaunt from his fellow undead.

Then, however, a colossal spider, gnashing mandibles dripping venom, ring of eyes gleaming, materialized beside Ysval. One of Aoth's fellow battle wizards had evidently summoned it. The spider pounced on the shadowy entity. The serrated jaws ripped him.

Ysval tore the creature off him and smashed it down on its back. As it started to heave itself upright, he thrust out his hand at it, malign power shivered through the air, and the arachnid stopped moving.

But Mirror's form once more appeared as steady and stable as it ever did, and as Ysval finished with the spider, Nymia rode by him and bashed him with her mace.

We're like a swarm of wasps attacking a man, Aoth thought. Individually, we're puny in comparison, but it's hard for him to defend himself against all of us at once.

Perhaps, his arrogance and manifest fury notwithstanding, Ysval also believed his foes might ultimately overwhelm him, for he brandished his fist, and ragged tendrils of shadow blazed outward from his body. His opponents stumbled and reeled. He lashed out with claw and tail, flinging them backward, giving himself room to spread his wings and spring into the air.

No, thought Aoth, you don't get to break away and work your magic without interference. You have to stay on the ground where everyone can pound on you.

"Get him," he said, and Brightwing dived.

Ysval heard or sensed them coming and turned to face them. When he met the gaze of the nighthaunt's moon white eyes, Aoth felt a jolt of dread, and angry at his reaction, he promised himself it was the last time. One way or another, this filthy thing was never going to scare him again.

Then Brightwing froze. Thanks to their psychic bond, Aoth could tell his familiar was still alive and conscious. Indeed, she wasn't even wounded, but Ysval had somehow paralyzed her, and now she wasn't swooping but falling. The nighthaunt laughed.

Why shouldn't he? Now that the griffon couldn't shift her wings, her plummeting trajectory wouldn't take her and Aoth within reach of him.

Aoth charged his lance with all the power it could hold then hurled it like a javelin. The long, heavy weapon wasn't designed for use as a missile, but perhaps some god sharpened his eye and strengthened his arm, maybe Kossuth, avenging the treacherous murder of his Burning Braziers, because the spear plunged into Ysval's shoulder.

To how much effect, it was impossible to say, because Aoth and Brightwing fell past him an instant later. The mage started rattling off a counterspell that might, if poor Chathi's patron deity saw fit to grant a second boon, cleanse the griffon's clenched muscles of their affliction.

Unfortunately, Aoth didn't have time to finish. He and Brightwing slammed down hard on a rooftop, which crunched and buckled beneath them but didn't give way entirely.

The impact spiked pain up the length of his body, but rather to his surprise, he survived it, and Brightwing did too. He could only assume that, despite her paralysis, her wings had caught enough air to keep them from falling at maximum speed.

Some yards away, Ysval crashed onto the street with the lance still sticking out of his body. He immediately sought to scramble to his feet, so obviously neither the spear nor the fall had killed him, but as Aoth had hoped, the injury to his shoulder had at least deprived him of the use of his wings.

Evidently recovered from the stunning effect of the burst of shadow, Bareris and Mirror rushed Ysval and cut at him relentlessly. The nighthaunt managed one more snatch with his talons and a final strike with his tail then toppled onto his side and lay motionless.

•• •• •• •• •• •• •• •• •• •• •• •• ••

Some part of Bareris realized Ysval was dead. Nonetheless, he couldn't stop hacking at the corpse, not until a phantom streaked across his field of vision and tore a knight from the saddle.

Bareris looked up. Having existed for their allotted span, the floating barriers had begun to wink out of existence, and the ghosts were rushing through the openings, swarming on the griffon riders like soft, gleaming leeches attacking a party of swimmers.

The plan indicated that as soon as Ysval died, someone

who possessed the necessary magic was supposed to dispel the unnatural gloom enveloping the fortress. It didn't seem to be happening. Was any of that select group of spellcasters still alive? If so, immersed in the chaos of battle, struggling to fend off the foes assailing him, had he even perceived that the moment for action had arrived?

Bareris drew a deep breath and bellowed loudly as only a bard could. "Break the darkness! Now! Now! Now!" On the other side of the battlefield, Milsantos's trumpeter blew the call intended to communicate the same message.

For several heartbeats, it appeared no one heard, at least no one with the power to respond in the appropriate manner. Then, however, the sky brightened from black to blue in an instant. Bareris flinched and squinted at the sudden blaze of sunlight that scoured the wraiths from the air.

He wasn't certain they'd all perished. Perhaps some endured as mere disembodied awareness or potential, like Mirror at his most ethereal, but even if so, they lacked the power to manifest until night returned.

Of course, the Keep of Thazar still harbored ghouls and animate corpses, creatures able to tolerate daylight even if it pained them, so the battle was far from over. Still, Bareris was now certain he and his allies were going to win. Considered as revenge, it wasn't enough. It could never be enough, but it was a start, and weary to the bone though he was, he strode back toward the breached wall and the muddled din of the fight still raging there in search of something else to kill. For some reason impervious to the purifying sun, Mirror fell into step beside him.

chapter fourteen

17 Kythorn, the Year of Risen Elfkin

Aoth took a swallow of beer, belched, and said, "One nice thing about the undead: When they occupy a fortress, they don't drink up all the ale."

In truth, he had good reason to be glad of it. So many priests had died when Szass Tam's torches exploded that after the battle, healing magic had been in short supply. As a captain and war mage, he hadn't had any difficulty or qualms about commandeering the services of a cleric to knit his broken bones and Brightwing's too, but bruises, however painful, were a different matter. Nymia and many other officers he'd known wouldn't have hesitated to order up a second dose of healing to ease them, but he couldn't, not when there were legionnaires likely to die for want of a priest's attention. He simply bore the discomfort as best he could, and alcohol helped, as it helped so many things in life.

Seated on the other side of the shabby little parlor that comprised the greater portion of their billet, methodically honing a dagger, Bareris raised his head and asked, "How soon, do you think, will we head up into the mountains?"

Aoth sighed. His new friend's response had nothing to do with what he himself had said, but at least he'd answered. Half the time, when someone spoke to him, he didn't.

"It's hard to say. You know as well as I do, an army needs time to put itself back in order after a big, hard fight, and when the tharchions are ready to attack this underground fortress you tell of, it might be easier to reach it through the portal in Delhumide."

"No." The dagger whispered against the whetstone. "The necromancers know an intruder found and used it already. I doubt it's there anymore."

"Well, you could be right." In actuality, Aoth wasn't certain Nymia and Milsantos would decide to go hunting "Xingax" and his cohorts by any route. The zulkirs hadn't ordered them to, a march over the Sunrise Mountains would be difficult, and who knew if Bareris could even find the wizards' lair again? But he had a hunch the bard wasn't ready to hear that.

Bareris glowered. "You sound as if you don't even want to go."

"I won't want to go anywhere for the next couple of days. You wouldn't either, if you'd come out of the battle banged up like me. Anyway, I'm a legionnaire. I go where my tharchion sends me."

"What about Chathi?"

"I liked her. I miss her, but it won't keep me from living the rest of my life. She wouldn't want that. I doubt your Tammith would have wanted it for you, either."

"You don't understand. You can't. You were only with Chathi a short time. My whole life centered on Tammith."

"It's grand to love and be loved, but a man needs to stand at the center of his own life."

"I only wanted to make her happy, yet I failed her in everything." Bareris laughed. "By the Harp, that's a mild way of putting it, isn't it? Failed her. I *destroyed* her."

"A priest would say you set her soul free. Certainly, you did everything you could for her. It's a miracle you were even able to track her."

"If I'd never left Bezantur—"

"And if I'd figured out the torches were dangerous a few breaths sooner, Chathi might still be alive. Whenever things go wrong, you can always find an if, but what's the point of brooding over it? You're only torturing yourself."

Bareris stood up and reached for his sword belt, which hung on a peg on the wall with Aoth's lance leaning beside it. "I'm going for a walk."

"My friend, if I've said anything to offend you, I'm sorry."

Bareris shook his head. "It isn't that. It's just . . . " He slid the newly sharpened knife into its sheath then buckled on his weapons. "I just need to be alone."

•• •• •• •• •• •• •• •• •• •• •• •• ••

Malark was as tired as he could recall ever being, even during the first months of his monastic training, and accordingly eager to reach his destination. Even so, he brought his flying horse down to the trail for the final leg of the journey up the valley. If the undead were still in possession of the Keep of Thazar, he'd be at least slightly less conspicuous approaching at ground level, and if the legionnaires had succeeded in retaking the place, he didn't want them mistaking him for a wraith. By now, they were likely wary of most anything that flew.

His steed snorted, expressing its displeasure at descending. When first created, it hadn't displayed emotion, nor had its black coat felt so much like actual horsehair. Malark wondered if, over time, simply by virtue of being perceived and employed, an illusory creature could become more real.

The question intrigued him, but now was not the time to ponder it. He'd do better to focus his attention on his surroundings, lest some skeleton or dread warrior notice him before he spotted it.

He crested a rise and the castle came into view, with a portion of the curtain wall demolished and an army, or the overflow of one, camped around it. He smiled, for the force was plainly composed of living men and orcs. Minute with distance though they were, he could see them moving freely about in the sunlight, and downwind, he could smell their cook fires and latrines. In addition to which, the banners of Thay, Pyarados, and Thazalhar flew from spires inside the fortress.

He cantered on into the encampment, where, it seemed to him, a general air of lethargic exhaustion prevailed. Still, it wasn't long before someone realized he was a stranger and came to ask his business.

"I'm an emissary from Tharchion Flass," he answered, "and I need to see Nymia Focar and Milsantos Daramos immediately."

•• •• •• •• •• •• •• •• •• •• •• •• •• ••

Nymia had heard reports of Dmitra Flass's outlander lieutenant but had never met him before, so she studied him curiously. Despite what had evidently been a wearisome journey, he kneeled without any show of stiffness or soreness, and the regard of his striking green eyes bespoke intellect and self-possession. Her initial impression was that he appeared as competent as his reputation indicated.

"Rise," said Milsantos, "and tell us your business."

He and Nymia had taken a room near the top of the central

keep to serve as their command center, and weather permitting, threw open the casements to admit fresh air and illumination. This afternoon the old man sat in a chair near one of the west windows, and the golden sigils on his breastplate—Nymia wondered fleetingly if, when on campaign, he ever dispensed entirely with the weight, heat, and general discomfort of plate armor—gleamed in a shaft of sunlight.

"Thank you," said Malark. "I understand you've been busy retaking the valley and castle. May I ask how much you know about what's been happening elsewhere in Thay?"

"Szass Tam," said Milsantos, "asked his fellow zulkirs to make him regent, but they declined."

Malark smiled. "I'm glad to find you so well informed. It will save us at least a little time, and we don't have much to spare, but I imagine there are facts you haven't had the opportunity to learn. Szass Tam manipulated recent events to increase the likelihood of the other zulkirs acceding to his request. Among other machinations, he murdered Druxus Rhym and Aznar Thrul, tampered with the transmuters' election, betrayed a Thayan army to the Rashemi, and fomented riots in the major cities. All deeds that furthered his plan in one way or another."

No, Nymia thought, I don't want to hear this. She and Milsantos had defeated the undead marauders Szass Tam's followers had created as the lich himself had charged her to do, even though it meant taking necromancers captive and destroying their dread-warrior servants. But in the aftermath, everything had seemed to be all right. Though Szass Tam almost certainly knew what the armies of Pyarados and Thazalhar had accomplished, he hadn't come rushing to exact retribution. She'd dared to hope she might actually emerge from this mad, paradoxical situation unscathed.

Yet here was the small man with the spot on his chin telling her secrets she was better off not knowing and almost certainly with the intent of enmeshing her in new dangers and ambiguities. She could have joyfully bashed in his skull with her mace and chucked the corpse out one of the casements.

Frowning, Milsantos fingered a rune on his armor. "We didn't know all that, but it doesn't surprise me, because we have discovered that Red Wizards of Necromancy created and directed the raiders we've been fighting."

Nymia wanted to bash him too. Why did you tell him that? she thought. It's bad enough that we know, worse to prattle about it to one of Dmitra's agents.

"That makes sense," said Malark. "Initially, it gave him another opportunity to play the savior, and after his fellow zulkirs rejected his proposal, it likewise served the next phase of his scheme."

"You speak," said Milsantos, "as if you know what that is."

"I do," said Malark. "After the vote, when it became clear Szass Tam was still playing his games, Tharchion Flass gave me the task of figuring out what his new purpose is. In time, it occurred to me that in the wake of their botched invasion of Rashemen, he likely commands the complete loyalty of Tharchions Kren and Odesseiron, and that reflection led to a rather alarming supposition. Employing an unnaturally swift steed, I rode far to learn if it could possibly be true. It is. I discovered the legions of Gauros and Surthay, newly augmented by a massive infusion of undead warriors, marching south."

"You're telling us," Milsantos said, "that since his fellow zulkirs refused to vote Szass Tam a throne, he means to seize it by force of arms."

"Yes, and now your army, which includes the Burning Braziers, is on the wrong side of the realm to oppose him."

Milsantos rose and gestured to a map of Thay spread on one of the trestles tables. "Show me the northerners' route."

Malark advanced to the table, and nerves taut as bowstrings,

Nymia reluctantly stood and approached for a better look as well.

Using his fingertip, the outlander traced a path along the vellum chart. "As best I can reconstruct it, they swung west through the sparsely inhabited part of Eltabbar and have now headed south into Lapendrar."

Milsantos nodded. "In their place, I'd do the same. Pyras Autorian is loyal to Szass Tam, but it would still be arduous to drag an army up the Second Escarpment, across the peaks of the Thaymount, then down the cliffs once more. You'd be seen, too, by someone hostile to your intentions. Too many Red Wizards have estates in the highlands, and on the south half of the plateau, the fiefs and towns are packed in too close for a host to sneak through."

"That's true," Nymia said, "but surely someone noticed them marching through Lapendrar. Hezass Nymar may not have a strong enough army to oppose them, but why didn't he warn the council of their coming? Why did one of Dmitra's agents have to venture forth and discover this for himself?"

"I can hazard a guess," said Malark. "Hezass Nymar dances to Szass Tam's piping as well, though maybe not to the point of lending his own relatively meager forces to the lich's scheme. That I simply couldn't tell, and Szass Tam may not want them anyway. Someone has to hold the Aglarondan border. But at least to the extent of granting free passage to Tharchions Odesseiron and Kren and keeping their progress a secret." He smiled. "The priest's probably glad he chose to govern from Escalant instead of residing in Lapendrar proper. If the necromancers fail, he can claim afterward that he didn't know what was going on."

Milsantos grunted. "If we're going to speculate, let's do it about something important. Where are Kren and Odesseiron headed? It can't be the capital, or they would have circled east instead of west. It has to be Bezantur. Take it and you pretty much control the whole south of the realm and all access to the sea. You've taken a giant step toward winning your war almost before it's begun."

"Tharchion Flass agrees with you," said Malark, "particularly since the city and all Priador are in a vulnerable condition. Their tharchion is dead and I'm informed that now the commander of his legion and city guard is too. Apparently the Shadowmasters assassinated him. Szass Tam must have hired them."

"What I want to know," Nymia said, "is why you, a servant of Dmitra Flass, have ridden all the way to the eastern edge of Thay to tell us these things. The last I heard, she too was Szass Tam's faithful follower."

"Until recently, yes. She's since decided the prudent course is to cast her lot with six zulkirs rather than one."

"Still," said Milsantos, "that doesn't quite explain what you're doing here."

"If Priador can't defend itself, someone else has to."

"Meaning us?" Nymia asked. "You said it yourself: We're on the wrong side of the country."

"But you're prepared to march and fight, seeing as how you've been doing it for tendays already. Your men know how to combat the undead. Your have the most formidable war priests in Thay at your disposal.

"In contrast, many another legion is still nestled in the garrison it's occupied more or less peacefully ever since the new trade policy began. After all Szass Tam has done to win their regard, many a soldier reveres or fears him and is reluctant to take up arms against him. Indeed, at this point, it's an open question just how many tharchions will stand with the council."

Milsantos snorted. "Your argument isn't as strong as you imagine. We fought hard to retake this fortress. We'd benefit greatly from a few more days of rest. On top of which, the fire priests are dead. The arms Szass Tam furnished turned against them."

Malark smiled in apparent admiration. "Thus depriving us of perhaps our most potent weapon against specters and the like."

"Still," the old man said, "it may be that you've come to the right people. Let's assume that in time the council can field a sufficient force to oppose the northerners. The immediate task, then, is to slow down the enemy advance and keep them from reaching Bezantur before that happens. Nymia, your griffon riders have the mobility and skills required."

"Damn it!" Nymia exploded, then caught herself. It was neither dignified nor prudent for two tharchions to argue in front of an inferior, particularly one who'd no doubt report the discussion word for word to one of their compatriots. "Messenger, wait outside."

"Of course." Malark bowed, withdrew, and closed the door behind him

"I take it," Milsantos said, "that you don't care for my suggestion."

"How dare you assume," she gritted, "without a word of discussion between us, that I have any intention of fighting Szass Tam?"

"Ah," he said. "Perhaps that was presumptuous of me, and I apologize, but I think Dmitra Flass's notion is sound: Six zulkirs are stronger than one."

"Even when the one is Szass Tam?"

"Well, we can hope so."

"Even when we know for certain he already controls Gauros, Surthay, High Thay, and Lapendrar, and we don't know if any other tharchions except Dmitra—assuming we can even trust that duplicitous slut—mean to oppose him? What if we march against him, and it turns out we're the only ones?"

Milsantos smiled. "It will be inconvenient to say the least. Still, we'll have the other six zulkirs and the orders of wizardry they command."

"Until some of them deem it advantageous to switch sides. You know what they're like."

"Yes. I do. So what's your thought?"

"It's not as if the outlander brought us actual orders from the council. Despite the airs she puts on, Dmitra is our peer, not our superior."

"True. Apparently she begrudged the time it would have taken to palaver with the zulkirs."

"That means we aren't obligated to do anything. We can stay put here in the east and let everybody else slaughter one another in Priador."

Milsantos pulled a wry face. "It's tempting. You and I have survived a long while by keeping our noses out of the zulkirs' squabbles, but I fear it's not possible anymore. The old rivalries have flared into actual war, and if you don't choose a side, both will regard you as an enemy."

"Let's say you're right. In that case, I want to back the winning side. Just how certain are you it will be the council?"

"To be honest, not certain at all, but I'm willing to play my hunch. In addition to which, I've seen quite a bit of the undead of late, enough to sicken me. I don't want a lich as sole ruler of my homeland."

Nymia sighed. "Nor do I. He unleashed his pet horrors on my tharch, ordered me to dispose of them, then betrayed and crippled our army at the worst possible moment. At this point, I hate and mistrust him too much to support him."

"We're agreed, then."

"Yes, curse you. I can have the Griffon Legion in the air before dusk, but it's going to be a nightmare getting the rest of the army ready for a forced march. We'll be lucky if the wretches don't mutiny." A thought struck her. "We're still holding all those necromancers prisoner. If we try to take them with us, they'll slow us down, and if we leave them behind, lightly guarded, they're apt to escape despite their bonds and gags."

"Then we'll have to kill them."

She ran her hand over her scalp. "Just kill a band of Red Wizards."

Milsantos grinned. "Don't tell me you've never felt the urge."

•• •• •• •• •• •• •• •• •• •• •• •• •• ••

Squinting, Aoth scrutinized the mountainsides, but it was Brightwing who spotted the would-be travelers and pointed them out to him. Sword swinging at his side, bow slung across his back, Bareris was climbing a narrow, rocky trail. Diminished by sunlight and the absence of combat to the merest suggestion of murk, Mirror flowed along behind him.

Brightwing furled her wings, swooped, and landed in front of them, effectively blocking the path, though that wasn't Aoth's precise intention. At Bareris's back on the valley floor, small as a dollhouse with distance, the Keep of Thazar and the surrounding encampment bustled with activity occasioned by the impending departure. The sight reminded Aoth of an anthill.

"I have men to oversee," he said, "and my own packing to attend to. I don't have time to chase you."

Bareris shrugged. "Then you shouldn't have."

"Should I let you throw your life away? As soon as I realized your belongings were gone, I guessed what you intended, and it's crazy. Even if you can find it again, you can't attack a necromancers' stronghold by yourself."

"I'm not by myself. Mirror decided to stick with me."

"It's still crazy."

"My quarrel is with Xingax and his confederates. If you legionnaires no longer mean to go after them, that's my bad luck, but it doesn't change what I need to do."

"I understand why you want to destroy Xingax, but you

should save your fiercest hatred for Szass Tam. He's the one who bears ultimate responsibility for Tammith's transformation. Xingax was simply carrying out his orders."

Bareris's mouth tightened. "I suppose that's true."

"Then come west with the army, idiot! If you want to punish Szass Tam in the only way that folk like us have any hope of hurting him, the time to do it is now. If we don't keep him from taking Bezantur, there'll be no stopping him later. You can hunt down Xingax another day."

Bareris stood pondering for a heartbeat or two then said, "All right. Under one condition."

Aoth snorted. "I go out of my way to keep a lunatic from committing suicide, and he wants to bargain with me. What is it you want?"

"A griffon. Surely there's at least one that lost its master in the battle. Let me fly west with you."

"Have you ever ridden a griffon?"

"No, but you can teach me, and I can use song to establish a bond with my steed. You've seen me do it before."

Now it was Aoth's turn to consider. Bareris—and Mirror—could prove invaluable in the actions to come, but those same skirmishes would be perilous for a novice rider.

"Please," Bareris said. "A moment ago, you called me a madman. I know you were joking, but sometimes I truly do feel as if my mind is going to break. It's not quite as bad when I'm striking blows against those who corrupted Tammith, and I'll fare better fighting alongside you than trudging for days merely hoping for a battle at the end of the trek."

"Very well," said Aoth. "We'll find a masterless griffon and see if you can charm it."

"Which is more," Brightwing said, "than you ever did for me."

chapter fifteen

22–27 Kythorn, the Year of Risen Elfkin

The road to Priador ran roughly parallel to the First Escarpment, and the legions of the north straggled along it for miles. Bareris knew he and his comrades had no choice but to leave the body of the enemy host unmolested, at least while the sun burned in the sky. They didn't dare risk attacking such a superior force.

Outriders, however, were a different matter, and when an army lost those, it was reduced to creeping blind. Accordingly, the Griffon Legion, or what remained of it after the campaign through Pyarados and up the Pass of Thazar, had divided into smaller bands to hunt enemy scouts.

Aoth whistled and pointed with his lance. Following the gesture, Bareris saw the horsemen on the plain. The griffon riders dived, Bareris's eager mount furling its wings before he even gave the signal.

The northerners spotted them descending. A couple fled, perhaps because their horses panicked. The rest, evidently realizing they couldn't outrun griffons, scrambled to ready their bows.

An arrow streaked upward, and Bareris's steed veered to dodge it. He was slow shifting his weight to facilitate the maneuver, and the griffon screeched in annoyance.

The shaft still missed them, though, and an instant later, the griffon plunged down atop the archer and his piebald horse, driving its claws into their bodies and smashing them to the ground.

Bareris cast about. On all sides, griffons, the warriors on their backs essentially superfluous, shredded their shrieking targets with beak and talon. They hadn't gotten all the outriders, though. A necromancer with a scarlet robe peeking out from under his cloak howled words of power and swept his arms through mystic passes. His hands left smears of darkness on the air.

Bareris shouted at him. Striking hard as a hammer, the sound knocked the Red Wizard out of the saddle and ruined his spell-casting. Brightwing sprang, and Aoth thrust his lance into the warlock's chest.

"We need to catch the ones who ran," said Aoth.

Bareris bumped his mount's flanks with his heels, and the griffon lashed its wings and leaped into the air. They raced in pursuit of the surviving scouts then saw there was no need to hurry. A shadow in the sunlight, eyes and other features barely discernible in his smear of a face, Mirror stood over the bodies of the northerners and their horses.

Bareris realized he ought to strip the corpses. Riding his flying steed, Malark Springhill had accompanied the griffon riders west, and though he'd eventually split off to attend to some project of his own, he'd first urged them to obtain the trappings of warriors from Gauros and Surthay whenever possible. These should do nicely. Thanks to the way Mirror's spectral sword dispatched its victims, they weren't even bloody or torn.

Malark cleared his throat. It seemed a gentler away of announcing his presence than abruptly casting his reflection into a lady's mirror.

It still startled her, though. Seated at her dressing table, one bright blue eye painted, the other not and therefore looking smaller than its mate, Nephis Sepret lurched around, then sighed and pressed a hand to her bosom when she saw who'd interrupted her at her toilet.

"Someday," she said, "you must tell me how you sneak in here without the servants knowing."

He waved his hand to indicate the glittering gold-and-sapphire jewelry she'd laid out for herself. "That's a lot of finery, considering that the autharch is otherwise engaged."

She smiled. "His fickleness doesn't mean I have to be lonely."

Charmed despite himself as usual by her beauty and brazenness, Malark smiled back. "You play a dangerous game, Saer."

"As opposed to spying for you and Dmitra Flass?" Nephis turned back to the mirror and brushed blue pigment across the remaining eyelid. "From time to time, I need the touch of a *young* man, and I can handle Ramas. That's what makes me valuable, isn't it?"

"In fact, it makes you important. I assume you've kept abreast of recent events, the murders of two zulkirs, Szass Tam's failed bid for a regency, and all the rest of it, but what you don't know is that the lich is marching legions south to gain himself a throne by force of arms. Their intended route leads through Anhaurz on the way to Bezantur."

She twisted back around. "You aren't serious."

"Yes, I am. The question is, how fast will His Omnipotence's host cover the distance? Fast enough to reach the coast all but unopposed, or slowly enough for his rivals to field an adequate force to intercept him?"

"The new bridge," she said.

Malark nodded. "Very good. If the autharch allows it to stand, Szass Tam's warriors can cross the Lapendrar quickly. If he knocks it down, they'll still get across eventually, but it will cost them precious time. From what you've told me of Ramas Ankhalab, I assume that once he learns of the northerners' approach, his inclination will be to demolish the span."

"Yes," Nephis said. "The fool long ago gave his loyalty to Aznar Thrul and his faction and hasn't wavered since, but don't worry. He may spend the occasional night with another trollop—and thank Sune for that, or when would I scratch my own itches?—but he's still besotted with me. I can persuade him to do whatever I want."

Malark hesitated for a heartbeat. "I haven't instructed you to take any particular action as of yet."

She snorted. "Did you think you had to? Szass Tam saved my father's life and restored his honor. He helped my brother gain entry to the order of Necromancy and shielded So-Kehur when the other apprentices wanted to hurt him. I'd do anything to help him."

He sighed. "I knew you'd say that." And it was a pity Szass Tam and Dmitra Flass no longer shared a common purpose. "I'll say farewell then. Just be ready to counsel the autharch when he receives word of the northern army."

She pouted. "Must you go so soon? Why not linger a while and help me scratch my itches?"

"I wish I could, but I have another message to deliver. Good-bye, my friend."

He crept back to her music room with its harp and lutes, then climbed out a window and down the wall. He slipped into a shadowy bower where he could stand and ponder unobserved.

The note he carried inside his tunic read:

Milord Autharch,

Your mistress Lady Nephis is untrue. She intends a tryst with a lover in the Carnelian Suite this very night. She employs a talisman of invisibility to keep such assignations, so those who go to catch her in the act should deploy the appropriate countermagic.

If the lord of the city was as jealous and choleric as Nephis had always claimed, the message should serve to end her influence over him for good and all. The only question was how to deliver it without being noticed. Fortunately, such problems rarely stymied Malark for long, and after a few more breaths, the solution came to him.

•• •• •• •• •• •• •• •• •• •• •• •• •• •• ••

The inn stood midway between two tax stations. Aoth suspected the proprietor had liked it that way, liked not having a publican looking over his shoulder every time he rented bed space or sold a mug of ale.

Cowering before armed intruders in the caravanserai's common room, doing his inadequate best to shield his wife and three children with his pudgy body, he didn't look as if he liked it anymore. To all appearances, he would have given almost anything for a garrison of legionnaire protectors close at hand.

The family's manifest terror gave Aoth a pang of guilt, for after all, they weren't enemy warriors and had nothing to do with Szass Tam and his ambitions. They just happened to be in the wrong place at the wrong time. But war was made of such injustices.

"You have to clear out," he said, "and stay gone for a while."

The innkeeper, whose round, dark face seemed made for jollity rather than dread, swallowed. "Sir, please, I don't understand. This place is our home, and our living, too. It's all we have."

A griffon rider lifted his sword and stepped forward. "Fine, imbecile, you had your chance."

"Halt!" Aoth snapped, and then, when the soldier obeyed, returned his attention to the innkeeper. "You see how it is. You can take your coin with you, and anything else you can carry, but you must leave, and keep away till the end of the summer anyway. Believe me, you'll be safer that way."

The innkeeper's wife whispered in his ear, and then he said, "All right. We'll get our things."

"Just be quick about it," Aoth replied.

They were, and before long, they slunk out into the pounding rain that was almost unheard of in Thay, except for late at night. Aoth assumed the council's weather wizards were responsible. It was yet another ploy to slow the northerners' advance, in part by turning Lapendrar's roads to muck.

Unfortunately, the rain also made for cold flying with diminished visibility, but the Griffon Legion would simply have to cope. Aoth turned to his men and said, "Let's get to it. Poison the beer barrels, and the well, too."

The warrior who'd threatened the innkeeper cocked his head. "You don't think finding the inn deserted will make the bastards suspicious?"

"Common folk often flee the approach of an army," Aoth replied. "If it makes the northerners leery enough to refrain from pilfering an unattended keg of ale, they're not like any soldiers I ever knew."

• • • • • • • • • • • • • • • • • •

Dmitra surveyed the zulkirs seated around the table. It seemed to her that every face betrayed worry, no matter how the mage lords tried to mask it, and why not? They all had plenty to worry about.

"Your Omnipotences," she said, "thank you for agreeing to meet with me."

"You should thank us," Samas Kul said, round face and fat neck a mottled red, "for by the Golden Coin, I don't know why I came. Some of us listened to you before, and as a result we're at war with Szass Tam!"

"Whereas if we hadn't heeded," Lallara snapped, waspish as ever, "the lich would be king already."

"That might be better than the alternative."

"No," said Nevron, glowering and smelling of sulfur, "it's not. I will never bend my knee to Szass Tam. I'd sooner drown the entire realm in hellfire."

Yaphyll's lips quirked into an impish smile. "It would be nice if we could chart a middle course. A tactic that avoids both surrender and ash."

"Your loyal servants in the Griffon Legion," Dmitra said, "are doing their best to hinder Szass Tam's advance. Unfortunately, a number of other companies are dawdling when they should be rushing to prepare for war. In some cases, they fear to take sides in a quarrel among zulkirs. In others, they're contemplating fighting for the lich.

"You have similar problems among the nobles and commoners," she continued. "Many are loath to exert themselves or make any sacrifices to assist the defense. Some merely await the opportunity to work against you as spies and saboteurs."

"We already knew Szass Tam did an exemplary job of endearing himself to the masses," Nevron growled. "Do you have a remedy?"

"I hope so, Your Omnipotence," Dmitra replied. "You six must forsake the seeming security of your castles and speak directly with lesser folk: the captains, the lords, and whomever."

Nevron glared at her. "You mean plead for their help?"

"Of course not. You are their masters, now and forever. The

problem is, so is Szass Tam. You need to loom as large in their thoughts as he does, so command them as always, but do it in person. Don't count on them to obey your deputies with the same diligence and alacrity they'd show to you."

Samas Kul snorted. "I don't have the proper physique for chasing frantically about the realm."

"Perhaps you should consider turning into something leaner," Yaphyll replied. "That's what transmutation's all about, or so I'm told."

"In truth, Your Omnipotence," Dmitra said, "I didn't envision *you* doing a great deal of traveling. With an army marching against it, its tharchion and the commander of its legions assassinated, and the Shadowmasters still lurking about to hinder efforts at defense, nowhere in the realm needs more sorting out than Bezantur. You're the zulkir who lives there and heads up the guild that made the city rich. You can set matters right if anyone can, but not by hiding behind fortress walls."

"Walls have their uses," Lauzoril said in his usual prissy, tepid manner. "Szass Tam or his proxies have murdered two zulkirs already. Now you propose that the rest of us expose ourselves unnecessarily."

"Understand," said Mythrellan, her body patterned in brown and tan diamonds like snakeskin, "we have reason to fear traitors even within the ranks of our own orders. But I don't suppose I have to explain that to you."

"I infer," Dmitra said, "you're alluding to the fact that though I'm an illusionist, for a long while I gave my greatest loyalty to Szass Tam instead of your exalted self. What can I say, except that I recall a time when you too were pleased to have him as an ally."

Yaphyll chortled. "As were Lallara, Samas, and I, so let's forgo deploring old miscalculations and address current needs, to which end I'll say I believe Dmitra Flass is right. Whatever our concerns about our personal safety, we need to take the southern tharchs in hand while we still can."

"I'm glad to hear you say so," Dmitra said, "for I have even more to recommend."

Samas Kul snorted. "What else can there be?"

"You're all used to Szass Tam working through agents and subordinates. As you do. As lords everywhere do. But I know him, and I promise you that when his army undertakes a major battle, he'll fight alongside his vassals. Obviously, his wizardry will all but guarantee a victory—unless we have archmages fighting on our side, too."

The zulkirs exchanged glances. Dmitra felt as if she could read their thoughts. None was especially eager to risk himself on a battlefield, where, if Lady Luck turned against him, even the most formidable spellcaster could fall. Their underlings were supposed to face such hazards for them. But chiefly they all flinched from the prospect of a duel of spells with Szass Tam. The lich was their superior, and whether or not any of them would ever concede it aloud, they knew it.

The moment stretched on until Lallara suddenly banged her fist on the table. "Damn us for cowards! It's six against one, isn't it?"

Yaphyll grinned. "It is, and I think that if we're sensible, we must either fight as hard as we can or flee into exile. I'm not disposed to the latter. I just refurnished the south wing of my palace."

"Fine," Samas Kul spat. "I'll tend to Bezantur and all the rest of it, but it's a bitter jest that I finally rise to be a zulkir, and then, instantly, everything turns to dung."

Dmitra could see they were all of one mind, and she breathed a sigh of relief. Her masters cared for nothing but their own self-interest, which meant their brittle accord could fracture at any time, but for the moment at least, they'd follow where she led.

For the time being, the rain had dwindled to a drizzle. Bareris supposed that was good. It wouldn't wash the pigment off his face or the faces of his companions.

Unfortunately, his garments were already soaked, and a letup in the downpour couldn't stop him feeling cold nor exhausted. The days and nights of flying and fighting almost without sleep had taken their toll. He crooned a restorative charm under his breath, and a tingle of vitality and alertness thrilled along his nerves.

Off to the north of the enemy encampment, light flashed, dazzling in the night. Aoth and Brightwing had swooped in to cast their fire magic. The supply wagons were as wet as everything else, and Aoth hadn't been certain the spell would actually suffice to set them ablaze, but the wavering yellow glow persisted, proof that he'd succeeded. Horses screamed, and men clamored.

With luck, the fire had distracted everyone, even sentries. Bareris, Malark, and ten comrades, all clad in the trappings of the enemy and each with gray stain on his skin and streaks of amber phosphorescence above his eyes, jumped up from their hiding places and sprinted toward the perimeter of the camp.

They got inside without anyone raising an alarm, and then they were just zombies shambling mindlessly about, waiting for some necromancer to command them. At least that was how it was supposed to look.

Several enemy legionnaires stood babbling and gawking in the direction of the fire. Bareris and his companions circled to take them from behind. He eased his sword from its scabbard and slid it into a warrior's back. Malark broke a man's neck with a gentle-looking thump from the heel of his hand.

Somebody saw and yelled a warning. Northerners scurried

to grab their weapons and shields. Bareris and his comrades slaughtered several more, then it was time to go. Their disguises wouldn't bear scrutiny for long, nor could they hope to stand against all the foes within easy reach of them. They cut their way clear and fled back into the night toward the spot where their griffons—and Malark's flying horse—waited to bear them to safety.

The loss of supplies should hinder the enemy a little. The confusion and dismay arising from the perception that some of their own undead warriors had rebelled might flummox them yet a little more. Anything to delay the advance for even another dozen heartbeats.

.. ..

For one terrifying instant, Aoth dreamed he'd fallen from Brightwing's back, then woke to find it so. Fortunately, however, in reality, he hadn't been riding her across the sky but using her for a pillow, and she'd dumped his head and shoulders onto the cold, wet ground when she sprang to her feet. Now she stood staring into the trees and the darkness like a hound on a point.

Stiff, sore, and grainy-eyed, Aoth grabbed his lance and clambered upright. "What is it?"

"I don't know," the griffon replied. "Something terrible."

A shadow appeared between two oaks. "That's rather harsh."

Aoth borrowed Brightwing's eyes so he too could see in the dark, and the murky figure became a gaunt, dark-eyed man. The newcomer walked with a straight, unadorned ebony staff, and the fingers peeking from the sleeves of his wizard's robes were shriveled and flaking.

For a heartbeat, Aoth could only stand and stare, frozen by the certainty his life had come to an end. Then he started to level his spear and drew breath to chant. He was a warrior and could at least go down fighting.

"Don't!" Brightwing screeched. "He isn't attacking!"

Szass Tam smiled. "Your familiar has good instincts, Captain Fezim. At the risk of sounding immodest, I'm . . . formidable. When I kill with my own hands, the victim tends to be a fellow archmage, a demigod, or a whole army. Anything less is scarcely worth the bother, which is not to suggest that your brave and resourceful company doesn't merit *some* sort of attention."

Aoth swallowed. "I don't understand."

"I'd like a parley with you and your fellow officers." Szass Tam gestured toward the heart of the grove, where the exhausted griffon riders had camped in the evidently vain hope the trees would conceal them from hostile eyes. His sleeve slipped down toward his wrist, revealing more of his withered hand. "Will you grant me safe conduct?"

"Yes," said Aoth.

He felt as if he were still mired in a dream, and it was somehow impossible to say anything else. He led Szass Tam toward his slumbering, snoring comrades. Brightwing followed, positioning herself behind the lich so she could pounce on him if it became necessary to protect her master, even though Aoth could feel she shared his conviction that Szass Tam could crush them like ants whenever he chose.

Szass Tam surveyed the sleeping men and griffons. "Do you want to wake them or should I?"

"I'll do it," Aoth replied. "Get up, everyone!" The mundane quality of the words made the moment feel that much more unreal.

Men groaned and rolled over, rubbed their eyes and threw off their covers, then faltered as Aoth had done when they saw who'd tracked them down. Rather, all but one of them did. Bareris leaped up, drew his sword, and sprang, all in a single blur of motion. Aoth lunged to interpose himself between the bard and Szass Tam but saw he wouldn't make it in time.

Bareris's sword flashed at the necromancer's head, and Szass Tam caught in his hand. The enchanted weapon should have cut the skeletal fingers off, but instead, Aoth saw some sort of malignancy flash up the blade. The sword shattered, and Bareris crumpled.

Sword in hand, vaguely resembling Aoth at this particular moment, Mirror streaked at the lich. Szass Tam simply looked at the ghost, and Mirror froze into a statue of shimmer and murk.

Warriors snatched up their weapons, and griffons gathered themselves to spring. They were all afraid of Szass Tam, but now that a fight had broken out, none intended to stand idle while the lich struck down their comrades. Nor, for that matter, did Aoth. He charged his lance with power.

Szass Tam flourished his staff. Patterns of rainbow-colored light shimmered into existence around his body, then flowed into another configuration, and another after that. The ongoing process was fascinating, so much so that despite the urgencies of the moment, Aoth could only stand and stare. No doubt his comrades felt the same compulsion.

"I entered your camp under sign of truce," Szass Tam said, "and this swordsman and the ghost had no right to attack me. Even so, I've done them no permanent harm. Now will you grant me the parley I seek, or should I smite you all while you stand helpless?"

It was difficult even to think, let alone talk, while transfixed by the shifting lights, but Aoth managed to force the words out. "You can have your talk. No one else will raise his hand to you."

"Good," said the necromancer, and his halo faded away. "Now, who are your fellow officers?" The folk in question stepped forward, some only after a moment's hesitation. Szass

Tam gestured to a patch of clear ground a few yards away. "It looks as if we have room to sit and talk over there. Shall we?"

The officers exchanged looks then moved in the direction the zulkir had indicated. Aoth surmised that the situation felt as surreal and impossible to control to them as it did to him. He started after them.

"Help me over there," Bareris croaked.

Aoth snorted. "You already had your chance to be stupid."

"If you gave Szass Tam a truce, I was wrong to break it, and I'm sorry, but I have to hear what he has to say."

"Don't make me regret it." Aoth hauled Bareris to his feet, draped the bard's arm across his shoulders, and essentially carried him to the clear spot. As far as he could see, Bareris didn't have any actual wounds. Szass Tam had simply burned away his strength.

The necromancer smiled sardonically as Aoth set Bareris back down on the ground. "I trust the inclusion of this gentleman won't prevent us from enjoying a civil conversation."

"He'll behave himself," said Aoth. He paused, waiting for somebody senior to himself to assume the role of chief spokesman for the Griffon Legion, then he realized no one else intended to put himself forward. "What is it you want to say to us, Your Omnipotence?"

"I suppose," the lich replied, sitting cross-legged on the grass like any ordinary person, "I should begin by congratulating you. Your campaign of harassment slowed my army sufficiently to achieve your purpose."

Despite his fear of the lich, Aoth felt a pang of satisfaction. "So you won't take Bezantur without a hard fight."

"Alas," said Szass Tam, "I won't take it at all, at least not this month nor the next. My fellow zulkirs have a sizable force maneuvering to intercept me, and they're reportedly willing to commit their own persons to the battle. I'd have to fight them with the Lapendrar at my back, hindering my retreat if I should need to make one, and even if I won, Samas Kul has Bezantur ready to resist a siege. All things considered, my tharchions and I believe the superior strategy is to withdraw."

"Then we won," said Malark.

Of them all, he seemed most at ease in the lich's presence, perhaps because, serving as Dmitra Flass's lieutenant, he'd seen the creature often. Or maybe it was simply because few things seemed to daunt or even surprise him.

"In a sense," said Szass Tam, "but it's time to consider *what* you've won. By balking me, you've simply condemned Thay to a long war instead of a short one, a protracted struggle as destructive as only the wizardry of archmages can devise. That's of little practical consequence to me. I'll still win in the end, and immortal as I am, I'll have all the time I need to rebuild. But I would have preferred to spare humbler folk the miseries that now await them."

Aoth shrugged. "I don't know about any of that. I just know we had to follow our orders and do our duty."

"Why," asked Szass Tam, "do you believe your duty lies with the other zulkirs instead of me?"

"That," said Malark, smiling, "is a good question, Your Omnipotence, for obviously, nothing you've done is illegal, treasonous, or wrong. It can't be, because a zulkir's will is itself the definition of what's proper."

"As I recall," Szass Tam said, "you hail from the Moonsea. Perhaps it amuses you to mock our Thayan way of thinking."

"By no means," said Malark. "I simply meant to convey that I follow your logic. I recognize your authority is as legitimate as the council's, and the choice between you is essentially an arbitrary one."

"Then why not join me," said the lich, "and undo a portion of the harm you've caused? You could. You could strike a crippling blow before the council realizes you've switched sides, and afterward I'll treat you well. You'll hold high honors in the Thay to come, whereas if you cleave to your present course, you'll only reap disaster and defeat."

"That may be," said Malark. "I certainly wouldn't wager against you, Your Omnipotence, but even knowing the decision's not particularly sensible, I prefer to oppose you."

Szass Tam cocked his head. "Why?"

"Without intending any insult, I have to confess the undead repulse me. Everything should live and die in its season, so I'm not partial to the idea of a lich king, and likewise not averse to the idea of this long war you promise. It promises to be quite a spectacle."

"I'm against you, too," said Aoth, though the words made him feel as if he were slipping his neck into a noose. "I swore my oath to Nymia Focar, so if she stands with the council, so do I." He hesitated. "Actually, there's more to it than that. I saw what your undead raiders did in Pyarados to the 'humbler folk' you say you'd like to spare. I saw the torches explode in the hands of the priests who trusted you, and it all just sticks in my craw a little."

"I regret those deaths," said Szass Tam, "but they were necessary to further a greater good."

"What 'greater good?'" Aoth demanded. "You already ruled Thay, or near enough. The other zulkirs followed your lead more often than not. Why must you wear an actual crown even if it brings ruin on the land?"

Szass Tam hesitated. "It's a little complicated."

"Not for me," Bareris gritted. "Your servants destroyed the woman I loved and hundreds of innocents like her. You made yourself the enemy of your own people, and we'd all be crazy to give you our trust or fealty ever again."

"You gentlemen disappoint me," said the lich. "Is there none among you with any breadth or clarity of thought? Does it truly matter if a few peasants perished a day or a decade early? Everyone suffers and dies in the end, and the world rolls on just the same without him. That's the sad, shabby way of things as they are." He looked at Bareris. "In a year or two, you'll forget all about this lass you think you adored."

"You're wrong," said Bareris. "I'll never forget her, and I'll make sure you don't, either."

Szass Tam looked around the circle of captains. "I'll ask once more: Are you all of one mind? Does no one believe the Griffon Legion ought to side with the eldest and most powerful zulkir? The wizard whom, in your private thoughts, you already considered the one true master of Thay?"

Apparently no one did. Probably more than one of them questioned the wisdom of his choice, but awed and frightened by the lich, they'd kept mum while Aoth, Malark, and Bareris presented a united front, and now, perhaps, it was easier to remain silent than dissent.

"So be it then. Just don't say I didn't give you a chance." Szass Tam rose, and Aoth tensed. Truce or no, it wouldn't astonish him if the necromancer, his offer spurned, lashed out with some terrible spell.

Instead he simply nodded goodnight and turned his back to them as if they were trusted friends then strolled toward the perimeter of the camp.

"Your Omnipotence!" Malark called.

Szass Tam glanced back around. "Yes?"

"May I ask one question?"

"Go ahead, though I don't promise an answer you'll understand."

"Tell us why you killed Druxus Rhym."

"How astute of you to wonder. Suffice it to say, I spoke of necessary sacrifices, and poor Druxus's was the most vital and regrettable of all." Szass Tam took another step, and then, abruptly, he was gone, vanished between one instant and the next.

Aoth realized he was holding his breath and let it out. "That was . . . interesting. What did we just do?"

Malark grinned. "Signed our own death warrants, probably."

"I wish I believed you were wrong." Aoth turned to the other officers. "Get the men moving. We have to clear out. Maybe Szass Tam didn't feel like dirtying his own hands slaughtering us, but now that he knows where we are, he could still send wraiths and skin kites down on our heads."

epilogue

2 Flamerule, the Year of Risen Elfkin

Night after night, the bats ranged this way and that, attacking scaly little kobolds, shaggy mountain sheep, and whatever other prey they could find. Gradually, the blood replenished their strength.

The one direction they didn't want to fly was north. They couldn't remember precisely why, but they had a sense that if they traveled in that direction, something fundamental would change and existence would become abhorrent.

Yet over time, they did drift north. They simply couldn't help it.

At last they reached the wide round shaft plunging deep into the earth. They realized they'd seen it before, and the entity floating above the rim of the well also. He looked like a huge, malformed fetus, and impossible as it seemed, he was even more grotesque than formerly. His eyes were more ill-matched, with one approximately human and the other globular and white.

The same was true of his hands. One remained a puny, rotting thing, but its mate was now enormous, ink black, and possessed of long talons. A ring of sutures revealed that someone had stitched it on.

The bats made one final effort to flee but only in their thoughts. Their will was so thoroughly constrained that even as they struggled, they swooped to the rim of the well, swirled together, and became a single being.

With unity came memory, and Tammith realized who and what she was. Anguish rose inside her.

"Daughter!" Xingax crowed. "This is wonderful! I was certain I'd lost you, but then I felt you returning to me."

She yearned to attack him, yearned, too, to put an end to herself and knew she could do neither.

"You must tell me," said Xingax, "how did you survive?"

"He cut me apart," she said dully. Bareris had, her love, and had been right to do it. "It was horrible, but it didn't kill me, and somehow I turned the pieces into bats and flew inside a house. I made it just before the sunlight came."

Xingax smiled. "I told you you're special."

"I'm vile!" she spat. "You changed me to fight in an army, and we lost. The other creatures died. Let me die too."

He pouted. "I'd hoped that by now you would have put such foolish notions behind you. Our master didn't lose his whole army, just a fraction of it, and of course you'll continue to serve with the host that remains. I predict that in time you'll rise to be one of its greatest champions. Now come below. You can have your pick of the slaves, and that will make you feel better."

personages of thay

The Zulkirs

Aznar Thrul (Evocation); also tharchion of Priador

Druxus Rhym (Transmutation)

Lallara (Abjuration)

Lauzoril (Enchantment)

Mythrellan (Illusion)

Nevron (Conjuration)

Szass Tam (Necromancy)

Yaphyll (Divination)

The Tharchions

Azhir Kren (Gauros)

Dimon (Tyraturos); also a priest of Bane

Dmitra Flass (Eltabbar); also a Red Wizard of Illusion and
princess of Mulmaster; "the First Princess of Thay"

Hezass Nymar (Lapendrar); also Eternal Flame of the temple
of Kossuth in Escalant

Homen Odesseiron (Surthay)

Invarri Metron (Delhumide)

Milsantos Daramos (Thazalhar)

Nymia Focar (Pyarados)

Pyras Autorian (Thaymount)

Thessaloni Canos (Alaor)

Others

Iphegor Nath, High Flamelord of the Church of Kossuth

Ramas Ankhalab, autharch of Anhaurz

Samas Kul, Master of the Guild of Foreign Trade; also a Red
Wizard of Transmutation

Shabella the Pale, Guildmistress of the Temple of Mask in
Bezantur; also chief of that city's thieves' guild

WELCOME TO THE

WORLD

Created by Keith Baker and developed by Bill Slavicsek and James Wyatt, EBERRON® is the latest setting designed for the DUNGEONS & DRAGONS® Roleplaying game, novels, comic books, and electronic games.

ANCIENT, WIDESPREAD MAGIC

Magic pervades the EBERRON world. Artificers create wonders of engineering and architecture. Wizards and sorcerers use their spells in war and peace. Magic also leaves its mark—the coveted dragonmark—on members of a gifted aristocracy. Some use their gifts to rule wisely and well, but too many rule with ruthless greed, seeking only to expand their own dominance.

INTRIGUE AND MYSTERY

A land ravaged by generations of war. Enemy nations that fought each other to a standstill over countless, bloody battlefields now turn to subtler methods of conflict. While nations scheme and merchants bicker, priceless secrets from the past lie buried and lost in the devastation, waiting to be tracked down by intrepid scholars and rediscovered by audacious adventurers.

SWASHBUCKLING ADVENTURE

The EBERRON setting is no place for the timid. Courage, strength, and quick thinking are needed to survive and prosper in this land of peril and high adventure.

During the Last War, Gaven was an
adventurer, searching the darkest reaches
of the underworld. But an encounter with
a powerful artifact forever changed him,
breaking his mind and landing him in the
deepest cell of the darkest prison in
all the world.

THE DRACONIC PROPHECIES

BOOK I

When war looms on the horizon, some see it as more
than renewed hostilities between nations. Some see the
fulfillment of an ancient prophecy—one that promises
both the doom and salvation of the world. And Gaven may
be the key to it all.

THE STORM DRAGON

The first EBERRON hardcover by veteran game designer and
the author of *In the Claws of the Tiger*:

James Wyatt

SEPTEMBER 2007